The Complete Short Stories

Volume Two

ROALD DAHL

PENGUIN BOOKS

PENGUIN BOOKS

Published by the Penguin Group
Penguin Books Ltd, 80 Strand, London WC2R ORL, England
Penguin Group (USA) Inc., 375 Hudson Street, New York, New York 10014, USA
Penguin Group (Canada), 90 Eglinton Avenue East, Suite 700, Toronto, Ontario, Canada M4P 2Y3
(a division of Pearson Penguin Canada Inc.)
Penguin Ireland, 25 St Stephen's Green, Dublin 2, Ireland (a division of Penguin Books Ltd)
Penguin Group (Australia), 707 Collins Street, Melbourne, Victoria 3008, Australia
(a division of Pearson Australia Group Pty Ltd)
Penguin Books India Pvt Ltd, 11 Community Centre, Panchsheel Park, New Delhi – 110 017, India
Penguin Group (NZ), 67 Apollo Drive, Rosedale, Auckland 0632, New Zealand
(a division of Pearson New Zealand Ltd)
Penguin Books (South Africa) (Pty) Ltd, Block D, Rosebank Office Park,
181 Jan Smuts Avenue, Parktown North, Gauteng 2193, South Africa

Penguin Books Ltd, Registered Offices: 80 Strand, London WC2R ORL, England

www.penguin.com

These stories have been previously published in a variety of publications.
Details of each story's original publication are provided at the start of
each chapter and constitute an extension of this copyright page
This collection first published in Penguin Books 2013

001

Copyright © Roald Dahl Nominee Ltd, 1954, 1958, 1959, 1960, 1965,
1966, 1974, 1977, 1980, 1986, 1987, 1988
Introduction copyright © Anthony Horowitz, 2013
All rights reserved

The moral right of the copyright holders has been asserted

Set in 12.5/14.75pt Garamond MT Std
Typeset by Jouve (UK), Milton Keynes
Printed in Great Britain by Clays Ltd, St Ives plc

ISBN: 978-1-405-91011-8

www.greenpenguin.co.uk

PENGUIN BOOKS

The Complete Short Stories: Volume Two

Roald Dahl is best known for his mischievous, wildly inventive stories for children. But throughout his life he was also a prolific and acclaimed writer of stories for adults. These sinister, surprising tales continue to entertain, amuse and shock generations of readers even today.

Contents

v

CONTENTS

Introduction
by Anthony Horowitz

It's extraordinary how Roald Dahl's success continues even over twenty years after his death. He still sells a million books a year, and more people borrow his books from public libraries than they do books by Charles Dickens or plays by William Shakespeare. He has a hugely successful musical based on one of his titles (*Matilda*) on the London stage, and as I write this there's another one (*Charlie and the Chocolate Factory*) on the way. Hollywood producers fall over each other to turn his work into films, the best of which – *The Fantastic Mr Fox* – had George Clooney and Meryl Streep in lead roles. Children from all over the world make a pilgrimage to his museum in Great Missenden. He even has a special day named after him.

Dahl always was the master. Long before Harry Potter made children's books fashionable (and profitable), Dahl was out there with his own unique tone of voice. It is hardly surprising that he is one of the very few writers who even have their own adjective. When you say 'Dahlesque', people know exactly what you mean. Back in 1979, when my own first children's book was published, this could be quite daunting. The truth is that at that time very few other authors got a word in edgeways; he wasn't just dominant, he was monolithic. And with good reason.

By then he had written four real masterpieces, books that broke down the barrier between adult author and child reader and released young fiction from the dreary expectations of didacticism, morality and condescension. *James and the Giant Peach*, the two *Charlie* novels, *Danny the Champion of the World* – these were books to be relished. They had a completely new language. They were perhaps the first books that your parents didn't need to recommend. Children found them for themselves.

And it didn't end there. Roald Dahl had already written the screenplay for one of the best ever James Bond films – *You Only Live Twice*. And if that wasn't enough, a TV series had just started that had silhouettes of naked women dancing around to a catchy theme tune followed by Dahl himself, sitting in an armchair, introducing his *Tales of the Unexpected*, as they were called. The television series made an enormous impact at the time, bringing together a panoply of heavyweight stars including Cyril Cusack, John Mills, John Gielgud, Joseph Cotten and Janet Leigh. It was based on some of the stories you will find in this book.

I have to say that I'm slightly amused to find myself introducing this collection. I read the stories in my early twenties, shortly after I'd started at York University, and even wrote to Dahl, suggesting that they would make a great TV series . . . which at least shows prescience on my behalf. He wrote me a very nice letter back saying that they were already in production, and there aren't many writers of his stature who would have taken the time. Today, part of me feels that I've finally been invited to the dinner party . . . though only as the butler. Even so, I am more than happy to be here. I have always loved the stories and I'm glad to share them with a new generation.

Some of them are more familiar than others. 'William and Mary' is one of the most memorable, if only because of the last image, the unspeakable fate that befalls William Pearl who has actually died – after a fashion – before the story begins. Alfred Knopf, Dahl's publisher, said it made him physically sick when he read it. It's unusual to think of Dahl as a sci-fi author, but of course personal circumstance forced him to take an interest in medicine and he tells an unlikely tale with complete authority. I cannot think of anyone who has taken the petty annoyances of an unhappy marriage and spun them to such extremes.

In the same arena, there's the sad tale of Mrs Bixby and her efforts to hang on to a mink coat ('Mrs Bixby and the Colonel's Coat'), and Cyril Boggis with his plan to steal a priceless Chippendale commode ('Parson's Pleasure'). This latter was the part played by John Gielgud. Both these stories take quite small incidents and spin out of them a narrative that illuminates – if that's the right word – something about the human condition, albeit its murkier side. In essence, shouldn't a short story aspire to do exactly that? This collection also houses an undisputed masterpiece of short-story writing, 'Pig'. Donald Sturrock, Dahl's first-rate biographer, describes it as 'the most misanthropic tale he ever penned' and it's worth considering for a moment as it contains so many of the hallmarks we have come to know as Dahlesque.

There's a nurse called McPottle and an aunt called Glosspan. The hero's parents are hastily killed in bizarre circumstances, in this case gunned down by 'cops, all of whom had received medals before for killing robbers'. Brought up as a vegetarian, the hero (whose name is Lexington) has the misfortune to visit Manhattan, where he tastes meat for the first time. 'What I have here on my plate is without doubt the most delicious thing I have ever tasted.' Dahl wrote about chocolate in much the same way, and indeed a love of food pervades his writing. He even produced a couple of cookery books. And yet 'Pig' is not exactly a children's story. Lexington's discovery leads him to yet another gruesome fate. Nobody in their right mind would want to be a character in a Roald Dahl short story. Lexington's demise is described with that glee and relish you find in all Dahl's best work, and at the same time it seems almost completely random.

Which begs the question: who are these stories actually for? I'm not sure it's easy to say, and it may be that even Dahl wasn't entirely certain himself when he wrote them. One or two of them – 'The Wonderful Story of Henry Sugar', for example – are delightful and inoffensive and were supposedly aimed at 'older children'. I also love the energy and humour of 'The Hitch-hiker', which has as its main character a brilliant pickpocket called Michael Fish, a man who could have appeared in any of Dahl's major novels. But others are more troubling. What are we to make of 'Bitch', for example? It's got a splendid set-up with the mad olfactory chemist, Henry Biotte, creating a new perfume that will change the world. Once again, Dahl has clearly done his research, and the whole premise could be said to have foreshadowed Patrick Süskind's brilliant novel *Perfume*, which turned up ten years later. But 'Bitch' makes for uncomfortable reading as it leads to what is effectively rape, even if it's rape with a smile. 'I looked down and saw that my beloved sexual organ was three feet long and thick to match.' It may not be quite what lovers of *Matilda* expect.

Some of these stories are so macabre that you have to wonder what was going on in the head of the man who wrote them. In 'Georgy Porgy' the hero – a 31-year-old vicar – has a phobia about women caused by seeing a rabbit devour its newborn baby. The conclusion to this cheerful tale will certainly keep you awake at night. And I'm not quite sure what to make of 'The Swan', either. We're used to seeing bullies in Dahl's work, but although Raymond and Ernie might be distantly related to such villains as Boggis, Bunce and Bean (*The Fantastic Mr Fox*), they take cruelty and sadism to a whole new level. At the same time, this story has one of the strangest and most poetical endings you'll ever come across. It's fair to say that no one else has ever written anything like it.

Whatever my own – occasional – misgivings, I think it's excellent that Penguin has chosen to include so many disparate stories in this collection. Roald Dahl had an extraordinary imagination, and here it is revealed in all its diverse manifestations. Sly, shocking, disturbing, mischievous or downright malevolent, Dahl caters to every taste. If you read Dahl as a child, here is a chance to reacquaint yourself with him. There are very few authors writing what might be called 'crossover' fiction, which is to say, building a bridge between young and adult fiction, but that is just what Dahl achieves. He finds the child in the adult and the adult in the child and, with a little smile, he sticks the knife in both.

The Way Up to Heaven

First published in the *New Yorker*,
27 February 1954

All her life, Mrs Foster had had an almost pathological
fear of missing a train, a plane, a boat or even a theatre
curtain. In other respects, she was not a particularly
nervous woman, but the mere thought of being late on
occasions like these would throw her into such a state of
nerves that she would begin to twitch. It was nothing
much – just a tiny vellicating muscle in the corner of the
left eye, like a secret wink – but the annoying thing was
that it refused to disappear until an hour or so after the
train or plane or whatever it was had been safely caught.

It is really extraordinary how in certain people a simple
apprehension about a thing like catching a train can grow
into a serious obsession. At least half an hour before it
was time to leave the house for the station, Mrs Foster
would step out of the elevator all ready to go, with hat and
coat and gloves, and then, being quite unable to sit down,
she would flutter and fidget about from room to room
until her husband, who must have been well aware of her
state, finally emerged from his privacy and suggested in a
cool dry voice that perhaps they had better get going now,
had they not?

Mr Foster may possibly have had a right to be irritated
by this foolishness of his wife's, but he could have had no

1

excuse for increasing her misery by keeping her waiting unnecessarily. Mind you, it is by no means certain that this is what he did, yet whenever they were to go somewhere, his timing was so accurate – just a minute or two late, you understand – and his manner so bland that it was hard to believe he wasn't purposely inflicting a nasty private little torture of his own on the unhappy lady. And one thing he must have known – that she would never dare to call out and tell him to hurry. He had disciplined her too well for that. He must also have known that if he was prepared to wait even beyond the last moment of safety, he could drive her nearly into hysterics. On one or two special occasions in the later years of their married life, it seemed almost as though he had *wanted* to miss the train simply in order to intensify the poor woman's suffering.

Assuming (though one cannot be sure) that the husband was guilty, what made his attitude doubly unreasonable was the fact that, with the exception of this one small irrepressible foible, Mrs Foster was and always had been a good and loving wife. For over thirty years, she had served him loyally and well. There was no doubt about this. Even she, a very modest woman, was aware of it, and although she had for years refused to let herself believe that Mr Foster would ever consciously torment her, there had been times recently when she had caught herself beginning to wonder.

Mr Eugene Foster, who was nearly seventy years old, lived with his wife in a large six-storey house on East Sixty-second Street, and they had four servants. It was a gloomy place, and few people came to visit them. But on this particular morning in January, the house had come alive and there was a great deal of bustling about. One maid was distributing bundles of dust sheets to every room, while another was draping them over the furniture. The butler was bringing down suitcases and putting them in the hall. The cook kept popping up from the kitchen to have a word with the butler, and Mrs Foster herself, in an old-fashioned fur coat and with a black hat on the top of her head, was flying from room to room and pretending to supervise these operations. Actually, she was thinking of nothing at all except that she was going to miss her plane if her husband didn't come out of his study soon and get ready.

'What time is it, Walker?' she said to the butler as she passed him.

'It's ten minutes past nine, Madam.'

'And has the car come?'

'Yes, Madam, it's waiting. I'm just going to put the luggage in now.'

'It takes an hour to get to Idlewild,' she said. 'My plane leaves at eleven. I have to be there half an hour beforehand for the formalities. I shall be late. I just *know* I'm going to be late.'

'I think you have plenty of time, Madam,' the butler said kindly. 'I warned Mr Foster that you must leave at nine fifteen. There's still another five minutes.'

'Yes, Walker, I know, I know. But get the luggage in quickly, will you please?'

She began walking up and down the hall, and whenever the butler came by, she asked him the time. This, she kept telling herself, was the *one* plane she must not miss. It had taken her months to persuade her husband to allow her to go. If she missed it, he might easily decide that she should cancel the whole thing. And the trouble was that he insisted on coming to the airport to see her off.

'Dear God,' she said aloud, 'I'm going to miss it. I know, I know, I *know* I'm going to miss it.' The little muscle beside the left eye was twitching madly now. The eyes themselves were very close to tears.

'What time is it, Walker?'

'It's eighteen minutes past, Madam.'

'Now I really *will* miss it!' she cried. 'Oh, I wish he would come!'

This was an important journey for Mrs Foster. She was going all alone to Paris to visit her daughter, her only child, who was married to a Frenchman. Mrs Foster didn't care much for the Frenchman, but she was fond of her daughter, and, more than that, she had developed a great yearning to set eyes on her three grandchildren. She knew them only from the many photographs that she had received and that she kept putting up all over the house. They were beautiful, these children. She doted on them, and each time a new picture arrived, she would carry it away and sit with it for a long time, staring at it lovingly and searching the small faces for signs of that old satisfying blood likeness that meant so much. And now, lately, she had come more and more to feel that she did not really wish to live out her days in a place where she could not be near these children, and have them visit her, and take them for walks, and buy them presents, and watch them grow. She knew, of course, that it was wrong and in

a way disloyal to have thoughts like these while her husband was still alive. She knew also that although he was no
longer active in his many enterprises, he would never consent to leave New York and live in Paris. It was a miracle
that he had ever agreed to let her fly over there alone for
six weeks to visit them. But, oh, how she wished she could
live there always, and be close to them!

'Walker, what time is it?'

'Twenty-two minutes past, Madam.'

As he spoke, a door opened and Mr Foster came into
the hall. He stood for a moment, looking intently at his
wife, and she looked back at him – at this diminutive but
still quite dapper old man with the huge bearded face that
bore such an astonishing resemblance to those old photographs of Andrew Carnegie.

'Well,' he said, 'I suppose perhaps we'd better get going
fairly soon if you want to catch that plane.'

'*Yes*, dear – *yes*! Everything's ready. The car's waiting.'

'That's good,' he said. With his head over to one side,
he was watching her closely. He had a peculiar way of
cocking the head and then moving it in a series of small,
rapid jerks. Because of this and because he was clasping
his hands up high in front of him, near the chest, he was
somehow like a squirrel standing there – a quick clever old
squirrel from the Park.

'Here's Walker with your coat, dear. Put it on.'

'I'll be with you in a moment,' he said. 'I'm just going to
wash my hands.'

She waited for him, and the tall butler stood beside her,
holding the coat and the hat.

'Walker, will I miss it?'

'No, Madam,' the butler said. 'I think you'll make it all right.'

Then Mr Foster appeared again, and the butler helped him on with his coat. Mrs Foster hurried outside and got into the hired Cadillac. Her husband came after her, but he walked down the steps of the house slowly, pausing half-way to observe the sky and to sniff the cold morning air.

'It looks a bit foggy,' he said as he sat down beside her in the car. 'And it's always worse out there at the airport. I shouldn't be surprised if the flight's cancelled already.'

'Don't say that, dear – *please*.'

They didn't speak again until the car had crossed over the river to Long Island.

'I arranged everything with the servants,' Mr Foster said. 'They're all going off today. I gave them half pay for six weeks and told Walker I'd send him a telegram when we wanted them back.'

'Yes,' she said. 'He told me.'

'I'll move into the club tonight. It'll be a nice change staying at the club.'

'Yes, dear. I'll write to you.'

'I'll call in at the house occasionally to see that every-thing's all right and to pick up the mail.'

'But don't you really think Walker should stay there all the time to look after things?' she asked meekly.

'Nonsense. It's quite unnecessary. And anyway, I'd have to pay him full wages.'

'Oh yes,' she said. 'Of course.'

'What's more, you never know what people get up to

when they're left alone in a house,' Mr Foster announced, and with that he took out a cigar and, after snipping off the end with a silver cutter, lit it with a gold lighter.

She sat still in the car with her hands clasped together tight under the rug.

'Will you write to me?' she asked.

'I'll see,' he said. 'But I doubt it. You know I don't hold with letter-writing unless there's something specific to say.'

'Yes, dear, I know. So don't you bother.'

They drove on, along Queens Boulevard, and as they approached the flat marshland on which Idlewild is built, the fog began to thicken and the car had to slow down.

'Oh dear!' cried Mrs Foster. 'I'm *sure* I'm going to miss it now! What time is it?'

'Stop fussing,' the old man said. 'It doesn't matter anyway. It's bound to be cancelled now. They never fly in this sort of weather. I don't know why you bothered to come out.'

She couldn't be sure, but it seemed to her that there was suddenly a new note in his voice, and she turned to look at him. It was difficult to observe any change in his expression under all that hair. The mouth was what counted. She wished, as she had so often before, that she could see the mouth clearly. The eyes never showed anything except when he was in a rage.

'Of course,' he went on, 'if by any chance it *does* go, then I agree with you – you'll be certain to miss it now. Why don't you resign yourself to that?'

She turned away and peered through the window at the fog. It seemed to be getting thicker as they went along, and now she could only just make out the edge of the road and the margin of grassland beyond it. She knew that her husband was still looking at her. She glanced back at him again, and this time she noticed with a kind of horror that he was staring intently at the little place in the corner of her left eye where she could feel the muscle twitching.

'Won't you?' he said.

'Won't I what?'

'Be sure to miss it now if it goes. We can't drive fast in this muck.'

He didn't speak to her any more after that. The car crawled on and on. The driver had a yellow lamp directed on to the edge of the road and this helped him to keep going. Other lights, some white and some yellow, kept coming out of the fog towards them, and there was an especially bright one that followed close behind them all the time.

Suddenly, the driver stopped the car.

'There!' Mr Foster cried. 'We're stuck. I knew it.'

'No, sir,' the driver said, turning round. 'We made it. This is the airport.'

Without a word, Mrs Foster jumped out and hurried through the main entrance into the building. There was a mass of people inside, mostly disconsolate passengers standing around the ticket counters. She pushed her way through and spoke to the clerk.

'Yes,' he said. 'Your flight is temporarily postponed.

8

But please don't go away. We're expecting this weather to clear any moment.'

She went back to her husband who was still sitting in the car and told him the news. 'But don't you wait, dear,' she said. 'There's no sense in that.'

'I won't,' he answered. 'So long as the driver can get me back. Can you get me back, driver?'

'I think so,' the man said.

'Is the luggage out?'

'Yes, sir.'

'Good-bye, dear,' Mrs Foster said, leaning into the car and giving her husband a small kiss on the coarse grey fur of his cheek.

'Good-bye,' he answered. 'Have a good trip.'

The car drove off, and Mrs Foster was left alone.

The rest of the day was a sort of nightmare for her. She sat for hour after hour on a bench, as close to the airline counter as possible, and every thirty minutes or so she would get up and ask the clerk if the situation had changed. She always received the same reply – that she must continue to wait, because the fog might blow away at any moment. It wasn't until after six in the evening that the loudspeakers finally announced that the flight had been postponed until eleven o'clock the next morning.

Mrs Foster didn't quite know what to do when she heard this news. She stayed sitting on her bench for at least another half-hour, wondering, in a tired, hazy sort of way, where she might go to spend the night. She hated to leave the airport. She didn't wish to see her husband. She was terrified that in one way or another he would eventually manage to prevent her from getting to France. She would have liked to remain just where she was, sitting on the bench the whole night through. That would be the safest. But she was already exhausted, and it didn't take her long to realize that this was a ridiculous thing for an elderly lady to do. So in the end she went to a phone and called the house.

Her husband, who was on the point of leaving for the club, answered it himself. She told him the news, and asked whether the servants were still there.

'They've all gone,' he said.

'In that case, dear, I'll just get myself a room somewhere for the night. And don't you bother yourself about it at all.'

'That would be foolish,' he said. 'You've got a large house here at your disposal. Use it.'

'But, dear, it's *empty.*'

'Then I'll stay with you myself.'

'There's no food in the house. There's nothing.'

'Then eat before you come in. Don't be so stupid, woman. Everything you do, you seem to want to make a fuss about it.'

'Yes,' she said. 'I'm sorry. I'll get myself a sandwich here, and then I'll come on in.'

Outside, the fog had cleared a little, but it was still a long, slow drive in the taxi, and she didn't arrive back at the house on Sixty-second Street until fairly late.

Her husband emerged from his study when he heard her coming in. 'Well,' he said, standing by the study door, 'how was Paris?'

THE WAY UP TO HEAVEN

'We leave at eleven in the morning,' she answered. 'It's definite.'

'You mean if the fog clears.'

'It's clearing now. There's a wind coming up.'

'You look tired,' he said. 'You must have had an anxious day.'

'It wasn't very comfortable. I think I'll go straight to bed.'

'I've ordered a car for the morning,' he said. 'Nine o'clock.'

'Oh, thank you, dear. And I certainly hope you're not going to bother to come all the way out again to see me off.'

'No,' he said slowly. 'I don't think I will. But there's no reason why you shouldn't drop me at the club on your way.'

She looked at him, and at that moment he seemed to be standing a long way off from her, beyond some borderline. He was suddenly so small and far away that she couldn't be sure what he was doing, or what he was thinking, or even what he was.

'The club is downtown,' she said. 'It isn't on the way to the airport.'

'But you'll have plenty of time, my dear. Don't you want to drop me at the club?'

'Oh, yes – of course.'

'That's good. Then I'll see you in the morning at nine.'

She went up to her bedroom on the third floor, and she was so exhausted from her day that she fell asleep soon after she lay down.

Next morning, Mrs Foster was up early, and by eight thirty she was downstairs and ready to leave.

Shortly after nine, her husband appeared. 'Did you make any coffee?' he asked.

'No, dear. I thought you'd get a nice breakfast at the club. The car is here. It's been waiting. I'm all ready to go.'

They were standing in the hall – they always seemed to be meeting in the hall nowadays – she with her hat and coat and purse, he in a curiously cut Edwardian jacket with high lapels.

'Your luggage?'

'It's at the airport.'

'Ah yes,' he said. 'Of course. And if you're going to take me to the club first, I suppose we'd better get going fairly soon, hadn't we?'

'Yes!' she cried. 'Oh, yes – *please*!'

'I'm just going to get a few cigars. I'll be right with you. You get in the car.'

She turned and went out to where the chauffeur was standing, and he opened the car door for her as she approached.

'What time is it?' she asked him.

'About nine fifteen.'

Mr Foster came out five minutes later, and watching him as he walked slowly down the steps, she noticed that his legs were like goat's legs in those narrow stovepipe trousers that he wore. As on the day before, he paused halfway down to sniff the air and to examine the sky. The weather was still not quite clear, but there was a wisp of sun coming through the mist.

'Perhaps you'll be lucky this time,' he said as he settled himself beside her in the car.

'Hurry, please,' she said to the chauffeur. 'Don't bother about the rug. I'll arrange the rug. Please get going. I'm late.'

The man went back to his seat behind the wheel and started the engine.

'*Just* a moment!' Mr Foster said suddenly. 'Hold it a moment, chauffeur, will you?'

'What is it, dear?' She saw him searching the pockets of his overcoat.

'I had a little present I wanted you to take to Ellen,' he said. 'Now, where on earth is it? I'm sure I had it in my hand as I came down.'

'I never saw you carrying anything. What sort of present?'

'A little box wrapped up in white paper. I forgot to give it to you yesterday. I don't want to forget it today.'

'A little box!' Mrs Foster cried. 'I never saw any little box!' She began hunting frantically in the back of the car.

Her husband continued searching through the pockets of his coat. Then he unbuttoned the coat and felt around in his jacket. 'Confound it,' he said, 'I must've left it in my bedroom. I won't be a moment.'

'Oh, *please*!' she cried. 'We haven't got time! *Please* leave it! You can mail it. It's only one of those silly combs anyway. You're always giving her combs.'

'And what's wrong with combs, may I ask?' he said, furious that she should have forgotten herself for once.

'Nothing, dear, I'm sure. But . . .'

'Stay here!' he commanded. 'I'm going to get it.'

'Be quick, dear! Oh, *please* be quick!'

She sat still, waiting and waiting.

'Chauffeur, what time is it?'

The man had a wristwatch, which he consulted. 'I make it nearly nine thirty.'

'Can we get to the airport in an hour?'

'Just about.'

At this point, Mrs Foster suddenly spotted a corner of something white wedged down in the crack of the seat on the side where her husband had been sitting. She reached over and pulled out a small paper-wrapped box, and at the same time she couldn't help noticing that it was wedged down firm and deep, as though with the help of a pushing hand.

'Here it is!' she cried. 'I've found it! Oh dear, and now he'll be up there forever searching for it! Chauffeur, quickly – run in and call him down, will you please?'

The chauffeur, a man with a small rebellious Irish mouth, didn't care very much for any of this, but he climbed out of the car and went up the steps to the front door of the house. Then he turned and came back. 'Door's locked,' he announced. 'You got a key?'

'Yes – wait a minute.' She began hunting madly in her purse. The little face was screwed up tight with anxiety, the lips pushed outwards like a sprout.

'Here it is! No – I'll go myself. It'll be quicker. I know where he'll be.'

She hurried out of the car and up the steps to the front

door, holding the key in one hand. She slid the key into the keyhole and was about to turn it – and then she stopped. Her head came up, and she stood there absolutely motionless, her whole body arrested right in the middle of all this hurry to turn the key and get into the house, and she waited – five, six, seven, eight, nine, ten seconds, she waited. The way she was standing there, with her head in the air and the body so tense, it seemed as though she were listening for the repetition of some sound that she had heard a moment before from a place far away inside the house.

Yes – quite obviously she was listening. Her whole attitude was a *listening* one. She appeared actually to be moving one of her ears closer and closer to the door. Now it was right up against the door, and for still another few seconds she remained in that position, head up, ear to door, hand on key, about to enter but not entering, trying instead, or so it seemed, to hear and to analyse these sounds that were coming faintly from this place deep within the house.

Then, all at once, she sprang to life again. She withdrew the key from the door and came running back down the steps.

'It's too late!' she cried to the chauffeur. 'I can't wait for him, I simply can't. I'll miss the plane. Hurry now, driver, hurry! To the airport!'

The chauffeur, had he been watching her closely, might have noticed that her face had turned absolutely white and that the whole expression had suddenly altered. There was no longer that rather soft and silly look. A peculiar hardness had settled itself upon the features. The little mouth, usually so flabby, was now tight and thin, the eyes were bright, and the voice, when she spoke, carried a new note of authority.

'Hurry, driver, hurry!'

'Isn't your husband travelling with you?' the man asked, astonished.

'Certainly not! I was only going to drop him at the club. It won't matter. He'll understand. He'll get a cab. Don't sit there talking, man. *Get going!* I've got a plane to catch for Paris!'

With Mrs Foster urging him from the back seat, the man drove fast all the way, and she caught her plane with a few minutes to spare. Soon she was high up over the Atlantic, reclining comfortably in her aeroplane chair, listening to the hum of the motors, heading for Paris at last. The new mood was still with her. She felt remarkably strong and, in a queer sort of way, wonderful. She was a trifle breathless with it all, but this was more from pure astonishment at what she had done than anything else, and as the plane flew farther and farther away from New York and East Sixty-second Street, a great sense of calmness began to settle upon her. By the time she reached Paris, she was just as strong and cool and calm as she could wish.

She met her grandchildren, and they were even more beautiful in the flesh than in their photographs. They were like angels, she told herself, so beautiful they were. And every day she took them for walks, and fed them cakes, and bought them presents, and told them charming stories.

Once a week, on Tuesdays, she wrote a letter to her husband – a nice, chatty letter – full of news and gossip, which always ended with the words 'Now be sure to take your meals regularly, dear, although this is something I'm afraid you may not be doing when I'm not with you.'

When the six weeks were up, everybody was sad that she had to return to America, to her husband. Everybody, that is, except her. Surprisingly, she didn't seem to mind as much as one might have expected, and when she kissed them all good-bye, there was something in her manner and in the things she said that appeared to hint at the possibility of a return in the not too distant future.

However, like the faithful wife she was, she did not overstay her time. Exactly six weeks after she had arrived, she sent a cable to her husband and caught the plane back to New York.

Arriving at Idlewild, Mrs Foster was interested to observe that there was no car to meet her. It is possible that she might even have been a little amused. But she was extremely calm and did not overtip the porter who helped her into a taxi with her baggage.

New York was colder than Paris, and there were lumps of dirty snow lying in the gutters of the streets. The taxi drew up before the house on Sixty-second Street, and Mrs Foster persuaded the driver to carry her two large cases to the top of the steps. Then she paid him off and rang the bell. She waited, but there was no answer. Just to make sure, she rang again, and she could hear it tinkling shrilly far away in the pantry, at the back of the house. But still no one came.

So she took out her own key and opened the door herself.

The first thing she saw as she entered was a great pile of mail lying on the floor where it had fallen after being slipped through the letterbox. The place was dark and cold. A dust sheet was still draped over the grandfather clock. In spite of the cold, the atmosphere was peculiarly oppressive, and there was a faint but curious odour in the air that she had never smelled before.

She walked quickly across the hall and disappeared for a moment round the corner to the left, at the back. There was something deliberate and purposeful about this action; she had the air of a woman who is off to investigate a rumour or to confirm a suspicion. And when she returned a few seconds later, there was a little glimmer of satisfaction on her face.

She paused in the centre of the hall, as though wondering what to do next. Then suddenly, she turned and went across into her husband's study. On the desk she found his address book, and after hunting through it for a while she picked up the phone and dialled a number.

'Hello,' she said. 'Listen – this is Nine East Sixty-second Street . . . Yes, that's right. Could you send someone round as soon as possible, do you think? Yes, it seems to be stuck between the second and third floors. At least, that's where the indicator's pointing . . . Right away? Oh, that's very kind of you. You see, my legs aren't any too good for walking up a lot of stairs. Thank you so much. Good-bye.'

She replaced the receiver and sat there at her husband's desk, patiently waiting for the man who would be coming soon to repair the elevator.

Parson's Pleasure

First published in *Esquire* (April 1958)

Mr Boggis was driving the car slowly, leaning back comfortably in the seat with one elbow resting on the sill of the open window. How beautiful the countryside, he thought; how pleasant to see a sign or two of summer once again. The primroses especially. And the hawthorn. The hawthorn was exploding white and pink and red along the hedges and the primroses were growing underneath in little clumps, and it was beautiful.

He took one hand off the wheel and lit himself a cigarette. The best thing now, he told himself, would be to make for the top of Brill Hill. He could see it about half a mile ahead. And that must be the village of Brill, that cluster of cottages among the trees right on the very summit. Excellent. Not many of his Sunday sections had a nice elevation like that to work from.

He drove up the hill and stopped the car just short of the summit on the outskirts of the village. Then he got out and looked around. Down below, the countryside was spread out before him like a huge green carpet. He could see for miles. It was perfect. He took a pad and pencil from his pocket, leaned against the back of the car, and allowed his practised eye to travel slowly over the landscape.

He could see one medium farmhouse over on the right,

back in the fields, with a track leading to it from the road. There was another larger one beyond it. There was a house surrounded by tall elms that looked as though it might be a Queen Anne, and there were two likely farms away over on the left. Five places in all. That was about the lot in this direction.

Mr Boggis drew a rough sketch on his pad showing the position of each so that he'd be able to find them easily when he was down below, then he got back into the car and drove up through the village to the other side of the hill. From there he spotted six more possibles – five farms and one big white Georgian house. He studied the Georgian house through his binoculars. It had a clean prosperous look, and the garden was well ordered. That was a pity. He ruled it out immediately. There was no point in calling on the prosperous.

In this square then, in this section, there were ten possibles in all. Ten was a nice number, Mr Boggis told himself. Just the right amount for a leisurely afternoon's work. What time was it now? Twelve o'clock. He would have liked a pint of beer in the pub before he started, but on Sundays they didn't open until one. Very well, he would have it later. He glanced at the notes on his pad. He decided to take the Queen Anne first, the house with the elms. It had looked nicely dilapidated through the binoculars. The people there could probably do with some money. He was always lucky with Queen Annes, anyway. Mr Boggis climbed back into the car, released the handbrake, and began cruising slowly down the hill without the engine.

Apart from the fact that he was at this moment disguised in the uniform of a clergyman, there was nothing very sinister about Mr Cyril Boggis. By trade he was a dealer in antique furniture, with his own shop and showroom in the King's Road, Chelsea. His premises were not large, and generally he didn't do a great deal of business, but because he always bought cheap, very very cheap, and sold very very dear, he managed to make quite a tidy little income every year. He was a talented salesman, and when buying or selling a piece he could slide smoothly into whichever mood suited the client best. He could become grave and charming for the aged, obsequious for the rich, sober for the godly, masterful for the weak, mischievous for the widow, arch and saucy for the spinster. He was well aware of his gift, using it shamelessly on every possible occasion; and often, at the end of an unusually good performance, it was as much as he could do to prevent himself from turning aside and taking a bow or two as the thundering applause of the audience went rolling through the theatre.

In spite of this rather clownish quality of his, Mr Boggis was not a fool. In fact, it was said of him by some that he probably knew as much about French, English and Italian furniture as anyone else in London. He also had surprisingly good taste, and he was quick to recognize and reject an ungraceful design, however genuine the article might be. His real love, naturally, was for the work of the great eighteenth-century English designers, Ince, Mayhew, Chippendale, Robert Adam, Manwaring, Inigo Jones, Hepplewhite, Kent, Johnson, George Smith, Lock, Sheraton and the rest of them, but even with these he occasionally drew the line. He refused, for example, to allow a single piece from Chippendale's Chinese or Gothic period to come into his showroom, and the same was true of some of the heavier Italian designs of Robert Adam.

During the past few years, Mr Boggis had achieved considerable fame among his friends in the trade by his ability to produce unusual and often quite rare items with astonishing regularity. Apparently the man had a source of supply that was almost inexhaustible, a sort of private warehouse, and it seemed that all he had to do was to drive out to it once a week and help himself. Whenever they asked him where he got the stuff, he would smile knowingly and wink and murmur something about a little secret.

The idea behind Mr Boggis's little secret was a simple one, and it had come to him as a result of something that had happened on a certain Sunday afternoon nearly nine years before, while he was driving in the country.

He had gone out in the morning to visit his old mother, who lived in Sevenoaks, and on the way back the fan-belt on his car had broken, causing the engine to overheat and the water to boil away. He had got out of the car and walked to the nearest house, a smallish farm building about fifty yards off the road, and had asked the woman who answered the door if he could please have a jug of water.

While he was waiting for her to fetch it, he happened to glance in through the door to the living-room, and there, not five yards from where he was standing, he spotted something that made him so excited the sweat began to come out all over the top of his head. It was a large oak armchair of a type that he had only seen once before in his life. Each arm, as well as the panel at the back, was supported by a row of eight beautifully turned spindles. The back panel itself was decorated by an inlay of the most delicate floral design, and the head of a duck was carved to lie along half the length of either arm. Good God, he thought. This thing is late fifteenth century!

He poked his head in further through the door, and there, by heavens, was another of them on the other side of the fireplace!

He couldn't be sure, but two chairs like that must be worth at least a thousand pounds up in London. And oh, what beauties they were!

When the woman returned, Mr Boggis introduced himself and straight away asked if she would like to sell her chairs.

Dear me, she said. But why on earth should she want to sell her chairs?

No reason at all, except that he might be willing to give her a pretty nice price.

And how much would he give? They were definitely not for sale, but just out of curiosity, just for fun, you know, how much would he give?

Thirty-five pounds.

How much?

Thirty-five pounds.

Dear me, thirty-five pounds. Well, well, that was very interesting. She'd always thought they were valuable. They were very old. They were very comfortable too. She couldn't possibly do without them, not possibly. No, they were not for sale but thank you very much all the same.

They weren't really so very old, Mr Boggis told her, and they wouldn't be at all easy to sell, but it just happened that he had a client who rather liked that sort of thing. Maybe he could go up another two pounds – call it thirty-seven. How about that?

They bargained for half an hour, and of course in the end Mr Boggis got the chairs and agreed to pay her something less than a twentieth of their value.

That evening, driving back to London in his old station-wagon with the two fabulous chairs tucked away snugly in the back, Mr Boggis had suddenly been struck by what seemed to him to be a most remarkable idea.

Look here, he said. If there is good stuff in one farm-house, then why not in others? Why shouldn't he search for it? Why shouldn't he comb the countryside? He could do it on Sundays. In that way, it wouldn't interfere with his work at all. He never knew what to do with his Sundays.

So Mr Boggis bought maps, large-scale maps of all the counties around London, and with a fine pen he divided each of them up into a series of squares. Each of these squares covered an actual area of five miles by five, which was about as much territory, he estimated, as he could cope with on a single Sunday, were he to comb it thoroughly. He didn't want the towns and the villages. It was the comparatively isolated places, the large farmhouses and the rather dilapidated country mansions, that he was looking for; and in this way, if he did one square each Sunday, fifty-two squares a year, he would gradually cover every farm and every country house in the home counties.

But obviously there was a bit more to it than that. Country folk are a suspicious lot. So are the impoverished rich. You can't go about ringing their bells and expecting them to show you around their houses just for the asking, because they won't do it. That way you would never get beyond the front door. How then was he to gain admittance? Perhaps it would be best if he didn't let them know he was a dealer at all. He could be the telephone man, the plumber, the gas inspector. He could even be a clergyman . . .

From this point on, the whole scheme began to take on a more practical aspect. Mr Boggis ordered a large quantity of superior cards on which the following legend was engraved:

THE REVEREND
CYRIL WINNINGTON BOGGIS

President of the Society	*In association with*
for the Preservation of	*The Victoria and*
Rare Furniture	*Albert Museum*

From now on, every Sunday, he was going to be a nice old parson spending his holiday travelling around on a labour of love for the 'Society', compiling an inventory of the treasures that lay hidden in the country homes of England. And who in the world was going to kick him out when they heard that one?

Nobody.

And then, once he was inside, if he happened to spot something he really wanted, well – he knew a hundred different ways of dealing with that.

Rather to Mr Boggis's surprise, the scheme worked. In fact, the friendliness with which he was received in one house after another through the countryside was, in the beginning, quite embarrassing, even to him. A slice of cold pie, a glass of port, a cup of tea, a basket of plums, even a full sit-down Sunday dinner with the family, such things were constantly being pressed upon him. Sooner or later, of course, there had been some bad moments and a number of unpleasant incidents, but then nine years is more than four hundred Sundays, and that adds up to a great quantity of houses visited. All in all, it had been an interesting, exciting and lucrative business.

And now it was another Sunday and Mr Boggis was operating in the county of Buckinghamshire, in one of the most northerly squares on his map, about ten miles from Oxford, and as he drove down the hill and headed for his first house, the dilapidated Queen Anne, he began to get the feeling that this was going to be one of his lucky days.

He parked the car about a hundred yards from the gates and got out to walk the rest of the way. He never liked people to see his car until after a deal was completed. A dear old clergyman and a large station-wagon somehow never seemed quite right together. Also the short walk gave him time to examine the property closely from the outside and to assume the mood most likely to be suitable for the occasion.

Mr Boggis strode briskly up the drive. He was a small

fat-legged man with a belly. The face was round and rosy, quite perfect for the part, and the two large brown eyes that bulged out at you from this rosy face gave an impression of gentle imbecility. He was dressed in a black suit with the usual parson's dog-collar round his neck, and on his head a soft black hat. He carried an old oak walking-stick which lent him, in his opinion, a rather rustic easy-going air.

He approached the front door and rang the bell. He heard the sound of footsteps in the hall and the door opened and suddenly there stood before him, or rather above him, a gigantic woman dressed in riding-breeches. Even through the smoke of her cigarette he could smell the powerful odour of stables and horse manure that clung about her.

'Yes?' she asked, looking at him suspiciously. 'What is it you want?'

Mr Boggis, who half expected her to whinny any moment, raised his hat, made a little bow, and handed her his card. 'I do apologize for bothering you,' he said, and then he waited, watching her face as she read the message.

'I don't understand,' she said, handing back the card. 'What is it you want?'

Mr Boggis explained about the Society for the Preservation of Rare Furniture.

'This wouldn't by any chance be something to do with the Socialist Party?' she asked, staring at him fiercely from under a pair of pale bushy brows.

From then on, it was easy. A Tory in riding-breeches,

male or female, was always a sitting duck for Mr Boggis. He spent two minutes delivering an impassioned eulogy on the extreme Right Wing Conservative Party, then two more denouncing the Socialists. As a clincher, he made particular reference to the Bill that the Socialists had once introduced for the abolition of bloodsports in the country, and went on to inform his listener that his idea of heaven – 'though you better not tell the bishop, my dear' – was a place where one could hunt the fox, the stag and the hare with large packs of tireless hounds from morn till night every day of the week, including Sundays.

Watching her as he spoke, he could see the magic beginning to do its work. The woman was grinning now, showing Mr Boggis a set of enormous, slightly yellow teeth. 'Madam,' he cried, 'I beg of you, *please* don't get me started on Socialism.' At that point, she let out a great guffaw of laughter, raised an enormous red hand, and slapped him so hard on the shoulder that he nearly went over.

'Come in!' she shouted. 'I don't know what the hell you want, but come on in!'

Unfortunately, and rather surprisingly, there was nothing of any value in the whole house, and Mr Boggis, who never wasted time on barren territory, soon made his excuses and took his leave. The whole visit had taken less than fifteen minutes, and that, he told himself as he climbed back into his car and started off for the next place, was exactly as it should be.

From now on, it was all farmhouses, and the nearest was about half a mile up the road. It was a large half-timbered brick building of considerable age, and there was a magnificent pear tree still in blossom covering almost the whole of the south wall.

Mr Boggis knocked on the door. He waited, but no one came. He knocked again, but still there was no answer, so he wandered round the back to look for the farmer among the cowsheds. There was no one there either. He guessed that they must all still be in church, so he began peering in the windows to see if he could spot anything interesting. There was nothing in the dining-room. Nothing in the library either. He tried the next window, the living-room, and there, right under his nose, in the little alcove that the window made, he saw a beautiful thing, a semicircular card-table in mahogany, richly veneered and in the style of Hepplewhite, built around 1780.

'Ah-ha,' he said aloud, pressing his face hard against the glass. 'Well done, Boggis.'

But that was not all. There was a chair there as well, a single chair, and if he were not mistaken it was of an even finer quality than the table. Another Hepplewhite, wasn't it? And oh, what a beauty! The lattices on the back were finely carved with the honeysuckle, the husk and the pat-erae, the caning on the seat was original, the legs were very gracefully turned and the two back ones had that peculiar outward splay that meant so much. It was an exquisite chair. 'Before this day is done,' Mr Boggis said softly, 'I shall have the pleasure of sitting down upon that lovely seat.' He never bought a chair without doing this. It was a favourite test of his, and it was always an intriguing sight to see him lowering himself delicately into the seat, wait-ing for the 'give', expertly gauging the precise but infinitesimal degree of shrinkage that the years had caused in the mortise and dovetail joints.

But there was no hurry, he told himself. He would return here later. He had the whole afternoon before him.

The next farm was situated some way back in the fields, and in order to keep his car out of sight, Mr Boggis had to leave it on the road and walk about six hundred yards along a straight track that led directly into the back yard of the farmhouse. This place, he noticed as he approached, was a good deal smaller than the last, and he didn't hold out much hope for it. It looked rambling and dirty, and some of the sheds were clearly in bad repair.

There were three men standing in a close group in a corner of the yard, and one of them had two large black greyhounds with him, on leashes. When the men caught sight of Mr Boggis walking forward in his black suit and parson's collar, they stopped talking and seemed suddenly to stiffen and freeze, becoming absolutely still, motionless, three faces turned towards him, watching him suspiciously as he approached.

The oldest of the three was a stumpy man with a wide frog-mouth and small shifty eyes, and although Mr Boggis didn't know it, his name was Rummins and he was the owner of the farm.

The tall youth beside him, who appeared to have something wrong with one eye, was Bert, the son of Rummins.

The shortish flat-faced man with a narrow corrugated brow and immensely broad shoulders was Claud. Claud had dropped in on Rummins in the hope of getting a piece of pork or ham out of him from the pig that had been killed the day before. Claud knew about the killing – the noise of it had carried far across the fields – and he also knew that a man should have a government permit to do that sort of thing, and that Rummins didn't have one.

'Good afternoon,' Mr Boggis said. 'Isn't it a lovely day.'

None of the three men moved. At that moment they were all thinking precisely the same thing – that somehow or other this clergyman, who was certainly not the local fellow, had been sent to poke his nose into their business and to report what he found to the government.

'What beautiful dogs,' Mr Boggis said. 'I must say I've never been greyhound-racing myself, but they tell me it's a fascinating sport.'

Again the silence, and Mr Boggis glanced quickly from Rummins to Bert, then to Claud, then back again to Rummins, and he noticed that each of them had the same peculiar expression on his face, something between a jeer and a challenge, with a contemptuous curl to the mouth, and a sneer around the nose.

'Might I inquire if you are the owner?' Mr Boggis asked, undaunted, addressing himself to Rummins.

'What is it you want?'

'I do apologize for troubling you, especially on a Sunday.'

Mr Boggis offered his card and Rummins took it and held it up close to his face. The other two didn't move, but their eyes swivelled over to one side, trying to see.

'And what exactly might you be wanting?' Rummins asked.

For the second time that morning, Mr Boggis explained at some length the aims and ideals of the Society for the Preservation of Rare Furniture.

'We don't have any,' Rummins told him when it was over. 'You're wasting your time.'

'Now, just a minute, sir,' Mr Boggis said, raising a finger. 'The last man who said that to me was an old farmer down in Sussex, and when he finally let me into his house, d'you know what I found? A dirty-looking old chair in the corner of the kitchen, and it turned out to be worth *four hundred pounds*! I showed him how to sell it, and he bought himself a new tractor with the money.'

'What on earth are you talking about?' Claud said. 'There ain't no chair in the world worth four hundred pound.'

'Excuse me,' Mr Boggis answered primly, 'but there are plenty of chairs in England worth more than twice that figure. And you know where they are? They're tucked away in the farms and cottages all over the country, with the owners using them as steps and ladders and standing on them with hobnailed boots to reach a pot of jam out of the top cupboard or to hang a picture. This is the truth I'm telling you, my friend.'

Rummins shifted uneasily on his feet. 'You mean to say all you want to do is go inside and stand there in the middle of the room and look around?'

'Exactly,' Mr Boggis said. He was at last beginning to sense what the trouble might be. 'I don't want to pry into your cupboards or into your larder. I just want to look at the furniture to see if you happen to have any treasures here, and then I can write about them in our Society magazine.'

'You know what I think?' Rummins said, fixing him with his small wicked eyes. 'I think you're after buying the stuff yourself. Why else would you be going to all this trouble?'

'Oh, dear me. I only wish I had the money. Of course, if I saw something that I took a great fancy to, and it wasn't beyond my means, I might be tempted to make an offer. But alas, that rarely happens.'

'Well,' Rummins said, 'I don't suppose there's any harm in your taking a look around if that's all you want.' He led the way across the yard to the back door of the farm-house, and Mr Boggis followed him; so did the son, Bert, and Claud with his two dogs. They went through the kitchen, where the only furniture was a cheap deal table with a dead chicken lying on it, and they emerged into a fairly large, exceedingly filthy living-room.

And there it was! Mr Boggis saw it at once, and he stopped dead in his tracks and gave a little shrill gasp of shock. Then he stood there for five, ten, fifteen seconds at least, staring like an idiot, unable to believe, not daring to believe what he saw before him. It *couldn't* be true, not possibly! But the longer he stared, the more true it began to seem. After all, there it was standing against the wall right in front of him, as real and as solid as the house itself. And who in the world could possibly make a mistake about a thing like that? Admittedly it was painted white, but that made not the slightest difference. Some idiot had done that. The paint could easily be stripped off. But good God! Just look at it! And in a place like this!

At that point, Mr Boggis became aware of the three men, Rummins, Bert and Claud, standing together in a group over by the fireplace, watching him intently. They had seen him stop and gasp and stare, and they must have seen his face turning red, or maybe it was white, but in any event they had seen enough to spoil the whole goddam business if he didn't do something about it quick. In a flash, Mr Boggis clapped one hand over his heart, staggered to the nearest chair, and collapsed into it, breathing heavily.

'What's the matter with you?' Claud asked.

'It's nothing,' he gasped. 'I'll be all right in a minute. Please – a glass of water. It's my heart.'

Bert fetched him the water, handed it to him, and stayed close beside him, staring down at him with a fatuous leer on his face.

'I thought maybe you were looking at something,' Rummins said. The wide frog-mouth widened a fraction farther into a crafty grin, showing the stubs of several broken teeth.

'No, no,' Mr Boggis said. 'Oh dear me, no. It's just my heart. I'm so sorry. It happens every now and then. But it goes away quite quickly. I'll be all right in a couple of minutes.'

He *must* have time to think, he told himself. More important still, he must have time to compose himself thoroughly before he said another word. Take it gently, Boggis. And whatever you do, keep calm. These people may be ignorant, but they are not stupid. They are suspicious and wary and sly. And if it is really true – no it *can't* be, it *can't* be true . . .

He was holding one hand up over his eyes in a gesture of pain, and now, very carefully, secretly, he made a little crack between two of the fingers and peeked through.

Sure enough, the thing was still there, and on this occasion he took a good long look at it. Yes – he had been right the first time! There wasn't the slightest doubt about it! It was really unbelievable!

What he saw was a piece of furniture that any expert would have given almost anything to acquire. To a layman, it might not have appeared particularly impressive, especially when covered over as it was with dirty white paint, but to Mr Boggis it was a dealer's dream. He knew, as does every other dealer in Europe and America, that among the most celebrated and coveted examples of eighteenth-century English furniture in existence are the three famous pieces known as 'The Chippendale Commodes'. He knew their history backwards – that the first was 'discovered' in 1920, in a house at Moreton-on-the-Marsh, and was sold at Sotheby's the same year; that the other two turned up in the same auction rooms a year later, both coming out of Rainham Hall, Norfolk. They all fetched enormous prices. He couldn't quite remember the exact figure for the first one, or even the second, but he knew for certain that the last one to be sold had fetched thirty-nine hundred guineas. And that was in 1921! Today the same piece would surely be worth ten thousand pounds. Some man, Mr Boggis couldn't remember his name, had made a study of these commodes fairly recently and had proved that all three must have come from the same workshop, for the veneers were all from the same log, and the same set of templates had been used in the construction of each. No invoices had been found for any of them, but all the experts were agreed that these three commodes could have been executed only by Thomas Chippendale himself, with his own hands, at the most exalted period in his career.

And here, Mr Boggis kept telling himself as he peered cautiously through the crack in his fingers, here was the fourth Chippendale Commode! And *he* had found it! He would be rich! He would also be famous! Each of the other three was known throughout the furniture world by a special name – the Chastleton Commode, the First Rainham Commode, the Second Rainham Commode. This one would go down in history as the Boggis Commode! Just imagine the faces of the boys up there in London when they got a look at it tomorrow morning! And the luscious offers coming in from the big fellows over in the West End – Frank Partridge, Mallett, Jetley and the rest of them! There would be a picture of it in *The Times*, and it would say, 'The very fine Chippendale Commode which was recently discovered by Mr Cyril Boggis, a London dealer . . .' Dear God, what a stir he was going to make!

This one here, Mr Boggis thought, was almost exactly similar to the Second Rainham Commode. (All three, the Chastleton and the two Rainhams, differed from one another in a number of small ways.) It was a most impressive handsome affair built in the French Rococo style of Chippendale's Director period, a kind of large fat chest-of-drawers set upon four carved and fluted legs that raised it about a foot from the ground. There were six drawers in all, two long ones in the middle and two shorter ones on either side. The serpentine front was magnificently ornamented along the top and sides and bottom, and also vertically between each set of drawers, with intricate carvings of festoons and scrolls and clusters. The brass handles, although partly obscured by white paint, appeared to be superb. It was, of course, a rather 'heavy' piece, but the design had been executed with such elegance and grace that the heaviness was in no way offensive.

'How're you feeling now?' Mr Boggis heard someone saying.

'Thank you, thank you, I'm much better already. It passes quickly. My doctor says it's nothing to worry about really so long as I rest for a few minutes whenever it happens. Ah yes,' he said, raising himself slowly to his feet. 'That's better. I'm all right now.'

A trifle unsteadily, he began to move around the room examining the furniture, one piece at a time, commenting upon it briefly. He could see at once that apart from the commode it was a very poor lot.

'Nice oak table,' he said. 'But I'm afraid it's not old enough to be of any interest. Good comfortable chairs, but quite modern, yes, quite modern. Now this cupboard, well, it's rather attractive, but again, not valuable. This chest-of-drawers' – he walked casually past the Chippendale Commode and gave it a little contemptuous flip with his fingers – 'worth a few pounds, I dare say, but no more. A rather crude reproduction, I'm afraid. Probably made in Victorian times. Did you paint it white?'

'Yes,' Rummins said. 'Bert did it.'

'A very wise move. It's considerably less offensive in white.'

'That's a strong piece of furniture,' Rummins said. 'Some nice carving on it too.'

'Machine-carved,' Mr Boggis answered superbly, bending down to examine the exquisite craftsmanship. 'You can tell it a mile off. But still, I suppose it's quite pretty in its way. It has its points.'

He began to saunter off, then he checked himself and turned slowly back again. He placed the tip of one finger against the point of his chin, laid his head over to one side, and frowned as though deep in thought.

'You know what?' he said, looking at the commode, speaking so casually that his voice kept trailing off. 'I've just remembered . . . I've been wanting a set of legs something like that for a long time. I've got a rather curious table in my own little home, one of those low things that people put in front of the sofa, sort of a coffee-table, and last Michaelmas, when I moved house, the foolish movers damaged the legs in the most shocking way. I'm very fond of that table. I always keep my big Bible on it, and all my sermon notes.'

He paused, stroking his chin with the finger. 'Now I was just thinking. These legs on your chest-of-drawers might be very suitable. Yes, they might indeed. They could easily be cut off and fixed on to my table.'

He looked around and saw the three men standing absolutely still, watching him suspiciously, three pairs of eyes, all different but equally mistrusting, small pig-eyes for Rummins, large slow eyes for Claud, and two odd eyes for Bert, one of them very queer and boiled and misty pale, with a little black dot in the centre, like a fish-eye on a plate.

Mr Boggis smiled and shook his head. 'Come, come, what on earth am I saying? I'm talking as though I owned the piece myself. I do apologize.'

'What you mean to say is you'd like to buy it,' Rummins said.

'Well . . .' Mr Boggis glanced back at the commode, frowning. 'I'm not sure. I might . . . and then again . . . on second thoughts . . . no . . . I think it might be a bit too much trouble. It's not worth it. I'd better leave it.'

'How much were you thinking of offering?' Rummins asked.

'Not much, I'm afraid. You see, this is not a genuine antique. It's merely a reproduction.'

'I'm not so sure about that,' Rummins told him. 'It's been in *here* over twenty years, and before that it was up at the Manor House. I bought it there myself at auction when the old Squire died. You can't tell me that thing's new.'

'It's not exactly new, but it's certainly not more than about sixty years old.'

'It's more than that,' Rummins said. 'Bert, where's that bit of paper you once found at the back of one of them drawers? That old bill.'

The boy looked vacantly at his father.

Mr Boggis opened his mouth, then quickly shut it again without uttering a sound. He was beginning literally to shake with excitement, and to calm himself he walked over to the window and stared out at a plump brown hen pecking around for stray grains of corn in the yard.

'It was in the back of that drawer underneath all them rabbit-snares,' Rummins was saying. 'Go on and fetch it out and show it to the parson.'

When Bert went forward to the commode, Mr Boggis turned round again. He couldn't stand not watching him. He saw him pull out one of the big middle drawers, and he noticed the beautiful smooth way in which the drawer slid open. He saw Bert's hand dipping inside and rummaging around among a lot of wires and strings.

'You mean this?' Bert lifted out a piece of folded yellowing paper and carried it over to the father, who unfolded it and held it up close to his face.

'You can't tell me this writing ain't bloody old,' Rummins said, and he held the paper out to Mr Boggis, whose whole arm was shaking as he took it. It was brittle and it crackled slightly between his fingers. The writing was in a long sloping copperplate hand:

Edward Montagu, Esq.   *Dr*
                                    To Thos. Chippendale
A large mahogany Commode Table of exceeding fine wood, very rich carvd, set upon fluted legs, two very neat shapd long drawers in the middle part and two ditto on each side, with rich chasd Brass Handles and Ornaments, the whole compleatly finished in the most exquisite taste . . . £87

Mr Boggis was holding on to himself tight and fighting to

suppress the excitement that was spinning round inside him and making him dizzy. Oh God, it was wonderful! With the invoice, the value had climbed even higher. What in heaven's name would it fetch now? Twelve thousand pounds? Fourteen? Maybe fifteen or even twenty? Who knows?

Oh, boy!

He tossed the paper contemptuously on to the table and said quietly, 'It's exactly what I told you, a Victorian reproduction. This is simply the invoice that the seller – the man who made it and passed it off as an antique – gave to his client. I've seen lots of them. You'll notice that he doesn't say he made it himself. That would give the game away.'

'Say what you like,' Rummins announced, 'but that's an old piece of paper.'

'Of course it is, my dear friend. It's Victorian, late Victorian. About eighteen ninety. Sixty or seventy years old. I've seen hundreds of them. That was a time when masses of cabinet-makers did nothing else but apply themselves to faking the fine furniture of the century before.'

'Listen, Parson,' Rummins said, pointing at him with a thick dirty finger, 'I'm not saying as how you may not know a fair bit about this furniture business, but what I *am* saying is this: How on earth can you be so mighty sure it's a fake when you haven't even seen what it looks like underneath all that paint?'

'Come here,' Mr Boggis said. 'Come over here and I'll show you.' He stood beside the commode and waited for them to gather round. 'Now, anyone got a knife?'

Claud produced a horn-handled pocket knife, and Mr Boggis took it and opened the smallest blade. Then, working with apparent casualness but actually with extreme care, he began chipping off the white paint from a small area on the top of the commode. The paint flaked away cleanly from the old hard varnish underneath, and when he had cleared away about three square inches, he stepped back and said, 'Now, take a look at that!'

It was beautiful – a warm little patch of mahogany, glowing like a topaz, rich and dark with the true colour of its two hundred years.

'What's wrong with it?' Rummins asked.

'It's processed! Anyone can see that!'

'How can you see it, Mister? You tell us.'

'Well, I must say that's a trifle difficult to explain. It's chiefly a matter of experience. My experience tells me that without the slightest doubt this wood has been processed with lime. That's what they use for mahogany, to give it that dark aged colour. For oak, they use potash salts, and for walnut it's nitric acid, but for mahogany it's always lime.'

The three men moved a little closer to peer at the wood. There was a slight stirring of interest among them now. It was always intriguing to hear about some new form of crookery or deception.

'Look closely at the grain. You see that touch of orange in among the dark red-brown. That's the sign of lime.'

They leaned forward, their noses close to the wood, first Rummins, then Claud, then Bert.

'And then there's the patina,' Mr Boggis continued.

'The what?'

He explained to them the meaning of this word as applied to furniture.

'My dear friends, you've no idea the trouble these rascals will go to to imitate the hard beautiful bronze-like appearance of genuine patina. It's terrible, really terrible, and it makes me quite sick to speak of it!' He was spitting each word sharply off the tip of the tongue and making a sour mouth to show his extreme distaste. The men waited, hoping for more secrets.

'The time and trouble that some mortals will go to in order to deceive the innocent!' Mr Boggis cried. 'It's perfectly disgusting! D'you know what they did here, my friends? I can recognize it clearly. I can almost *see* them doing it, the long, complicated ritual of rubbing the wood with linseed oil, coating it over with French polish that has been cunningly coloured, brushing it down with pumice-stone and oil, beeswaxing it with a wax that contains dirt and dust, and finally giving it the heat treatment to crack the polish so that it looks like two-hundred-year-old varnish! It really upsets me to contemplate such knavery!'

The three men continued to gaze at the little patch of dark wood.

'Feel it!' Mr Boggis ordered. 'Put your fingers on it! There, how does it feel, warm or cold?'

'Feels cold,' Rummins said.

'Exactly, my friend! It happens to be a fact that faked patina is always cold to the touch. Real patina has a curiously warm feel to it.'

'This feels normal,' Rummins said, ready to argue.

'No, sir, it's cold. But of course it takes an experienced and sensitive fingertip to pass a positive judgement. You couldn't really be expected to judge this any more than I could be expected to judge the quality of your barley. Everything in life, my dear sir, is experience.'

The men were staring at this queer moon-faced clergyman with the bulging eyes, not quite so suspiciously now because he did seem to know a bit about his subject. But they were still a long way from trusting him.

Mr Boggis bent down and pointed to one of the metal drawer-handles on the commode. 'This is another place where the fakers go to work,' he said. 'Old brass normally has a colour and character all of its own. Did you know that?'

They stared at him, hoping for still more secrets.

'But the trouble is that they've become exceedingly skilled at matching it. In fact it's almost impossible to tell the difference between "genuine old" and "faked old". I don't mind admitting that it has me guessing. So there's not really any point in our scraping the paint off these handles. We wouldn't be any the wiser.'

'How can you possibly make new brass look like old?' Claud said. 'Brass doesn't rust, you know.'

'You are quite right, my friend. But these scoundrels have their own secret methods.'

'Such as what?' Claud asked. Any information of this nature was valuable, in his opinion. One never knew when it might come in handy.

'All they have to do,' Mr Boggis said, 'is to place these

THE COMPLETE SHORT STORIES

handles overnight in a box of mahogany shavings satur-
ated in sal ammoniac. The sal ammoniac turns the metal
green, but if you rub off the green, you will find underneath it a fine soft silvery-warm lustre, a lustre identical to
that which comes with very old brass. Oh, it is so bestial,
the things they do! With iron they have another trick.'

'What do they do with iron?' Claud asked, fascinated.

'Iron's easy,' Mr Boggis said. 'Iron locks and plates and
hinges are simply buried in common salt and they come
out all rusted and pitted in no time.'

'All right,' Rummins said. 'So you admit you can't tell
about the handles. For all you know, they may be hundreds and hundreds of years old. Correct?'

'Ah,' Mr Boggis whispered, fixing Rummins with two
big bulging brown eyes. 'That's where you're wrong. Watch
this.'

From his jacket pocket, he took out a small screwdriver.
At the same time, although none of them saw him do it,
he also took out a little brass screw which he kept well
hidden in the palm of his hand. Then he selected one
of the screws in the commode – there were four to each
handle – and began carefully scraping all traces of white
paint from its head. When he had done this, he started
slowly to unscrew it.

'If this is a genuine old brass screw from the eighteenth
century,' he was saying, 'the spiral will be slightly uneven
and you'll be able to see quite easily that it has been hand-
cut with a file. But if this brasswork is faked from more
recent times, Victorian or later, then obviously the screw
will be of the same period. It will be a mass-produced,

machine-made article. Anyone can recognize a machine-made screw. Well, we shall see.'

It was not difficult, as he put his hands over the old screw and drew it out, for Mr Boggis to substitute the new one hidden in his palm. This was another little trick of his, and through the years it had proved a most rewarding one. The pockets of his clergyman's jacket were always stocked with a quantity of cheap brass screws of various sizes.

'There you are,' he said, handing the modern screw to Rummins. 'Take a look at that. Notice the exact evenness of the spiral? See it? Of course you do. It's just a cheap common little screw that you yourself could buy today in any ironmonger's in the country.'

The screw was handed round from the one to the other, each examining it carefully. Even Rummins was impressed now.

Mr Boggis put the screwdriver back in his pocket together with the fine hand-cut screw that he'd taken from the commode, and then he turned and walked slowly past the three men towards the door.

'My dear friends,' he said, pausing at the entrance to the kitchen, 'it was so good of you to let me peep inside your little home – so kind. I do hope I haven't been a terrible old bore.'

Rummins glanced up from examining the screw. 'You didn't tell us what you were going to offer,' he said.

'Ah,' Mr Boggis said. 'That's quite right. I didn't, did I? Well, to tell you the honest truth, it's all a bit too much trouble. I think I'll leave it.'

'How much would you give?'

'You mean that you really wish to part with it?'

'I didn't say I wished to part with it. I asked you how much.'

Mr Boggis looked across at the commode, and he laid his head first to one side, then to the other, and he frowned, and pushed out his lips, and shrugged his shoulders, and gave a little scornful wave of the hand as though to say the thing was hardly worth thinking about really, was it?

'Shall we say . . . ten pounds. I think that would be fair.'

'Ten pounds!' Rummins cried. 'Don't be so ridiculous, Parson, *please*!'

'It's worth more'n that for firewood!' Claud said, disgusted.

'Look here at the bill!' Rummins went on, stabbing that precious document so fiercely with his dirty forefinger that Mr Boggis became alarmed. 'It tells you exactly what it cost! Eighty-seven pounds! And that's when it was new. Now it's antique it's worth double!'

'If you'll pardon me, no, sir, it's not. It's a second-hand reproduction. But I'll tell you what, my friend – I'm being rather reckless, I can't help it – I'll go up as high as fifteen pounds. How's that?'

'Make it fifty,' Rummins said.

A delicious little quiver like needles ran all the way down the back of Mr Boggis's legs and then under the soles of his feet. He had it now. It was his. No question about that. But the habit of buying cheap, as cheap as it was humanly possible to buy, acquired by years of necessity and practice, was too strong in him now to permit him to give in so easily.

'My dear man,' he whispered softly, 'I only *want* the legs. Possibly I could find some use for the drawers later on, but the rest of it, the carcass itself, as your friend so rightly said, it's firewood, that's all.'

'Make it thirty-five,' Rummins said.

'I *couldn't*, sir, I *couldn't*! It's not worth it. And I simply mustn't allow myself to haggle like this about a price. It's all wrong. I'll make you one final offer, and then I must go. Twenty pounds.'

'I'll take it,' Rummins snapped. 'It's yours.'

'Oh dear,' Mr Boggis said, clasping his hands. 'There I go again. I should never have started this in the first place.'

'You can't back out now, Parson. A deal's a deal.'

'Yes, yes, I know.'

'How're you going to take it?'

'Well, let me see. Perhaps if I were to drive my car up into the yard, you gentlemen would be kind enough to help me load it?'

'In a car? This thing'll never go in a car! You'll need a truck for this!'

'I don't think so. Anyway, we'll see. My car's on the road. I'll be back in a jiffy. We'll manage it somehow, I'm sure.'

Mr Boggis walked out into the yard and through the gate and then down the long track that led across the field towards the road. He found himself giggling quite uncontrollably, and there was a feeling inside him as though hundreds and hundreds of tiny bubbles were rising up from his stomach and bursting merrily in the top of his head, like sparkling-water. All the buttercups in the field were suddenly turning into golden sovereigns, glistening in the sunlight. The ground was littered with them, and he swung off the track on to the grass so that he could walk among them and tread on them and hear the little metallic tinkle they made as he kicked them around with his toes. He was finding it difficult to stop himself from breaking into a run. But clergymen never run; they walk slowly. Walk slowly, Boggis. Keep calm, Boggis. There's no hurry now. The commode is yours! Yours for twenty pounds, and it's worth fifteen or twenty thousand! The Boggis Commode! In ten minutes it'll be loaded into your car – it'll go in easily – and you'll be driving back to London and singing all the way! Mr Boggis driving the Boggis Commode home in the Boggis car. Historic occasion. What *wouldn't* a newspaperman give to get a picture of that! Should he arrange it? Perhaps he should. Wait and see. Oh, glorious day! Oh, lovely sunny summer day! Oh, glory be!

Back in the farmhouse, Rummins was saying, 'Fancy that old bastard giving twenty pound for a load of junk like this.'

'You did very nicely, Mr Rummins,' Claud told him. 'You think he'll pay you?'

'We don't put it in the car till he do.'

'And what if it won't go in the car?' Claud asked. 'You know what I think, Mr Rummins? You want my honest opinion? I think the bloody thing's too big to go in the car. And then what happens? Then he's going to say to hell with it and just drive off without it and you'll never see him again. Nor the money either. He didn't seem all that keen on having it, you know.'

Rummins paused to consider this new and rather alarming prospect.

'How can a thing like that possibly go in a car?' Claud went on relentlessly. 'A parson never has a big car anyway. You ever seen a parson with a big car, Mr Rummins?'

'Can't say I have.'

'Exactly! And now listen to me. I've got an idea. He told us, didn't he, that it was only the legs he was wanting. Right? So all we've got to do is to cut 'em off quick right here on the spot before he comes back, then it'll be sure to go in the car. All we're doing is saving him the trouble of cutting them off himself when he gets home. How about it, Mr Rummins?' Claud's flat bovine face glimmered with a mawkish pride.

'It's not such a bad idea at that,' Rummins said, looking at the commode. 'In fact it's a bloody good idea. Come on then, we'll have to hurry. You and Bert carry it out into the yard. I'll get the saw. Take the drawers out first.'

Within a couple of minutes, Claud and Bert had carried the commode outside and had laid it upside down in the yard amidst the chicken droppings and cow dung and mud. In the distance, halfway across the field, they could see a small black figure striding along the path towards the road. They paused to watch. There was something rather comical about the way in which this figure was conducting itself. Every now and again it would break into a trot, then it did a kind of hop, skip and jump, and once it seemed as though the sound of a cheerful song came rippling faintly to them from across the meadow.

'I reckon he's balmy,' Claud said, and Bert grinned darkly, rolling his misty eye slowly round in its socket.

Rummins came waddling over from the shed, squat and frog-like, carrying a long saw. Claud took the saw away from him and went to work.

'Cut 'em close,' Rummins said. 'Don't forget he's going to use 'em on another table.'

The mahogany was hard and very dry, and as Claud worked, a fine red dust sprayed out from the edge of the saw and fell softly to the ground. One by one, the legs came off, and when they were all severed, Bert stooped down and arranged them carefully in a row.

Claud stepped back to survey the results of his labour. There was a longish pause.

'Just let me ask you one question, Mr Rummins,' he said slowly. 'Even now, could *you* put that enormous thing into the back of a car?'

'Not unless it was a van.'

'Correct!' Claud cried. 'And parsons don't have vans, you know. All they've got usually is piddling little Morris Eights or Austin Sevens.'

'The legs is all he wants,' Rummins said. 'If the rest of it won't go in, then he can leave it. He can't complain. He's got the legs.'

'Now you know better'n that, Mr Rummins,' Claud said patiently. 'You know damn well he's going to start knocking the price if he don't get every single bit of this into the car. A parson's just as cunning as the rest of 'em when it comes to money, don't you make any mistake about that. Especially this old boy. So why don't we give him his firewood now and be done with it. Where d'you keep the axe?'

'I reckon that's fair enough,' Rummins said. 'Bert, go fetch the axe.'

Bert went into the shed and fetched a tall woodcutter's axe and gave it to Claud. Claud spat on the palms of his hands and rubbed them together. Then, with a long-armed high-swinging action, he began fiercely attacking the legless carcass of the commode.

It was hard work, and it took several minutes before he had the whole thing more or less smashed to pieces.

'I'll tell you one thing,' he said, straightening up, wiping his brow. 'That was a bloody good carpenter put this job together and I don't care what the parson says.'

'We're just in time!' Rummins called out. 'Here he comes!'

The Champion of the World

First published in the *New Yorker*,
31 January 1959

All day, in between serving customers, we had been crouching over the table in the office of the filling-station, preparing the raisins. They were plump and soft and swollen from being soaked in water, and when you nicked them with a razor-blade the skin sprang open and the jelly stuff inside squeezed out as easily as you could wish.

But we had a hundred and ninety-six of them to do altogether and the evening was nearly upon us before we had finished.

'Don't they look marvellous!' Claud cried, rubbing his hands together hard. 'What time is it, Gordon?'

'Just after five.'

Through the window we could see a station-wagon pulling up at the pumps with a woman at the wheel and about eight children in the back eating ice-creams.

'We ought to be moving soon,' Claud said. 'The whole thing'll be a washout if we don't arrive before sunset, you realize that.' He was getting twitchy now. His face had the same flushed and pop-eyed look it got before a dog-race or when there was a date with Clarice in the evening.

We both went outside and Claud gave the woman the number of gallons she wanted. When she had gone, he remained standing in the middle of the driveway squinting anxiously up at the sun which was now only the width of a man's hand above the line of trees along the crest of the ridge on the far side of the valley.

'All right,' I said. 'Lock up.'

He went quickly from pump to pump, securing each nozzle in its holder with a small padlock.

'You'd better take off that yellow pullover,' he said.

'Why should I?'

'You'll be shining like a bloody beacon out there in the moonlight.'

'I'll be all right.'

'You will not,' he said. 'Take it off, Gordon, please. I'll see you in three minutes.' He disappeared into his caravan behind the filling-station, and I went indoors and changed my yellow pullover for a blue one.

When we met again outside, Claud was dressed in a pair of black trousers and a dark-green turtleneck sweater. On his head he wore a brown cloth cap with the peak pulled down low over his eyes, and he looked like an apache actor out of a nightclub.

'What's under there?' I asked, seeing the bulge at his waistline.

He pulled up his sweater and showed me two thin but very large white cotton sacks which were bound neat and tight around his belly. 'To carry the stuff,' he said darkly.

'I see.'

'Let's go,' he said.

'I still think we ought to take the car.'

'It's too risky. They'll see it parked.'

'But it's over three miles up to that wood.'

'Yes,' he said. 'And I suppose you realize we can get six months in the clink if they catch us.'

'You never told me that.'

'Didn't I?'

'I'm not coming,' I said. 'It's not worth it.'

'The walk will do you good, Gordon. Come on.'

It was a calm sunny evening with little wisps of brilliant white cloud hanging motionless in the sky, and the valley was cool and very quiet as the two of us began walking together along the grass verge on the side of the road that ran between the hills towards Oxford.

'You got the raisins?' Claud asked.

'They're in my pocket.'

'Good,' he said. 'Marvellous.'

Ten minutes later we turned left off the main road into a narrow lane with high hedges on either side and from now on it was all uphill.

'How many keepers are there?' I asked.

'Three.'

Claud threw away a half-finished cigarette. A minute later he lit another.

'I don't usually approve of new methods,' he said. 'Not on this sort of a job.'

'Of course.'

'But by God, Gordon, I think we're on to a hot one this time.'

'You do?'

'There's no question about it.'

'I hope you're right.'

'It'll be a milestone in the history of poaching,' he said.

56

'But don't you go telling a single soul how we've done it, you understand. Because if this ever leaked out we'd have every bloody fool in the district doing the same thing and there wouldn't be a pheasant left.'

'I won't say a word.'

'You ought to be very proud of yourself,' he went on. 'There's been men with brains studying this problem for hundreds of years and not one of them's ever come up with anything even a quarter as artful as you have. Why didn't you tell me about it before?'

'You never invited my opinion,' I said.

And that was the truth. In fact, up until the day before, Claud had never even offered to discuss with me the sacred subject of poaching. Often enough, on a summer's evening when work was finished, I had seen him with cap on head sliding quietly out of his caravan and disappearing up the road towards the woods; and sometimes, watching him through the windows of the filling-station, I would find myself wondering exactly what he was going to do, what wily tricks he was going to practise all alone up there under the trees in the dead of night. He seldom came back until very late, and never, absolutely never did he bring any of the spoils with him personally on his return. But the following afternoon – and I couldn't imagine how he did it – there would always be a pheasant or a hare or a brace of partridges hanging up in the shed behind the filling-station for us to eat.

This summer he had been particularly active, and during the last couple of months he had stepped up the tempo to a point where he was going out four and sometimes five

THE COMPLETE SHORT STORIES

nights a week. But that was not all. It seemed to me that recently his whole attitude towards poaching had undergone a subtle and mysterious change. He was more purposeful about it now, more tight-lipped and intense than before, and I had the impression that this was not so much a game any longer as a crusade, a sort of private war that Claud was waging single-handed against an invisible and hated enemy.

But who?

I wasn't sure about this, but I had a suspicion that it was none other than the famous Mr Victor Hazel himself, the owner of the land and the pheasants. Mr Hazel was a local brewer with an unbelievably arrogant manner. He was rich beyond words, and his property stretched for miles along either side of the valley. He was a self-made man with no charm at all and precious few virtues. He loathed all persons of humble station, having once been one of them himself, and he strove desperately to mingle with what he believed were the right kind of folk. He rode to hounds and gave shooting-parties and wore fancy waistcoats, and every weekday he drove an enormous black Rolls-Royce past the filling-station on his way to the brewery. As he flashed by, we would sometimes catch a glimpse of the great glistening brewer's face above the wheel, pink as a ham, all soft and inflamed from drinking too much beer.

Anyway, yesterday afternoon, right out of the blue, Claud had suddenly said to me, 'I'll be going on up to Hazel's woods again tonight. Why don't you come along?'

'Who, me?'

'It's about the last chance this year for pheasants,' he had said. 'The shooting-season opens Saturday and the birds'll be scattered all over the place after that – if there's any left.'

'Why the sudden invitation?' I had asked, greatly suspicious.

'No special reason, Gordon. No reason at all.'

'Is it risky?'

He hadn't answered this.

'I suppose you keep a gun or something hidden away up there?'

'A gun!' he cried, disgusted. 'Nobody ever *shoots* pheasants, didn't you know that? You've only got to fire a *cap-pistol* in Hazel's woods and the keepers'll be on you.'

'Then how do you do it?'

'Ah,' he said, and the eyelids drooped over the eyes, veiled and secretive.

There was a long pause. Then he said, 'Do you think you could keep your mouth shut if I was to tell you a thing or two?'

'Definitely.'

'I've never told this to anyone else in my whole life, Gordon.'

'I am greatly honoured,' I said. 'You can trust me completely.'

He turned his head, fixing me with pale eyes. The eyes were large and wet and ox-like, and they were so near to me that I could see my own face reflected upside down in the centre of each.

'I am now about to let you in on the three best ways in

the world of poaching a pheasant,' he said. 'And seeing that you're the guest on this little trip, I am going to give you the choice of which one you'd like us to use tonight. How's that?'

'There's a catch in this.'

'There's no catch, Gordon. I swear it.'

'All right, go on.'

'Now, here's the thing,' he said. 'Here's the first big secret.' He paused and took a long suck at his cigarette. 'Pheasants,' he whispered softly, 'is *crazy* about raisins.'

'Raisins?'

'Just ordinary raisins. It's like a mania with them. My dad discovered that more than forty years ago just like he discovered all three of these methods I'm about to describe to you now.'

'I thought you said your dad was a drunk.'

'Maybe he was. But he was also a great poacher, Gordon. Possibly the greatest there's ever been in the history of England. My dad studied poaching like a scientist.'

'Is that so?'

'I mean it. I really mean it.'

'I believe you.'

'Do you know,' he said, 'my dad used to keep a whole flock of prime cockerels in the back yard purely for experimental purposes.'

'Cockerels?'

'That's right. And whenever he thought up some new stunt for catching a pheasant, he'd try it out on a cockerel first to see how it worked. That's how he discovered about raisins. It's also how he invented the horsehair method.'

Claud paused and glanced over his shoulder as though to make sure that there was nobody listening. 'Here's how it's done,' he said. 'First you take a few raisins and you soak them overnight in water to make them nice and plump and juicy. Then you get a bit of good stiff horsehair and you cut it up into half-inch lengths. Then you push one of these lengths of horsehair through the middle of each raisin so that there's about an eighth of an inch of it sticking out on either side. You follow?'

'Yes.'

'Now – the old pheasant comes along and eats one of these raisins. Right? And you're watching him from behind a tree. So what then?'

'I imagine it sticks in his throat.'

'That's obvious, Gordon. But here's the amazing thing. Here's what my dad discovered. The moment this happens, the bird *never moves his feet again*! He becomes absolutely rooted to the spot, and there he stands pumping his silly neck up and down just like it was a piston, and all you've got to do is walk calmly out from the place where you're hiding and pick him up in your hands.'

'I don't believe that.'

'I swear it,' he said. 'Once a pheasant's had the horsehair you can fire a rifle in his ear and he won't even jump. It's just one of those unexplainable little things. But it takes a genius to discover it.'

He paused, and there was a gleam of pride in his eye now as he dwelt for a moment or two upon the memory of his father, the great inventor.

'So that's Method Number One,' he said. 'Method

Number Two is even more simple still. All you do is you have a fishing line. Then you bait the hook with a raisin and you fish for the pheasant just like you fish for a fish. You pay out the line about fifty yards and you lie there on your stomach in the bushes waiting till you get a bite. Then you haul him in.'

'I don't think your father invented that one.'

'It's very popular with fishermen,' he said, choosing not to hear me. 'Keen fishermen who can't get down to the seaside as often as they want. It gives them a bit of the old thrill. The only trouble is it's rather noisy. The pheasant squawks like hell as you haul him in, and then every keeper in the wood comes running.'

'What is Method Number Three?' I asked.

'Ah,' he said. 'Number Three's a real beauty. It was the last one my dad ever invented before he passed away.'

'His final great work?'

'Exactly, Gordon. And I can even remember the very day it happened, a Sunday morning it was, and suddenly my dad comes into the kitchen holding a huge white cockerel in his hands and he says, "I think I've got it!" There's a little smile on his face and a shine of glory in his eyes and he comes in very soft and quiet and he puts the bird down right in the middle of the kitchen table and he says, "By God I think I've got a good one this time!" "A good what?" Mum says, looking up from the sink. "Horace, take that filthy bird off my table." The cockerel has a funny little paper hat over its head, like an ice-cream cone upside down, and my dad is pointing to it proudly. "Stroke him," he says. "He won't move an inch." The cockerel starts scratching away at the paper hat with one of its feet, but the hat seems to be stuck on with glue and it won't come off. "No bird in the world is going to run away once you cover up his eyes," my dad says, and he starts poking the cockerel with his finger and pushing it around on the table, but it doesn't take the slightest bit of notice. "You can have this one," he says, talking to Mum. "You can kill it and dish it up for dinner as a celebration of what I have just invented." And then straight away he takes me by the arm and marches me quickly out the door and off we go over the fields and up into the big forest the other side of Haddenham which used to belong to the Duke of Buckingham, and in less than two hours we get five lovely fat pheasants with no more trouble than it takes to go out and buy them in a shop.'

Claud paused for breath. His eyes were huge and moist and dreamy as they gazed back into the wonderful world of his youth.

'I don't quite follow this,' I said. 'How did he get the paper hats over the pheasants' heads up in the woods?'

'You'd never guess it.'

'I'm sure I wouldn't.'

'Then here it is. First of all you dig a little hole in the ground. Then you twist a piece of paper into the shape of a cone and you fit this into the hole, hollow end upwards, like a cup. Then you smear the paper cup all around the inside with bird-lime and drop in a few raisins. At the same time you lay a trail of raisins along the ground leading up to it. Now – the old pheasant comes pecking along the trail, and when he gets to the hole he pops his head inside to gobble the raisins and the next thing he knows he's got a paper hat stuck over his eyes and he can't see a thing. Isn't it marvellous what some people think of, Gordon? Don't you agree?'

'Your dad was a genius,' I said.

'Then take your pick. Choose whichever one of the three methods you fancy and we'll use it tonight.'

'You don't think they're all just a trifle on the crude side, do you?'

'Crude!' he cried, aghast. 'Oh my God! And who's been having roasted pheasant in the house nearly every single day for the last six months and not a penny to pay?'

He turned and walked away towards the door of the workshop. I could see that he was deeply pained by my remark.

'Wait a minute,' I said. 'Don't go.'

'You want to come or don't you?'

'Yes, but let me ask you something first. I've just had a bit of an idea.'

'Keep it,' he said. 'You are talking about a subject you don't know the first thing about.'

'Do you remember that bottle of sleeping-pills the doc gave me last month when I had a bad back?'

'What about them?'

'Is there any reason why those wouldn't work on a pheasant?'

Claud closed his eyes and shook his head pityingly from side to side.

'Wait,' I said.

'It's not worth discussing,' he said. 'No pheasant in the

world is going to swallow those lousy red capsules. Don't you know any better than that?'

'You are forgetting the raisins,' I said. 'Now listen to this. We take a raisin. Then we soak it till it swells. Then we make a tiny slit in one side of it with a razor-blade. Then we hollow it out a little. Then we open up one of my red capsules and pour all the powder into the raisin. Then we get a needle and cotton and very carefully we sew up the slit. Now . . .'

Out of the corner of my eye, I saw Claud's mouth slowly beginning to open.

'Now,' I said. 'We have a nice clean-looking raisin with two and a half grains of seconal inside it, and let me tell *you* something now. That's enough dope to knock the average *man* unconscious, never mind about *birds*!'

I paused for ten seconds to allow the full impact of this to strike home.

'What's more, with this method we could operate on a really grand scale. We could prepare *twenty* raisins if we felt like it, and all we'd have to do is scatter them around the feeding-grounds at sunset and then walk away. Half an hour later we'd come back, and the pills would be beginning to work, and the pheasants would be up in the trees by then, roosting, and they'd be starting to feel groggy, and they'd be wobbling and trying to keep their balance, and soon every pheasant that had eaten *one single raisin* would keel over unconscious and fall to the ground. My dear boy, they'd be dropping out of the trees like apples, and all we'd have to do is walk around picking them up!'

Claud was staring at me, rapt.

'Oh Christ,' he said softly.

'And they'd never catch us either. We'd simply stroll through the woods dropping a few raisins here and there as we went, and even if they were *watching* us they wouldn't notice anything.'

'Gordon,' he said, laying a hand on my knee and gazing at me with eyes large and bright as two stars. 'If this thing works, it will *revolutionize* poaching.'

'I'm glad to hear it.'

'How many pills have you got left?' he asked.

'Forty-nine. There were fifty in the bottle and I've only used one.'

'Forty-nine's not enough. We want at least two hundred.'

'Are you mad!' I cried.

He walked slowly away and stood by the door with his back to me, gazing at the sky.

'Two hundred's the bare minimum,' he said quietly. 'There's really not much point in doing it unless we have two hundred.'

What is it now, I wondered. What the hell's he trying to do?

'This is the last chance we'll have before the season opens,' he said.

'I couldn't possibly get any more.'

'You wouldn't want us to come back empty-handed, would you?'

'But why so *many*?'

Claud turned his head and looked at me with large

innocent eyes. 'Why not?' he said gently. 'Do you have any objection?'

My God, I thought suddenly. The crazy bastard is out to wreck Mr Victor Hazel's opening-day shooting-party.

'You get us two hundred of those pills,' he said, 'and then it'll be worth doing.'

'I can't.'

'You could try, couldn't you?'

Mr Hazel's party took place on the first of October every year and it was a very famous event. Debilitated gentlemen in tweed suits, some with titles and some who were merely rich, motored in from miles around with their gun-bearers and dogs and wives, and all day long the noise of shooting rolled across the valley. There were always enough pheasants to go round, for each summer the woods were methodically restocked with dozens and dozens of young birds at incredible expense. I had heard it said that the cost of rearing and keeping each pheasant up to the time when it was ready to be shot was well over five pounds (which is approximately the price of two hundred loaves of bread). But to Mr Hazel it was worth every penny of it. He became, if only for a few hours, a big cheese in a little world and even the Lord Lieutenant of the County slapped him on the back and tried to remember his first name when he said good-bye.

'How would it be if we just reduced the dose?' Claud asked. 'Why couldn't we divide the contents of one capsule among four raisins?'

'I suppose you could if you wanted to.'

'But would a quarter of a capsule be strong enough for each bird?'

One simply had to admire the man's nerve. It was dangerous enough to poach a single pheasant up in those woods at this time of year and here he was planning to knock off the bloody lot.

'A quarter would be plenty,' I said.

'You're sure of that?'

'Work it out for yourself. It's all done by bodyweight. You'd still be giving about twenty times more than is necessary.'

'Then we'll quarter the dose,' he said, rubbing his hands. He paused and calculated for a moment. 'We'll have one hundred and ninety-six raisins!'

'Do you realize what that involves?' I said. 'They'll take hours to prepare.'

'What of it!' he cried. 'We'll go tomorrow instead. We'll soak the raisins overnight and then we'll have all morning and afternoon to get them ready.'

And that was precisely what we did.

Now, twenty-four hours later, we were on our way. We had been walking steadily for about forty minutes and we were nearing the point where the lane curved round to the right and ran along the crest of the hill towards the big wood where the pheasants lived. There was about a mile to go.

'I don't suppose by any chance these keepers might be carrying guns?' I asked.

'All keepers carry guns,' Claud said.

I had been afraid of that.

'It's for the vermin mostly.'

'Ah.'

'Of course there's no guarantee they won't take a pot at a poacher now and again.'

'You're joking.'

'Not at all. But they only do it from behind. Only when you're running away. They like to pepper you in the legs at about fifty yards.'

'They can't do that!' I cried. 'It's a criminal offence!'

'So is poaching,' Claud said.

We walked on awhile in silence. The sun was below the high hedge on our right now and the lane was in shadow.

'You can consider yourself lucky this isn't thirty years ago,' he went on. 'They used to shoot you on sight in those days.'

'Do you believe that?'

'I know it,' he said. 'Many's the night when I was a nipper I've gone into the kitchen and seen my old dad lying face downwards on the table and Mum standing over him digging the grapeshot out of his buttocks with a potato knife.'

'Stop,' I said. 'It makes me nervous.'

'You believe me, don't you?'

'Yes, I believe you.'

'Towards the end he was so covered in tiny little white scars he looked exactly like it was snowing.'

'Yes,' I said. 'All right.'

'Poacher's arse, they used to call it,' Claud said. 'And there wasn't a man in the whole village who didn't have a bit of it one way or another. But my dad was the champion.'

'Good luck to him,' I said.

'I wish to hell he was here now,' Claud said, wistful. 'He'd have given anything in the world to be coming with us on this job tonight.'

'He could take my place,' I said. 'Gladly.'

We had reached the crest of the hill and now we could see the wood ahead of us, huge and dark with the sun going down behind the trees and little sparks of gold shining through.

'You'd better let me have those raisins,' Claud said.

I gave him the bag and he slid it gently into his trouser pocket.

'No talking once we're inside,' he said. 'Just follow me and try not to go snapping any branches.'

Five minutes later we were there. The lane ran right up to the wood itself and then skirted the edge of it for about three hundred yards with only a little hedge between. Claud slipped through the hedge on all fours and I followed.

It was cool and dark inside the wood. No sunlight came in at all.

'This is spooky,' I said.

'Ssshh!'

Claud was very tense. He was walking just ahead of me, picking his feet up high and putting them down gently on the moist ground. He kept his head moving all the time, the eyes sweeping slowly from side to side, searching for danger. I tried doing the same, but soon I began to see a keeper behind every tree, so I gave it up.

Then a large patch of sky appeared ahead of us in the

roof of the forest and I knew that this must be the clearing. Claud had told me that the clearing was the place where the young birds were introduced into the woods in early July, where they were fed and watered and guarded by the keepers, and where many of them stayed from force of habit until the shooting began.

'There's always plenty of pheasants in the clearing,' he had said.

'Keepers too, I suppose.'

'Yes, but there's thick bushes all around and that helps.'

We were now advancing in a series of quick crouching spurts, running from tree to tree and stopping and waiting and listening and running on again, and then at last we were kneeling safely behind a big clump of alder right on the edge of the clearing and Claud was grinning and nudging me in the ribs and pointing through the branches at the pheasants.

The place was absolutely stiff with birds. There must have been two hundred of them at least strutting around among the tree-stumps.

'You see what I mean?' Claud whispered.

It was an astonishing sight, a sort of poacher's dream come true. And how close they were! Some of them were not more than ten paces from where we knelt. The hens were plump and creamy-brown and they were so fat their breast-feathers almost brushed the ground as they walked. The cocks were slim and beautiful, with long tails and brilliant red patches around the eyes, like scarlet spectacles. I glanced at Claud. His big ox-like face was transfixed in ecstasy. The mouth was slightly open and the eyes had a kind of glazy look about them as they stared at the pheasants.

I believe that all poachers react in roughly the same way as this on sighting game. They are like women who sight large emeralds in a jeweller's window, the only difference being that the women are less dignified in the methods they employ later on to acquire the loot. Poacher's arse is nothing to the punishment that a female is willing to endure.

'Ah-ha,' Claud said softly. 'You see the keeper?'

'Where?'

'Over the other side, by that big tree. Look carefully.'

'My God!'

'It's all right. He can't see *us*.'

We crouched close to the ground, watching the keeper. He was a smallish man with a cap on his head and a gun under his arm. He never moved. He was like a little post standing there.

'Let's go,' I whispered.

The keeper's face was shadowed by the peak of his cap, but it seemed to me that he was looking directly at us.

'I'm not staying here,' I said.

'Hush,' Claud said.

Slowly, never taking his eyes from the keeper, he reached into his pocket and brought out a single raisin. He placed it in the palm of his right hand, and then quickly, with a little flick of the wrist, he threw the raisin high into the air. I watched it as it went sailing over the bushes and I saw it land within a yard or so of two henbirds standing together beside an old tree-stump. Both birds turned their heads sharply at the drop of the raisin. Then one of them hopped over and made a quick peck at the ground and that must have been it.

I glanced up at the keeper. He hadn't moved.

Claud threw a second raisin into the clearing; then a third, and a fourth, and a fifth.

At this point, I saw the keeper turn away his head in order to survey the wood behind him.

Quick as a flash, Claud pulled the paper bag out of his pocket and tipped a huge pile of raisins into the cup of his right hand.

'Stop,' I said.

But with a great sweep of the arm he flung the whole handful high over the bushes into the clearing.

They fell with a soft little patter, like raindrops on dry leaves, and every single pheasant in the place must either have seen them coming or heard them fall. There was a flurry of wings and a rush to find the treasure.

The keeper's head flicked round as though there were a spring inside his neck. The birds were all pecking away madly at the raisins. The keeper took two quick paces forward and for a moment I thought he was going in to investigate. But then he stopped, and his face came up and his eyes began travelling slowly around the perimeter of the clearing.

'Follow me,' Claud whispered. 'And *keep down.*' He started crawling away swiftly on all fours, like some kind of a monkey.

I went after him. He had his nose close to the ground and his huge tight buttocks were winking at the sky and it was easy to see now how poacher's arse had come to be an occupational disease among the fraternity.

We went along like this for about a hundred yards.

'Now run,' Claud said.

We got to our feet and ran, and a few minutes later we emerged through the hedge into the lovely open safety of the lane.

'It went marvellous,' Claud said, breathing heavily. 'Didn't it go absolutely marvellous?' The big face was scarlet and glowing with triumph.

'It was a mess,' I said.

'What!' he cried.

'Of course it was. We can't possibly go back now. That keeper knows there was someone there.'

'He knows nothing,' Claud said. 'In another five minutes it'll be pitch dark inside the wood and he'll be sloping off home to his supper.'

'I think I'll join him.'

'You're a great poacher,' Claud said. He sat down on the grassy bank under the hedge and lit a cigarette.

The sun had set now and the sky was a pale smoke blue, faintly glazed with yellow. In the woods behind us the shadows and the spaces in between the trees were turning from grey to black.

'How long does a sleeping-pill take to work?' Claud asked.

'Look out,' I said. 'There's someone coming.'

The man had appeared suddenly and silently out of the dusk and he was only thirty yards away when I saw him.

'Another bloody keeper,' Claud said.

We both looked at the keeper as he came down the lane towards us. He had a shotgun under his arm and there was a black Labrador walking at his heels. He stopped when he was a few paces away and the dog stopped with him and stayed behind him, watching us through the keeper's legs.

'Good evening,' Claud said, nice and friendly.

This one was a tall bony man about forty with a swift eye and a hard cheek and hard dangerous hands.

'I know you,' he said softly, coming closer. 'I know the both of you.'

Claud didn't answer this.

'You're from the fillin'-station. Right?'

His lips were thin and dry, with some sort of a brownish crust over them.

'You're Cubbage and Hawes and you're from the fillin'-station on the main road. Right?'

'What are we playing?' Claud said. 'Twenty Questions?'

The keeper spat out a big gob of spit and I saw it go floating through the air and land with a plop on a patch of dry dust six inches from Claud's feet. It looked like a little baby oyster lying there.

'Beat it,' the man said. 'Go on. Get out.'

Claud sat on the bank smoking his cigarette and looking at the gob of spit.

'Go on,' the man said. 'Get out.'

When he spoke, the upper lip lifted above the gum and I could see a row of small discoloured teeth, one of them black, the others quince and ochre.

'This happens to be a public highway,' Claud said. 'Kindly do not molest us.'

The keeper shifted the gun from his left arm to his right.

'You're loiterin',' he said, 'with intent to commit a felony. I could run you in for that.'

'No you couldn't,' Claud said.

All this made me rather nervous.

'I've had my eye on you for some time,' the keeper said, looking at Claud.

'It's getting late,' I said. 'Shall we stroll on?'

Claud flipped away his cigarette and got slowly to his feet. 'All right,' he said. 'Let's go.'

We wandered off down the lane the way we had come, leaving the keeper standing there, and soon the man was out of sight in the half-darkness behind us.

'That's the head keeper,' Claud said. 'His name is Rabbetts.'

'Let's get the hell out,' I said.

'Come in here,' Claud said.

There was a gate on our left leading into a field and we climbed over it and sat down behind the hedge.

'Mr Rabbetts is also due for his supper,' Claud said. 'You mustn't worry about him.'

We sat quietly behind the hedge waiting for the keeper to walk past us on his way home. A few stars were showing and a bright three-quarter moon was coming up over the hills behind us in the east.

'Here he is,' Claud whispered. 'Don't move.'

The keeper came loping softly up the lane with the dog padding quick and soft-footed at his heels, and we watched them through the hedge as they went by.

'He won't be coming back tonight,' Claud said.

'How do you know that?'

'A keeper never waits for you in the wood if he knows where you live. He goes to your house and hides outside and watches for you to come back.'

'That's worse.'

'No, it isn't, not if you dump the loot somewhere else before you go home. He can't touch you then.'

'What about the other one, the one in the clearing?'

'He's gone too.'

'You can't be sure of that.'

'I've been studying these bastards for months, Gordon, honest I have. I know all their habits. There's no danger.'

Reluctantly I followed him back into the wood. It was pitch dark in there now and very silent, and as we moved cautiously forward the noise of our footsteps seemed to go echoing around the walls of the forest as though we were walking in a cathedral.

'Here's where we threw the raisins,' Claud said.

I peered through the bushes.

The clearing lay dim and milky in the moonlight.

'You're quite sure the keeper's gone?'

'I *know* he's gone.'

I could just see Claud's face under the peak of his cap, the pale lips, the soft pale cheeks, and the large eyes with a little spark of excitement dancing slowly in each.

'Are they roosting?'

'Yes.'

'Whereabouts?'

'All around. They don't go far.'

'What do we do next?'

'We stay here and wait. I brought you a light,' he added, and he handed me one of those small pocket flashlights shaped like a fountain-pen. 'You may need it.'

I was beginning to feel better. 'Shall we see if we can spot some of them sitting in the trees?' I said.

'No.'

'I should like to see how they look when they're roosting.'

'This isn't a nature-study,' Claud said. 'Please be quiet.'

We stood there for a long time waiting for something to happen.

'I've just had a nasty thought,' I said. 'If a bird can keep its balance on a branch when it's asleep, then surely there isn't any reason why the pills should make it fall down.'

Claud looked at me quick.

'After all,' I said, 'it's not dead. It's still only sleeping.'

'It's doped,' Claud said.

'But that's just a *deeper* sort of sleep. Why should we expect it to fall down just because it's in a *deeper* sleep?'

There was a gloomy silence.

'We should've tried it with chickens,' Claud said. 'My dad would've done that.'

'Your dad was a genius,' I said.

At that moment there came a soft thump from the wood behind us.

'Hey!'

'Ssshh!'

We stood listening.

Thump.

78

'There's another!'

It was a deep muffled sound as though a bag of sand had been dropped from about shoulder height.

Thump!

'They're pheasants!' I cried.

'Wait!'

'I'm sure they're pheasants!'

Thump! Thump!

'You're right!'

We ran back into the wood.

'Where were they?'

'Over here! Two of them were over here!'

'I thought they were this way.'

'Keep looking!' Claud shouted. 'They can't be far.'

We searched for about a minute.

'Here's one!' he called.

When I got to him he was holding a magnificent cock-bird in both hands. We examined it closely with our flashlights.

'It's doped to the gills,' Claud said. 'It's still alive, I can feel its heart, but it's doped to the bloody gills.'

Thump!

'There's another!'

Thump! Thump!

'Two more!'

Thump!

Thump! Thump! Thump!

'Jesus Christ!'

Thump! Thump! Thump! Thump!

Thump! Thump!

All around us the pheasants were starting to rain down out of the trees. We began rushing around madly in the dark, sweeping the ground with our flashlights.

Thump! Thump! Thump! This lot fell almost on top of me. I was right under the tree as they came down and I found all three of them immediately – two cocks and a hen. They were limp and warm, the feathers wonderfully soft in the hand.

'Where shall I put them?' I called out. I was holding them by the legs.

'Lay them here, Gordon! Just pile them up here where it's light!'

Claud was standing on the edge of the clearing with the moonlight streaming down all over him and a great bunch of pheasants in each hand. His face was bright, his eyes big and bright and wonderful, and he was staring around him like a child who has just discovered that the whole world is made of chocolate.

Thump!

Thump! Thump!

'I don't like it,' I said. 'It's too many.'

'It's beautiful!' he cried and he dumped the birds he was carrying and ran off to look for more.

Thump! Thump! Thump! Thump!

Thump!

It was easy to find them now. There were one or two lying under every tree. I quickly collected six more, three in each hand, and ran back and dumped them with the others. Then six more. Then six more after that.

And still they kept falling.

Claud was in a whirl of ecstasy now, dashing about like a mad ghost under the trees. I could see the beam of his flashlight waving around in the dark and each time he found a bird he gave a little yelp of triumph.

Thump! Thump! Thump!

'That bugger Hazel ought to hear this!' he called out.

'Don't shout,' I said. 'It frightens me.'

'What's that?'

'Don't *shout*. There might be keepers.'

'Screw the keepers!' he cried. 'They're all eating!'

For three or four minutes, the pheasants kept on falling. Then suddenly they stopped.

'Keep searching!' Claud shouted. 'There's plenty more on the ground!'

'Don't you think we ought to get out while the going's good?'

'No,' he said.

We went on searching. Between us we looked under every tree within a hundred yards of the clearing, north, south, east and west, and I think we found most of them in the end. At the collecting-point there was a pile of pheasants as big as a bonfire.

'It's a miracle,' Claud was saying. 'It's a bloody miracle.' He was staring at them in a kind of trance.

'We'd better just take half a dozen each and get out quick,' I said.

'I would like to count them, Gordon.'

'There's no time for that.'

'I must count them.'

'No,' I said. 'Come on.'

'One . . .
'Two . . .
'Three . . .
'Four . . .'

He began counting them very carefully, picking up each bird in turn and laying it carefully to one side. The moon was directly overhead now and the whole clearing was brilliantly illuminated.

'I'm not standing around here like this,' I said. I walked back a few paces and hid myself in the shadows, waiting for him to finish.

'A hundred and seventeen . . . a hundred and eighteen . . . a hundred and nineteen . . . *a hundred and twenty*!' he cried. '*One hundred and twenty birds!* It's an all-time record!'

I didn't doubt it for a moment.

'The most my dad ever got in one night was fifteen and he was drunk for a week afterwards!'

'You're the champion of the world,' I said. 'Are you ready now?'

'One minute,' he answered and he pulled up his sweater and proceeded to unwind the two big white cotton sacks from around his belly. 'Here's yours,' he said, handing one of them to me. 'Fill it up quick.'

The light of the moon was so strong I could read the small print along the base of the sack. J. W. CRUMP, it said. KESTON FLOUR MILLS, LONDON SW17.

'You don't think that bastard with the brown teeth is watching us this very moment from behind a tree?'

'There's no chance of that,' Claud said. 'He's down at

the filling-station like I told you, waiting for us to come home.'

We started loading the pheasants into the sacks. They were soft and floppy-necked and the skin underneath the feathers was still warm.

'There'll be a taxi waiting for us in the lane,' Claud said.

'What?'

'I always go back in a taxi, Gordon, didn't you know that?'

I told him I didn't.

'A taxi is anonymous,' Claud said. 'Nobody knows who's inside a taxi except the driver. My dad taught me that.'

'Which driver?'

'Charlie Kinch. He's only too glad to oblige.'

We finished loading the pheasants, and I tried to hump my bulging sack on to my shoulder. My sack had about sixty birds inside it, and it must have weighed a hundred-weight and a half, at least. 'I can't carry this,' I said. 'We'll have to leave some of them behind.'

'Drag it,' Claud said. 'Just pull it behind you.'

We started off through the pitch-black woods, pulling the pheasants behind us. 'We'll never make it all the way back to the village like this,' I said.

'Charlie's never let me down yet,' Claud said.

We came to the margin of the wood and peered through the hedge into the lane. Claud said, 'Charlie boy' very softly and the old man behind the wheel of the taxi not five yards away poked his head out into the moonlight and gave us a sly toothless grin. We slid through the hedge, dragging the sacks after us along the ground.

'Hullo!' Charlie said. 'What's this?'

'It's cabbages,' Claud told him. 'Open the door.'

Two minutes later we were safely inside the taxi, cruising slowly down the hill towards the village.

It was all over now bar the shouting. Claud was triumphant, bursting with pride and excitement, and he kept leaning forward and tapping Charlie Kinch on the shoulder and saying, 'How about it, Charlie? How about this for a haul?' and Charlie kept glancing back pop-eyed at the huge bulging sacks lying on the floor between us and saying, 'Jesus Christ, man, how did you do it?'

'There's six brace of them for you, Charlie,' Claud said. And Charlie said, 'I reckon pheasants is going to be a bit scarce up at Mr Victor Hazel's opening-day shoot this year,' and Claud said, 'I imagine they are, Charlie, I imagine they are.'

'What in God's name are you going to do with a hundred and twenty pheasants?' I asked.

'Put them in cold storage for the winter,' Claud said. 'Put them in with the dogmeat in the deep-freeze at the filling-station.'

'Not tonight, I trust?'

'No, Gordon, not tonight. We leave them at Bessie's house tonight.'

'Bessie who?'

'Bessie Organ.'

'Bessie *Organ*!'

'Bessie always delivers my game, didn't you know that?'

'I don't know anything,' I said. I was completely stunned. Mrs Organ was the wife of the Reverend Jack Organ, the local vicar.

'Always choose a respectable woman to deliver your game,' Claud announced. 'That's correct, Charlie, isn't it?'

'Bessie's a right smart girl,' Charlie said.

We were driving through the village now and the street-lamps were still on and the men were wandering home from the pubs. I saw Will Prattley letting himself in quietly by the side-door of his fishmonger's shop and Mrs Prattley's head was sticking out of the window just above him, but he didn't know it.

'The vicar is very partial to roasted pheasant,' Claud said.

'He hangs it eighteen days,' Charlie said, 'then he gives it a couple of good shakes and all the feathers drop off.'

The taxi turned left and swung in through the gates of the vicarage. There were no lights on in the house and nobody met us. Claud and I dumped the pheasants in the coal shed at the rear, and then we said good-bye to Charlie Kinch and walked back in the moonlight to the filling-station, empty-handed. Whether or not Mr Rabbetts was watching us as we went in, I do not know. We saw no sign of him.

'Here she comes,' Claud said to me the next morning.

'Who?'

'Bessie – Bessie Organ.' He spoke the name proudly and with a slight proprietary air, as though he were a general referring to his bravest officer.

I followed him outside.

'Down there,' he said, pointing.

Far away down the road I could see a small female figure advancing towards us.

'What's she pushing?' I asked.

Claud gave me a sly look.

'There's only one safe way of delivering game,' he announced, 'and that's under a baby.'

'Yes,' I murmured, 'yes, of course.'

'That'll be young Christopher Organ in there, aged one and a half. He's a lovely child, Gordon.'

I could just make out the small dot of a baby sitting high up in the pram, which had its hood folded down.

'There's sixty or seventy pheasants at least under that little nipper,' Claud said happily. 'You just imagine that.'

'You can't put sixty or seventy pheasants in a pram.'

'You can if it's got a deep well underneath it, and if you take out the mattress and pack them in tight, right up to the top. All you need then is a sheet. You'll be surprised how little room a pheasant takes up when it's limp.'

We stood beside the pumps waiting for Bessie Organ to arrive. It was one of those warm windless September mornings with a darkening sky and a smell of thunder in the air.

'Right through the village bold as brass,' Claud said. 'Good old Bessie.'

'She seems in rather a hurry to me.'

Claud lit a new cigarette from the stub of the old one. 'Bessie is never in a hurry,' he said.

'She certainly isn't walking normal,' I told him. 'You look.'

He squinted at her through the smoke of his cigarette.

Then he took the cigarette out of his mouth and looked again.

'Well?' I said.

'She does seem to be going a tiny bit quick, doesn't she?' he said carefully.

'She's going damn quick.'

There was a pause. Claud was beginning to stare very hard at the approaching woman.

'Perhaps she doesn't want to be caught in the rain, Gordon. I'll bet that's exactly what it is, she thinks it's going to rain and she don't want the baby to get wet.'

'Why doesn't she put the hood up?'

He didn't answer this.

'She's *running*!' I cried. 'Look!' Bessie had suddenly broken into a full sprint.

Claud stood very still, watching the woman; and in the silence that followed I fancied I could hear a baby screaming.

'What's up?'

He didn't answer.

'There's something wrong with that baby,' I said. 'Listen.'

At this point, Bessie was about two hundred yards away from us but closing fast.

'Can you hear him now?' I said.

'Yes.'

'He's yelling his head off.'

The small shrill voice in the distance was growing louder every second, frantic, piercing, non-stop, almost hysterical.

'He's having a fit,' Claud announced.

'I think he must be.'

'That's why she's running, Gordon. She wants to get him in here quick and put him under a cold tap.'

'I'm sure you're right,' I said. 'In fact I know you're right. Just listen to that noise.'

'If it isn't a fit, you can bet your life it's something like it.'

'I quite agree.'

Claud shifted his feet uneasily on the gravel of the driveway. 'There's a thousand and one different things keep happening every day to little babies like that,' he said.

'Of course.'

'I knew a baby once who caught his fingers in the spokes of the pram wheel. He lost the lot. It cut them clean off.'

'Yes.'

'Whatever it is,' Claud said, 'I wish to Christ she'd stop running.'

A long truck loaded with bricks came up behind Bessie and the driver slowed down and poked his head out the window to stare. Bessie ignored him and flew on, and she was so close now I could see her big red face with the mouth wide open, panting for breath. I noticed she was wearing white gloves on her hands, very prim and dainty, and there was a funny little white hat to match perched right on the top of her head, like a mushroom.

Suddenly, out of the pram, straight up into the air, flew an enormous pheasant!

Claud let out a cry of horror.

The fool in the truck going along beside Bessie started roaring with laughter.

The pheasant flapped around drunkenly for a few

seconds, then it lost height and landed in the grass by the side of the road.

A grocer's van came up behind the truck and began hooting to get by. Bessie kept running.

Then – *whoosh!* – a second pheasant flew up out of the pram.

Then a third, and a fourth. Then a fifth.

'My God!' I said. 'It's the pills! They're wearing off!'

Claud didn't say anything.

Bessie covered the last fifty yards at a tremendous pace, and she came swinging into the driveway of the filling-station with birds flying up out of the pram in all directions.

'What the hell's going on?' she cried.

'Go round the back!' I shouted. 'Go round the back!' But she pulled up sharp against the first pump in the line, and before we could reach her she had seized the screaming infant in her arms and dragged him clear.

'No! No!' Claud cried, racing towards her. 'Don't lift the baby! Put him back! Hold down the sheet!' But she wasn't even listening, and with the weight of the child suddenly lifted away, a great cloud of pheasants rose up out of the pram, fifty or sixty of them, at least, and the whole sky above us was filled with huge brown birds flapping their wings furiously to gain height.

Claud and I started running up and down the driveway waving our arms to frighten them off the premises. 'Go away!' we shouted. 'Shoo! Go away!' But they were too dopey still to take any notice of us and within half a minute down they came again and settled themselves like a swarm of locusts all over the front of my filling-station. The place was covered with them. They sat wing to wing along the edges of the roof and on the concrete canopy that came out over the pumps, and a dozen at least were clinging to the sill of the office window. Some had flown down on to the rack that held the bottles of lubricating-oil, and others were sliding about on the bonnets of my second-hand cars. One cockbird with a fine tail was perched superbly on top of a petrol pump, and quite a number, those that were too drunk to stay aloft, simply squatted in the driveway at our feet, fluffing their feathers and blinking their small eyes.

Across the road, a line of cars had already started forming behind the brick-lorry and the grocery-van, and people were opening their doors and getting out and beginning to cross over to have a closer look. I glanced at my watch. It was twenty to nine. Any moment now, I thought, a large black car is going to come streaking along the road from the direction of the village, and the car will be a Rolls, and the face behind the wheel will be the great glistening brewer's face of Mr Victor Hazel.

'They near pecked him to pieces!' Bessie was shouting, clasping the screaming baby to her bosom.

'You go on home, Bessie,' Claud said, white in the face.

'Lock up,' I said. 'Put out the sign. We've gone for the day.'

The Landlady

First published in the *New Yorker*,
28 November 1959

Billy Weaver had travelled down from London on the slow afternoon train, with a change at Reading on the way, and by the time he got to Bath it was about nine o'clock in the evening and the moon was coming up out of a clear starry sky over the houses opposite the station entrance. But the air was deadly cold and the wind was like a flat blade of ice on his cheeks.

'Excuse me,' he said, 'but is there a fairly cheap hotel not too far away from here?'

'Try the Bell and Dragon,' the porter answered, pointing down the road. 'They might take you in. It's about a quarter of a mile along on the other side.'

Billy thanked him and picked up his suitcase and set out to walk the quarter-mile to the Bell and Dragon. He had never been to Bath before. He didn't know anyone who lived there. But Mr Greenslade at the Head Office in London had told him it was a splendid town. 'Find your own lodgings,' he had said, 'and then go along and report to the Branch Manager as soon as you've got yourself settled.'

Billy was seventeen years old. He was wearing a new navy-blue overcoat, a new brown trilby hat, and a new brown suit, and he was feeling fine. He walked briskly down the street. He was trying to do everything briskly these days. Briskness, he had decided, was *the* one common characteristic of all successful businessmen. The big shots up at Head Office were absolutely fantastically brisk all the time. They were amazing.

There were no shops on this wide street that he was walking along, only a line of tall houses on each side, all of them identical. They had porches and pillars and four or five steps going up to their front doors, and it was obvious that once upon a time they had been very swanky residences. But now, even in the darkness, he could see that the paint was peeling from the woodwork on their doors and windows, and that the handsome white façades were cracked and blotchy from neglect.

Suddenly, in a downstairs window that was brilliantly illuminated by a street-lamp not six yards away, Billy caught sight of a printed notice propped up against the glass in one of the upper panes. It said BED AND BREAKFAST. There was a vase of yellow chrysanthemums, tall and beautiful, standing just underneath the notice.

He stopped walking. He moved a bit closer. Green curtains (some sort of velvety material) were hanging down on either side of the window. The chrysanthemums looked wonderful beside them. He went right up and peered through the glass into the room, and the first thing he saw was a bright fire burning in the hearth. On the carpet in front of the fire, a pretty little dachshund was curled up asleep with its nose tucked into its belly. The room itself, so far as he could see in the half-darkness, was filled with pleasant furniture. There was a baby-grand piano and a big sofa and several plump armchairs; and in one corner he spotted a large parrot in a cage. Animals were usually a good sign in a place like this, Billy told himself; and all in all, it looked to him as though it would be a pretty decent house to stay in. Certainly it would be more comfortable than the Bell and Dragon.

On the other hand, a pub would be more congenial than a boarding-house. There would be beer and darts in the evenings, and lots of people to talk to, and it would probably be a good bit cheaper, too. He had stayed a couple of nights in a pub once before and he had liked it. He had never stayed in any boarding-houses, and, to be perfectly honest, he was a tiny bit frightened of them. The name itself conjured up images of watery cabbage, rapacious landladies, and a powerful smell of kippers in the living-room.

After dithering about like this in the cold for two or three minutes, Billy decided that he would walk on and take a look at the Bell and Dragon before making up his mind. He turned to go.

And now a queer thing happened to him. He was in the act of stepping back and turning away from the window when all at once his eye was caught and held in the most peculiar manner by the small notice that was there. BED AND BREAKFAST, it said. BED AND BREAKFAST, BED AND BREAKFAST, BED AND BREAKFAST. Each word was like a large black eye staring at him through the glass, holding him, compelling him, forcing him to stay where he was and not to walk away from that house, and the next thing he knew, he was actually moving across from the window to the front door of the house, climbing the steps that led up to it, and reaching for the bell.

He pressed the bell. Far away in a back room he heard it ringing, and then *at once* – it must have been at once because he hadn't even had time to take his finger from the bell-button – the door swung open and a woman was standing there.

Normally you ring the bell and you have at least a half-minute's wait before the door opens. But this dame was like a jack-in-the-box. He pressed the bell – and out she popped! It made him jump.

She was about forty-five or fifty years old, and the moment she saw him, she gave him a warm welcoming smile.

'*Please* come in,' she said pleasantly. She stepped aside, holding the door wide open, and Billy found himself automatically starting forward. The compulsion or, more accurately, the desire to follow after her into that house was extraordinarily strong.

'I saw the notice in the window,' he said, holding himself back.

'Yes, I know.'

'I was wondering about a room.'

'It's *all* ready for you, my dear,' she said. She had a round pink face and very gentle blue eyes.

'I was on my way to the Bell and Dragon,' Billy told her. 'But the notice in your window just happened to catch my eye.'

'My dear boy,' she said, 'why don't you come in out of the cold?'

'How much do you charge?'

'Five and sixpence a night, including breakfast.'

It was fantastically cheap. It was less than half of what he had been willing to pay.

'If that is too much,' she added, 'then perhaps I can reduce it just a tiny bit. Do you desire an egg for breakfast? Eggs are expensive at the moment. It would be sixpence less without the egg.'

'Five and sixpence is fine,' he answered. 'I should like very much to stay here.'

'I knew you would. Do come in.'

She seemed terribly nice. She looked exactly like the mother of one's best school-friend welcoming one into the house to stay for the Christmas holidays. Billy took off his hat, and stepped over the threshold.

'Just hang it there,' she said, 'and let me help you with your coat.'

There were no other hats or coats in the hall. There were no umbrellas, no walking-sticks – nothing.

'We have it *all* to ourselves,' she said, smiling at him over her shoulder as she led the way upstairs. 'You see, it isn't very often I have the pleasure of taking a visitor into my little nest.'

The old girl is slightly dotty, Billy told himself. But at five and sixpence a night, who gives a damn about that? 'I should've thought you'd be simply swamped with applicants,' he said politely.

'Oh, I am, my dear, I am, of course I am. But the trouble is that I'm inclined to be just a teeny weeny bit choosy and particular – if you see what I mean.'

'Ah, yes.'

'But I'm always ready. Everything is always ready day and night in this house just on the off-chance that an acceptable young gentleman will come along. And it is such a pleasure, my dear, such a very great pleasure when now and again I open the door and I see someone standing there who is just *exactly* right.' She was halfway up the stairs, and she paused with one hand on the stair-rail, turning her head and smiling down at him with pale lips. 'Like you,' she added, and her blue eyes travelled slowly all the way down the length of Billy's body, to his feet, and then up again.

On the second-floor landing she said to him, 'This floor is mine.'

They climbed up another flight. 'And this one is *all* yours,' she said. 'Here's your room. I do hope you'll like it.' She took him into a small but charming front bedroom, switching on the light as she went in.

'The morning sun comes right in the window, Mr Perkins. It *is* Mr Perkins, isn't it?'

'No,' he said. 'It's Weaver.'

'Mr Weaver. How nice. I've put a water-bottle between the sheets to air them out, Mr Weaver. It's such a comfort to have a hot water-bottle in a strange bed with clean sheets, don't you agree? And you may light the gas fire at any time if you feel chilly.'

'Thank you,' Billy said. 'Thank you ever so much.' He noticed that the bedspread had been taken off the bed, and that the bedclothes had been neatly turned back on one side, all ready for someone to get in.

'I'm so glad you appeared,' she said, looking earnestly into his face. 'I was beginning to get worried.'

'That's all right,' Billy answered brightly. 'You mustn't worry about me.' He put his suitcase on the chair and started to open it.

'And what about supper, my dear? Did you manage to get anything to eat before you came here?'

'I'm not a bit hungry, thank you,' he said. 'I think I'll just go to bed as soon as possible because tomorrow I've got to get up rather early and report to the office.'

'Very well, then. I'll leave you now so that you can unpack. But before you go to bed, would you be kind enough to pop into the sitting-room on the ground floor and sign the book? Everyone has to do that because it's the law of the land, and we don't want to go breaking any laws at *this* stage in the proceedings, do we?' She gave him a little wave of the hand and went quickly out of the room and closed the door.

Now, the fact that his landlady appeared to be slightly off her rocker didn't worry Billy in the least. After all, she not only was harmless – there was no question about that – but she was also quite obviously a kind and generous soul. He guessed that she had probably lost a son in the war, or something like that, and had never gotten over it.

So a few minutes later, after unpacking his suitcase and washing his hands, he trotted downstairs to the ground floor and entered the living-room. His landlady wasn't there, but the fire was glowing in the hearth, and the little dachshund was still sleeping soundly in front of it. The room was wonderfully warm and cosy. I'm a lucky fellow, he thought, rubbing his hands. This is a bit of all right.

He found the guest-book lying open on the piano, so he took out his pen and wrote down his name and address. There were only two other entries above his on the page, and, as one always does with guest-books, he started to read them. One was a Christopher Mulholland from Cardiff. The other was Gregory W. Temple from Bristol.

That's funny, he thought suddenly. Christopher Mulholland. It rings a bell.

Now where on earth had he heard that rather unusual name before?

Was it a boy at school? No. Was it one of his sister's numerous young men, perhaps, or a friend of his father's? No, no, it wasn't any of those. He glanced down again at the book.

Christopher Mulholland   *231 Cathedral Road, Cardiff*
Gregory W. Temple   *27 Sycamore Drive, Bristol*

As a matter of fact, now he came to think of it, he wasn't at all sure that the second name didn't have almost as much of a familiar ring about it as the first.

'Gregory Temple?' he said aloud, searching his memory. 'Christopher Mulholland? . . .'

'Such charming boys,' a voice behind him answered, and he turned and saw his landlady sailing into the room with a large silver tea-tray in her hands. She was holding it well out in front of her, and rather high up, as though the tray were a pair of reins on a frisky horse.

'They sound somehow familiar,' he said.

'They do? How interesting.'

'I'm almost positive I've heard those names before somewhere. Isn't that odd? Maybe it was in the newspapers. They weren't famous in any way, were they? I mean famous cricketers or footballers or something like that?'

'Famous,' she said, setting the tea-tray down on the low table in front of the sofa. 'Oh no, I don't think they were famous. But they were incredibly handsome, both of them, I can promise you that. They were tall and young and handsome, my dear, just exactly like you.'

Once more, Billy glanced down at the book. 'Look here,' he said, noticing the dates. 'This last entry is over two years old.'

'It is?'

'Yes, indeed. And Christopher Mulholland's is nearly a year before that – more than *three years* ago.'

'Dear me,' she said, shaking her head and heaving a dainty little sigh. 'I would never have thought it. How time does fly away from us all, doesn't it, Mr Wilkins?'

'It's Weaver,' Billy said. 'W-e-a-v-e-r.'

'Oh, of course it is!' she cried, sitting down on the sofa. 'How silly of me. I do apologize. In one ear and out the other, that's me, Mr Weaver.'

'You know something?' Billy said. 'Something that's really quite extraordinary about all this?'

'No, dear, I don't.'

'Well, you see, both of these names – Mulholland and Temple – I not only seem to remember each one of them separately, so to speak, but somehow or other, in some peculiar way, they both appear to be sort of connected together as well. As though they were both famous for the same sort of thing, if you see what I mean — like . . . well . . . like Dempsey and Tunney, for example, or Churchill and Roosevelt.'

'How amusing,' she said. 'But come over here now, dear, and sit down beside me on the sofa and I'll give you a nice cup of tea and a ginger biscuit before you go to bed.'

'You really shouldn't bother,' Billy said. 'I didn't mean you to do anything like that.' He stood by the piano, watching her as she fussed about with the cups and saucers. He noticed that she had small, white, quickly moving hands, and red fingernails.

'I'm almost positive it was in the newspapers I saw them,' Billy said. 'I'll think of it in a second. I'm sure I will.'

There is nothing more tantalizing than a thing like this that lingers just outside the borders of one's memory. He hated to give up.

'Now wait a minute,' he said. 'Wait just a minute. Mulholland . . . Christopher Mulholland . . . wasn't *that* the name of the Eton schoolboy who was on a walking-tour through the West Country, and then all of a sudden . . .'

'Milk?' she said. 'And sugar?'

'Yes, please. And then all of a sudden . . .'

'Eton schoolboy?' she said. 'Oh no, my dear, that can't possibly be right because *my* Mr Mulholland was certainly not an Eton schoolboy when he came to me. He was a Cambridge undergraduate. Come over here now and sit next to me and warm yourself in front of this lovely fire. Come on. Your tea's all ready for you.' She patted the empty place beside her on the sofa, and she sat there smiling at Billy and waiting for him to come over.

He crossed the room slowly, and sat down on the edge of the sofa. She placed his teacup on the table in front of him.

'*There* we are,' she said. 'How nice and cosy this is, isn't it?'

Billy started sipping his tea. She did the same. For half a minute or so, neither of them spoke. But Billy knew that she was looking at him. Her body was half turned towards him, and he could feel her eyes resting on his face, watching him over the rim of her teacup. Now and again, he caught a whiff of a peculiar smell that seemed to emanate directly from her person. It was not in the least unpleasant, and it reminded him – well, he wasn't quite sure what it reminded him of. Pickled walnuts? New leather? Or was it the corridors of a hospital?

At length, she said, 'Mr Mulholland was a great one for his tea. Never in my life have I seen anyone drink as much tea as dear, sweet Mr Mulholland.'

'I suppose he left fairly recently,' Billy said. He was still puzzling his head about the two names. He was positive now that he had seen them in the newspapers – in the headlines.

'Left?' she said, arching her brows. 'But my dear boy, he never left. He's still here. Mr Temple is also here. They're on the fourth floor, both of them together.'

Billy set his cup down slowly on the table and stared at his landlady. She smiled back at him, and then she put out one of her white hands and patted him comfortingly on the knee. 'How old are you, my dear?' she asked.

'Seventeen.'

'Seventeen!' she cried. 'Oh, it's the perfect age! Mr Mulholland was also seventeen. But I think he was a trifle shorter than you are; in fact I'm sure he was, and his teeth weren't *quite* so white. You have the most beautiful teeth, Mr Weaver, did you know that?'

'They're not as good as they look,' Billy said. 'They've got simply masses of fillings in them at the back.'

'Mr Temple, of course, was a little older,' she said, ignoring his remark. 'He was actually twenty-eight. And yet I never would have guessed it if he hadn't told me, never in my whole life. There wasn't a *blemish* on his body.'

'A what?' Billy said.

'His skin was *just* like a baby's.'

There was a pause. Billy picked up his teacup and took another sip of his tea, then he set it down again gently in its saucer. He waited for her to say something else, but she seemed to have lapsed into another of her silences. He sat there staring straight ahead of him into the far corner of the room, biting his lower lip.

'That parrot,' he said at last. 'You know something? It had me completely fooled when I first saw it through the window. I could have sworn it was alive.'

'Alas, no longer.'

'It's most terribly clever the way it's been done,' he said. 'It doesn't look in the least bit dead. Who did it?'

'I did.'

'*You* did?'

'Of course,' she said. 'And have you met my little Basil as well?' She nodded towards the dachshund curled up so comfortably in front of the fire. Billy looked at it. And suddenly, he realized that this animal had all the time been just as silent and motionless as the parrot. He put out a hand and touched it gently on the top of its back. The back was hard and cold, and when he pushed the hair to one side with his fingers, he could see the skin underneath, greyish-black and dry and perfectly preserved.

'Good gracious me,' he said. 'How absolutely fascinating.' He turned away from the dog and stared with deep admiration at the little woman beside him on the sofa. 'It must be most awfully difficult to do a thing like that.'

'Not in the least,' she said. 'I stuff *all* my little pets myself when they pass away. Will you have another cup of tea?'

'No, thank you,' Billy said. The tea tasted faintly of bitter almonds, and he didn't much care for it.

'You did sign the book, didn't you?'

'Oh yes.'

'That's good. Because later on, if I happen to forget what you were called, then I could always come down here and look it up. I still do that almost every day with Mr Mulholland and Mr . . . Mr . . .'

'Temple,' Billy said. 'Gregory Temple. Exuse my asking, but haven't there been *any* other guests here except them in the last two or three years?'

Holding her teacup high in one hand, inclining her head slightly to the left, she looked up at him out of the corners of her eyes and gave him another gentle little smile.

'No, my dear,' she said. 'Only you.'

Genesis and Catastrophe

A True Story

First published as 'A Fine Son' in *Playboy*
(December 1959)

'Everything is normal,' the doctor was saying. 'Just lie back and relax.' His voice was miles away in the distance and he seemed to be shouting at her.

'You have a son.'

'What?'

'You have a fine son. You understand that, don't you? A fine son. Did you hear him crying?'

'Is he all right, Doctor?'

'Of course he is all right.'

'Please let me see him.'

'You'll see him in a moment.'

'You are certain he is all right?'

'I am quite certain.'

'Is he still crying?'

'Try to rest. There is nothing to worry about.'

'Why has he stopped crying, Doctor? What happened?'

'Don't excite yourself, please. Everything is normal.'

'I want to see him. Please let me see him.'

'Dear lady,' the doctor said, patting her hand. 'You have a fine strong healthy child. Don't you believe me when I tell you that?'

'What is the woman over there doing to him?'

'Your baby is being made to look pretty for you,' the doctor said. 'We are giving him a little wash, that is all. You must spare us a moment or two for that.'

'You swear he is all right?'

'I swear it. Now lie back and relax. Close your eyes. Go on, close your eyes. That's right. That's better. Good girl . . .'

'I have prayed and prayed that he will live, Doctor.'

'Of course he will live. What are you talking about?'

'The others didn't.'

'What?'

'None of my other ones lived, Doctor.'

The doctor stood beside the bed looking down at the pale exhausted face of the young woman. He had never seen her before today. She and her husband were new people in the town. The innkeeper's wife, who had come up to assist in the delivery, had told him that the husband worked at the local customs-house on the border and that the two of them had arrived quite suddenly at the inn with one trunk and one suitcase about three months ago. The husband was a drunkard, the innkeeper's wife had said, an arrogant, overbearing, bullying little drunkard, but the young woman was gentle and religious. And she was very sad. She never smiled. In the few weeks that she had been here, the innkeeper's wife had never once seen her smile. Also there was a rumour that this was the husband's third marriage, that one wife had died and that the other had divorced him for unsavoury reasons. But that was only a rumour.

The doctor bent down and pulled the sheet up a little

higher over the patient's chest. 'You have nothing to worry about,' he said gently. 'This is a perfectly normal baby.'

'That's exactly what they told me about the others. But I lost them all, Doctor. In the last eighteen months I have lost all three of my children, so you mustn't blame me for being anxious.'

'Three?'

'This is my fourth . . . in four years.'

The doctor shifted his feet uneasily on the bare floor.

'I don't think you know what it means, Doctor, to lose them all, all three of them, slowly, separately, one by one. I keep seeing them. I can see Gustav's face now as clearly as if he were lying here beside me in the bed. Gustav was a lovely boy, Doctor. But he was always ill. It is terrible when they are always ill and there is nothing you can do to help them.'

'I know.'

The woman opened her eyes, stared up at the doctor for a few seconds, then closed them again.

'My little girl was called Ida. She died a few days before Christmas. That is only four months ago. I just wish you could have seen Ida, Doctor.'

'You have a new one now.'

'But Ida was so beautiful.'

'Yes,' the doctor said. 'I know.'

'How can you know?' she cried.

'I am sure that she was a lovely child. But this new one is also like that.' The doctor turned away from the bed and walked over to the window and stood there looking out. It was a wet grey April afternoon, and across the street he could see the red roofs of the houses and the huge rain-drops splashing on the tiles.

'Ida was two years old, Doctor . . . and she was so beautiful I was never able to take my eyes off her from the time I dressed her in the morning until she was safe in bed again at night. I used to live in holy terror of something happening to that child. Gustav had gone and my little Otto had also gone and she was all I had left. Sometimes I used to get up in the night and creep over to the cradle and put my ear close to her mouth just to make sure that she was breathing.'

'Try to rest,' the doctor said, going back to the bed. 'Please try to rest.' The woman's face was white and bloodless, and there was a slight bluish-grey tinge around the nostrils and the mouth. A few strands of damp hair hung down over her forehead, sticking to the skin.

'When she died . . . I was already pregnant again when that happened, Doctor. This new one was a good four months on its way when Ida died. "I don't want it!" I shouted after the funeral. "I won't have it! I have buried enough children!" And my husband . . . he was strolling among the guests with a big glass of beer in his hand . . . he turned around quickly and said, "I have news for you, Klara, I have good news." Can you imagine that, Doctor? We have just buried our third child and he stands there with a glass of beer in his hand and tells me that he has good news. "Today I have been posted to Braunau," he says, "so you can start packing at once. This will be a new start for you, Klara," he says. "It will be a new place and you can have a new doctor . . ."'

'Please don't talk any more.'

'You *are* the new doctor, aren't you, Doctor?'

'That's right.'

'And here we are in Braunau.'

'Yes.'

'I am frightened, Doctor.'

'Try not to be frightened.'

'What chance can the fourth one have now?'

'You must stop thinking like that.'

'I can't help it. I am certain there is something inherited that causes my children to die in this way. There must be.'

'That is nonsense.'

'Do you know what my husband said to me when Otto was born, Doctor? He came into the room and he looked into the cradle where Otto was lying and he said, "Why do *all* my children have to be so small and weak?"'

'I am sure he didn't say that.'

'He put his head right into Otto's cradle as though he were examining a tiny insect and he said, "All I am saying is why can't they be better *specimens*? That's all I am saying." And three days after that, Otto was dead. We baptized him quickly on the third day and he died the same evening. And then Gustav died. And then Ida died. All of them died, Doctor ... and suddenly the whole house was empty ...'

'Don't think about it now.'

'Is this one so very small?'

'He is a normal child.'

'But small?'

'He is a little small, perhaps. But the small ones are

often a lot tougher than the big ones. Just imagine, Frau Hitler, this time next year he will be almost learning how to walk. Isn't that a lovely thought?'

She didn't answer this.

'And two years from now he will probably be talking his head off and driving you crazy with his chatter. Have you settled on a name for him yet?'

'A name?'

'Yes.'

'I don't know. I'm not sure. I think my husband said that if it was a boy we were going to call him Adolfus.'

'That means he would be called Adolf.'

'Yes. My husband likes Adolf because it has a certain similarity to Alois. My husband is called Alois.'

'Excellent.'

'Oh no!' she cried, starting up suddenly from the pillow. 'That's the same question they asked me when Otto was born! It means he is going to die! You are going to baptize him at once!'

'Now, now,' the doctor said, taking her gently by the shoulders. 'You are quite wrong. I promise you you are wrong. I was simply being an inquisitive old man, that is all. I love talking about names. I think Adolfus is a particularly fine name. It is one of my favourites. And look – here he comes now.'

The innkeeper's wife, carrying the baby high up on her enormous bosom, came sailing across the room towards the bed. 'Here is the little beauty!' she cried, beaming. 'Would you like to hold him, my dear? Shall I put him beside you?'

'Is he well wrapped?' the doctor asked. 'It is extremely cold in here.'

'Certainly he is well wrapped.'

The baby was tightly swaddled in a white woollen shawl, and only the tiny pink head protruded. The innkeeper's wife placed him gently on the bed beside the mother. 'There you are,' she said. 'Now you can lie there and look at him to your heart's content.'

'I think you will like him,' the doctor said, smiling. 'He is a fine little baby.'

'He has the most lovely hands!' the innkeeper's wife claimed. 'Such long delicate fingers!'

The mother didn't move. She didn't even turn her head to look.

'Go on!' cried the innkeeper's wife. 'He won't bite you!'

'I am frightened to look. I don't dare to believe that I have another baby and that he is all right.'

'Don't be so stupid.'

Slowly, the mother turned her head and looked at the small, incredibly serene face that lay on the pillow beside her.

'Is this my baby?'

'Of course.'

'Oh . . . oh . . . but he is beautiful.'

The doctor turned away and went over to the table and began putting his things into his bag. The mother lay on the bed gazing at the child and smiling and touching him and making little noises of pleasure. 'Hello, Adolfus,' she whispered. 'Hello, my little Adolf . . .'

'Ssshh!' said the innkeeper's wife. 'Listen! I think your husband is coming.'

The doctor walked over to the door and opened it and looked out into the corridor.

'Herr Hitler?'

'Yes.'

'Come in, please.'

A small man in a dark-green uniform stepped softly into the room and looked around him.

'Congratulations,' the doctor said. 'You have a son.'

The man had a pair of enormous whiskers meticulously groomed after the manner of the Emperor Franz Josef, and he smelled strongly of beer. 'A son?'

'Yes.'

'How is he?'

'He is fine. So is your wife.'

'Good.' The father turned and walked with a curious little prancing stride over to the bed where his wife was lying. 'Well, Klara,' he said, smiling through his whiskers. 'How did it go?' He bent down to take a look at the baby. Then he bent lower. In a series of quick jerky movements, he bent lower and lower until his face was only about twelve inches from the baby's head. The wife lay sideways on the pillow, staring up at him with a kind of supplicating look.

'He has the most marvellous pair of lungs,' the innkeeper's wife announced. 'You should have heard him screaming just after he came into this world.'

'But my God, Klara . . .'

'What is it, dear?'

'This one is even smaller than Otto was!'

The doctor took a couple of quick paces forward. 'There is nothing wrong with that child,' he said.

Slowly, the husband straightened up and turned away from the bed and looked at the doctor. He seemed bewildered and stricken. 'It's no good lying, Doctor,' he said. 'I know what it means. It's going to be the same all over again.'

'Now you listen to me,' the doctor said.

'But do you *know* what happened to the others, Doctor?'

'You must forget about the others, Herr Hitler. Give this one a chance.'

'But so small and weak!'

'My dear sir, he has only just been born.'

'Even so . . .'

'What are you trying to do?' cried the innkeeper's wife. 'Talk him into his grave?'

'That's enough!' the doctor said sharply.

The mother was weeping now. Great sobs were shaking her body.

The doctor walked over to the husband and put a hand on his shoulder. 'Be good to her,' he whispered. 'Please. It is very important.' Then he squeezed the husband's shoulder hard and began pushing him forward surreptitiously to the edge of the bed. The husband hesitated. The doctor squeezed harder, signalling to him urgently through fingers and thumb. At last, reluctantly, the husband bent down and kissed his wife lightly on the cheek.

'All right, Klara,' he said. 'Now stop crying.'

'I have prayed so hard that he will live, Alois.'

'Yes.'

'Every day for months I have gone to the church and begged on my knees that this one will be allowed to live.'

'Yes, Klara, I know.'

'Three dead children is all that I can stand, don't you realize that?'

'Of course.'

'He *must* live, Alois. He *must*, he *must* . . . Oh God, be merciful unto him now . . .'

Mrs Bixby and the Colonel's Coat

First published in *Nugget* (1959)

America is the land of opportunity for women. Already they own about eighty-five per cent of the wealth of the nation. Soon they will have it all. Divorce has become a lucrative process, simple to arrange and easy to forget; and ambitious females can repeat it as often as they please and parlay their winnings to astronomical figures. The husband's death also brings satisfactory rewards and some ladies prefer to rely upon this method. They know that the waiting period will not be unduly protracted, for overwork and hypertension are bound to get the poor devil before long, and he will die at his desk with a bottle of benzedrines in one hand and a packet of tranquillizers in the other.

Succeeding generations of youthful American males are not deterred in the slightest by this terrifying pattern of divorce and death. The higher the divorce rate climbs, the more eager they become. Young men marry like mice, almost before they have reached the age of puberty, and a large proportion of them have at least two ex-wives on the payroll by the time they are thirty-six years old. To support these ladies in the manner to which they are accustomed, the men must work like slaves, which is of course precisely what they are. But now at last, as they approach their premature middle age, a sense of disillusionment and fear begins to creep slowly into their hearts, and in the evenings they take to huddling together in little groups, in clubs and bars, drinking their whiskies and swallowing their pills, and trying to comfort one another with stories.

The basic theme of these stories never varies. There are always three main characters – the husband, the wife and the dirty dog. The husband is a decent clean-living man, working hard at his job. The wife is cunning, deceitful and lecherous, and she is invariably up to some sort of jiggery-pokery with the dirty dog. The husband is too good a man even to suspect her. Things look black for the husband. Will the poor man ever find out? Must he be a cuckold for the rest of his life? Yes, he must. But wait! Suddenly, by a brilliant manoeuvre, the husband completely turns the tables on his monstrous spouse. The woman is flabbergasted, stupefied, humiliated, defeated. The audience of men around the bar smiles quietly to itself and takes a little comfort from the fantasy.

There are many of these stories going around, these wonderful wishful-thinking dreamworld inventions of the unhappy male, but most of them are too fatuous to be worth repeating, and far too fruity to be put down on paper. There is one, however, that seems to be superior to the rest, particularly as it has the merit of being true. It is extremely popular with twice- or thrice-bitten males in search of solace, and if you are one of them, and if you haven't heard it before, you may enjoy the way it comes out. The story is called 'Mrs Bixby and the Colonel's Coat', and it goes something like this:

Dr and Mrs Bixby lived in a smallish apartment some-where in New York City. Dr Bixby was a dentist who made an average income. Mrs Bixby was a big vigorous woman with a wet mouth. Once a month, always on Friday afternoons, Mrs Bixby would board the train at Pennsylvania Station and travel to Baltimore to visit her old aunt. She would spend the night with the aunt and return to New York on the following day in time to cook supper for her husband. Dr Bixby accepted this arrange-ment good-naturedly. He knew that Aunt Maude lived in Baltimore, and that his wife was very fond of the old lady, and certainly it would be unreasonable to deny either of them the pleasure of a monthly meeting.

'Just so long as you don't ever expect me to accompany you,' Dr Bixby had said in the beginning.

'Of course not, darling,' Mrs Bixby had answered. 'After all, she is not *your* aunt. She's mine.'

So far so good.

At it turned out, however, the aunt was little more than a convenient alibi for Mrs Bixby. The dirty dog, in the shape of a gentleman known as the Colonel, was lurking slyly in the background, and our heroine spent the greater part of her Baltimore time in this scoundrel's company. The Colonel was exceedingly wealthy. He lived in a charm-ing house on the outskirts of the town. No wife or family encumbered him, only a few discreet and loyal servants, and in Mrs Bixby's absence he consoled himself by riding his horses and hunting the fox.

Year after year, this pleasant alliance between Mrs Bixby and the Colonel continued without a hitch. They met so seldom – twelve times a year is not much when you come to think of it – that there was little or no chance of their growing bored with one another. On the contrary, the long wait between meetings only made the heart grow fonder, and each separate occasion became an exciting reunion.

'Tally-ho!' the Colonel would cry each time he met her at the station in the big car. 'My dear, I'd almost forgotten how ravishing you looked. Let's go to earth.'

Eight years went by.

It was just before Christmas, and Mrs Bixby was standing on the station in Baltimore waiting for the train to take her back to New York. This particular visit which had just ended had been more than usually agreeable, and she was in a cheerful mood. But then the Colonel's company always did that to her these days. The man had a way of making her feel that she was altogether a rather remarkable woman, a person of subtle and exotic talents, fascinating beyond measure; and what a very different thing that was from the dentist husband at home who never succeeded in making her feel that she was anything but a sort of eternal patient, someone who dwelt in the waiting-room, silent among the magazines, seldom if ever nowadays to be called in to suffer the finicky precise ministrations of those clean pink hands.

'The Colonel asked me to give you this,' a voice beside her said. She turned and saw Wilkins, the Colonel's groom, a small wizened dwarf with grey skin, and he was pushing a large flattish cardboard box into her arms.

'Good gracious me!' she cried, all of a flutter. 'My

heavens, what an enormous box! What is it, Wilkins? Was there a message? Did he send me a message?'

'No message,' the groom said, and he walked away.

As soon as she was on the train, Mrs Bixby carried the box into the privacy of the Ladies' Room and locked the door. How exciting this was! A Christmas present from the Colonel. She started to undo the string. 'I'll bet it's a dress,' she said aloud. 'It might even be two dresses. Or it might be a whole lot of beautiful underclothes. I won't look. I'll just feel around and try to guess what it is. I'll try to guess the colour as well, and exactly what it looks like. Also how much it cost.'

She shut her eyes tight and slowly lifted off the lid. Then she put one hand down into the box. There was some tissue paper on top; she could feel it and hear it rustling. There was also an envelope or a card of some sort. She ignored this and began burrowing underneath the tissue paper, the fingers reaching out delicately, like tendrils.

'My God,' she cried suddenly. 'It can't be true!'

She opened her eyes wide and stared at the coat. Then she pounced on it and lifted it out of the box. Thick layers of fur made a lovely noise against the tissue paper as they unfolded, and when she held it up and saw it hanging to its full length, it was so beautiful it took her breath away.

Never had she seen mink like this before. It *was* mink, wasn't it? Yes, of course it was. But what a glorious colour! The fur was almost pure black. At first she thought it *was* black; but when she held it closer to the window she saw that there was a touch of blue in it as well, a deep rich blue, like cobalt. Quickly she looked at the label. It said simply, WILD LABRADOR MINK. There was nothing else, no sign of where it had been bought or anything. But that, she told herself, was probably the Colonel's doing. The wily old fox was making darn sure he didn't leave any tracks. Good for him. But what in the world could it have cost? She hardly dared to think. Four, five, six thousand dollars? Possibly more.

She just couldn't take her eyes off it. Nor, for that matter, could she wait to try it on. Quickly she slipped off her own plain red coat. She was panting a little now, she couldn't help it, and her eyes were stretched very wide. But oh God, the feel of that fur! And those huge wide sleeves with their thick turned-up cuffs! Who was it had once told her that they always used female skins for the arms and male skins for the rest of the coat? Someone had told her that. Joan Rutfield, probably; though how *Joan* would know anything about *mink* she couldn't imagine.

The great black coat seemed to slide on to her almost of its own accord, like a second skin. Oh boy! It was the queerest feeling! She glanced into the mirror. It was fantastic. Her whole personality had suddenly changed completely. She looked dazzling, radiant, rich, brilliant, voluptuous, all at the same time. And the sense of power that it gave her! In this coat she could walk into any place she wanted and people would come scurrying around her like rabbits. The whole thing was just too wonderful for words!

Mrs Bixby picked up the envelope that was still lying in the box. She opened it and pulled out the Colonel's letter:

I once heard you saying you were fond of mink so I got you this.
I'm told it's a good one. Please accept it with my sincere good
wishes as a parting gift. For my own personal reasons I shall not
be able to see you any more. Good-bye and good luck.

Well!

Imagine that!

Right out of the blue, just when she was feeling so happy.

No more Colonel.

What a dreadful shock.

She would miss him enormously.

Slowly, Mrs Bixby began stroking the lovely soft black fur of the coat. What you lose on the swings you get back on the roundabouts.

She smiled and folded the letter, meaning to tear it up and throw it out the window, but in folding it she noticed that there was something written on the other side:

P.S. Just tell them that nice generous aunt of yours gave it to you
for Christmas.

Mrs Bixby's mouth, at that moment stretched wide in a silky smile, snapped back like a piece of elastic.

'The man must be mad!' she cried. 'Aunt Maude doesn't have that sort of money. She couldn't possibly give me this.'

But if Aunt Maude didn't give it to her, then who did?

Oh God! In the excitement of finding the coat and trying it on, she had completely overlooked this vital aspect.

In a couple of hours she would be in New York. Ten minutes after that she would be home, and the husband would be there to greet her; and even a man like Cyril, dwelling as he did in a dark phlegmy world of root canals, bicuspids and caries, would start asking a few questions if his wife suddenly waltzed in from a week-end wearing a six-thousand-dollar mink coat.

You know what I think, she told herself. I think that goddam Colonel has done this on purpose just to torture me. He knew perfectly well Aunt Maude didn't have enough money to buy this. He knew I wouldn't be able to keep it.

But the thought of parting with it now was more than Mrs Bixby could bear.

'I've *got* to have this coat!' she said aloud. 'I've got to have this coat! I've got to have this coat!'

Very well, my dear. You shall have the coat. But don't panic. Sit still and keep calm and start thinking. You're a clever girl, aren't you? You've fooled him before. The man never has been able to see much further than the end of his own probe, you know that. So just sit absolutely still and *think*. There's lots of time.

Two and a half hours later, Mrs Bixby stepped off the train at Pennsylvania Station and walked quickly to the exit. She was wearing her old red coat again now and carrying the cardboard box in her arms. She signalled for a taxi.

'Driver,' she said, 'would you know of a pawnbroker that's still open around here?'

The man behind the wheel raised his brows and looked back at her, amused.

'Plenty along Sixth Avenue,' he answered.

'Stop at the first one you see, then, will you please?' She got in and was driven away.

Soon the taxi pulled up outside a shop that had three brass balls hanging over the entrance.

'Wait for me, please,' Mrs Bixby said to the driver, and she got out of the taxi and entered the shop.

There was an enormous cat crouching on the counter eating fishheads out of a white saucer. The animal looked up at Mrs Bixby with bright yellow eyes, then looked away again and went on eating. Mrs Bixby stood by the counter, as far away from the cat as possible, waiting for someone to come, staring at the watches, the shoe buckles, the enamel brooches, the old binoculars, the broken spectacles, the false teeth. Why did they always pawn their teeth, she wondered.

'Yes?' the proprietor said, emerging from a dark place in the back of the shop.

'Oh, good evening,' Mrs Bixby said. She began to untie the string round the box. The man went up to the cat and started stroking it along the top of its back, and the cat went on eating the fishheads.

'Isn't it silly of me?' Mrs Bixby said. 'I've gone and lost my pocketbook, and this being Saturday, the banks are all closed until Monday and I've simply got to have some money for the week-end. This is quite a valuable coat, but I'm not asking much. I only want to borrow enough on it to tide me over till Monday. Then I'll come back and redeem it.'

The man waited, and said nothing. But when she pulled

out the mink and allowed the beautiful thick fur to fall over the counter, his eyebrows went up and he drew his hand away from the cat and came over to look at it. He picked it up and held it out in front of him.

'If only I had a watch on me or a ring,' Mrs Bixby said, 'I'd give you that instead. But the fact is I don't have a thing with me other than this coat.' She spread out her fingers for him to see.

'It looks new,' the man said, fondling the soft fur.

'Oh yes, it is. But, as I said, I only want to borrow enough to tide me over till Monday. How about fifty dollars?'

'I'll loan you fifty dollars.'

'It's worth a hundred times more than that, but I know you'll take good care of it until I return.'

The man went over to a drawer and fetched a ticket and placed it on the counter. The ticket looked like one of those labels you tie on to the handle of your suitcase, the same shape and size exactly, and the same stiff brownish paper. But it was perforated across the middle so that you could tear it in two, and both halves were identical.

'Name?' he asked.

'Leave that out. And the address.'

She saw the man pause, and she saw the nib of the pen hovering over the dotted line, waiting.

'You don't *have* to put the name and address, do you?'

The man shrugged and shook his head and the pen-nib moved on down to the next line.

'It's just that I'd rather not,' Mrs Bixby said. 'It's purely personal.'

'You'd better not lose this ticket, then.'

'I won't lose it.'

'You realize that anyone who gets hold of it can come in and claim the article?'

'Yes, I know that.'

'Simply on the number.'

'Yes, I know.'

'What do you want me to put for a description?'

'No description either, thank you. It's not necessary. Just put the amount I'm borrowing.'

The pen-nib hesitated again, hovering over the dotted line beside the word ARTICLE.

'I think you ought to put a description. A description is always a help if you want to sell the ticket. You never know, you might want to sell it sometime.'

'I don't want to sell it.'

'You might have to. Lots of people do.'

'Look,' Mrs Bixby said. 'I'm not broke, if that's what you mean. I simply lost my purse. Don't you understand?'

'You have it your own way then,' the man said. 'It's your coat.'

At this point an unpleasant thought struck Mrs Bixby. 'Tell me something,' she said. 'If I don't have a description on my ticket, how can I be sure you'll give me back the coat and not something else when I return?'

'It goes in the books.'

'But all I've got is a number. So actually you could hand me any old thing you wanted, isn't that so?'

'Do you want a description or don't you?' the man asked.

'No,' she said. 'I trust you.'

The man wrote 'fifty dollars' opposite the word VALUE on both sections of the ticket, then he tore it in half along the perforations and slid the lower portion across the counter. He took a wallet from the inside pocket of his jacket and extracted five ten-dollar bills. 'The interest is three per cent a month,' he said.

'Yes, all right. And thank you. You'll take good care of it, won't you?'

The man nodded but said nothing.

'Shall I put it back in the box for you?'

'No,' the man said.

Mrs Bixby turned and went out of the shop on to the street where the taxi was waiting. Ten minutes later, she was home.

'Darling,' she said as she bent over and kissed her husband. 'Did you miss me?'

Cyril Bixby laid down the evening paper and glanced at the watch on his wrist. 'It's twelve and a half minutes past six,' he said. 'You're a bit late, aren't you?'

'I know. It's those dreadful trains. Aunt Maude sent you her love as usual. I'm dying for a drink, aren't you?'

The husband folded his newspaper into a neat rectangle and placed it on the arm of his chair. Then he stood up and crossed over to the sideboard. His wife remained in the centre of the room pulling off her gloves, watching him carefully, wondering how long she ought to wait. He had his back to her now, bending forward to measure the gin, putting his face right up close to the measurer and peering into it as though it were a patient's mouth.

It was funny how small he always looked after the Colonel. The Colonel was huge and bristly, and when you were near to him he smelled faintly of horseradish. This one was small and neat and bony and he didn't really smell of anything at all, except peppermint drops, which he sucked to keep his breath nice for the patients.

'See what I've bought for measuring the vermouth,' he said, holding up a calibrated glass beaker. 'I can get it to the nearest milligram with this.'

'Darling, how clever.'

I really must try to make him change the way he dresses, she told herself. His suits are just too ridiculous for words. There had been a time when she thought they were wonderful, those Edwardian jackets with high lapels and six buttons down the front, but now they merely seemed absurd. So did the narrow stovepipe trousers. You had to have a special sort of face to wear things like that, and Cyril just didn't have it. His was a long bony countenance with a narrow nose and a slightly prognathous jaw, and when you saw it coming up out of the top of one of those tightly fitting old-fashioned suits it looked like a caricature of Sam Weller. He probably thought it looked like Beau Brummell. It was a fact that in the office he invariably greeted female patients with his white coat unbuttoned so that they would catch a glimpse of the trappings underneath; and in some obscure way this was obviously meant to convey the impression that he was a bit of a dog. But Mrs Bixby knew better. The plumage was a bluff. It meant nothing. It reminded her of an ageing peacock strutting on the lawn with only half its feathers left. Or one of those fatuous self-fertilizing flowers – like the dandelion. A dandelion never has to get fertilized for the setting of its seed, and all those brilliant yellow petals are just a waste of time, a boast, a masquerade. What's that word the biologists use? Subsexual. A dandelion is subsexual. So, for that matter, are the summer broods of water fleas. It sounds a bit like Lewis Carroll, she thought – water fleas and dandelions and dentists.

'Thank you, darling,' she said, taking the martini and seating herself on the sofa with her handbag on her lap. 'And what did *you* do last night?'

'I stayed on in the office and cast a few inlays. I also got my accounts up to date.'

'Now really, Cyril, I think it's high time you let other people do your donkey work for you. You're much too important for that sort of thing. Why don't you give the inlays to the mechanic?'

'I prefer to do them myself. I'm extremely proud of my inlays.'

'I know you are, darling, and I think they're absolutely wonderful. They're the best inlays in the whole world. But I don't want you to burn yourself out. And why doesn't that Pulteney woman do the accounts? That's part of her job, isn't it?'

'She does do them. But I have to price everything up first. She doesn't know who's rich and who isn't.'

'This martini is perfect,' Mrs Bixby said, setting down her glass on the side table. 'Quite perfect.' She opened her bag and took out a handkerchief as if to blow her nose.

'Oh look!' she cried, seeing the ticket. 'I forgot to show you this! I found it just now on the seat of my taxi. It's got a number on it, and I thought it might be a lottery ticket or something, so I kept it.'

She handed the small piece of stiff brown paper to her husband, who took it in his fingers and began examining it minutely from all angles, as though it were a suspect tooth.

'You know what this is?' he said slowly.

'No dear, I don't.'

'It's a pawn ticket.'

'A what?'

'A ticket from a pawnbroker. Here's the name and address of the shop – somewhere on Sixth Avenue.'

'Oh dear, I *am* disappointed. I was hoping it might be a ticket for the Irish Sweep.'

'There's no reason to be disappointed,' Cyril Bixby said. 'As a matter of fact this could be rather amusing.'

'Why could it be amusing, darling?'

He began explaining to her exactly how a pawn ticket worked, with particular reference to the fact that anyone possessing the ticket was entitled to claim the article. She listened patiently until he had finished his lecture.

'You think it's worth claiming?' she asked.

'I think it's worth finding out what it is. You see this figure of fifty dollars that's written here? You know what that means?'

'No, dear, what does it mean?'

'It means that the item in question is almost certain to be something quite valuable.'

'You mean it'll be worth fifty dollars?'

'More like five hundred.'

'Five hundred!'

'Don't you understand?' he said. 'A pawnbroker never gives you more than about a tenth of the real value.'

'Good gracious! I never knew that.'

'There's a lot of things you don't know, my dear. Now you listen to me. Seeing that there's no name and address of the owner . . .'

'But surely there's something to say who it belongs to?'

'Not a thing. People often do that. They don't want anyone to know they've been to a pawnbroker. They're ashamed of it.'

'Then you think we can keep it?'

'Of course we can keep it. This is now *our* ticket.'

'You mean *my* ticket,' Mrs Bixby said firmly. 'I found it.'

'My dear girl, what *does* it matter? The important thing is that we are now in a position to go and redeem it any time we like for only fifty dollars. How about that?'

'Oh, what fun!' she cried. 'I think it's terribly exciting, especially when we don't even know what it is. It could be *anything*, isn't that right, Cyril? Absolutely anything!'

'It could indeed, although it's most likely to be either a ring or a watch.'

'But wouldn't it be marvellous if it was a *real* treasure? I mean something *really* old, like a wonderful old vase or a Roman statue.'

'There's no knowing what it might be, my dear. We shall just have to wait and see.'

'I think it's absolutely fascinating! Give me the ticket

and I'll rush over first thing Monday morning and find out!'

'I think I'd better do that.'

'Oh no!' she cried. 'Let *me* do it!'

'I think not. I'll pick it up on my way to work.'

'But it's *my* ticket! *Please* let me do it, Cyril! Why should *you* have all the fun?'

'You don't know these pawnbrokers, my dear. You're liable to get cheated.'

'I wouldn't get cheated, honestly I wouldn't. Give it to me, please.'

'Also you have to have fifty dollars,' he said, smiling. 'You have to pay out fifty dollars in cash before they'll give it to you.'

'I've got that,' she said. 'I think.'

'I'd rather you didn't handle it, if you don't mind.'

'But Cyril, *I found* it. It's mine. Whatever it is, it's mine, isn't that right?'

'Of course it's yours, my dear. There's no need to get so worked up about it.'

'I'm not. I'm just excited, that's all.'

'I suppose it hasn't occurred to you that this might be something entirely masculine – a pocket-watch, for example, or a set of shirt-studs. It isn't only women that go to pawnbrokers, you know.'

'In that case I'll give it to you for Christmas,' Mrs Bixby said magnanimously. 'I'll be delighted. But if it's a woman's thing, I want it myself. Is that agreed?'

'That sounds very fair. Why don't you come with me when I collect it?'

Mrs Bixby was about to say yes to this, but caught herself just in time. She had no wish to be greeted like an old customer by the pawnbroker in her husband's presence.

'No,' she said slowly. 'I don't think I will. You see, it'll be even more thrilling if I stay behind and wait. Oh, I do hope it isn't going to be something that neither of us wants.'

'You've got a point there,' he said. 'If I don't think it's worth fifty dollars, I won't even take it.'

'But you said it would be worth five hundred.'

'I'm quite sure it will. Don't worry.'

'Oh, Cyril, I can hardly wait! Isn't it exciting?'

'It's amusing,' he said, slipping the ticket into his waistcoat pocket. 'There's no doubt about that.'

Monday morning came at last, and after breakfast Mrs Bixby followed her husband to the door and helped him on with his coat.

'Don't work too hard, darling,' she said.

'No, all right.'

'Home at six?'

'I hope so.'

'Are you going to have time to go to that pawnbroker?' she asked.

'My God, I forgot all about it. I'll take a cab and go there now. It's on my way.'

'You haven't lost the ticket, have you?'

'I hope not,' he said, feeling in his waistcoat pocket. 'No, here it is.'

'And you have enough money?'

'Just about.'

'Darling,' she said, standing close to him and straightening his tie, which was perfectly straight. 'If it happens to be something nice, something you think I might like, will you telephone me as soon as you get to the office?'

'If you want me to, yes.'

'You know, I'm sort of hoping it'll be something for you, Cyril. I'd much rather it was for you than for me.'

'That's very generous of you, my dear. Now I must run.'

About an hour later, when the telephone rang, Mrs Bixby was across the room so fast she had the receiver off the hook before the first ring had finished.

'I got it!' he said.

'You did! Oh, Cyril, what was it? Was it something good?'

'Good!' he cried. 'It's fantastic! You wait till you get your eyes on this! You'll swoon!'

'Darling, what is it? Tell me quick!'

'You're a lucky girl, that's what you are.'

'It's for me, then?'

'Of course it's for you. Though how in the world it ever got to be pawned for only fifty dollars I'll be damned if I know. Someone's crazy.'

'Cyril! Stop keeping me in suspense! I can't bear it!'

'You'll go mad when you see it.'

'What is it?'

'Try to guess.'

Mrs Bixby paused. Be careful, she told herself. Be very careful now.

'A necklace,' she said.

'Wrong.'

'A diamond ring.'

'You're not even warm. I'll give you a hint. It's something you can wear.'

'Something I can wear? You mean like a hat?'

'No, it's not a hat,' he said, laughing.

'For goodness' sake, Cyril! Why don't you tell me?'

'Because I want it to be a surprise. I'll bring it home with me this evening.'

'You'll do nothing of the sort!' she cried. 'I'm coming right down there to get it now!'

'I'd rather you didn't do that.'

'Don't be so silly, darling. Why shouldn't I come?'

'Because I'm too busy. You'll disorganize my whole morning schedule. I'm half an hour behind already.'

'Then I'll come in the lunch hour. All right?'

'I'm not having a lunch hour. Oh well, come at one thirty then, while I'm having a sandwich. Good-bye.'

At half past one precisely, Mrs Bixby arrived at Dr Bixby's place of business and rang the bell. Her husband, in his white dentist's coat, opened the door himself.

'Oh, Cyril, I'm so excited!'

'So you should be. You're a lucky girl, did you know that?' He led her down the passage and into the surgery.

'Go and have your lunch, Miss Pulteney,' he said to the assistant, who was busy putting instruments into the sterilizer. 'You can finish that when you come back.' He waited until the girl had gone, then he walked over to a closet that he used for hanging up his clothes and stood in front of it, pointing with his finger. 'It's in there,' he said. 'Now – shut your eyes.'

Mrs Bixby did as she was told. Then she took a deep breath and held it, and in the silence that followed she could hear him opening the cupboard door and there was a soft swishing sound as he pulled out a garment from among the other things hanging there.

'All right! You can look!'

'I don't dare to,' she said, laughing.

'Go on. Take a peek.'

Coyly, beginning to giggle, she raised one eyelid a fraction of an inch, just enough to give her a dark blurry view of the man standing there in his white overalls holding something up in the air.

'Mink!' he cried. 'Real mink!'

At the sound of the magic word she opened her eyes quick, and at the same time she actually started forward in order to clasp the coat in her arms.

But there was no coat. There was only a ridiculous little fur neckpiece dangling from her husband's hand.

'Feast your eyes on that!' he said, waving it in front of her face.

Mrs Bixby put a hand up to her mouth and started backing away. I'm going to scream, she told herself. I just know it. I'm going to scream.

'What's the matter, my dear? Don't you like it?' He stopped waving the fur and stood staring at her, waiting for her to say something.

'Why yes,' she stammered. 'I . . . I . . . think it's . . . it's lovely . . . really lovely.'

'Quite took your breath away for a moment there, didn't it?'

'Yes, it did.'

'Magnificent quality,' he said. 'Fine colour, too. You know something, my dear? I reckon a piece like this would cost you two or three hundred dollars at least if you had to buy it in a shop.'

'I don't doubt it.'

There were two skins, two narrow mangy-looking skins with their heads still on them and glass beads in their eye sockets and little paws hanging down. One of them had the rear end of the other in its mouth, biting it.

'Here,' he said. 'Try it on.' He leaned forward and draped the thing round her neck, then stepped back to admire. 'It's perfect. It really suits you. It isn't everyone who has mink, my dear.'

'No, it isn't.'

'Better leave it behind when you go shopping or they'll all think we're millionaires and start charging us double.'

'I'll try to remember that, Cyril.'

'I'm afraid you mustn't expect anything else for Christmas. Fifty dollars was rather more than I was going to spend anyway.'

He turned away and went over to the basin and began washing his hands. 'Run along now, my dear, and buy yourself a nice lunch. I'd take you out myself but I've got old man Gorman in the waiting-room with a broken clasp on his denture.'

Mrs Bixby moved towards the door.

I'm going to kill that pawnbroker, she told herself. I'm going right back there to the shop this very minute and I'm going to throw this filthy neckpiece right in his face and if he refuses to give me back my coat I'm going to kill him.

'Did I tell you I was going to be late home tonight?' Cyril Bixby said, still washing his hands.

'No.'

'It'll probably be at least eight thirty the way things look at the moment. It may even be nine.'

'Yes, all right. Good-bye.' Mrs Bixby went out, slamming the door behind her.

At that precise moment, Miss Pulteney, the secretary-assistant, came sailing past her down the corridor on her way to lunch.

'Isn't it a gorgeous day?' Miss Pulteney said as she went by, flashing a smile. There was a lilt in her walk, a little whiff of perfume attending her, and she looked like a queen, just exactly like a queen in the beautiful black mink coat that the Colonel had given to Mrs Bixby.

Pig

First published in *Kiss, Kiss* (1960)

I

Once upon a time, in the City of New York, a beautiful baby boy was born into this world, and the joyful parents named him Lexington.

No sooner had the mother returned home from the hospital carrying Lexington in her arms than she said to her husband, 'Darling, now you must take me out to a most marvellous restaurant for dinner so that we can celebrate the arrival of our son and heir.'

Her husband embraced her tenderly and told her that any woman who could produce such a beautiful child as Lexington deserved to go absolutely any place she wanted. But was she strong enough yet, he inquired, to start running around the city late at night?

No, she said, she wasn't. But what the hell.

So that evening they both dressed themselves up in fancy clothes, and leaving little Lexington in care of a trained infant's nurse who was costing them twenty dollars a day and was Scottish into the bargain, they went out to the finest and most expensive restaurant in town. There they each ate a giant lobster and drank a bottle of champagne between them, and after that, they went on to a nightclub, where they drank another bottle of champagne and then sat holding hands for several hours while they recalled and discussed and admired each individual physical feature of their lovely newborn son.

They arrived back at their house on the East Side of Manhattan at around two o'clock in the morning and the husband paid off the taxi-driver and then began feeling in his pockets for the key to the front door. After a while, he announced that he must have left it in the pocket of his other suit, and he suggested they ring the bell and get the nurse to come down and let them in. An infant's nurse at twenty dollars a day must expect to be hauled out of bed occasionally in the night, the husband said.

So he rang the bell. They waited. Nothing happened. He rang it again, long and loud. They waited another minute. Then they both stepped back on to the street and shouted the nurse's name (McPottle) up at the nursery windows on the third floor, but there was still no response. The house was dark and silent. The wife began to grow apprehensive. Her baby was imprisoned in this place, she told herself. Alone with McPottle. And who was McPottle? They had known her for two days, that was all, and she had a thin mouth, a small disapproving eye, and a starchy bosom, and quite clearly she was in the habit of sleeping much too soundly for safety. If she couldn't hear the front-door bell, then how on earth did she expect to hear a baby crying? Why, this very second the poor thing might be swallowing its tongue or suffocating on its pillow.

'He doesn't use a pillow,' the husband said. 'You are not to worry. But I'll get you in if that's what you want.' He was feeling rather superb after all the champagne, and now he bent down and undid the laces of one of his black patent-leather shoes, and took it off. Then, holding it by the toe, he flung it hard and straight right through the dining-room window on the ground floor.

'There you are,' he said, grinning. 'We'll deduct it from McPottle's wages.'

He stepped forward and very carefully put a hand through the hole in the glass and released the catch. Then he raised the window.

'I shall lift you in first, little mother,' he said, and he took his wife round the waist and lifted her off the ground. This brought her big red mouth up level with his own, and very close, so he started kissing her. He knew from experience that women like very much to be kissed in this position, with their bodies held tight and their legs dangling in the air, so he went on doing it for quite a long time, and she wiggled her feet, and made loud gulping noises down in her throat. Finally, the husband turned her round and began easing her gently through the open window into the dining-room. At this point, a police patrol car came nosing silently along the street towards them. It stopped about thirty yards away, and three cops of Irish extraction leaped out of the car and started running in the direction of the husband and wife, brandishing revolvers.

'Stick 'em up!' the cops shouted. 'Stick 'em up!' But it was impossible for the husband to obey this order without letting go of his wife, and had he done this she would either have fallen to the ground or would have been left dangling half in and half out of the house, which is a terribly uncomfortable position for a woman; so he continued gallantly to push her upwards and inwards through the window. The cops, all of whom had received medals before for killing robbers, opened fire immediately, and although they were still running, and although the wife in particular was presenting them with a very small target indeed, they succeeded in scoring several direct hits on each body – sufficient anyway to prove fatal in both cases.

Thus, when he was no more then twelve days old, little Lexington became an orphan.

II

The news of this killing, for which the three policemen subsequently received citations, was eagerly conveyed to all relatives of the deceased couple by newspaper reporters, and the next morning, the closest of these relatives, as well as a couple of undertakers, three lawyers and a priest, climbed into taxis and set out for the house with the broken window. They assembled in the living-room, men and women both, and they sat around in a circle on the sofas and armchairs, smoking cigarettes and sipping sherry and debating what on earth should be done now with the baby upstairs, the orphan Lexington.

It soon became apparent that none of the relatives was particularly keen to assume responsibility for the child, and the discussions and arguments continued all through the day. Everybody declared an enormous, almost an irresistible desire to look after him, and would have done so with the greatest of pleasure were it not for the fact that their apartment was too small, or that they already had one baby and couldn't possibly afford another, or that they wouldn't know what to do with the poor little thing when they went abroad in the summer, or that they were getting on in years, which surely would be most unfair to the boy when he grew up, and so on and so forth. They all knew, of course, that the father had been heavily in debt for a long time and that the house was mortgaged and that consequently there would be no money at all to go with the child.

They were still arguing like mad at six in the evening when suddenly, in the middle of it all, an old aunt of the deceased father (her name was Glosspan) swept in from Virginia, and without even removing her hat and coat, not even pausing to sit down, ignoring all offers of a martini, a whisky, a sherry, she announced firmly to the assembled relatives that she herself intended to take sole charge of the infant boy from then on. What was more, she said, she would assume full financial responsibility on all counts, including education, and everyone else could go on back home where they belonged and give their consciences a rest. So saying, she trotted upstairs to the nursery and snatched Lexington from his cradle and swept out of the house with the baby clutched tightly in her arms, while the relatives simply sat and stared and smiled and looked relieved, and McPottle the nurse stood stiff with disapproval at the head of the stairs, her lips compressed, her arms folded across her starchy bosom.

And thus it was that the infant Lexington, when he was thirteen days old, left the City of New York and travelled southward to live with his Great Aunt Glosspan in the State of Virginia.

III

Aunt Glosspan was nearly seventy when she became guardian to Lexington, but to look at her you would never have guessed it for one minute. She was as sprightly as a woman half her age, with a small, wrinkled, but still quite beautiful face and two lovely brown eyes that sparkled at you in the nicest way. She was also a spinster, though you would never have guessed that either, for there was nothing spinsterish about Aunt Glosspan. She was never bitter or gloomy or irritable; she didn't have a moustache; and she wasn't in the least bit jealous of other people, which in itself is something you can seldom say about either a spinster or a virgin lady, although of course it is not known for certain whether Aunt Glosspan qualified on both counts.

But she was an eccentric old woman, there was no doubt about that. For the past thirty years she had lived a strange isolated life all by herself in a tiny cottage high up on the slopes of the Blue Ridge Mountains, several miles from the nearest village. She had five acres of pasture, a plot for growing vegetables, a flower garden, three cows, a dozen hens and a fine cockerel.

And now she had little Lexington as well.

She was a strict vegetarian and regarded the consumption of animal flesh as not only unhealthy and disgusting, but horribly cruel. She lived upon lovely clean foods like milk, butter, eggs, cheese, vegetables, nuts, herbs and fruit, and she rejoiced in the conviction that no living creature would be slaughtered on her account, not even a shrimp. Once, when a brown hen of hers passed away in the prime of life from being eggbound, Aunt Glosspan was so distressed that she nearly gave up egg-eating altogether.

She knew not the first thing about babies, but that didn't worry her in the least. At the railway station in New York, while waiting for the train that would take her and Lexington back to Virginia, she bought six feeding-bottles, two dozen diapers, a box of safety pins, a carton of milk for the journey and a small paper-covered book called *The Care of Infants*. What more could anyone want? And when the train got going, she fed the baby some milk, changing its nappies after a fashion, and laid it down on the seat to sleep. Then she read *The Care of Infants* from cover to cover.

'There is no problem here,' she said, throwing the book out the window. 'No problem at all.'

And curiously enough there wasn't. Back home in the cottage everything went just as smoothly as could be. Little Lexington drank his milk and belched and yelled and slept exactly as a good baby should, and Aunt Glosspan glowed with joy whenever she looked at him, and showered him with kisses all day long.

IV

By the time he was six years old, young Lexington had grown into a most beautiful boy with long golden hair and deep blue eyes the colour of cornflowers. He was bright and cheerful, and already he was learning to help his old aunt in all sorts of different ways around the property, collecting the eggs from the chicken house, turning the handle of the butter churn, digging up potatoes in the vegetable garden, and searching for wild herbs on the side of the mountain. Soon, Aunt Glosspan told herself, she would have to start thinking about his education.

But she couldn't bear the thought of sending him away to school. She loved him so much now that it would kill her to be parted from him for any length of time. There was, of course, that village school down in the valley, but it was a dreadful-looking place, and if she sent him there she just knew they would start forcing him to eat meat the very first day he arrived.

'You know what, my darling?' she said to him one day when he was sitting on a stool in the kitchen watching her make cheese. 'I don't really see why I shouldn't give you your lessons myself.'

The boy looked up at her with his large blue eyes, and gave her a lovely trusting smile. 'That would be nice,' he said.

'And the very first thing I should do would be to teach you how to cook.'

'I think I would like that, Aunt Glosspan.'

'Whether you like it or not, you're going to have to learn some time,' she said. 'Vegetarians like us don't have nearly so many foods to choose from as ordinary people, and therefore they must learn to be doubly expert with what they have.'

'Aunt Glosspan,' the boy said, 'what *do* ordinary people eat that we don't?'

'Animals,' she answered, tossing her head in disgust.

'You mean *live* animals?'

'No,' she said. 'Dead ones.'

The boy considered this for a moment.

'You mean when they die they *eat* them instead of *burying* them?'

'They don't wait for them to die, my pet. They kill them.'

'How do they kill them, Aunt Glosspan?'

'They usually slit their throats with a knife.'

'But what *kind* of animals?'

'Cows and pigs mostly, and sheep.'

'Cows!' the boy cried. 'You mean like Daisy and Snowdrop and Lily?'

'Exactly, my dear.'

'But *how* do they eat them, Aunt Glosspan?'

'They cut them up into bits and they cook the bits. They like it best when it's all red and bloody and sticking to the bones. They love to eat lumps of cow's flesh with the blood oozing out of it.'

'Pigs too?'

'They adore pigs.'

'Lumps of bloody pig's meat,' the boy said. 'Imagine that. What else do they eat, Aunt Glosspan?'

'Chickens.'

'Chickens!'

'Millions of them.'

'Feathers and all?'

'No, dear, not the feathers. Now run along outside and get Aunt Glosspan a bunch of chives, will you, my darling?'

Shortly after that, the lessons began. They covered five subjects, reading, writing, geography, arithmetic and cooking, but the latter was by far the most popular with both teacher and pupil. In fact, it very soon became apparent that young Lexington possessed a truly remarkable talent in this direction. He was a born cook. He was dextrous and quick. He could handle his pans like a juggler. He could slice a single potato into twenty paper-thin slivers in less time than it took his aunt to peel it. His palate was exquisitely sensitive, and he could taste a pot of strong onion soup and immediately detect the presence of a single tiny leaf of sage. In so young a boy, all this was a bit bewildering to Aunt Glosspan, and to tell the truth she didn't quite know what to make of it. But she was proud as proud could be, all the same, and predicted a brilliant future for the child.

'What a mercy it is,' she said, 'that I have such a wonderful little fellow to look after me in my dotage.' And a couple of years later, she retired from the kitchen for good, leaving Lexington in sole charge of all household cooking. The boy was now ten years old, and Aunt Glosspan was nearly eighty.

V

With the kitchen to himself, Lexington straight away began experimenting with dishes of his own invention. The old favourites no longer interested him. He had a violent urge to create. There were hundreds of fresh ideas in his head. 'I will begin,' he said, 'by devising a chestnut soufflé.' He made it and served it up for supper that very night. It was terrific. 'You are a genius!' Aunt Glosspan cried, leaping up from her chair and kissing him on both cheeks. 'You will make history!'

From then on, hardly a day went by without some new delectable creation being set upon the table. There was Brazil-nut soup, hominy cutlets, vegetable ragout, dandelion omelette, cream-cheese fritters, stuffed-cabbage surprise, stewed foggage, shallots *à la bonne femme*, beetroot mousse piquant, prunes Stroganoff, Dutch rarebit, turnips on horseback, flaming spruce-needle tarts, and many many other beautiful compositions. Never before in her life, Aunt Glosspan declared, had she tasted such food as this; and in the mornings, long before lunch was due, she would go out on to the porch and sit there in her rocking-chair, speculating about the coming meal, licking her chops, sniffing the aromas that came wafting out through the kitchen window.

'What's that you're making in there today, boy?' she would call out.

'Try to guess, Aunt Glosspan.'

'Smells like a bit of salsify fritters to me,' she would say, sniffing vigorously.

Then out he would come, this ten-year-old child, a little grin of triumph on his face, and in his hands a big steaming pot of the most heavenly stew made entirely of parsnips and lovage.

'You know what you ought to do,' his aunt said to

him, gobbling the stew. 'You ought to set yourself down this very minute with paper and pencil and write a cooking-book.'

He looked at her across the table, chewing his parsnips slowly.

'Why not?' she cried. 'I've taught you how to write and I've taught you how to cook and now all you've got to do is put the two things together. You write a cooking-book, my darling, and it'll make you famous the whole world over.'

'All right,' he said. 'I will.'

And that very day, Lexington began writing the first page of that monumental work which was to occupy him for the rest of his life. He called it *Eat Good and Healthy*.

VI

Seven years later, by the time he was seventeen, he had recorded over nine thousand different recipes, all of them original, all of them delicious.

But now, suddenly, his labours were interrupted by the tragic death of Aunt Glosspan. She was afflicted in the night by a violent seizure, and Lexington, who had rushed into her bedroom to see what all the noise was about, found her lying on her bed yelling and cussing and twisting herself up into all manner of complicated knots. Indeed, she was a terrible sight to behold, and the agitated youth danced round her in his pyjamas, wringing his hands, and wondering what on earth he should do. Finally, in an effort to cool her down, he fetched a bucket of water from the pond in the cow field and tipped it over her head, but this only intensified the paroxysms, and the old lady expired within the hour.

'This is really too bad,' the poor boy said, pinching her several times to make sure that she was dead. 'And how sudden! How quick and sudden! Why only a few hours ago she seemed in the very best of spirits. She even took three large helpings of my most recent creation, devilled mushroom-burgers, and told me how succulent it was.'

After weeping bitterly for several minutes, for he had loved his aunt very much, he pulled himself together and carried her outside and buried her behind the cowshed.

The next day, while tidying up her belongings, he came across an envelope that was addressed to him in Aunt Glosspan's handwriting. He opened it and drew out two fifty-dollar bills and a letter. 'Darling boy,' the letter said.

I know that you have never yet been down the mountain since you were thirteen days old, but as soon as I die you must put on a pair of shoes and a clean shirt and walk down to the village and find the doctor. Ask the doctor to give you a death certificate to prove that I am dead. Then take this certificate to my lawyer, a man called Mr Samuel Zuckermann, who lives in New York City and who has a copy of my will. Mr Zuckermann will arrange everything. The cash in this envelope is to pay the doctor for the certificate and to cover the cost of your journey to New York. Mr Zuckermann will give you more money when you get there, and it

THE COMPLETE SHORT STORIES

is my earnest wish that you use it to further your researches into
culinary and vegetarian matters, and that you continue to work
upon that great book of yours until you are satisfied that it is
complete in every way. Your loving aunt – Glosspan.

Lexington, who had always done everything his aunt told him, pocketed the money, put on a pair of shoes and a clean shirt, and went down the mountain to the village where the doctor lived.

'Old Glosspan?' the doctor said. 'My God, is *she* dead?'

'Certainly she's dead,' the youth answered. 'If you will come back home with me now I'll dig her up and you can see for yourself.'

'How deep did you bury her?' the doctor asked.

'Six or seven feet down, I should think.'

'And how long ago?'

'Oh, about eight hours.'

'Then she's dead,' the doctor announced. 'Here's the certificate.'

VII

Our hero now set out for the City of New York to find Mr Samuel Zuckermann. He travelled on foot, and he slept under hedges, and he lived on berries and wild herbs, and it took him sixteen days to reach the metropolis.

'What a fabulous place this is!' he cried as he stood at the corner of Fifty-seventh Street and Fifth Avenue, staring around him. 'There are no cows or chickens anywhere, and none of the women looks in the least like Aunt Glosspan.'

As for Mr Samuel Zuckermann, he looked like nothing that Lexington had ever seen before.

He was a small spongy man with livid jowls and a huge magenta nose, and when he smiled, bits of gold flashed at you marvellously from lots of different places inside his mouth. In his luxurious office, he shook Lexington warmly by the hand and congratulated him upon his aunt's death.

'I suppose you knew that your dearly beloved guardian was a woman of considerable wealth?' he said.

'You mean the cows and the chickens?'

'I mean half a million bucks,' Mr Zuckermann said.

'How much?'

'Half a million dollars, my boy. And she's left it all to you.' Mr Zuckermann leaned back in his chair and clasped his hands over his spongy paunch. At the same time, he began secretly working his right forefinger in through his waistcoat and under his shirt so as to scratch the skin around the circumference of his navel – a favourite exercise of his, and one that gave him a peculiar pleasure. 'Of course, I shall have to deduct fifty per cent for my services,' he said, 'but that still leaves you with two hundred and fifty grand.'

'I am rich!' Lexington cried. 'This is wonderful! How soon can I have the money?'

'Well,' Mr Zuckermann said, 'luckily for you, I happen to be on rather cordial terms with the tax authorities around here, and I am confident that I shall be able to persuade them to waive all death duties and back taxes.'

'How kind you are,' murmured Lexington.

'I shall naturally have to give somebody a small honorarium.'

'Whatever you say, Mr Zuckermann.'

'I think a hundred thousand would be sufficient.'

'Good gracious, isn't that rather excessive?'

'Never undertip a tax-inspector or a policeman,' Mr Zuckermann said. 'Remember that.'

'But how much does it leave for me?' the youth asked meekly.

'One hundred and fifty thousand. But then you've got the funeral expenses to pay out of that.'

'*Funeral* expenses?'

'You've got to pay the funeral parlour. Surely you know that?'

'But I buried her myself, Mr Zuckermann, behind the cowshed.'

'I don't doubt it,' the lawyer said. 'So what?'

'I never used a funeral parlour.'

'Listen,' Mr Zuckermann said patiently. 'You may not know it, but there is a law in this State which says that no beneficiary under a will may receive a single penny of his inheritance until the funeral parlour has been paid in full.'

'You mean that's a *law*?'

'Certainly it's a law, and a very good one it is, too. The funeral parlour is one of our great national institutions. It must be protected at all cost.'

Mr Zuckermann himself, together with a group of public-spirited doctors, controlled a corporation that owned a chain of nine lavish funeral parlours in the city, not to mention a casket factory in Brooklyn and a post-graduate school for embalmers in Washington Heights. The celebration of death was therefore a deeply religious affair in Mr Zuckermann's eyes. In fact, the whole business affected him profoundly, almost as profoundly, one might say, as the birth of Christ affected the shopkeeper.

'You had no right to go out and bury your aunt like that,' he said. 'None at all.'

'I'm very sorry, Mr Zuckermann.'

'Why, it's downright subversive.'

'I'll do whatever you say, Mr Zuckermann. All I want to know is how much I'm going to get in the end, when everything's paid.'

There was a pause. Mr Zuckermann sighed and frowned and continued secretly to run the tip of his finger round the rim of his navel.

'Shall we say fifteen thousand?' he suggested, flashing a big gold smile. 'That's a nice round figure.'

'Can I take it with me this afternoon?'

'I don't see why not.'

So Mr Zuckermann summoned his chief cashier and told him to give Lexington fifteen thousand dollars out of the petty cash, and to obtain a receipt. The youth, who by this time was delighted to be getting anything at all, accepted the money gratefully and stowed it away in his knapsack. Then he shook Mr Zuckermann warmly by the hand, thanked him for all his help, and went out of the office.

'The whole world is before me!' our hero cried as he emerged into the street. 'I now have fifteen thousand dollars to see me through until my book is published. And after that, of course, I shall have a great deal more.' He stood on the pavement, wondering which way to go. He turned left and began strolling slowly down the street, staring at the sights of the city.

'What a revolting smell,' he said, sniffing the air. 'I can't stand this.' His delicate olfactory nerves, tuned to receive only the most delicious kitchen aromas, were being tortured by the stench of the diesel-oil fumes pouring out of the backs of the buses.

'I must get out of this place before my nose is ruined altogether,' he said. 'But first, I've simply got to have something to eat. I'm starving.' The poor boy had had nothing but berries and wild herbs for the past two weeks, and now his stomach was yearning for solid food. I'd like a nice hominy cutlet, he told himself. Or maybe a few juicy salsify fritters.

He crossed the street and entered a small restaurant. The place was hot inside, and dark and silent. There was a strong smell of cooking-fat and cabbage water. The only other customer was a man with a brown hat on his head, crouching intently over his food, who did not look up as Lexington came in.

Our hero seated himself at a corner table and hung his knapsack on the back of his chair. This, he told himself, is going to be most interesting. In all my seventeen years I have tasted only the cooking of two people, Aunt Glosspan and myself – unless one counts Nurse McPottle, who must have heated my bottle a few times when I was an infant. But I am now about to sample the art of a new chef altogether, and perhaps, if I am lucky, I may pick up a couple of useful ideas for my book.

A waiter approached out of the shadows at the back, and stood beside the table.

'How do you do,' Lexington said. 'I should like a large hominy cutlet please. Do it twenty-five seconds each side, in a very hot skillet with sour cream, and sprinkle a pinch of lovage on it before serving – unless of course your chef knows of a more original method, in which case I should be delighted to try it.'

The waiter laid his head over to one side and looked carefully at his customer. 'You want the roast pork and cabbage?' he asked. 'That's all we got left.'

'Roast what and cabbage?'

The waiter took a soiled handkerchief from his trouser pocket and shook it open with a violent flourish, as though he were cracking a whip. Then he blew his nose loud and wet.

'You want it or don't you?' he said, wiping his nostrils.

'I haven't the foggiest idea what it is,' Lexington replied, 'but I should love to try it. You see, I am writing a cooking-book and . . .'

'One pork and cabbage!' the waiter shouted, and some-where in the back of the restaurant, far away in the darkness, a voice answered him.

The waiter disappeared. Lexington reached into his knapsack for his personal knife and fork. These were a present from Aunt Glosspan, given him when he was six years old, made of solid silver, and he had never eaten with any other instruments since. While waiting for the food to arrive, he polished them lovingly with a piece of soft muslin.

Soon the waiter returned carrying a plate on which there lay a thick greyish-white slab of something hot. Lexington leaned forward anxiously to smell it as it was put down before him. His nostrils were wide open now to receive the scent, quivering and sniffing.

'But this is absolute heaven!' he exclaimed. 'What an aroma! It's tremendous!'

The waiter stepped back a pace, watching his customer carefully.

'Never in my life have I smelled anything as rich and wonderful as this!' our hero cried, seizing his knife and fork. 'What on earth is it made of?'

The man in the brown hat looked around and stared, then returned to his eating. The waiter was backing away towards the kitchen.

Lexington cut off a small piece of the meat, impaled it on his silver fork, and carried it up to his nose so as to smell it again. Then he popped it into his mouth and began to chew it slowly, his eyes half closed, his body tense.

'This is fantastic!' he cried. 'It is a brand-new flavour! Oh, Glosspan, my beloved Aunt, how I wish you were with me now so you could taste this remarkable dish! Waiter! Come here at once! I want you!'

The astonished waiter was now watching from the other end of the room, and he seemed reluctant to move any closer.

'If you will come and talk to me I will give you a present,'

Lexington said, waving a hundred-dollar bill. 'Please come over here and talk to me.'

The waiter sidled cautiously back to the table, snatched away the money, and held it up close to his face, peering at it from all angles. Then he slipped it quickly into his pocket.

'What can I do for you, my friend?' he asked.

'Look,' Lexington said. 'If you will tell me what this delicious dish is made of, and exactly how it is prepared, I will give you another hundred.'

'I already told you,' the man said. 'It's pork.'

'And what exactly is pork?'

'You never had roast pork before?' the waiter asked, staring.

'For heaven's sake, man, tell me what it is and stop keeping me in suspense like this.'

'It's pig,' the waiter said. 'You just bung it in the oven.'

'*Pig!*'

'All pork is pig. Didn't you know that?'

'You mean *this* is *pig's meat*?'

'I guarantee it.'

'But ... but ... that's impossible,' the youth stammered. 'Aunt Glosspan, who knew more about food than anyone else in the world, said that meat of any kind was disgusting, revolting, horrible, foul, nauseating and beastly. And yet this piece that I have here on my plate is without a doubt the most delicious thing that I have ever tasted. Now how on earth do you explain that? Aunt Glosspan certainly wouldn't have told me it was revolting if it wasn't.'

'Maybe your aunt didn't know how to cook it,' the waiter said.

'Is that possible?'

'You're damn right it is. Especially with pork. Pork has to be very well done or you can't eat it.'

'Eureka!' Lexington cried. 'I'll bet that's exactly what happened! She did it wrong!' He handed the man another hundred-dollar bill. 'Lead me to the kitchen,' he said. 'Introduce me to the genius who prepared this meat.'

Lexington was at once taken into the kitchen, and there he met the cook who was an elderly man with a rash on one side of his neck.

'This will cost you another hundred,' the waiter said.

Lexington was only too glad to oblige, but this time he gave the money to the cook. 'Now listen to me,' he said, 'I have to admit that I am really rather confused by what the waiter has just been telling me. Are you quite positive that the delectable dish which I have just been eating was prepared from pig's flesh?'

The cook raised his right hand and began scratching the rash on his neck.

'Well,' he said, looking at the waiter and giving him a sly wink, 'all I can tell you is that I *think* it was pig's meat.'

'You mean you're not sure?'

'One can't ever be sure.'

'Then what else could it have been?'

'Well,' the cook said, speaking very slowly and still staring at the waiter. 'There's just a chance, you see, that it might have been a piece of human stuff.'

'You mean a man?'

'Yes.'

'Good heavens.'

'Or a woman. It could have been either. They both taste the same.'

'Well – now you really do surprise me,' the youth declared.

'One lives and learns.'

'Indeed one does.'

'As a matter of fact, we've been getting an awful lot of it just lately from the butcher's in place of pork,' the cook declared.

'Have you really?'

'The trouble is, it's almost impossible to tell which is which. They're both very good.'

'The piece I had just now was simply superb.'

'I'm glad you liked it,' the cook said. 'But to be quite honest, I think that was a bit of pig. In fact, I'm almost sure it was.'

'You are?'

'Yes, I am.'

'In that case, we shall have to assume that you are right,' Lexington said. 'So now will you please tell me – and here is another hundred dollars for your trouble – will you please tell me precisely how you prepared it?'

The cook, after pocketing the money, launched out upon a colourful description of how to roast a loin of pork, while the youth, not wanting to miss a single word of so great a recipe, sat down at the kitchen table and recorded every detail in his notebook.

'Is that all?' he asked when the cook had finished.

THE COMPLETE SHORT STORIES

'That's all.'

'But there must be more to it than that, surely?'

'You got to get a good piece of meat to start off with,' the cook said. 'That's half the battle. It's got to be a good hog and it's got to be butchered right, otherwise it'll turn out lousy whichever way you cook it.'

'Show me how,' Lexington said. 'Butcher me one now so I can learn.'

'We don't butcher pigs in the kitchen,' the cook said. 'That lot you just ate came from a packing-house over in the Bronx.'

'Then give me the address!'

The cook gave him the address, and our hero, after thanking them both many times for all their kindnesses, rushed outside and leaped into a taxi and headed for the Bronx.

VIII

The packing-house was a big four-storey brick building, and the air around it smelled sweet and heavy, like musk. At the main entrance gates, there was a large notice which said VISITORS WELCOME AT ANY TIME, and thus encouraged, Lexington walked through the gates and entered a cobbled yard which surrounded the building itself. He then followed a series of signposts (THIS WAY FOR THE GUIDED TOURS), and came eventually to a small corrugated-iron shed set well apart from the main building (VISITORS WAITING-ROOM). After knocking politely on the door, he went in.

160

There were six other people ahead of him in the waiting-room. There was a fat mother with her two little boys aged about nine and eleven. There was a bright-eyed young couple who looked as though they might be on their honeymoon. And there was a pale woman with long white gloves, who sat very upright, looking straight ahead with her hands folded on her lap. Nobody spoke. Lexington wondered whether they were all writing cooking-books, like himself, but when he put this question to them aloud, he got no answer. The grown-ups merely smiled mysteriously to themselves and shook their heads, and the two children stared at him as though they were seeing a lunatic.

Soon, the door opened and a man with a merry pink face popped his head into the room and said, 'Next, please.' The mother and the two boys got up and went out.

About ten minutes later, the same man returned. 'Next, please,' he said again, and the honeymoon couple jumped up and followed him outside.

Two new visitors came in and sat down – a middle-aged husband and a middle-aged wife, the wife carrying a wicker shopping-basket containing groceries.

'Next, please,' said the guide, and the woman with the long white gloves got up and left.

Several more people came in and took their places on the stiff-backed wooden chairs.

Soon the guide returned for the third time, and now it was Lexington's turn to go outside.

'Follow me, please,' the guide said, leading the youth across the yard towards the main building.

'How exciting this is!' Lexington cried, hopping from one foot to the other. 'I only wish that my dear Aunt Glosspan could be with me now to see what I am going to see.'

'I myself only do the preliminaries,' the guide said. 'Then I shall hand you over to someone else.'

'Anything you say,' cried the ecstatic youth.

First they visited a large penned-in area at the back of the building where several hundred pigs were wandering around. 'Here's where they start,' the guide said. 'And over there's where they go in.'

'Where?'

'Right there.' The guide pointed to a long wooden shed that stood against the outside wall of the factory. 'We call it the shackling-pen. This way, please.'

Three men wearing long rubber boots were driving a dozen pigs into the shackling-pen just as Lexington and the guide approached, so they all went in together.

'Now,' the guide said, 'watch how they shackle them.'

Inside, the shed was simply a bare wooden room with no roof, but there was a steel cable with hooks on it that kept moving slowly along the length of one wall, parallel with the ground, about three feet up. When it reached the end of the shed, this cable suddenly changed direction and climbed vertically upwards through the open roof towards the top floor of the main building.

The twelve pigs were huddled together at the far end of the pen, standing quietly, looking apprehensive. One of the men in rubber boots pulled a length of metal chain down from the wall and advanced upon the nearest animal, approaching it from the rear. Then he bent down and quickly looped one end of the chain around one of the animal's hind legs. The other end he attached to a hook on the moving cable as it went by. The cable kept moving. The chain tightened. The pig's leg was pulled up and back, and then the pig itself began to be dragged backwards. But it didn't fall down. It was rather a nimble pig, and somehow it managed to keep its balance on three legs, hopping from foot to foot and struggling against the pull of the chain, but going back and back all the time until at the end of the pen where the cable changed direction and went vertically upwards, the creature was suddenly jerked off its feet and borne aloft. Shrill protests filled the air.

'Truly a fascinating process,' Lexington said. 'But what was that funny cracking noise it made as it went up?'

'Probably the leg,' the guide answered. 'Either that or the pelvis.'

'But doesn't that matter?'

'Why should it matter?' the guide asked. 'You don't eat the bones.'

The rubber-booted men were busy shackling the rest of the pigs, and one after another they were hooked to the moving cable and hoisted up through the roof, protesting loudly as they went.

'There's a good deal more to this recipe than just picking herbs,' Lexington said. 'Aunt Glosspan would never have made it.'

At this point, while Lexington was gazing skyward at the last pig to go up, a man in rubber boots approached him quietly from behind and looped one end of a chain round the youth's own left ankle, hooking the other end to the moving belt. The next moment, before he had time to realize what was happening, our hero was jerked off his feet and dragged backwards along the concrete floor of the shackling-pen.

'Stop!' he cried. 'Hold everything! My leg is caught!'

But nobody seemed to hear him, and five seconds later, the unhappy young man was jerked off the floor and hoisted vertically upwards through the open roof of the pen, dangling upside down by one ankle, and wriggling like a fish.

'Help!' he shouted. 'Help! There's been a frightful mistake! Stop the engines! Let me down!'

The guide removed a cigar from his mouth and looked up serenely at the rapidly ascending youth, but he said nothing. The men in rubber boots were already on their way out to collect the next batch of pigs.

'Oh save me!' our hero cried. 'Let me down! Please let me down!' But he was now approaching the top floor of the building where the moving belt curled over like a snake and entered a large hole in the wall, a kind of doorway without a door; and there, on the threshold, waiting to greet him, clothed in a dark-stained yellow rubber apron, and looking for all the world like Saint Peter at the Gates of Heaven, the sticker stood.

Lexington saw him only from upside down, and very briefly at that, but even so he noticed at once the expression of absolute peace and benevolence on the man's face, the cheerful twinkle in the eyes, the little wistful smile, and the dimples in his cheeks – and all this gave him hope.

'Hi there,' the sticker said, smiling.

'Quick! Save me!' our hero cried.

'With pleasure,' the sticker said, and taking Lexington gently by one ear with his left hand, he raised his right hand and deftly slit open the boy's jugular vein with a knife.

The belt moved on. Lexington went with it. Everything was still upside down and the blood was pouring out of his throat and getting into his eyes, but he could still see after a fashion, and he had a blurred impression of being in an enormously long room, and at the far end of the room there was a great smoking cauldron of water, and there were dark figures, half hidden in the steam, dancing round the edge of it, brandishing long poles. The conveyor-belt seemed to be travelling right over the top of the cauldron, and the pigs seemed to be dropping down one by one into the boiling water, and one of the pigs seemed to be wearing long white gloves on its front feet.

Suddenly our hero started to feel very sleepy, but it wasn't until his good strong heart had pumped the last drop of blood from his body that he passed on out of this, the best of all possible worlds, into the next.

Royal Jelly

First published in *Kiss Kiss* (1960)

'It worries me to death, Albert, it really does,' Mrs Taylor said.

She kept her eyes fixed on the baby who was now lying absolutely motionless in the crook of her left arm.

'I just know there's something wrong.'

The skin on the baby's face had a pearly translucent quality, and was stretched very tightly over the bones.

'Try again,' Albert Taylor said.

'It won't do any good.'

'You have to keep trying, Mabel,' he said.

She lifted the bottle out of the saucepan of hot water and shook a few drops of milk on to the inside of her wrist, testing for temperature.

'Come on,' she whispered. 'Come on, my baby. Wake up and take a bit more of this.'

There was a small lamp on the table close by that made a soft yellow glow all around her.

'Please,' she said. 'Take just a weeny bit more.'

The husband watched her over the top of his magazine. She was half dead with exhaustion, he could see that, and the pale oval face, usually so grave and serene, had taken on a kind of pinched and desperate look. But even so, the drop of her head as she gazed down at the child was curiously beautiful.

'You see,' she murmured. 'It's no good. She won't have it.'

She held the bottle up to the light, squinting at the calibrations.

'One ounce again. That's all she's taken. No – it isn't even that. It's only three quarters. It's not enough to keep body and soul together, Albert, it really isn't. It worries me to death.'

'I know,' he said.

'If only they could *find out* what was wrong.'

'There's nothing wrong, Mabel. It's just a matter of time.'

'Of course there's something wrong.'

'Dr Robinson says no.'

'Look,' she said, standing up. 'You can't tell me it's natural for a six-weeks-old child to weigh less, less by more than *two whole pounds* than she did when she was born! Just look at those legs! They're nothing but skin and bone!'

The tiny baby lay limply on her arm, not moving.

'Dr Robinson said you was to stop worrying, Mabel. So did that other one.'

'Ha!' she said. 'Isn't that wonderful! I'm to stop worrying!'

'Now, Mabel.'

'What does he want me to do? Treat it as some sort of a joke?'

'He didn't say that.'

'I hate doctors! I hate them all!' she cried, and she swung away from him and walked quickly out of the room towards the stairs, carrying the baby with her.

Albert Taylor stayed where he was and let her go.

In a little while he heard her moving about in the bedroom directly over his head, quick nervous footsteps going tap tap tap on the linoleum above. Soon the footsteps would stop, and then he would have to get up and follow her, and when he went into the bedroom he would find her sitting beside the cot as usual, staring at the child and crying softly to herself and refusing to move.

'She's starving, Albert,' she would say.

'Of course she's not starving.'

'She *is* starving. I know she is. And Albert?'

'Yes?'

'I believe you know it too, but you won't admit it. Isn't that right?'

Every night now it was like this.

Last week they had taken the child back to the hospital, and the doctor had examined it carefully and told them that there was nothing the matter.

'It took us nine years to get this baby, Doctor,' Mabel had said. 'I think it would kill me if anything should happen to her.'

That was six days ago and since then it had lost another five ounces.

But worrying about it wasn't going to help anybody, Albert Taylor told himself. One simply had to trust the doctor on a thing like this. He picked up the magazine that was still lying on his lap and glanced idly down the list of contents to see what it had to offer this week:

All his life Albert Taylor had been fascinated by anything that had to do with bees. As a small boy he used often to catch them in his bare hands and go running with them into the house to show to his mother, and sometimes he would put them on his face and let them crawl about over his cheeks and neck, and the astonishing thing about it all was that he never got stung. On the contrary, the bees seemed to enjoy being with him. They never tried to fly away, and to get rid of them he would have to brush them off gently with his fingers. Even then they would frequently return and settle again on his arm or hand or knee, any place where the skin was bare.

His father, who was a bricklayer, said there must be some witch's stench about the boy, something noxious that came oozing out through the pores of the skin, and that no good would ever come of it, hypnotizing insects like that. But the mother said it was a gift given him by God, and even went so far as to compare him with St Francis and the birds.

As he grew older, Albert Taylor's fascination with bees developed into an obsession, and by the time he was twelve he had built his first hive. The following summer he had captured his first swarm. Two years later, at the age of fourteen, he had no less than five hives standing neatly in a row against the fence in his father's small back yard, and already – apart from the normal task of producing honey – he was practising the delicate and complicated business of rearing his own queens, grafting larvae into artificial cell cups, and all the rest of it.

He never had to use smoke when there was work to do inside a hive, and he never wore gloves on his hands or a net over his head. Clearly there was some strange sympathy between this boy and the bees, and down in the village, in the shops and pubs, they began to speak about him with a certain kind of respect, and people started coming up to the house to buy his honey.

When he was eighteen, he had rented one acre of rough pasture alongside a cherry orchard down the valley about a mile from the village, and there he had set out to establish his own business. Now, eleven years later, he was still in the same spot, but he had six acres of ground instead of one, two hundred and forty well-stocked hives, and a small house that he'd built mainly with his own hands. He had married at the age of twenty and that, apart from the fact that it had taken them over nine years to get a child, had also been a success. In fact everything had gone pretty well for Albert until this strange little baby girl came along and started frightening them out of their wits by refusing to eat properly and losing weight every day.

He looked up from the magazine and began thinking about his daughter.

This evening, for instance, when she had opened her eyes at the beginning of the feed, he had gazed into them and seen something that frightened him to death – a kind of misty vacant stare, as though the eyes themselves were not connected to the brain at all but were just lying loose in their sockets like a couple of small grey marbles.

Did those doctors really know what they were talking about?

He reached for an ashtray and started slowly picking the ashes out from the bowl of his pipe with a matchstick.

One could always take her along to another hospital, somewhere in Oxford perhaps. He might suggest that to Mabel when he went upstairs.

He could still hear her moving around in the bedroom, but she must have taken off her shoes now and put on slippers because the noise was very faint.

He switched his attention back to the magazine and went on with his reading. He finished an article called 'Experiences in the Control of Nosema', then turned over the page and began reading the next one, 'The Latest on Royal Jelly'. He doubted very much whether there would be anything in this that he didn't know already:

'What is this wonderful substance called royal jelly?'

He reached for the tin of tobacco on the table beside him and began filling his pipe, still reading.

Royal jelly is a glandular secretion produced by the nurse bees to feed the larvae immediately they have hatched

THE COMPLETE SHORT STORIES

from the egg. The pharyngeal glands of bees produce this substance in much the same way as the mammary glands of vertebrates produce milk. The fact is of great biological interest because no other insects in the world are known to have evolved such a process.

All old stuff, he told himself, but for want of anything better to do, he continued to read.

Royal jelly is fed in concentrated form to all bee larvae for the first three days after hatching from the egg: but beyond that point, for all those who are destined to become drones or workers, this precious food is greatly diluted with honey and pollen. On the other hand, the larvae which are destined to become queens are fed throughout the whole of their larval period on a concentrated diet of pure royal jelly. Hence the name.

Above him, up in the bedroom, the noise of the footsteps had stopped altogether. The house was quiet. He struck a match and put it to his pipe.

Royal jelly must be a substance of tremendous nourishing power, for on this diet alone, the honey-bee larva increases in weight fifteen hundred times in five days.

That was probably about right, he thought, although for some reason it had never occurred to him to consider larval growth in terms of weight before.

This is as if a seven-and-a-half-pound baby should increase in that time to five tons.

Albert Taylor stopped and read that sentence again. He read it a third time.

This is as if a seven-and-a-half-pound baby . . .

'Mabel!' he cried, jumping up from his chair. 'Mabel! Come here!'

He went out into the hall and stood at the foot of the stairs calling for her to come down.

There was no answer.

He ran up the stairs and switched on the light on the landing. The bedroom door was closed. He crossed the landing and opened it and stood in the doorway looking into the dark room. 'Mabel,' he said. 'Come downstairs a moment, will you please? I've just had a bit of an idea. It's about the baby.'

The light from the landing behind him cast a faint glow over the bed and he could see her dimly now, lying on her stomach with her face buried in the pillow and her arms up over her head. She was crying again.

'Mabel,' he said, going over to her, touching her shoulder. 'Please come down a moment. This may be important.'

'Go away,' she said. 'Leave me alone.'

'Don't you want to hear about my idea?'

'Oh, Albert, I'm *tired*,' she sobbed. 'I'm so tired I don't know what I'm doing any more. I don't think I can go on. I don't think I can stand it.'

There was a pause. Albert Taylor turned away from her and walked slowly over to the cradle where the baby was lying, and peered in. It was too dark for him to see the child's face, but when he bent down close he could hear the sound of breathing, very faint and quick. 'What time is the next feed?' he asked.

'Two o'clock, I suppose.'

'And the one after that?'

'Six in the morning.'

'I'll do them both,' he said. 'You go to sleep.'

She didn't answer.

'You get properly into bed, Mabel, and go straight to sleep, you understand? And stop worrying. I'm taking over completely for the next twelve hours. You'll give yourself a nervous breakdown going on like this.'

'Yes,' she said. 'I know.'

'I'm taking the nipper and myself *and* the alarm clock into the spare room this very moment, so you just lie down and relax and forget all about us. Right?' Already he was pushing the cradle out through the door.

'Oh, Albert,' she sobbed.

'Don't you worry about a thing. Leave it to me.'

'Albert . . .'

'Yes?'

'I love you, Albert.'

'I love you too, Mabel. Now go to sleep.'

Albert Taylor didn't see his wife again until nearly eleven o'clock the next morning.

'Good *gracious* me!' she cried, rushing down the stairs in dressing-gown and slippers. 'Albert! Just look at the time!

I must have slept twelve hours at least! Is everything all right? What happened?'

He was sitting quietly in his armchair, smoking a pipe and reading the morning paper. The baby was in a sort of carrier cot on the floor at his feet, sleeping.

'Hullo, dear,' he said, smiling.

She ran over to the cot and looked in. 'Did she take anything, Albert? How many times have you fed her? She was due for another one at ten o'clock, did you know that?'

Albert Taylor folded the newspaper neatly into a square and put it away on the side table. 'I fed her at two in the morning,' he said, 'and she took about half an ounce, no more. I fed her again at six and she did a bit better that time, two ounces . . .'

'*Two ounces!* Oh, Albert, that's marvellous!'

'And we just finished the last feed ten minutes ago. There's the bottle on the mantelpiece. Only one ounce left. She drank three. How's that?' He was grinning proudly, delighted with his achievement.

The woman quickly got down on her knees and peered at the baby.

'Don't she look better?' he asked eagerly. 'Don't she look fatter in the face?'

'It may sound silly,' the wife said, 'but I actually think she does. Oh, Albert, you're a marvel! How did you do it?'

'She's turning the corner,' he said. 'That's all it is. Just like the doctor prophesied, she's turning the corner.'

'I pray to God you're right, Albert.'

'Of course I'm right. From now on, you watch her go.'

The woman was gazing lovingly at the baby.

'You look a lot better yourself too, Mabel.'

'I feel wonderful. I'm sorry about last night.'

'Let's keep it this way,' he said. 'I'll do all the night feeds in future. You do the day ones.'

She looked up at him across the cot, frowning. 'No,' she said. 'Oh no, I wouldn't allow you to do that.'

'I don't want you to have a breakdown, Mabel.'

'I won't, not now I've had some sleep.'

'Much better we share it.'

'No, Albert. This is my job and I intend to do it. Last night won't happen again.'

There was a pause. Albert Taylor took the pipe out of his mouth and examined the grain on the bowl. 'All right,' he said. 'In that case I'll just relieve you of the donkey work, I'll do all the sterilizing and the mixing of the food and getting everything ready. That'll help you a bit, anyway.'

She looked at him carefully, wondering what could have come over him all of a sudden.

'You see, Mabel, I've been thinking . . .'

'Yes, dear.'

'I've been thinking that up until last night I've never even raised a finger to help you with this baby.'

'That isn't true.'

'Oh yes it is. So I've decided that from now on I'm going to do *my* share of the work. I'm going to be the feed-mixer and the bottle-sterilizer. Right?'

'It's very sweet of you, dear, but I really don't think it's necessary . . .'

'Come on!' he cried. 'Don't change the luck! I done it the last three times and just *look* what happened! When's the next one? Two o'clock, isn't it?'

'Yes.'

'It's all mixed,' he said. 'Everything's all mixed and ready and all you've got to do when the time comes is to go out there to the larder and take it off the shelf and warm it up. That's *some* help, isn't it?'

The woman got up off her knees and went over to him and kissed him on the cheek. 'You're such a nice man,' she said. 'I love you more and more every day I know you.'

Later, in the middle of the afternoon, when Albert was outside in the sunshine working among the hives, he heard her calling to him from the house.

'Albert!' she shouted. 'Albert, come here!' She was running through the buttercups towards him.

He started forward to meet her, wondering what was wrong.

'Oh, Albert! Guess what!'

'What?'

'I've just finished giving her the two-o'clock feed and she's taken the whole lot!'

'No!'

'Every drop of it! Oh, Albert, I'm so happy! She's going to be all right! She's turned the corner just like you said!' She came up to him and threw her arms round his neck and hugged him, and he clapped her on the back and laughed and said what a marvellous little mother she was.

'Will you come in and watch the next one and see if she does it again, Albert?'

He told her he wouldn't miss it for anything, and she hugged him again, then turned and ran back to the house, skipping over the grass and singing all the way.

Naturally, there was a certain amount of suspense in the air as the time approached for the six-o'clock feed. By five thirty both parents were already seated in the living-room waiting for the moment to arrive. The bottle with the milk formula in it was standing in a saucepan of warm water on the mantelpiece. The baby was asleep in its carrier cot on the sofa.

At twenty minutes to six it woke up and started screaming its head off.

'There you are!' Mrs Taylor cried. 'She's asking for the bottle. Pick her up quick, Albert, and hand her to me here. Give me the bottle first.'

He gave her the bottle, then placed the baby on the woman's lap. Cautiously, she touched the baby's lips with the end of the nipple. The baby seized the nipple between its gums and began to suck ravenously with a rapid powerful action.

'Oh, Albert, isn't it wonderful?' she said, laughing.

'It's terrific, Mabel.'

In seven or eight minutes, the entire contents of the bottle had disappeared down the baby's throat.

'You clever girl,' Mrs Taylor said. 'Four ounces again.'

Albert Taylor was leaning forward in his chair, peering intently into the baby's face. 'You know what?' he said. 'She even seems as though she's put on a touch of weight already. What do you think?'

The mother looked down at the child.

'Don't she seem bigger and fatter to you, Mabel, than she was yesterday?'

'Maybe she does, Albert. I'm not sure. Although actually there couldn't be any *real* gain in such a short time as this. The important thing is that she's eating normally.'

'She's turned the corner,' Albert said. 'I don't think you need worry about her any more.'

'I certainly won't.'

'You want me to go up and fetch the cradle back into our own bedroom, Mabel?'

'Yes, please,' she said.

Albert went upstairs and moved the cradle. The woman followed with the baby, and after changing its nappy, she laid it gently down on its bed. Then she covered it with sheet and blanket.

'Doesn't she look lovely, Albert?' she whispered. 'Isn't that the most beautiful baby you've ever seen in your *entire* life?'

'Leave her be now, Mabel,' he said. 'Come on downstairs and cook us a bit of supper. We both deserve it.'

After they had finished eating, the parents settled themselves in armchairs in the living-room, Albert with his magazine and his pipe, Mrs Taylor with her knitting. But this was a very different scene from the one of the night before. Suddenly, all tensions had vanished. Mrs Taylor's handsome oval face was glowing with pleasure, her cheeks were pink, her eyes were sparkling bright, and her mouth was fixed in a little dreamy smile of pure content. Every now and again she would glance up from her knitting and gaze affectionately at her husband. Occasionally, she would stop the clicking of her needles altogether for a few seconds and sit quite still, looking at the ceiling, listening for a cry or a whimper from upstairs. But all was quiet.

'Albert,' she said after a while.

'Yes, dear?'

'What was it you were going to tell me last night when you came rushing up to the bedroom? You said you had an idea for the baby.'

Albert Taylor lowered the magazine on to his lap and gave her a long sly look.

'Did I?' he said.

'Yes.' She waited for him to go on, but he didn't.

'What's the big joke?' she asked. 'Why are you grinning like that?'

'It's a joke all right,' he said.

'Tell it to me, dear.'

'I'm not sure I ought to,' he said. 'You might call me a liar.'

She had seldom seen him looking so pleased with himself as he was now, and she smiled back at him, egging him on.

'I'd just like to see your face when you hear it, Mabel, that's all.'

'Albert, what *is* all this?'

He paused, refusing to be hurried.

'You do think the baby's better, don't you?' he asked.

'Of course I do.'

'You agree with me that all of a sudden she's feeding marvellously and looking one hundred per cent different?'

'I do, Albert, yes.'

'That's good,' he said, the grin widening. 'You see, it's me that did it.'

'Did what?'

'I cured the baby.'

'Yes, dear, I'm sure you did.' Mrs Taylor went right on with her knitting.

'You don't believe me, do you?'

'Of course I believe you, Albert. I give you all the credit, every bit of it.'

'Then how did I do it?'

'Well,' she said, pausing a moment to think. 'I suppose it's simply that you're a brilliant feed-mixer. Ever since you started mixing the feeds she's got better and better.'

'You mean there's some sort of an art in mixing the feeds?'

'Apparently there is.' She was knitting away and smiling quietly to herself, thinking how funny men were.

'I'll tell you a secret,' he said. 'You're absolutely right. Although, mind you, it isn't so much *how* you mix it that counts. It's what you put in. You realize that, don't you, Mabel?'

Mrs Taylor stopped knitting and looked up sharply at her husband. 'Albert,' she said, 'don't tell me you've been putting things into that child's milk?'

He sat there grinning.

'Well, have you or haven't you?'

'It's possible,' he said.

'I don't believe it.'

He had a strange fierce way of grinning that showed his teeth.

'Albert,' she said. 'Stop playing with me like this.'

'Yes, dear, all right.'

'You haven't *really* put anything into her milk, have you? Answer me properly, Albert. This could be serious with such a tiny baby.'

'The answer is yes, Mabel.'

'*Albert Taylor!* How could you?'

'Now don't get excited,' he said. 'I'll tell you all about it if you really want me to, but for heaven's sake keep your hair on.'

'It was beer!' she cried. 'I just know it was beer!'

'Don't be so daft, Mabel, please.'

'Then what was it?'

Albert laid his pipe down carefully on the table beside him and leaned back in his chair. 'Tell me,' he said, 'did you ever by any chance happen to hear me mentioning something called royal jelly?'

'I did not.'

'It's magic,' he said. 'Pure magic. And last night I suddenly got the idea that if I was to put some of this into the baby's milk . . .'

'How *dare* you!'

'Now, Mabel, you don't even know what it is yet.'

'I don't care what it is,' she said. 'You can't go putting foreign bodies like that into a tiny baby's milk. You must be mad.'

'It's perfectly harmless, Mabel, otherwise I wouldn't have done it. It comes from bees.'

'I might have guessed that.'

'And it's so precious that practically no one can afford to take it. When they do, it's only one little drop at a time.'

'And how much did you give to our baby, might I ask?'

'Ah,' he said, 'that's the whole point. That's where the difference lies. I reckon that our baby, just in the last four feeds, has already swallowed about fifty times as much royal jelly as anyone else in the world has ever swallowed before. How about that?'

'Albert, stop pulling my leg.'

'I swear it,' he said proudly.

She sat there staring at him, her brow wrinkled, her mouth slightly open.

'You know what this stuff actually costs, Mabel, if you want to buy it? There's a place in America advertising it for sale this very moment for something like five hundred dollars a pound jar! *Five hundred dollars!* That's more than gold, you know!'

She hadn't the faintest idea what he was talking about.

'I'll prove it,' he said, and he jumped up and went across to the large bookcase where he kept all his literature about bees. On the top shelf, the back numbers of the *American Bee Journal* were neatly stacked alongside those of the *British Bee Journal*, *Beecraft*, and other magazines. He took down the last issue of the *American Bee Journal* and turned to a page of small classified advertisements at the back.

'Here you are,' he said. 'Exactly as I told you. "We sell royal jelly – $480 per lb jar wholesale."'

He handed her the magazine so she could read it herself.

'Now do you believe me? This is an actual shop in New York, Mabel. It says so.'

'It doesn't say you can go stirring it into the milk of a practically newborn baby,' she said. 'I don't know what's come over you, Albert, I really don't.'

'It's curing her, isn't it?'

'I'm not so sure about that, now.'

'Don't be so damn silly, Mabel. You know it is.'

'Then why haven't other people done it with *their* babies?'

'I keep telling you,' he said. 'It's too expensive. Practically nobody in the world can afford to buy royal jelly just for *eating* except maybe one or two multimillionaires. The people who buy it are the big companies that make women's face creams and things like that. They're using it as a stunt. They mix a tiny pinch of it into a big jar of face cream and it's selling like hot cakes for absolutely enormous prices. They claim it takes out the wrinkles.'

'And does it?'

'Now how on earth would I know that, Mabel? Anyway,' he said, returning to his chair, 'that's not the point. The point is this. It's done so much good to our little baby just in the last few hours that I think we ought to go right on giving it to her. Now don't interrupt, Mabel. Let me finish. I've got two hundred and forty hives out there and if I turn over maybe a hundred of them to making royal jelly, we ought to be able to supply her with all she wants.'

'Albert Taylor,' the woman said, stretching her eyes wide and staring at him. 'Have you gone out of your mind?'

'Just hear me through, will you please?'

'I forbid it,' she said, 'absolutely. You're not to give my baby another drop of that horrid jelly, you understand?'

'Now, Mabel . . .'

'And quite apart from that, we had a shocking honey crop last year, and if you go fooling around with those hives now, there's no telling what might not happen.'

'There's nothing wrong with my hives, Mabel.'

'You know very well we had only half the normal crop last year.'

'Do me a favour, will you?' he said. 'Let me explain some of the marvellous things this stuff does.'

'You haven't even told me what it is yet.'

'All right, Mabel. I'll do that too. Will you listen? Will you give me a chance to explain it?'

She sighed and picked up her knitting once more. 'I suppose you might as well get it off your chest, Albert. Go on and tell me.'

He paused, a bit uncertain now how to begin. It wasn't going to be easy to explain something like this to a person with no detailed knowledge of apiculture at all.

'You know, don't you,' he said, 'that each colony has only one queen?'

'Yes.'

'And that this queen lays all the eggs?'

'Yes, dear. That much I know.'

'All right. Now the queen can actually lay two different kinds of eggs. You didn't know that, but she can. It's what we call one of the miracles of the hive. She can lay eggs that produce drones, and she can lay eggs that produce workers. Now if that isn't a miracle, Mabel, I don't know what is.'

'Yes, Albert, all right.'

'The drones are the males. We don't have to worry about them. The workers are all females. So is the queen, of course. But the workers are unsexed females, if you see what I mean. Their organs are completely undeveloped, whereas the queen is tremendously sexy. She can actually lay her own weight in eggs in a single day.'

He hesitated, marshalling his thoughts.

'Now what happens is this. The queen crawls around on the comb and lays her eggs in what we call cells. You know all those hundreds of little holes you see in a honeycomb? Well, a brood comb is just about the same except the cells don't have honey in them, they have eggs. She lays one egg to each cell, and in three days each of these eggs hatches out into a tiny grub. We call it a larva.

'Now, as soon as this larva appears, the nurse bees – they're young workers – all crowd round and start feeding it like mad. And you know what they feed it on?'

'Royal jelly,' Mabel answered patiently.

'Right!' he cried. 'That's exactly what they do feed it on. They get this stuff out of a gland in their heads and they start pumping it into the cell to feed the larva. And what happens then?'

He paused dramatically, blinking at her with his small watery-grey eyes. Then he turned slowly in his chair and reached for the magazine that he had been reading the night before.

'You want to know what happens then?' he asked, wetting his lips.

'I can hardly wait.'

'"Royal jelly,"' he read aloud, '"must be a substance of tremendous nourishing power, for on this diet alone, the honey-bee larva increases in weight *fifteen hundred times* in five days!"'

'How much?'

'*Fifteen hundred times*, Mabel. And you know what that means if you put it in terms of a human being? It means,' he said, lowering his voice, leaning forward, fixing her with those small pale eyes, 'it means that in five days a baby weighing seven and a half pounds to start off with would increase in weight to *five tons*!'

For the second time, Mrs Taylor stopped knitting.

'Now you mustn't take that too literally, Mabel.'

'Who says I mustn't?'

'It's just a scientific way of putting it, that's all.'

'Very well, Albert. Go on.'

'But that's only half the story,' he said. 'There's more to come. The really amazing thing about royal jelly, I haven't told you yet. I'm going to show you now how it can transform a plain dull-looking little worker bee with practically no sex organs at all into a great big beautiful fertile queen.'

'Are you saying our baby is dull-looking and plain?' she asked sharply.

'Now don't go putting words into my mouth, Mabel, please. Just listen to this. Did you know that the queen bee and the worker bee, although they are completely different when they grow up, are both hatched out of exactly the same kind of egg?'

'I don't believe that,' she said.

'It's true as I'm sitting here, Mabel, honest it is. Any time the bees want a queen to hatch out of the egg instead of a worker, they can do it.'

'How?'

'Ah,' he said, shaking a thick forefinger in her direction. 'That's just what I'm coming to. That's the secret of the whole thing. Now – what do *you* think it is, Mabel, that makes this miracle happen?'

'Royal jelly,' she answered. 'You already told me.'

'Royal jelly it is!' he cried, clapping his hands and bouncing up on his seat. His big round face was glowing with excitement now, and two vivid patches of scarlet had appeared high up on each cheek.

'Here's how it works. I'll put it very simply for you. The bees want a new queen. So they build an extra-large cell, a queen cell we call it, and they get the old queen to lay one of her eggs in there. The other one thousand nine hundred and ninety-nine eggs she lays in ordinary worker cells. Now. As soon as these eggs hatch out into larvae, the nurse bees rally round and start pumping in the royal jelly. All of them get it, workers as well as queen. But here's the vital thing, Mabel, so listen carefully. Here's where the difference comes. The worker larvae only receive this special marvellous food for the *first three days* of their larval life. After that they have a complete change of diet. What really happens is they get weaned, except that it's not like an ordinary weaning because it's so sudden. After the third day they're put straight away on to more or less routine bees' food – a mixture of honey and pollen – and then about two weeks later they emerge from the cells as workers.

'But not so the larva in the queen cell! This one gets royal jelly *all the way through its larval life*. The nurse bees simply pour it into the cell, so much so in fact that the little larva is literally floating in it. And that's what makes it into a queen!'

'You can't prove it,' she said.

'Don't talk so damn silly, Mabel, please. Thousands of people have proved it time and time again, famous scientists in every country in the world. All you have to do is take a larva out of a worker cell and put it in a queen cell – that's what we call grafting – and just so long as the nurse bees keep it well supplied with royal jelly, then presto! – it'll grow up into a queen! And what makes it more marvellous still is the absolutely enormous difference between a queen and a worker when they grow up. The abdomen is a different shape. The sting is different. The legs are different. The . . .'

'In what way are the legs different?' she asked, testing him.

'The legs? Well, the workers have little pollen baskets on their legs for carrying the pollen. The queen has none. Now here's another thing. The queen has fully developed sex organs. The workers don't. And most amazing of all, Mabel, the queen lives for an average of four to six years. The worker hardly lives that many months. And all this difference simply because one of them got royal jelly and the other didn't!'

'It's pretty hard to believe,' she said, 'that a food can do all that.'

'Of course it's hard to believe. It's another of the miracles of the hive. In fact it's the biggest ruddy miracle of them all. It's such a hell of a big miracle that it's baffled the greatest men of science for hundreds of years. Wait a moment. Stay there. Don't move.'

Again he jumped up and went over to the bookcase and started rummaging among the books and magazines.

'I'm going to find you a few of the reports. Here we are. Here's one of them. Listen to this.' He started reading aloud from a copy of the *American Bee Journal*:

'"Living in Toronto at the head of a fine research laboratory given to him by the people of Canada in recognition of his truly great contribution to humanity in the discovery of insulin, Dr Frederick A. Banting became curious about royal jelly. He requested his staff to do a basic fractional analysis . . ."'

He paused.

'Well, there's no need to read it all, but here's what happened. Dr Banting and his people took some royal jelly from queen cells that contained two-day-old larvae, and then they started analysing it. And what d'you think they found?'

'They found,' he said, 'that royal jelly contained phenols, sterols, glycerils, dextrose, *and* – now here it comes – and eighty to eighty-five per cent *unidentified* acids!'

He stood beside the bookcase with the magazine in his hand, smiling a funny little furtive smile of triumph, and his wife watched him, bewildered.

He was not a tall man; he had a thick plump pulpy-looking body that was built close to the ground on abbreviated legs. The legs were slightly bowed. The head was huge and round, covered with bristly short-cut hair, and the greater part of the face – now that he had given up shaving altogether – was hidden by a brownish yellow fuzz about an inch long. In one way and another, he was rather grotesque to look at, there was no denying that.

'Eighty to eighty-five per cent,' he said, 'unidentified acids. Isn't that fantastic?' He turned back to the bookshelf and began hunting through the other magazines.

'What does it mean, unidentified acids?'

'That's the whole point! No one knows! Not even Banting could find out. You've heard of Banting?'

'No.'

'He just happens to be about the most famous living doctor in the world today, that's all.'

Looking at him now as he buzzed around in front of the bookcase with his bristly head and his hairy face and his plump pulpy body, she couldn't help thinking that somehow, in some curious way, there was a touch of the bee about this man. She had often seen women grow to look like the horses that they rode, and she had noticed that people who bred birds or bull terriers or pomeranians frequently resembled in some small but startling manner the creature of their choice. But up until now it had never occurred to her that her husband might look like a bee. It shocked her a bit.

'And did Banting ever try to eat it,' she asked, 'this royal jelly?'

'Of course he didn't eat it, Mabel. He didn't have enough for that. It's too precious.'

'You know something?' she said, staring at him but smiling a little all the same. 'You're getting to look just a teeny bit like a bee yourself, did you know that?'

He turned and looked at her.

'I suppose it's the beard mostly,' she said. 'I do wish you'd stop wearing it. Even the colour is sort of bee-ish, don't you think?'

'What the hell are you talking about, Mabel?'

'Albert,' she said. 'Your language.'

'Do you want to hear any more of this or don't you?'

'Yes, dear, I'm sorry. I was only joking. Do go on.'

He turned away again and pulled another magazine out of the bookcase and began leafing through the pages. 'Now just listen to this, Mabel. "In 1939, Heyl experimented with twenty-one-day-old rats, injecting them with royal jelly in varying amounts. As a result, he found a precocious follicular development of the ovaries directly in proportion to the quantity of royal jelly injected."'

'There!' she cried. 'I knew it!'

'Knew what?'

'I knew something terrible would happen.'

'Nonsense. There's nothing wrong with that. Now here's another, Mabel. "Still and Burdett found that a male rat which hitherto had been unable to breed, upon receiving a minute daily dose of royal jelly, became a father many times over."'

'Albert,' she cried, 'this stuff is *much* too strong to give to a baby! I don't like it at all.'

'Nonsense, Mabel.'

'Then why do they only try it out on rats, tell me that? Why don't some of these famous scientists take it themselves? They're too clever, that's why. Do you think Dr Banting is going to risk finishing up with precious ovaries? Not him.'

'But they *have* given it to people, Mabel. Here's a whole article about it. Listen.' He turned the page and again began reading from the magazine. '"In Mexico, in 1953, a group of enlightened physicians began prescribing minute doses of royal jelly for such things as cerebral neuritis, arthritis, diabetes, autointoxication from tobacco, impotence in men, asthma, croup and gout ... There are stacks of signed testimonials ... A celebrated stockbroker in Mexico City contracted a particularly stubborn case of psoriasis. He became physically unattractive. His clients began to forsake him. His business began to suffer. In desperation he turned to royal jelly – one drop with every meal – and presto! – he was cured in a fortnight. A waiter in the Café Jena, also in Mexico City, reported that his father, after taking minute doses of this wonder substance in capsule form, sired a healthy boy child at the age of ninety. A bullfight promoter in Acapulco, finding himself landed with a rather lethargic-looking bull, injected it with one gram of royal jelly (an excessive dose) just before it entered the arena. Thereupon, the beast became so swift and savage that it promptly dispatched two picadors, three horses and a matador, and finally ... "'

'Listen!' Mrs Taylor said, interrupting him. 'I think the baby's crying.'

Albert glanced up from his reading. Sure enough, a lusty yelling noise was coming from the bedroom above.

'She must be hungry,' he said.

His wife looked at the clock. 'Good gracious me!' she cried, jumping up. 'It's past her time again already! You mix the feed, Albert, quickly, while I bring her down! But hurry! I don't want to keep her waiting.'

In half a minute, Mrs Taylor was back, carrying the screaming infant in her arms. She was flustered now, still quite unaccustomed to the ghastly non-stop racket that a healthy baby makes when it wants its food. 'Do be quick, Albert!' she called, settling herself in the armchair and arranging the child on her lap. 'Please hurry!'

Albert entered from the kitchen and handed her the bottle of warm milk. 'It's just right,' he said. 'You don't have to test it.'

She hitched the baby's head a little higher in the crook of her arm, then pushed the rubber teat straight into the wide-open yelling mouth. The baby grabbed the teat and began to suck. The yelling stopped. Mrs Taylor relaxed.

'Oh, Albert, isn't she lovely?'

'She's terrific, Mabel – thanks to royal jelly.'

'Now, dear, I don't want to hear another word about that nasty stuff. It frightens me to death.'

'You're making a big mistake,' he said.

'We'll see about that.'

The baby went on sucking the bottle.

'I do believe she's going to finish the whole lot again, Albert.'

'I'm sure she is,' he said.

And a few minutes later, the milk was all gone.

'Oh, what a good girl you are!' Mrs Taylor cried, as very gently she started to withdraw the nipple. The baby sensed what she was doing and sucked harder, trying to hold on. The woman gave a quick little tug, and *plop*, out it came.

'Waa! Waa! Waa! Waa! Waa!' the baby yelled.

'Nasty old wind,' Mrs Taylor said, hoisting the child on to her shoulder and patting its back.

It belched twice in quick succession.

'There you are, my darling, you'll be all right now.'

For a few seconds, the yelling stopped. Then it started again.

'Keep belching her,' Albert said. 'She's drunk it too quick.'

His wife lifted the baby back on to her shoulder. She rubbed its spine. She changed it from one shoulder to the other. She lay it on its stomach on her lap. She sat it up on her knee. But it didn't belch again, and the yelling became louder and more insistent every minute.

'Good for the lungs,' Albert Taylor said, grinning. 'That's the way they exercise their lungs, Mabel, did you know that?'

'There, there, there,' the wife said, kissing it all over the face. 'There, there, there.'

They waited another five minutes, but not for one moment did the screaming stop.

'Change the nappy,' Albert said. 'It's got a wet nappy, that's all it is.' He fetched a clean one from the kitchen, and Mrs Taylor took the old one off and put the new one on.

This made no difference at all.

'Waa! Waa! Waa! Waa! Waa!' the baby yelled.

'You didn't stick the safety pin through the skin, did you, Mabel?'

'Of course I didn't,' she said, feeling under the nappy with her fingers to make sure.

The parents sat opposite one another in their armchairs, smiling nervously, watching the baby on the mother's lap, waiting for it to tire and stop screaming.

'You know what?' Albert Taylor said at last.

'What?'

'I'll bet she's still hungry. I'll bet all she wants is another swig at that bottle. How about me fetching her an extra lot?'

'I don't think we ought to do that, Albert.'

'It'll do her good,' he said, getting up from his chair. 'I'm going to warm her up a second helping.'

He went into the kitchen, and was away several minutes. When he returned he was holding a bottle brimful of milk.

'I made her a double,' he announced. 'Eight ounces. Just in case.'

'Albert! Are you mad! Don't you know it's just as bad to overfeed as it is to underfeed?'

'You don't have to give her the lot, Mabel. You can stop any time you like. Go on,' he said, standing over her. 'Give her a drink.'

Mrs Taylor began to tease the baby's lip with the end of the nipple. The tiny mouth closed like a trap over the rubber teat and suddenly there was silence in the room. The baby's whole body relaxed and a look of absolute bliss came over its face as it started to drink.

'There you are, Mabel! What did I tell you?'

The woman didn't answer.

'She's ravenous, that's what she is. Just look at her suck.'

Mrs Taylor was watching the level of the milk in the bottle. It was dropping fast, and before long three or four ounces out of the eight had disappeared.

'There,' she said. 'That'll do.'

'You can't pull it away now, Mabel.'

'Yes, dear. I must.'

'Go on, woman. Give her the rest and stop fussing.'

'But *Albert* . . .'

'She's famished, can't you see that? Go on, my beauty,' he said. 'You finish that bottle.'

'I don't like it, Albert,' the wife said, but she didn't pull the bottle away.

'She's making up for lost time, Mabel, that's all she's doing.'

Five minutes later the bottle was empty. Slowly, Mrs Taylor withdrew the nipple, and this time there was no protest from the baby, no sound at all. It lay peacefully on the mother's lap, the eyes glazed with contentment, the mouth half open, the lips smeared with milk.

'Twelve whole ounces, Mabel!' Albert Taylor said. 'Three times the normal amount! Isn't that amazing!'

The woman was staring down at the baby. And now the old anxious tight-lipped look of the frightened mother was slowly returning to her face.

'What's the matter with *you*?' Albert asked. 'You're not worried by that, are you? You can't expect her to get back to normal on a lousy four ounces, don't be ridiculous.'

'Come here, Albert,' she said.

'What?'

'I said come here.'

He went over and stood beside her.

'Take a good look and tell me if you see anything different.'

He peered closely at the baby. 'She seems bigger, Mabel, if that's what you mean. Bigger and fatter.'

'Hold her,' she ordered. 'Go on, pick her up.'

He reached out and lifted the baby up off the mother's lap. 'Good God!' he cried. 'She weighs a ton!'

'Exactly.'

'Now isn't that marvellous!' he cried, beaming. 'I'll bet she must almost be back to normal already!'

'It frightens me, Albert. It's too quick.'

'Nonsense, woman.'

'It's that disgusting jelly that's done it,' she said. 'I hate the stuff.'

'There's nothing disgusting about royal jelly,' he answered, indignant.

'Don't be a fool, Albert! You think it's *normal* for a child to start putting on weight at this speed?'

'You're never satisfied!' he cried. 'You're scared stiff

when she's losing and now you're absolutely terrified because she's gaining! What's the matter with you, Mabel?'

The woman got up from her chair with the baby in her arms and started towards the door. 'All I can say is,' she said, 'it's lucky I'm here to see you don't give her any more of it, that's all I can say.' She went out, and Albert watched her through the open door as she crossed the hall to the foot of the stairs and started to ascend, and when she reached the third or fourth step she suddenly stopped and stood quite still for several seconds as though remembering something. Then she turned and came down again rather quickly and re-entered the room.

'Albert,' she said.

'Yes?'

'I assume there wasn't any royal jelly in this last feed we've just given her?'

'I don't see why you should assume that, Mabel.'

'Albert!'

'What's wrong?' he asked, soft and innocent.

'How *dare* you!' she cried.

Albert Taylor's great bearded face took on a pained and puzzled look. 'I think you ought to be very glad she's got another big dose of it inside her,' he said. 'Honest I do. And this *is* a big dose, Mabel, believe you me.'

The woman was standing just inside the doorway clasping the sleeping baby in her arms and staring at her husband with huge eyes. She stood very erect, her body absolutely stiff with fury, her face paler, more tight-lipped than ever.

'You mark my words,' Albert was saying, 'you're going

to have a nipper there soon that'll win first prize in any baby show in the *entire* country. Hey, why don't you weigh her now and see what she is? You want me to get the scales, Mabel, so you can weigh her?'

The woman walked straight over to the large table in the centre of the room and laid the baby down and quickly started taking off its clothes. 'Yes!' she snapped. 'Get the scales!' Off came the little nightgown, then the undervest.

Then she unpinned the nappy and she drew it away and the baby lay naked on the table.

'But Mabel!' Albert cried. 'It's a miracle! She's fat as a puppy!'

Indeed, the amount of flesh the child had put on since the day before was astounding. The small sunken chest with the rib-bones showing all over it was now plump and round as a barrel, and the belly was bulging high in the air. Curiously, though, the arms and legs did not seem to have grown in proportion. Still short and skinny, they looked like little sticks protruding from a ball of fat.

'Look!' Albert said. 'She's even beginning to get a bit of fuzz on the tummy to keep her warm!' He put out a hand and was about to run the tips of his fingers over the powdering of silky yellowy-brown hairs that had suddenly appeared on the baby's stomach.

'*Don't you touch her!*' the woman cried. She turned and faced him, her eyes blazing, and she looked suddenly like some kind of a little fighting bird with her neck arched over towards him as though she were about to fly at his face and peck his eyes out.

'Now wait a minute,' he said, retreating.

'You must be mad!' she cried.

'Now wait just one minute, Mabel, will you please, because if you're still thinking this stuff is dangerous ... That is what you're thinking, isn't it? All right, then. Listen carefully. I shall now proceed to *prove* to you once and for all, Mabel, that royal jelly is absolutely harmless to human beings, even in enormous doses. For example – why do you think we had only half the usual honey crop last summer? Tell me that.'

His retreat, walking backwards, had taken him three or four yards away from her, where he seemed to feel more comfortable.

'The reason we had only half the usual crop last summer,' he said slowly, lowering his voice, 'was because I turned one hundred of my hives over to the production of royal jelly.'

'You *what?*'

'Ah,' he whispered. 'I thought that might surprise you a bit. And I've been making it ever since right under your very nose.' His small eyes were glinting at her, and a slow sly smile was creeping round the corners of his mouth.

'You'll never guess the reason, either,' he said. 'I've been afraid to mention it up to now because I thought it might ... well ... sort of embarrass you.'

There was a slight pause. He had his hands clasped high in front of him, level with his chest, and he was rubbing one palm against the other, making a soft scraping noise.

'You remember that bit I read you out of the magazine? That bit about the rat? Let me see now, how does it go? "Still and Burdett found that a male rat which hitherto had been unable to breed ... "' He hesitated, the grin widening, showing his teeth.

'You get the message, Mabel?'

She stood quite still, facing him.

'The very first time I ever read that sentence, Mabel, I jumped straight out of my chair and I said to myself if it'll work with a lousy rat, I said, then there's no reason on earth why it shouldn't work with Albert Taylor.'

He paused again, craning his head forward and turning one ear slightly in his wife's direction, waiting for her to say something. But she didn't.

'And here's another thing,' he went on. 'It made me feel so absolutely marvellous, Mabel, and so sort of completely different to what I was before that I went right on taking it even after you'd announced the joyful tidings. *Buckets* of it I must have swallowed during the last twelve months.'

The big heavy haunted-looking eyes of the woman were moving intently over the man's face and neck. There was no skin showing at all on the neck, not even at the sides below the ears. The whole of it, to a point where it disappeared into the collar of the shirt, was covered all the way round with those shortish silky hairs, yellowly black.

'Mind you,' he said, turning away from her, gazing lovingly now at the baby, 'it's going to work far better on a tiny infant than on a fully developed man like me. You've only got to look at her to see that, don't you agree?'

The woman's eyes travelled slowly downwards and

settled on the baby. The baby was lying naked on the table, fat and white and comatose, like some gigantic grub that was approaching the end of its larval life and would soon emerge into the world complete with mandibles and wings.

'Why don't you cover her up, Mabel?' he said. 'We don't want our little queen to catch a cold.'

William and Mary

First published in *Kiss Kiss* (1960)

William Pearl did not leave a great deal of money when he died, and his will was a simple one. With the exception of a few small bequests to relatives, he left all his property to his wife.

The solicitor and Mrs Pearl went over it together in the solicitor's office, and when the business was completed, the widow got up to leave. At that point, the solicitor took a sealed envelope from the folder on his desk and held it out to his client.

'I have been instructed to give you this,' he said. 'Your husband sent it to us shortly before he passed away.' The solicitor was pale and prim, and out of respect for a widow he kept his head on one side as he spoke, looking downwards. 'It appears that it might be something personal, Mrs Pearl. No doubt you'd like to take it home with you and read it in privacy.'

Mrs Pearl accepted the envelope and went out into the street. She paused on the pavement, feeling the thing with her fingers. A letter of farewell from William? Probably, yes. A formal letter. It was bound to be formal – stiff and formal. The man was incapable of acting otherwise. He had never done anything informal in his life.

My dear Mary, I trust that you will not permit my departure from this world to upset you too much, but that you will continue to

204

*observe those precepts which have guided you so well during our
partnership together. Be diligent and dignified in all things. Be
thrifty with your money. Be very careful that you do not . . . et
cetera, et cetera.*

A typical William letter.

Or was it possible that he might have broken down at
the last moment and written her something beautiful?
Maybe this was a beautiful tender message, a sort of love
letter, a lovely warm note of thanks to her for giving him
thirty years of her life and for ironing a million shirts and
cooking a million meals and making a million beds, something that she could read over and over again, once a day
at least, and she would keep it for ever in the box on her
dressing-table together with her brooches.

There is no knowing what people will do when they are
about to die, Mrs Pearl told herself, and she tucked the
envelope under her arm and hurried home.

She let herself in the front door and went straight to
the living-room and sat down on the sofa without removing her hat or coat. Then she opened the envelope and
drew out the contents. These consisted, she saw, of some
fifteen or twenty sheets of lined white paper, folded over
once and held together at the top left-hand corner by a
clip. Each sheet was covered with the small, neat, forward-
sloping writing that she knew so well, but when she noticed
how much of it there was, and in what a neat businesslike
manner it was written, and how the first page didn't even
begin in the nice way a letter should, she began to get
suspicious.

She looked away. She lit herself a cigarette. She took one puff and laid the cigarette in the ashtray.

If this is about what I am beginning to suspect it is about, she told herself, then I don't want to read it.

Can one refuse to read a letter from the dead?

Yes.

Well . . .

She glanced over at William's empty chair on the other side of the fireplace. It was a big brown leather armchair, and there was a depression on the seat of it, made by his buttocks over the years. Higher up, on the backrest, there was a dark oval stain on the leather where his head had rested. He used to sit reading in that chair and she would be opposite him on the sofa, sewing on buttons or mending socks or putting a patch on the elbow of one of his jackets, and every now and then a pair of eyes would glance up from the book and settle on her, watchful, but strangely impersonal, as if calculating something. She had never liked those eyes. They were ice blue, cold, small, and rather close together, with two deep vertical lines of disapproval dividing them. All her life they had been watching her. And even now, after a week alone in the house, she sometimes had an uneasy feeling that they were still there, following her around, staring at her from doorways, from empty chairs, through a window at night.

Slowly she reached into her handbag and took out her spectacles and put them on. Then, holding the pages up high in front of her so that they caught the late afternoon light from the window behind, she started to read:

This note, my dear Mary, is entirely for you, and will be given you shortly after I am gone.

Do not be alarmed by the sight of all this writing. It is nothing but an attempt on my part to explain to you precisely what Landy is going to do to me, and why I have agreed that he should do it, and what are his theories and his hopes. You are my wife and you have a right to know these things. In fact you must know them. During the past few days I have tried very hard to speak with you about Landy, but you have steadfastly refused to give me a hearing. This, as I have already told you, is a very foolish attitude to take, and I find it not entirely an unselfish one either. It stems mostly from ignorance, and I am absolutely convinced that if only you were made aware of all the facts, you would immediately change your view. That is why I am hoping that when I am no longer with you, and your mind is less distracted, you will consent to listen to me more carefully through these pages. I swear to you that when you have read my story, your sense of antipathy will vanish, and enthusiasm will take its place. I even dare to hope that you will become a little proud of what I have done.

As you read on, you must forgive me, if you will, for the coolness of my style, but this is the only way I know of getting my message over to you clearly. You see, as my time draws near, it is natural that I begin to brim with every kind of sentimentality under the sun. Each day I grow more extravagantly wistful, especially in the evenings, and unless I watch myself closely my emotions will be overflowing on to these pages.

I have a wish, for example, to write something about you and what a satisfactory wife you have been to me through the years, and I am promising myself that if there is time, and I still have the strength, I shall do that next.

I have a yearning also to speak about this Oxford of mine where I have been living and teaching for the past seventeen years, to tell something about the glory of the place and to explain, if I can, a little of what it has meant to have been allowed to work in its midst. All the things and places that I loved so well keep crowding in on me now in this gloomy bedroom. They are bright and beautiful as they always were, and today, for some reason, I can see them more clearly than ever. The path around the lake in the gardens of Worcester College, where Lovelace used to walk. The gateway at Pembroke. The view westward over the town from Magdalen Tower. The great hall at Christ Church. The little rockery at St John's where I have counted more than a dozen varieties of campanula, including the rare and dainty C. waldsteiniana. *But there, you see! I haven't even begun and already I'm falling into the trap. So let me get started now; and let you read it slowly, my dear, without any of that sense of sorrow or disapproval that might otherwise embarrass your understanding. Promise me now that you will read it slowly, and that you will put yourself in a cool and patient frame of mind before you begin.*

The details of the illness that struck me down so suddenly in my middle life are known to you. I need not waste time upon them — except to admit at once how foolish I was not to have gone earlier to my doctor. Cancer is one of the few remaining diseases that these modern drugs cannot cure. A surgeon can operate if it has not spread too far; but with me, not only did I leave it too late, but the thing had the effrontery to attack me in the pancreas, making both surgery and survival equally impossible.

So here I was with somewhere between one and six months left to live, growing more melancholy every hour — and then, all of a sudden, in comes Landy.

That was six weeks ago, on a Tuesday morning, very early, long before your visiting time, and the moment he entered I knew there was some sort of madness in the wind. He didn't creep in on his toes, sheepish and embarrassed, not knowing what to say, like all my other visitors. He came in strong and smiling, and he strode up to the bed and stood there looking down at me with a wild bright glimmer in his eyes, and he said, 'William, my boy, this is perfect. You're just the one I want!'

Perhaps I should explain to you here that although John Landy has never been to our house, and you have seldom if ever met him, I myself have been friendly with him for at least nine years. I am, of course, primarily a teacher of philosophy, but as you know I've lately been dabbling a good deal in psychology as well. Landy's interests and mine have therefore slightly overlapped. He is a magnificent neurosurgeon, one of the finest, and recently he has been kind enough to let me study the results of some of his work, especially the varying effects of prefrontal lobotomies upon different types of psychopath. So you can see that when he suddenly burst in on me Tuesday morning, we were by no means strangers to one another.

'Look,' he said, pulling up a chair beside the bed. 'In a few weeks you're going to be dead. Correct?'

Coming from Landy, the question didn't seem especially unkind. In a way it was refreshing to have a visitor brave enough to touch upon the forbidden subject.

'You're going to expire right here in this room, and then they'll take you out and cremate you.'

'Bury me,' I said.

'That's even worse. And then what? Do you believe you'll go to heaven?'

'I doubt it,' I said, 'though it would be comforting to think so.'

'Or hell, perhaps?'

'I don't really see why they should send me there.'

'You never know, my dear William.'

'What's all this about?' I asked.

'Well,' he said, and I could see him watching me carefully, 'personally, I don't believe that after you're dead you'll ever hear of yourself again – unless . . .' and here he paused and smiled and leaned closer '. . . unless, of course, you have the sense to put yourself into my hands. Would you care to consider a proposition?'

The way he was staring at me, and studying me, and appraising me with a queer kind of hungriness, I might have been a piece of prime beef on the counter and he had bought it and was waiting for them to wrap it up.

'I'm really serious about it, William. Would you care to consider a proposition?'

'I don't know what you're talking about.'

'Then listen and I'll tell you. Will you listen to me?'

'Go on then, if you like. I doubt I've got very much to lose by hearing it.'

'On the contrary, you have a great deal to gain – especially after you're dead.'

I am sure he was expecting me to jump when he said this, but for some reason I was ready for it. I lay quite still, watching his face and that slow white smile of his that always revealed the gold clasp of an upper denture curled round the canine on the left side of his mouth.

'This is a thing, William, that I've been working on quietly for some years. One or two others here at the hospital have been *helping me, especially Morrison, and we've completed a number of fairly successful trials with laboratory animals. I'm at the stage now where I'm ready to have a go with a man. It's a big idea, and it may sound a bit far-fetched at first, but from a surgical point of view there doesn't seem to be any reason why it shouldn't be more or less practicable.'*

Landy leaned forward and placed both his hands on the edge of my bed. He has a good face, handsome in a bony sort of way, and with none of the usual doctor's look about it. You know that look, most of them have it. It glimmers at you out of their eyeballs like a dull electric sign and it reads ONLY I CAN SAVE YOU. *But John Landy's eyes were wide and bright and little sparks of excitement were dancing in the centres of them.*

'Quite a long time ago,' he said, 'I saw a short medical film that had been brought over from Russia. It was a rather gruesome thing, but interesting. It showed a dog's head completely severed from the body, but with the normal blood supply being maintained through the arteries and veins by means of an artificial heart. Now the thing is this: that dog's head, sitting there all alone on a sort of tray, was alive. The brain was functioning. They proved it by several tests. For example, when food was smeared on the dog's lips, the tongue would come out and lick it away; and the eyes would follow a person moving across the room.

'It seemed reasonable to conclude from this that the head and the brain did not need to be attached to the rest of the body in order to remain alive — provided, of course, that a supply of properly oxygenated blood could be maintained.

'Now then. My own thought, which grew out of seeing this film, was to remove the brain from the skull of a human and keep it alive and functioning as an independent unit for an

unlimited period after he is dead. You *brain, for example, after* you *are dead.'*

'*I don't like that,*' I said.

'*Don't interrupt, William. Let me finish. So far as I can tell from subsequent experiments, the brain is a peculiarly self-supporting object. It manufactures its own cerebrospinal fluid. The magic processes of thought and memory which go on inside it are manifestly not impaired by the absence of limbs or trunk or even of skull, provided, as I say, that you keep pumping in the right kind of oxygenated blood under the proper conditions.*

'*My dear William, just think for a moment of your own brain. It is in perfect shape. It is crammed full of a lifetime of learning. It has taken you years of work to make it what it is. It is just beginning to give out some first-rate original ideas. Yet soon it is going to have to die along with the rest of your body simply because your silly little pancreas is lousy with cancer.*'

'*No thank you,*' I said to him. '*You can stop there. It's a repulsive idea, and even if you could do it, which I doubt, it would be quite pointless. What possible use is there in keeping my brain alive if I couldn't talk or see or hear or feel? Personally, I can think of nothing more unpleasant.*'

'*I believe that you* would *be able to communicate with us,*' Landy said. '*And we might even succeed in giving you a certain amount of vision. But let's take this slowly. I'll come to all that later on. The fact remains that you're going to die fairly soon whatever happens; and my plans would not involve touching you at all until* after *you are dead. Come now, William. No true philosopher could object to lending his dead body to the cause of science.*'

'That's not putting it quite straight,' I answered. 'It seems to me there'd be some doubt as to whether I were dead or alive by the time you'd finished with me.'

'Well,' he said, smiling a little, 'I suppose you're right about that. But I don't think you ought to turn me down quite so quickly, before you know a bit more about it.'

'I said I don't want to hear it.'

'Have a cigarette,' he said, holding out his case.

'I don't smoke, you know that.'

He took one himself and lit it with a tiny silver lighter that was no bigger than a shilling piece. 'A present from the people who make my instruments,' he said. 'Ingenious, isn't it?'

I examined the lighter, then handed it back.

'May I go on?' he asked.

'I'd rather you didn't.'

'Just lie still and listen. I think you'll find it quite interesting.'

There were some blue grapes on a plate beside my bed. I put the plate on my chest and began eating the grapes.

'At the very moment of death,' Landy said, 'I should have to be standing by so that I could step in immediately and try to keep your brain alive.'

'You mean leaving it in the head?'

'To start with, yes. I'd have to.'

'And where would you put it after that?'

'If you want to know, in a sort of basin.'

'Are you really serious about this?'

'Certainly I'm serious.'

'All right. Go on.'

'I suppose you know that when the heart stops and the brain is deprived of fresh blood and oxygen, its tissues die very rapidly.

Anything from four to six minutes and the whole thing's dead. Even after three minutes you may get a certain amount of damage. So I should have to work rapidly to prevent this from happening. But with the help of the machine, it should all be quite simple.'

'What machine?'

'The artificial heart. We've got a nice adaptation here of the one originally devised by Alexis Carrel and Lindbergh. It oxygenates the blood, keeps it at the right temperature, pumps it in at the right pressure, and does a number of other little necessary things. It's really not at all complicated.'

'Tell me what you would do at the moment of death,' I said. 'What is the first thing you would do?'

'Do you know anything about the vascular and venous arrangements of the brain?'

'No.'

'Then listen. It's not difficult. The blood supply to the brain is derived from two main sources, the internal carotid arteries and the vertebral arteries. There are two of each, making four arteries in all. Got that?'

'Yes.'

'And the return system is even simpler. The blood is drained away by only two large veins, the internal jugulars. So you have four arteries going up – they go up the neck, of course – and two veins coming down. Around the brain itself they naturally branch out into other channels, but those don't concern us. We never touch them.'

'All right,' I said. 'Imagine that I've just died. Now what would you do?'

'I should immediately open your neck and locate the four arteries, the carotids and the vertebrals. I should then perfuse them, which means that I'd stick a large hollow needle into each. These four needles would be connected by tubes to the artificial heart.

'Then, working quickly, I would dissect out both the left and right internal jugular veins and hitch these also to the heart machine to complete the circuit. Now switch on the machine, which is already primed with the right type of blood, and there you are. The circulation through your brain would be restored.'

'I'd be like that Russian dog.'

'I don't think you would. For one thing, you'd certainly lose consciousness when you died, and I very much doubt whether you would come to again for quite a long time — if indeed you came to at all. But, conscious or not, you'd be in a rather interesting position, wouldn't you? You'd have a cold dead body and a living brain.'

Landy paused to savour this delightful prospect. The man was so entranced and bemused by the whole idea that he evidently found it impossible to believe I might not be feeling the same way.

'We could now afford to take our time,' he said. 'And believe me, we'd need it. The first thing we'd do would be to wheel you to the operating-room, accompanied of course by the machine, which must never stop pumping. The next problem . . .'

'All right,' I said. 'That's enough. I don't have to hear the details.'

'Oh but you must,' he said. 'It is important that you should know precisely what is going to happen to you all the way through. You see, afterwards, when you regain consciousness, it will be much more satisfactory from your point of view if you are able to *remember exactly* where *you are and* how *you came to be there. If only for your own peace of mind you should know that. You agree?'*

I lay still on the bed, watching him.

'So the next problem would be to remove your brain, intact and undamaged, from your dead body. The body is useless. In fact it has already started to decay. The skull and the face are also useless. They are both encumbrances and I don't want them around. All I want is the brain, the clean beautiful brain, alive and perfect. So when I get you on the table I will take a saw, a small oscillating saw, and with this I shall proceed to remove the whole vault of your skull. You'd still be unconscious at that point so I wouldn't have to bother with anaesthetic.'

'Like hell you wouldn't,' I said.

'You'd be out cold, I promise you that, William. Don't forget you died just a few minutes before.'

'Nobody's sawing off the top of my skull without an anaes-thetic,' I said.

Landy shrugged his shoulders. 'It makes no difference to me,' he said. 'I'll be glad to give you a little procaine if you want it. If it will make you any happier I'll infiltrate the whole scalp with procaine, the whole head, from the neck up.'

'Thanks very much,' I said.

'You know,' he went on, 'it's extraordinary what sometimes happens. Only last week a man was brought in unconscious, and I opened his head without any anaesthetic at all and removed a small blood clot. I was still working inside the skull when he woke up and began talking.

'"Where am I?" he asked.

'"You're in hospital."

216

' "Well," he said. "Fancy that."

' "Tell me," I asked him, "is this bothering you, what I'm doing?"

' "No," he answered. "Not at all. What are you doing?"

' "I'm just removing a blood clot from your brain."

' "You are?"

' "Just lie still. Don't move. I'm nearly finished."

' "So that's the bastard been giving me all those headaches," the man said.'

Landy paused and smiled, remembering the occasion. 'That's word for word what the man said,' he went on, 'although the next day he couldn't even recollect the incident. It's a funny thing, the brain.'

'I'll have the procaine,' I said.

'As you wish, William. And now, as I say, I'd take a small oscillating saw and carefully remove your complete calvarium — the whole vault of the skull. This would expose the top half of the brain, or rather the outer covering in which it is wrapped. You may or may not know that there are three separate coverings round the brain itself — the outer one called the dura mater or dura, the middle one called the arachnoid, and the inner one called the pia mater or pia. Most laymen seem to have the idea that the brain is a naked thing floating around in fluid in your head. But it isn't. It's wrapped up neatly in these three strong coverings, and the cerebrospinal fluid actually flows within the little gap between the two inner coverings, known as the subarachnoid space. As I told you before, this fluid is manufactured by the brain, and it drains off into the venous system by osmosis.

'I myself would leave all three coverings — don't they have lovely names, the dura, the arachnoid, and the pia? — I'd leave them all *intact. There are many reasons for this, not least among them being the fact that within the dura run the venous channels that drain the blood from the brain into the jugular.*

'Now,' he went on, 'we've got the upper half of your skull off so that the top of the brain, wrapped in its outer covering, is exposed. The next step is the really tricky one: to release the whole package so that it can be lifted cleanly away, leaving the stubs of the four supply arteries and the two veins hanging underneath ready to be re-connected to the machine. This is an immensely lengthy and complicated business involving the delicate chipping away of much bone, the severing of many nerves, and the cutting and tying of numerous blood vessels. The only way I could do it with any hope of success would be by taking a rongeur and slowly biting off the rest of your skull, peeling it off downwards like an orange until the sides and underneath of the brain covering are fully exposed. The problems involved are highly technical and I won't go into them, but I feel fairly sure that the work can be done. It's simply a question of surgical skill and patience. And don't forget that I'd have plenty of time, as much as I wanted, because the artificial heart would be continually pumping away alongside the operating-table, keeping the brain alive.

'Now, let's assume that I've succeeded in peeling off your skull and removing everything else that surrounds the sides of the brain. That leaves it connected to the body only at the base, mainly by the spinal column and by the two large veins and the four arteries that are supplying it with blood. So what next?

'I would sever the spinal column just above the first cervical vertebra, taking great care not to harm the two vertebral arteries which are in that area. But you must remember that the dura or outer covering is open at this place to receive the spinal column, so

I'd have to close this opening by sewing the edges of the dura together. There'd be no problem there.

'At this point, I would be ready for the final move. To one side, on a table, I'd have a basin of a special shape, and this would be filled with what we call Ringer's Solution. That is a special kind of fluid we use for irrigation in neurosurgery. I would now cut the brain completely loose by severing the supply arteries and the veins. Then I would simply pick it up in my hands and transfer it to the basin. This would be the only other time during the whole proceeding when the blood flow would be cut off; but once it was in the basin, it wouldn't take a moment to re-connect the stubs of the arteries and veins to the artificial heart.

'So there you are,' Landy said. 'Your brain is now in the basin, and still alive, and there isn't any reason why it shouldn't stay alive for a very long time, years and years perhaps, provided we looked after the blood and the machine.'

'But would it function?'

'My dear William, how should I know? I can't even tell you whether it would ever regain consciousness.'

'And if it did?'

'There now! That would be fascinating!'

'Would it?' I said, and I must admit I had my doubts.

'Of course it would! Lying there with all your thinking processes working beautifully, and your memory as well . . .'

'And not being able to see or feel or smell or hear or talk,' I said.

'Ah!' he cried. 'I knew I'd forgotten something! I never told you about the eye. Listen. I am going to try to leave one of your optic nerves intact, as well as the eye itself. The optic nerve is a little thing about the thickness of a clinical thermometer and about two

inches in length as it stretches between the brain and the eye. The beauty of it is that it's not really a nerve at all. It's an outpouching of the brain itself, and the dura or brain covering extends along it and is attached to the eyeball. The back of the eye is therefore in very close contact with the brain, and cerebrospinal fluid flows right up to it.

'All this suits my purpose very well, and makes it reasonable to suppose that I could succeed in preserving one of your eyes. I've already constructed a small plastic case to contain the eyeball, instead of your own socket, and when the brain is in the basin, submerged in Ringer's Solution, the eyeball in its case will float on the surface of the liquid.'

'Staring at the ceiling,' I said.

'I suppose so, yes. I'm afraid there wouldn't be any muscles there to move it around. But it might be sort of fun to lie there so quietly and comfortably peering out at the world from your basin.'

'Hilarious,' I said. 'How about leaving me an ear as well?'

'I'd rather not try an ear this time.'

'I want an ear,' I said. 'I insist upon an ear.'

'No.'

'I want to listen to Bach.'

'You don't understand how difficult it would be,' Landy said gently. 'The hearing apparatus – the cochlea, as it's called – is a far more delicate mechanism than the eye. What's more, it is encased in bone. So is a part of the auditory nerve that connects it with the brain. I couldn't possibly chisel the whole thing out intact.'

'Couldn't you leave it encased in the bone and bring the bone to the basin?'

'No,' he said firmly. 'This thing is complicated enough already. And anyway, if the eye works, it doesn't matter all that much about your hearing. We can always hold up messages for you to read. You really must leave me to decide what is possible and what isn't.'

'I haven't yet said that I'm going to do it.'

'I know, William, I know.'

'I'm not sure I fancy the idea very much.'

'Would you rather be dead, altogether?'

'Perhaps I would. I don't know yet. I wouldn't be able to talk, would I?'

'Of course not.'

'Then how would I communicate with you? How would you know that I'm conscious?'

'It would be easy for us to know whether or not you regain consciousness,' Landy said. 'The ordinary electroencephalograph could tell us that. We'd attach the electrodes directly to the frontal lobes of your brain, there in the basin.'

'And you could actually tell?'

'Oh, definitely. Any hospital could do that part of it.'

'But I couldn't communicate with you.'

'As a matter of fact,' Landy said, 'I believe you could. There's a man up in London called Wertheimer who's doing some interesting work on the subject of thought communication, and I've been in touch with him. You know, don't you, that the thinking brain throws off electrical and chemical discharges? And that these discharges go out in the form of waves, rather like radio waves?'

'I know a bit about it,' I said.

'*Well, Wertheimer has constructed an apparatus somewhat similar to the encephalograph, though far more sensitive, and he maintains that within certain narrow limits it can help him to interpret the actual things that a brain is thinking. It produces a kind of graph which is apparently decipherable into words or thoughts. Would you like me to ask Wertheimer to come and see you?*'

'*No,*' *I said. Landy was already taking it for granted that I was going to go through with this business, and I resented his attitude.* Go away now and leave me alone,' *I told him.* '*You won't get anywhere by trying to rush me.*'

He stood up at once and crossed to the door.

'*One question,*' *I said.*

He paused with a hand on the doorknob. '*Yes, William?*'

'*Simply this. Do you yourself honestly believe that when my brain is in that basin, my mind will be able to function exactly as it is doing at present? Do you believe that I will be able to think and reason as I can now? And will the power of memory remain?*'

'*I don't see why not,*' *he answered.* '*It's the same brain. It's alive. It's undamaged. In fact, it's completely untouched. We haven't even opened the dura. The big difference, of course, would be that we've severed every single nerve that leads into it – except for the one optic nerve – and this means that your thinking would no longer be influenced by your senses. You'd be living in an extraordinarily pure and detached world. Nothing to bother you at all, not even pain. You couldn't possibly feel pain because there wouldn't be any nerves to feel it with. In a way, it would be an almost perfect situation. No worries or fears or pains or hunger or thirst. Not even any desires. Just your memories and your*' *thoughts, and if the remaining eye happened to function, then you could read books as well. It all sounds rather pleasant to me.'*

'It does, does it?'

'Yes, William, it does. And particularly for a Doctor of Philosophy. It would be a tremendous experience. You'd be able to reflect upon the ways of the world with a detachment and a serenity that no man had ever attained before. And who knows what might not happen then! Great thoughts and solutions might come to you, great ideas that could revolutionize our way of life! Try to imagine, if you can, the degree of concentration that you'd be able to achieve!'

'And the frustration,' I said.

'Nonsense. There couldn't be any frustration. You can't have frustration without desire, and you couldn't possibly have any desire. Not physical desire, anyway.'

'I should certainly be capable of remembering my previous life in the world, and I might desire to return to it.'

'What, to this mess! Out of your comfortable basin and back into this madhouse!'

'Answer one more question,' I said. 'How long do you believe you could keep it alive?'

'The brain? Who knows? Possibly for years and years. The conditions would be ideal. Most of the factors that cause deterioration would be absent, thanks to the artificial heart. The blood-pressure would remain constant at all times, an impossible condition in real life. The temperature would also be constant. The chemical composition of the blood would be near perfect. There would be no impurities in it, no virus, no bacteria, nothing. Of course it's foolish to guess, but I believe that a brain might live for two or three hundred years in circumstances like these. Good-bye

for now,' he said. 'I'll drop in and see you tomorrow.' He went out quickly, leaving me, as you might guess, in a fairly disturbed state of mind.

My immediate reaction after he had gone was one of revulsion towards the whole business. Somehow, it wasn't at all nice. There was something basically repulsive about the idea that I myself, with all my mental faculties intact, should be reduced to a small slimy grey blob lying in a pool of water. It was monstrous, obscene, unholy. Another thing that bothered me was the feeling of helplessness that I was bound to experience once Landy had got me into the basin. There could be no going back after that, no way of protesting or explaining. I would be committed for as long as they could keep me alive.

And what, for example, if I could not stand it? What if it turned out to be terribly painful? What if I became hysterical?

No legs to run away on. No voice to scream with. Nothing. I'd just have to grin and bear it for the next two centuries.

No mouth to grin with either.

At this point, a curious thought struck me, and it was this: Does not a man who has had a leg amputated often suffer from the delusion that the leg is still there? Does he not tell the nurse that the toes he doesn't have any more are itching like mad, and so on and so forth? I seemed to have heard something to that effect quite recently.

Very well. On the same premise, was it not possible that my brain, lying there alone in that basin, might not suffer from a similar delusion in regard to my body? In which case, all my usual aches and pains could come flooding over me and I wouldn't even be able to take an aspirin to relieve them. One moment I might be imagining that I had the most excruciating cramp in my leg, or a *violent indigestion, and a few minutes later, I might easily get the feeling that my poor bladder – you know me – was so full that if I didn't get to emptying it soon it would burst.*

Heaven forbid.

I lay there for a long time thinking these horrid thoughts. Then quite suddenly, round about midday, my mood began to change. I became less concerned with the unpleasant aspect of the affair and found myself able to examine Landy's proposals in a more reasonable light. Was there not, after all, I asked myself, something a bit comforting in the thought that my brain might not necessarily have to die and disappear in a few weeks' time? There was indeed. I am rather proud of my brain. It is a sensitive, lucid and uberous organ. It contains a prodigious store of information, and it is still capable of producing imaginative and original theories. As brains go, it is a damn good one, though I say it myself. Whereas my body, my poor old body, the thing that Landy wants to throw away – well, even you, my dear Mary, will have to agree with me that there is really nothing about that which is worth preserving any more.

I was lying on my back eating a grape. Delicious it was, and there were three little seeds in it which I took out of my mouth and placed on the edge of the plate.

'I'm going to do it,' I said quietly. 'Yes, by God, I'm going to do it. When Landy comes back to see me tomorrow I shall tell him straight out that I'm going to do it.'

It was as quick as that. And from then on, I began to feel very much better. I surprised everyone by gobbling an enormous lunch, and shortly after that you came in to visit me as usual.

But how well I looked, you told me. How bright and well and chirpy. Had anything happened? Was there some good news?

Yes, I said, there was. And then, if you remember, I bade you sit down and make yourself comfortable, and I started out immediately to explain to you as gently as I could what was in the wind.

Alas, you would have none of it. I had hardly begun telling you the barest details when you flew into a fury and said that the thing was revolting, disgusting, horrible, unthinkable, and when I tried to go on, you marched out of the room.

Well, Mary, as you know, I have tried to discuss this subject with you many times since then, but you have consistently refused to give me a hearing. Hence this note, and I can only hope that you will have the good sense to permit yourself to read it. It has taken me a long time to write. Two weeks have gone by since I started to scribble the first sentence, and I'm now a good deal weaker than I was then. I doubt I have the strength to say much more. Certainly I won't say good-bye, because there's a chance, just a tiny chance, that if Landy succeeds in his work I may actually see you again later, that is if you can bring yourself to come and visit me.

I am giving orders that these pages shall not be delivered to you until a week after I am gone. By now, therefore, as you sit reading them, seven days have already elapsed since Landy did the deed. You yourself may even know what the outcome has been. If you don't, if you have purposely kept yourself apart and have refused to have anything to do with it — which I suspect may be the case — please change your mind now and give Landy a call to see how things went with me. That is the least you can do. I have told him that he may expect to hear from you on the seventh day.

Your faithful husband
William

P.S. Be good when I am gone, and always remember that it is harder to be a widow than a wife. Do not drink cocktails. Do not waste money. Do not smoke cigarettes. Do not eat pastry. Do not use lipstick. Do not buy a television apparatus. Keep my rose beds and my rockery well weeded in the summers. And incidentally I suggest that you have the telephone disconnected now that I shall have no further use for it.

W.

Mrs Pearl laid the last page of the manuscript slowly down on the sofa beside her. Her little mouth was pursed up tight and there was a whiteness around her nostrils.

But really! You would think a widow was entitled to a bit of peace after all these years.

The whole thing was just too awful to think about. Beastly and awful. It gave her the shudders.

She reached for her bag and found herself another cigarette. She lit it, inhaling the smoke deeply and blowing it out in clouds all over the room. Through the smoke she could see her lovely television set, brand new, lustrous, huge, crouching defiantly but also a little self-consciously on top of what used to be William's worktable.

What would he say, she wondered, if he could see that now?

She paused, to remember the last time he had caught her smoking a cigarette. That was about a year ago, and she was sitting in the kitchen by the open window having a quick one before he came home from work. She'd had the radio on loud playing dance music and she had turned round to pour herself another cup of coffee and there he was standing in the doorway, huge and grim, staring down at her with those awful eyes, a little black dot of fury blazing in the centre of each.

For four weeks after that, he had paid the housekeeping bills himself and given her no money at all, but of course he wasn't to know that she had over six pounds stashed away in a soap-flake carton in the cupboard under the sink.

'What is it?' she had said to him once during supper. 'Are you worried about me getting lung cancer?'

'I am not,' he had answered.

'Then why can't I smoke?'

'Because I disapprove, that's why.'

He had also disapproved of children, and as a result they had never had any of them either.

Where was he now, this William of hers, the great disapprover?

Landy would be expecting her to call up. Did she *have* to call Landy?

Well, not really, no.

She finished her cigarette, then lit another one immediately from the old stub. She looked at the telephone that was sitting on the worktable beside the television set. William had asked her to call. He had specifically requested that she telephone Landy as soon as she had read the letter. She hesitated, fighting hard now against that old ingrained sense of duty that she didn't quite yet dare to shake off. Then, slowly, she got to her feet and crossed over to the phone on the worktable. She found a number in the book, dialled it, and waited.

'I want to speak to Dr Landy, please.'

'Who is calling?'

'Mrs Pearl. Mrs William Pearl.'

'One moment, please.'

Almost at once, Landy was on the other end of the wire.

'Mrs Pearl?'

'This is Mrs Pearl.'

There was a slight pause.

'I am so glad you called at last, Mrs Pearl. You are quite well, I hope?' The voice was quiet, unemotional, courteous. 'I wonder if you would care to come over here to the hospital? Then we can have a little chat. I expect you are very eager to know how it all came out.'

She didn't answer.

'I can tell you now that everything went pretty smoothly, one way and another. Far better, in fact, than I was entitled to hope. It is not only alive, Mrs Pearl, it is conscious. It recovered consciousness on the second day. Isn't that interesting?'

She waited for him to go on.

'And the eye is seeing. We are sure of that because we get an immediate change in the deflections on the encephalograph when we hold something up in front of it. And now we're giving it the newspaper to read every day.'

'Which newspaper?' Mrs Pearl asked sharply.

'The *Daily Mirror*. The headlines are larger.'

'He hates the *Mirror*. Give him *The Times*.'

There was a pause, then the doctor said, 'Very well, Mrs Pearl. We'll give it *The Times*. We naturally want to do all we can to keep it happy.'

'*Him*,' she said. 'Not *it*. *Him!*'

'Him,' the doctor said. 'Yes, I beg your pardon. To keep him happy. That's one reason why I suggested you should come along here as soon as possible. I think it would be good for him to see you. You could indicate how delighted you were to be with him again – smile at him and blow him a kiss and all that sort of thing. It's bound to be a comfort to him to know that you are standing by.'

There was a long pause.

'Well,' Mrs Pearl said at last, her voice suddenly very meek and tired. 'I suppose I had better come on over and see how he is.'

'Good. I knew you would. I'll wait here for you. Come straight up to my office on the second floor. Good-bye.'

Half an hour later, Mrs Pearl was at the hospital.

'You mustn't be surprised by what he looks like,' Landy said as he walked beside her down a corridor.

'No, I won't.'

'It's bound to be a bit of a shock to you at first. He's not very prepossessing in his present state, I'm afraid.'

'I didn't marry him for his looks, Doctor.'

Landy turned and stared at her. What a queer little woman this was, he thought, with her large eyes and her sullen, resentful air. Her features, which must have been quite pleasant once, had now gone completely. The mouth was slack, the cheeks loose and flabby, and the whole face gave the impression of having slowly but surely sagged to pieces through years and years of joyless married life. They walked on for a while in silence.

'Take your time when you get inside,' Landy said. 'He

won't know you're in there until you place your face directly above his eye. The eye is always open, but he can't move it at all, so the field of vision is very narrow. At present we have it looking straight up at the ceiling. And of course he can't hear anything. We can talk together as much as we like. It's in here.'

Landy opened a door and ushered her into a small square room.

'I wouldn't go too close yet,' he said, putting a hand on her arm. 'Stay back here a moment with me until you get used to it all.'

There was a biggish white enamel bowl about the size of a wash-basin standing on a high white table in the centre of the room, and there were half a dozen thin plastic tubes coming out of it. These tubes were connected with a whole lot of glass piping in which you could see the blood flowing to and from the heart machine. The machine itself made a soft rhythmic pulsing sound.

'He's in there,' Landy said, pointing to the basin, which was too high for her to see into. 'Come just a little closer. Not too near.'

He led her two paces forward.

By stretching her neck, Mrs Pearl could now see the surface of the liquid inside the basin. It was clear and still, and on it there floated a small oval capsule, about the size of a pigeon's egg.

'That's the eye in there,' Landy said. 'Can you see it?'

'Yes.'

'So far as we can tell, it is still in perfect condition. It's his right eye, and the plastic container has a lens on it similar to the one he used in his own spectacles. At this moment he's probably seeing quite as well as he did before.'

'The ceiling isn't much to look at,' Mrs Pearl said.

'Don't worry about that. We're in the process of working out a whole programme to keep him amused, but we don't want to go too quickly at first.'

'Give him a good book.'

'We will, we will. Are you feeling all right, Mrs Pearl?'

'Yes.'

'Then we'll go forward a little more, shall we, and you'll be able to see the whole thing.'

He led her forward until they were standing only a couple of yards from the table, and now she could see right down into the basin.

'There you are,' Landy said. 'That's William.'

He was far larger than she had imagined he would be, and darker in colour. With all the ridges and creases running over his surface, he reminded her of nothing so much as an enormous pickled walnut. She could see the stubs of the four big arteries and the two veins coming out from the base of him and the neat way in which they were joined to the plastic tubes; and with each throb of the heart machine, all the tubes gave a little jerk in unison as the blood was pushed through them.

'You'll have to lean over,' Landy said, 'and put your pretty face right above the eye. He'll see you then, and you can smile at him and blow him a kiss. If I were you I'd say a few nice things as well. He won't actually hear them, but I'm sure he'll get the general idea.'

'He hates people blowing kisses at him,' Mrs Pearl said.

'I'll do it my own way if you don't mind.' She stepped up to the edge of the table, leaned forward until her face was directly over the basin, and looked straight down into William's eye.

'Hallo, dear,' she whispered. 'It's me – Mary.'

The eye, bright as ever, stared back at her with a peculiar, fixed intensity.

'How are you, dear?' she said.

The plastic capsule was transparent all the way round so that the whole of the eyeball was visible. The optic nerve connecting the underside of it to the brain looked like a short length of grey spaghetti.

'Are you feeling all right, William?'

It was a queer sensation peering into her husband's eye when there was no face to go with it. All she had to look at was the eye, and she kept staring at it, and gradually it grew bigger and bigger, and in the end it was the only thing that she could see – a sort of face in itself. There was a network of tiny red veins running over the white surface of the eyeball, and in the ice-blue of the iris there were three or four rather pretty darkish streaks radiating from the pupil in the centre. The pupil was large and black, with a little spark of light reflecting from one side of it.

'I got your letter, dear, and came over at once to see how you were. Dr Landy says you are doing wonderfully well. Perhaps if I talk slowly you can understand a little of what I am saying by reading my lips.'

There was no doubt that the eye was watching her.

'They are doing everything possible to take care of you,

dear. This marvellous machine thing here is pumping away all the time and I'm sure it's a lot better than those silly old hearts all the rest of us have. Ours are liable to break down any moment, but yours will go on for ever.'

She was studying the eye closely, trying to discover what there was about it that gave it such an unusual appearance.

'You seem fine, dear, just fine. Really you do.'

It looked ever so much nicer, this eye, than either of his eyes used to look, she told herself. There was a softness about it somewhere, a calm, kindly quality that she had never seen before. Maybe it had to do with the dot in the very centre, the pupil. William's pupils used always to be tiny black pinheads. They used to glint at you, stabbing into your brain, seeing right through you, and they always knew at once what you were up to and even what you were thinking. But this one she was looking at now was large and soft and gentle, almost cowlike.

'Are you quite sure he's conscious?' she asked, not looking up.

'Oh yes, completely,' Landy said.

'And he *can* see me?'

'Perfectly.'

'Isn't that marvellous? I expect he's wondering what happened.'

'Not at all. He knows perfectly well where he is and why he's there. He can't possibly have forgotten that.'

'You mean he *knows* he's in this basin?'

'Of course. And if only he had the power of speech, he would probably be able to carry on a perfectly normal conversation with you this very minute. So far as I can see, there should be absolutely no difference mentally between this William here and the one you used to know back home.'

'Good *gracious* me,' Mrs Pearl said, and she paused to consider this intriguing aspect.

You know what, she told herself, looking behind the eye now and staring hard at the great grey pulpy walnut that lay so placidly under the water. I'm not at all sure that I don't prefer him as he is at present. In fact, I believe that I could live very comfortably with this kind of a William. I could cope with this one.

'Quiet, isn't he?' she said.

'Naturally he's quiet.'

No arguments and criticisms, she thought, no constant admonitions, no rules to obey, no ban on smoking cigarettes, no pair of cold disapproving eyes watching me over the top of a book in the evenings, no shirts to wash and iron, no meals to cook – nothing but the throb of the heart machine, which was rather a soothing sound anyway and certainly not loud enough to interfere with television.

'Doctor,' she said. 'I do believe I'm suddenly getting to feel the most enormous affection for him. Does that sound queer?'

'I think it's quite understandable.'

'He looks so helpless and silent lying there under the water in his little basin.'

'Yes, I know.'

'He's like a baby, that's what he's like. He's exactly like a little baby.'

THE COMPLETE SHORT STORIES

Landy stood still behind her, watching.

'There,' she said softly, peering into the basin. 'From now on Mary's going to look after you *all* by herself and you've nothing to worry about in the world. When can I have him back home, Doctor?'

'I beg your pardon?'

'I said when can I have him back – back in my own house?'

'You're joking,' Landy said.

She turned her head slowly round and looked directly at him. 'Why should I joke?' she asked. Her face was bright, her eyes round and bright as two diamonds.

'He couldn't possibly be moved.'

'I don't see why not.'

'This is an experiment, Mrs Pearl.'

'It's my husband, Dr Landy.'

A funny little nervous half-smile appeared on Landy's mouth. 'Well . . .' he said.

'It *is* my husband, you know.' There was no anger in her voice. She spoke quietly, as though merely reminding him of a simple fact.

'That's rather a tricky point,' Landy said, wetting his lips. 'You're a widow now, Mrs Pearl. I think you must resign yourself to that fact.'

She turned away suddenly from the table and crossed over to the window. 'I mean it,' she said, fishing in her bag for a cigarette. 'I want him back.'

Landy watched her as she put the cigarette between her lips and lit it. Unless he were very much mistaken, there was something a bit odd about this woman, he thought.

She seemed almost pleased to have her husband over there in the basin.

He tried to imagine what his own feelings would be if it were *his* wife's brain lying there and *her* eye staring up at him out of that capsule.

He wouldn't like it.

'Shall we go back to my room now?' he said.

She was standing by the window, apparently quite calm and relaxed, puffing her cigarette.

'Yes, all right.'

On her way past the table she stopped and leaned over the basin once more. 'Mary's leaving now, sweetheart,' she said. 'And don't you worry about a single thing, you understand? We're going to get you right back home where we can look after you properly just as soon as we possibly can. And listen, dear . . .' At this point she paused and carried the cigarette to her lips, intending to take a puff.

Instantly the eye flashed.

She was looking straight into it at the time, and right in the centre of it she saw a tiny but brilliant flash of light, and the pupil contracted into a minute black pinpoint of absolute fury.

At first she didn't move. She stood bending over the basin, holding the cigarette up to her mouth, watching the eye.

Then very slowly, deliberately, she put the cigarette between her lips and took a long suck. She inhaled deeply, and she held the smoke inside her lungs for three or four seconds; then suddenly, *whoosh*, out it came through her nostrils in two thin jets which struck the water in the basin and billowed out over the surface in a thick blue cloud, enveloping the eye.

Landy was over by the door, with his back to her, waiting. 'Come on, Mrs Pearl,' he called.

'Don't look so cross, William,' she said softly. 'It isn't any good looking cross.'

Landy turned his head to see what she was doing.

'Not any more it isn't,' she whispered. 'Because from now on, my pet, you're going to do just exactly what Mary tells you. Do you understand that?'

'Mrs Pearl,' Landy said, moving towards her.

'So don't be a naughty boy again, will you, my precious,' she said, taking another pull at the cigarette. 'Naughty boys are liable to get punished most severely nowadays, you ought to know that.'

Landy was beside her now, and he took her by the arm and began drawing her firmly but gently away from the table.

'Good-bye, darling,' she called. 'I'll be back soon.'

'That's enough, Mrs Pearl.'

'Isn't he sweet?' she cried, looking up at Landy with big bright eyes. 'Isn't he darling? I just can't wait to get him home.'

Georgy Porgy

First published in *Kiss Kiss* (1960)

Without in any way wishing to blow my own trumpet, I think that I can claim to being in most respects a moderately well-matured and rounded individual. I have travelled a good deal. I am adequately read. I speak Greek and Latin. I dabble in science. I can tolerate a mildly liberal attitude in the politics of others. I have compiled a volume of notes upon the evolution of the madrigal in the fifteenth century. I have witnessed the death of a large number of persons in their beds; and in addition, I have influenced, at least I hope I have, the lives of quite a few others by the spoken word delivered from the pulpit.

Yet in spite of all this, I must confess that I have never in my life – well, how shall I put it? – I have never really had anything much to do with women.

To be perfectly honest, up until three weeks ago I had never so much as laid a finger on one of them except perhaps to help her over a stile or something like that when the occasion demanded. And even then I always tried to ensure that I touched only the shoulder or the waist or some other place where the skin was covered, because the one thing I never could stand was actual contact between my skin and theirs. Skin touching skin, my skin, that is, touching the skin of a female, whether it were leg, neck, face, hand or merely finger, was so repugnant to me that

I invariably greeted a lady with my hands clasped firmly behind my back to avoid the inevitable handshake.

I could go further than that and say that any sort of physical contact with them, even when the skin wasn't bare, would disturb me considerably. If a woman stood close to me in a queue so that our bodies touched, or if she squeezed in beside me on a bus seat, hip to hip and thigh to thigh, my cheeks would begin burning like mad and little prickles of sweat would start coming out all over the crown of my head.

This condition is all very well in a schoolboy who has just reached the age of puberty. With him it is simply Dame Nature's way of putting on the brakes and holding the lad back until he is old enough to behave himself like a gentleman. I approve of that.

But there was no reason on God's earth why I, at the ripe old age of thirty-one, should continue to suffer a similar embarrassment. I was well trained to resist temptation, and I was certainly not given to vulgar passions.

Had I been even the slightest bit ashamed of my own personal appearance, then that might possibly have explained the whole thing. But I was not. On the contrary, and though I say it myself, the fates had been rather kind to me in that regard. I stood exactly five and a half feet tall in my stockinged feet, and my shoulders, though they sloped downwards a little from the neck, were nicely in balance with my small neat frame. (Personally, I've always thought that a little slope on the shoulder lends a subtle and faintly aesthetic air to a man who is not overly tall, don't you agree?) My features were regular, my teeth were in excellent condition (protruding only a smallish amount from the upper jaw), and my hair, which was an unusually brilliant ginger-red, grew thickly all over my scalp. Good heavens above, I had seen men who were perfect shrimps in comparison with me displaying an astonishing aplomb in their dealings with the fairer sex. And oh, how I envied them! How I longed to do likewise – to be able to share in a few of those pleasant little rituals of contact that I observed continually taking place between men and women – the touching of hands, the peck on the cheek, the linking of arms, the pressure of knee against knee or foot against foot under the dining-table, and most of all, the full-blown violent embrace that comes when two of them join together on the floor – for a dance.

But such things were not for me. Alas, I had to spend my time avoiding them instead. And this, my friends, was easier said than done, even for a humble curate in a small country region far from the fleshpots of the metropolis.

My flock, you understand, contained an inordinate number of ladies. There were scores of them in the parish, and the unfortunate thing about it was that at least sixty per cent of them were spinsters, completely untamed by the benevolent influence of holy matrimony.

I tell you I was jumpy as a squirrel.

One would have thought that with all the careful training my mother had given me as a child, I should have been capable of taking this sort of thing well in my stride; and no doubt I would have done if only she had lived long enough to complete my education. But alas, she was killed when I was still quite young.

She was a wonderful woman, my mother. She used to wear huge bracelets on her wrists, five or six of them at a time, with all sorts of things hanging from them and tinkling against each other as she moved. It didn't matter where she was, you could always find her by listening for the noise of those bracelets. It was better than a cowbell. And in the evenings she used to sit on the sofa in her black trousers with her feet tucked up underneath her, smoking endless cigarettes from a long black holder. And I'd be crouching on the floor, watching her.

'You want to taste my martini, George?' she used to ask.

'Now stop it, Clare,' my father would say. 'If you're not careful you'll stunt the boy's growth.'

'Go on,' she said. 'Don't be frightened of it. Drink it.'

I always did everything my mother told me.

'That's enough,' my father said. 'He only has to know what it tastes like.'

'Please don't interfere, Boris. This is *very* important.'

My mother had a theory that nothing in the world should be kept secret from a child. Show him everything. Make him *experience* it.

'I'm not going to have any boy of mine going around whispering dirty secrets with other children and having to guess about this thing and that simply because no one will tell him.'

Tell him everything. Make him listen.

'Come over here, George, and I'll tell you what there is to know about God.'

She never read stories to me at night before I went to

bed; she just 'told' me things instead. And every evening it was something different.

'Come over here, George, because now I'm going to tell you about Mohammed.'

She would be sitting on the sofa in her black trousers with her legs crossed and her feet tucked up underneath her, and she'd beckon to me in a queer languorous manner with the hand that held the long black cigarette-holder, and the bangles would start jingling all the way up her arm.

'If you must have a religion I suppose Mohammedanism is as good as any of them. It's all based on keeping healthy. You have lots of wives, and you mustn't ever smoke or drink.'

'Why mustn't you smoke or drink, Mummy?'

'Because if you've got lots of wives you have to keep healthy and virile.'

'What is virile?'

'I'll go into that tomorrow, my pet. Let's deal with one subject at a time. Another thing about the Mohammedan is that he never never gets constipated.'

'Now, Clare,' my father would say, looking up from his book. 'Stick to the facts.'

'My dear Boris, you don't know anything about it. Now if only *you* would try bending forward and touching the ground with your forehead morning, noon and night every day, facing Mecca, you might have a bit less trouble in that direction yourself.'

I used to love listening to her, even though I could only understand about half of what she was saying. She really was telling me secrets, and there wasn't anything more exciting than that.

'Come over here, George, and I'll tell you precisely how your father makes his money.'

'Now, Clare, that's quite enough.'

'Nonsense, darling. Why make a *secret* out of it with the child? He'll only imagine something much much worse.'

I was exactly ten years old when she started giving me detailed lectures on the subject of sex. This was the biggest secret of them all, and therefore the most enthralling.

'Come over here, George, because now I'm going to tell you how you came into this world, right from the very beginning.'

I saw my father glance up quietly, and open his mouth wide the way he did when he was going to say something vital, but my mother was already fixing him with those brilliant shining eyes of hers, and he went slowly back to his book without uttering a sound.

'Your poor father is embarrassed,' she said, and she gave me her private smile, the one that she gave to nobody else, only to me – the one-sided smile where just one corner of her mouth lifted slowly upwards until it made a lovely long wrinkle that stretched right up to the eye itself, and became a sort of wink-smile instead.

'Embarrassment, my pet, is the one thing that I want you never to feel. And don't think for a moment that your father is embarrassed only because of *you*.'

My father started wriggling about in his chair.

'My God, he's even embarrassed about things like that when he's alone with me, his own wife.'

'About things like what?' I asked.

At that point my father got up and quietly left the room.

I think it must have been about a week after this that my mother was killed. It may possibly have been a little later, ten days or a fortnight, I can't be sure. All I know is that we were getting near the end of this particular series of 'talks' when it happened; and because I myself was personally involved in the brief chain of events that led up to her death, I can still remember every single detail of that curious night just as clearly as if it were yesterday. I can switch it on in my memory any time I like and run it through in front of my eyes exactly as though it were the reel of a cinema film; and it never varies. It always ends at precisely the same place, no more and no less, and it always begins in the same peculiarly sudden way, with the screen in darkness, and my mother's voice somewhere above me, calling my name:

'George! Wake up, George, wake up!'

And then there is a bright electric light dazzling in my eyes, and right from the very centre of it, but far away, the voice is still calling to me:

'George, wake up and get out of bed and put your dressing-gown on! Quickly! You're coming downstairs. There's something I want you to see. Come on, child, come on! Hurry up! And put your slippers on. We're going outside.'

'Outside?'

'Don't argue with me, George. Just do as you're told.' I am so sleepy I can hardly see to walk, but my mother takes me firmly by the hand and leads me downstairs and out through the front door into the night where the cold air is like a sponge of water in my face, and I open my eyes wide and see the lawn all sparkling with frost and the cedar tree with its tremendous arms standing black against a thin small moon. And overhead a great mass of stars is wheeling up into the sky.

We hurry across the lawn, my mother and I, her bracelets all jingling like mad and me having to trot to keep up with her. Each step I take I can feel the crisp frosty grass crunching softly underfoot.

'Josephine has just started having her babies,' my mother says. 'It's a perfect opportunity. You shall watch the whole process.'

There is a light burning in the garage when we get there, and we go inside. My father isn't there, nor is the car, and the place seems huge and bare, and the concrete floor is freezing cold through the soles of my bedroom slippers. Josephine is reclining on a heap of straw inside the low wire cage in one corner of the room – a large blue rabbit with small pink eyes that watch us suspiciously as we go towards her. The husband, whose name is Napoleon, is now in a separate cage in the opposite corner, and I notice that he is standing up on his hind legs scratching impatiently at the netting.

'Look!' my mother cries. 'She's just having the first one! It's almost out!'

We both creep closer to Josephine, and I squat down beside the cage with my face right up against the wire. I am fascinated. Here is one rabbit coming out of another. It is magical and rather splendid. It is also very quick.

'Look how it comes out all neatly wrapped up in its own little cellophane bag!' my mother is saying.

'And just look how she's taking care of it now! The poor darling doesn't have a face-flannel, and even if she did she couldn't hold it in her paws, so she's washing it with her tongue instead.'

The mother rabbit rolls her small pink eyes anxiously in our direction, and then I see her shifting position in the straw so that her body is between us and the young one.

'Come round the other side,' my mother says. 'The silly thing has moved. I do believe she's trying to hide her baby from us.'

We go round the other side of the cage. The rabbit follows us with her eyes. A couple of yards away the buck is prancing madly up and down, clawing at the wire.

'Why is Napoleon so excited?' I ask.

'I don't know, dear. Don't you bother about him. Watch Josephine. I expect she'll be having another one soon. Look how carefully she's washing that little baby! She's treating it just like a human mother treats hers! Isn't it funny to think that I did almost exactly the same sort of thing to you once?'

The big blue doe is still watching us, and now, again, she pushes the baby away with her nose and rolls slowly over to face the other way. Then she goes on with her licking and cleaning.

'Isn't it wonderful how a mother knows instinctively just what she has to do?' my mother says. 'Now you just imagine, my pet, that that baby is *you*, and Josephine is *me* – wait a minute, come back over here again so you can get a better look.'

We creep back round the cage to keep the baby in view.

'See how she's fondling it and kissing it all over! There! She's *really* kissing it now, isn't she! Exactly like me and you!'

I peer closer. It seems a queer way of kissing to me.

'Look!' I scream. 'She's eating it!'

And sure enough, the head of the baby rabbit is now disappearing swiftly into the mother's mouth.

'Mummy! Quick!'

But almost before the sound of my scream has died away, the whole of that tiny pink body has vanished down the mother's throat.

I swing quickly round, and the next thing I know I'm looking straight into my own mother's face, not six inches above me, and no doubt she is trying to say something or it may be that she is too astonished to say anything, but all I see is the mouth, the huge red mouth opening wider and wider and wider until it is just a great big round gaping hole with a black black centre, and I scream again, and this time I can't stop. Then suddenly out come her hands, and I can feel her skin touching mine, the long cold fingers closing tightly over my fists, and I jump back and jerk myself free and rush blindly out into the night. I run down the drive and through the front gates, screaming all the way, and then, above the noise of my own voice I can hear the jingle of bracelets coming up behind me in the dark, getting louder and louder as she keeps gaining on me all the way down the long hill to the bottom of the lane and over the bridge on to the main road where the cars are streaming by at sixty miles an hour with headlights blazing.

Then somewhere behind me I hear a screech of tyres skidding on the road surface, and then there is silence, and I notice suddenly that the bracelets aren't jingling behind me any more.

Poor mother.

If only she could have lived a little longer.

I admit that she gave me a nasty fright with those rabbits, but it wasn't her fault, and anyway queer things like that were always happening between her and me. I had come to regard them as a sort of toughening process that did me more good than harm. But if only she could have lived long enough to complete my education, I'm sure I should never have had all that trouble I was telling you about a few minutes ago.

I want to get on with that now. I didn't mean to begin talking about my mother. She doesn't have anything to do with what I originally started out to say. I won't mention her again.

I was telling you about the spinsters in my parish. It's an ugly word, isn't it – spinster? It conjures up the vision either of a stringy old hen with a puckered mouth or of a huge ribald monster shouting around the house in riding-breeches. But these were not like that at all. They were a clean, healthy, well-built group of females, the majority of them highly bred and surprisingly wealthy, and I feel sure that the average unmarried man would have been gratified to have them around.

In the beginning, when I first came to the vicarage, I didn't have too bad a time. I enjoyed a measure of protection, of course, by reason of my calling and my cloth. In addition, I myself adopted a cool dignified attitude that was calculated to discourage familiarity. For a few months, therefore, I was able to move freely among my parishioners, and no one took the liberty of linking her arm in mine at a charity bazaar, or of touching my fingers with hers as she passed me the cruet at suppertime. I was very happy. I was feeling better than I had in years. Even that little nervous habit I had of flicking my earlobe with my forefinger when I talked began to disappear.

This was what I call my first period, and it extended over approximately six months. Then came trouble.

I suppose I should have known that a healthy male like myself couldn't hope to evade embroilment indefinitely simply by keeping a fair distance between himself and the ladies. It just doesn't work. If anything it has the opposite effect.

I would see them eyeing me covertly across the room at a whist drive, whispering to one another, nodding, running their tongues over their lips, sucking at their cigarettes, plotting the best approach, but always whispering, and sometimes I overheard snatches of their talk – 'What a shy person . . . he's just a trifle nervous, isn't he . . . he's much too tense . . . he needs companionship . . . he wants loosening up . . . we must teach him how to relax.' And then slowly, as the weeks went by, they began to stalk me. I knew they were doing it. I could feel it happening although at first they did nothing definite to give themselves away.

That was my second period. It lasted for the best part of a year and was very trying indeed. But it was paradise compared with the third and final phase.

For now, instead of sniping at me sporadically from far away, the attackers suddenly came charging out of the wood with bayonets fixed. It was terrible, frightening. Nothing is more calculated to unnerve a man than the swift unexpected assault. Yet I am not a coward. I will stand my ground against any single individual of my own size under any circumstances. But this onslaught, I am now convinced, was conducted by vast numbers operating as one skilfully co-ordinated unit.

The first offender was Miss Elphinstone, a large woman with moles. I had dropped in on her during the afternoon to solicit a contribution towards a new set of bellows for the organ, and after some pleasant conversation in the library she had graciously handed me a cheque for two guineas. I told her not to bother to see me to the door and I went out into the hall to get my hat. I was about to reach for it when all at once – she must have come tiptoeing up behind me – all at once I felt a bare arm sliding through mine, and one second later her fingers were entwined in my own, and she was squeezing my hand hard, in out, in out, as though it were the bulb of a throat-spray.

'Are you really so Very Reverend as you're always pretending to be?' she whispered.

Well!

All I can tell you is that when that arm of hers came sliding in under mine, it felt exactly as though a cobra was coiling itself round my wrist. I leaped away, pulled open the front door, and fled down the drive without looking back.

The very next day we held a jumble sale in the village

hall (again to raise money for the new bellows), and towards the end of it I was standing in a corner quietly drinking a cup of tea and keeping an eye on the villagers crowding round the stalls when all of a sudden I heard a voice beside me saying, 'Dear me, what a hungry look you have in those eyes of yours.' The next instant a long curvaceous body was leaning up against mine and a hand with red fingernails was trying to push a thick slice of coconut cake into my mouth.

'Miss Prattley,' I cried. 'Please!'

But she'd got me up against the wall, and with a teacup in one hand and a saucer in the other I was powerless to resist. I felt the sweat breaking out all over me and if my mouth hadn't quickly become full of the cake she was pushing into it, I honestly believe I would have started to scream.

A nasty incident, that one; but there was worse to come.

The next day it was Miss Unwin. Now Miss Unwin happened to be a close friend of Miss Elphinstone's *and* of Miss Prattley's, and this of course should have been enough to make me very cautious. Yet who would have thought that she of all people, Miss Unwin, that quiet gentle little mouse who only a few weeks before had presented me with a new hassock exquisitely worked in needlepoint with her own hands, who would have thought that *she* would ever have taken a liberty with anyone? So when she asked me to accompany her down to the crypt to show her the Saxon murals, it never entered my head that there was devilry afoot. But there was.

I don't propose to describe this encounter; it was too

painful. And the ones which followed were no less savage. Nearly every day from then on, some new outrageous incident would take place. I became a nervous wreck. At times I hardly knew what I was doing. I started reading the burial service at young Gladys Pitcher's wedding. I dropped Mrs Harris's new baby into the font during the christening and gave it a nasty ducking. An uncomfortable rash that I hadn't had in over two years reappeared on the side of my neck, and that annoying business with my ear-lobe came back worse than ever before. Even my hair began coming out in my comb. The faster I retreated, the faster they came after me. Women are like that. Nothing stimulates them quite so much as a display of modesty or shyness in a man. And they become doubly persistent if underneath it all they happen to detect – and here I have a most difficult confession to make – if they happen to detect, as they did in me, a little secret gleam of longing shining in the backs of the eyes.

You see, actually I was mad about women.

Yes, I know. You will find this hard to believe after all that I have said, but it was perfectly true. You must understand that it was only when they touched me with their fingers or pushed up against me with their bodies that I became alarmed. Providing they remained at a safe distance, I could watch them for hours on end with the same peculiar fascination that you yourself might experience in watching a creature you couldn't bear to touch – an octopus, for example, or a long poisonous snake. I loved the smooth white look of a bare arm emerging from a sleeve, curiously naked like a peeled banana. I could get enormously excited just from watching a girl walk across the room in a tight dress; and I particularly enjoyed the back view of a pair of legs when the feet were in rather high heels – the wonderful braced-up look behind the knees, with the legs themselves very taut as though they were made of strong elastic stretched out almost to breaking-point, but not quite. Sometimes, in Lady Birdwell's drawing-room, sitting near the window on a summer's afternoon, I would glance over the rim of my teacup towards the swimming-pool and become agitated beyond measure by the sight of a little patch of sunburned stomach bulging between the top and bottom of a two-piece bathing-suit.

There is nothing wrong in having thoughts like these. All men harbour them from time to time. But they did give me a terrible sense of guilt. Is it me, I kept asking myself, who is unwittingly responsible for the shameless way in which these ladies are now behaving? Is it the gleam in my eye (which I cannot control) that is constantly rousing their passions and egging them on? Am I unconsciously giving them what is sometimes known as the come-hither signal every time I glance their way? Am I?

Or is this brutal conduct of theirs inherent in the very nature of the female?

I had a pretty fair idea of the answer to this question, but that was not good enough for me. I happen to possess a conscience that can never be consoled by guesswork; it has to have proof. I simply had to find out who was really the guilty party in this case – me or them – and with this object in view, I now decided to perform a simple experiment of my own invention, using Snelling's rats.

A year or so previously I had had some trouble with an objectionable choirboy named Billy Snelling. On three consecutive Sundays this youth had brought a pair of white rats into church and had let them loose on the floor during my sermon. In the end I had confiscated the animals and carried them home and placed them in a box in the shed at the bottom of the vicarage garden. Purely for humane reasons I had then proceeded to feed them, and as a result, but without any further encouragement from me, the creatures began to multiply very rapidly. The two became five, and the five became twelve.

It was at this point that I decided to use them for research purposes. There were exactly equal numbers of males and females, six of each, so that conditions were ideal.

I first isolated the sexes, putting them into two separate cages, and I left them like that for three whole weeks. Now a rat is a very lascivious animal, and any zoologist will tell you that for them this is an inordinately long period of separation. At a guess I would say that one week of enforced celibacy for a rat is equal to approximately one year of the same treatment for someone like Miss Elphinstone or Miss Prattley; so you can see that I was doing a pretty fair job in reproducing actual conditions.

When the three weeks were up, I took a large box that was divided across the centre by a little fence, and I placed the females on one side and the males on the other. The fence consisted of nothing more than three single strands of naked wire, one inch apart, but there was a powerful electric current running through the wires.

To add a touch of reality to the proceedings, I gave

each female a name. The largest one, who also had the longest whiskers, was Miss Elphinstone. The one with a short thick tail was Miss Prattley. The smallest of them all was Miss Unwin, and so on. The males, all six of them, were *ME*.

I now pulled up a chair and sat back to watch the result.

All rats are suspicious by nature, and when I first put the two sexes together in the box with only the wire between them, neither side made a move. The males stared hard at the females through the fence. The females stared back, waiting for the males to come forward. I could see that both sides were tense with yearning. Whiskers quivered and noses twitched and occasionally a long tail would flick sharply against the wall of the box.

After a while, the first male detached himself from his group and advanced gingerly towards the fence, his belly close to the ground. He touched a wire and was immediately electrocuted. The remaining eleven rats froze, motionless.

There followed a period of nine and a half minutes during which neither side moved; but I noticed that while all the males were now staring at the dead body of their colleague, the females had eyes only for the males.

Then suddenly Miss Prattley with the short tail could stand it no longer. She came bounding forward, hit the wire, and dropped dead.

The males pressed their bodies closer to the ground and gazed thoughtfully at the two corpses by the fence. The females also seemed to be quite shaken, and there was another wait, with neither side moving.

Now it was Miss Unwin who began to show signs of impatience. She snorted audibly and twitched a pink mobile nose-end from side to side, then suddenly she started jerking her body quickly up and down as though she were doing push-ups. She glanced round at her remaining four companions, raised her tail high in the air as much as to say 'Here I go, girls,' and with that she advanced briskly to the wire, pushed her head through it, and was killed.

Sixteen minutes later, Miss Foster made her first move. Miss Foster was a woman in the village who bred cats, and recently she had had the effrontery to put up a large sign outside her house in the High Street, saying FOSTER'S CATTERY. Through long association with the creatures she herself seemed to have acquired all their most noxious characteristics, and whenever she came near me in a room I could detect, even through the smoke of her Russian cigarette, a faint but pungent aroma of cat. She had never struck me as having much control over her baser instincts, and it was with some satisfaction, therefore, that I watched her now as she foolishly took her own life in a last desperate plunge towards the masculine sex.

A Miss Montgomery-Smith came next, a small determined woman who had once tried to make me believe that she had been engaged to a bishop. She died trying to creep on her belly under the lowest wire, and I must say I thought this a very fair reflection upon the way in which she lived her life.

And still the five remaining males stayed motionless, waiting.

The fifth female to go was Miss Plumley. She was a devious one who was continually slipping little messages addressed to me into the collection bag. Only the Sunday before, I had been in the vestry counting the money after morning service and had come across one of them tucked inside a folded ten-shilling note. 'Your poor throat sounded hoarse today during the sermon,' it said. 'Let me bring you a bottle of my own cherry pectoral to soothe it down. Most affectionately, Eunice Plumley.'

Miss Plumley ambled slowly up to the wire, sniffed the centre strand with the tip of her nose, came a fraction too close, and received two hundred and forty volts of alternating current through her body.

The five males stayed where they were, watching the slaughter.

And now only Miss Elphinstone remained on the feminine side.

For a full half-hour neither she nor any of the others made a move. Finally one of the males stirred himself slightly, took a step forward, hesitated, thought better of it, and slowly sank back into a crouch on the floor.

This must have frustrated Miss Elphinstone beyond measure, for suddenly, with eyes blazing, she rushed forward and took a flying leap at the wire. It was a spectacular jump and she nearly cleared it; but one of her hind legs grazed the top strand, and thus she also perished with the rest of her sex.

I cannot tell you how much good it did me to watch this simple and, though I say it myself, this rather ingenious experiment. In one stroke I had laid open the incredibly lascivious, stop-at-nothing nature of the female. My own sex was vindicated; my own conscience was cleared. In a trice, all those awkward little flashes of guilt from which I had continually been suffering flew out the window. I felt suddenly very strong and serene in the knowledge of my own innocence.

For a few moments I toyed with the absurd idea of electrifying the black iron railings that ran round the vicarage garden; or perhaps just the gate would be enough. Then I would sit back comfortably in a chair in the library and watch through the window as the real Misses Elphinstone and Prattley and Unwin came forward one after the other and paid the final penalty for pestering an innocent male.

Such foolish thoughts!

What I must actually do now, I told myself, was to weave round me a sort of invisible electric fence constructed entirely out of my own personal moral fibre. Behind this I would sit in perfect safety while the enemy, one after another, flung themselves against the wire.

I would begin by cultivating a brusque manner. I would speak crisply to all women, and refrain from smiling at them. I would no longer step back a pace when one of them advanced upon me. I would stand my ground and glare at her, and if she said something that I considered suggestive, I would make a sharp retort.

It was in this mood that I set off the very next day to attend Lady Birdwell's tennis party.

I was not a player myself, but her ladyship had graciously invited me to drop in and mingle with the guests when play was over at six o'clock. I believe she thought that it lent a certain tone to a gathering to have a clergyman present, and she was probably hoping to persuade me to repeat the performance I gave the last time I was there, when I sat at the piano for a full hour and a quarter after supper and entertained the guests with a detailed description of the evolution of the madrigal through the centuries.

I arrived at the gates on my cycle promptly at six o'clock and pedalled up the long drive towards the house. This was the first week of June, and the rhododendrons were massed in great banks of pink and purple all the way along on either side. I was feeling unusually blithe and dauntless. The previous day's experiment with the rats had made it impossible now for anyone to take me by surprise. I knew exactly what to expect and I was armed accordingly. All round me the little fence was up.

'Ah, good evening, Vicar,' Lady Birdwell cried, advancing upon me with both arms outstretched.

I stood my ground and looked her straight in the eye. 'How's Birdwell?' I said. 'Still up in the city?'

I doubt whether she had ever before in her life heard Lord Birdwell referred to thus by someone who had never even met him. It stopped her dead in her tracks. She looked at me queerly and didn't seem to know how to answer.

'I'll take a seat if I may,' I said, and walked past her towards the terrace where a group of nine or ten guests were settled comfortably in cane chairs, sipping their drinks. They were mostly women, the usual crowd, all of them dressed in white tennis clothes, and as I strode in among them, my own sober black suiting seemed to give me, I thought, just the right amount of separateness for the occasion.

The ladies greeted me with smiles. I nodded to them and sat down in a vacant chair, but I didn't smile back.

'I think perhaps I'd better finish my story another time,' Miss Elphinstone was saying. 'I don't believe the vicar would approve.' She giggled and gave me an arch look. I knew she was waiting for me to come out with my usual little nervous laugh and to say my usual little sentence about how broad-minded I was; but I did nothing of the sort. I simply raised one side of my upper lip until it shaped itself into a tiny curl of contempt (I had practised in the mirror that morning), and then I said sharply, in a loud voice, 'Mens sana in corpore sano.'

'What's that?' she cried. 'Come again, Vicar.'

'A clean mind in a healthy body,' I answered. 'It's a family motto.'

There was an odd kind of silence for quite a long time after this. I could see the women exchanging glances with one another, frowning, shaking their heads.

'The vicar's in the dumps,' Miss Foster announced. She was the one who bred cats. 'I think the vicar needs a drink.'

'Thank you,' I said, 'but I never imbibe. You know that.'

'Then do let me fetch you a nice cooling glass of fruit cup?'

This last sentence came softly and rather suddenly from someone just behind me, to my right, and there was a note of such genuine concern in the speaker's voice that I turned around.

I saw a lady of singular beauty whom I had met only once before, about a month ago. Her name was Miss Roach, and I remembered that she had struck me then as being a person far out of the usual run. I had been particularly impressed by her gentle and reticent nature; and the fact that I had felt comfortable in her presence proved beyond doubt that she was not the sort of person who would try to impinge herself upon me in any way.

'I'm sure you must be tired after cycling all that distance,' she was saying now.

I swivelled right round in my chair and looked at her carefully. She was certainly a striking person – unusually muscular for a woman, with broad shoulders and powerful arms and a huge calf bulging on each leg. The flush of the afternoon's exertions was still upon her, and her face glowed with a healthy red sheen.

'Thank you so much, Miss Roach,' I said, 'but I never touch alcohol in any form. Maybe a small glass of lemon squash . . .'

'The fruit cup is only made of fruit, Padre.'

How I loved a person who called me 'Padre'. The word has a military ring about it that conjures up visions of stern discipline and officer rank.

'Fruit cup?' Miss Elphinstone said. 'It's harmless.'

'My dear man, it's nothing but vitamin C,' Miss Foster said.

'Much better for you than fizzy lemonade,' Lady Birdwell said. 'Carbon dioxide attacks the lining of the stomach.'

'I'll get you some,' Miss Roach said, smiling at me pleasantly. It was a good open smile, and there wasn't a trace of guile or mischief from one corner of the mouth to the other.

She stood up and walked over to the drink table. I saw her slicing an orange, then an apple, then a cucumber, then a grape, and dropping the pieces into a glass. Then she poured in a large quantity of liquid from a bottle whose label I couldn't quite read without my spectacles, but I fancied that I saw the name JIM on it, or TIM, or PIM, or some such word.

'I hope there's enough left,' Lady Birdwell called out. 'Those greedy children of mine do love it so.'

'Plenty,' Miss Roach answered, and she brought the drink to me and set it on the table.

Even without tasting it I could easily understand why children adored it. The liquid itself was dark amber-red and there were great hunks of fruit floating around among the ice cubes; and on top of it all, Miss Roach had placed a sprig of mint. I guessed that the mint had been put there specially for me, to take some of the sweetness away and to lend a touch of grown-upness to a concoction that was otherwise so obviously for youngsters.

'Too sticky for you, Padre?'

'It's delectable,' I said, sipping it. 'Quite perfect.'

It seemed a pity to gulp it down quickly after all the trouble Miss Roach had taken to make it, but it was so refreshing I couldn't resist.

'Do let me make you another?'

I liked the way she waited until I had set the glass on the table, instead of trying to take it out of my hand.

'I wouldn't eat the mint if I were you,' Miss Elphinstone said.

'I'd better get another bottle from the house,' Lady Birdwell called out. 'You're going to need it, Mildred.'

'Do that,' Miss Roach replied. 'I drink gallons of the stuff myself,' she went on, speaking to me. 'And I don't think you'd say that I'm exactly what you might call emaciated.'

'No indeed,' I answered fervently. I was watching her again as she mixed me another brew, noticing how the muscles rippled under the skin of the arm that raised the bottle. Her neck also was uncommonly fine when seen from behind; not thin and stringy like the necks of a lot of these so-called modern beauties, but thick and strong with a slight ridge running down either side where the sinews bulged. It wasn't easy to guess the age of a person like this, but I doubted whether she could have been more than forty-eight or -nine.

I had just finished my second big glass of fruit cup when I began to experience a most peculiar sensation. I seemed to be floating up out of my chair, and hundreds of little warm waves came washing in under me, lifting me higher and higher. I felt as buoyant as a bubble, and everything around me seemed to be bobbing up and down and swirling gently from side to side. It was all very pleasant, and I was overcome by an almost irresistible desire to break into song.

'Feeling happy?' Miss Roach's voice sounded miles and miles away, and when I turned to look at her, I was astonished to see how near to me she really was. She, also, was bobbing up and down.

'Terrific,' I answered. 'I'm feeling absolutely terrific.'

Her face was large and pink, and it was so close to me now that I could see the pale carpet of fuzz covering both her cheeks, and the way the sunlight caught each tiny separate hair and made it shine like gold. All of a sudden I found myself wanting to put out a hand and stroke those cheeks of hers with my fingers. To tell the truth, I wouldn't have objected in the least if she had tried to do the same to me.

'Listen,' she said softly. 'How about the two of us taking a little stroll down the garden to see the lupins?'

'Fine,' I answered. 'Lovely. Anything you say.'

There is a small Georgian summer-house alongside the croquet lawn in Lady Birdwell's garden, and the very next thing I knew, I was sitting inside it on a kind of chaise longue and Miss Roach was beside me. I was still bobbing up and down, and so was she, and so, for that matter, was the summer-house, but I was feeling wonderful. I asked Miss Roach if she would like me to give her a song.

'Not now,' she said, encircling me with her arms and squeezing my chest against hers so hard that it hurt.

'Don't,' I said, melting.

'That's better,' she kept saying. 'That's much better, isn't it?'

Had Miss Roach or any other female tried to do this sort of thing to me an hour before, I don't quite know what would have happened. I think I would probably have fainted. I might even have died. But here I was now, the same old me, actually relishing the contact of those enormous bare arms against my body! Also – and this was the most amazing thing of all – I was beginning to feel the urge to reciprocate.

I took the lobe of her left ear between my thumb and forefinger, and tugged it playfully.

'Naughty boy,' she said.

I tugged harder and squeezed it a bit at the same time. This roused her to such a pitch that she began to grunt and snort like a hog. Her breathing became loud and stertorous.

'Kiss me,' she ordered.

'What?' I said.

'Come on, kiss me.'

At that moment, I saw her mouth. I saw this great mouth of hers coming slowly down on top of me, starting to open, and coming closer and closer, and opening wider and wider; and suddenly my whole stomach began to roll right over inside me and I went stiff with terror.

'No!' I shrieked. 'Don't!'

I can only tell you that I had never in all my life seen anything more terrifying than that mouth. I simply could not *stand* it coming at me like that. Had it been a red-hot iron someone was pushing into my face I wouldn't have been nearly so petrified, I swear I wouldn't. The strong arms were around me, pinning me down so that I couldn't move, and the mouth kept getting larger and larger, and then all at once it was right on top of me, huge and wet and cavernous, and the next second – I was inside it.

I was right inside this enormous mouth, lying on my stomach along the length of the tongue, with my feet somewhere around the back of the throat; and I knew instinctively that unless I got myself out again at once I was going to be swallowed alive – just like that baby rabbit. I could feel my legs being drawn down the throat by some kind of suction, and quickly I threw up my arms and grabbed hold of the lower front teeth and held on for dear life. My head was near the mouth-entrance, and I could actually look right out between the lips and see a little patch of the world outside – sunlight shining on the polished wooden floor of the summer-house, and on the floor itself a gigantic foot in a white tennis shoe.

I had a good grip with my fingers on the edge of the teeth, and in spite of the suction, I was managing to haul myself up slowly towards the daylight when suddenly the upper teeth came down on my knuckles and started chopping away at them so fiercely I had to let go. I went sliding back down the throat, feet first, clutching madly at this and that as I went, but everything was so smooth and slippery I couldn't get a grip. I glimpsed a bright flash of gold on the left as I slid past the last of the molars, and then three inches farther on I saw what must have been the uvula above me, dangling like a thick red stalactite from the roof of the throat. I grabbed at it with both hands but the thing slithered through my fingers and I went on down.

I remember screaming for help, but I could barely hear the sound of my own voice above the noise of the wind that was caused by the throat-owner's breathing. There seemed to be a gale blowing all the time, a queer erratic gale that blew alternately very cold (as the air came in) and very hot (as it went out again).

I managed to get my elbows hooked over a sharp fleshy

ridge – I presume the epiglottis – and for a brief moment I hung there, defying the suction and scrabbling with my feet to find a foothold on the wall of the larynx; but the throat gave a huge heaving swallow that jerked me away, and down I went again.

From then on, there was nothing else for me to catch hold of, and down and down I went until soon my legs were dangling below me in the upper reaches of the stomach, and I could feel the slow powerful pulsing of peristalsis dragging away at my ankles, pulling me down and down and down . . .

Far above me, outside in the open air, I could hear the distant babble of women's voices:

'It's not true . . .'

'But my dear Mildred, how awful . . .'

'The man must be mad . . .'

'Your poor mouth, just look at it . . .'

'A sex maniac . . .'

'A sadist . . .'

'Someone ought to write to the bishop . . .'

And then Miss Roach's voice, louder than the others, swearing and screeching like a parakeet:

'He's damn lucky I didn't kill him, the little bastard! . . . I said to him, listen, I said, if ever I happen to want any of my teeth extracted, I'll go to a dentist, not to a goddam vicar . . . It isn't as though I'd given him any encouragement either! . . .'

'Where is he now, Mildred?'

'God knows. In the bloody summer-house, I suppose.'

'Hey girls, let's go and root him out!'

Oh dear, oh dear. Looking back on it all now, some three weeks later, I don't know how I ever came through the nightmare of that awful afternoon without taking leave of my senses.

A gang of witches like that is a very dangerous thing to fool around with, and had they managed to catch me in the summer-house right then and there when their blood was up, they would likely as not have torn me limb from limb on the spot.

Either that, or I should have been frog-marched down to the police station with Lady Birdwell and Miss Roach leading the procession through the main street of the village.

But of course they didn't catch me.

They didn't catch me then, and they haven't caught me yet, and if my luck continues to hold, I think I've got a fair chance of evading them altogether – or anyway for a few months, until they forget about the whole affair.

As you might guess, I am having to keep entirely to myself and to take no part in public affairs or social life. I find that writing is a most salutary occupation at a time like this, and I spend many hours each day playing with sentences. I regard each sentence as a little wheel, and my ambition lately has been to gather several hundred of them together at once and to fit them all end to end, with the cogs interlocking, like gears, but each wheel a different size, each turning at a different speed. Now and again I try to put a really big one right next to a very small one in such a way that the big one, turning slowly, will make the small one spin so fast that it hums. Very tricky, that.

I also sing madrigals in the evenings, but I miss my own harpsichord terribly.

All the same, this isn't such a bad place, and I have made myself as comfortable as I possibly can. It is a small chamber situated in what is almost certainly the primary section of the duodenal loop, just before it begins to run vertically downwards in front of the right kidney. The floor is quite level – indeed it was the first level place I came to during that horrible descent down Miss Roach's throat – and that's the only reason I managed to stop at all. Above me, I can see a pulpy sort of opening that I take to be the pylorus, where the stomach enters the small intestine (I can still remember some of those diagrams my mother used to show me), and below me, there is a funny little hole in the wall where the pancreatic duct enters the lower section of the duodenum.

It is all a trifle bizarre for a man of conservative tastes like myself. Personally I prefer oak furniture and parquet flooring. But there is anyway one thing here that pleases me greatly, and that is the walls. They are lovely and soft, like a sort of padding, and the advantage of this is that I can bounce up against them as much as I wish without hurting myself.

There are several other people about, which is rather surprising, but thank God they are every one of them males. For some reason or other, they all wear white coats, and they bustle around pretending to be very busy and important. In actual fact, they are an uncommonly ignorant bunch of fellows. They don't even seem to realize where they *are*. I try to tell them, but they refuse to listen.

Sometimes I get so angry and frustrated with them that I lose my temper and start to shout; and then a sly mistrustful look comes over their faces and they begin backing slowly away, and saying, 'Now then. Take it easy. Take it easy, Vicar, there's a good boy. Take it easy.'

What sort of talk is that?

But there is one oldish man – he comes in to see me every morning after breakfast – who appears to live slightly closer to reality than the others. He is civil and dignified, and I imagine he is lonely because he likes nothing better than to sit quietly in my room and listen to me talk. The only trouble is that whenever we get on to the subject of our whereabouts, he starts telling me that he's going to help me to escape. He said it again this morning, and we had quite an argument about it.

'But can't you see,' I said patiently, 'I don't *want* to escape.'

'My dear Vicar, why ever not?'

'I keep telling you – because they're all searching for me outside.'

'Who?'

'Miss Elphinstone and Miss Roach and Miss Prattley and all the rest of them.'

'What nonsense.'

'Oh yes they are! And I imagine they're after *you* as well, but you won't admit it.'

'No, my friend, they are not after me.'

'Then may I ask precisely what you are doing down here?'

A bit of a stumper for him, that one. I could see he didn't know how to answer it.

'I'll bet you were fooling around with Miss Roach and got yourself swallowed up just the same as I did. I'll bet that's exactly what happened, only you're ashamed to admit it.'

He looked suddenly so wan and defeated when I said this that I felt sorry for him.

'Would you like me to sing you a song?' I asked.

But he got up without answering and went quietly out into the corridor.

'Cheer up,' I called after him. 'Don't be depressed. There is always some balm in Gilead.'

The Visitor

First published in *Playboy* (May 1965)

Not long ago, a large wooden case was deposited at the door of my house by the railway delivery service. It was an unusually strong and well-constructed object, and made of some kind of dark red hardwood, not unlike mahogany. I lifted it with great difficulty on to a table in the garden, and examined it carefully. The stencilling on one side said that it had been shipped from Haifa by the m/v *Waverley Star*, but I could find no sender's name or address. I tried to think of somebody living in Haifa or thereabouts who might be wanting to send me a magnificent present. I could think of no one. I walked slowly to the toolshed, still pondering the matter deeply, and returned with a hammer and screwdriver. Then I began gently to prise open the top of the case.

Behold, it was filled with books! Extraordinary books! One by one, I lifted them all out (not yet looking inside any of them) and stacked them in three tall piles on the table. There were twenty-eight volumes altogether, and very beautiful they were indeed. Each of them was identically and superbly bound in rich green morocco, with the initials O.H.C. and a Roman numeral (I to XXVIII) tooled in gold upon the spine.

I took up the nearest volume, number XVI, and opened it. The unlined white pages were filled with a neat small

273

handwriting in black ink. On the title page was written '1934'. Nothing else. I took up another volume, number XXI. It contained more manuscript in the same handwriting, but on the title page it said '1939'. I put it down and pulled out Vol. 1, hoping to find a preface of some kind there, or perhaps the author's name. Instead, I found an envelope inside the cover. The envelope was addressed to me. I took out the letter it contained and glanced quickly at the signature. 'Oswald Hendryks Cornelius', it said.

It was Uncle Oswald!

No member of the family had heard from Uncle Oswald for over thirty years. The letter was dated 10 March 1964, and until its arrival, we could only assume that he still existed. Nothing was really known about him except that he lived in France, that he travelled a great deal, that he was a wealthy bachelor with unsavoury but glamorous habits who steadfastly refused to have anything to do with his own relatives. The rest was all rumour and hearsay, but the rumours were so splendid and the hearsay so exotic that Oswald had long since become a shining hero and a legend to us all.

'My dear boy,' the letter began

I believe that you and your three sisters are my closest surviving blood relations. You are therefore my rightful heirs, and because I have made no will, all that I leave behind me when I die will be yours. Alas, I have nothing to leave. I used to have quite a lot, and the fact that I have recently disposed of it all in my own way is none of your business. As consolation, though, I am sending you

my private diaries. These, I think, ought to remain in the family.
They cover all the best years of my life, and it will do you no harm
to read them. But if you show them around or lend them out to
strangers, you do so at your own great peril. If you publish them,
then that, I should imagine, would be the end of both you and
your publisher simultaneously. For you must understand that
thousands of the heroines whom I mention in the diaries are still
only half dead, and if you were foolish enough to splash their
lily-white reputations with scarlet print, they would have your head
on a salver in two seconds flat, and probably roast it in the oven
for good measure. So you'd better be careful. I only met you once.
That was years ago, in 1921, when your family was living in that
large ugly house in South Wales. I was your big uncle and you
were a very small boy, about five years old. I don't suppose you
remember the young Norwegian nursemaid you had then.
A remarkably clean, well-built girl she was, and exquisitely
shaped even in her uniform with its ridiculous starchy white shield
concealing her lovely bosom. The afternoon I was there, she was
taking you for a walk in the woods to pick bluebells, and I
asked if I might come along. And when we got well into the
middle of the woods, I told you I'd give you a bar of chocolate if
you could find your own way home. And you did (see Vol. III).
You were a sensible child. Farewell – Oswald Hendryks
Cornelius.

The sudden arrival of the diaries caused much excitement in the family, and there was a rush to read them. We
were not disappointed. It was astonishing stuff – hiliarious,
witty, exciting, and often quite touching as well. The man's

vitality was unbelievable. He was always on the move, from city to city, from country to country, from woman to woman, and in between the women, he would be searching for spiders in Kashmir or tracking down a blue porcelain vase in Nanking. But the women always came first. Wherever he went, he left an endless trail of females in his wake, females ruffled and ravished beyond words, but purring like cats.

Twenty-eight volumes with exactly three hundred pages to each volume take a deal of reading, and there are precious few writers who could hold an audience over a distance like that. But Oswald did it. The narrative never seemed to lose its flavour, the pace seldom slackened, and almost without exception, every single entry, whether it was long or short, and whatever the subject, became a marvellous little individual story that was complete in itself. And at the end of it all, when the last page of the last volume had been read, one was left with the rather breathless feeling that this might just possibly be one of the major autobiographical works of our time.

If it were regarded solely as a chronicle of a man's amorous adventures, then without a doubt there was nothing to touch it. Casanova's *Memoirs* read like a parish magazine in comparison, and the famous lover himself, beside Oswald, appears positively undersexed.

There was social dynamite on every page; Oswald was right about that. But he was surely wrong in thinking that the explosions would all come from the women. What about their husbands, the humiliated cock-sparrows, the cuckolds? The cuckold, when aroused, is a very fierce bird indeed, and there would be thousands upon thousands of them rising up out of the bushes if *The Cornelius Diaries*, unabridged, saw the light of day while they were still alive. Publication, therefore, was right out of the question.

A pity, this. Such a pity, in fact, that I thought something ought to be done about it. So I sat down and reread the diaries from beginning to end in the hope that I might discover at least one complete passage which could be printed and published without involving both the publisher and myself in serious litigation. To my joy, I found no less than six. I showed them to a lawyer. He said he thought they *might* be 'safe', but he wouldn't guarantee it. One of them – 'The Sinai Desert Episode' – seemed 'safer' than the other five, he added.

So I have decided to start with that one and to offer it for publication right away, at the end of this short preface. If it is accepted and all goes well, then perhaps I shall release one or two more.

The Sinai entry is from the last volume of all, Vol. XXVIII, and is dated 24 August 1946. In point of fact, it is the *very last entry* of the last volume of all, the last thing Oswald ever wrote, and we have no record of where he went or what he did after that date. One can only guess. You shall have the entry verbatim in a moment, but first of all, and so that you may more easily understand some of the things Oswald says and does in his story, let me try to tell you a little about the man himself. Out of the mass of confession and opinion contained in those twenty-eight volumes, there emerges a fairly clear picture of his character.

At the time of the Sinai episode, Oswald Hendryks Cornelius was fifty-one years old, and he had, of course, never been married. 'I am afraid,' he was in the habit of saying, 'that I have been blessed, or should I call it burdened, with an uncommonly fastidious nature.'

In some ways, this was true, but in others, and especially in so far as marriage was concerned, the statement was the exact opposite of the truth.

The real reason Oswald had refused to get married was simply that he had never in his life been able to confine his attentions to one particular woman for longer than the time it took to conquer her. When that was done, he lost interest and looked around for another victim.

A normal man would hardly consider this a valid reason for remaining single, but Oswald was not a normal man. He was not even a normally polygamous man. He was, to be honest, such a wanton and incorrigible philanderer that no bride on earth would have put up with him for more than a few days, let alone for the duration of a honeymoon – although heaven knows there were enough who would have been willing to give it a try.

He was a tall, narrow person with a fragile and faintly aesthetic air. His voice was soft, his manner was courteous, and at first sight he seemed more like a gentleman-in-waiting to the Queen than a celebrated rapscallion. He never discussed his amorous affairs with other men, and a stranger, though he might sit and talk with him all evening, would be unable to observe the slightest sign of deceit in Oswald's clear blue eyes. He was, in fact, precisely the sort of man that an anxious father would be likely to choose to escort his daughter safely home.

But sit Oswald beside a *woman*, a woman who interested him, and instantaneously his eyes would change, and as he looked at her, a small dangerous spark would begin dancing slowly in the very centre of each pupil; and then he would set about her with his conversation, talking to her rapidly and cleverly and almost certainly more wittily than anyone else had ever done before. This was a gift he had, a most singular talent, and when he put his mind to it, he could make his words coil themselves round and round the listener until they held her in some sort of a mild hypnotic spell.

But it wasn't only his fine talk and the look in his eyes that fascinated the women. It was also his nose. (In Vol. xiv, Oswald includes, with obvious relish, a note written to him by a certain lady in which she describes such things as this in great detail.) It appears that when Oswald was aroused, something odd would begin to happen around the edges of his nostrils, a tightening of the rims, a visible flaring which enlarged the nostril holes and revealed whole areas of the bright red skin inside. This created a queer, wild, animalistic impression, and although it may not sound particularly attractive when described on paper, its effect upon the ladies was electric.

Almost without exception, women were drawn towards Oswald. In the first place, he was a man who refused to be owned at any price, and this automatically made him desirable. Add to this the unusual combination of a first-rate intellect, an abundance of charm and a reputation for excessive promiscuity, and you have a potent recipe.

Then again, and forgetting for a moment the disreputable and licentious angle, it should be noted that there were a number of other surprising facets to Oswald's character that in themselves made him a rather intriguing person. There was, for example, very little that he did not know about nineteenth-century Italian opera, and he had written a curious little manual upon the three composers Donizetti, Verdi and Ponchielli. In it, he listed by name all the important mistresses that these men had had during their lives, and he went on to examine, in a most serious vein, the relationship between creative passion and carnal passion, and the influence of the one upon the other, particularly as it affected the works of these composers.

Chinese porcelain was another of Oswald's interests, and he was acknowledged as something of an international authority in this field. The blue vases of the Tchin-Hoa period were his special love, and he had a small but exquisite collection of these pieces.

He also collected spiders and walking-sticks.

His collection of spiders, or more accurately, his collection of Arachnida, because it included scorpions and pedipalps, was possibly as comprehensive as any outside a museum, and his knowledge of the hundreds of genera and species was impressive. He maintained, incidentally (and probably correctly), that spiders' silk was superior in quality to the ordinary stuff spun by silkworms, and he never wore a tie that was made of any other material. He possessed about forty of these ties altogether, and in order to acquire them in the first place, and in order also to be able to add two new ties a year to his wardrobe, he had to keep thousands and thousands of *Arana* and *Epeira diademata* (the common English garden spiders) in an old conservatory in the garden of his country house outside Paris, where they bred and multiplied at approximately the same rate as they ate one another. From them, he collected the raw thread himself – no one else would enter that ghastly glasshouse – and sent it to Avignon, where it was reeled and thrown and scoured and dyed and made into cloth. From Avignon, the cloth was delivered directly to Sulka, who were enchanted by the whole business, and only too glad to fashion ties out of such a rare and wonderful material.

'But you can't *really* like spiders?' the women visitors would say to Oswald as he displayed his collection.

'Oh, but I adore them,' he would answer. 'Especially the females. They remind me so much of certain human females that I know. They remind me of my very favourite human females.'

'What nonsense, darling.'

'Nonsense? I think not.'

'It's rather insulting.'

'On the contrary, my dear, it is the greatest compliment I could pay. Did you not know, for instance, that the female spider is so savage in her love-making that the male is very lucky indeed if he escapes with his life at the end of it all. Only if he is exceedingly agile and marvellously ingenious will he get away in one piece.'

'Now, *Oswald*!'

'And the crab spider, my beloved, the teeny-weeny little crab spider is so dangerously passionate that her lover has to tie her down with intricate loops and knots of his own thread before he dares to embrace her . . .'

'Oh, *stop* it, Oswald, this *minute*!' the women would cry, their eyes shining.

Oswald's collection of walking-sticks was something else again. Every one of them had belonged either to a distinguished or a disgusting person, and he kept them all in his Paris apartment, where they were displayed in two long racks standing against the walls of the passage (or should one call it the highway?) which led from the living-room to the bedroom. Each stick had its own little ivory label above it, saying Sibelius, Milton, King Farouk, Dickens, Robespierre, Puccini, Oscar Wilde, Franklin Roosevelt, Goebbels, Queen Victoria, Toulouse-Lautrec, Hindenburg, Tolstoy, Laval, Sarah Bernhardt, Goethe, Voroshiloff, Cézanne, Tojo . . . There must have been over a hundred of them in all, some very beautiful, some very plain, some with gold or silver tops, and some with curly handles.

'Take down the Tolstoy,' Oswald would say to a pretty visitor. 'Go on, take it down . . . that's right . . . and now . . . now rub your own palm gently over the knob that has been worn to a shine by the great man himself. Is it not rather wonderful, the mere contact of your skin with that spot?'

'It is, rather, isn't it.'

'And now take the Goebbels and do the same thing. Do it properly, though. Allow your palm to fold tightly over the handle . . . good . . . and now . . . now lean your weight on it, lean hard, exactly as the little deformed doctor used to do . . . there . . . that's it . . . now stay like that for a minute or so and then tell me if you do not feel a thin finger of ice creeping all the way up your arm and into your chest.'

'It's terrifying!'

'Of course it is. Some people pass out completely. They keel right over.'

Nobody ever found it dull to be in Oswald's company, and perhaps that, more than anything else, was the reason for his success.

We come now to the Sinai episode. Oswald, during that month, had been amusing himself by motoring at a fairly leisurely pace down from Khartoum to Cairo. His car was a superlative prewar Lagonda which had been carefully stored in Switzerland during the war years, and as you can imagine, it was fitted with every kind of gadget under the sun. On the day before Sinai (23 August 1946), he was in Cairo, staying at Shepheard's Hotel, and that evening, after a series of impudent manoeuvres, he had succeeded in getting hold of a Moorish lady of supposedly aristocratic descent, called Isabella. Isabella happened to be the jealously guarded mistress of none other than a certain notorious and dyspeptic Royal Personage (there was still a monarchy in Egypt then). This was a typically Oswaldian move.

But there was more to come. At midnight, he drove the lady out to Giza and persuaded her to climb with him in the moonlight right to the very top of the great pyramid of Cheops.

'. . . There can be no safer place,' he wrote in the diary,

> nor a more romantic one, than the apex of a pyramid on a warm night when the moon is full. The passions are stirred not only by the magnificent view but also by that curious sensation of power that surges within the body whenever one surveys the world from a great height. And as for safety – this pyramid is exactly 481 feet high, which is 115 feet higher than the dome of St Paul's Cathedral, and from the summit one can observe all the approaches with the greatest of ease. No other boudoir on earth can offer this facility. None has so many emergency exits, either, so that if some sinister figure should happen to come clambering up in pursuit on one side of the pyramid, one has only to slip calmly and quietly down the other . . .

As it happened, Oswald had a very narrow squeak indeed that night. Somehow, the palace must have got word of the little affair, for Oswald, from his lofty moon-lit pinnacle, suddenly observed *three* sinister figures, not one, closing in on three different sides, and starting to climb. But luckily for him, there is a fourth side to the great pyramid of Cheops, and by the time those Arab thugs had reached the top, the two lovers were already at the bottom and getting into the car.

The entry for 24 August takes up the story at exactly this point. It is reproduced here word for word and comma for comma as Oswald wrote it. Nothing has been altered or added or taken away:

24 August 1946

'He'll chop off Isabella's head if he catch her now,' Isabella said.

'Rubbish,' I answered, but I reckoned she was probably right.

'He'll chop off Oswald's head, too,' she said.

'Not mine, dear lady. I shall be a long way away from here when daylight comes. I'm heading straight up the Nile for Luxor immediately.'

We were driving quickly away from the pyramids now. It was about two thirty a.m.

'To Luxor?' she said.

'Yes.'

'And Isabella is going with you.'

'No,' I said.

'Yes,' she said.

'It is against my principles to travel with a lady,' I said.

I could see some lights ahead of us. They came from the Mena House Hotel, a place where tourists stay out in the desert, not far from the pyramids. I drove fairly close to the hotel and stopped the car.

'I'm going to drop you here,' I said. 'We had a fine time.'

'So you won't take Isabella to Luxor?'

'I'm afraid not,' I said. 'Come on, hop it.'

She started to get out of the car, then she paused with one foot on the road, and suddenly she swung round and poured out upon me a torrent of language so filthy yet so fluent that I had heard nothing like it from the lips of a lady since . . . well, since 1931, in Marrakesh, when the greedy old Duchess of Glasgow put her hand into a chocolate box and got nipped by a scorpion I happened to have placed there for safe-keeping (Vol. XIII, 5 June 1931).

'You are disgusting,' I said.

Isabella leaped out and slammed the door so hard the whole car jumped on its wheels. I drove off very fast. Thank heaven I was rid of her. I cannot abide bad manners in a pretty girl.

As I drove, I kept one eye on the mirror, but as yet no car seemed to be following me. When I came to the outskirts of Cairo, I began threading my way through the side roads, avoiding the centre of the city. I was not particularly worried. The royal watch-dogs were unlikely to carry the matter much further. All the same, it would have been foolhardy to go back to Shepheard's at this point. It wasn't necessary anyway, because all my baggage, except for a small valise, was with me in the car. I never leave suitcases behind me in my room when I go out of an evening in a foreign city. I like to be mobile.

I had no intention, of course, of going to Luxor. I wanted now to get away from Egypt altogether. I didn't like the country at all. Come to think of it, I never had. The place made me feel uncomfortable in my skin. It was the dirtiness of it all, I think, and the putrid smells. But then let us face it, it really is a rather squalid country; and I have a powerful suspicion, though I hate to say it, that the Egyptians wash themselves less thoroughly than any other peoples in the world – with the possible exception of the Mongolians. Certainly they do not wash their crockery to my taste. There was, believe it or not, a long, crusted, coffee-coloured lipmark stamped upon the rim of the cup they placed before me at breakfast yesterday. Ugh! It was repulsive! I kept staring at it and wondering whose slobbery lower lip had done the deed.

I was driving now through the narrow dirty streets of the eastern suburbs of Cairo. I knew precisely where I was going. I had made up my mind about that before I was even halfway down the pyramid with Isabella. I was going to Jerusalem. It was no distance to speak of, and it was a city that I always enjoyed. Furthermore, it was the quickest way out of Egypt. I would proceed as follows:

1. Cairo to Ismailia. About three hours driving. Sing an opera on the way, as usual. Arrive Ismailia 6–7 a.m. Take a room and have a two-hour sleep. Then shower, shave and breakfast.

2. At 10 a.m., cross over the Suez Canal by the Ismailia bridge and take the desert road across Sinai to the Palestine border. Make a search for scorpions en route in the Sinai Desert. Time, about four hours, arriving Palestine border 2 p.m.

3. From there, continue straight on to Jerusalem via Beersheba, reaching the King David Hotel in time for cocktails and dinner.

It was several years since I had travelled that particular road, but I remembered that the Sinai Desert was an outstanding place for scorpions. I badly wanted another female opisthophthalmus, a large one. My present specimen had the fifth segment of its tail missing, and I was ashamed of it.

It didn't take me long to find the main road to Ismailia, and as soon as I was on it, I settled the Lagonda down to a steady sixty-five miles an hour. The road was narrow, but it had a smooth surface, and there was no traffic. The Delta country lay bleak and dismal around me in the moonlight, the flat treeless fields, the ditches running between, and the black soil everywhere. It was inexpressibly dreary.

But it didn't worry *me*. I was no part of it. I was completely isolated in my own luxurious little shell, as snug as a hermit crab and travelling a lot faster. Oh, how I do love to be on the move, winging away to new people and new places and leaving the old ones far behind! Nothing in the world exhilarates me more than that. And how I despise the average citizen, who settles himself down upon one tiny spot of land with one asinine woman, to breed and stew and rot in that condition unto his life's end. And always with the same woman! I simply cannot *believe* that any man in his senses would put up with just one female day after day and year after year. Some of them, of course, don't. But millions pretend they do.

I myself have never, absolutely never permitted an intimate relationship to last for more than twelve hours. That is the furthest limit. Even eight hours is stretching it a bit, to my mind. Look what happened, for example, with Isabella. While we were upon the summit of the pyramid, she was a lady of scintillating parts, as pliant and playful as a puppy, and had I left her there to the mercy of those three Arab thugs, and skipped down on my own, all would have been well. But I foolishly stuck by her and helped her to descend, and as a result, the lovely lady turned into a vulgar screeching trollop, disgusting to behold.

What a world we live in! One gets no thanks these days for being chivalrous.

The Lagonda moved on smoothly through the night. Now for an opera. Which one should it be this time? I was in the mood for a Verdi. What about *Aida*? Of course! It must be *Aida* – the Egyptian opera! Most appropriate.

I began to sing. I was in exceptionally good voice tonight. I let myself go. It was delightful; and as I drove through the small town of Bilbeis, I was Aida herself, singing '*Numei pietà*', the beautiful concluding passage of the first scene.

Half an hour later, at Zagazig, I was Amonasro begging the King of Egypt to save the Ethiopian captives with '*Ma tu, re, tu signore possente*'.

Passing through El Abbasa, I was Rhadames, rendering '*Fuggiam gli adori nospiti*', and now I opened all the windows of the car so that this incomparable love song might reach the ears of the fellaheen snoring in their hovels along the roadside, and perhaps mingle with their dreams.

As I pulled into Ismailia, it was six o'clock in the morning and the sun was already climbing high in a milky-blue heaven, but I myself was in the terrible sealed-up dungeon with Aida, singing, '*O terra, addio; addio valle di pianti!*'

How swiftly the journey had gone. I drove to an hotel. The staff was just beginning to stir. I stirred them up some more and got the best room available. The sheets and blanket on the bed looked as though they had been slept in by twenty-five unwashed Egyptians on twenty-five consecutive nights, and I tore them off with my own hands (which I scrubbed immediately afterward with antiseptic soap) and replaced them with my personal bedding. Then I set my alarm and slept soundly for two hours.

For breakfast I ordered a poached egg on a piece of toast. When the dish arrived – and I tell you, it makes my stomach curdle just to write about it – there was a *gleaming, curly, jet-black hair*, three inches long, lying diagonally across the yolk of my poached egg. It was too much. I leaped up from the table and rushed out of the dining-room. '*Addio!*' I cried, flinging some money at the cashier as I went by, '*Addio valle di pianti!*' And with that I shook the filthy dust of the hotel from my feet.

Now for the Sinai Desert. What a welcome change that would be. A real desert is one of the least contaminated places on earth, and Sinai was no exception. The road across it was a narrow strip of black tarmac about a hundred and forty miles long, with only a single filling-station and a group of huts at the halfway mark, at a place called B'ir Rawd Salim. Otherwise there was nothing but pure uninhabited desert all the way. It would be very hot at this time of year, and it was essential to carry drinking water in case of a breakdown. I therefore pulled up outside a kind of general store in the main street of Ismailia to get my emergency canister refilled.

I went in and spoke to the proprietor. The man had a nasty case of trachoma. The granulation on the under surfaces of his eyelids was so acute that the lids themselves were raised right up off the eyeballs – a beastly sight. I asked him if he would sell me a gallon of *boiled* water. He thought I was mad, and madder still when I insisted on following him back into his grimy kitchen to make sure that he did things properly. He filled a kettle with tap-water and placed it on a paraffin stove. The stove had a tiny little smoky yellow flame. The proprietor seemed very proud of the stove and of its performance. He stood admiring it, his head on one side. Then he suggested that I might prefer to go back and wait in the shop. He would bring me the water, he said, when it was ready. I refused to leave. I stood there watching the kettle like a lion, waiting for the water to boil; and while I was doing this, the breakfast scene suddenly started coming back to me in all its horror – the egg, the yolk and the hair. Whose hair was it that had lain embedded in the slimy yolk of my egg at breakfast? Undoubtedly it was the cook's hair. And when, pray, had the cook last washed his head? He had probably never washed his head. Very well, then. He was almost certainly verminous. But that in itself would not cause a hair to fall out. What *did* cause the cook's hair, then, to fall out on to my poached egg this morning as he transferred the egg from the pan to the plate? There is a reason for all things, and in this case the reason was obvious. The cook's scalp was infested with purulent seborrhoeic impetigo. And the hair itself, the long black hair that I might so easily have swallowed had I been less alert, was therefore swarming with millions and millions of living pathogenic cocci whose exact scientific name I have, happily, forgotten.

Can I, you ask, be absolutely sure that the cook had purulent seborrhoeic impetigo? Not absolutely sure – no. But if he hadn't, then he certainly had ringworm instead.

And what did that mean? I knew only too well what it meant. It meant that ten million microsporons had been clinging and clustering round that awful hair, waiting to go into my mouth.

I began to feel sick.

'The water boils,' the shopkeeper said triumphantly.

'Let it boil,' I told him. 'Give it eight minutes more. What is it you want me to get – typhus?'

Personally, I never drink plain water by itself if I can help it, however pure it may be. Plain water has no flavour at all. I take it, of course, as tea or as coffee, but even then I try to arrange for bottled Vichy or Malvern to be used in the preparation. I avoid tap-water. Tap-water is diabolical stuff. Often it is nothing more nor less than reclaimed sewage.

'Soon this water will be boiled away in steam,' the proprietor said, grinning at me with green teeth.

I lifted the kettle myself and poured the contents into my canister.

Back in the shop, I bought six oranges, a small watermelon and a slab of well-wrapped English chocolate. Then I returned to the Lagonda. Now at last I was away.

A few minutes later, I had crossed the sliding bridge that went over the Suez Canal just above Lake Timsah, and ahead of me lay the flat blazing desert and the little tarmac road stretching out before me like a black ribbon all the way to the horizon. I settled the Lagonda down to the usual steady sixty-five miles an hour, and I opened the windows wide. The air that came in was like the breath of an oven. The time was almost noon, and the sun was throwing its heat directly on to the roof of the car. My thermometer inside registered 103°. But as you know, a touch of warmth never bothers me so long as I am sitting still and am wearing suitable clothes – in this case a pair of cream-coloured linen slacks, a white Aertex shirt and a spider's-silk tie of the loveliest rich moss-green. I felt perfectly comfortable and at peace with the world.

For a minute or two I played with the idea of performing another opera en route – I was in the mood for *La Gioconda* – but after singing a few bars of the opening chorus, I began to perspire slightly; so I rang down the curtain, and lit a cigarette instead.

I was now driving through some of the finest scorpion country in the world, and I was eager to stop and make a search before I reached the halfway filling-station at B'ir Rawd Salim. I had so far met not a single vehicle nor seen a living creature since leaving Ismailia an hour before. This pleased me. Sinai was authentic desert. I pulled up on the side of the road and switched off the engine. I was thirsty, so I ate an orange. Then I put my white topee on my head, and eased myself slowly out of the car, out of my comfortable hermit-crab shell and into the sunlight. For a full minute I stood motionless in the middle of the road, blinking at the brilliance of the surroundings.

There was a blazing sun, a vast hot sky and beneath it all on every side a great pale sea of yellow sand that was not quite of this world. There were mountains now in the distance on the south side of the road, bare, pale, tanagra-coloured mountains faintly glazed with blue and purple, that rose up suddenly out of the desert and faded away in a haze of heat against the sky. The stillness was over-powering. There was no sound at all, no voice of bird or insect anywhere, and it gave me a queer godlike feeling to be standing there alone in the middle of such a splendid, hot, inhuman landscape – as though I were on another planet altogether, on Jupiter or Mars, or in some place more distant and desolate still, where never would the grass grow nor the clouds turn red.

I went to the boot of the car and took out my killing-box, my net and my trowel. Then I stepped off the road into the soft burning sand. I walked slowly for about a hundred yards into the desert, my eyes searching the ground. I was not looking for scorpions but the lairs of scorpions. The scorpion is a cryptozoic and nocturnal creature that hides all through the day either under a stone or in a burrow, according to its type. Only after the sun has gone down does it come out to hunt for food.

The one I wanted, opisthophthalmus, was a burrower, so I wasted no time turning over stones. I searched only for burrows. After ten or fifteen minutes, I had found none; but already the heat was getting to be too much for me, and I decided reluctantly to return to the car. I walked back very slowly, still watching the ground, and I had reached the road and was in the act of stepping on to it when all at once, in the sand, not more than twelve inches from the edge of the tarmac, I caught sight of a scorpion's burrow.

I put the killing-box and the net on the ground beside me. Then, with my little trowel, I began very cautiously to scrape away the sand all round the hole. This was an operation that never failed to excite me. It was like a treasure hunt – a treasure hunt with just the right amount of danger accompanying it to stir the blood. I could feel my heart beating away in my chest as I probed deeper and deeper into the sand.

And suddenly . . . there she was!

Oh, my heavens, what a whopper! A gigantic female scorpion, not opisthophthalmus, as I saw immediately, but pandinus, the other large African burrower. And clinging to her back – this was too good to be true! – swarming all over her, were one, two, three, four, five . . . a total of fourteen tiny babies! The mother was six inches long at least! Her children were the size of small revolver bullets. She had seen me now, the first human she had ever seen in her life, and her pincers were wide open, her tail was curled high over her back like a question mark, ready to strike. I took up the net, and slid it swiftly underneath her, and scooped her up. She twisted and squirmed, striking wildly in all directions with the end of her tail. I saw a single drop of venom fall through the mesh on to the sand. Quickly, I transferred her, together with all the offspring, to the killing-box, and closed the lid. Then I fetched the ether from the car, and poured it through the little gauze hole in the top of the box until the pad inside was well soaked.

How splendid she would look in my collection! The babies would, of course, fall away from her as they died, but I would stick them on again with glue in more or less their correct positions; and then I would be the proud possessor of a huge female pandinus with her own fourteen offspring on her back! I was extremely pleased.

I lifted the killing-box (I could feel her thrashing about furiously inside) and placed it in the boot, together with the net and trowel. Then I returned to my seat in the car, lit a cigarette, and drove on.

The more contented I am, the slower I drive. I drove quite slowly now, and it must have taken me nearly an hour more to reach B'ir Rawd Salim, the halfway station. It was a most unenticing place. On the left, there was a single gasoline pump and a wooden shack. On the right, there were three more shacks, each about the size of a potting-shed. The rest was desert. There was not a soul in sight. The time was twenty minutes before two in the afternoon, and the temperature inside the car was 106°.

What with the nonsense of getting the water boiled before leaving Ismailia, I had forgotten completely to fill up with gasoline before leaving, and my gauge was now registering slightly less than two gallons. I'd cut it rather fine – but no matter. I pulled in alongside the pump, and waited. Nobody appeared. I pressed the horn button, and the four tuned horns on the Lagonda shouted their wonderful '*Son gia mille e tre!*' across the desert. Nobody appeared. I pressed again.

Son gia mille e tre

sang the horns. Mozart's phrase sounded magnificent in these surroundings. But still nobody appeared. The inhabitants of B'ir Rawd Salim didn't give a damn, it seemed, about my friend Don Giovanni and the one thousand and three women he had deflowered in Spain.

At last, after I had played the horns no less than six times, the door of the hut behind the gasoline pump opened and a tallish man emerged and stood on the threshold, doing up his buttons with both hands. He took his time over this, and not until he had finished did he glance up at the Lagonda. I looked back at him through my open window. I saw him take the first step in my direction . . . he took it very, very slowly . . . Then he took a second step . . .

My God! I thought at once. The spirochetes have got him!

He had the slow, wobbly walk, the loose-limbed, high-stepping gait of a man with locomotor ataxia. With each step he took, the front foot was raised high in the air before him and brought down violently to the ground, as though he were stamping on a dangerous insect.

I thought: I had better get out of here. I had better start the motor and get the hell out of here before he reaches me. But I knew I couldn't. I *had* to have the gasoline. I sat in the car staring at the awful creature as he came stamping laboriously over the sand. He must have had the revolting disease for years and years, otherwise it wouldn't have developed into ataxia. *Tabes dorsalis*, they call it in professional circles, and pathologically this means that the victim is suffering from degeneration of the posterior columns of the spinal cord. But ah my foes and oh my friends, it is really a lot worse than that; it is a slow and merciless consuming of the actual nerve fibres of the body by syphilitic toxins.

The man – the Arab, I shall call him – came right up to the door of my side of the car and peered in through the open window. I leaned away from him, praying that he would come not an inch closer. Without a doubt, he was one of the most blighted humans I had ever seen. His face had the eroded, eaten-away look of an old wood-carving when the worm has been at it, and the sight of it made me wonder how many other diseases the man was suffering from, besides syphilis.

'Salaam,' he mumbled.

'Fill up the tank,' I told him.

He didn't move. He was inspecting the interior of the Lagonda with great interest. A terrible feculent odour came wafting in from his direction.

'Come along!' I said sharply. 'I want some gasoline!'

He looked at me and grinned. It was more of a leer than a grin, an insolent mocking leer that seemed to be saying, 'I am the king of the gasoline pump at B'ir Rawd Salim! Touch me if you dare!' A fly had settled in the corner of one of his eyes. He made no attempt to brush it away.

'You want gasoline?' he said, taunting me.

I was about to swear at him, but I checked myself just in time, and answered politely, 'Yes please, I would be very grateful.'

He watched me slyly for a few moments to be sure I wasn't mocking him, then he nodded as though satisfied now with my behaviour. He turned away and started slowly towards the rear of the car. I reached into the door-pocket for my bottle of Glenmorangie. I poured myself a stiff one, and sat sipping it. The man's face had been within a yard of my own; his foetid breath had come pouring into the car . . . and who knows how many billions of airborne viruses might not have come pouring in with it? On such an occasion it is a fine thing to sterilize the mouth and throat with a drop of Highland whisky. The whisky is also a solace. I emptied the glass, and poured myself another. Soon I began to feel less alarmed. I noticed the watermelon lying on the seat beside me. I decided that a slice of it at this moment would be refreshing. I took my knife from its case and cut out a thick section. Then, with the point of the knife, I carefully picked out all the black seeds, using the rest of the melon as a receptacle.

I sat drinking the whisky and eating the melon. Both were delicious.

'Gasoline is done,' the dreadful Arab said, appearing at the window. 'I check water now, and oil.'

I would have preferred him to keep his hands off the Lagonda altogether, but rather than risk an argument, I said nothing. He went clumping off towards the front of the car, and his walk reminded me of a drunken Hitler Stormtrooper doing the goosestep in very slow motion.

Tabes dorsalis, as I live and breathe.

The only other disease to induce that queer highstepping gait is chronic beriberi. Well – he probably had that one, too. I cut myself another slice of watermelon, and concentrated for a minute or so on taking out the seeds with the knife. When I looked up again, I saw that the Arab had raised the bonnet of the car on the right-hand side, and was bending over the engine. His head and shoulders were out of sight, and so were his hands and arms. What on earth was the man doing? The oil dipstick was on the other side. I rapped on the windshield. He seemed not to hear me. I put my head out of the window and shouted, 'Hey! Come out of there!'

Slowly, he straightened up, and as he drew his right arm out of the bowels of the engine, I saw that he was holding in his fingers something that was long and black and curly and very thin.

'Good God!' I thought. 'He's found a snake in there!'

He came round to the window, grinning at me and holding the object out for me to see; and only then, as I got a closer look, did I realize that it was not a snake at all – *it was the fan-belt of my Lagonda!*

All the awful implications of suddenly being stranded in this outlandish place with this disgusting man came flooding over me as I sat there staring dumbly at my broken fan-belt.

'You can see,' the Arab was saying, 'it was hanging on by a single thread. A good thing I noticed it.'

I took it from him and examined it closely. 'You cut it!' I cried.

'Cut it?' he answered softly. 'Why should I cut it?'

To be perfectly honest, it was impossible for me to judge whether he had or had not cut it. If he had, then he had also taken the trouble to fray the severed ends with some instrument to make it look like an ordinary break. Even so, my guess was that he *had* cut it, and if I was right then the implications were more sinister than ever.

'I suppose you know I can't go on without a fan-belt?'
I said.

He grinned again with that awful mutilated mouth,
showing ulcerated gums. 'If you go now,' he said, 'you will
boil over in three minutes.'

'So what do you suggest?'

'I shall get you another fan-belt.'

'You will?'

'Of course. There is a telephone here, and if you will
pay for the call, I will telephone to Ismailia. And if they
haven't got one in Ismailia, I will telephone to Cairo.
There is no problem.'

'No problem!' I shouted, getting out of the car. 'And
when, pray, do you think the fan-belt is going to arrive in
this ghastly place?'

'There is a mail-truck comes through every morning
about ten o'clock. You would have it tomorrow.'

The man had all the answers. He never even had to
think before replying.

This bastard, I thought, *has cut fan-belts before.*

I was very alert now, and watching him closely.

'They will not have a fan-belt for a machine of this
make in Ismailia,' I said. 'It would have to come from the
agents in Cairo. I will telephone them myself.' The fact
that there was a telephone gave me some comfort. The
telephone poles had followed the road all the way across
the desert, and I could see the two wires leading into the
hut from the nearest pole. 'I will ask the agents in Cairo to
set out immediately for this place in a special vehicle,' I
said.

The Arab looked along the road towards Cairo, some two hundred miles away. 'Who is going to drive six hours here and six hours back to bring a fan-belt?' he said. 'The mail will be just as quick.'

'Show me the telephone,' I said, starting towards the hut. Then a nasty thought struck me, and I stopped.

How could I possibly use this man's contaminated instrument? The earpiece would have to be pressed against my ear, and the mouthpiece would almost certainly touch my mouth; and I didn't give a damn what the doctors said about the impossibility of catching syphilis from remote contact. A syphilitic mouthpiece was a syphilitic mouthpiece, and you wouldn't catch *me* putting it anywhere near *my* lips, thank you very much. I wouldn't even enter his hut.

I stood there in the sizzling heat of the afternoon and looked at the Arab with his ghastly diseased face, and the Arab looked back at me, as cool and unruffled as you please.

'You want the telephone?' he asked.

'No,' I said. 'Can you read English?'

'Oh, yes.'

'Very well. I shall write down for you the name of the agents and the name of this car, and also my own name. They know me there. You will then tell them what is wanted. And listen . . . tell them to dispatch a special car immediately at my expense. I will pay them well. And if they won't do that, tell them they *have* to get the fan-belt to Ismailia in time to catch the mail-truck. You understand?'

'There is no problem,' the Arab said.

So I wrote down what was necessary on a piece of paper and gave it to him. He walked away with that slow, stamping tread towards the hut, and disappeared inside. I closed the bonnet of the car. Then I went back and sat in the driver's seat to think things out.

I poured myself another whisky, and lit a cigarette. There must be *some* traffic on this road. Somebody would surely come along before nightfall. But would that help me? No, it wouldn't – unless I were prepared to hitch a ride and leave the Lagonda and all my baggage behind to the tender mercies of the Arab. Was I prepared to do that? I didn't know. Probably yes. But if I were forced to stay the night, I would lock myself in the car and try to keep awake as much as possible. On no account would I enter the shack where that creature lived. Nor would I touch his food. I had whisky and water, and I had half a watermelon and a slab of chocolate. That was ample.

The heat was pretty bad. The thermometer in the car was still around 104°. It was hotter outside in the sun. I was perspiring freely. My God, what a place to get stranded in! And what a companion!

After about fifteen minutes, the Arab came out of the hut. I watched him all the way to the car.

'I talked to garage in Cairo,' he said, pushing his face through the window. 'Fan-belt will arrive tomorrow by mail-truck. Everything arranged.'

'Did you ask them about sending it at once?'

'They said impossible,' he answered.

'You're sure you asked them?'

303

He inclined his head to one side and gave me that sly insolent grin. I turned away and waited for him to go. He stayed where he was. 'We have house for visitors,' he said. 'You can sleep there very nice. My wife will make food, but you will have to pay.'

'Who else is here besides you and your wife?'

'Another man,' he said. He waved an arm in the direction of the three shacks across the road, and I turned and saw a man standing in the doorway of the middle shack, a short wide man who was dressed in dirty khaki slacks and shirt. He was standing absolutely motionless in the shadow of the doorway, his arms dangling at his sides. He was looking at me.

'Who is he?' I said.

'Saleh.'

'What does he do?'

'He helps.'

'I will sleep in the car,' I said. 'And it will not be necessary for your wife to prepare food. I have my own.' The Arab shrugged and turned away and started back towards the shack where the telephone was. I stayed in the car. What else could I do? It was just after two thirty. In three or four hours' time it would start to get a little cooler. Then I could take a stroll and maybe hunt up a few scorpions. Meanwhile, I had to make the best of things as they were. I reached into the back of the car where I kept my box of books and, without looking, I took out the first one I touched. The box contained thirty or forty of the best books in the world, and all of them could be reread a hundred times and would improve with each reading.

It was immaterial which one I got. It turned out to be *The Natural History of Selborne*. I opened it at random . . .

. . . We had in this village more than twenty years ago an idiot boy, whom I well remember, who, from a child, showed a strong propensity to bees; they were his food, his amusement, his sole object. And as people of this cast have seldom more than one point of view, so this lad exerted all his few faculties on this one pursuit. In winter he dozed away his time, within his father's house, by the fireside, in a kind of torpid state, seldom departing from the chimney-corner; but in the summer he was all alert, and in quest of his game in the fields, and on sunny banks. Honey-bees, bumble-bees, wasps, were his prey wherever he found them; he had no apprehensions from their stings, but would seize them *nudis manibus*, and at once disarm them of their weapons, and suck their bodies for the sake of their honey-bags. Sometimes he would fill his bosom, between his shirt and his skin, with a number of these captives, and sometimes confine them to bottles. He was a very *merops apiaster*, or bee-bird, and very injurious to men that kept bees; for he would slide into their bee-gardens, and, sitting down before the stools, would rap with his fingers on the hives, and so take the bees as they came out. He has been known to overturn hives for the sake of honey, of which he is passionately fond. Where metheglin was making, he would linger around the tubs and vessels, begging a draught of what he called bee-wine. As he ran about, he used to make a humming noise with his lips, resembling the buzzing of bees . . .

I glanced up from the book and looked around me. The motionless man across the road had disappeared. There was nobody in sight. The silence was eerie, and the stillness, the utter stillness and desolation of the place was profoundly oppressive. I knew I was being watched. I knew that every little move I made, every sip of whisky and every puff of a cigarette, was being carefully noticed. I detest violence and I never carry a weapon. But I could have done with one now. For a while, I toyed with the idea of starting the motor and driving on down the road until the engine boiled over. But how far would I get? Not very far in this heat and without a fan. One mile, perhaps, or two at the most . . .

No – to hell with it. I would stay where I was and read my book.

It must have been about an hour later that I noticed a small dark speck moving towards me along the road in the far distance, coming from the Jerusalem direction. I laid aside my book without taking my eyes away from the speck. I watched it growing bigger and bigger. It was travelling at a great speed, at a really amazing speed. I got out of the Lagonda and hurried to the side of the road and stood there, ready to signal the driver to stop.

Closer and closer it came, and when it was about a quarter of a mile away, it began to slow down. Suddenly, I noticed the shape of its radiator. It was a *Rolls-Royce*! I raised an arm and kept it raised, and the big green car with a man at the wheel pulled in off the road and stopped beside my Lagonda.

I felt absurdly elated. Had it been a Ford or a Morris,

I would have been pleased enough, but I would not have been elated. The fact that it was a Rolls – a Bentley would have done equally well, or an Isotta, or another Lagonda – was a virtual guarantee that I would receive all the assistance I required; for whether you know it or not, there is a powerful brotherhood existing among people who own very costly automobiles. They respect one another automatically, and the reason they respect one another is simply that wealth respects wealth. In point of fact, there is nobody in the world that a very wealthy person respects more than another very wealthy person, and because of this, they naturally seek each other out wherever they go. Recognition signals of many kinds are used among them. With the female, the wearing of massive jewels is perhaps the most common; but the costly automobile is also much favoured, and is used by both sexes. It is a travelling placard, a public declaration of affluence, and as such, it is also a card of membership to that excellent unofficial society, the Very-Wealthy-People's Union. I am a member myself of long standing, and am delighted to be one. When I meet another member, as I was about to do now, I feel an immediate rapport. I respect him. We speak the same language. He is one of *us*. I had good reason, therefore, to be elated.

The driver of the Rolls climbed out and came towards me. He was a small dark man with olive skin, and he wore an immaculate white linen suit. Probably a Syrian, I thought. Just possibly a Greek. In the heat of the day he looked as cool as could be.

'Good afternoon,' he said. 'Are you having trouble?'

I greeted him, and then, bit by bit, I told him everything that had happened.

'My dear fellow,' he said in perfect English, 'but my *dear fellow*, how very distressing. What rotten luck. This is no place to get stranded in.'

'It isn't, is it?'

'And you say that a new fan-belt has definitely been ordered?'

'Yes,' I answered, 'if I can rely upon the proprietor of this establishment.'

The Arab, who had emerged from his shack almost before the Rolls had come to a stop, now joined us, and the stranger proceeded to question him swiftly in Arabic about the steps he had taken on my behalf. It seemed to me that the two knew each other pretty well, and it was clear that the Arab was in great awe of the new arrival. He was practically crawling along the ground in his presence.

'Well – that seems to be all right,' the stranger said at last, turning to me. 'But quite obviously you won't be able to move on from here until tomorrow morning. Where were you headed for?'

'Jerusalem,' I said. 'And I don't relish the idea of spending the night in this infernal spot.'

'I should say not, my dear man. That would be most uncomfortable.' He smiled at me, showing exceptionally white teeth. Then he took out a cigarette case, and offered me a cigarette. The case was gold, and on the outside of it there was a thin line of green jade inlaid diagonally from corner to corner. It was a beautiful thing. I accepted the cigarette. He lit it for me, then lit his own.

The stranger took a long pull at his cigarette, inhaling deeply. Then he tilted back his head and blew the smoke up into the sun. 'We shall both get heat-stroke if we stand around here much longer,' he said. 'Will you permit me to make a suggestion?'

'But of course.'

'I do hope you won't consider it presumptuous, coming from a complete stranger . . .'

'Please . . .'

'You can't possibly remain here, so I suggest you come back and stay the night in my house.'

There! The Rolls-Royce was smiling at the Lagonda – smiling at it as it would never have smiled at a Ford or a Morris!

'You mean in Ismailia?' I said.

'No, no,' he answered, laughing. 'I live just around the corner, just over there.' He waved a hand in the direction he had come from.

'But surely you were going to Ismailia? I wouldn't want you to change your plans on my behalf.'

'I wasn't going to Ismailia at all,' he said. 'I was coming down here to collect the mail. My house – and this may surprise you – is quite close to where we are standing. You see that mountain? That's Maghara. I'm immediately behind it.'

I looked at the mountain. It lay about ten miles to the north, a yellow rocky lump, perhaps two thousand feet high. 'Do you really mean that you have a house in the middle of all this . . . this wasteland?' I asked.

'You don't believe me?' he said, smiling.

'Of course I believe you,' I answered. 'Nothing surprises me any more. Except, perhaps,' and here I smiled back at him, 'except when I meet a stranger in the middle of the desert, and he treats me like a brother. I am overwhelmed by your offer.'

'Nonsense, my dear fellow. My motives are entirely selfish. Civilized company is not easy to come by in these parts. I am quite thrilled at the thought of having a guest for dinner. Permit me to introduce myself – Abdul Aziz.' He made a quick little bow.

'Oswald Cornelius,' I said. 'It is a great pleasure.' We shook hands.

'I live partly in Beirut,' he said.

'I live in Paris.'

'Charming. And now – shall we go? Are you ready?'

'But my car,' I said. 'Can I leave it here safely?'

'Have no fear about that. Omar is a friend of mine. He's not much to look at, poor chap, but he won't let you down if you're with me. And the other one, Saleh, is a good mechanic. He'll fit your new fan-belt when it arrives tomorrow. I'll tell him now.'

Saleh, the man from across the road, had walked over while we were talking. Mr Aziz gave him his instructions. He then spoke to both men about guarding the Lagonda. He was brief and incisive. Omar and Saleh stood bowing and scraping. I went across to the Lagonda to get a suitcase. I needed a change of clothes badly.

'Oh, by the way,' Mr Aziz called over to me, 'I usually put on a black tie for dinner.'

'Of course,' I murmured, quickly pushing back my first choice of suitcase and taking another.

'I do it for the ladies mostly. They seem to like dressing themselves up for dinner.'

I turned sharply and looked at him, but he was already getting into his car.

'Ready?' he said.

I took the suitcase and placed it in the back of the Rolls. Then I climbed into the front seat beside him, and we drove off.

During the drive, we talked casually about this and that. He told me that his business was in carpets. He had offices in Beirut and Damascus. His forefathers, he said, had been in the trade for hundreds of years.

I mentioned that I had a seventeenth-century Damascus carpet on the floor of my bedroom in Paris.

'You don't mean it!' he cried, nearly swerving off the road with excitement. 'Is it silk and wool, with the warp made entirely of silk? And has it got a ground of gold and silver threads?'

'Yes,' I said. 'Exactly.'

'But my dear fellow! You mustn't put a thing like that on the floor!'

'It is touched only by bare feet,' I said.

That pleased him. It seemed that he loved carpets almost as much as I loved the blue vases of Tchin-Hoa.

Soon we turned left off the tarred road on to a hard stony track and headed straight over the desert towards the mountain. 'This is my private driveway,' Mr Aziz said. 'It is five miles long.'

'You are even on the telephone,' I said, noticing the poles that branched off the main road to follow his private drive.

And then suddenly a queer thought struck me.

That Arab at the filling-station . . . he also was on the telephone . . .

Might not this, then, explain the fortuitous arrival of Mr Aziz?

Was it possible that my lonely host had devised a clever method of shanghai-ing travellers off the road in order to provide himself with what he called 'civilized company' for dinner? Had he, in fact, given the Arab standing instructions to immobilize the cars of all likely-looking persons one after the other as they came along? 'Just cut the fan-belt, Omar. Then phone me up quick. But make sure it's a decent-looking fellow with a good car. Then I'll pop along and see if I think he's worth inviting to the house . . .'

It was ridiculous, of course.

'I think,' my companion was saying, 'that you are wondering why in the world I should choose to have a house out here in a place like this.'

'Well, yes. I am a bit.'

'Everyone does,' he said.

'*Everyone*,' I said.

'Yes,' he said.

Well, well, I thought – everyone.

'I live here,' he said, 'because I have a peculiar affinity

with the desert. I am drawn to it the same way as a sailor is drawn to the sea. Does that seem so very strange to you?'

'No,' I answered, 'it doesn't seem strange at all.'

He paused and took a pull at his cigarette. Then he said, 'That is one reason. But there is another. Are you a family man, Mr Cornelius?'

'Unfortunately not,' I answered cautiously.

'I am,' he said. 'I have a wife and a daughter. Both of them, in my eyes at any rate, are very beautiful. My daughter is just eighteen. She has been to an excellent boarding-school in England, and she is now . . .' he shrugged . . . 'she is now just sitting around and waiting until she is old enough to get married. But this waiting period – what does one do with a beautiful young girl during that time? I can't let her loose. She is far too desirable for that. When I take her to Beirut, I see the men hanging around her like wolves waiting to pounce. It drives me nearly out of my mind. I know all about men, Mr Cornelius. I know how they behave. It is true, of course, that I am not the only father who has had this problem. But the others seem somehow able to face it and accept it. They let their daughters go. They just turn them out of the house and look the other way. I cannot do that. I simply *cannot bring* myself to do it! I refuse to allow her to be mauled by every Achmed, Ali and Hamil that comes along. And that, you see, is the other reason why I live in the desert – to protect my lovely child for a few more years from the wild beasts. Did you say that you had no family at all, Mr Cornelius?'

'I'm afraid that's true.'

'Oh.' He seemed disappointed. 'You mean you've never been married?'

'Well . . . no,' I said. 'No, I haven't.' I waited for the next inevitable question. It came about a minute later.

'Have you never *wanted* to get married and have children?'

They all asked that one. It was simply another way of saying, 'Are you, in that case, homosexual?'

'Once,' I said. 'Just once.'

'What happened?'

'There was only one person ever in my life, Mr Aziz . . . and after she went . . .' I sighed.

'You mean she died?'

I nodded, too choked up to answer.

'My dear fellow,' he said. 'Oh, I am so sorry. Forgive me for intruding.'

We drove on for a while in silence.

'It's amazing,' I murmured, 'how one loses all interest in matters of the flesh after a thing like that. I suppose it's the shock. One never gets over it.'

He nodded sympathetically, swallowing it all.

'So now I just travel around trying to forget. I've been doing it for years . . .'

We had reached the foot of Mount Maghara now and were following the track as it curved round the mountain towards the side that was invisible from the road – the north side. 'As soon as we round the next bend you'll see the house,' Mr Aziz said.

We rounded the bend . . . and there it was! I blinked

and stared, and I tell you that for the first few seconds I literally could not believe my eyes. I saw before me a white castle – I mean it – a *tall, white castle* with turrets and towers and little spires all over it, standing like a fairy-tale in the middle of a small splash of green vegetation on the lower slope of the blazing-hot, bare, yellow mountain! It was fantastic! It was straight out of Hans Christian Andersen or Grimm. I had seen plenty of romantic-looking Rhine and Loire valley castles in my time, but never before had I seen anything with such a slender, graceful, fairy-tale quality as this! The greenery, as I observed when we drew closer, was a pretty garden of lawns and date-palms, and there was a high white wall going all the way round to keep out the desert.

'Do you approve?' my host asked, smiling.

'It's fabulous!' I said. 'It's like all the fairy-tale castles in the world made into one.'

'That's exactly what it is!' he cried. 'It's a fairy-tale castle! I built it especially for my daughter, my beautiful Princess.'

And the beautiful Princess is imprisoned within its walls by her strict and jealous father, King Abdul Aziz, who refuses to allow her the pleasures of masculine company. But watch out, for here comes Prince Oswald Cornelius to the rescue! Unbeknownst to the King, he is going to ravish the beautiful Princess, and make her very happy.

'You have to admit it's different,' Mr Aziz said.

'It is that.'

'It is also nice and private. I sleep very peacefully here. So does the Princess. No unpleasant young men are likely to come climbing in through *those* windows during the night.'

'Quite so,' I said.

'It used to be a small oasis,' he went on. 'I bought it from the government. We have ample water for the house, the swimming-pool and three acres of garden.'

We drove through the main gates, and I must say it was wonderful to come suddenly into a miniature paradise of green lawns and flowerbeds and palm trees. Everything was in perfect order, and water-sprinklers were playing on the lawns. When we stopped at the front door of the house, two servants in spotless gallabiyahs and scarlet tarbooshes ran out immediately, one to each side of the car, to open the doors for us.

Two servants? But would both of them have come out like that unless they'd been expecting *two* people? I doubted it. More and more, it began to look as though my odd little theory about being shanghaied as a dinner guest was turning out to be correct. It was all very amusing.

My host ushered me in through the front door, and at once I got that lovely shivery feeling that comes over the skin as one walks suddenly out of intense heat into an air-conditioned room. I was standing in the hall. The floor was of green marble. On my right, there was a wide archway leading to a large room, and I received a fleeting impression of cool white walls, fine pictures and superlative Louis XV furniture. What a place to find oneself in, in the middle of the Sinai Desert!

And now a woman was coming slowly down the stairs. My host had turned away to speak to the servants, and he didn't see her at once, so when she reached the bottom step, the woman paused, and she laid her naked arm like a white anaconda along the rail of the banister, and there she stood, looking at me as though she were Queen Semiramis on the steps of Babylon, and I was a candidate who might or might not be to her taste. Her hair was jet-black, and she had a figure that made me wet my lips.

When Mr Aziz turned and saw her, he said, 'Oh darling, there you are. I've brought you a guest. His car broke down at the filling-station – such rotten luck – so I asked him to come back and stay the night. Mr Cornelius . . . my wife.'

'How very nice,' she said quietly, coming forward.

I took her hand and raised it to my lips. 'I am overcome by your kindness, madame,' I murmured. There was, upon that hand of hers, a diabolical perfume. It was almost exclusively animal. The subtle, sexy secretions of the sperm-whale, the male musk-deer and the beaver were all there, pungent and obscene beyond words; they dominated the blend completely, and only faint traces of the clean vegetable oils – lemon, cajuput and zeroli – were allowed to come through. It was superb! And another thing I noticed in the flash of that first moment was this: when I took her hand, she did not, as other women do, let it lie limply across my palm like a fillet of raw fish. Instead, she placed her thumb *underneath* my hand, with the fingers on top; and thus she was able to – and I swear she did – exert a gentle but suggestive pressure upon my hand as I administered the conventional kiss.

'Where is Diana?' asked Mr Aziz.

'She's out by the pool,' the woman said. And turning to me, 'Would *you* like a swim, Mr Cornelius? You must be roasted after hanging around that awful filling-station.'

She had huge velvet eyes, so dark they were almost black, and when she smiled at me, the end of her nose moved upwards, distending the nostrils.

There and then, Prince Oswald Cornelius decided that he cared not one whit about the beautiful Princess who was held captive in the castle by the jealous King. He would ravish the Queen instead.

'Well . . .' I said.

'I'm going to have one,' Mr Aziz said.

'Let's all have one,' his wife said. 'We'll lend you a pair of trunks.'

I asked if I might go up to my room first and get out a clean shirt and clean slacks to put on after the swim, and my hostess said, 'Yes, of course,' and told one of the servants to show me the way. He took me up two flights of stairs, and we entered a large white bedroom which had in it an exceptionally large double-bed. There was a well-equipped bathroom leading off to one side, with a pale-blue bathtub and a bidet to match. Everywhere, things were scrupulously clean and very much to my liking. While the servant was unpacking my case, I went over to the window and looked out, and I saw the great blazing desert sweeping in like a yellow sea all the way from the horizon until it met the white garden wall just below me, and there, within the wall, I could see the swimming-pool, and beside the pool there was a girl lying on her back in the shade of a big pink parasol. The girl was wearing a white swimming-costume, and she was reading a book. She had long slim legs and black hair. She was the Princess.

What a set-up, I thought. The white castle, the comfort, the cleanliness, the air-conditioning, the two dazzlingly beautiful females, the watchdog husband, and a whole evening to work in! The situation was so perfectly designed for my entertainment that it would have been impossible to improve upon it. The problems that lay ahead appealed to me very much. A simple straightforward seduction did not amuse me any more. There was no artistry in that sort of thing; and I can assure you that had I been able, by waving a magic wand, to make Mr Abdul Aziz, the jealous watchdog, disappear for the night, I would not have done so. I wanted no pyrrhic victories.

When I left the room, the servant accompanied me. We descended the first flight of stairs, and then, on the landing of the floor below my own, I paused and said casually, 'Does the whole family sleep on this floor?'

'Oh, yes,' the servant said. 'That is the master's room there' – indicating a door – 'and next to it is Mrs Aziz. Miss Diana is opposite.'

Three separate rooms. All very close together. Virtually impregnable. I tucked the information away in my mind and went on down to the pool. My host and hostess were there before me.

'This is my daughter, Diana,' my host said.

The girl in the white swimming-suit stood up and I kissed her hand. 'Hello, Mr Cornelius,' she said.

She was using the same heavy animal perfume as her mother – ambergris, musk and castor! What a smell it had – bitchy, brazen and marvellous! I sniffed at it like a dog. She was, I thought, even more beautiful than the parent, if that were possible. She had the same large velvety eyes, the same black hair, and the same shape of face; but her legs were unquestionably longer, and there was something about her body that gave it a slight edge over the older woman's: it was more sinuous, more snaky and almost certain to be a good deal more flexible. But the older woman, who was probably thirty-seven and looked no more than twenty-five, had a spark in her eye that her daughter could not possibly match.

Eeny, meeny, miny, mo – just a little while ago, Prince Oswald had sworn that he would ravish the Queen alone, and to hell with the Princess. But now that he had seen the Princess in the flesh, he did not know which one to prefer. Both of them, in their different ways, held forth a promise of innumerable delights, the one innocent and eager, the other expert and voracious. The truth of the matter was that he would like to have them both – the Princess as an hors d'œuvre, and the Queen as the main dish.

'Help yourself to a pair of trunks in the changing-room, Mr Cornelius,' Mrs Aziz was saying, so I went into the hut and changed, and when I came out again the three of them were already splashing about in the water. I dived in and joined them. The water was so cold it made me gasp.

'I thought that would surprise you,' Mr Aziz said, laughing. 'It's cooled. I keep it at sixty-five degrees. It's more refreshing in this climate.'

Later, when the sun began dropping lower in the sky, we all sat around in our wet swimming-clothes while a servant brought us pale, ice-cold martinis, and it was at this point that I began, very slowly, very cautiously, to seduce the two ladies in my own particular fashion. Normally, when I am given a free hand, this is not especially difficult for me to do. The curious little talent that I happen to possess – the ability to hypnotize a woman with words – very seldom lets me down. It is not, of course, done only with words. The words themselves, the innocuous, superficial words, are spoken only by the mouth, whereas the real message, the improper and exciting promise, comes from all the limbs and organs of the body, and is transmitted through the eyes. More than that I cannot honestly tell you about how it is done. The point is that it works. It works like cantharides. I believe that I could sit down opposite the Pope's wife, if he had one, and within fifteen minutes, were I to try hard enough, she would be leaning towards me over the table with her lips apart and her eyes glazed with desire. It is a minor talent, not a great one, but I am none the less thankful to have had it bestowed upon me, and I have done my best at all times to see that it has not been wasted.

So the four of us, the two wondrous women, the little man and myself, sat close together in a semicircle beside the swimming-pool, lounging in deck-chairs and sipping our drinks and feeling the warm six o'clock sunshine upon our skin. I was in good form. I made them laugh a great deal. The story about the greedy old Duchess of Glasgow putting her hand in the chocolate box and getting nipped by one of my scorpions had the daughter falling out of her chair with mirth; and when I described in detail the interior of my spider breeding-house in the garden outside Paris, both ladies began wriggling with revulsion and pleasure.

It was at this stage that I noticed the eyes of Mr Abdul

Aziz resting upon me in a good-humoured, twinkling kind of way. 'Well, well,' the eyes seemed to be saying, 'we are glad to see that you are not quite so disinterested in women as you led us to believe in the car . . . Or is it, perhaps, that these congenial surroundings are helping you to forget that great sorrow of yours at last . . .' Mr Aziz smiled at me, showing his pure white teeth. It was a friendly smile. I gave him a friendly smile back. What a friendly little fellow he was. He was genuinely delighted to see me paying so much attention to the ladies. So far, then, so good.

I shall skip very quickly over the next few hours, for it was not until after midnight that anything really tremendous happened to me. A few brief notes will suffice to cover the intervening period:

At seven o'clock, we all left the swimming-pool and returned to the house to dress for dinner.

At eight o'clock, we assembled in the big living-room to drink another cocktail. The two ladies were both superbly turned out, and sparkling with jewels. Both of them wore low-cut, sleeveless evening-dresses which had come, without any doubt at all, from some great fashion house in Paris. My hostess was in black, her daughter in pale blue, and the scent of that intoxicating perfume was everywhere about them. What a pair they were! The older woman had that slight forward hunch to her shoulders which one sees only in the most passionate and practised of females; for in the same way as a horsey woman will become bandy-legged from sitting constantly upon a horse, so a woman of great passion will develop a curious roundness of the shoulders from continually embracing men. It is an occupational deformity, and the noblest of them all.

The daughter was not yet old enough to have acquired this singular badge of honour, but with her it was enough for me simply to stand back and observe the shape of her body and to notice the splendid sliding motion of her thighs underneath the tight silk dress as she wandered about the room. She had a line of tiny soft golden hairs growing all the way up the exposed length of her spine, and when I stood behind her it was difficult to resist the temptation of running my knuckles up and down those lovely vertebrae.

At eight thirty, we moved into the dining-room. The dinner that followed was a really magnificent affair, but I shall waste no time here describing food or wine. Throughout the meal I continued to play most delicately and insidiously upon the sensibilities of the women, employing every skill that I possessed; and by the time the dessert arrived, they were melting before my eyes like butter in the sun.

After dinner we returned to the living-room for coffee and brandy, and then, at my host's suggestion, we played a couple of rubbers of bridge.

By the end of the evening, I knew for certain that I had done my work well. The old magic had not let me down. Either of the two ladies, should circumstances permit, was mine for the asking. I was not deluding myself over this. It was a straightforward, obvious fact. It stood out a mile. The face of my hostess was bright with excitement, and whenever she looked at me across the card table, those huge dark velvety eyes would grow bigger and bigger, and the nostrils would dilate, and the mouth would open slightly to reveal the tip of a moist pink tongue squeezing through between the teeth. It was a marvellously lascivious gesture, and more than once it caused me to trump my own trick. The daughter was less daring but equally direct. Each time her eyes met mine, and that was often enough, she would raise her brows just the tiniest fraction of a centimetre, as though asking a question; then she would make a quick sly little smile, supplying the answer.

'I think it's time we all went to bed,' Mr Aziz said, examining his watch. 'It's after eleven. Come along, my dears.'

Then a queer thing happened. At once, without a second's hesitation and without another glance in my direction, both ladies rose and made for the door! It was astonishing. It left me stunned. I didn't know what to make of it. It was the quickest thing I'd ever seen. And yet it wasn't as though Mr Aziz had spoken angrily. His voice, to me at any rate, had sounded as pleasant as ever. But now he was already turning out the lights, indicating clearly that he wished me also to retire. What a blow! I had expected at least to receive a whisper from either the wife or the daughter before we separated for the night, just a quick three or four words telling me where to go and when; but instead, I was left standing like a fool beside the card table while the two ladies glided out of the room.

My host and I followed them up the stairs. On the landing of the first floor, the mother and daughter stood side by side, waiting for me.

'Goodnight, Mr Cornelius,' my hostess said.

'Goodnight, Mr Cornelius,' the daughter said.

'Goodnight, my dear fellow,' Mr Aziz said. 'I do hope you have everything you want.'

They turned away, and there was nothing for me to do but continue slowly, reluctantly, up the second flight of stairs to my own room. I entered it and closed the door. The heavy brocade curtains had already been drawn by one of the servants, but I parted them and leaned out of the window to take a look at the night. The air was still and warm, and a brilliant moon was shining over the desert. Below me, the swimming-pool in the moonlight looked something like an enormous glass mirror lying flat on the lawn, and beside it I could see the four deck-chairs we had been sitting in earlier.

Well, well, I thought. What happens now?

One thing I knew I must not do in this house was to venture out of my room and go prowling around the corridors. That would be suicide. I had learned many years ago that there are three breeds of husband with whom one must never take unnecessary risks – the Bulgarian, the Greek and the Syrian. None of them, for some reason, resents you flirting quite openly with his wife, but he will kill you at once if he catches you getting into her bed. Mr Aziz was a Syrian. A degree of prudence was therefore essential, and if any move were going to be made now, it must be made not by me but by one of the two women, for only she (or they) would know precisely what was safe and what was dangerous. Yet I had to admit that after witnessing the way in which my host had called them both to heel four minutes ago, there was very little hope of further action in the near future. The trouble was, though, that I had gotten myself so infernally steamed up.

I undressed and took a long cold shower. That helped. Then, because I have never been able to sleep in the moonlight, I made sure that the curtains were tightly drawn together. I got into bed, and for the next hour or so I lay reading some more of Gilbert White's *Natural History of Selborne*. That also helped, and at last, somewhere between midnight and one a.m., there came a time when I was able to switch out the light and prepare myself for sleep without altogether too many regrets.

I was just beginning to doze off when I heard some tiny sounds. I recognized them at once. They were sounds that I had heard many times before in my life, and yet they were still, for me, the most thrilling and evocative in the whole world. They consisted of a series of little soft metallic noises, of metal grating gently against metal, and they were made, they were always made by somebody who was very slowly, very cautiously, turning the handle of one's door from the outside. Instantly, I became wide awake. But I did not move. I simply opened my eyes and stared in the direction of the door; and I can remember wishing at that moment for a gap in the curtain, for just a small thin shaft of moonlight to come in from outside so that I could at least catch a glimpse of the shadow of the lovely form that was about to enter. But the room was as dark as a dungeon.

I did not hear the door open. No hinge squeaked. But suddenly a little gust of air swept through the room and rustled the curtains and a moment later I heard the soft thud of wood against wood as the door was carefully closed again. Then came the click of the latch as the handle was released.

Next, I heard feet tiptoeing towards me over the carpet.

For one horrible second, it occurred to me that this might just possibly be Mr Abdul Aziz creeping in upon me with a long knife in his hand, but then all at once a warm extensile body was bending over mine, and a woman's voice was whispering in my ear, '*Don't make a sound!*'

'My dearest beloved,' I said, wondering which one of them it was, 'I knew you'd . . .' Instantly her hand came over my mouth.

'*Please!*' she whispered. '*Not another word!*'

I didn't argue. My lips had many better things to do than that. So had hers.

Here I must pause. This is not like me at all – I know that. But just for once, I wish to be excused a detailed description of the great scene that followed. I have my own reasons for this and I beg you to respect them. In any case, it will do you no harm to exercise your own imagination for a change, and if you wish, I will stimulate it a little by saying simply and truthfully that of the many thousands and thousands of women I have known in my time, none has transported me to greater extremes of ecstasy than this lady of the Sinai Desert. Her dexterity was amazing. Her passion was intense. Her range was unbelievable. At every turn, she was ready with some new and intricate manoeuvre. And to cap it all, she possessed the subtlest and most recondite style I have ever encountered. She was a great artist. She was a genius.

All this, you will probably say, indicated clearly that my visitor must have been the older woman. You would be wrong. It indicated nothing. True genius is a gift of birth. It has very little to do with age; and I can assure you I had no way of knowing for certain which of them it was in the darkness of that room. I wouldn't have bet a penny on it either way. At one moment, after some particularly boisterous cadenza, I would be convinced it was the wife. *It must be the wife!* Then suddenly the whole tempo would begin to change, and the melody would become so childlike and innocent that I found myself swearing it was the daughter. *It must be the daughter!*

Maddening it was not to know the true answer. It tantalized me. It also humbled me, for, after all, a connoisseur, a supreme connoisseur, should always be able to guess the vintage without seeing the label on the bottle. But this one really had me beat. At one point, I reached for cigarettes, intending to solve the mystery in the flare of a match, but her hand was on me in a flash, and cigarettes and matches both were snatched away and flung across the room. More than once, I began to whisper the question itself into her ear, but I never got three words out before the hand shot up again and smacked itself over my mouth. Rather violently, too.

Very well, I thought. Let it be for now. Tomorrow morning, downstairs in the daylight, I shall know by the glow on the face, by the way the eyes look back into mine, and by a hundred other little tell-tale signs. I shall also know by the marks that my teeth have made on the left side of the neck, above the dress line. A rather wily move, that one, I thought, and so perfectly timed – my vicious bite was administered during the height of her passion – that she never for one moment realized the significance of the act.

It was altogether a most memorable night, and at least four hours must have gone by before she gave me a final fierce embrace, and slipped out of the room as quickly as she had come in.

The next morning I did not awaken until after ten o'clock. I got out of bed and drew open the curtains. It was another brilliant, hot, desert day. I took a leisurely bath, then dressed myself as carefully as ever. I felt relaxed and chipper. It made me very happy to think that I could still summon a woman to my room with my eyes alone, even in middle-age. And what a woman! It would be fascinating to find out which one of them she was. I would soon know.

I made my way slowly down the two flights of stairs.

'Good morning, my dear fellow, good morning!' Mr Aziz said, rising from a small desk he had been writing at in the living-room. 'Did you have a good night?'

'Excellent, thank you,' I answered, trying not to sound smug.

He came and stood close to me, smiling with his very white teeth. His shrewd little eyes rested on my face and moved over it slowly, as though searching for something.

'I have good news for you,' he said. 'They called up from B'ir Rawd Salim five minutes ago and said your new fan-belt had arrived by the mail-truck. Saleh is fitting it on now. It'll be ready in an hour. So when you've had some breakfast, I'll drive you over and you can be on your way.'

I told him how grateful I was.

'We'll be sorry to see you go,' he said. 'It's been an immense pleasure for all of us having you drop in like this, an immense pleasure.'

I had my breakfast alone in the dining-room. Afterwards, I returned to the living-room to smoke a cigarette while my host continued writing at his desk.

'Do forgive me,' he said. 'I just have a couple of things to finish here. I won't be long. I've arranged for your case to be packed and put in the car, so you have nothing to worry about. Sit down and enjoy your cigarette. The ladies ought to be down any minute now.'

The wife arrived first. She came sailing into the room looking more than ever like the dazzling Queen Semiramis of the Nile, and the first thing I noticed about her was the pale-green chiffon scarf knotted casually round her neck! Casually but carefully! So carefully that no part of the skin of the neck was visible. The woman went straight over to her husband and kissed him on the cheek. 'Good morning, my darling,' she said.

You cunning beautiful bitch, I thought.

'Good *morning*, Mr Cornelius,' she said gaily, coming over to sit in the chair opposite mine. 'Did you have a good night? I do hope you had everything you wanted.'

Never in my life have I seen such a sparkle in a woman's eyes as I saw in hers that morning, nor such a glow of pleasure in a woman's face.

'I had a very good night indeed, thank *you*,' I answered, showing her that I knew.

She smiled and lit a cigarette. I glanced over at Mr Aziz,

who was still writing away busily at the desk with his back to us. He wasn't paying the slightest attention to his wife or to me. He was, I thought, exactly like all the other poor cuckolds that I had ever created. Not one of them would believe that it could happen to him, not right under his own nose.

'Good morning, everybody!' cried the daughter, sweeping into the room. 'Good morning, Daddy! Good morning, Mummy!' She gave them each a kiss. 'Good morning, Mr Cornelius!' She was wearing a pair of pink slacks and a rust-coloured blouse, and I'll be damned if she didn't also have a scarf tied carelessly but carefully round her neck! A chiffon scarf!

'Did you have a decent night?' she asked, perching herself like a young bride on the arm of my chair, arranging herself in such a way that one of her thighs rested against my forearm. I leaned back and looked at her closely. She looked back at me and winked. She actually winked! Her face was glowing and sparkling every bit as much as her mother's, and if anything, she seemed even more pleased with herself than the older woman.

I felt pretty confused. Only one of them had a bite mark to conceal, yet both of them had covered their necks with scarves. I conceded that this might be a coincidence, but on the face of it, it looked much more like a conspiracy to me. It looked as though they were both working closely together to keep me from discovering the truth. But what an extraordinarily screwy business! And what was the purpose of it all? And in what other peculiar ways, might I ask, did they plot and plan together among themselves? Had they drawn lots or something the night before? Or did they simply take it in turns with visitors? I *must* come back again, I told myself, for another visit as soon as possible just to see what happens the next time. In fact, I might motor down specially from Jerusalem in a day or two. It would be easy, I reckoned, to get myself invited again.

'Are you ready, Mr Cornelius?' Mr Aziz said, rising from his desk.

'Quite ready,' I answered.

The ladies, sleek and smiling, led the way outside to where the big green Rolls-Royce was waiting. I kissed their hands and murmured a million thanks to each of them. Then I got into the front seat beside my host, and we drove off. The mother and daughter waved. I lowered my window and waved back. Then we were out of the garden and into the desert, following the stony yellow track as it skirted the base of Mount Maghara, with the telegraph poles marching along beside us.

During the journey, my host and I conversed pleasantly about this and that. I was at pains to be as agreeable as possible because my one object now was to get myself invited to stay at the house again. If I didn't succeed in getting *him* to ask *me*, then I should have to ask *him*. I would do it at the last moment. 'Good-bye, my dear friend,' I would say, gripping him warmly by the throat. 'May I have the pleasure of dropping in to see you again if I happen to be passing this way?' And of course he would say yes.

'Did you think I exaggerated when I told you my daughter was beautiful?' he asked me.

'You understated it,' I said. 'She's a raving beauty. I do congratulate you. But your wife is no less lovely. In fact, between the two of them they almost swept me off my feet,' I added, laughing.

'I noticed that,' he said, laughing with me. 'They're a couple of very naughty girls. They do so love to flirt with other men. But why should I mind? There's no harm in flirting.'

'None whatsoever,' I said.

'I think it's gay and fun.'

'It's charming,' I said.

In less than half an hour we had reached the main Ismailia–Jerusalem road. Mr Aziz turned the Rolls on to the black tarmac strip and headed for the filling-station at seventy miles an hour. In a few minutes we would be there. So now I tried moving a little closer to the subject of another visit, fishing gently for an invitation. 'I can't get over your house,' I said. 'I think it's simply wonderful.'

'It is nice, isn't it?'

'I suppose you're bound to get pretty lonely out there, on and off, just the three of you together?'

'It's no worse than anywhere else,' he said. 'People get lonely wherever they are. A desert, or a city – it doesn't make much difference, really. But we do have visitors, you know. You'd be surprised at the number of people who drop in from time to time. Like you, for instance. It was a great pleasure having you with us, my dear fellow.'

'I shall never forget it,' I said. 'It is a rare thing to find kindness and hospitality of that order nowadays.'

I waited for him to tell me that I must come again, but he didn't. A little silence sprang up between us, a slightly uneasy little silence. To bridge it, I said, 'I think yours is the most thoughtful paternal gesture I've ever heard of in my life.'

'Mine?'

'Yes. Building a house right out there in the back of beyond and living in it just for your daughter's sake, to protect her. I think it's remarkable.'

I saw him smile, but he kept his eyes on the road and said nothing. The filling-station and the group of huts were now in sight about a mile ahead of us. The sun was high and it was getting hot inside the car.

'Not many fathers would put themselves out to that extent,' I went on.

Again he smiled, but somewhat bashfully this time, I thought. And then he said, 'I don't deserve *quite* as much credit as you like to give me, really I don't. To be absolutely honest with you, that pretty daughter of mine isn't the only reason for my living in such splendid isolation.'

'I know that.'

'You do?'

'You told me. You said the other reason was the desert. You loved it, you said, as a sailor loves the sea.'

'So I did. And it's quite true. But there's still a third reason.'

'Oh, and what is that?'

He didn't answer me. He sat quite still with his hands on the wheel and his eyes fixed on the road ahead.

'I'm sorry,' I said. 'I shouldn't have asked the question. It's none of my business.'

'No, no, that's quite all right,' he said. 'Don't apologize.'

I stared out of the window at the desert. 'I think it's hotter than yesterday,' I said. 'It must be well over a hundred already.'

'Yes.'

I saw him shifting a little in his seat, as though trying to get comfortable, and then he said, 'I don't really see why I shouldn't tell you the truth about that house. You don't strike me as being a gossip.'

'Certainly not,' I said.

We were close to the filling-station now, and he had slowed the car down almost to walking-speed to give himself time to say what he had to say. I could see the two Arabs standing beside my Lagonda, watching us.

'That daughter,' he said at length, 'the one you met – she isn't the only daughter I have.'

'Oh, really?'

'I've got another who is five years older than she.'

'And just as beautiful, no doubt,' I said. 'Where does she live? In Beirut?'

'No, she's in the house.'

'In which house? Not the one we've just left?'

'Yes.'

'But I never saw her!'

'Well,' he said, turning suddenly to watch my face, 'maybe not.'

'But why?'

'She has leprosy.'

I jumped.

'Yes, I know,' he said, 'it's a terrible thing. She has the worst kind, too, poor girl. It's called anaesthetic leprosy. It is highly resistant, and almost impossible to cure. If only it were the nodular variety, it would be much easier. But it isn't, and there you are. So when a visitor comes to the house, she keeps to her own apartment, on the third floor . . .'

The car must have pulled into the filling-station about then because the next thing I can remember was seeing Mr Abdul Aziz sitting there looking at me with those small clever black eyes of his, and he was saying, 'But my dear fellow, you mustn't alarm yourself like this. Calm yourself down, Mr Cornelius, calm yourself down! There's absolutely nothing in the world for you to worry about. It is not a very contagious disease. You have to have the most *intimate* contact with the person in order to catch it . . .'

I got out of the car very slowly and stood in the sunshine. The Arab with the diseased face was grinning at me and saying, 'Fan-belt all fixed now. Everything fine.' I reached into my pocket for cigarettes, but my hand was shaking so violently I dropped the packet on the ground. I bent down and retrieved it. Then I got a cigarette out and managed to light it. When I looked up again, I saw the green Rolls-Royce already half a mile down the road, and going away fast.

The Last Act

First published in *Playboy* (January 1966)

Anna was in the kitchen washing a head of Boston lettuce for the family supper when the doorbell rang. The bell itself was on the wall directly above the sink, and it never failed to make her jump if it rang when she happened to be near. For this reason, neither her husband nor any of the children ever used it. It seemed to ring extra loud this time, and Anna jumped extra high.

When she opened the door, two policemen were standing outside. They looked at her out of pale waxen faces, and she looked back at them, waiting for them to say something.

She kept looking at them, but they didn't speak or move. They stood so still and so rigid that they were like two wax figures somebody had put on her doorstep as a joke. Each of them was holding his helmet in front of him in his two hands.

'What is it?' Anna asked.

They were both young, and they were wearing leather gauntlets up to their elbows. She could see their enormous motor-cycles propped up along the edge of the sidewalk behind them, and dead leaves were falling around the motor-cycles and blowing along the sidewalk and the whole of the street was brilliant in the yellow light of a clear, gusty September evening. The taller of the two policemen shifted uneasily on his feet. Then he said quietly, 'Are you Mrs Cooper, ma'am?'

'Yes, I am.'

The other said, 'Mrs Edmund J. Cooper?'

'Yes.' And then slowly it began to dawn upon her that these men, neither of whom seemed anxious to explain his presence, would not be behaving as they were unless they had some distasteful duty to perform.

'Mrs Cooper,' she heard one of them saying, and from the way he said it, as gently and softly as if he were comforting a sick child, she knew at once that he was going to tell her something terrible. A great wave of panic came over her, and she said, 'What happened?'

'We have to inform you, Mrs Cooper . . .'

The policeman paused, and the woman, watching him, felt as though her whole body were shrinking and shrinking and shrinking inside its skin.

'. . . that your husband was involved in an accident on the Hudson River Parkway at approximately five forty-five this evening, and died in the ambulance . . .'

The policeman who was speaking produced the crocodile wallet she had given Ed on their twentieth wedding anniversary, two years back, and as she reached out to take it, she found herself wondering whether it might not still be warm from having been close to her husband's chest only a short while ago.

'If there's anything we can do,' the policeman was saying, 'like calling up somebody to come over . . . some friend or relative maybe . . .'

Anna heard his voice drifting away, then fading out

altogether, and it must have been about then that she began to scream. Soon she became hysterical, and the two policemen had their hands full trying to control her until the doctor arrived some forty minutes later and injected something into her arm.

She was no better, though, when she woke up the following morning. Neither her doctor nor her children were able to reason with her in any way at all, and had she not been kept under almost constant sedation for the next few days, she would undoubtedly have taken her own life. In the brief lucid periods between drug-takings, she acted as though she were demented, calling out her husband's name and telling him that she was coming to join him as soon as she possibly could. It was terrible to listen to her. But in defence of her behaviour, it should be said at once that this was no ordinary husband she had lost.

Anna Greenwood had married Ed Cooper when they were both eighteen, and over the time they were together, they grew to be closer and more dependent upon each other than it is possible to describe in words. Every year that went by, their love became more intense and overwhelming, and towards the end, it had reached such a ridiculous peak that it was almost impossible for them to endure the daily separation caused by Ed's departure for the office in the mornings. When he returned at night he would rush through the house to seek her out, and she, who had heard the noise of the front door slamming, would drop everything and rush simultaneously in his direction, meeting him head on, recklessly, at full speed, perhaps halfway up the stairs, or on the landing, or between the kitchen and the hall; and as they came together, he would take her in his arms and hug her and kiss her for minutes on end as though she were yesterday's bride. It was wonderful. It was so utterly unbelievably wonderful that one is very nearly able to understand why she should have had no desire and no heart to continue living in a world where her husband did not exist any more.

Her three children, Angela (twenty), Mary (nineteen) and Billy (seventeen and a half), stayed around her constantly right from the start of the catastrophe. They adored their mother, and they certainly had no intention of letting her commit suicide if they could help it. They worked hard and with loving desperation to convince her that life could still be worth living, and it was due entirely to them that she managed in the end to come out of the nightmare and climb back slowly into the ordinary world.

Four months after the disaster, she was pronounced 'moderately safe' by the doctors, and she was able to return, albeit rather listlessly, to the old routine of running the house and doing the shopping and cooking the meals for her grown-up children.

But then what happened?

Before the snows of that winter had melted away, Angela married a young man from Rhode Island and went off to live in the suburbs of Providence.

A few months later, Mary married a fair-haired giant from a town called Slayton, in Minnesota, and away she flew for ever and ever and ever. And although Anna's heart was now beginning to break all over again into tiny

pieces, she was proud to think that neither of the two girls
had the slightest inkling of what was happening to her.
('Oh, Mummy, isn't it wonderful!' 'Yes, my darling, I think
it's the most beautiful wedding there's ever been! I'm even
more excited than you are!' etc. etc.)

And then, to put the lid on everything, her beloved
Billy, who had just turned eighteen, went off to begin his
first year at Yale.

So all at once, Anna found herself living in a completely empty house.

It is an awful feeling, after twenty-three years of boisterous, busy, magical family life, to come down alone to
breakfast in the mornings, to sit there in silence with a
cup of coffee and a piece of toast, and to wonder what you
are going to do with the day that lies ahead. The room you
are sitting in, which has heard so much laughter, and seen
so many birthdays, so many Christmas trees, so many
presents being opened, is quiet now and feels curiously
cold. The air is heated and the temperature itself is normal, but the place still makes you shiver. The clock has
stopped because you were never the one who wound it in
the first place. A chair stands crooked on its legs, and you
sit staring at it, wondering why you hadn't noticed it
before. And when you glance up again, you have a sudden
panicky feeling that all the four walls of the room have
begun creeping in upon you very very slowly when you
weren't looking.

In the beginning, she would carry her coffee cup over
to the telephone and start calling up friends. But all her
friends had husbands and children, and although they

were always as nice and warm and cheerful as they could possibly be, they simply could not spare the time to sit and chat with a desolate lady from across the way first thing in the morning. So then she started calling up her married daughters instead.

They, also, were sweet and kind to her at all times, but Anna detected, very soon, a subtle change in their attitudes towards her. She was no longer number one in their lives. They had husbands now, and were concentrating everything upon them. Gently but firmly, they were moving their mother into the background. It was quite a shock. But she knew they were right. They were absolutely right. She was no longer entitled to impinge upon their lives or to make them feel guilty for neglecting her.

She saw Dr Jacobs regularly, but he wasn't really any help. He tried to get her to talk and she did her best, and sometimes he made little speeches to her full of oblique remarks about sex and sublimation. Anna never properly understood what he was driving at, but the burden of his song appeared to be that she should get herself another man.

She took to wandering around the house and fingering things that used to belong to Ed. She would pick up one of his shoes and put her hand into it and feel the little dents that the ball of his foot and his toes had made upon the sole. She found a sock with a hole in it, and the pleasure it gave her to darn that sock was indescribable. Occasionally, she took out a shirt, a tie and a suit, and laid them on the bed, all ready for him to wear, and once, one rainy Sunday morning, she made an Irish stew . . .

It was hopeless to go on.

So how many pills would she need to make absolutely sure of it this time? She went upstairs to her secret store and counted them. There were only nine. Was that enough? She doubted that it was. Oh, hell. The one thing she was not prepared to face all over again was failure – the rush to the hospital, the stomach-pump, the seventh floor of the Payne Whitney Pavilion, the psychiatrists, the humiliation, the misery of it all . . .

In that case, it would have to be the razor-blade. But the trouble with the razor-blade was that it had to be done properly. Many people failed miserably when they tried to use the razor-blade on the wrist. In fact, nearly all of them failed. They didn't cut deep enough. There was a big artery down there somewhere that simply had to be reached. Veins were no good. Veins made plenty of mess, but they never quite managed to do the trick. Then again, the razor-blade was not an easy thing to hold, not if one had to make a firm incision, pressing it right home all the way, deep deep down. But *she* wouldn't fail. The ones who failed were the ones who actually *wanted* to fail. She wanted to succeed.

She went to the cupboard in the bathroom, searching for blades. There weren't any. Ed's razor was still there, and so was hers. But there was no blade in either of them, and no little packet lying alongside. That was understandable. Such things had been removed from the house on an earlier occasion. But there was no problem. Anyone could buy a packet of razor-blades.

She returned to the kitchen and took the calendar down

from the wall. She chose 23 September, which was Ed's birthday, and wrote r-b (for razor-blades) against the date. She did this on 9 September, which gave her exactly two weeks' grace to put her affairs in order. There was much to be done – old bills to be paid, a new will to be written, the house to be tidied up, Billy's college fees to be taken care of for the next four years, letters to the children, to her own parents, to Ed's mother, and so on and so forth.

Yet, busy as she was, she found that those two weeks, those fourteen long days, were going far too slowly for her liking. She wanted to use the blade, and eagerly every morning she counted the days that were left. She was like a child counting the days before Christmas. For wherever it was that Ed Cooper had gone when he died, even if it were only to the grave, she was impatient to join him.

It was in the middle of this two-week period that her friend Elizabeth Paoletti came calling on her at eight thirty one morning. Anna was making coffee in the kitchen at the time, and she jumped when the bell rang and jumped again when it gave a second long blast.

Liz came sweeping in through the front door, talking non-stop as usual. 'Anna, my darling woman, I need your help! Everyone's down with flu at the office. You've *got* to come! Don't argue with me! I know you can type and I know you haven't got a damn thing in the world to do all day except mope. Just grab your hat and purse and let's get going. Hurry up, girl, hurry up! I'm late as it is!'

Anna said, 'Go away, Liz. Leave me alone.'

'The cab is waiting,' Liz said.

'Please,' Anna said, 'don't try to bully me now. I'm not coming.'

'You are coming,' Liz said. 'Pull yourself together. Your days of glorious martyrdom are over.'

Anna continued to resist, but Liz wore her down, and in the end she agreed to go along just for a few hours.

Elizabeth Paoletti was in charge of an adoption society, one of the best in the city. Nine of the staff were down with flu. Only two were left, excluding herself. 'You don't know a thing about the work,' she said in the cab, 'but you're just going to have to help us all you can . . .'

The office was bedlam. The telephones alone nearly drove Anna mad. She kept running from one cubicle to the next, taking messages that she did not understand. And there were girls in the waiting-room, young girls with ashen stony faces, and it became part of her duty to type their answers on an official form.

'The father's name?'

'Don't know.'

'You've no idea?'

'What's the father's name got to do with it?'

'My dear, if the father is known, then his consent has to be obtained as well as yours before the child can be offered for adoption.'

'You're quite sure about that?'

'Jesus, I told you, didn't I?'

At lunchtime, somebody brought her a sandwich, but there was no time to eat it. At nine o'clock that night, exhausted and famished and considerably shaken by some of the knowledge she had acquired, Anna staggered home, took a stiff drink, fried up some eggs and bacon, and went to bed.

'I'll call for you at eight o'clock tomorrow morning,' Liz had said. 'And for God's sake be ready.' Anna was ready. And from then on she was hooked.

It was as simple as that.

All she'd needed right from the beginning was a good hard job of work to do, and plenty of problems to solve – other people's problems instead of her own.

The work was arduous and often quite shattering emotionally, but Anna was absorbed by every moment of it, and within about – we are skipping right forward now – within about a year and a half, she began to feel moderately happy once again. She was finding it more and more difficult to picture her husband vividly, to see him precisely as he was when he ran up the stairs to meet her, or when he sat across from her at supper in the evenings. The exact sound of his voice was becoming less easy to recall, and even the face itself, unless she glanced at a photograph, was no longer sharply etched in the memory. She still thought about him constantly, but she discovered that she could do so now without bursting into tears, and when she looked back on the way she had behaved a while ago, she felt slightly embarrassed. She started taking a mild interest in her clothes and in her hair, she returned to using lipstick and to shaving the hair from her legs. She enjoyed her food, and when people smiled at her, she smiled right back at them and meant it. In other words, she was back in the swim once again. She was pleased to be alive.

It was at this point that Anna had to go down to Dallas on office business.

Liz's office did not normally operate beyond state lines, but in this instance, a couple who had adopted a baby through the agency had subsequently moved away from New York and gone to live in Texas. Now, five months after the move, the wife had written to say that she no longer wanted to keep the child. Her husband, she announced, had died of a heart attack soon after they'd arrived in Texas. She herself had remarried almost at once, and her new husband 'found it impossible to adjust to an adopted baby . . .'

Now this was a serious situation, and quite apart from the welfare of the child itself, there were all manner of legal obligations involved.

Anna flew down to Dallas in a plane that left New York very early, and she arrived before breakfast. After checking in at her hotel, she spent the next eight hours with the persons concerned in the affair, and by the time she had done all that could be done that day, it was around four thirty in the afternoon and she was utterly exhausted. She took a cab back to the hotel, and went up to her room. She called Liz on the phone to report the situation, then she undressed and soaked herself for a long time in a warm bath. Afterwards, she wrapped up in a towel and lay on the bed, smoking a cigarette.

Her efforts on behalf of the child had so far come to nothing. There had been two lawyers there who had treated her with absolute contempt. How she hated them. She detested their arrogance and their softly spoken hints that nothing she might do would make the slightest difference to their client. One of them kept his feet up on the table all the way through the discussion, and both of them had rolls of fat on their bellies, and the fat spilled out into their shirts like liquid and hung in huge folds over their belted trouser-tops.

Anna had visited Texas many times before in her life, but until now she had never gone there alone. Her visits had always been with Ed, keeping him company on business trips; and during those trips, he and she had often spoken about the Texans in general and about how difficult it was to like them. One could ignore their coarseness and their vulgarity. It wasn't that. But there was, it seemed, a quality of ruthlessness still surviving among these people, something quite brutal, harsh, inexorable, that it was impossible to forgive. They had no bowels of compassion, no pity, no tenderness. The only so-called virtue they possessed – and this they paraded ostentatiously and endlessly to strangers – was a kind of professional benevolence. It was plastered all over them. Their voices, their smiles, were rich and syrupy with it. But it left Anna cold. It left her quite, quite cold inside.

'Why do they love acting so tough?' she used to ask.

'Because they're children,' Ed would answer. 'They're dangerous children who go about trying to imitate their grandfathers. Their grandfathers *were* pioneers. These people aren't.'

It seemed that they lived, these present-day Texans, by a sort of egotistic will, push and be pushed. Everybody was pushing. Everybody was being pushed. And it was all very fine for a stranger in their midst to step aside and announce firmly, 'I will *not* push, and I will *not* be pushed.' That was impossible. It was especially impossible in Dallas. Of all the cities in the state, Dallas was the one that had always disturbed Anna the most. It was such a godless city, she thought, such a rapacious, gripped, iron, godless city. It was a place that had run amok with its money, and no amount of gloss and phony culture and syrupy talk could hide the fact that the great golden fruit was rotten inside.

Anna lay on the bed with her bath towel around her. She was alone in Dallas this time. There was no Ed with her now to envelop her in his incredible strength and love; and perhaps it was because of this that she began, all of a sudden, to feel slightly uneasy. She lit a second cigarette and waited for the uneasiness to pass. It didn't pass; it got worse. A hard little knot of fear was gathering itself in the top of her stomach, and there it stayed, growing bigger every minute. It was an unpleasant feeling, the kind one might experience if one were alone in the house at night and heard, or thought one heard, a footstep in the next room.

In this place there were a million footsteps, and she could hear them all.

She got off the bed and went over to the window, still wrapped in her towel. Her room was on the twenty-second floor, and the window was open. The great city lay pale and milky-yellow in the evening sunshine. The street below was solid with automobiles. The sidewalk was filled with people. Everybody was hustling home from work, pushing and being pushed. She felt the need of a friend. She wanted very badly to have someone to talk to at this moment. She would have liked a house to go to, a house with a family – a wife and husband and children and rooms full of toys, and the husband and wife would fling their arms around her at the front door and cry out, 'Anna! How marvellous to see you! How long can you stay? A week, a month, a year?'

All of a sudden, as so often happens in situations like this, her memory went *click*, and she said aloud, 'Conrad Kreuger! Good heavens above! *He* lives in Dallas . . . at least he used to . . .'

She hadn't seen Conrad since they were classmates in high school, in New York. They were both about seventeen then, and Conrad had been her beau, her love, her everything. For over a year they had gone around together, and each of them had sworn eternal loyalty to the other, with marriage in the near future. Then suddenly Ed Cooper had flashed into her life, and that, of course, had been the end of the romance with Conrad. But Conrad did not seem to have taken the break too badly. It certainly couldn't have *shattered* him, because not more than a month or two later he had started going strong with another girl in the class . . .

Now what was *her* name?

A big handsome bosomy girl she was, with flaming red hair and a peculiar name, a very old-fashioned name. What was it? Arabella? No, not Arabella. Ara-something, though. Araminty? Yes! Araminty it was! And what is more, within a year or so, Conrad Kreuger had married

Araminty and had carried her back with him to Dallas, the place of his birth.

Anna went over to the bedside table and picked up the telephone directory.

Kreuger, Conrad P., MD.

That was Conrad all right. He had always said he was going to be a doctor. The book gave an office number and a residence number.

Should she phone him?

Why not?

She glanced at her watch. It was five twenty. She lifted the receiver and gave the number of his office.

'Doctor Kreuger's surgery,' a girl's voice answered.

'Hello,' Anna said. 'Is Doctor Kreuger there?'

'The doctor is busy right now. May I ask who's calling?'

'Will you please tell him that Anna Greenwood telephoned him.'

'Who?'

'Anna Greenwood.'

'Yes, Miss Greenwood. Did you wish for an appointment?'

'No, thank you.'

'Is there something I can do for you?'

Anna gave the name of her hotel, and asked her to pass it on to Dr Kreuger.

'I'll be very glad to,' the secretary said. 'Good-bye, Miss Greenwood.'

'Good-bye,' Anna said. She wondered whether Dr Conrad P. Kreuger would remember her name after all these years. She believed he would. She lay back again on the bed and began trying to recall what Conrad himself used to look like. Extraordinarily handsome, that he was. Tall ... lean ... big-shouldered ... with almost pure-black hair ... and a marvellous face ... a strong carved face like one of those Greek heroes, Perseus or Ulysses. Above all, though, he had been a very gentle boy, a serious, decent, quiet, gentle boy. He had never kissed her much – only when he said good-bye in the evenings. And he'd never gone in for necking, as all the others had. When he took her home from the movies on Saturday nights, he used to park his old Buick outside her house and sit there in the car beside her, just talking and talking about the future, his future and hers, and how he was going to go back to Dallas to become a famous doctor. His refusal to indulge in necking and all the nonsense that went with it had impressed her no end. He respects me, she used to say. He loves me. And she was probably right. In any event, he had been a nice man, a nice good man. And had it not been for the fact that Ed Cooper was a super-nice, super-good man, she was sure she would have married Conrad Kreuger.

The telephone rang. Anna lifted the receiver. 'Yes,' she said. 'Hello.'

'Anna Greenwood?'

'Conrad Kreuger!'

'My dear Anna! What a fantastic surprise. Good gracious me. After all these years.'

'It's a long time, isn't it.'

'It's a lifetime. Your voice sounds just the same.'

'So does yours.'

'What brings you to our fair city? Are you staying long?'

'No, I have to go back tomorrow. I hope you didn't mind my calling you.'

'Hell, no, Anna. I'm delighted. Are you all right?'

'Yes, I'm fine. I'm fine now. I had a bad time of it for a bit after Ed died . . .'

'What!'

'He was killed in an automobile two and a half years ago.'

'Oh gee, Anna, I *am* sorry. How terrible. I . . . I don't know what to say . . .'

'Don't say anything.'

'You're okay now?'

'I'm fine. Working like a slave.'

'That's the girl . . .'

'How's . . . how's Araminty?'

'Oh, she's fine.'

'Any children?'

'One,' he said. 'A boy. How about you?'

'I have three, two girls and a boy.'

'Well, well, what d'you know! Now listen, Anna . . .'

'I'm listening.'

'Why don't I run over to the hotel and buy you a drink? I'd like to do that. I'll bet you haven't changed one iota.'

'I look old, Conrad.'

'You're lying.'

'I feel old, too.'

'You want a good doctor?'

'Yes. I mean no. Of course I don't. I don't want any more doctors. All I need is . . . well . . .'

THE COMPLETE SHORT STORIES

'Yes?'

'This place worries me, Conrad. I guess I need a friend. That's all I need.'

'You've got one. I have just one more patient to see, and then I'm free. I'll meet you down in the bar, the something room, I've forgotten what it's called, at six, in about half an hour. Will that suit you?'

'Yes,' she said. 'Of course. And . . . thank you, Conrad.' She replaced the receiver, then got up from the bed, and began to dress.

She felt mildly flustered. Not since Ed's death had she been out and had a drink alone with a man. Dr Jacobs would be pleased when she told him about it on her return. He wouldn't congratulate her madly, but he would certainly be pleased. He'd say it was a step in the right direction, a beginning. She still went to him regularly, and now that she had gotten so much better, his oblique references had become far less oblique and he had more than once told her that her depressions and suicidal tendencies would never completely disappear until she had actually and physically 'replaced' Ed with another man.

'But it is impossible to replace a person one has loved to distraction,' Anna had said to him the last time he had brought up the subject. 'Heavens above, doctor, when Mrs Crummlin-Brown's parakeet died last month, her *parakeet*, mind you, not her husband, she was so shook up about it, she swore she'd never have another bird again!'

'Mrs Cooper,' Dr Jacobs had said, 'one doesn't normally have sexual intercourse with a parakeet.'

'Well . . . no . . .'

'That's why it doesn't have to be replaced. But when a husband dies, and the surviving wife is still an active and a healthy woman, she will invariably get a replacement within three years if she possibly can. And vice versa.'

Sex. It was about the only thing that sort of doctor ever thought about. He had sex on the brain.

By the time Anna had dressed and taken the elevator downstairs, it was ten minutes after six. The moment she walked into the bar, a man stood up from one of the tables. It was Conrad. He must have been watching the door. He came across the floor to meet her. He was smiling nervously. Anna was smiling, too. One always does.

'Well, well,' he said. 'Well well well,' and she, expecting the usual peck on the cheek, inclined her face upwards towards his own, still smiling. But she had forgotten how formal Conrad was. He simply took her hand in his and shook it – once. 'This *is* a surprise,' he said. 'Come and sit down.'

The room was the same as any other hotel drinking-room. It was lit by dim lights, and filled with many small tables. There was a saucer of peanuts on each table, and there were leather bench-seats all around the walls. The waiters were rigged out in white jackets and maroon pants. Conrad led her to a corner table, and they sat down facing each other. A waiter was standing over them at once.

'What will you have?' Conrad asked.

'Could I have a martini?'

'Of course. Vodka?'

'No, gin, please.'

'One gin martini,' he said to the waiter. 'No. Make it

two. I've never been much of a drinker, Anna, as you probably remember, but I think this calls for a celebration.'

The waiter went away. Conrad leaned back in his chair and studied her carefully. 'You look pretty good,' he said.

'You look pretty good yourself, Conrad,' she told him. And so he did. It was astonishing how little he had aged in twenty-five years. He was just as lean and handsome as he'd ever been – in fact, more so. His black hair was still black, his eye was clear, and he looked altogether like a man who was no more than thirty years old.

'You *are* older than me, aren't you?' he said.

'What sort of a question is that?' she said, laughing. 'Yes, Conrad, I am exactly one year older than you. I'm forty-two.'

'I thought you were.' He was still studying her with the utmost care, his eyes travelling all over her face and neck and shoulders. Anna felt herself blushing.

'Are you an enormously successful doctor?' she asked. 'Are you the best in town?'

He cocked his head over to one side, right over, so that the ear almost touched the top of the shoulder. It was a mannerism that Anna had always liked. 'Successful?' he said. 'Any doctor can be successful these days in a big city – financially, I mean. But whether or not I am absolutely first rate at my job is another matter. I only hope and pray that I am.'

The drinks arrived and Conrad raised his glass and said, 'Welcome to Dallas, Anna. I'm so pleased you called me up. It's good to see you again.'

'It's good to see you, too, Conrad,' she said, speaking the truth.

He looked at her glass. She had taken a huge first gulp, and the glass was now half empty. 'You prefer gin to vodka?' he asked.

'I do,' she said, 'yes.'

'You ought to change over.'

'Why?'

'Gin is not good for females.'

'It's not?'

'It's very bad for them.'

'I'm sure it's just as bad for males,' she said.

'Actually, no. It isn't nearly so bad for males as it is for females.'

'Why is it bad for females?'

'It just is,' he said. 'It's the way they're built. What kind of work are you engaged in, Anna? And what brought you all the way down to Dallas? Tell me about you.'

'Why is gin bad for females?' she said, smiling at him.

He smiled back at her and shook his head, but he didn't answer.

'Go on,' she said.

'No, let's drop it.'

'You can't leave me up in the air like this,' she said. 'It's not fair.'

After a pause, he said, 'Well, if you really want to know, gin contains a certain amount of the oil which is squeezed out of juniper berries. They use it for flavouring.'

'What does it do?'

'Plenty.'

'Yes, but what?'

'Horrible things.'

'Conrad, don't be shy. I'm a big girl now.'

He was still the same old Conrad, she thought, still as diffident, as scrupulous, as shy as ever. For that she liked him. 'If this drink is really doing horrible things to me,' she said, 'then it is unkind of you not to tell me what those things are.'

Gently, he pinched the lobe of his left ear with the thumb and forefinger of his right hand. Then he said, 'Well, the truth of the matter is, Anna, oil of juniper has a direct inflammatory effect upon the uterus.'

'Now come on!'

'I'm not joking.'

'Mother's ruin,' Anna said. 'It's an old wives' tale.'

'I'm afraid not.'

'But you're talking about women who are pregnant.'

'I'm talking about all women, Anna.' He had stopped smiling now, and he was speaking quite seriously. He seemed to be concerned about her welfare.

'What do you specialize in?' she asked him. 'What kind of medicine? You haven't told me that.'

'Gynaecology and obstetrics.'

'Ah-ha!'

'Have you been drinking gin for many years?' he asked.

'Oh, about twenty,' Anna said.

'Heavily?'

'For heaven's sake, Conrad, stop worrying about my insides. I'd like another martini, please.'

'Of course.'

He called the waiter and said, 'One vodka martini.'

'No,' Anna said, 'gin.'

He sighed and shook his head and said, 'Nobody listens to her doctor these days.'

'You're not my doctor.'

'No,' he said. 'I'm your friend.'

'Let's talk about your wife,' Anna said. 'Is she still as beautiful as ever?'

He waited a few moments, then he said, 'Actually, we're divorced.'

'Oh, no!'

'Our marriage lasted for the grand total of two years. It was hard work to keep it going even that long.'

For some reason, Anna was profoundly shocked. 'But she was such a beautiful girl,' she said. 'What happened?'

'Everything happened, everything you could possibly think of that was bad.'

'And the child?'

'She got him. They always do.' He sounded very bitter. 'She took him back to New York. He comes to see me once a year, in the summer. He's twenty years old now. He's at Princeton.'

'Is he a fine boy?'

'He's a wonderful boy,' Conrad said. 'But I hardly know him. It isn't much fun.'

'And you never married again?'

'No, never. But that's enough about me. Let's talk about you.'

Slowly, gently, he began to draw her out on the subject of her health and the bad times she had gone through after Ed's death. She found she didn't mind talking to him about it, and she told him more or less the whole story.

'But what makes your doctor think you're not completely cured?' he said. 'You don't look very suicidal to me.'

'I don't think I am. Except that sometimes, not often, mind you, but just occasionally, when I get depressed, I have the feeling that it wouldn't take such a hell of a big push to send me over the edge.'

'In what way?'

'I kind of start edging towards the bathroom cupboard.'

'What do you have in the bathroom cupboard?'

'Nothing very much. Just the ordinary equipment a girl has for shaving her legs.'

'I see.' Conrad studied her face for a few moments, then he said, 'Is that how you were feeling just now when you called me?'

'Not quite. But I'd been thinking about Ed. And that's always a bit dangerous.'

'I'm glad you called.'

'So am I,' she said.

Anna was getting to the end of her second martini. Conrad changed the subject and began talking about his practice. She was watching him rather than listening to him. He was so damned handsome it was impossible not to watch him. She put a cigarette between her lips, then offered the pack to Conrad.

'No thanks,' he said. 'I don't.' He picked up a book of matches from the table and gave her a light, then he blew out the match and said, 'Are those cigarettes mentholated?'

'Yes, they are.'

She took a deep drag, and blew the smoke slowly up into the air. 'Now go ahead and tell me that they're going to shrivel up my entire reproductive system,' she said.

He laughed and shook his head.

'Then why did you ask?'

'Just curious, that's all.'

'You're lying. I can tell it from your face. You were about to give me the figures for the incidence of lung cancer in heavy smokers.'

'Lung cancer has nothing to do with menthol, Anna,' he said, and he smiled and took a tiny sip of his original martini, which he had so far hardly touched. He set the glass back carefully on the table. 'You still haven't told me what work you are doing,' he went on, 'or why you came to Dallas.'

'Tell me about menthol first. If it's even half as bad as the juice of the juniper berry, I think I ought to know about it quick.'

He laughed and shook his head.

'Please!'

'No, ma'am.'

'Conrad, you simply cannot start things up like this and then drop them. It's the second time in five minutes.'

'I don't want to be a medical bore,' he said.

'You're not being a bore. These things are fascinating. Come on! Tell! Don't be mean.'

It was pleasant to be sitting there feeling moderately high on two big martinis, and making easy talk with this graceful man, this quiet, comfortable, graceful person. He was not being coy. Far from it. He was simply being his normal scrupulous self.

'Is it something shocking?' she asked.

'No. You couldn't call it that.'

'Then go ahead.'

He picked up the packet of cigarettes still lying in front of her, and studied the label. 'The point is this,' he said. 'If you inhale menthol, you absorb it into the bloodstream. And that isn't good, Anna. It does things to you. It has certain very definite effects upon the central nervous system. Doctors still prescribe it occasionally.'

'I know that,' she said. 'Nose-drops and inhalations.'

'That's one of its minor uses. Do you know the other?'

'You rub it on the chest when you have a cold.'

'You can if you like, but it wouldn't help.'

'You put it in ointment and it heals cracked lips.'

'That's camphor.'

'So it is.'

He waited for her to have another guess.

'Go ahead and tell me,' she said.

'It may surprise you a bit.'

'I'm ready to be surprised.'

'Menthol,' Conrad said, 'is a well-known anti-aphrodisiac.'

'A what?'

'It suppresses sexual desire.'

'Conrad, you're making these things up.'

'I swear to you I'm not.'

'Who uses it?'

'Very few people nowadays. It has too strong a flavour. Saltpetre is much better.'

'Ah yes. I know about saltpetre.'

'What do you know about saltpetre?'

'They give it to prisoners,' Anna said. 'They sprinkle it on their cornflakes every morning to keep them quiet.'

'They also use it in cigarettes,' Conrad said.

'You mean prisoners' cigarettes?'

'I mean *all* cigarettes.'

'That's nonsense.'

'Is it?'

'Of course it is.'

'Why do you say that?'

'Nobody would stand for it,' she said.

'They stand for cancer.'

'That's quite different, Conrad. How do you know they put saltpetre in cigarettes?'

'Have you never wondered,' he said, 'what makes a cigarette go on burning when you lay it in the ashtray? Tobacco doesn't burn of its own accord. Any pipe smoker will tell you that.'

'They use special chemicals,' she said.

'Exactly; they use saltpetre.'

'Does saltpetre burn?'

'Sure it burns. It used to be one of the prime ingredients of old-fashioned gunpowder. Fuses, too. It makes very good fuses. That cigarette of yours is a first-rate slow-burning fuse, is it not?'

Anna looked at her cigarette. Though she hadn't drawn on it for a couple of minutes, it was still smouldering away and the smoke was curling upwards from the tip in a slim blue-grey spiral.

'So this has menthol in it *and* saltpetre?' she said.

'Absolutely.'

'And they're *both* anti-aphrodisiacs?'

'Yes. You're getting a double dose.'

'It's ridiculous, Conrad. It's too little to make any difference.'

He smiled but didn't answer this.

'There's not enough there to inhibit a cockroach,' she said.

'That's what you think, Anna. How many do you smoke a day?'

'About thirty.'

'Well,' he said, 'I guess it's none of my business.' He paused, and then he added, 'But you and I would be a lot better off today if it was.'

'Was what?'

'My business.'

'Conrad, what *do* you mean?'

'I'm simply saying that if you, once upon a time, hadn't suddenly decided to drop me, none of this misery would have happened to either of us. We'd still be happily married to each other.'

His face had suddenly taken on a queer sharp look.

'Drop you?'

'It was quite a shock, Anna.'

'Oh dear,' she said, 'but everybody drops everybody else at that age, don't they?'

'I wouldn't know,' Conrad said.

'You're not cross with me still, are you, for doing that?'

'Cross!' he said. 'Good God, Anna! Cross is what children get when they lose a toy! I lost a wife!'

She stared at him, speechless.

'Tell me,' he went on, 'didn't you have any idea how I felt at the time?'

'But, Conrad, we were so *young*.'

'It destroyed me, Anna. It just about destroyed me.'

'But how . . .'

'How what?'

'How, if it meant so much, could you turn right around and get engaged to somebody else a few weeks later?'

'Have you never heard of the rebound?' he asked.

She nodded, gazing at him in dismay.

'I was wildly in love with you, Anna.'

She didn't answer.

'I'm sorry,' he said. 'That was a silly outburst. Please forgive me.'

There was a long silence.

Conrad was leaning back in his chair, studying her from a distance. She took another cigarette from the pack, and lit it. Then she blew out the match and placed it carefully in the ashtray. When she glanced up again, he was still watching her. There was an intent, far look in his eyes.

'What are you thinking about?' she asked.

He didn't answer.

'Conrad,' she said, 'do you still hate me for doing what I did?'

'Hate you?'

'Yes, hate me. I have a queer feeling that you do. I'm sure you do, even after all these years.'

'Anna,' he said.

'Yes, Conrad?'

He hitched his chair closer to the table, and leaned forward. 'Did it ever cross your mind . . .'

He stopped.

She waited.

He was looking so intensely earnest all of a sudden that she leaned forward herself.

'Did what cross my mind?' she asked.

'The fact that you and I . . . that both of us . . . have a bit of unfinished business.'

She stared at him.

He looked back at her, his eyes as bright as two stars. 'Don't be shocked,' he said, 'please.'

'Shocked?'

'You look as though I'd just asked you to jump out of the window with me.'

The room was full of people now, and it was very noisy. It was like being at a cocktail party. You had to shout to be heard.

Conrad's eyes waited on her, impatient, eager.

'I'd like another martini,' she said.

'Must you?'

'Yes,' she said, 'I must.'

In her whole life, she had been made love to by only one man – her husband, Ed.

And it had always been wonderful.

Three thousand times?

She thought more. Probably a good deal more. Who counts?

Assuming, though, for the sake of argument, that the

exact figure (for there has to be an exact figure) was three thousand, six hundred and eighty . . .

. . . and knowing that every single time it happened it was an act of pure, passionate, authentic love-making between the same man and the same woman . . .

. . . then how in heaven's name could an entirely new man, an unloved stranger, hope to come in suddenly on the three thousand, six hundred and eighty-*first* time and be even halfway acceptable?

He'd be a trespasser.

All the memories would come rushing back. She would be lying there suffocated by memories.

She had raised this very point with Dr Jacobs during one of her sessions a few months back, and old Jacobs had said, 'There will be no nonsense about memories, my dear Mrs Cooper. I wish you would forget that. Only the present will exist.'

'But how do I get there?' she had said. 'How can I summon up enough nerve suddenly to go upstairs to a bedroom and take off my clothes in front of a new man, a stranger, in cold blood? . . .'

'Cold blood!' he had cried. 'Good God, woman, it'll be boiling hot!' And later he had said, 'Do at any rate try to believe me, Mrs Cooper, when I tell you that any woman who has been deprived of sexual congress after more than twenty years of practice – of uncommonly frequent practice in your case, if I understand you correctly – any woman in those circumstances is going to suffer continually from severe psychological disturbances until the routine is re-established. You are feeling a lot better, I know that, but it is my duty to inform you that you are by no means back to normal . . .'

To Conrad, Anna said, 'This isn't by any chance a therapeutic suggestion, is it?'

'A *what*?'

'A therapeutic suggestion.'

'What in the world do you mean?'

'It sounds exactly like a plot hatched up by my Dr Jacobs.'

'Look,' he said, and now he leaned right across the table and touched her left hand with the tip of one finger. 'When I knew you before, I was too damn young and nervous to make that sort of a proposition, much as I wanted to. I didn't think there was any particular hurry then, anyway. I figured we had a whole lifetime before us. I wasn't to know you were going to drop me.'

Her martini arrived. Anna picked it up and began to drink it fast. She knew exactly what it was going to do to her. It was going to make her float. A third martini always did that. Give her a third martini and within seconds her body would become completely weightless and she would go floating around the room like a wisp of hydrogen gas.

She sat there holding the glass with both hands as though it were a sacrament. She took another gulp. There was not much of it left now. Over the rim of her glass she could see Conrad watching her with disapproval as she drank. She smiled at him radiantly.

'You're not against the use of anaesthetics when you operate, are you?' she asked.

'Please, Anna, don't talk like that.'

'I am beginning to float,' she said.

'So I see,' he answered. 'Why don't you stop there?'

'What did you say?'

'I said, why don't you stop?'

'Do you want me to tell you why?'

'No,' he said. He made a little forward movement with his hands as though he were going to take her glass away from her, so she quickly put it to her lips and tipped it high, holding it there for a few seconds to allow the last drop to run out. When she looked at Conrad again, he was placing a ten-dollar bill on the waiter's tray, and the waiter was saying, 'Thank *you*, sir. Thank you indeed,' and the next thing she knew she was floating out of the room and across the lobby of the hotel with Conrad's hand cupped lightly under one of her elbows, steering her towards the elevators. They floated up to the twenty-second floor, and then along the corridor to the door of her bedroom. She fished the key out of her purse and unlocked the door and floated inside. Conrad followed, closing the door behind him. Then very suddenly, he grabbed hold of her and folded her up in his enormous arms and started kissing her with great gusto.

She let him do it.

He kissed her all over her mouth and cheeks and neck, taking deep breaths in between the kisses. She kept her eyes open, watching him in a queer detached sort of way, and the view she got reminded her vaguely of the blurry close-up view of a dentist's face when he is working on an upper back tooth.

Then all of a sudden, Conrad put his tongue into one of her ears. The effect of this upon her was electric. It was as though a live two-hundred-volt plug had been pushed into an empty socket, and all the lights came on and the bones began to melt and the hot molten sap went running down into her limbs and she exploded into a frenzy. It was the kind of marvellous, wanton, reckless, flaming frenzy that Ed used to provoke in her so very often in the olden days by just a touch of the hand here and there. She flung her arms around Conrad's neck and started kissing him back with far more gusto than he had ever kissed her, and although he looked at first as though he thought she were going to swallow him alive, he soon recovered his balance.

Anna hadn't the faintest idea how long they stood there embracing and kissing with such violence, but it must have been for quite a while. She felt such happiness, such . . . such *confidence* again at last, such sudden overwhelming confidence in herself that she wanted to tear off her clothes and do a wild dance for Conrad in the middle of the room. But she did no such foolish thing. Instead, she simply floated away to the edge of the bed and sat down to catch her breath. Conrad quickly sat down beside her. She leaned her head against his chest and sat there glowing all over while he gently stroked her hair. Then she undid one button of his shirt and slid her hand inside and laid it against his chest. Through the ribs, she could feel the beating of his heart.

'What do I see here?' Conrad said.

'What do you see where, my darling?'

'On your scalp. You want to watch this, Anna.'

'You watch it for me, dearest.'

'Seriously,' he said, 'you know what this looks like? It looks like a tiny touch of androgenic alopecia.'

'Good.'

'No, it is not good. It's actually an inflammation of the hair follicles, and it causes baldness. It's quite common on women in their later years.'

'Oh, shut up, Conrad,' she said, kissing him on the side of the neck. 'I have the most gorgeous hair.'

She sat up and pulled off his jacket. Then she undid his tie and threw it across the room.

'There's a little hook on the back of my dress,' she said. 'Undo it, please.'

Conrad unhooked the hook, then unzipped the zipper and helped her to get out of the dress. She had on a rather nice pale-blue slip. Conrad was wearing an ordinary white shirt, as doctors do, but it was now open at the neck, and this suited him. His neck had a little ridge of sinewy muscle running up vertically on either side, and when he turned his head the muscle moved under the skin. It was the most beautiful neck Anna had ever seen.

'Let's do this very very slowly,' she said. 'Let's drive ourselves crazy with anticipation.'

His eyes rested a moment on her face, then travelled away, all the way down the length of her body, and she saw him smile.

'Shall we be very stylish and dissipated, Conrad, and order a bottle of champagne? I can ask room service to bring it up, and you can hide in the bathroom when they come in.'

'No,' he said. 'You've had enough to drink already. Stand up, please.'

The tone of his voice caused her to stand up at once.

'Come here,' he said.

She went close to him. He was still sitting on the bed, and now, without getting up, he reached forward and began to take off the rest of her clothes. He did this slowly and deliberately. His face had become suddenly rather pale.

'Oh, darling,' she said, 'how marvellous! You've got that famous thing! A real thick clump of hair growing out of each of your ears! You know what that means, don't you? It's *the* absolutely positive sign of enormous virility!' She bent down and kissed him on the ear. He went on taking off her clothes – the bra, the shoes, the girdle, the pants, and finally the stockings, all of which he dropped in a heap on the floor. The moment he had peeled off her last stocking and dropped it, he turned away. He turned right away from her as though she didn't exist, and now he began to undress himself.

It was rather odd to be standing so close to him in nothing but her own skin and him not even giving her a second look. But perhaps men did these things. Ed might have been an exception. How could *she* know? Conrad took off his white shirt first, and after folding it very carefully, he stood up and carried it to a chair and laid it on one of the arms. He did the same with his undershirt. Then he sat down again on the edge of the bed and started removing his shoes. Anna remained quite still, watching him. His sudden change of mood, his silence, his curious intensity, were making her a bit afraid. But they were also exciting her. There was a stealth, almost a menace in his movements, as though he were some splendid animal treading softly towards the kill. A leopard.

She became hypnotized watching him. She was watching his fingers, the surgeon's fingers, as they untied and loosened the laces of the left shoe, easing it off the foot, and placing it neatly half under the bed. The right shoe came next. Then the left sock and the right sock, both of them being folded together and laid with the utmost precision across the toes of the shoes. Finally the fingers moved up to the top of the trousers, where they undid one button and then began to manipulate the zipper. The trousers, when taken off, were folded along the creases, then carried over to the chair. The underpants followed.

Conrad, now naked, walked slowly back to the edge of the bed, and sat. Then at last, he turned his head and noticed her. She stood waiting ... and trembling. He looked her slowly up and down. Then abruptly, he shot out a hand and took her by the wrist, and with a sharp pull he had her sprawled across the bed.

The relief was enormous. Anna flung her arms around him and held on to him tightly, oh so tightly, for fear that he might go away. She was in mortal fear that he might go away and not come back. And there they lay, she holding on to him as though he were the only thing left in the world to hold on to, and he, strangely quiet, watchful, intent, slowly disentangling himself and beginning to touch her now in a number of different places with those fingers of his, those expert surgeon's fingers. And once again she flew into a frenzy.

The things he did to her during the next few moments were terrible and exquisite. He was, she knew, merely getting her ready, preparing her, or as they say in the hospital, prepping her for the operation itself, but oh God, she had never known or experienced anything even remotely like this. And it was all exceedingly quick, for in what seemed to her no more than a few seconds, she had reached that excruciating point of no return where the whole room becomes compressed into a single tiny blinding speck of light that is going to explode and tear one to pieces at the slightest extra touch. At this stage, in a swift rapacious parabola, Conrad swung his body on top of her for the final act.

And now Anna felt her passion being drawn out of her as if a long live nerve were being drawn slowly out of her body, a long live thread of electric fire, and she cried out to Conrad to go on and on and on, and as she did so, in the middle of it all, somewhere above her, she heard another voice, and this other voice grew louder and louder, more and more insistent, demanding to be heard:

'I said are you *wearing* something?' the voice wanted to know.

'Oh darling, what is it?'

'I keep asking you, are you *wearing* something?'

'Who, me?'

'There's an obstruction here. You must be wearing a diaphragm or some other appliance.'

'Of course not, darling. Everything's wonderful. Oh, do be quiet.'

'Everything is *not* wonderful, Anna.'

Like a picture on a screen, the room swam back into focus. In the foreground was Conrad's face. It was suspended above her, on naked shoulders. The eyes were looking directly into hers. The mouth was still talking.

'If you're going to use a device, then for heaven's sake learn to introduce it in the proper manner. There is nothing so aggravating as careless positioning. The diaphragm has to be placed right back against the cervix.'

'But I'm not wearing anything!'

'You're not? Well, there's still an obstruction.'

Not only the room but the whole world as well seemed slowly to be sliding away from under her now.

'I feel sick,' she said.

'You what?'

'I feel sick.'

'Don't be childish, Anna.'

'Conrad, I'd like you to go, please. Go now.'

'What on earth are you talking about?'

'Go away from me, Conrad!'

'That's ridiculous, Anna. Okay, I'm sorry I spoke. Forget it.'

'*Go away!*' she cried. '*Go away! Go away! Go away!*'

She tried to push him away from her, but he was huge and strong and he had her pinned.

'Calm yourself,' he said. 'Relax. You can't suddenly change your mind like this, in the middle of everything. And for heaven's sake, don't start weeping.'

'Leave me alone, Conrad, I beg you.'

He seemed to be gripping her with everything he had, arms and elbows, hands and fingers, thighs and knees, ankles and feet. He was like a toad the way he gripped her. He was exactly like an enormous clinging toad, gripping and grasping and refusing to let go. She had seen a toad once doing precisely this. It was copulating with a frog on a stone beside a stream, and there it sat, motionless, repulsive, with an evil yellow gleam in its eye, gripping the frog with its two powerful front paws and refusing to let go . . .

'Now stop struggling, Anna. You're acting like a hysterical child. For God's sake, woman, what's eating you?'

'You're hurting me!' she cried.

'*Hurting* you?'

'It's hurting me terribly!'

She told him this only to get him away.

'You know why it's hurting?' he said.

'Conrad! Please!'

'Now wait a minute, Anna. Allow me to explain . . .'

'No!' she cried. 'I've had enough explaining!'

'My dear woman . . .'

'No!' She was struggling desperately to free herself, but he still had her pinned.

'The reason it hurts,' he went on, 'is that you are not manufacturing any fluid. The mucosa is virtually dry . . .'

'Stop!'

'The actual name is senile atrophic vaginitis. It comes with age, Anna. That's why it's called *senile* vaginitis. There's not much one can do . . .'

At that point, she started to scream. The screams were not very loud, but they were screams nevertheless, terrible, agonized stricken screams, and after listening to them for a few seconds, Conrad, in a single graceful movement, suddenly rolled away from her and pushed her to one side with both hands. He pushed her with such force that she fell on to the floor.

She climbed slowly to her feet, and as she staggered into the bathroom, she was crying 'Ed! . . . Ed! . . . Ed! . . .' in a queer supplicating voice. The door shut.

Conrad lay very still listening to the sounds that came from behind the door. At first, he heard only the sobbing of the woman, but a few seconds later, above the sobbing, he heard the sharp metallic click of a cupboard being opened. Instantly, he sat up and vaulted off the bed and began to dress himself with great speed. His clothes, so neatly folded, lay ready at hand, and it took him no more than a couple of minutes to put them on. When that was done, he crossed to the mirror and wiped the lipstick off his face with a handkerchief. He took a comb from his pocket and ran it through his fine black hair. He walked once round the bed to see if he had forgotten anything, and then, carefully, like a man who is tiptoeing from a room where a child is sleeping, he moved out into the corridor, closing the door softly behind him.

The Great Switcheroo

First published in *Playboy* (April 1974)

There were about forty people at Jerry and Samantha's cocktail party that evening. It was the usual crowd, the usual discomfort, the usual appalling noise. People had to stand very close to one another and shout to make themselves heard. Many were grinning, showing capped white teeth. Most of them had a cigarette in the left hand, a drink in the right.

I moved away from my wife Mary and her group. I headed for the small bar in the far corner, and when I got there, I sat down on a bar-stool and faced the room. I did this so that I could look at the women. I settled back with my shoulders against the bar-rail, sipping my Scotch and examining the women one by one over the rim of my glass.

I was studying not their figures but their faces, and what interested me there was not so much the face itself but the big red mouth in the middle of it all. And even then, it wasn't the whole mouth but only the lower lip. The lower lip, I had recently decided, was the great revealer. It gave away more than the eyes. The eyes hid their secrets. The lower lip hid very little. Take, for example, the lower lip of Jacinth Winkleman, who was standing nearest to me. Notice the wrinkles on that lip, how some were parallel and some radiated outwards. No two people had the same pattern of lip-wrinkles, and come to think of it, you could catch a criminal that way if you had his lip-print on file and he had taken a drink at the scene of the crime. The lower lip is what you suck and nibble when you're ruffled, and Martha Sullivan was doing that right now as she watched from a distance her fatuous husband slobbering over Judy Martinson. You lick it when lecherous. I could see Ginny Lomax licking hers with the tip of her tongue as she stood beside Ted Dorling and gazed up into his face. It was a deliberate lick, the tongue coming out slowly and making a slow wet wipe along the entire length of the lower lip. I saw Ted Dorling looking at Ginny's tongue, which was what she wanted him to do.

It really does seem to be a fact, I told myself, as my eyes wandered from lower lip to lower lip across the room, that all the less attractive traits of the human animal, arrogance, rapacity, gluttony, lasciviousness and the rest of them, are clearly signalled in that little carapace of scarlet skin. But you have to know the code. The protuberant or bulging lower lip is supposed to signify sensuality. But this is only half true in men and wholly untrue in women. In women, it is the thin line you should look for, the narrow blade with the sharply delineated bottom edge. And in the nymphomaniac there is a tiny just visible crest of skin at the top centre of the lower lip.

Samantha, my hostess, had that.

Where was she now, Samantha?

Ah, there she was, taking an empty glass out of a guest's hand. Now she was heading my way to refill it.

'Hello, Vic,' she said. 'You all alone?'

She's a nympho-bird all right, I told myself. But a very rare example of the species, because she is entirely and utterly monogamous. She is a married monogamous nympho-bird who stays for ever in her own nest.

She is also the fruitiest female I have ever set eyes upon in my whole life.

'Let me help you,' I said, standing up and taking the glass from her hand. 'What's wanted in here?'

'Vodka on the rocks,' she said. 'Thanks, Vic.' She laid a lovely long white arm upon the top of the bar and she leaned forward so that her bosom rested on the bar-rail, squashing upwards. 'Oops,' I said, pouring vodka outside the glass.

Samantha looked at me with huge brown eyes, but said nothing.

'I'll wipe it up,' I said.

She took the refilled glass from me and walked away. I watched her go. She was wearing black pants. They were so tight around the buttocks that the smallest mole or pimple would have shown through the cloth. But Samantha Rainbow had not a blemish on her bottom. I caught myself licking my own lower lip. That's right, I thought. I want her. I lust after that woman. But it's too risky to try. It would be suicide to make a pass at a girl like that. First of all, she lives next door, which is too close. Secondly, as I have already said, she is monogamous. Thirdly, she is thick as a thief with Mary, my own wife. They exchange dark female secrets. Fourthly, her husband Jerry is my very old and good friend, and not even I, Victor Hammond, though I am churning with lust, would dream of

THE GREAT SWITCHEROO

trying to seduce the wife of a man who is my very old and trusty friend.

Unless . . .

It was at this point, as I sat on the bar-stool letching over Samantha Rainbow, that an interesting idea began to filter quietly into the centre of my brain. I remained still, allowing the idea to expand. I watched Samantha across the room, and began fitting her into the framework of the idea. Oh, Samantha, my gorgeous and juicy little jewel, I shall have you yet.

But could anybody seriously hope to get away with a crazy lark like that?

No, not in a million nights.

One couldn't even *try* it unless Jerry agreed. So why think about it?

Samantha was standing about six yards away, talking to Gilbert Mackesy. The fingers of her right hand were curled around a tall glass. The fingers were long and almost certainly dexterous.

Assuming, just for the fun of it, that Jerry did agree, then even so, there would still be gigantic snags along the way. There was, for example, the little matter of physical characteristics. I had seen Jerry many times at the club having a shower after tennis, but right now I couldn't for the life of me recall the necessary details. It wasn't the sort of thing one noticed very much. Usually, one didn't even look.

Anyway, it would be madness to put the suggestion to Jerry point-blank. I didn't know him *that* well. He might be horrified. He might even turn nasty. There could be an

381

ugly scene. I must test him out, therefore, in some subtle fashion.

'You know something,' I said to Jerry about an hour later when we were sitting together on the sofa having a last drink. The guests were drifting away and Samantha was by the door saying goodbye to them. My own wife Mary was out on the terrace talking to Bob Swain. I could see through the open french windows. 'You know something funny?' I said to Jerry as we sat together on the sofa.

'What's funny?' Jerry asked me.

'A fellow I had lunch with today told me a fantastic story. Quite unbelievable.'

'What story?' Jerry said. The whisky had begun to make him sleepy.

'This man, the one I had lunch with, had a terrific letch after the wife of his friend who lived nearby. And his friend had an equally big letch after the wife of the man I had lunch with. Do you see what I mean?'

'You mean two fellers who lived close to each other both fancied each other's wives.'

'Precisely,' I said.

'Then there was no problem,' Jerry said.

'There was a very big problem,' I said. 'The wives were both very faithful and honourable women.'

'Samantha's the same,' Jerry said. 'She wouldn't look at another man.'

'Nor would Mary,' I said. 'She's a fine girl.'

Jerry emptied his glass and set it down carefully on the sofa-table. 'So what happened in your story?' he said. 'It sounds dirty.'

'What happened,' I said, 'was that these two randy sods cooked up a plan which made it possible for each of them to ravish the other's wife without the wives ever knowing it. If you can believe such a thing.'

'With chloroform?' Jerry said.

'Not at all. They were fully conscious.'

'Impossible,' Jerry said. 'Someone's been pulling your leg.'

'I don't think so,' I said. 'From the way this man told it to me, with all the little details and everything, I don't think he was making it up. In fact, I'm sure he wasn't. And listen, they didn't do it just once, either. They've been doing it every two or three weeks for months!'

'And the wives don't know?'

'They haven't a clue.'

'I've got to hear this,' Jerry said. 'Let's get another drink first.'

We crossed to the bar and refilled our glasses, then returned to the sofa.

'You must remember,' I said, 'that there had to be a tremendous lot of preparation and rehearsal beforehand. And many intimate details had to be exchanged to give the plan a chance of working. But the essential part of the scheme was simple:

'They fixed a night, call it Saturday. On that night the husbands and wives were to go up to bed as usual, at say eleven or eleven thirty.

'From then on, normal routine would be preserved. A little reading, perhaps, a little talking, then out with the lights.

'After lights out, the husbands would at once roll over

and pretend to go to sleep. This was to discourage their wives from getting fresh, which at this stage must on no account be permitted. So the wives went to sleep. But the husbands stayed awake. So far so good.

'Then at precisely one a.m., by which time the wives would be in a good deep sleep, each husband would slip quietly out of bed, put on a pair of bedroom slippers and creep downstairs in his pyjamas. He would open the front door and go out into the night, taking care not to close the door behind him.

'They lived,' I went on, 'more or less across the street from one another. It was a quiet suburban neighbour- hood and there was seldom anyone about at that hour. So these two furtive pyjama-clad figures would pass each other as they crossed the street, each one heading for another house, another bed, another woman.'

Jerry was listening to me carefully. His eyes were a little glazed from drink, but he was listening to every word.

'The next part,' I said, 'had been prepared very thor- oughly by both men. Each knew the inside of his friend's house almost as well as he knew his own. He knew how to find his way in the dark both downstairs and up without knocking over the furniture. He knew his way to the stairs and exactly how many steps there were to the top and which of them creaked and which didn't. He knew on which side of the bed the woman upstairs was sleeping.

'Each took off his slippers and left them in the hall, then up the stairs he crept in his bare feet and pyjamas. This part of it, according to my friend, was rather excit- ing. He was in a dark silent house that wasn't his own, and on his way to the main bedroom he had to pass no less than three children's bedrooms where the doors were always left slightly open.'

'Children!' Jerry cried. 'My God, what if one of them had woken up and said, "Daddy, is that you?"'

'That was all taken care of,' I said. 'Emergency procedure would then come into effect immediately. Also if the wife, just as he was creeping into her room, woke up and said, "Darling, what's wrong? Why are you wandering about?"; then again, emergency procedure.'

'What emergency procedure?' Jerry said.

'Simple,' I answered. 'The man would immediately dash downstairs and out the front door and across to his own house and ring the bell. This was a signal for the other character, no matter what he was doing at the time, also to rush downstairs at full speed and open the door and let the other fellow in while he went out. This would get them both back quickly to their proper houses.'

'With egg all over their faces,' Jerry said.

'Not at all,' I said.

'That doorbell would have woken the whole house,' Jerry said.

'Of course,' I said. 'And the husband, returning upstairs in his pyjamas, would merely say, "I went to see who the hell was ringing the bell at this ungodly hour. Couldn't find anyone. It must have been a drunk."'

'What about the other guy?' Jerry asked. 'How does he explain why he rushed downstairs when his wife or child spoke to him?'

'He would say, "I heard someone prowling abo

'Jesus,' Jerry said.

'Each of these men,' I said, 'had to learn a new part. He had, in effect, to become an actor. He was impersonating another character.'

'Not so easy, that,' Jerry said.

'No problem at all, according to my friend. The only thing one had to watch out for was not to get carried away and start improvising. One had to follow the stage directions very carefully and stick to them.'

Jerry took another pull at his drink. He also took another look at Mary on the terrace. Then he leaned back against the sofa, glass in hand.

'These two characters,' he said. 'You mean they actually pulled it off?'

'I'm damn sure they did,' I said. 'They're still doing it. About once every three weeks.'

'Fantastic story,' Jerry said. 'And a damn crazy dangerous thing to do. Just imagine the sort of hell that would break loose if you were caught. Instant divorce. Two divorces, in fact. One on each side of the street. Not worth it.'

'Takes a lot of guts,' I said.

'The party's breaking up,' Jerry said. 'They're all going home with their goddamn wives.'

I didn't say any more after that. We sat there for a couple of minutes sipping our drinks while the guests began drifting towards the hall.

'Did he say it was fun, this friend of yours?' Jerry asked suddenly.

'He said it was a gas,' I answered. 'He said all the normal

pleasures got intensified one hundred per cent because of the risk. He swore it was the greatest way of doing it in the world, impersonating the husband and the wife not knowing it.'

At that point, Mary came in through the french windows with Bob Swain. She had an empty glass in one hand and a flame-coloured azalea in the other. She had picked the azalea on the terrace.

'I've been watching you,' she said, pointing the flower at me like a pistol. 'You've hardly stopped talking for the last ten minutes. What's he been telling you, Jerry?'

'A dirty story,' Jerry said, grinning.

'He does that when he drinks,' Mary said.

'Good story,' Jerry said. 'But totally impossible. Get him to tell it to you sometime.'

'I don't like dirty stories,' Mary said. 'Come along, Vic. It's time we went.'

'Don't go yet,' Jerry said, fixing his eyes upon her splendid bosom. 'Have another drink.'

'No thanks,' she said. 'The children'll be screaming for their supper. I've had a lovely time.'

'Aren't you going to kiss me good night?' Jerry said, getting up from the sofa. He went for her mouth, but she turned her head quickly and he caught only the edge of her cheek.

'Go away, Jerry,' she said. 'You're drunk.'

'Not drunk,' Jerry said. 'Just lecherous.'

'Don't you get lecherous with me, my boy,' Mary said sharply. 'I hate that sort of talk.' She marched away across the room, carrying her bosom before her like a battering-ram.

'So long, Jerry,' I said. 'Fine party.'

Mary, full of dark looks, was waiting for me in the hall. Samantha was there, too, saying good-bye to the last guests – Samantha with her dexterous fingers and her smooth skin and her smooth, dangerous thighs. 'Cheer up, Vic,' she said to me, her white teeth showing. She looked like the creation, the beginning of the world, the first morning. 'Good night, Vic darling,' she said, stirring her fingers in my vitals.

I followed Mary out of the house. 'You feeling all right?' she asked.

'Yes,' I said. 'Why not?'

'The amount you drink is enough to make anyone feel ill,' she said.

There was a scrubby old hedge dividing our place from Jerry's and there was a gap in it we always used. Mary and I walked through the gap in silence. We went into the house and she cooked up a big pile of scrambled eggs and bacon, and we ate it with the children.

After the meal, I wandered outside. The summer evening was clear and cool and because I had nothing else to do I decided to mow the grass in the front garden. I got the mower out of the shed and started it up. Then I began the old routine of marching back and forth behind it. I like mowing grass. It is a soothing operation, and on our front lawn I could always look at Samantha's house going one way and think about her going the other.

I had been at it for about ten minutes when Jerry came strolling through the gap in the hedge. He was smoking a pipe and had his hands in his pockets and he stood on the edge of the grass, watching me. I pulled up in front of him, but left the motor ticking over.

'Hi, sport,' he said. 'How's everything?'

'I'm in the doghouse,' I said. 'So are you.'

'Your little wife,' he said, 'is just too goddam prim and prissy to be true.'

'Oh, I know that.'

'She rebuked me in my own house,' Jerry said.

'Not very much.'

'It was enough,' he said, smiling slightly.

'Enough for what?'

'Enough to make me want to get a little bit of my own back on her. So what would you think if I suggested you and I have a go at that thing your friend told you about at lunch?'

When he said this, I felt such a surge of excitement my stomach nearly jumped out of my mouth. I gripped the handles of the mower and started revving the engine.

'Have I said the wrong thing?' Jerry asked.

I didn't answer.

'Listen,' he said. 'If you think it's a lousy idea, let's just forget I ever mentioned it. You're not mad at me, are you?'

'I'm not mad at you, Jerry,' I said. 'It's just that it never entered my head that *we* should do it.'

'It entered mine,' he said. 'The set-up is perfect. We wouldn't even have to cross the street.' His face had gone suddenly bright and his eyes were shining like two stars. 'So what do you say, Vic?'

'I'm thinking,' I said.

'Maybe you don't fancy Samantha.'

'I don't honestly know,' I said.

'She's lots of fun,' Jerry said. 'I guarantee that.'

At this point, I saw Mary come out on to the front porch. 'There's Mary,' I said. 'She's looking for the children. We'll talk some more tomorrow.'

'Then it's a deal?'

'It could be, Jerry. But only on condition we don't rush it. I want to be dead sure everything is right before we start. Damn it all, this is a whole brand-new can of beans!'

'No, it's not!' he said. 'Your friend said it was a gas. He said it was easy.'

'Ah, yes,' I said. 'My friend. Of course. But each case is different.' I opened the throttle on the mower and went whirring away across the lawn. When I got to the far side and turned around, Jerry was already through the gap in the hedge and walking up to his front door.

The next couple of weeks was a period of high conspiracy for Jerry and me. We held secret meetings in bars and restaurants to discuss strategy, and sometimes he dropped into my office after work and we had a planning session behind the closed door. Whenever a doubtful point arose, Jerry would always say, 'How did your friend do it?' And I would play for time and say, 'I'll call him up and ask him about that one.'

After many conferences and much talk, we agreed upon the following main points:

1. That D Day should be a Saturday.
2. That on D Day evening we should take our wives out to a good dinner, the four of us together.

3. That Jerry and I should leave our houses and cross over through the gap in the hedge at precisely one a.m. Sunday morning.

4. That instead of lying in bed in the dark until one a.m. came along, we should both, as soon as our wives were asleep, go quietly downstairs to the kitchen and drink coffee.

5. That we should use the front doorbell idea if an emergency arose.

6. That the return cross-over time was fixed for two a.m.

7. That while in the wrong bed, questions (if any) from the woman must be answered by an 'Uh-uh' sounded with the lips closed tight.

8. That I myself must immediately give up cigarettes and take to a pipe so that I would 'smell' the same as Jerry.

9. That we should at once start using the same brand of hair oil and after-shave lotion.

10. That as both of us normally wore our wristwatches in bed, and they were much the same shape, it was decided not to exchange. Neither of us wore rings.

11. That each man must have something unusual about him that the woman would identify positively with her own husband. We therefore invented what became known as 'The Sticking Plaster Ploy'. It worked like this: on D Day evening, when the couples arrived back in their own homes immediately after the dinner, each husband would make a point of going to the

kitchen to cut himself a piece of cheese. At the same time, he would carefully stick a large piece of plaster over the tip of the forefinger of his right hand. Having done this, he would hold up the finger and say to his wife, 'I cut myself. It's nothing, but it was bleeding a bit.' Thus, later on, when the men have switched beds, each woman will be made very much aware of the plaster-covered finger (the man would see to that), and will associate it directly with her own husband. An important psychological ploy, this, calculated to dissipate any tiny suspicion that might enter the mind of either female.

So much for the basic plans. Next came what we referred to in our notes as 'Familiarization with the Layout'. Jerry schooled me first. He gave me three hours' training in his own house one Sunday afternoon when his wife and children were out. I had never been into their bedroom before. On the dressing table were Samantha's perfumes, her brushes, and all her other little things. A pair of her stockings was draped over the back of a chair. Her night-dress, white and blue, was hanging behind the door leading to the bathroom.

'Okay,' Jerry said. 'It'll be pitch dark when you come in. Samantha sleeps on this side, so you must tiptoe around the end of the bed and slide in on the other side, over there. I'm going to blindfold you and let you practise.'

At first, with the blindfold on, I wandered all over the room like a drunk. But after about an hour's work, I was able to negotiate the course pretty well. But before Jerry would finally pass me out, I had to go blindfold all the way from the front door through the hall, up the stairs, past the children's rooms, into Samantha's room and finish up in exactly the right place. And I had to do it silently, like a thief. All this took three hours of hard work, but I got it in the end.

The following Sunday morning when Mary had taken our children to church, I was able to give Jerry the same sort of work-out in my house. He learned the ropes faster than me, and within an hour he had passed the blindfold test without placing a foot wrong.

It was during this session that we decided to disconnect each woman's bedside lamp as we entered the bedroom. So Jerry practised finding the plug and pulling it out with his blindfold on, and the following week-end, I was able to do the same in Jerry's house.

Now came by far the most important part of our training. We called it 'Spilling the Beans', and it was here that both of us had to describe in every detail the procedure we adopted when making love to our own wives. We agreed not to worry ourselves with any exotic variations that either of us might or might not occasionally practise. We were concerned only with teaching one another the most commonly used routine, the one least likely to arouse suspicion.

The session took place in my office at six o'clock on a Wednesday evening, after the staff had gone home. At first, we were both slightly embarrassed, and neither of us wanted to begin. So I got out the bottle of whisky, and after a couple of stiff drinks, we loosened up and the teach-in started. While Jerry talked I took notes, and vice versa. At the end of it all, it turned out that the only real difference between Jerry's routine and my own was one of tempo. But what a difference it was! He took things (if what he said was to be believed) in such a leisurely fashion and he prolonged the moments to such an extravagant degree that I wondered privately to myself whether his partner did not sometimes go to sleep in the middle of it all. My job, however, was not to criticize but to copy, and I said nothing.

Jerry was not so discreet. At the end of my personal description, he had the temerity to say, 'Is that really what you do?'

'What do you mean?' I asked.

'I mean is it all over and done with as quickly as that?'

'Look,' I said. 'We aren't here to give each other lessons. We're here to learn the facts.'

'I know that,' he said. 'But I'm going to feel a bit of an ass if I copy your style exactly. My God, you go through it like an express train whizzing through a country station!'

I stared at him, mouth open.

'Don't look so surprised,' he said. 'The way you told it to me, anyone would think . . .'

'Think what?' I said.

'Oh, forget it,' he said.

'Thank you,' I said. I was furious. There are two things in this world at which I happen to know I excel. One is driving an automobile and the other is you-know-what. So to have him sit there and tell me I didn't know how to behave with my own wife was a monstrous piece of effrontery. It was he who didn't know, not me. Poor Samantha. What she must have had to put up with over the years.

'I'm sorry I spoke,' Jerry said. He poured more whisky into our glasses. 'Here's to the great switcheroo!' he said. 'When do we go?'

'Today is Wednesday,' I said. 'How about this coming Saturday?'

'Christ,' Jerry said.

'We ought to do it while everything's still fresh in our minds,' I said. 'There's an awful lot to remember.'

Jerry walked to the window and looked down at the traffic in the street below. 'Okay,' he said, turning around. 'Next Saturday it shall be!' Then we drove home in our separate cars.

'Jerry and I thought we'd take you and Samantha out to dinner Saturday night,' I said to Mary. We were in the kitchen and she was cooking hamburgers for the children.

She turned around and faced me, frying-pan in one hand, spoon in the other. Her blue eyes looked straight into mine. 'My Lord, Vic,' she said. 'How nice. But what are we celebrating?'

I looked straight back at her and said, 'I thought it would be a change to see some new faces. We're always meeting the same old bunch of people in the same old houses.'

She took a step forward and kissed me on the cheek. 'What a good man you are,' she said. 'I love you.'

'Don't forget to phone the baby-sitter.'

'No, I'll do it tonight,' she said.

Thursday and Friday passed very quickly, and suddenly it was Saturday. It was D Day. I woke up feeling madly excited. After breakfast, I couldn't sit still, so I decided to go out and wash the car. I was in the middle of this when Jerry came strolling through the gap in the hedge, pipe in mouth.

'Hi, sport,' he said. 'This is the day.'

'I know that,' I said. I also had a pipe in my mouth. I was forcing myself to smoke it, but I had trouble keeping it alight, and the smoke burned my tongue.

'How're you feeling?' Jerry asked.

'Terrific,' I said. 'How about you?'

'I'm nervous,' he said.

'Don't be nervous, Jerry.'

'This is one hell of a thing we're trying to do,' he said. 'I hope we pull it off.'

I went on polishing the windshield. I had never known Jerry to be nervous of anything before. It worried me a bit.

'I'm damn glad we're not the first people ever to try it,' he said. 'If no one had ever done it before, I don't think I'd risk it.'

'I agree,' I said.

'What stops me being too nervous,' he said, 'is the fact that your friend found it so fantastically easy.'

'My friend said it was a cinch,' I said. 'But for Chrissake, Jerry, don't be nervous when the time comes. That would be disastrous.'

'Don't worry,' he said. 'But Jesus, it's exciting, isn't it?'

'It's exciting all right,' I said.

'Listen,' he said. 'We'd better go easy on the booze tonight.'

'Good idea,' I said. 'See you at eight thirty.'

At half past eight, Samantha, Jerry, Mary and I drove in Jerry's car to Billy's Steak House. The restaurant, despite its name, was high-class and expensive, and the girls had put on long dresses for the occasion. Samantha was wearing something green that didn't start until it was halfway down her front, and I had never seen her looking lovelier. There were candles on our table. Samantha was seated opposite me and whenever she leaned forward with her face close to the flame, I could see that tiny crest of skin at the top centre of her lower lip. 'Now,' she said as she accepted a menu from the waiter, 'I wonder what I'm going to have tonight.'

Ho-ho-ho, I thought, that's a good question.

Everything went fine in the restaurant and the girls enjoyed themselves. When we arrived back at Jerry's house, it was eleven forty-five, and Samantha said, 'Come in and have a nightcap.'

'Thanks,' I said, 'but it's a bit late. And the baby-sitter has to be driven home.' So Mary and I walked across to our house, and *now*, I told myself as I entered the front door, *from now on* the countdown begins. I must keep a clear head and forget nothing.

While Mary was paying the baby-sitter, I went to the fridge and found a piece of Canadian cheddar. I took a knife from the drawer and a strip of plaster from the cupboard. I stuck the plaster around the tip of the forefinger of my right hand and waited for Mary to turn around.

'I cut myself,' I said, holding up the finger for her to see. 'It's nothing, but it was bleeding a bit.'

'I'd have thought you'd had enough to eat for the evening,' was all she said. But the plaster registered on her mind and my first little job had been done.

I drove the baby-sitter home and by the time I got back up to the bedroom it was round about midnight and Mary was already half asleep with her light out. I switched out the light on my side of the bed and went into the bathroom to undress. I pottered about in there for ten minutes or so and when I came out, Mary, as I had hoped, was well and truly sleeping. There seemed no point in getting into bed beside her. So I simply pulled back the covers a bit on my side to make it easier for Jerry, then with my slippers on, I went downstairs to the kitchen and switched on the electric kettle. It was now twelve seventeen. Forty-three minutes to go.

At twelve thirty-five, I went upstairs to check on Mary and the kids. Everyone was sound asleep.

At twelve fifty-five, five minutes before zero hour, I went up again for a final check. I went right up close to Mary's bed and whispered her name. There was no answer. Good. *That's it! Let's go!*

I put a brown raincoat over my pyjamas. I switched off the kitchen light so that the whole house was in darkness. I put the front door lock on the latch. And then, feeling an enormous sense of exhilaration, I stepped silently out into the night.

There were no lamps on our street to lighten the darkness. There was no moon or even a star to be seen. It was a black black night, but the air was warm and there was a little breeze blowing from somewhere.

I headed for the gap in the hedge. When I got very close, I was able to make out the hedge itself and find the gap. I stopped there, waiting. Then I heard Jerry's footsteps coming towards me.

'Hi, sport,' he whispered. 'Everything okay?'

'All ready for you,' I whispered back.

He moved on. I heard his slippered feet padding softly over the grass as he went towards my house. I went towards his.

I opened Jerry's front door. It was even darker inside than out. I closed the door carefully. I took off my raincoat and hung it on the doorknob. I removed my slippers and placed them against the wall by the door. I literally could not see my hands before my face. Everything had to be done by touch.

My goodness, I was glad Jerry had made me practise blindfold for so long. It wasn't my feet that guided me now but my fingers. The fingers of one hand or another were never for a moment out of contact with something, a wall, the banister, a piece of furniture, a window-curtain. And I knew or thought I knew exactly where I was all the time. But it was an awesome eerie feeling trespassing on tiptoe through someone else's house in the middle of the night. As I fingered my way up the stairs, I found myself thinking of the burglars who had broken into our front room last winter and stolen the television set. When the police came next morning, I pointed out to them an enormous turd lying in the snow outside the garage. 'They nearly always do that,' one of the cops told me. 'They can't help it. They're scared.'

I reached the top of the stairs. I crossed the landing with my right fingertips touching the wall all the time. I started down the corridor, but paused when my hand found the door of the first children's room. The door was slightly open. I listened. I could hear young Robert Rainbow, aged eight, breathing evenly inside. I moved on. I found the door to the second children's bedroom. This one belonged to Billy, aged six and Amanda, three. I stood listening. All was well.

The main bedroom was at the end of the corridor, about four yards on. I reached the door. Jerry had left it open, as planned. I went in. I stood absolutely still just inside the door, listening for any sign that Samantha might be awake. All was quiet. I felt my way around the wall until I reached Samantha's side of the bed. Immediately, I knelt on the floor and found the plug connecting her bedside lamp. I drew it from its socket and laid it on the carpet. Good. Much safer now. I stood up. I couldn't see Samantha, and at first I couldn't hear anything either. I bent low over the bed. Ah yes, I could hear her breathing. Suddenly I caught a whiff of the heavy musky perfume she had been using that evening, and I felt the blood rushing to my groin. Quickly I tiptoed around the big bed, keeping two fingers in gentle contact with the edge of the bed the whole way.

All I had to do now was get in. I did so, but as I put my

weight upon the mattress, the creaking of the springs underneath sounded as though someone was firing a rifle in the
room. I lay motionless, holding my breath. I could hear my
heart thumping away like an engine in my throat. Samantha
was facing away from me. She didn't move. I pulled the
covers up over my chest and turned towards her. A female
glow came out of her to me. Here we go, then! *Now!*

I slid a hand over and touched her body. Her nightdress
was warm and silky. I rested the hand gently on her hips.
Still she didn't move. I waited a minute or so, then I
allowed the hand that lay upon the hip to steal onwards
and go exploring. Slowly, deliberately, and very accurately,
my fingers began the process of setting her on fire.

She stirred. She turned on to her back. Then she murmured sleepily, 'Oh, dear . . . Oh, my goodness me . . . Good
heavens, darling!'

I, of course, said nothing. I just kept on with the job.

A couple of minutes went by.

She was lying quite still.

Another minute passed. Then another. She didn't move
a muscle.

I began to wonder how much longer it would be before
she caught alight.

I persevered.

But why the silence? Why this absolute and total immo-
bility, this frozen posture?

Suddenly it came to me. I had forgotten completely
about Jerry! I was so hotted up, I had forgotten all about
his own personal routine! I was doing it my way, not his!
His way was far more complex than mine. It was ridicu-

lously elaborate. It was quite unnecessary. But it was what she was used to. And now she was noticing the difference and trying to figure out what on earth was going on.

But it was too late to change direction now. I must keep going.

I kept going. The woman beside me was like a coiled spring lying there. I could feel the tension under her skin. I began to sweat.

Suddenly, she uttered a queer little groan.

More ghastly thoughts rushed through my mind. Could she be ill? Was she having a heart attack? Ought I to get the hell out quick?

She groaned again, louder this time. Then all at once, she cried out, 'Yes-yes-yes-yes-yes!' and like a bomb whose slow fuse had finally reached the dynamite, she exploded into life. She grabbed me in her arms and went for me with such incredible ferocity, I felt I was being set upon by a tiger.

Or should I say tigress?

I never dreamed a woman could do the things Samantha did to me then. She was a whirlwind, a dazzling frenzied whirlwind that tore me up by the roots and spun me around and carried me high into the heavens, to places I did not know existed.

I myself did not contribute. How could I? I was helpless. I was the palm tree spinning in the heavens, the lamb in the claws of the tiger. It was as much as I could do to keep breathing.

Thrilling it was, all the same, to surrender to the hands of a violent woman, and for the next ten, twenty, thirty minutes — how would I know? — the storm raged on. But

I have no intention here of regaling the reader with bizarre details. I do not approve of washing juicy linen in public. I am sorry, but there it is. I only hope that my reticence will not create too strong a sense of anticlimax. Certainly, there was nothing anti about my own climax, and in the final searing paroxysm I gave a shout which should have awakened the entire neighbourhood. Then I collapsed. I crumpled up like a drained wineskin.

Samantha, as though she had done no more than drink a glass of water, simply turned away from me and went right back to sleep.

Phew!

I lay still, recuperating slowly.

I had been right, you see, about that little thing on her lower lip, had I not?

Come to think of it, I had been right about more or less everything that had to do with this incredible escapade. What a triumph! I felt wonderfully relaxed and well-spent.

I wondered what time it was. My watch was not a luminous one. I'd better go. I crept out of bed. I felt my way, a trifle less cautiously this time, around the bed, out of the bedroom, along the corridor, down the stairs and into the hall of the house. I found my raincoat and slippers. I put them on. I had a lighter in the pocket of my raincoat. I used it and read the time. It was eight minutes before two. Later than I thought, I opened the front door and stepped out into the black night.

My thoughts now began to concentrate upon Jerry. Was he all right? Had he gotten away with it? I moved through the darkness towards the gap in the hedge.

'Hi, sport,' a voice whispered beside me.

'Jerry!'

'Everything okay?' Jerry asked.

'Fantastic,' I said. 'Amazing. What about you?'

'Same with me,' he said. I caught the flash of his white teeth grinning at me in the dark. 'We made it, Vic!' he whispered, touching my arm. 'You were right! It worked! It was sensational!'

'See you tomorrow,' I whispered. 'Go home.'

We moved apart. I went through the hedge and entered my house. Three minutes later, I was safely back in my own bed, and my own wife was sleeping soundly along-side me.

The next morning was Sunday. I was up at eight thirty and went downstairs in pyjamas and dressing-gown, as I always do on a Sunday, to make breakfast for the family. I had left Mary sleeping. The two boys, Victor, aged nine, and Wally, seven, were already down.

'Hi, Daddy,' Wally said.

'I've got a great new breakfast,' I announced.

'What?' both boys said together. They had been into town and fetched the Sunday paper and were now reading the comics.

'We make some buttered toast and we spread orange marmalade on it,' I said. 'Then we put strips of crisp bacon on top of the marmalade.'

'*Bacon!*' Victor said. 'With *orange marmalade!*'

'I know. But you wait till you try it. It's wonderful.'

I dished out the grapefruit juice and drank two glasses of it myself. I set another on the table for Mary when she came down. I switched on the electric kettle, put the bread in the toaster, and started to fry the bacon. At this point, Mary came into the kitchen. She had a flimsy peach-coloured chiffon thing over her nightdress.

'Good morning,' I said, watching her over my shoulder as I manipulated the frying-pan.

She did not answer. She went to her chair at the kitchen table and sat down. She started to sip her juice. She looked neither at me nor at the boys. I went on frying the bacon.

'Hi, Mummy,' Wally said.

She didn't answer this either.

The smell of the bacon fat was beginning to turn my stomach.

'I'd like some coffee,' Mary said, not looking around. Her voice was very odd.

'Coming right up,' I said. I pushed the frying-pan away from the heat and quickly made a cup of black instant coffee. I placed it before her.

'Boys,' she said, addressing the children, 'would you please do your reading in the other room till breakfast is ready.'

'Us?' Victor said. 'Why?'

'Because I say so.'

'Are we doing something wrong?' Wally asked.

'No, honey, you're not. I just want to be left alone for a moment with Daddy.'

I felt myself shrink inside my skin. I wanted to run. I wanted to rush out the front door and go running down the street and hide.

'Get yourself a coffee, Vic,' she said, 'and sit down.'

Her voice was quite flat. There was no anger in it. There was just nothing. And she still wouldn't look at me. The boys went out, taking the comic section with them.

'Shut the door,' Mary said to them.

I put a spoonful of powdered coffee into my cup and poured boiling water over it. I added milk and sugar. The silence was shattering. I crossed over and sat down in my chair opposite her. It might just as well have been an electric chair, the way I was feeling.

'Listen, Vic,' she said, looking into her coffee cup. 'I want to get this said before I lose my nerve and then I won't be able to say it.'

'For heaven's sake, what's all the drama about?' I asked. 'Has something happened?'

'Yes, Vic, it has.'

'What?'

Her face was pale and still and distant, unconscious of the kitchen around her.

'Come on, then, out with it,' I said bravely.

'You're not going to like this very much,' she said, and her big blue haunted-looking eyes rested a moment on my face, then travelled away.

'What am I not going to like very much?' I said. The sheer terror of it all was beginning to stir my bowels. I felt the same way as those burglars the cops had told me about.

'You know I hate talking about love-making and all that sort of thing,' she said. 'I've never once talked to you about it all the time we've been married.'

'That's true,' I said.

She took a sip of her coffee, but she wasn't tasting it. 'The point is this,' she said. 'I've never liked it. If you really want to know, I've hated it.'

'Hated what?' I asked.

'Sex,' she said. 'Doing it.'

'Good Lord!' I said.

'It's never given me even the slightest little bit of pleasure.'

This was shattering enough in itself, but the real cruncher was still to come, I felt sure of that.

'I'm sorry if that surprises you,' she added.

I couldn't think of anything to say, so I kept quiet.

Her eyes rose again from the coffee cup and looked into mine, watchful, as if calculating something, then fell again. 'I wasn't ever going to tell you,' she said. 'And I never would have if it hadn't been for last night.'

I said very slowly, 'What about last night?'

'Last night,' she said, 'I suddenly found out what the whole crazy thing is all about.'

'You did?'

She looked full at me now, and her face was as open as a flower. 'Yes,' she said. 'I surely did.'

I didn't move.

'Oh darling!' she cried, jumping up and rushing over and giving me an enormous kiss. 'Thank you so much for last night! You were marvellous! And I was marvellous! We were both marvellous! Don't look so embarrassed, my darling! You ought to be proud of yourself! You were fantastic! I love you! I do! I do!'

I just sat there.

She leaned close to me and put an arm around my shoulders. 'And now,' she said softly, 'now that you have ... I don't quite know how to say this ... now that you have sort of discovered what it is I *need*, everything is going to be so marvellous from now on!'

I still sat there. She went slowly back to her chair. A big tear was running down one of her cheeks. I couldn't think why.

'I was right to tell you, wasn't I?' she said, smiling through her tears.

'Yes,' I said. 'Oh, yes.' I stood up and went over to the cooker so that I wouldn't be facing her. Through the kitchen window, I caught sight of Jerry crossing his garden with the Sunday paper under his arm. There was a lilt in his walk, a little prance of triumph in each pace he took, and when he reached the steps of his front porch, he ran up them two at a time.

The Butler

First published in *Travel and Leisure* (May 1974)
with the title 'The Butler Did It'

As soon as George Cleaver had made his first million, he and Mrs Cleaver moved out of their small suburban villa into an elegant London house. They acquired a French chef called Monsieur Estragon and an English butler called Tibbs, both wildly expensive. With the help of these two experts, the Cleavers set out to climb the social ladder and began to give dinner parties several times a week on a lavish scale.

But these dinners never seemed quite to come off. There was no animation, no spark to set the conversation alight, no style at all. Yet the food was superb and the service faultless.

'What the heck's wrong with our parties, Tibbs?' Mr Cleaver said to the butler. 'Why don't nobody never loosen up and let themselves go?'

Tibbs inclined his head to one side and looked at the ceiling. 'I hope, sir, you will not be offended if I offer a small suggestion.'

'What is it?'

'It's the wine, sir.'

'What about the wine?'

'Well, sir, Monsieur Estragon serves superb food.

Superb food should be accompanied by superb wine. But you serve them a cheap and very odious Spanish red.'

'Then why in heaven's name didn't you say so before, you twit?' cried Mr Cleaver. 'I'm not short of money. I'll give them the best flipping wine in the world if that's what they want! What *is* the best wine in the world?'

'Claret, sir,' the butler replied, 'from the greatest *châteaux* in Bordeaux – Lafite, Latour, Haut-Brion, Margaux, Mouton-Rothschild and Cheval Blanc. And from only the very greatest vintage years, which are, in my opinion, 1906, 1914, 1929 and 1945. Cheval Blanc was also magnificent in 1895 and 1921, and Haut-Brion in 1906.'

'Buy them all!' said Mr Cleaver. 'Fill the flipping cellar from top to bottom!'

'I can try, sir,' the butler said. 'But wines like these are extremely rare and cost a fortune.'

'I don't give a hoot what they cost!' said Mr Cleaver. 'Just go out and get them!'

That was easier said than done. Nowhere in England or in France could Tibbs find any wine from 1895, 1906, 1914 or 1921. But he did manage to get hold of some twenty-nines and forty-fives. The bills for these wines were astronomical. They were in fact so huge that even Mr Cleaver began to sit up and take notice. And his interest quickly turned into outright enthusiasm when the butler suggested to him that a knowledge of wine was a very considerable social asset. Mr Cleaver bought books on the subject and read them from cover to cover. He also learned a great deal from Tibbs himself, who taught him, among other things, just how wine should properly be tasted. 'First, sir, you sniff it long and deep, with your nose right inside the top of the glass, like this. Then you take a mouthful and you open your lips a tiny bit and suck in air, letting the air bubble through the wine. Watch me do it. Then you roll it vigorously around your mouth. And finally you swallow it.'

In due course, Mr Cleaver came to regard himself as an expert on wine, and inevitably he turned into a colossal bore. 'Ladies and gentlemen,' he would announce at dinner, holding up his glass, 'this is a Margaux '29! The greatest year of the century! Fantastic bouquet! Smells of cowslips! And notice especially the after taste and how the tiny trace of tannin gives it that glorious astringent quality! Terrific, ain't it?'

The guests would nod and sip and mumble a few praises, but that was all.

'What's the matter with the silly twerps?' Mr Cleaver said to Tibbs after this had gone on for some time. 'Don't none of them appreciate a great wine?'

The butler laid his head to one side and gazed upward. 'I think they *would* appreciate it, sir,' he said, 'if they were able to taste it. But they can't.'

'What the heck d' you mean, they can't taste it?'

'I believe, sir, that you have instructed Monsieur Estragon to put liberal quantities of vinegar in the salad-dressing.'

'What's wrong with that? I like vinegar.'

'Vinegar,' the butler said, 'is the enemy of wine. It destroys the palate. The dressing should be made of pure olive oil and a little lemon juice. Nothing else.'

'Hogwash!' said Mr Cleaver.

'As you wish, sir.'

'I'll say it again, Tibbs. You're talking hogwash. The vinegar don't spoil my palate one bit.'

'You are very fortunate, sir,' the butler murmured, backing out of the room.

That night at dinner, the host began to mock his butler in front of the guests. 'Mister Tibbs,' he said, 'has been trying to tell me I can't taste my wine if I put vinegar in the salad-dressing. Right, Tibbs?'

'Yes, sir,' Tibbs replied gravely.

'And I told him hogwash. Didn't I, Tibbs?'

'Yes, sir.'

'This wine,' Mr Cleaver went on, raising his glass, 'tastes to me exactly like a Château Lafite '45, and what's more it is a Château Lafite '45.'

Tibbs, the butler, stood very still and erect near the sideboard, his face pale. 'If you'll forgive me, sir,' he said, 'that is not a Lafite '45.'

Mr Cleaver swung round in his chair and stared at the butler. 'What the heck d'you mean,' he said. 'There's the empty bottles beside you to prove it!'

These great clarets, being old and full of sediment, were always decanted by Tibbs before dinner. They were served in cut-glass decanters, while the empty bottles, as is the custom, were placed on the sideboard. Right now, two empty bottles of Lafite '45 were standing on the sideboard for all to see.

'The wine you are drinking, sir,' the butler said quietly, 'happens to be that cheap and rather odious Spanish red.'

Mr Cleaver looked at the wine in his glass, then at the

butler. The blood was coming to his face now, his skin was turning scarlet. 'You're lying, Tibbs!' he said.

'No sir, I'm not lying,' the butler said. 'As a matter of fact, I have never served you any other wine but Spanish red since I've been here. It seemed to suit you very well.'

'Don't believe him!' Mr Cleaver cried out to his guests. 'The man's gone mad.'

'Great wines,' the butler said, 'should be treated with reverence. It is bad enough to destroy the palate with three or four cocktails before dinner, as you people do, but when you slosh vinegar over your food into the bargain, then you might just as well be drinking dishwater.'

Ten outraged faces around the table stared at the butler. He had caught them off balance. They were speechless.

'This,' the butler said, reaching out and touching one of the empty bottles lovingly with his fingers, 'this is the last of the forty-fives. The twenty-nines have already been finished. But they were glorious wines. Monsieur Estragon and I enjoyed them immensely.'

The butler bowed and walked quite slowly from the room. He crossed the hall and went out of the front door of the house into the street where Monsieur Estragon was already loading their suitcases into the boot of the small car which they owned together.

Bitch

First published in *Playboy* (July 1974)

I have so far released for publication only one episode from Uncle Oswald's diaries. It concerned, as some of you may remember, a carnal encounter between my uncle and a Syrian female leper in the Sinai Desert. Six years have gone by since its publication and nobody has yet come forward to make trouble. I am therefore encouraged to release a second episode from these curious pages. My lawyer has advised against it. He points out that some of the people concerned are still living and are easily recognizable. He says I will be sued mercilessly. Well, let them sue. I am proud of my uncle. He knew how life should be lived. In a preface to the first episode I said that Casanova's *Memoirs* read like a parish magazine beside Uncle Oswald's diaries, and that the great lover himself, when compared with my uncle, appears positively undersexed. I stand by that, and given time I shall prove it to the world. Here then is a little episode from Volume XXIII, precisely as Uncle Oswald wrote it:

Paris
Wednesday

Breakfast at ten. I tried the honey. It was delivered yesterday in an early Sèvres sucrier which had that lovely canary-coloured ground known as *jonquille*. 'From Suzie,'

417

the note said, 'and thank you.' It is nice to be appreciated. And the honey was interesting. Suzie Jolibois had, among other things, a small farm south of Casablanca, and was fond of bees. Her hives were set in the midst of a planta-tion of *Cannabis indica*, and the bees drew their nectar exclusively from this source. They lived, those bees, in a state of perpetual euphoria and were disinclined to work. The honey was therefore very scarce. I spread a third piece of toast. The stuff was almost black. It had a pun-gent aroma. The telephone rang. I put the receiver to my ear and waited. I never speak first when called. After all, I'm not phoning them. They're phoning me.

'Oswald! Are you there?'

I knew the voice. 'Yes, Henri,' I said. 'Good morning.'

'Listen!' he said, speaking fast and sounding excited. 'I think I've got it! I'm almost certain I've got it! Forgive me if I'm out of breath, but I've just had a rather fantastic experience. It's all right now. Everything's fine. Will you come over?'

'Yes,' I said. 'I'll come over.' I replaced the receiver and poured myself another cup of coffee. Had Henri really done it at last? If he had, then I wanted to be around to share the fun.

I must pause here to tell you how I met Henri Biotte. Some three years ago I drove down to Provence to spend a summer weekend with a lady who was interesting to me simply because she possessed an extraordinarily powerful muscle in a region where other women have no muscles at all. An hour after my arrival, I was strolling alone on the lawn beside the river when a small dark man approached me. He had black hairs on the backs of his hands and he made me a little bow and said, 'Henri Biotte, a fellow guest.'

'Oswald Cornelius,' I said.

Henri Biotte was as hairy as a goat. His chin and cheeks were covered with bristly black hair and thick tufts of it were sprouting from his nostrils. 'May I join you?' he said, falling into step beside me and starting immediately to talk. And what a talker he was! How Gallic, how excitable. He walked with a mad little hop, and his fingers flew as if he wanted to scatter them to the four winds of heaven, and his words went off like firecrackers, with terrific speed. He was a Belgian chemist, he said, working in Paris. He was an olfactory chemist. He had devoted his life to the study of olfaction.

'You mean smell?' I said.

'Yes, yes!' he cried. 'Exactly! I am an expert on smells. I know more about smells than anyone else in the world!'

'Good smells or bad?' I asked, trying to slow him down.

'Good smells, lovely smells, glorious smells!' he said. 'I make them! I can make any smell you want!'

He went on to tell me he was the chief perfume blender to one of the great couturiers in the city. And his nose, he said, placing a hairy finger on the tip of his hairy proboscis, probably looked just like any other nose, did it not? I wanted to tell him it had more hairs sprouting from the noseholes than wheat from the prairies and why didn't he get his barber to snip them out, but instead I confessed politely that I could see nothing unusual about it.

'Quite so,' he said. 'But in actual fact it is a smelling

organ of phenomenal sensitivity. With two sniffs it can detect the presence of a single drop of macrocylic musk in a gallon of geranium oil.'

'Extraordinary,' I said.

'On the Champs Elysées,' he went on, 'which is a wide thoroughfare, my nose can identify the precise perfume being used by a woman walking on the other side of the street.'

'With the traffic in between?'

'With heavy traffic in between,' he said.

He went on to name two of the most famous perfumes in the world, both of them made by the fashion house he worked for. 'Those are my personal creations,' he said modestly. 'I blended them myself. They have made a fortune for the celebrated old bitch who runs the business.'

'But not for you?'

'Me! I am but a poor miserable employee on a salary,' he said, spreading his palms and hunching his shoulders so high they touched his earlobes. 'One day, though, I shall break away and pursue my dream.'

'You have a dream?'

'I have a glorious, tremendous, exciting dream, my dear sir!'

'Then why don't you pursue it?'

'Because first I must find a man farsighted enough and wealthy enough to back me.'

Ah-ha, I thought, so that's what it's all about. 'With a reputation like yours, that shouldn't be too difficult,' I said.

'The sort of rich man I seek is hard to find,' he said.

'He must be a sporty gambler with a very keen appetite for the bizarre.'

That's me, you clever little bugger, I thought. 'What is this dream you wish to pursue?' I asked him. 'Is it making perfumes?'

'My dear fellow!' he cried. 'Anyone can make *perfumes*! I'm talking about *the* perfume! The *only* one that counts!'

'Which would that be?'

'Why, the *dangerous* one, of course! And when I have made it, I shall rule the world!'

'Good for you,' I said.

'I am not joking, Monsieur Cornelius. Would you permit me to explain what I am driving at?'

'Go ahead.'

'Forgive me if I sit down,' he said, moving towards a bench. 'I had a heart attack last April and I have to be careful.'

'I'm sorry to hear that.'

'Oh, don't be sorry. All will be well so long as I don't overdo things.'

It was a lovely afternoon and the bench was on the lawn near the riverbank and we sat down on it. Beside us, the river flowed slow and smooth and deep, and there were little clouds of water-flies hovering over the surface. Across the river there were willows along the bank and beyond the willows an emerald-green meadow, yellow with buttercups, and a single cow grazing. The cow was brown and white.

'I will tell you what kind of perfume I wish to make,' he

said. 'But it is essential I explain a few other things to you on the way or you will not fully understand. So please bear with me a while.' One hand lay limp upon his lap, the hairy part upwards. It looked like a black rat. He was stroking it gently with the fingers of the other hand.

'Let us consider first,' he said, 'the phenomenon that occurs when a dog meets a bitch in heat. The dog's sexual drive is tremendous. All self-control disappears. He has only one thought in his head, which is to fornicate on the spot, and unless he is prevented by force, he will do so. But do you know what it is that causes this tremendous sex-drive in a dog?'

'Smell,' I said.

'Precisely, Monsieur Cornelius. Odorous molecules of a special conformation enter the dog's nostrils and stimulate his olfactory nerve-endings. This causes urgent signals to be sent to the olfactory bulb and thence to the higher brain centres. It is *all* done by smell. If you sever a dog's olfactory nerve, he will lose interest in sex. This is also true of many other mammals, but it is not true of man. Smell has nothing to do with the sexual appetite of the human male. He is stimulated in this respect by sight, by tactility and by his lively imagination. Never by smell.'

'What about perfume?' I said.

'It's all rubbish!' he answered. 'All those expensive scents in small bottles, the ones I make, they have no aphrodisiac effect at all upon a man. Perfume was never intended for that purpose. In the old days, women used it to conceal the fact that they stank. Today, when they no longer stink, they use it purely for narcissistic reasons.

They enjoy putting it on and smelling their own good
smells. Men hardly notice the stuff. I promise you that.'

'I do,' I said.

'Does it stir you physically?'

'No, not physically. Aesthetically, yes.'

'You enjoy the smell. So do I. But there are plenty of
other smells I enjoy more – the bouquet of a good Lafite,
the scent of a fresh Comice pear, or the smell of the air
blowing in from the sea on the Brittany coast.'

A trout jumped high in midstream and the sunlight
flashed on its body. 'You must forget,' said Monsieur
Biotte, 'all the nonsense about musk and ambergris and
the testicular secretions of the civet cat. We make our perfumes from chemicals these days. If I want a musky odour
I will use ethylene sebacate. Phenylacetic acid will give me
civet and benzaldehyde will provide the smell of almonds.
No sir, I am no longer interested in mixing up chemicals
to make pretty smells.'

For some minutes his nose had been running slightly,
wetting the black hairs in his nostrils. He noticed it and
produced a handkerchief and gave it a blow and a wipe.
'What I intend to do,' he said, 'is to produce a perfume
which will have the same electrifying effect upon a man as
the scent of a bitch in heat has upon a dog! One whiff and
that'll be it! The man will lose all control. He'll rip off his
pants and ravish the lady on the spot!'

'We could have some fun with that,' I said.

'We could rule the world!' he cried.

'Yes, but you told me just now that smell has nothing to
do with the sexual appetite of the human male.'

'It doesn't,' he said. 'But it used to. I have evidence that in the period of the post-glacial drift, when primitive man was far more closely related to the ape than he is now, he still retained the ape-like characteristic of jumping on any right-smelling female he ran across. And later, in the Palaeolithic and Neolithic periods, he continued to become sexually animated by smell, but to a lesser and lesser degree. By the time the higher civilizations had come along in Egypt and China around 10,000 BC, evolution had played its part and had completely suppressed man's ability to be stimulated sexually by smell. Am I boring you?'

'Not at all. But tell me, does that mean an actual physical change has taken place in man's smelling apparatus?'

'Absolutely not,' he said, 'otherwise there'd be nothing we could do about it. The little mechanism that enabled our ancestors to smell these subtle odours is still there. I happen to know it is. Listen, you've seen how some people can make their ears move a tiny bit?'

'I can do it myself,' I said, doing it.

'You see,' he said, 'the ear-moving muscle is still there. It's a leftover from the time when man used to be able to cock his ears forwards for better hearing, like a dog. He lost that ability over a hundred thousand years ago, but the muscle remains. And the same applies to our smelling apparatus. The mechanism for smelling those secret smells is still there, but we have lost the ability to use it.'

'How can you be so certain it's still there?' I asked.

'Do you know how our smelling system works?' he said.

'Not really.'

424

'Then I shall tell you, otherwise I cannot answer your question. Attend closely, please. Air is sucked in through the nostrils and passes the three baffle-shaped turbinate bones in the upper part of the nose. There it gets warmer and filtered. This warm air now travels up and over two clefts that contain the smelling organs. These organs are patches of yellowish tissue, each about an inch square. In this tissue are embedded the nerve-fibres and nerve-endings of the olfactory nerve. Every nerve-ending consists of an olfactory cell bearing a cluster of tiny hair-like filaments. These filaments act as receivers. "Receptors" is a better word. And when the receptors are tickled or stimulated by odorous molecules, they send signals to the brain. If, as you come downstairs in the morning, you sniff into your nostrils the odorous molecules of frying bacon, these will stimulate your receptors, the receptors will flash a signal along the olfactory nerve to the brain, and the brain will interpret it in terms of the character and intensity of the odour. And that is when you cry out, "Ah-ha, bacon for breakfast!"'

'I never eat bacon for breakfast,' I said.

He ignored this.

'These receptors,' he went on, 'these tiny hair-like filaments are what concern us. And now you are going to ask me how on earth they can tell the difference between one odorous molecule and another, between say peppermint and camphor?'

'How can they?' I said. I was interested in this.

'Attend more closely than ever now, please,' he said. 'At the end of each receptor is an indentation, a sort of cup, except that it isn't round. This is the "receptor site". Imagine now thousands of these little hair-like filaments with tiny cups at their extremities, all waving about like the tendrils of sea anemones and waiting to catch in their cups any odorous molecules that pass by. That, you see, is what actually happens. When you sniff a certain smell, the odorous molecules of the substance which made that smell go rushing around inside your nostrils and get caught by the little cups, the receptor sites. Now the important thing to remember is this. Molecules come in all shapes and sizes. Equally, the little cups or receptor sites are also differently shaped. Thus, the molecules lodge only in the receptor sites which fit them. Pepperminty molecules go only into special pepperminty receptor sites. Camphor molecules, which have a quite different shape, will fit only into the special camphor receptor sites, and so on. It's rather like those toys for small children where they have to fit variously shaped pieces into the right holes.'

'Let me see if I understand you,' I said. 'Are you saying that my brain will know it is a pepperminty smell simply because the molecule has lodged in a pepperminty reception site?'

'Precisely.'

'But you are surely not suggesting there are differently shaped receptor sites for every smell in the world?'

'No,' he said, 'as a matter of fact, man has only seven differently shaped sites.'

'Why only seven?'

'Because our sense of smell recognizes only seven

426

"pure primary odours". All the rest are "complex odours" made up by mixing the primaries.'

'Are you sure of that?'

'Positive. Our sense of taste has even less. It recognizes only four primaries – sweet, sour, salt and bitter! All other tastes are mixtures of these.'

'What are the seven pure primary odours?' I asked him.

'Their names are of no importance to us,' he said. 'Why confuse the issue.'

'I'd like to hear them.'

'All right,' he said. 'They are camphoraceous, pungent, musky, ethereal, floral, pepperminty and putrid. Don't look so sceptical, please. This isn't *my* discovery. Very learned scientists have worked on it for years. And their conclusions are quite accurate, *except in one respect.*'

'What's that?'

'*There is an eighth pure primary odour which they don't know about, and an eighth receptor site to receive the curiously shaped molecules of that odour!*'

'Ah-ha-ha!' I said. 'I see what you're driving at.'

'Yes,' he said, 'the eighth pure primary odour is the sexual stimulant that caused primitive man to behave like a dog thousands of years ago. It has a very peculiar molecular structure.'

'Then you know what it is?'

'Of course I know what it is.'

'And you say we still retain the receptor sites for these peculiar molecules to fit into?'

'Absolutely.'

'This mysterious smell,' I said, 'does it ever reach our own nostrils nowadays?'

'Frequently.'

'Do we smell it? I mean, are we aware of it?'

'No.'

'You mean the molecules don't get caught in the receptor sites?'

'They do, my dear fellow, they do. But nothing happens. No signal is sent off to the brain. The telephone line is out of action. It's like that ear muscle. The mechanism is still there, but we've lost the ability to use it properly.'

'And what do you propose to do about that?' I asked.

'I shall reactivate it,' he said. 'We are dealing with nerves here, not muscles. And these nerves are not dead or injured, they're merely dormant. I shall probably increase the intensity of the smell a thousandfold, and add a catalyst.'

'Go on,' I said.

'That's enough.'

'I should like to hear more,' I said.

'Forgive me for saying so, Monsieur Cornelius, but I don't think you know enough about organoleptic quality to follow me any further. The lecture is over.'

Henri Biotte sat smug and quiet on the bench beside the river stroking the back of one hand with the fingers of the other. The tufts of hair sprouting from his nostrils gave him a pixie look, but that was camouflage. He struck me rather as a dangerous and dainty little creature, someone who lurked behind stones with a sharp eye and a sting in his tail, waiting for the lone traveller to come by. Surreptitiously I searched his face. The mouth interested me. The lips had a magenta tinge, possibly something to do with his heart trouble. The lower lip was caruncular and pendulous. It bulged out in the middle like a purse, and could easily have served as a receptacle for small coins. The skin of the lip seemed to be blown up very tight, as though by air, and it was constantly wet, not from licking but from an excess of saliva in the mouth.

And there he sat, this Monsieur Henri Biotte, smiling a wicked little smile and waiting patiently for me to react. He was a totally amoral man, that much was clear, but then so was I. He was also a wicked man, and although I cannot in all honesty claim wickedness as one of my own virtues, I find it irresistible in others. A wicked man has a lustre all his own. Then again, there was something diabolically splendid about a person who wished to set back the sex habits of civilized man half a million years.

Yes, he had me hooked. So there and then, sitting beside the river in the garden of the lady from Provence, I made an offer to Henri. I suggested he should leave his present employment forthwith and set himself up in a small laboratory. I would pay all the bills for this little venture as well as making good his salary. It would be a five-year contract, and we would go fifty-fifty on anything that came out of it.

Henri was ecstatic. 'You mean it?' he cried. 'You are serious?'

I held out my hand. He grasped it in both of his and shook it vigorously. It was like shaking hands with a yak. 'We shall control mankind!' he said. 'We'll be the gods of the earth!' He flung his arms around me and embraced me and kissed me first on one cheek, then on the other. Oh, this awful Gallic kissing. Henri's lower lip felt like the wet underbelly of a toad against my skin. 'Let's keep the celebrations until later,' I said, wiping myself dry with a linen handkerchief.

Henri Biotte made apologies and excuses to his hostess and rushed back to Paris that night. Within a week he had given up his old job and had rented three rooms to serve as a laboratory. These were on the third floor of a house on the Left Bank, on the Rue de Cassette, just off the Boulevard Raspaille. He spent a great deal of my money equipping the place with complicated apparatus, and he even installed a large cage into which he put two apes, a male and a female. He also took on an assistant, a clever and moderately presentable young lady called Jeanette. And with all that, he set to work.

You should understand that for me this little venture was of no great importance. I had plenty of other things to amuse me. I used to drop in on Henri maybe a couple of times a month to see how things were going, but otherwise I left him entirely to himself. My mind wasn't on his job. I hadn't the patience for that kind of research. And when results failed to come quickly, I began to lose all interest. Even the pair of over-sexed apes ceased to amuse me after a while.

Only once did I derive any pleasure from my visits to his laboratory. As you must know by now, I can seldom resist even a moderately presentable woman. And so, on a certain rainy Thursday afternoon, while Henri was busy applying electrodes to the olfactory organs of a frog in one room, I found myself applying something infinitely more agreeable to Jeanette in the other room. I had not, of course, expected anything out of the ordinary from this little frolic. I was acting more out of habit than anything else. But my goodness, what a surprise I got! Beneath her white overall, this rather austere research chemist turned out to be a sinewy and flexible female of immense dexterity. The experiments she performed, first with the oscillator, then with the high-speed centrifuge, were absolutely breathtaking. In fact, not since that Turkish tightrope walker in Ankara (see Vol. XXI) had I experienced anything quite like it. Which all goes to show for the thousandth time that women are as inscrutable as the ocean. You never know what you have under your keel, deep water or shallow, until you have heaved the lead.

I did not bother to visit the laboratory again after that. You know my rule. I never return to a female a second time. With me at any rate, women invariably pull out all the stops during the first encounter, and a second meeting can therefore be nothing more than the same old tune on the same old fiddle. Who wants that? Not me. So when I suddenly heard Henri's voice calling urgently to me over the telephone that morning at breakfast, I had almost forgotten his existence.

I drove through the fiendish Paris traffic to the Rue de Cassette. I parked the car and took the tiny elevator to the third floor. Henri opened the door of the laboratory. 'Don't move!' he cried. 'Stay right where you are!' He scuttled away and returned in a few seconds holding a little tray upon which lay two greasy-looking red rubber objects. 'Noseplugs,' he said. 'Put them in, please. Like me. Keep out the molecules. Go on, ram them in tight. You'll have to breathe through your mouth, but who cares?'

Each noseplug had a short length of blue string attached to its blunt lower end, presumably for pulling it back out of the nostril. I could see the two bits of blue string dangling from Henri's nostrils. I inserted my own noseplugs. Henri inspected them. He rammed them in tighter with his thumb. Then he went dancing back into the lab, waving his hairy hands and crying out, 'Come in now, my dear Oswald! Come in, come in! Forgive my excitement, but this is a great day for me!' The plugs in his nose made him speak as though he had a bad cold. He hopped over to a cupboard and reached inside. He brought out one of those small square bottles made of very thick glass that hold about an ounce of perfume. He carried it over to where I stood, cupping his hands around it as though it were a tiny bird. 'Look! Here it is! The most precious fluid in the entire world!'

This is the sort of rubbishy overstatement I dislike intensely. 'So you think you've done it?' I said.

'I know I've done it, Oswald! I am certain I've done it!'

'Tell me what happened.'

'That's not so easy,' he said. 'But I can try.'

He placed the little bottle carefully on the bench. 'I had left this particular blend, Number 1076, to distil overnight,' he went on. 'That was because only one drop of distillate is produced every half-hour. I had it dripping into a sealed beaker to prevent evaporation. All these fluids are extremely volatile. And so, soon after I arrived at eight thirty this morning, I went over to Number 1076 and lifted the seal from the beaker. I took a tiny sniff. Just one tiny sniff. Then I replaced the seal.'

'And then?'

'Oh, my God, Oswald, it was fantastic! I completely lost control of myself! I did things I would never in a million years have dreamed of doing!'

'Such as what?'

'My dear fellow, I went completely wild! I was like a wild beast, an animal! I was not human! The civilizing influences of centuries simply dropped away! I was Neolithic!'

'What did you do?'

'I can't remember the next bit very clearly. It was all so quick and violent. But I became overwhelmed by the most terrifying sensation of lust it is possible to imagine. Everything else was blotted out of my mind. All I wanted was a woman. I felt that if I didn't get hold of a woman immediately, I would explode.'

'Lucky Jeanette,' I said, glancing towards the next room. 'How is she now?'

'Jeanette left me over a year ago,' he said. 'I replaced her with a brilliant young chemist called Simone Gautier.'

'Lucky Simone, then.'

'No, no!' Henri cried. 'That was the awful thing! She hadn't arrived! Today of all days, she was late for work! I began to go mad. I dashed out into the corridor and down the stairs. I was like a dangerous animal. I was hunting for a woman, any woman, and heaven help her when I found her!'

'And who did you find?'

'Nobody, thank God. Because suddenly, I regained my senses. The effect had worn off. It was very quick, and I was standing alone on the second-floor landing. I felt cold. But I knew at once exactly what had happened. I ran back upstairs and re-entered this room with my nostrils pinched tightly between finger and thumb. I went straight to the drawer where I stored the noseplugs. Ever since I started working on this project, I have kept a supply of noseplugs ready for just such an occasion. I rammed in the plugs. Now I was safe.'

'Can't the molecules get up into the nose through the mouth?' I asked him.

'They can't reach the receptor sites,' he said. 'That's why you can't smell through your mouth. So I went over to the apparatus and switched off the heat. I then transferred the tiny quantity of precious fluid from the beaker to this very solid airtight bottle you see here. In it there are precisely eleven cubic centimetres of Number 1076.'

'Then you telephoned me.'

'Not immediately no. Because at that point, Simone arrived. She took one look at me and ran into the next room, screaming.'

'Why did she do that?'

'My God, Oswald, I was standing there stark naked and I hadn't realized it. I must have ripped off all my clothes!'

'Then what?'

'I got dressed again. After that, I went and told Simone exactly what had happened. When she heard the truth, she became as excited as me. Don't forget, we've been working on this together for over a year now.'

'Is she still here?'

'Yes. She's next door in the other lab.'

It was quite a story Henri had told me. I picked up the little square bottle and held it against the light. Through the thick glass I could see about half an inch of fluid, pale and pinkish-grey, like the juice of a ripe quince.

'Don't drop it,' Henri said. 'Better put it down.' I put it down. 'The next step,' he went on, 'will be to make an accurate test under scientific conditions. For that I shall have to spray a measured quantity on to a woman and then let a man approach her. It will be necessary for me to observe the operation at close range.'

'You are a dirty old man,' I said.

'I am an olfactory chemist,' he said primly.

'Why don't I go out into the street with my noseplugs in,' I said, 'and spray some on to the first woman who comes along. You can watch from the window here. It ought to be fun.'

'It would be fun all right,' Henri said. 'But not very scientific. I must make the tests indoors under controlled conditions.'

'And I will play the male part,' I said.

'No, Oswald.'

'What do you mean, no. I insist.'

'Now listen to me,' Henri said. 'We have not yet found out what will happen when a woman is present. This stuff is very powerful, I am certain of that. And you, my dear sir, are not exactly young. It could be extremely dangerous. It could drive you beyond the limit of your endurance.'

I was stung. 'There are no limits to my endurance,' I said.

'Rubbish,' Henri said. 'I refuse to take chances. That is why I have engaged the fittest and strongest young man I could find.'

'You mean you've already done this?'

'Certainly I have,' Henri said. 'I am excited and impatient. I want to get on. The boy will be here any minute.'

'Who is he?'

'A professional boxer.'

'Good God.'

'His name is Pierre Lacaille. I am paying him one thousand francs for the job.'

'How did you find him?'

'I know a lot more people than you think, Oswald. I am not a hermit.'

'Does the man know what he's in for?'

'I have told him that he is to participate in a scientific experiment that has to do with the psychology of sex. The less he knows the better.'

'And the woman? Who will you use there?'

'Simone, of course,' Henri said. 'She is a scientist in her own right. She will be able to observe the reactions of the male even more closely than me.'

'That she will,' I said. 'Does she realize what might happen to her?'

'Very much so. And I had one hell of a job persuading her to do it. I had to point out that she would be participating in a demonstration that will go down in history. It will be talked about for hundreds of years.'

'Nonsense,' I said.

'My dear sir, through the centuries there are certain great epic moments of scientific discovery that are never forgotten. Like the time when Dr Horace Wells of Hartford, Connecticut, had a tooth pulled out in 1844.'

'What was so historic about that?'

'Dr Wells was a dentist who had been playing about with nitrous oxide gas. One day, he got a terrible toothache. He knew the tooth would have to come out, and he called in another dentist to do the job. But first he persuaded his colleague to put a mask over his face and turn on the nitrous oxide. He became unconscious and the tooth was extracted and he woke up again as fit as a flea. Now *that*, Oswald, was the first operation ever performed in the world under general anaesthesia. It started something big. We shall do the same.'

At this point, the doorbell rang. Henri grabbed a pair of noseplugs and carried them with him to the door. And there stood Pierre, the boxer. But Henri would not allow him to enter until the plugs were rammed firmly up his nostrils. I believe the fellow came thinking he was going to act in a blue film, but the business with the plugs must have quickly disillusioned him. Pierre Lacaille was a bantamweight, small, muscular and wiry. He had a flat face and a bent nose. He was about twenty-two and not very bright.

Henri introduced me, then ushered us straight into the adjoining laboratory where Simone was working. She was

437

standing by the lab bench in a white overall, writing something in a notebook. She looked up at us through thick glasses as we came in. The glasses had a white plastic frame.

'Simone,' Henri said, 'this is Pierre Lacaille.' Simone looked at the boxer but said nothing. Henri didn't bother to introduce me.

Simone was a slim thirtyish woman with a pleasant scrubbed face. Her hair was brushed back and plaited into a bun. This, together with the white spectacles, the white overall and the white skin of her face, gave her a quaint antiseptic air. She looked as though she had been sterilized for thirty minutes in an autoclave and should be handled with rubber gloves. She gazed at the boxer with large brown eyes.

'Let's get going,' Henri said. 'Are you ready?'

'I don't know what's going to happen,' the boxer said. 'But I'm ready.' He did a little dance on his toes.

Henri was also ready. He had obviously worked the whole thing out before I arrived. 'Simone will sit in that chair,' he said, pointing to a plain wooden chair set in the middle of the laboratory. 'And you, Pierre, will stand on the six-metre mark with your noseplugs still in.'

There were chalk lines on the floor indicating various distances from the chair, from half a metre up to six metres.

'I shall begin by spraying a small quantity of liquid on to the lady's neck,' Henri went on addressing the boxer. 'You will then remove your noseplugs and start walking slowly towards her.' To me he said, 'I wish first of all to

discover the effective range, the exact distance he is from
the subject when the molecules hit.'

'Does he start with his clothes on?' I asked.

'Exactly as he is now.'

'And is the lady expected to co-operate or to resist?'

'Neither. She must be a purely passive instrument in
his hands.'

Simone was still looking at the boxer. I saw her slide the
end of her tongue slowly over her lips.

'This perfume,' I said to Henri, 'does it have any effect
upon a woman?'

'None whatsoever,' he said. 'That is why I am sending
Simone out now to prepare the spray.' The girl went into
the main laboratory, closing the door behind her.

'So you spray something on the girl and I walk towards
her,' the boxer said. 'What happens then?'

'We shall have to wait and see,' Henri said. 'You are not
worried, are you?'

'Me, worried?' the boxer said. 'About a woman?'

'Good boy,' Henri said. Henri was becoming very excited.
He went hopping from one end of the room to the other,
checking and rechecking the position of the chair on its
chalk mark and moving all breakables such as glass bea-
kers and bottles and test-tubes off the bench on to a high
shelf. 'This isn't the ideal place,' he said, 'but we must
make the best of it.' He tied a surgeon's mask over the
lower part of his face, then handed one to me.

'Don't you trust the noseplugs?'

'It's just an extra precaution,' he said. 'Put it on.'

The girl returned carrying a tiny stainless-steel spray-gun.

She gave the gun to Henri. Henri took a stop-watch from his pocket. 'Get ready, please,' he said. 'You, Pierre, stand over there on the six-metre mark.' Pierre did so. The girl seated herself in the chair. It was a chair without arms. She sat very prim and upright in her spotless white overall with her hands folded on her lap, her knees together. Henri stationed himself behind the girl. I stood to one side. 'Are we ready?' Henri cried.

'Wait,' said the girl. It was the first word she had spoken. She stood up, removed her spectacles, placed them on a high shelf, then returned to her seat. She smoothed the white overall along her thighs, then clasped her hands together and laid them again on her lap.

'Are we ready now?' Henri said.

'Let her have it,' I said. 'Shoot.'

Henri aimed the little spray-gun at an area of bare skin just below Simone's ear. He pulled the trigger. The gun made a soft hiss and a fine misty spray came out of its nozzle.

'Pull your noseplugs out!' Henri called to the boxer as he skipped quickly away from the girl and took up a position next to me. The boxer caught hold of the strings dangling from his nostrils and pulled. The vaselined plugs slid out smoothly.

'Come on, come on!' Henri shouted. 'Start moving! Drop the plugs on the floor and come forwards slowly!' The boxer took a pace forwards. 'Not so fast!' Henri cried. 'Slowly does it! That's better! Keep going! Keep going! Don't stop!' He was crazy with excitement, and I must admit I was getting a bit worked up myself. I glanced at the girl. She was crouching in the chair, just a few yards away from the boxer, tense, motionless, watching his every move, and I found myself thinking about a white female rat I had once seen in a cage with a huge python. The python was going to swallow the rat and the rat knew it, and the rat was crouching very low and still, hypnotized, transfixed, utterly fascinated by the slow advancing movements of the snake.

The boxer edged forwards.

As he passed the five-metre mark, the girl unclasped her hands. She laid them palms downwards on her thighs. Then she changed her mind and placed them more or less underneath her buttocks, gripping the seat of the chair on either side, bracing herself, as it were, against the coming onslaught.

The boxer had just passed the two-metre mark when the smell hit him. He stopped dead. His eyes glazed and he swayed on his legs as though he had been tapped on the head with a mallet. I thought he was going to keel over, but he didn't. He stood there swaying gently from side to side like a drunk. Suddenly he started making noises through his nostrils, queer little snorts and grunts that reminded me of a pig sniffing around its trough. Then without any warning at all, he sprang at the girl. He ripped off her white overall, her dress and her underclothes. After that, all hell broke loose.

There is little point in describing exactly what went on during the next few minutes. You can guess most of it anyway. I do have to admit, though, that Henri had probably been right in choosing an exceptionally fit and healthy young man. I hate to say it, but I doubt my middle-aged body could have stood up to the incredibly violent gymnastics the boxer seemed driven to perform. I am not a voyeur. I hate that sort of thing. But in this case, I stood there absolutely transfixed. The sheer animal ferocity of the man was frightening. He was like a wild beast. And right in the middle of it all, Henri did an interesting thing. He produced a revolver and rushed up to the boxer and shouted, 'Get away from that girl! Leave her alone or I'll shoot you!' The boxer ignored him, so Henri fired a shot just over the top of his head and yelled, 'I mean it, Pierre! I shall kill you if you don't stop!' The boxer didn't even look up.

Henri was hopping and dancing about the room and shouting, 'It's fantastic! It's magnificent! Unbelievable! It works! It works! We've done it, my dear Oswald! We've done it!'

The action stopped as quickly as it had begun. The boxer suddenly let go of the girl, stood up, blinked a few times, and then said, 'Where the hell am I? What happened?'

Simone, who seemed to have come through it all with no bones broken, jumped up, grabbed her clothes, and ran into the next room. 'Thank you, mademoiselle,' said Henri as she flew past him.

The interesting thing was that the bemused boxer hadn't the faintest idea what he had been doing. He stood there naked and covered with sweat, gazing around the room and trying to figure out how in the world he came to be in that condition.

'What did I do?' he asked. 'Where's the girl?'

'You were terrific!' Henri shouted, throwing him a towel. 'Don't worry about a thing! The thousand francs is all yours!'

Just then the door flew open and Simone, still naked, ran back into the lab. 'Spray me again!' she cried. 'Oh, Monsieur Henri, spray me just one more time!' Her face was alight, her eyes shining brilliantly.

'The experiment is over,' Henri said. 'Go away and dress yourself.' He took her firmly by the shoulders and pushed her back into the other room. Then he locked the door.

Half an hour later, Henri and I sat celebrating our success in a small café down the street. We were drinking coffee and brandy. 'How long did it go on?' I asked.

'Six minutes and thirty-two seconds,' Henri said.

I sipped my brandy and watched the people strolling by on the sidewalk. 'What's the next move?'

'First, I must write up my notes,' Henri said. 'Then we shall talk about the future.'

'Does anyone else know the formula?'

'Nobody.'

'What about Simone?'

'She doesn't know it.'

'Have you written it down?'

'Not so anyone else could understand it. I shall do that tomorrow.'

'Do it first thing,' I said. 'I'll want a copy. What shall we call the stuff? We need a name.'

'What do you suggest?'

'*Bitch*,' I said. 'Let's call it *Bitch*.' Henri smiled and nodded his head slowly. I ordered more brandy. 'It would be great stuff for stopping a riot,' I said. 'Much better than tear-gas. Imagine the scene if you sprayed it on an angry mob.'

'Nice,' Henri said. 'Very nice.'

'Another thing we could do, we could sell it to very fat, very rich women at fantastic prices.'

'We could do that,' Henri answered.

'Do you think it would cure loss of virility in men?' I asked him.

'Of course,' Henri said. 'Impotence would go out the window.'

'What about octogenarians?'

'Them, too,' he said, 'though it would kill them at the same time.'

'And marriages on the rocks?'

'My dear fellow,' Henri said. 'The possibilities are legion.'

At that precise moment, the seed of an idea came sneaking slowly into my mind. As you know, I have a passion for politics. And my strongest passion, although I am English, is for the politics of the United States of America. I have always thought it is over there, in that mighty and mixed-up nation, that the destinies of mankind must surely lie. And right now, there was a President in office whom I could not stand. He was an evil man who pursued evil polices. Worse than that, he was a humourless and unattractive creature. So why didn't I, Oswald Cornelius, remove him from office?

The idea appealed to me.

'How much *Bitch* have you got in the lab at the moment?'
I asked.

'Exactly ten cubic centimetres,' Henri said.

'And how much is one dose?'

'We used one cc for our test.'

'That's all I want,' I said. 'One cc. I'll take it home with
me today. And a set of noseplugs.'

'No,' Henri said. 'Let's not play around with it at this
stage. It's too dangerous.'

'It is my property,' I said. 'Half of it is mine. Don't forget our agreement.'

In the end, he had to give in. But he hated doing it. We
went back to the lab, inserted our noseplugs, and Henri
measured out precisely one cc of *Bitch* into a small scent
bottle. He sealed the stopper with wax and gave me the
bottle. 'I implore you to be discreet,' he said. 'This is probably
the most important scientific discovery of the century,
and it must not be treated as a joke.'

From Henri's place, I drove directly to the workshop
of an old friend, Marcel Brossollet. Marcel was an inventor
and manufacturer of tiny precise scientific gadgets. He did
a lot of work for surgeons, devising new types of heart-
valves and pacemakers and those little one-way valves that
reduce intra-cranial pressure in hydrocephalics.

'I want you to make me,' I said to Marcel, 'a capsule that
will hold exactly one cc of liquid. To this little capsule, there
must be attached a timing device that will split the capsule
and release the liquid at a predetermined moment. The entire
thing must not be more than half an inch long and half an
inch thick. The smaller the better. Can you manage that?'

'Very easily,' Marcel said. 'A thin plastic capsule, a tiny section of razor-blade to split the capsule, a spring to flip the razor-blade, and the usual pre-set alarm system on a very small ladies' watch. Should the capsule be fillable?'

'Yes. Make it so I myself can fill it and seal it up. Can I have it in a week?'

'Why not?' Marcel said. 'It is very simple.'

The next morning brought dismal news. That lecherous little slut Simone had apparently sprayed herself with the entire remaining stock of *Bitch*, over nine cubic centimetres of it, the moment she arrived at the lab! She had then sneaked up behind Henri, who was just settling himself at his desk to write up his notes.

I don't have to tell you what happened next. And worst of all, the silly girl had forgotten that Henri had a serious heart condition. Damn it, he wasn't even allowed to climb a flight of stairs. So when the molecules hit him the poor fellow didn't stand a chance. He was dead within a minute, killed in action as they say, and that was that.

The infernal woman might at least have waited until he had written down the formula. As it was, Henri left not a single note. I searched the lab after they had taken away his body, but I found nothing. So now more than ever, I was determined to make good use of the only remaining cubic centimetre of *Bitch* in the world.

A week later, I collected from Marcel Brossollet a beautiful little gadget. The timing device consisted of the smallest watch I had ever seen, and this, together with the capsule and all the other parts, had been secured to a tiny aluminium plate three eighths of an inch square. Marcel showed me how to fill and seal the capsule and set the timer. I thanked him and paid the bill.

As soon as possible, I travelled to New York. In Manhattan, I put up at the Plaza Hotel. I arrived there at about three in the afternoon. I took a bath, had a shave, and asked room service to send me up a bottle of Glenlivet and some ice. Feeling clean and comfortable in my dressing-gown, I poured myself a good strong drink of the delicious malt whisky, then settled down in a deep chair with the morning's *New York Times*. My suite overlooked Central Park, and through the open window I could hear the hum of traffic and the blaring of cab-drivers' horns on Central Park South. Suddenly, one of the smaller headlines on the front page of the paper caught my eye. It said, PRESIDENT ON TV TONIGHT. I read on.

The President is expected to make an important foreign policy statement when he speaks tonight at the dinner to be given in his honour by the Daughters of the American Revolution in the ballroom of the Waldorf Astoria . . .

My God, what a piece of luck!

I had been prepared to wait in New York for many weeks before I got a chance like this. The President of the United States does not often appear with a bunch of women on television. And that was exactly how I had to have him. He was an extraordinarily slippery customer. He had fallen into many a sewer and had always come out smelling of shit. Yet he managed every time to convince the nation that the smell was coming from someone else,

447

not him. So the way I figured it was this. A man who rapes a woman in full sight of twenty million viewers across the country would have a pretty hard time denying he ever did it.

I read on.

The President will speak for approximately twenty minutes, commencing at nine p.m. and all major TV networks will carry the speech. He will be introduced by Mrs Elvira Ponsonby, the incumbent President of the Daughters of the American Revolution. When interviewed in her suite at the Waldorf Towers, Mrs Ponsonby said . . .

It was perfect! Mrs Ponsonby would be seated on the President's right. At ten past nine precisely, with the President well into his speech and half the population of the United States watching, a little capsule nestling secretly in the region of Mrs Ponsonby's bosom would be punctured and half a centimetre of *Bitch* would come oozing out on to her gilt lamé ball-gown. The President's head would come up, he would sniff and sniff again, his eyes would bulge, his nostrils would flare, and he would start snorting like a stallion. Then suddenly he would turn and grab hold of Mrs Ponsonby. She would be flung across the dining-table and the President would leap on top of her, with the pie à la mode and strawberry shortcake flying in all directions.

I leaned back and closed my eyes, savouring the delicious scene. I saw the headlines in the papers the next morning:

PRESIDENT'S BEST PERFORMANCE TO DATE
PRESIDENTIAL SECRETS REVEALED TO NATION
PRESIDENT INAUGURATES BLUE TV

and so on.

He would be impeached the next day and I would slip quietly out of New York and head back to Paris. Come to think of it, I would be leaving tomorrow!

I checked the time. It was nearly four o'clock. I dressed myself without hurrying. I took the elevator down to the main lobby and strolled across to Madison Avenue. Somewhere around Sixty-second Street, I found a good florist's shop. There I bought a corsage of three massive orchid blooms all fastened together. The orchids were cattleyas, white and mauve splotches on them. They were particularly vulgar. So, undoubtedly, was Mrs Elvira Ponsonby. I had the shop pack them in a handsome box tied up with gold string. Then I strolled back to the Plaza, carrying the box, and went up to my suite.

I locked all doors leading to the corridor in case the maid should come in to turn back the bed. I got out the noseplugs and vaselined them carefully. I inserted them in my nostrils, ramming them home very hard. I tied a surgeon's mask over my lower face as an extra precaution, just as Henri had done. I was ready now for the next step.

With an ordinary nose-dropper, I transferred my precious cubic centimetre of *Bitch* from the scent bottle to the tiny capsule. The hand holding the dropper shook a little as I did this, but all went well. I sealed the capsule.

449

After that, I wound up the tiny watch and set it to the correct time. It was three minutes after five o'clock. Lastly, I set the timer to go off and break the capsule at ten minutes past nine.

The stems of the three huge orchid blooms had been tied together by the florist with a broad one-inch-wide white ribbon and it was a simple matter for me to remove the ribbon and secure my little capsule and timer to the orchid stems with cotton thread. When that was done, I wound the ribbon back around the stems and over my gadget. Then I retied the bow. It was a nice job.

Next, I telephoned the Waldorf and learned that the dinner was to begin at eight o'clock, but that the guests must be assembled in the ballroom by seven thirty before the President arrived.

At ten minutes to seven, I paid off my cab outside the Waldorf Towers entrance and walked into the building. I crossed the small lobby and placed my orchid box on the reception desk. I leaned over the desk, getting as close as possible to the clerk. 'I have to deliver this package to Mrs Elvira Ponsonby,' I whispered, using a slight American accent. 'It is a gift from the President.'

The clerk looked at me suspiciously.

'Mrs Ponsonby is introducing the President before he speaks tonight in the ballroom,' I added. 'The President wishes her to have this corsage right away.'

'Leave it here and I'll have it sent up to her suite,' the clerk said.

'No, you won't,' I told him. 'My orders are to deliver it in person. What's the number of her suite?'

The man was impressed. 'Mrs Ponsonby is in five-o-one,' he said.

I thanked him and went into the elevator. When I got out at the fifth floor and walked along the corridor, the elevator operator stayed and watched me. I rang the bell to five-o-one.

The door was opened by the most enormous female I had ever seen in my life. I have seen giant women in circuses. I have seen lady wrestlers and weight-lifters. I have seen the huge Masai women in the plains below Kilimanjaro. But never had I seen a female so tall and broad and thick as this one. Nor so thoroughly repugnant. She was groomed and dressed for the greatest occasion of her life, and in the two seconds that elapsed before either of us spoke, I was able to take most of it in – the metallic silver-blue hair with every strand glued into place, the brown pig-eyes, the long sharp nose sniffing for trouble, the curled lips, the prognathous jaw, the powder, the mascara, the scarlet lipstick and, most shattering of all, the massive shored-up bosom that projected like a balcony in front of her. It stuck out so far it was a miracle she didn't topple forwards with the weight of it all. And there she stood, this pneumatic giant, swathed from neck to ankles in the stars and stripes of the American flag.

'Mrs Elvira Ponsonby?' I murmured.

'I am Mrs Ponsonby,' she boomed. 'What do you want? I am extremely busy.'

'Mrs Ponsonby,' I said. 'The President has ordered me to deliver this to you in person.'

She melted immediately. 'The dear man!' she shouted.

'How perfectly gorgeous of him!' Two massive hands reached out to grab the box. I let her have it.

'My instructions are to make sure you open it before you go to the banquet,' I said.

'Sure I'll open it,' she said. 'Do I have to do it in front of you?'

'If you wouldn't mind.'

'Okay, come on in. But I don't have much time.'

I followed her into the living-room of the suite. 'I am to tell you,' I said, 'that it comes with all good wishes from one President to another.'

'Ha!' she roared. 'I like that! What a gorgeous man he is!' She untied the gold string of the box and lifted the lid. 'I guessed it!' she shouted. 'Orchids! How splendid! They're far grander than this poor little thing I'm wearing!'

I had been so dazzled by the galaxy of stars across her bosom that I hadn't noticed the single orchid pinned to the left-hand side.

'I must change over at once,' she said. 'The President will be expecting me to wear his gift.'

'He certainly will,' I said.

Now to give you an idea of how far her chest stuck out in front of her, I must tell you that when she reached forward to unpin the flower, she was only just able to touch it even with her arms fully extended. She fiddled around with the pin for quite a while, but she couldn't really see what she was doing and it wouldn't come undone. 'I'm terrified of tearing this gorgeous gown,' she said. 'Here, you do it.' She swung around and thrust her mammoth bust in my face. I hesitated. 'Go on!' she boomed. 'I don't have all night!' I went to it, and in the end I managed to get the pin unhooked from her dress.

'Now let's get the other one on,' she said.

I put aside the single orchid and lifted my own flowers carefully from the box.

'Have they got a pin?' she asked.

'I don't believe they have,' I said. That was something I'd forgotten.

'No matter,' she said. 'We'll use the old one.' She removed the safety pin from the first orchid, and then, before I could stop her, she seized the three orchids I was holding and jabbed the pin hard into the white ribbon around the stems. She jabbed it almost exactly into the spot where my little capsule of *Bitch* was lying hidden. The pin struck something hard and wouldn't go through. She jabbed it again. Again it struck metal. 'What the hell's under here?' she snorted.

'Let me do it!' I cried, but it was too late, because the wet stain of *Bitch* from the punctured capsule was already spreading over the white ribbon and one hundredth of a second later the smell hit me. It caught me smack under the nose and it wasn't actually like a smell at all because a smell is something intangible. You cannot feel a smell. But this stuff was palpable. It was solid. It felt as though some kind of fiery liquid were being squirted up my nostrils under high pressure. It was exceedingly uncomfortable. I could feel it pushing higher and higher, penetrating far beyond the nasal passages, forcing its way up behind the forehead and reaching for the brain. Suddenly the stars and stripes on Mrs Ponsonby's dress began to wobble and bobble about and then the whole room started wobbling and I could hear my heart thumping in my head. It felt as though I were going under an anaesthetic.

At that point, I must have blacked out completely, if only for a couple of seconds.

When I came round again, I was standing naked in a rosy room and there was a funny feeling in my groin. I looked down and saw that my beloved sexual organ was three feet long and thick to match. It was still growing. It was lengthening and swelling at a tremendous rate. At the same time, my body was shrinking. Smaller and smaller shrank my body. Bigger and bigger grew my astonishing organ, and it went on growing, by God, until it had enveloped my entire body and absorbed it within itself. I was now a gigantic perpendicular penis, seven feet tall and as handsome as they come.

I did a little dance around the room to celebrate my splendid new condition. On the way I met a maiden in a star-spangled dress. She was very big as maidens go. I drew myself up to my full height and declaimed in a loud voice:

> 'The summer's flower is to the summer sweet,
> It flourishes despite the summer's heat.
> But tell me truly, did you ever see
> A sexual organ quite so grand as me?'

The maiden leaped up and flung her arms as far around me as she could. Then cried out:

'Shall I compare thee to a summer's day?
Shall I . . . Oh dear, I know not what to say.
But all my life I've had an itch to kiss
A man who could erect himself like this.'

A moment later, the two of us were millions of miles
up in outer space, flying through the universe in a shower
of meteorites all red and gold. I was riding her bareback,
crouching forwards and gripping her tightly between my
thighs. 'Faster!' I shouted, jabbing long spurs into her
flanks. 'Go faster!' Faster and still faster she flew, spurting
and spinning around the rim of the sky, her mane streaming with sun, and snow waving out of her tail. The sense
of power I had was overwhelming. I was unassailable,
supreme. I was the Lord of the Universe, scattering the
planets and catching the stars in the palm of my hand and
tossing them away as though they were ping-pong balls.

Oh, ecstasy and ravishment! Oh, Jericho and Tyre and
Sidon! The walls came tumbling down and the firmament
disintegrated, and out of the smoke and fire of the explosion, the sitting-room in the Waldorf Towers came
swimming slowly back into my consciousness like a rainy
day. The place was a shambles. A tornado would have
done less damage. My clothes were on the floor. I started
dressing myself very quickly. I did it in about thirty seconds flat. And as I ran towards the door, I heard a voice
that seemed to be coming from somewhere behind an
upturned table in the far corner of the room. 'I don't
know who you are, young man,' it said. 'But you've certainly done me a power of good.'

Ah, Sweet Mystery of Life

First published in *The New York Times*
(September 1974)

My cow started bulling at dawn and the noise can drive you crazy if the cowshed is right under your window. So I got dressed early and phoned Claud at the filling-station to ask if he'd give me a hand to lead her down the steep hill and across the road over to Rummins's farm to have her serviced by Rummins's famous bull.

Claud arrived five minutes later and we tied a rope around the cow's neck and set off down the lane on this cool September morning. There were high hedges on either side of the lane and the hazel bushes had clusters of big ripe nuts all over them.

'You ever seen Rummins do a mating?' Claud asked me.

I told him I had never seen anyone do an official mating between a bull and a cow.

'Rummins does it special,' Claud said. 'There's nobody in the world does a mating the way Rummins does it.'

'What's so special about it?'

'You got a treat coming to you,' Claud said.

'So has the cow,' I said.

'If the rest of the world knew about what Rummins does at a mating,' Claud said, 'he'd be world famous. It would change the whole science of dairy-farming all over the world.'

'Why doesn't he tell them then?' I asked.

'I doubt he's ever even thought about it,' Claud said. 'Rummins isn't one to bother his head about things like that. He's got the best dairy-herd for miles around and that's all he cares about. He doesn't want the newspapers swarming all over his place asking questions, which is exactly what would happen if it ever got out.'

'Why don't you tell me about it,' I said.

We walked on in silence for a while, the cow pulling ahead.

'I'm surprised Rummins said yes to lending you his bull,' Claud said. 'I've never known him do that before.'

At the bottom of the lane we crossed the Aylesbury road and climbed up the hill on the other side of the valley towards the farm. The cow knew there was a bull up there somewhere and she was pulling harder than ever on the rope. We had to trot to keep up with her.

There were no gates at the farm entrance, just a wide gap and a cobbled yard beyond. Rummins, carrying a pail of milk across the yard, saw us coming. He set the pail down slowly and came over to meet us. 'She's ready then, is she?' he said.

'Been yelling her head off,' I said.

Rummins walked around my cow, examining her carefully. He was a short man, built squat and broad like a frog. He had a wide frog-mouth and broken teeth and shifty eyes, but over the years I had grown to respect him for his wisdom and the sharpness of his mind.

'All right then,' he said. 'What is it you want, a heifer calf or a bull?'

'Can I choose?'

'Of course you can choose.'

'Then I'll have a heifer,' I said, keeping a straight face. 'We want milk not beef.'

'Hey, Bert!' Rummins called out. 'Come and give us a hand!'

Bert emerged from the cowsheds. He was Rummins's youngest son, a tall boneless boy with a runny nose and something wrong with one eye. The eye was pale and misty-grey all over, like a boiled fish-eye, and it moved quite independently from the other eye. 'Get another rope,' Rummins said.

Bert fetched a rope and looped it around my cow's neck so that she now had two ropes holding her, my own and Bert's. 'He wants a heifer,' Rummins said. 'Face her into the sun.'

'Into the sun?' I said. 'There isn't any sun.'

'There's always sun,' Rummins said. 'Them bloody clouds don't make no difference. Come on now. Get a jerk on, Bert. Bring her round. Sun's over there.'

With Bert holding one rope and Claud and me holding the other, we manoeuvred the cow round until her head was facing directly towards the place in the sky where the sun was hidden behind the clouds.

'I told you it was different,' Claud whispered. 'You're going to see something soon you've never seen in your life before.'

'Hold her steady now!' Rummins ordered. 'Don't let her jump round!' Then he hurried over to a shed in the far corner of the yard and brought out the bull. He was an enormous beast, a black-and-white Friesian, with short legs and a body like a ten-ton truck. Rummins was leading it by a chain attached to a steel ring through the bull's nose.

'Look at them bangers on him,' Claud said. 'I'll bet you've never seen a bull with bangers like that before.'

'Tremendous,' I said. They were like a couple of cantaloupe melons in a carrier bag and they were almost dragging on the ground as the bull waddled forwards.

'You better stand back and leave the rope to me,' Claud said. 'You get right out of the way.' I was happy to comply.

The bull approached my cow slowly, staring at her with dangerous white eyes. Then he started snorting and pawing the ground with one foreleg.

'Hang on tight!' Rummins shouted to Bert and Claud. They were leaning back against their respective ropes, holding them very taut and at right angles to the cow.

'Come on, boy,' Rummins whispered softly to the bull. 'Go to it, lad.'

With surprising agility the bull heaved his front part up on to my cow's back and I caught a glimpse of a long scarlet penis, as thin as a rapier and just as stiff, and then it was inside the cow and the cow staggered and the bull heaved and snorted and in thirty seconds it was all over. The bull climbed down again slowly and stood there looking somewhat pleased with himself.

'Some bulls don't know where to put it,' Rummins said. 'But mine does. Mine could thread a needle with that dick of his.'

'Wonderful,' I said. 'A bull's eye.'

'That's exactly where the word come from,' Rummins said. 'A bull's eye. Come on, lad,' he said to the bull. 'You've had your lot for today.' He led the bull back to the shed and shut him in and when he returned I thanked him, and then I asked him if he really believed that facing the cow into the sun during the mating would produce a female calf.

'Don't be so damn silly,' he said. 'Of course I believe it. Facts is facts.'

'What do you mean facts is facts?'

'I mean what I say, mister. It's a certainty. That's right, ain't it, Bert?'

Bert swivelled his misty eye around in its socket and said, 'Too bloody true it's right.'

'And if you face her away from the sun does it get you a male?'

'Every single time,' Rummins said. I smiled and he saw it. 'You don't believe me, do you?'

'Not really,' I said.

'Come with me,' he said. 'And when you see what I'm going to show you, you'll bloody well have to believe me. You two stay here and watch that cow,' he said to Claud and Bert. Then he led me into the farmhouse. The room we went into was dark and small and dirty. From a drawer in the sideboard he produced a whole stack of thin exercise books. They were the kind children use at school. 'These is calving books,' he announced. 'And in here is a record of every mating that's ever been done on this farm since I first started thirty-two years ago.'

He opened a book at random and allowed me to look. There were four columns on each page: COW'S NAME, DATE OF MATING, DATE OF BIRTH, SEX OF CALF.

I glanced down the sex column. *Heifer*, it said. *Heifer, Heifer, Heifer, Heifer, Heifer.*

'We don't want no bull calves here,' Rummins said. 'Bull calves is a dead loss on a dairy farm.'

I turned over a page. *Heifer*, it said. *Heifer, Heifer, Heifer, Heifer, Heifer.*

'Hey,' I said. 'Here's a bull calf.'

'That's quite right,' Rummins said. 'Now take a look at what I wrote opposite that one at the time of the mating.' I glanced at column two. *Cow jumped round*, it said.

'Some of them gets fractious and you can't hold 'em steady,' Rummins said. 'So they finish up facing the other way. That's the only time I ever get a bull.'

'This is fantastic,' I said, leafing through the book.

'Of course it's fantastic,' Rummins said. 'It's one of the most fantastic things in the whole world. Do you actually know what I average on this farm? I average ninety-eight per cent heifers year in year out! Check it for yourself. Go on and check it. I'm not stopping you.'

'I'd like very much to check it,' I said. 'May I sit down?'

'Help yourself,' Rummins said. 'I've got work to do.' I found a pencil and paper and I proceeded to go through each one of the thirty-two little books with great care. There was one book for each year, from 1915 to 1946. There were approximately eighty calves a year born on the farm, and my final results over the thirty-two-year period were as follows:

Heifer calves 2, 516
Bull calves 56
Total calves born, including stillborn 2, 572

I went outside to look for Rummins. Claud had disappeared. He'd probably taken my cow home. I found Rummins in the dairy pouring milk into the separator. 'Haven't you ever told anyone about this?' I asked him.

'Never have,' he said.

'Why not?'

'I reckon it ain't nobody else's business.'

'But my dear man, this could transform the entire milk industry the world over.'

'It might,' he said. 'It might easily do that. It wouldn't do the beef business no harm either if they could get bulls every time.'

'How did you hear about it in the first place?'

'My old dad told me,' Rummins said. 'When I were about eighteen, my old dad said to me, "I'll tell you a secret," he said, "that'll make you rich." And he told me this.'

'Has it made you rich?'

'I ain't done too bad for myself, have I?' he said.

'But did your father offer any sort of explanation as to why it works?' I asked.

Rummins explored the inner rim of one nostril with the end of his thumb, holding the noseflap between thumb and forefinger as he did so. 'A very clever man, my old dad was,' he said. 'Very clever indeed. Of course he told me how it works.'

'How?'

'He explained to me that a cow don't have nothing to do with deciding the sex of the calf,' Rummins said. 'All a cow's got is an egg. It's the bull decides what the sex is going to be. The sperm of the bull.'

'Go on,' I said.

'According to my old dad, a bull has two different kinds of sperm, female sperm and male sperm. You follow me so far?'

'Yes,' I said. 'Keep going.'

'So when the old bull shoots off his sperm into the cow, a sort of swimming race takes place between the male and the female sperm to see which one can reach the egg first. If the female sperm wins, you get a heifer.'

'But what's the sun got to do with it?' I asked.

'I'm coming to that,' he said, 'so listen carefully. When an animal is standing on all fours like a cow, and when you face her head into the sun, then the sperm has also got to travel directly into the sun to reach the egg. Switch the cow around and they'll be travelling away from the sun.'

'So what you're saying,' I said, 'is that the sun exerts a pull of some sort on the female sperm and makes them swim faster than the male sperm.'

'Exactly!' cried Rummins. 'That's exactly it! It exerts a pull! It drags them forwards! That's why they always win! And if you turn the cow round the other way, it's pulling them backwards and the male sperm wins instead.'

'It's an interesting theory,' I said. 'But it hardly seems likely that the sun, which is millions of miles away, could exert a pull on a bunch of spermatozoa inside a cow.'

'You're talking rubbish!' cried Rummins. 'Absolute and

THE COMPLETE SHORT STORIES

utter rubbish! Don't the moon exert a pull on the bloody tides of the ocean to make 'em high and low? Of course it does! So why shouldn't the sun exert a pull on the female sperm?'

'I see your point.'

Suddenly Rummins seemed to have had enough. 'You'll have a heifer calf for sure,' he said, turning away. 'Don't you worry about that.'

'Mr Rummins,' I said.

'What?'

'Is there any reason why this shouldn't work with humans as well?'

'Of course it'll work with humans,' he said. 'Just so long as you remember everything's got to be pointed in the right direction. A cow ain't lying down you know. It's standing on all fours.'

'I see what you mean.'

'And it ain't no good doing it at night either,' he said, 'because the sun is shielded behind the earth and it can't influence anything.'

'That's true,' I said, 'but have you any sort of proof it works with humans?'

Rummins laid his head to one side and gave me another of his long sly broken-toothed grins. 'I've got four boys of my own, ain't I?' he said.

'So you have.'

'Ruddy girls ain't no use to me around here,' he said. 'Boys is what you want on a farm and I've got four of 'em, right?'

'Right,' I said, 'you're absolutely right.'

The Hitch-hiker

First published in *Atlantic Monthly*
(August 1977)

I had a new car. It was an exciting toy, a big BMW 3.3 Li, which means 3.3 litre, long wheelbase, fuel injection. It had a top speed of 129 mph and terrific acceleration. The body was pale blue. The seats inside were darker blue and they were made of leather, genuine soft leather of the finest quality. The windows were electrically operated and so was the sun-roof. The radio aerial popped up when I switched on the radio, and disappeared when I switched it off. The powerful engine growled and grunted impatiently at slow speeds, but at sixty miles an hour the growling stopped and the motor began to purr with pleasure.

I was driving up to London by myself. It was a lovely June day. They were haymaking in the fields and there were buttercups along both sides of the road. I was whispering along at seventy miles an hour, leaning back comfortably in my seat, with no more than a couple of fingers resting lightly on the wheel to keep her steady. Ahead of me I saw a man thumbing a lift. I touched the footbrake and brought the car to a stop beside him. I always stopped for hitch-hikers. I knew just how it used to feel to be standing on the side of a country road watching the cars go by. I hated the drivers for pretending they didn't see me, especially the ones in big cars with three empty seats. The large expensive cars seldom stopped. It was always the smaller ones that offered you a lift, or the old rusty ones, or the ones that were already crammed full of children and the driver would say, 'I think we can squeeze in one more.'

The hitch-hiker poked his head through the open window and said, 'Going to London, guv'nor?'

'Yes,' I said, 'jump in.'

He got in and I drove on.

He was a small ratty-faced man with grey teeth. His eyes were dark and quick and clever, like a rat's eyes, and his ears were slightly pointed at the top. He had a cloth cap on his head and he was wearing a greyish-coloured jacket with enormous pockets. The grey jacket, together with the quick eyes and the pointed ears, made him look more than anything like some sort of a huge human rat.

'What part of London are you headed for?' I asked him.

'I'm goin' right through London and out the other side,' he said. 'I'm goin' to Epsom, for the races. It's Derby Day today.'

'So it is,' I said. 'I wish I were going with you. I love betting on horses.'

'I never bet on horses,' he said. 'I don't even watch 'em run. That's a stupid silly business.'

'Then why do you go?' I asked.

He didn't seem to like that question. His little ratty face went absolutely blank and he sat there staring straight ahead at the road, saying nothing.

'I expect you help to work the betting machines or something like that,' I said.

'That's even sillier,' he answered. 'There's no fun working them lousy machines and selling tickets to mugs. Any fool could do that.'

There was a long silence. I decided not to question him any more. I remembered how irritated I used to get in my hitch-hiking days when drivers kept asking *me* questions. Where are you going? Why are you going there? What's your job? Are you married? Do you have a girl-friend? What's her name? How old are you? And so on and so forth. I used to hate it.

'I'm sorry,' I said. 'It's none of my business what you do. The trouble is, I'm a writer, and most writers are terrible nosey parkers.'

'You write books?' he asked.

'Yes.'

'Writin' books is OK,' he said. 'It's what I call a skilled trade. I'm in a skilled trade too. The folks I despise is them that spend all their lives doin' crummy old routine jobs with no skill in 'em at all. You see what I mean?'

'Yes.'

'The secret of life,' he said, 'is to become very very good at somethin' that's very very 'ard to do.'

'Like you,' I said.

'Exactly. You and me both.'

'What makes you think that *I'm* any good at my job?' I asked. 'There's an awful lot of bad writers around.'

'You wouldn't be drivin' about in a car like this if you weren't no good at it,' he answered. 'It must've cost a tidy packet, this little job.'

'It wasn't cheap.'

'What can she do flat out?' he asked.

'One hundred and twenty-nine miles an hour,' I told him.

'I'll bet she won't do it.'

'I'll bet she will.'

'All car makers is liars,' he said. 'You can buy any car you like and it'll never do what the makers say it will in the ads.'

'This one will.'

'Open 'er up then and prove it,' he said. 'Go on, guv'nor, open 'er right up and let's see what she'll do.'

There is a roundabout at Chalfont St Peter and immediately beyond it there's a long straight section of dual carriageway. We came out of the roundabout on to the carriageway and I pressed my foot down on the accelerator. The big car leaped forwards as though she'd been stung. In ten seconds or so, we were doing ninety.

'Lovely!' he cried. 'Beautiful! Keep goin'!'

I had the accelerator jammed right down against the floor and I held it there.

'One hundred!' he shouted ... 'A hundred and five! ... A hundred and ten! ... A hundred and fifteen! Go on! Don't slack off!'

I was in the outside lane and we flashed past several cars as though they were standing still – a green Mini, a big cream-coloured Citroën, a white Land Rover, a huge truck with a container on the back, an orange-coloured Volkswagen Minibus ...

'A hundred and twenty!' my passenger shouted, jumping up and down. 'Go on! Go on! Get 'er up to one-two-nine!'

At that moment, I heard the scream of a police siren. It

was so loud it seemed to be right inside the car, and then a policeman on a motor-cycle loomed up alongside us on the inside lane and went past us and raised a hand for us to stop.

'Oh, my sainted aunt!' I said. 'That's torn it!'

The policeman must have been doing about a hundred and thirty when he passed us, and he took plenty of time slowing down. Finally, he pulled into the side of the road and I pulled in behind him. 'I didn't know police motor-cycles could go as fast as that,' I said rather lamely.

'That one can,' my passenger said. 'It's the same make as yours. It's a BMW R90S. Fastest bike on the road. That's what they're usin' nowadays.'

The policeman got off his motor-cycle and leaned the machine sideways on to its prop stand. Then he took off his gloves and placed them carefully on the seat. He was in no hurry now. He had us where he wanted us and he knew it.

'This is real trouble,' I said. 'I don't like it one bit.'

'Don't talk to 'im any more than is necessary, you understand,' my companion said. 'Just sit tight and keep mum.'

Like an executioner approaching his victim, the policeman came strolling slowly towards us. He was a big meaty man with a belly, and his blue breeches were skintight around his enormous thighs. His goggles were pulled up on the helmet, showing a smouldering red face with wide cheeks.

We sat there like guilty schoolboys, waiting for him to arrive.

'Watch out for this man,' my passenger whispered. ''Ee looks mean as the devil.'

The policeman came round to my open window and placed one meaty hand on the sill. 'What's the hurry?' he said.

'No hurry, officer,' I answered.

'Perhaps there's a woman in the back having a baby and you're rushing her to hospital? Is that it?'

'No, officer.'

'Or perhaps your house is on fire and you're dashing home to rescue the family from upstairs?' His voice was dangerously soft and mocking.

'My house isn't on fire, officer.'

'In that case,' he said, 'you've got yourself into a nasty mess, haven't you? Do you know what the speed limit is in this country?'

'Seventy,' I said.

'And do you mind telling me exactly what speed you were doing just now?'

I shrugged and didn't say anything.

When he spoke next, he raised his voice so loud that I jumped. *'One hundred and twenty miles per hour!'* he barked. 'That's *fifty* miles an hour over the limit!'

He turned his head and spat out a big gob of spit. It landed on the wing of my car and started sliding down over my beautiful blue paint. Then he turned back again and stared hard at my passenger. 'And who are you?' he asked sharply.

'He's a hitch-hiker,' I said. 'I'm giving him a lift.'

'I didn't ask you,' he said. 'I asked him.'

"Ave I done somethin' wrong?' my passenger asked.
His voice was as soft and oily as haircream.

'That's more than likely,' the policeman answered. 'Anyway, you're a witness. I'll deal with you in a minute.
Driving-licence,' he snapped, holding out his hand.

I gave him my driving-licence.

He unbuttoned the left-hand breast-pocket of his tunic
and brought out the dreaded book of tickets. Carefully, he
copied the name and address from my licence. Then he
gave it back to me. He strolled round to the front of
the car and read the number from the number-plate and
wrote that down as well. He filled in the date, the time and
the details of my offence. Then he tore out the top copy
of the ticket. But before handing it to me, he checked that
all the information had come through clearly on his own
carbon copy. Finally, he replaced the book in his tunic
pocket and fastened the button.

'Now you,' he said to my passenger, and he walked
around to the other side of the car. From the other breast-
pocket he produced a small black notebook. 'Name?' he
snapped.

'Michael Fish,' my passenger said.

'Address?'

'Fourteen, Windsor Lane, Luton.'

'Show me something to prove this is your real name
and address,' the policeman said.

My passenger fished in his pockets and came out with
a driving-licence of his own. The policeman checked the
name and address and handed it back to him. 'What's your
job?' he asked sharply.

'I'm an 'od carrier.'

'A *what*?'

'An 'od carrier.'

'Spell it.'

'H-O-D C-A-...'

'That'll do. And what's a hod carrier, may I ask?'

'An 'od carrier, officer, is a person 'oo carries the cement
up the ladder to the bricklayer. And the 'od is what 'ee carries it in. It's got a long 'andle, and on the top you've got
two bits of wood set at an angle...'

'All right, all right. Who's your employer?'

'Don't 'ave one. I'm unemployed.'

The policeman wrote all this down in the black notebook. Then he returned the book to its pocket and did up
the button.

'When I get back to the station I'm going to do a little
checking up on you,' he said to my passenger.

'Me? What've I done wrong?' the rat-faced man asked.

'I don't like your face, that's all,' the policeman said.
'And we just might have a picture of it somewhere in our
files.' He strolled round the car and returned to my
window.

'I suppose you know you're in serious trouble,' he said
to me.

'Yes, officer.'

'You won't be driving this fancy car of yours again for
a very long time, not after *we've* finished with you. You
won't be driving *any* car again come to that for several
years. And a good thing, too. I hope they lock you up for
a spell into the bargain.'

'You mean prison?' I asked, alarmed.

'Absolutely,' he said, smacking his lips. 'In the clink. Behind the bars. Along with all the other criminals who break the law. *And* a hefty fine into the bargain. Nobody will be more pleased about that than me. I'll see you in court, both of you. You'll be getting a summons to appear.'

He turned away and walked over to his motor-cycle. He flipped the prop stand back into position with his foot and swung his leg over the saddle. Then he kicked the starter and roared off up the road out of sight.

'Phew!' I gasped. 'That's done it.'

'We was caught,' my passenger said. 'We was caught good and proper.'

'I was caught, you mean.'

'That's right,' he said. 'What you goin' to do now, guv'nor?'

'I'm going straight up to London to talk to my solicitor,' I said. I started the car and drove on.

'You mustn't believe what 'ee said to you about goin' to prison,' my passenger said. 'They don't put nobody in the clink just for speedin'.'

'Are you sure of that?' I asked.

'I'm positive,' he answered. 'They can take your licence away and they can give you a whoppin' big fine, but that'll be the end of it.'

I felt tremendously relieved.

'By the way,' I said, 'why did you lie to him?'

'Who, me?' he said. 'What makes you think I lied?'

'You told him you were an unemployed hod carrier. But you told *me* you were in a highly skilled trade.'

473

'So I am,' he said. 'But it don't pay to tell everythin' to a copper.'

'So what *do* you do?' I asked him.

'Ah,' he said slyly. 'That'd be tellin', wouldn't it?'

'Is it something you're ashamed of?'

'Ashamed?' he cried. 'Me, ashamed of my job? I'm about as proud of it as anybody could be in the entire world!'

'Then why won't you tell me?'

'You writers really is nosey parkers, aren't you?' he said. 'And you ain't goin' to be 'appy, I don't think, until you've found out exactly what the answer is?'

'I don't really care one way or the other,' I told him, lying.

He gave me a crafty little ratty look out of the sides of his eyes. 'I think you do care,' he said. 'I can see it in your face that you think I'm in some kind of a very peculiar trade and you're just achin' to know what it is.'

I didn't like the way he read my thoughts. I kept quiet and stared at the road ahead.

'You'd be right, too,' he went on. 'I *am* in a very peculiar trade. I'm in the queerest peculiar trade of 'em all.'

I waited for him to go on.

'That's why I 'as to be extra careful 'oo I'm talkin' to, you see. 'Ow am I to know, for instance, you're not another copper in plain clothes?'

'Do I look like a copper?'

'No,' he said. 'You don't. And you ain't. Any fool could tell that.'

He took from his pocket a tin of tobacco and a packet of cigarette papers and started to roll a cigarette. I was watching him out of the corner of one eye, and the speed with which he performed this rather difficult operation was incredible. The cigarette was rolled and ready in about five seconds. He ran his tongue along the edge of the paper, stuck it down and popped the cigarette between his lips. Then, as if from nowhere, a lighter appeared in his hand. The lighter flamed. The cigarette was lit. The lighter disappeared. It was altogether a remarkable performance.

'I've never seen anyone roll a cigarette as fast as that,' I said.

'Ah,' he said, taking a deep suck of smoke. 'So you noticed.'

'Of course I noticed. It was quite fantastic.'

He sat back and smiled. It pleased him very much that I had noticed how quickly he could roll a cigarette. 'You want to know what makes me able to do it?' he asked.

'Go on then.'

'It's because I've got fantastic fingers. These fingers of mine,' he said, holding up both hands high in front of him, 'are quicker and cleverer than the fingers of the best piano player in the world!'

'Are you a piano player?'

'Don't be daft,' he said. 'Do I look like a piano player?'

I glanced at his fingers. They were so beautifully shaped, so slim and long and elegant, they didn't seem to belong to the rest of him at all. They looked more like the fingers of a brain surgeon or a watchmaker.

'My job,' he went on, 'is a hundred times more difficult than playin' the piano. Any twerp can learn to do that. There's titchy little kids learnin' to play the piano in almost any 'ouse you go into these days. That's right, ain't it?'

'More or less,' I said.

'Of course it's right. But there's not one person in ten million can learn to do what I do. Not one in ten million! 'Ow about that?'

'Amazing,' I said.

'You're darn right it's amazin',' he said.

'I think I know what you do,' I said. 'You do conjuring tricks. You're a conjurer.'

'Me?' he snorted. 'A conjurer? Can you picture me goin' round crummy kids' parties makin' rabbits come out of top 'ats?'

'Then you're a card player. You get people into card games and deal yourself marvellous hands.'

'Me! A rotten card-sharper!' he cried. 'That's a miserable racket if ever there was one.'

'All right. I give up.'

I was taking the car along slowly now, at no more than forty miles an hour, to make quite sure I wasn't stopped again. We had come on to the main London–Oxford road and were running down the hill towards Denham.

Suddenly, my passenger was holding up a black leather belt in his hand. 'Ever seen this before?' he asked. The belt had a brass buckle of unusual design.

'Hey!' I said. 'That's mine, isn't it? It *is* mine! Where did you get it?'

He grinned and waved the belt gently from side to side.

'Where d'you think I got it?' he said. 'Off the top of your trousers, of course.'

I reached down and felt for my belt. It was gone.

'You mean you took it off me while we've been driving along?' I asked, flabbergasted.

He nodded, watching me all the time with those little black ratty eyes.

'That's impossible,' I said. 'You'd have to undo the buckle and slide the whole thing out through the loops all the way round. I'd have seen you doing it. And even if I hadn't seen you, I'd have felt it.'

'Ah, but you didn't, did you?' he said, triumphant. He dropped the belt on his lap, and now all at once there was a brown shoelace dangling from his fingers. 'And what about this, then?' he exclaimed, waving the shoelace.

'What about it?' I said.

'Anyone round 'ere missin' a shoelace?' he asked, grinning.

I glanced down at my shoes. The lace of one of them was missing. 'Good grief!' I said. 'How did you do that? I never saw you bending down.'

'You never saw nothin',' he said proudly. 'You never even saw me move an inch. And you know why?'

'Yes,' I said. 'Because you've got fantastic fingers.'

'Exactly right!' he cried. 'You catch on pretty quick, don't you?' He sat back and sucked away at his home-made cigarette, blowing the smoke out in a thin stream against the windshield. He knew he had impressed me greatly with those two tricks, and this made him very happy. 'I don't want to be late,' he said. 'What time is it?'

'There's a clock in front of you,' I told him.

'I don't trust car clocks,' he said. 'What does your watch say?'

I hitched up my sleeve to look at the watch on my wrist. It wasn't there. I looked at the man. He looked back at me, grinning.

'You've taken that, too,' I said.

He held out his hand and there was my watch lying in his palm. 'Nice bit of stuff, this,' he said. 'Superior quality. Eighteen-carat gold. Easy to flog, too. It's never any trouble gettin' rid of quality goods.'

'I'd like it back, if you don't mind,' I said rather huffily.

He placed the watch carefully on the leather tray in front of him. 'I wouldn't nick anything from you, guv'nor,' he said. 'You're my pal. You're giving me a lift.'

'I'm glad to hear it,' I said.

'All I'm doin' is answerin' your questions,' he went on. 'You asked me what I did for a livin' and I'm showin' you.'

'What else have you got of mine?'

He smiled again, and now he started to take from the pocket of his jacket one thing after another that belonged to me – my driving-licence, a key-ring with four keys on it, some pound notes, a few coins, a letter from my publishers, my diary, a stubby old pencil, a cigarette-lighter, and last of all, a beautiful old sapphire ring with pearls around it belonging to my wife. I was taking the ring up to the jeweller in London because one of the pearls was missing.

'Now *there's* another lovely piece of goods,' he said, turning the ring over in his fingers. 'That's eighteenth century, if I'm not mistaken, from the reign of King George the Third.'

'You're right,' I said, impressed. 'You're absolutely right.'

He put the ring on the leather tray with the other items.

'So you're a pickpocket,' I said.

'I don't like that word,' he answered. 'It's a coarse and vulgar word. Pickpockets is coarse and vulgar people who only do easy little amateur jobs. They lift money from blind old ladies.'

'What do you call yourself, then?'

'Me? I'm a fingersmith. I'm a professional fingersmith.' He spoke the words solemnly and proudly, as though he were telling me he was the President of the Royal College of Surgeons or the Archbishop of Canterbury.

'I've never heard that word before,' I said. 'Did you invent it?'

'Of course I didn't invent it,' he replied. 'It's the name given to them who's risen to the very top of the profession. You've 'eard of a goldsmith and a silversmith, for instance. They're experts with gold and silver. I'm an expert with my fingers, so I'm a fingersmith.'

'It must be an interesting job.'

'It's a marvellous job,' he answered. 'It's lovely.'

'And that's why you go to the races?'

'Race meetings is easy meat,' he said. 'You just stand around after the race, watchin' for the lucky ones to queue up and draw their money. And when you see someone collectin' a big bundle of notes, you simply follows after 'im and 'elps yourself. But don't get me wrong, guv'nor. I never takes nothin' from a loser. Nor from poor people neither. I only go after them as can afford it, the winners and the rich.'

'That's very thoughtful of you,' I said. 'How often do you get caught?'

'Caught?' he cried, disgusted. '*Me* get caught! It's only pickpockets get caught. Fingersmiths never. Listen, I could take the false teeth out of your mouth if I wanted to and you wouldn't even catch me!'

'I don't have false teeth,' I said.

'I know you don't,' he answered. 'Otherwise I'd 'ave 'ad 'em out long ago!'

I believed him. Those long slim fingers of his seemed able to do anything.

We drove on for a while without talking.

'That policeman's going to check up on you pretty thoroughly,' I said. 'Doesn't that worry you a bit?'

'Nobody's checkin' up on me,' he said.

'Of course they are. He's got your name and address written down most carefully in his black book.'

The man gave me another of his sly, ratty little smiles. 'Ah,' he said. 'So 'ee 'as. But I'll bet 'ee ain't got it all written down in 'is memory as well. I've never known a copper yet with a decent memory. Some of 'em can't even remember their own names.'

'What's memory got to do with it?' I asked. 'It's written down in his book, isn't it?'

'Yes, guv'nor, it is. But the trouble is, 'ee's lost the book. 'Ee's lost both books, the one with my name in it *and* the one with yours.'

In the long delicate fingers of his right hand, the man

was holding up in triumph the two books he had taken from the policeman's pockets. 'Easiest job I ever done,' he announced proudly.

I nearly swerved the car into a milk-truck, I was so excited.

'That copper's got nothin' on either of us now,' he said.

'You're a genius!' I cried.

''Ee's got no names, no addresses, no car number, no nothin',' he said.

'You're brilliant!'

'I think you'd better pull in off this main road as soon as possible,' he said. 'Then we'd better build a little bonfire and burn these books.'

'You're a fantastic fellow,' I exclaimed.

'Thank you, guv'nor,' he said. 'It's always nice to be appreciated.'

The Swan

First published in *The Wonderful Story of*
Henry Sugar (1977)

Ernie had been given a .22 rifle for his birthday. His father, who was already slouching on the sofa watching the telly at nine thirty on this Saturday morning, said, 'Let's see what you can pot, boy. Make yourself useful. Bring us back a rabbit for supper.'

'There's rabbits in that big field the other side of the lake,' Ernie said. 'I seen 'em.'

'Then go out and nab one,' the father said, picking breakfast from between his front teeth with a split matchstick. 'Go out and nab us a rabbit.'

'I'll get yer two,' Ernie said.

'And on the way back,' the father said, 'get me a quart bottle of brown ale.'

'Gimme the money, then,' Ernie said.

The father, without taking his eyes from the TV screen, fished in his pocket for a pound note. 'And don't try pinchin' the change like you did last time,' he said. 'You'll get a thick ear if you do, birthday or no birthday.'

'Don't worry,' Ernie said.

'And if you want to practise and get your eye in with that gun,' the father said, 'birds is best. See 'ow many spadgers you can knock down, right?'

'Right,' Ernie said. 'There's spadgers all the way up the lane in the 'edges. Spadgers is easy.'

'If you think spadgers is easy,' the father said, 'go get yourself a jenny wren. Jenny wrens is 'alf the size of spadgers and they never sit still for one second. Get yourself a jenny wren before you start shootin' yer mouth off about 'ow clever you is.'

'Now, Albert,' his wife said, looking up from the sink. 'That's not nice, shootin' little birds in the nestin' season. I don't mind rabbits, but little birds in the nestin' season is another thing altogether.'

'Shut your mouth,' the father said. 'Nobody's askin' your opinion. And listen to me, boy,' he said to Ernie. 'Don't go waving that thing about in the street because you ain't got no licence. Stick it down your trouser-leg till you're out in the country, right?'

'Don't worry,' Ernie said. He took the gun and the box of bullets and went out to see what he could kill. He was a big lout of a boy, fifteen years old this birthday. Like his truck-driver father, he had small slitty eyes set very close together near the top of the nose. His mouth was loose, the lips often wet. Brought up in a household where physical violence was an everyday occurrence, he was himself an extremely violent person. Most Saturday afternoons, he and a gang of friends travelled by train or bus to football matches, and if they didn't manage to get into a bloody fight before they returned home, they considered it a wasted day. He took great pleasure in catching small boys after school and twisting their arms behind their backs. Then he would order them to say insulting and filthy things about their own parents.

'Ow! Please don't, Ernie! Please!'

'Say it or I'll twist your arm off!'

They always said it. Then he would give the arm an extra twist and the victim would go off in tears.

Ernie's best friend was called Raymond. He lived four doors away, and he, too, was a big boy for his age. But while Ernie was heavy and loutish, Raymond was tall, slim and muscular.

Outside Raymond's house, Ernie put two fingers in his mouth and gave a long shrill whistle. Raymond came out. 'Look what I got for me birthday,' Ernie said, showing the gun.

'Cripes!' Raymond said. 'We can have some fun with that!'

'Come on, then,' Ernie said. 'We're goin' up to the big field the other side of the lake to get us a rabbit.'

The two boys set off. This was a Saturday morning in May, and the countryside was beautiful around the small village where the boys lived. The chestnut trees were in full flower and the hawthorn was white along the hedges. To reach the big rabbit field, Ernie and Raymond had first to walk down a narrow hedgy lane for half a mile. Then they must cross the railway line, and go round the big lake where wild ducks and moorhens and coots and ring-ouzels lived. Beyond the lake, over the hill and down the other side, lay the rabbit field. This was all private land belonging to Mr Douglas Highton and the lake itself was a sanctuary for waterfowl.

All the way up the lane, they took turns with the gun, potting at small birds in the hedges. Ernie got a bullfinch and a hedge-sparrow. Raymond got a second bullfinch, a whitethroat and a yellowhammer. As each bird was killed, they tied it by the legs to a line of string. Raymond never went anywhere without a big ball of string in his jacket pocket, and a knife. Now they had five little birds dangling on the line of string.

'You know something,' Raymond said. 'We can eat these.'

'Don't talk so daft,' Ernie said. 'There's not enough meat on one of those to feed a woodlouse.'

'There is, too,' Raymond said. 'The Frenchies eat 'em and so do the Eyeties. Mr Sanders told us about it in class. He said the Frenchies and the Eyeties put up nets and catch 'em by the million and then they eat 'em.'

'All right, then,' Ernie said. 'Let's see 'ow many we can get. Then we'll take 'em 'ome and put 'em in the rabbit stew.'

As they progressed up the lane, they shot at every little bird they saw. By the time they got to the railway line, they had fourteen small birds dangling on the line of string.

'Hey!' whispered Ernie, pointing with a long arm. 'Look over there!'

There was a group of trees and bushes alongside the railway line, and beside one of the bushes stood a small boy. He was looking up into the branches of an old tree through a pair of binoculars.

'You know who that is?' Raymond whispered back. 'It's that little twerp Watson.'

THE COMPLETE SHORT STORIES

'You're right!' Ernie whispered. 'It's Watson, the scum of the earth!'

Peter Watson was always the enemy. Ernie and Raymond detested him because he was nearly everything that they were not. He had a small frail body. His face was freckled and he wore spectacles with thick lenses. He was a brilliant pupil, already in the senior class at school although he was only thirteen. He loved music and played the piano well. He was no good at games. He was quiet and polite. His clothes, although patched and darned, were always clean. And his father did not drive a truck or work in a factory. He worked in the bank.

'Let's give the little perisher a fright,' Ernie whispered.

The two bigger boys crept up close to the small boy, who didn't see them because he still had binoculars to his eyes.

'*'Ands up!*' shouted Ernie, pointing the gun.

Peter Watson jumped. He lowered the binoculars and stared through his spectacles at the two intruders.

'Go on!' Ernie shouted. 'Stick 'em up!'

'I wouldn't point that gun if I were you,' Peter Watson said.

'*We're* givin' the orders round 'ere!' Ernie said.

'So stick 'em up,' Raymond said, 'unless you want a slug in the guts!'

Peter Watson stood quite still, holding the binoculars in front of him with both hands. He looked at Raymond. Then he looked at Ernie. He was not afraid, but he knew better than to play the fool with these two. He had suffered a good deal from their attentions over the years.

'What do you want?' he asked.

'*I want you to stick 'em up!*' Ernie yelled at him. 'Can't you understand English?'

Peter Watson didn't move.

'I'll count to five,' Ernie said. 'And if they're not up by then, you get it in the guts. One . . . Two . . . Three . . .'

Peter Watson raised his arms slowly above his head. It was the only sensible thing to do. Raymond stepped forwards and snatched the binoculars from his hands. 'What's this?' he snapped. 'Who you spyin' on?'

'Nobody.'

'Don't lie, Watson. Them things is used for spyin'! I'll bet you was spyin' on us! That's right, ain't it? Confess it!'

'I certainly wasn't spying on you.'

'Give 'im a clip over the ear,' Ernie said. 'Teach 'im not to lie to us.'

'I'll do that in a minute,' Raymond said. 'I'm just workin' meself up.'

Peter Watson considered the possibility of trying to escape. All he could do would be to turn and run, and that was pointless. They'd catch him in seconds. And if he shouted for help, there was no one to hear him. All he could do, therefore, was to keep calm and try to talk his way out of the situation.

'Keep them 'ands up!' Ernie barked, waving the barrel of the gun gently from side to side the way he had seen it done by gangsters on the telly. 'Go on, laddie, reach!'

Peter did as he was told.

'So 'oo was you spyin' on?' Raymond asked. 'Out with it!'

'I was watching a green woodpecker,' Peter said.

'A what?'

'A male green woodpecker. He was tapping the trunk of that old dead tree, searching for grubs.'

'Where is 'ee?' Ernie snapped, raising his gun. 'I'll 'ave 'im!'

'No, you won't,' Peter said, looking at the string of tiny birds slung over Raymond's shoulder. 'He flew off the moment you shouted. Woodpeckers are extremely timid.'

'What you watchin' 'im for?' Raymond asked suspiciously. 'What's the point? Don't you 'ave nothin' better to do?'

'It's fun watching birds,' Peter said. 'It's a lot more fun than shooting them.'

'Why, you cheeky little bleeder!' Ernie cried. 'So you don't like us shootin' birds, eh? Is that what you're sayin'?'

'I think it's absolutely pointless.'

'You don't like anything we do, isn't that right?' Raymond said.

Peter didn't answer.

'Well, let me tell *you* something,' Raymond went on. 'We don't like anything you do either.'

Peter's arms were beginning to ache. He decided to take a risk. Slowly, he lowered them to his sides.

'Up!' yelled Ernie. 'Get 'em up!'

'What if I refuse?'

'Blimey! You got a ruddy nerve, ain't you?' Ernie said. 'I'm tellin' you for the last time, if you don't stick 'em up I'll pull the trigger!'

'That would be a criminal act,' Peter said. 'It would be a case for the police.'

'And you'd be a case for the 'ospital!' Ernie said.

'Go ahead and shoot,' Peter said. 'Then they'll send you to Borstal. That's prison.'

He saw Ernie hesitate.

'You're really askin' for it, ain't you?' Raymond said.

'I'm simply asking to be left alone,' Peter said. 'I haven't done you any harm.'

'You're a stuck-up little squirt,' Ernie said. 'That's exactly what you are, a stuck-up little squirt.'

Raymond leaned over and whispered something in Ernie's ear. Ernie listened intently. Then he slapped his thigh and said, 'I like it! It's a great idea!'

Ernie placed his gun on the ground and advanced upon the small boy. He grabbed him and threw him to the ground. Raymond took the roll of string from his pocket and cut off a length of it. Together, they forced the boy's arms in front of him and tied his wrists together tight.

'Now the legs,' Raymond said. Peter struggled and received a punch in the stomach. That winded him and he lay still. Next, they tied his ankles together with more string. He was now trussed up like a chicken and completely helpless.

Ernie picked up his gun, and then, with his other hand, he grabbed one of Peter's arms. Raymond grabbed the other arm and together they began to drag the boy over the grass towards the railway lines.

Peter kept absolutely quiet. Whatever it was they were up to, talking to them wasn't going to help matters.

They dragged their victim down the embankment and on to the railway lines themselves. Then one took the arms and the other the feet and they lifted him up and laid him down again lengthwise right between two lines.

'You're mad!' Peter said. 'You can't do this!'

''Oo says we can't? This is just a little lesson we're teachin' you not to be cheeky.'

'More string,' Ernie said.

Raymond produced the ball of string and the two larger boys now proceeded to tie the victim down in such a way that he couldn't wriggle away from between the rails. They did this by looping string around each of his arms and then threading the string under the rails on either side. They did the same with his middle body and his ankles. When they had finished, Peter Watson was strung down helpless and virtually immobile between the rails. The only parts of his body he could move to any extent were his head and feet.

Ernie and Raymond stepped back to survey their handiwork. 'We done a nice job,' Ernie said.

'There's trains every 'arf 'our on this line,' Raymond said. 'We ain't gonna 'ave long to wait.'

'This is murder!' cried the small boy lying between the rails.

'No it ain't,' Raymond told him. 'It ain't anything of the sort.'

'Let me go! Please let me go! I'll be killed if a train comes along!'

'If you *are* killed, sonny boy,' Ernie said, 'it'll be your own ruddy fault and I'll tell you why. Because if you lift your 'ead up like you're doin' now, then you've 'ad it, chum! You keep down flat and you might just possibly get away with it. On the other 'and, you might not because I ain't exactly sure 'ow much clearance them trains've got underneath. You 'appen to know, Raymond, 'ow much clearance them trains got underneath?'

'Very little,' Raymond said. 'They're built ever so close to the ground.'

'Might be enough and it might not,' Ernie said.

'Let's put it this way,' Raymond said. 'It'd probably just about be enough for an *ordinary* person like me or you, Ernie. But Mister Watson 'ere I'm not so sure about and I'll tell you why.'

'Tell me,' Ernie said, egging him on.

'Mister Watson 'ere's got an extra big 'ead, that's why. 'Ee's so flippin' big-'eaded I personally think the bottom bit of the train's goin' to scrape 'im whatever 'appens. I'm not saying it's goin' to take 'is 'ead off, mind you. In fact, I'm pretty sure it ain't goin' to do that. But it's goin' to give 'is face a good old scrapin' over. You can be quite sure of that.'

'I think you're right,' Ernie said.

'It don't do,' Raymond said, 'to 'ave a great big swollen 'ead full of brains if you're lyin' on the railway line with a train comin' towards you. That's right, ain't it, Ernie?'

'That's right,' Ernie said.

The two bigger boys climbed back up the embankment and sat on the grass behind some bushes. Ernie produced a pack of cigarettes and they both lit up.

Peter Watson, lying helpless between the rails, realized now that they were not going to release him. These were dangerous, crazy boys. They lived for the moment and never considered the consequences. I must try to keep calm and think, Peter told himself. He lay there, quite still, weighing his chances. His chances were good. The highest part of his head was his nose. He estimated the end of his nose was sticking up about four inches above the rails. Was that too much? He wasn't quite sure what clearance these modern diesels had above the ground. It certainly wasn't very much. The back of his head was resting upon loose gravel in between two sleepers. He must try to burrow down a little into the gravel. So he began to wriggle his head from side to side, pushing the gravel away and gradually making for himself a small indentation, a hole in the gravel. In the end, he reckoned he had lowered his head an extra two inches. That would do for the head. But what about the feet? They were sticking up, too. He took care of that by swinging the two tied-together feet over to one side so they lay almost flat.

He waited for the train to come.

Would the driver see him? It was very unlikely, for this was the main line, London, Doncaster, York, Newcastle and Scotland, and they used huge long engines in which the driver sat in a cab way back and kept an eye open only for the signals. Along this stretch of the track trains travelled around eighty miles an hour. Peter knew that. He had sat on the bank many times watching them. When he was younger, he used to keep a record of their numbers in a little book, and sometimes the engines had names written on their sides in gold letters.

Either way, he told himself, it was going to be a terrifying business. The noise would be deafening, and the swish

THE SWAN

of the eighty-mile-an-hour wind wouldn't be much fun either. He wondered for a moment whether there would be any kind of vacuum created underneath the train as it rushed over him, sucking him upwards. There might well be. So whatever happened, he must concentrate everything upon pressing his entire body against the ground. Don't go limp. Keep stiff and tense and press down into the ground.

'How're you doin', rat-face!' one of them called out to him from the bushes above. 'What's it like waitin' for the execution?'

He decided not to answer. He watched the blue sky above his head where a single cumulus cloud was drifting slowly from left to right. And to keep his mind off the thing that was going to happen soon, he played a game that his father had taught him long ago on a hot summer's day when they were lying on their backs in the grass above the cliffs at Beachy Head. The game was to look for strange faces in the folds and shadows and billows of a cumulus cloud. If you looked hard enough, his father had said, you would always find a face of some sort up there. Peter let his eyes travel slowly over the cloud. In one place, he found a one-eyed man with a beard. In another, there was a long-chinned laughing witch. An aeroplane came across the cloud travelling from east to west. It was a small high-winged monoplane with a red fuselage. An old Piper Cub, he thought it was. He watched it until it disappeared.

And then, quite suddenly, he heard a curious little vibrating sound coming from the rails on either side of him. It was very soft, this sound, scarcely audible, a tiny little humming, thrumming whisper that seemed to be coming along the rails from far away.

That's a train, he told himself.

The vibrating along the rails grew louder, then louder still. He raised his head and looked down the long and absolutely straight railway line that stretched away for a mile or more into the distance. It was then that he saw the train. At first it was only a speck, a faraway black dot, but in those few seconds that he kept his head raised, the dot grew bigger and bigger, and it began to take shape, and soon it was no longer a dot but the big, square, blunt front-end of a diesel express. Peter dropped his head and pressed it down hard into the small hole he had dug for it in the gravel. He swung his feet over to one side. He shut his eyes tight and tried to sink his body into the ground.

The train came over him like an explosion. It was as though a gun had gone off in his head. And with the explosion came a tearing, screaming wind that was like a hurricane blowing down his nostrils and into his lungs. The noise was shattering. The wind choked him. He felt as if he were being eaten alive and swallowed up in the belly of a screaming murderous monster.

And then it was over. The train had gone. Peter opened his eyes and saw the blue sky and the big white cloud still drifting overhead. It was all over now and he had done it. He had survived.

'It missed 'im,' said a voice.

'What a pity,' said another voice.

He glanced sideways and saw the two large louts standing over him.

THE SWAN

'Cut 'im loose,' Ernie said.

Raymond cut the strings binding him to the rails on either side.

'Undo 'is feet so 'ee can walk, but keep 'is 'ands tied,' Ernie said.

Raymond cut the strings around his ankles.

'Get up,' Ernie said.

Peter got to his feet.

'You're still a prisoner, matey,' Ernie said.

'What about them rabbits?' Raymond asked. 'I thought we was goin' to try for a few rabbits?'

'Plenty of time for that,' Ernie answered. 'I just thought we'd push the little bleeder into the lake on the way.'

'Good,' Raymond said. 'Cool 'im down.'

'You've had your fun,' Peter Waston said. 'Why don't you let me go now?'

'Because you're a prisoner,' Ernie said. 'And you ain't just no ordinary prisoner neither. You're a spy. And you know what 'appens to spies when they get caught, don't you? They get put up against the wall and shot.'

Peter didn't say any more after that. There was no point at all in provoking those two. The less he said to them and the less he resisted them, the more chance he would have of escaping injury. He had no doubt whatsoever that in their present mood they were capable of doing him quite serious bodily harm. He knew for a fact that Ernie had once broken little Wally Simpson's arm after school and Wally's parents had gone to the police. He had also heard Raymond boasting about what he called 'putting the boot in' at the football matches they went to. This, he understood,

495

meant kicking someone in the face or body when he was lying on the ground. They were hooligans, these two, and from what Peter read in his father's newspaper nearly every day, they were not by any means on their own. It seemed the whole country was full of hooligans. They wrecked the interiors of trains, they fought pitched battles in the streets with knives and bicycle chains and metal clubs, they attacked pedestrains, especially other young boys walking alone, and they smashed up roadside cafés. Ernie and Raymond, though perhaps not quite yet fully qualified hooligans, were most definitely on their way.

Therefore, Peter told himself, he must continue to be passive. Do not insult them. Do not aggravate them in any way. And above all, do not try to take them on physically. Then, hopefully, in the end, they might become bored with this nasty little game and go off to shoot rabbits.

The two larger boys had each taken hold of one of Peter's arms and they were marching him across the next field towards the lake. The prisoner's wrists were still tied together in front of him. Ernie carried the gun in his spare hand. Raymond carried the binoculars he had taken from Peter. They came to the lake.

The lake was beautiful on this golden May morning. It was a long and fairly narrow lake with tall willow trees growing here and there along its banks. In the middle, the water was clear and clean, but nearer to the land there was a forest of reeds and bulrushes.

Ernie and Raymond marched their prisoner to the edge of the lake and there they stopped.

'Now then,' Ernie said. 'What I suggest is this. You take 'is arms and I take 'is legs and we'll swing the little perisher one two three as far out as we can into them nice muddy reeds. 'Ow's that?'

'I like it,' Raymond said. 'And leave 'is 'ands tied together, right?'

'Right,' Ernie said. "Ow's that with you, snot-nose?'

'If that's what you're going to do, I can't very well stop you,' Peter said, trying to keep his voice cool and calm.

'Just you try and stop us,' Ernie said, grinning, 'and then see what 'appens to you.'

'One last question,' Peter said. 'Did you ever take on somebody your own size?'

The moment he said it, he knew he had made a mistake. He saw the flush coming to Ernie's cheeks and there was a dangerous little spark dancing in his small black eyes.

Luckily, at that very moment, Raymond saved the situation. 'Hey! Lookit that bird swimmin' in the reeds over there!' he shouted, pointing. 'Let's 'ave 'im!'

It was a mallard drake, with a curvy spoon-shaped yellow beak and a head of emerald green with a white ring round its neck. 'Now those you really *can* eat,' Raymond went on. 'It's a wild duck.'

'I'll 'ave 'im!' Ernie cried. He let go of the prisoner's arm and lifted the gun to his shoulder.

'This is a bird sanctuary,' Peter said.

'A what?' Ernie asked, lowering the gun.

'Nobody shoots birds here. It's strictly forbidden.'

"Oo says it's forbidden?'

'The owner, Mr Douglas Highton.'

'You must be joking,' Ernie said and he raised the gun again. He fired. The duck crumpled in the water.

'Go get 'im,' Ernie said to Peter. 'Cut 'is 'ands free, Raymond, 'cause then 'ee can be our flippin' gun-dog and fetch the birds after we shoot 'em.'

Raymond took out his knife and cut the string binding the small boy's wrists.

'Go on!' Ernie snapped. 'Go get 'im!'

The killing of the beautiful duck had disturbed Peter very much. 'I refuse,' he said.

Ernie hit him across the face hard with his open hand. Peter didn't fall down, but a small trickle of blood began running out of one nostril.

'You dirty little perisher!' Ernie said. 'You just try refusin' me one more time and I'm goin' to make you a promise. And the promise is like this. You refuse me just one more time and I'm goin' to knock out every single one of them shiny white front teeth of yours, top and bottom. You understand that?'

Peter said nothing.

'Answer me!' Ernie barked. 'Do you understand that?'

'Yes,' Peter said quietly. 'I understand.'

'Get on with it, then!' Ernie shouted.

Peter walked down the bank, into the muddy water, through the reeds, and picked up the duck. He brought it back and Raymond took it from him and tied string around its legs.

'Now we got a retriever dog with us, let's see if we can't get us a few more of them ducks,' Ernie said. He strolled along the bank, gun in hand, searching the reeds. Suddenly he stopped. He crouched. He put a finger to his lips and said, 'Sshh!'

Raymond went over to join him. Peter stood a few yards away, his trousers covered in mud up to the knees.

'Lookit in there!' Ernie whispered, pointing into a dense patch of bulrushes. 'D'you see what I see?'

'Holy cats!' cried Raymond. 'What a beauty!'

Peter, peering from a little further away into the rushes, saw at once what they were looking at. It was a swan, a magnificent white swan sitting serenely upon her nest. The nest itself was a huge pile of reeds and rushes that rose up about two feet above the waterline, and upon the top of all this the swan was sitting like a great white lady of the lake. Her head was turned towards the boys on the bank, alert and watchful.

''Ow about *that*?' Ernie said. 'That's better'n ducks, ain't it?'

'You think you can get 'er?' Raymond said.

'Of course I can get 'er. I'll drill a 'ole right through 'er noggin!'

Peter felt a wild rage beginning to build up inside him. He walked up to the two bigger boys. 'I wouldn't shoot that swan if I were you,' he said, trying to keep his voice calm. 'Swans are the most protected birds in England.'

'And what's that got to do with it?' Ernie asked him, sneering.

'And I'll tell you something else,' Peter went on, throwing all caution away. 'Nobody shoots a bird sitting on its nest. Absolutely nobody! She may even have cygnets under her! You just can't do it!'

''Oo says we can't?' Raymond asked, sneering. 'Mister bleedin' snotty-nose Peter Watson, is that the one 'oo says it?'

'The whole country says it,' Peter answered. 'The law says it and the police say it and *everyone* says it!'

'I don't say it!' Ernie said, raising his gun.

'Don't!' screamed Peter. 'Please don't!'

Crack! The gun went off. The bullet hit the swan right in the middle of her elegant head and the long white neck collapsed on to the side of the nest.

'Got 'er!' cried Ernie.

'Hot shot!' shouted Raymond.

Ernie turned to Peter who was standing small and white-faced and absolutely rigid. 'Now go get 'er,' he ordered.

Once again, Peter didn't move.

Ernie came up close to the smaller boy and bent down and stuck his face right up to Peter's. 'I'm tellin' you for the last time,' he said, soft and dangerous. 'Go get 'er!'

Tears were running down Peter's face as he went slowly down the bank and entered the water. He waded out to the dead swan and picked it up tenderly with both hands. Underneath it were two tiny cygnets, their bodies covered with yellow down. They were huddling together in the centre of the nest.

'Any eggs?' Ernie shouted from the bank.

'No,' Peter answered. 'Nothing.' There was a chance, he felt, that when the male swan returned, it would continue to feed the young ones on its own if they were left in the nest. He certainly did not want to leave them to the tender mercies of Ernie and Raymond.

Peter carried the dead swan back to the edge of the lake. He placed it on the ground. Then he stood up and faced the two others. His eyes, still wet with tears, were blazing with fury. 'That was a filthy thing to do!' he shouted. 'It was a stupid pointless act of vandalism! You're a couple of ignorant idiots! It's you who ought to be dead instead of the swan! You're not fit to be alive!'

He stood there, as tall as he could stand, splendid in his fury, facing the two taller boys and not caring any longer what they did to him.

Ernie didn't hit him this time. He seemed just a tiny bit taken aback at first by this outburst, but he quickly recovered. And now his loose lips formed themselves into a sly, wet smirk and his small close-together eyes began to glint in a most malicious manner. 'So you like swans, is that right?' he asked softly.

'I like swans and I hate you!' Peter cried.

'And am I right in thinkin',' Ernie went on, still smirking, 'am I absolutely right in thinkin' that you wished this old swan down 'ere were alive instead of dead?'

'That's a stupid question!' Peter shouted.

''Ee needs a clip over the ear-'ole,' Raymond said.

'Wait,' Ernie said. 'I'm doin' this exercise.' He turned back to Peter. 'So if I could make this swan come alive and go flyin' round the sky all over again, then you'd be 'appy. Right?'

'That's another stupid question!' Peter cried out. 'Who d'you think you are?'

'I'll tell you 'oo I am,' Ernie said. 'I'm a magic man, that's 'oo I am. And just to make you 'appy and contented,

I am about to do a magic trick that'll make this dead swan come alive and go flyin' all over the sky once again.'

'Rubbish!' Peter said. 'I'm going.' He turned and started to walk away.

'Grab 'im!' Ernie said.

Raymond grabbed him.

'Leave me alone!' Peter cried out.

Raymond slapped him on the cheek, hard. 'Now, now,' he said. 'Don't fight with auntie, not unless you want to get 'urt.'

'Gimme your knife,' Ernie said, holding out his hand. Raymond gave him his knife.

Ernie knelt down beside the dead swan and stretched out one of its enormous wings. 'Watch this,' he said.

'What's the big idea?' Raymond asked.

'Wait and see,' Ernie said. And now, using the knife, he proceeded to sever the great white wing from the swan's body. There is a joint in the bone where the wing meets the side of the bird, and Ernie located this and slid the knife into the joint and cut through the tendon. The knife was very sharp and it cut well, and soon the wing came away all in one piece.

Ernie turned the swan over and severed the other wing.

'String,' he said, holding out his hand to Raymond.

Raymond, who was grasping Peter by the arm, was watching fascinated. 'Where'd you learn 'ow to butcher up a bird like that?' he asked.

'With chickens,' Ernie said. 'We used to nick chickens from up at Stevens Farm and cut 'em up into chicken parts and flog 'em to a shop in Aylesbury. Gimme the string.'

Raymond gave him the ball of string. Ernie cut off six pieces, each about a yard long.

There are a series of strong bones running along the top edge of a swan's wing, and Ernie took one of the wings and started tying one end of the bits of string all the way along the top edge of the great wing. When he had done this, he lifted the wing with the six string ends dangling from it and said to Peter, 'Stick out your arm.'

'You're absolutely mad!' the smaller boy shouted. 'You're demented!'

'Make 'im stick it out,' Ernie said to Raymond.

Raymond held up a clenched fist in front of Peter's face and dabbed it gently against his nose. 'You see this,' he said. 'Well I'm goin' to smash you right in the kisser with it unless you do exactly as you're told, see? Now, stick out your arm, there's a good little boy.'

Peter felt his resistance collapsing. He couldn't hold out against these people any longer. For a few seconds, he stared at Ernie. Ernie with the tiny close-together black eyes gave the impression he would be capable of doing just about anything if he got really angry. Ernie, Peter felt at that moment, might quite easily kill a person if he were to lose his temper. Ernie, the dangerous backward child, was playing games now and it would be very unwise to spoil his fun. Peter held out an arm.

Ernie then proceeded to tie the six string ends one by one to Peter's arm, and when he had finished, the white wing of the swan was securely attached along the entire length of the arm itself.

'Ow's that, eh?' Ernie said, stepping back and surveying his work.

'Now the other one,' Raymond said, catching on to what Ernie was doing. 'You can't expect 'im to go flyin' round the sky with only one wing, can you?'

'Second wing comin' up,' Ernie said. He knelt down again and tied six more lengths of string to the top bones of the second wing. Then he stood up again. 'Let's 'ave the other arm,' he said. Peter, feeling sick and ridiculous, held out his other arm. Ernie strapped the wing tightly along the length of it.

'Now!' Ernie cried, clapping his hands and dancing a little jig on the grass. 'Now we got ourselves a real live swan all over again! Didn't I tell you I was a magic man? Didn't I tell you I was goin' to do a magic trick and make this dead swan come alive and go flyin' all over the sky? Didn't I tell you that?'

Peter stood there in the sunshine beside the lake on this beautiful May morning, the enormous, limp and slightly bloodied wings dangling grotesquely at his sides. 'Have you finished?' he said.

'Swans don't talk,' Ernie said. 'Keep your flippin' beak shut! And save your energy, laddie, because you're goin' to need all the strength and energy you got when it comes to flyin' round in the sky.' Ernie picked up his gun from the ground, then he grabbed Peter by the back of the neck with his free hand and said, 'March!'

They marched along the bank of the lake until they

came to a tall and graceful willow tree. There they halted. The tree was a weeping willow, and the long branches hung down from a great height and almost touched the surface of the lake.

'And now the magic swan is goin' to show us a bit of magic flyin',' Ernie announced. 'So what you're goin' to do, Mister Swan, is to climb up to the very top of this tree, and when you get there you're goin' to spread out your wings like a clever little swannee-swan-swan and you're goin' to take off!'

'Fantastic!' cried Raymond. 'Terrific! I like it very much!'

'So do I,' Ernie said. 'Because now we're goin' to find out just exactly 'ow clever this clever little swannee-swan-swan really is. 'Ee's terribly clever at school, we all know that, and 'ee's top of the class and everything else that's lovely, but let's see just exactly 'ow clever 'ee is when 'ee's at the top of the tree! Right, Mister Swan?' He gave Peter a push towards the tree.

How much further could this madness go? Peter wondered. He was beginning to feel a little mad himself, as though nothing was real any more and none of it was actually happening. But the thought of being high up in the tree and out of reach of these hooligans at last was something that appealed to him greatly. When he was up there, he could stay up there. He doubted very much if they would bother to come up after him. And even if they did, he could surely climb away from them along a thin limb that would not take the weight of two people.

The tree was a fairly easy one to climb, with several low branches to give him a start up. He began climbing. The huge white wings dangling from his arms kept getting in the way, but it didn't matter. What mattered now to Peter was that every inch upwards was another inch away from his tormentors below. He had never been a great one for tree-climbing and he wasn't especially good at it, but nothing in the world was going to stop him from getting to the top of this one. And once he was there, he thought it unlikely they would even be able to see him because of the leaves.

'Higher!' shouted Ernie's voice. 'Keep goin'!'

Peter kept going, and eventually he arrived at a point where it was impossible to go higher. His feet were now standing on a branch that was about as thick as a person's wrist, and this particular branch reached far out over the lake and then curved gracefully downwards. All the branches above him were very thin and whippy, but the one he was holding on to with his hands was quite strong enough for the purpose. He stood there, resting after the climb. He looked down for the first time. He was very high up, at least fifty feet. But he couldn't see the two boys. They were no longer standing at the base of the tree. Was it possible they had gone away at last?

'All right, Mister Swan!' came the dreaded voice of Ernie. 'Now listen carefully!'

The two of them had walked some distance away from the tree to a point where they had a clear view of the small boy at the top. Looking down at them now, Peter realized how very sparse and slender the leaves of a willow tree were. They gave him almost no cover at all.

'Listen carefully, Mister Swan!' the voice was shouting.

'Start walking out along that branch you're standin' on! Keep goin' till you're right over the nice muddy water! Then you take off!'

Peter didn't move. He was fifty feet above them now and they weren't ever going to reach him again. From down below, there was a long silence. It lasted maybe half a minute. He kept his eyes on the two distant figures in the field. They were standing quite still, looking up at him.

'All right then, Mister Swan!' came Ernie's voice again. 'I'm gonna count to ten, right? And if you ain't spread them wings and flown away by then, I'm gonna shoot you down instead with this little gun! And that'll make two swans I've knocked off today instead of one! So here we go, Mister Swan! One! . . . Two! . . . Three! . . . Four! . . . Five! . . . Six! . . .'

Peter remained still. Nothing would make him move from now on.

'Seven! . . . Eight! . . . Nine! . . . Ten!'

Peter saw the gun coming up to the shoulder. It was pointing straight at him. Then he heard the *crack* of the rifle and the *zip* of the bullet as it whistled past his head. It was a frightening thing. But he still didn't move. He could see Ernie loading the gun with another bullet.

'Last chance!' yelled Ernie. 'The next one's gonna get you!'

Peter stayed put. He waited. He watched the boy who was standing among the buttercups in the meadow far below with the other boy beside him. The gun came up once again to the shoulder.

This time he heard the *crack* at the same instant the

bullet hit him in the thigh. There was no pain, but the force of it was devastating. It was as though someone had whacked him on the leg with a sledgehammer, and it knocked both feet off the branch he was standing on. He scrabbled with his hands to hang on. The small branch he was holding on to bent over and split.

Some people, when they have taken too much and have been driven beyond the point of endurance, simply crumble and give up. There are others, though they are not many, who will for some reason always be unconquerable. You meet them in time of war and also in time of peace. They have an indomitable spirit and nothing, neither pain nor torture nor threat of death, will cause them to give up.

Little Peter Watson was one of these. And as he fought and scrabbled to prevent himself from falling out of the top of that tree, it came to him suddenly that he was going to win. He looked up and he saw a light shining over the waters of the lake that was of such brilliance and beauty he was unable to look away from it. The light was beckoning him, drawing him on, and he dived towards the light and spread his wings.

Three different people reported seeing a great white swan circling over the village that morning, a schoolteacher called Emily Mead, a man who was replacing some tiles on the roof of the chemist's shop whose name was William Eyles, and a boy called John Underwood who was flying his model aeroplane in a nearby field.

And that morning, Mrs Watson, who was washing up some dishes in her kitchen sink, happened to glance up through the window at the exact moment when something huge and white came flopping down on to the lawn in her back garden. She rushed outside. She went down on her knees beside the small crumpled figure of her only son. 'Oh, my darling!' she cried, near to hysterics and hardly believing what she saw. 'My darling boy! What happened to you?'

'My leg hurts,' Peter said, opening his eyes. Then he fainted.

'It's bleeding!' she cried and she picked him up and carried him inside. Quickly she phoned for the doctor and the ambulance. And while she was waiting for help to come, she fetched a pair of scissors and began cutting the string that held the two great wings of the swan to her son's arms.

The Wonderful Story of Henry Sugar

First published in *The Wonderful
Story of Henry Sugar* (1977)

Henry Sugar was forty-one years old and unmarried.
He was also wealthy. He was wealthy because he had had
a rich father who was now dead. He was unmarried
because he was too selfish to share any of his money
with a wife.

He was six feet two inches tall, but he wasn't really as
good-looking as he thought he was.

He paid a great deal of attention to his clothes. He
went to an expensive tailor for his suits, to a shirtmaker
for his shirts, and to a bootmaker for his shoes.

He used a costly aftershave lotion on his face, and he
kept his hands soft with a cream that contained turtle oil.

His hairdresser trimmed his hair once every ten days,
and he always took a manicure at the same time.

His upper front teeth had been capped at incredible
expense because the originals had had a rather nasty yellowish tinge. A small mole had been removed from his
left cheek by a plastic surgeon.

He drove a Ferrari car which must have cost him about
the same as a country cottage.

He lived in London in the summer, but as soon as
the first frosts appeared in October, he was off to the

West Indies or the South of France, where he stayed with friends. All his friends were wealthy from inherited money.

Henry had never done a day's work in his life, and his personal motto, which he had invented himself, was this: *It is better to incur a mild rebuke than to perform an onerous task.* His friends thought this was hilarious.

Men like Henry Sugar are to be found drifting like seaweed all over the world. They can be seen especially in London, New York, Paris, Nassau, Montego Bay, Cannes and St Tropez. They are not particularly bad men. But they are not good men either. They are of no real importance. They are simply a part of the decoration.

All of them, all wealthy people of this type, have one peculiarity in common: they have a terrific urge to make themselves still wealthier than they already are. The million is never enough. Nor is the two million. Always, they have this insatiable longing to get more money. And that is because they live in constant terror of waking up one morning and finding there's nothing in the bank.

These people all employ the same methods for trying to increase their fortunes. They buy stocks and shares, and watch them going up and down. They play roulette and blackjack for high stakes in casinos. They bet on horses. They bet on just about everything. Henry Sugar had once staked a thousand pounds on the result of a tortoise race on Lord Liverpool's tennis lawn. And he had wagered double that sum with a man called Esmond Hanbury on an even sillier bet, which was as follows: they let Henry's dog out into the garden and they watched it through the window. But before the dog was let out, each man had to guess beforehand what would be the first object the dog would lift its leg against. Would it be a wall, a post, a bush, or a tree? Esmond chose a wall. Henry, who had been studying his dog's habits for days with a view to making this particular bet, chose a tree, and he won the money.

With ridiculous games such as these did Henry and his friends try to conquer the deadly boredom of being both idle and wealthy.

Henry himself, as you may have noticed, was not above cheating a little on these friends of his if he saw the chance. The bet with the dog was definitely not honest. Nor, if you want to know, was the bet on the tortoise race. Henry cheated on that one by secretly forcing a little sleeping-pill powder into the mouth of his opponent's tortoise an hour before the race.

And now that you've got a rough idea of the sort of person Henry Sugar was, I can begin my story.

One summer week-end, Henry drove down from London to Guildford to stay with Sir William Wyndham. The house was magnificent, and so were the grounds, but when Henry arrived on that Saturday afternoon, it was already pelting with rain. Tennis was out, croquet was out. So was swimming in Sir William's outdoor pool. The host and his guests sat glumly in the drawing-room, staring at the rain splashing against the windows. The very rich are enormously resentful of bad weather. It is the one discomfort that their money cannot do anything about.

Somebody in the room said, 'Let's have a game of canasta for lovely high stakes.'

The others thought that a splendid idea, but as there were five people in all, one would have to sit out. They cut the cards. Henry drew the lowest, the unlucky card.

The other four sat down and began to play. Henry was annoyed at being out of the game. He wandered out of the drawing-room into the great hall. He stared at the pictures for a few moments, then he walked on through the house, bored to death at having nothing to do. Finally, he mooched into the library.

Sir William's father had been a famous book collector, and all the four walls to this huge room were lined with books from floor to ceiling. Henry Sugar was not impressed. He wasn't even interested. The only books he read were detective novels and thrillers. He ambled aimlessly round the room, looking to see if he could find any of the sort of books he liked. But the ones in Sir William's library were all leather-bound volumes with names on them like Balzac, Ibsen, Voltaire, Johnson and Pepys. Boring rubbish, the whole lot of it, Henry told himself. And he was just about to leave when his eye was caught and held by a book that was quite different from all the others. It was so slim he would never have noticed it if it hadn't been sticking out a little from the ones on either side. And when he pulled it from the shelf, he saw that it was actually nothing more than a cardboard-covered exercise-book of the kind children use at school. The cover was dark blue, but there was nothing written on it. Henry opened the exercise-book. On the first page, hand-printed in ink, it said:

A REPORT ON AN INTERVIEW
WITH IMHRAT KHAN, THE MAN WHO
COULD SEE WITHOUT HIS EYES

by

Dr John F. Cartwright

BOMBAY, INDIA

DECEMBER, 1934

That sounds mildly interesting, Henry told himself. He turned over a page. What followed was all handwritten in black ink. The writing was clear and neat. Henry read the first two pages standing up. Suddenly, he found himself wanting to read on. This was good stuff. It was fascinating. He carried the little book over to a leather armchair by the window and settled himself comfortably. Then he started reading again from the beginning.

This is what Henry read in the little blue exercise-book:

I, John Cartwright, am a surgeon at Bombay General Hospital. On the morning of the second of December, 1934, I was in the Doctors' Rest Room having a cup of tea. There were three other doctors there with me, all having a well-earned tea-break. They were Dr Marshall, Dr Phillips and Dr Macfarlane. There was a knock on the door. 'Come in,' I said.

The door opened and an Indian came in who smiled at us and said, 'Excuse me, please. Could I ask you gentlemen a favour?'

The Doctors' Rest Room was a most private place. Nobody other than a doctor was allowed to enter it except in an emergency.

'This is a private room,' Dr Macfarlane said sharply.

'Yes, yes,' the Indian answered. 'I know that and I am very sorry to be bursting in like this, sirs, but I have a most interesting thing to show you.'

All four of us were pretty annoyed and we didn't say anything.

'Gentlemen,' he said. 'I am a man who can see without using his eyes.'

We still didn't invite him to go on. But we didn't kick him out either.

'You can cover my eyes in any way you wish,' he said, 'you can bandage my head with fifty bandages and I will still be able to read you a book.'

He seemed perfectly serious. I felt my curiosity beginning to stir. 'Come here,' I said. He came over to me. 'Turn round.' He turned round. I placed my hands firmly over his eyes, holding the lids closed. 'Now,' I said. 'One of the other doctors in the room is going to hold up some fingers. Tell me how many he's holding up.'

Dr Marshall held up seven fingers.

'Seven,' the Indian said.

'Once more,' I said.

Dr Marshall clenched both fists and hid all his fingers.

'No fingers,' the Indian said.

I removed my hands from his eyes. 'Not bad,' I said.

'Hold on,' Dr Marshall said. 'Let's try this.' There was

a white doctor's coat hanging from a peg on the door. Dr Marshall took it down and rolled it into a sort of long scarf. He then wound it round the Indian's head and held the ends tight at the back. 'Try him now,' Dr Marshall said.

I took a key from my pocket. 'What is this?' I asked.

'A key,' he answered.

I put the key back and held up an empty hand. 'What is this object?' I asked him.

'There isn't any object,' the Indian said. 'Your hand is empty.'

Dr Marshall removed the covering from the man's eyes. 'How do you do it?' he asked. 'What's the trick?'

'There is no trick,' the Indian said. 'It is a genuine thing that I have managed after years of training.'

'What sort of training?' I asked.

'Forgive me, sir,' he said. 'But that is a private matter.'

'Then why did you come here?' I asked.

'I came to request a favour of you,' he said.

The Indian was a tall man of about thirty with light brown skin, the colour of a coconut. He had a small black moustache. Also, there was a curious matting of black hair growing all over the outsides of his ears. He wore a white cotton robe, and he had sandals on his bare feet.

'You see, gentlemen,' he went on, 'I am at present earning my living by working in a travelling theatre, and we have just arrived here in Bombay. Tonight we give our opening performance.'

'Where do you give it?' I asked.

'In the Royal Palace Hall,' he answered. 'In Acacia

Street. I am the star performer. I am billed on the pro-gramme as "Imhrat Khan, the man who sees without his eyes". And it is my duty to advertise the show in a big way. If we don't sell tickets, we don't eat.'

'What does this have to do with us?' I asked him.

'Very interesting for you,' he said. 'Lots of fun. Let me explain. You see, whenever our theatre arrives in a new town, I myself go straight to the largest hospital and I ask the doctors there to bandage my eyes. I ask them to do it in the most expert fashion. They must make sure my eyes are completely covered many times over. It is important that this job is done by doctors, otherwise people will think I am cheating. Then, when I am fully bandaged, I go out into the streets and I do a dangerous thing.'

'What do you mean by that?' I asked.

'What I mean is that I do something that is extremely dangerous for someone who cannot see.'

'What do you do?' I asked.

'It is very interesting,' he said. 'And you will see me do it if you will be so kind as to bandage me up first. It would be a great favour to me if you will do this little thing, sirs.'

I looked at the other three doctors. Dr Phillips said he had to go back to his patients. Dr Macfarlane said the same. Dr Marshall said, 'Well, why not? It might be amus-ing. It won't take a minute.'

'I'm with you,' I said. 'But let's do the job properly. Let's make absolutely sure he can't peep.'

'You are extremely kind,' the Indian said. 'Please do whatever you wish.'

Dr Phillips and Dr Macfarlane left the room.

'Before we bandage him,' I said to Dr Marshall, 'let's first of all seal down his eyelids. When we've done that, we'll fill his eye-sockets with something soft and solid and sticky.'

'Such as what?' Dr Marshall asked.

'What about dough?'

'Dough would be perfect,' Dr Marshall said.

'Right,' I said. 'If you will nip down to the hospital bakery and get some dough, I'll take him into the surgery and seal his lids.'

I led the Indian out of the Rest Room and down the long hospital corridor to the surgery. 'Lie down there,' I said, indicating the high bed. He lay down. I took a small bottle from the cupboard. It had an eyedropper in the top. 'This is something called collodion,' I told him. 'It will harden over your closed eyelids so that it is impossible for you to open them.'

'How do I get it off afterwards?' he asked me.

'Alcohol will dissolve it quite easily,' I said. 'It's perfectly harmless. Close your eyes now.'

The Indian closed his eyes. I applied collodion over both lids. 'Keep them closed,' I said. 'Wait for it to harden.'

In a couple of minutes, the collodion had made a hard film over the eyelids, sticking them down tight. 'Try to open them,' I said.

He tried but couldn't.

Dr Marshall came in with a basin of dough. It was the ordinary white dough used for baking bread. It was nice and soft. I took a lump of the dough and plastered it over one of the Indian's eyes. I filled the whole socket and let the dough overlap on to the surrounding skin. Then I pressed the edges down hard. I did the same with the other eye.

'That isn't too uncomfortable, is it?' I asked.

'No,' the Indian said. 'It's fine.'

'You do the bandaging,' I said to Dr Marshall. 'My fingers are too sticky.'

'A pleasure,' Dr Marshall said. 'Watch this.' He took a thick wad of cotton-wool and laid it on top of the Indian's dough-filled eyes. The cotton-wool stuck to the dough and stayed in place. 'Sit up, please,' Dr Marshall said.

The Indian sat up on the bed.

Dr Marshall took a roll of three-inch bandage and proceeded to wrap it round and round the man's head. The bandage held the cotton-wool and the dough firmly in place. Dr Marshall pinned the bandage. After that, he took a second bandage and began to wrap that one not only around the man's eyes but around his entire face and head.

'Please to leave my nose free for breathing,' the Indian said.

'Of course,' Dr Marshall answered. He finished the job and pinned down the end of the bandage. 'How's that?' he asked.

'Splendid,' I said. 'There's no way he can possibly see through that.'

The whole of the Indian's head was now swathed in thick white bandage, and the only thing you could see was the end of his nose sticking out. He looked like a man who had had some terrible brain operation.

'How does that feel?' Dr Marshall asked him.

'It feels good,' the Indian said. 'I must compliment you gentlemen on doing such a fine job.'

'Off you go, then,' Mr Marshall said, grinning at me. 'Show us how clever you are at seeing things now.'

The Indian got off the bed and walked straight to the door. He opened the door and went out.

'Great Scott!' I said. 'Did you see that? He put his hand right on to the doorknob!'

Dr Marshall had stopped grinning. His face had suddenly gone white. 'I'm going after him,' he said, rushing for the door. I rushed for the door as well.

The Indian was walking quite normally along the hospital corridor. Dr Marshall and I were about five yards behind him. And very spooky it was to watch this man with the enormous white and totally bandaged head strolling casually along the corridor just like anyone else. It was especially spooky when you knew for a certainty that his eyelids were sealed, that his eye-sockets were filled with dough, and that there was a great wad of cotton-wool and bandages on top of that.

I saw a native orderly coming along the corridor towards the Indian. He was pushing a food-trolley. Suddenly the orderly caught sight of the man with the white head, and he froze. The bandaged Indian stepped casually to one side of the trolley and went on.

'He saw it!' I cried. 'He must have seen that trolley! He walked right round it! This is absolutely unbelievable!'

Dr Marshall didn't answer me. His cheeks were white, his whole face rigid with shocked disbelief.

The Indian came to the stairs and started to go down them.

He went down with no trouble at all. He didn't even put a hand on the stair-rail. Several people were coming up the stairs. Each one of them stopped, gasped, stared, and quickly got out of his way.

At the bottom of the stairs, the Indian turned right and headed for the doors that led out into the street. Dr Marshall and I kept close behind him.

The entrance to our hospital stands back a little from the street, and there is a rather grand series of steps leading down from the entrance into a small courtyard with acacia trees around it. Dr Marshall and I came out into the blazing sunshine and stood at the top of the steps. Below us, in the courtyard, we saw a crowd of maybe a hundred people. At least half of them were barefoot children, and as our white-headed Indian walked down the steps, they all cheered and shouted and surged towards him. He greeted them by holding both hands above his head.

Suddenly I saw the bicycle. It was over to one side at the bottom of the steps, and a small boy was holding it. The bicycle itself was quite ordinary, but on the back of it, fixed somehow to the rear wheel-frame, was a huge placard, about five feet square. On the placard were written the following words:

IMHRAT KHAN, THE MAN WHO SEES
WITHOUT HIS EYES!
TODAY MY EYES HAVE BEEN BANDAGED BY
HOSPITAL DOCTORS!

APPEARING TONIGHT AND
ALL THIS WEEK AT
THE ROYAL PALACE HALL
ACACIA STREET, AT 7 P.M.
DON'T MISS IT!
YOU WILL SEE MIRACLES PERFORMED

Our Indian had reached the bottom of the steps and now he walked straight over to the bicycle. He said something to the boy and the boy smiled. The Indian mounted the bicycle. The crowd made way for him. Then, lo and behold, this fellow with the blocked-up, bandaged eyes now proceeded to ride across the courtyard and straight out into the bustling honking traffic of the street beyond! The crowd cheered louder than ever. The barefoot children ran after him, squealing and laughing. For a minute or so, we were able to keep him in sight. We saw him ride superbly down the busy street with motor-cars whizzing past him and a bunch of children running in his wake. Then he turned a corner and was gone.

'I feel quite giddy,' Dr Marshall said. 'I can't bring myself to believe it.'

'We have to believe it,' I said. 'He couldn't possibly have removed the dough from under the bandages. We never let him out of our sight. And as for unsealing his eyelids, that job would take him five minutes with cotton-wool and alcohol.'

'Do you know what I think,' Dr Marshall said. 'I think we have witnessed a miracle.'

We turned and walked slowly back into the hospital.

*

For the rest of the day, I was kept busy with patients in the hospital. At six in the evening, I came off duty and drove back to my flat for a shower and a change of clothes. It was the hottest time of year in Bombay, and even after sundown the heat was like an open furnace. If you sat still in a chair and did nothing, the sweat would come seeping out of your skin. Your face glistened with dampness all day long and your shirt stuck to your chest. I took a long cool shower. I drank a whisky and soda sitting on the veranda, with only a towel round my waist. Then I put on some clean clothes.

At ten minutes to seven, I was outside the Royal Palace Hall in Acacia Street. It was not much of a place. It was one of those smallish seedy halls that can be hired inexpensively for meetings or dances. There was a fair-sized crowd of local Indians milling round outside the ticket office, and a large poster over the entrance proclaiming that THE INTERNATIONAL THEATRE COMPANY was performing every night that week. It said there would be jugglers and conjurers and acrobats and sword-swallowers and fire-eaters and snake-charmers and a one-act play entitled *The Rajah and the Tiger Lady*. But above all this and in far the largest letters, it said IMRAT KHAN, THE MIRACLE MAN WHO SEES WITHOUT HIS EYES.

I bought a ticket and went in.

The show lasted two hours. To my surprise, I thoroughly enjoyed it. All the performers were excellent. I liked the man who juggled with cooking-utensils. He had a saucepan, a frying-pan, a baking tray, a huge plate and a casserole pot all flying through the air at the same time.

The snake-charmer had a big green snake that stood almost on the tip of its tail and swayed to the music of his flute. The fire-eater ate fire and the sword-swallower pushed a thin pointed rapier at least four feet down his throat and into his stomach. Last of all, to a great fanfare of trumpets, our friend Imhrat Khan came on to do his act. The bandages we had put on him at the hospital had now been removed.

Members of the audience were called on to the stage to blindfold him with sheets and scarves and turbans, and in the end there was so much material wrapped around his head he could hardly keep his balance. He was then given a revolver. A small boy came out and stood at the left of the stage. I recognized him as the one who had held the bicycle outside the hospital that morning. The boy placed a tin can on the top of his head and stood quite still. The audience became deathly silent as Imhrat Khan took aim. He fired. The bang made us all jump. The tin can flew off the boy's head and clattered to the floor. The boy picked it up and showed the bullet-hole to the audience. Everyone clapped and cheered. The boy smiled.

Then the boy stood against a wooden screen and Imhrat Khan threw knives all around his body, most of them going very close indeed. This was a splendid act. Not many people could have thrown knives with such accuracy even with their eyes uncovered, but here he was, this extraordinary fellow, with his head so swathed in sheets it looked like a great snowball on a stick, and he was flicking the sharp knives into the screen within a hair's breadth of the boy's head. The boy smiled all the way through the act, and when it was over the audience stamped its feet and screamed with excitement.

Imhrat Khan's last act, though not so spectacular, was even more impressive. A metal barrel was brought on stage. The audience was invited to examine it, to make sure there were no holes. There were no holes. The barrel was then placed over Imhrat Khan's already bandaged head. It came down over his shoulders and as far as his elbows, pinning the upper part of his arms to his sides. But he could still hold out his forearms and his hands. Someone put a needle in one of his hands and a length of cotton thread in the other. With no false moves, he neatly threaded the cotton through the eye of the needle. I was flabbergasted.

As soon as the show was over, I made my way backstage. I found Mr Imhrat Khan in a small but clean dressing-room, sitting quietly on a wooden stool. The little Indian boy was unwinding the masses of scarves and sheets from around his head.

'Ah,' he said. 'It is my friend the doctor from the hospital. Come in, sir, come in.'

'I saw the show,' I said.

'And what did you think?'

'I liked it very much. I thought you were wonderful.'

'Thank you,' he said. 'That is a high compliment.'

'I must congratulate your assistant as well,' I said, nodding to the small boy. 'He is very brave.'

'He cannot speak English,' the Indian said. 'But I will tell him what you said.' He spoke rapidly to the boy in Hindustani and the boy nodded solemnly but said nothing.

'Look,' I said. 'I did you a small favour this morning. Would you do me one in return? Would you consent to come out and have supper with me?'

All the wrappings were off his head now. He smiled at me and said, 'I think you are feeling curious, doctor. Am I not right?'

'Very curious,' I said. 'I'd like to talk to you.'

Once again, I was struck by the peculiarly thick matting of black hair growing on the outsides of his ears. I had not seen anything quite like it on another person. 'I have never been questioned by a doctor before,' he said. 'But I have no objection. It would be a pleasure to have supper with you.'

'Shall I wait in the car?'

'Yes, please,' he said. 'I must wash myself and get out of these dirty clothes.'

I told him what my car looked like and said I would be waiting outside.

He emerged fifteen minutes later, wearing a clean white cotton robe and the usual sandals on his bare feet. And soon the two of us were sitting comfortably in a small restaurant that I sometimes went to because it made the best curry in the city. I drank beer with my curry. Imhrat Khan drank lemonade.

'I am not a writer,' I said to him. 'I am a doctor. But if you will tell me your story from the beginning, if you will explain to me how you developed this magical power of being able to see without your eyes, I will write it down as faithfully as I can. And then, perhaps, I can get it published in the *British Medical Journal* or even in some famous magazine. And because I *am* a doctor and not just some writer trying to sell a story for money, people will be far more inclined to take seriously what I say. It would help you, wouldn't it, to become better known?'

'It would help me very much,' he said. 'But why should you want to do this?'

'Because I am madly curious,' I answered. 'That is the only reason.'

Imhrat Khan took a mouthful of curried rice and chewed it slowly. Then he said, 'Very well, my friend. I will do it.'

'Splendid!' I cried. 'Let's go back to my flat as soon as we've finished eating and then we can talk without anyone disturbing us.'

We finished our meal. I paid the bill. Then I drove Imhrat Khan back to my flat.

In the living-room, I got out paper and pencils so that I could make notes. I have a sort of private shorthand of my own that I use for taking down the medical history of patients, and with it I am able to record most of what a person says if he doesn't speak too quickly. I think I got just about everything Imhrat Khan said to me that evening, word for word, and here it is. I give it to you exactly as he spoke it:

'I am an Indian, a Hindu,' said Imhrat Khan, 'and I was born in Akhnur, in Kashmir State, in 1905. My family is poor and my father worked as a ticket inspector on the railway. When I was a small boy of thirteen, an Indian conjurer comes to our school and gives a performance. His name, I remember, is Professor Moor – all conjurers in India call themselves "professor" – and his tricks are very good. I am tremendously impressed. I think it is real magic. I feel – how shall I call it – I feel a powerful wish to learn about this magic myself, so two days later I run away from home, determined to find and to follow my new hero, Professor Moor. I take all my savings, fourteen rupees, and only the clothes I am wearing. I am wearing a white dhoti and sandals. This is in 1918 and I am thirteen years old.

'I find out that Professor Moor has gone to Lahore, two hundred miles away, so all alone, I take a ticket, third class, and I get on the train and follow him. In Lahore, I discover the Professor. He is working at his conjuring in a very cheap-type show. I tell him of my admiration and offer myself to him as assistant. He accepts me. My pay? Ah yes, my pay is eight annas a day.

'The Professor teaches me to do the linking-rings trick and my job is to stand in the street before the theatre doing this trick and calling to the people to come in and see the show.

'For six whole weeks this is very fine. It is much better than going to school. But then what a terrible bombshell I receive when suddenly it comes to me that there is no real magic in Professor Moor, that all is trickery and quickness of the hand. Immediately the Professor is no longer my hero. I lose every bit of interest in my job, but at the same time my whole mind becomes filled with a very strong longing. I long above all things to find out about the real magic and to discover something about the strange power which is called yoga.

'To do this, I must find a yogi who is willing to let me become his disciple. This is not going to be easy. True yogis do not grow on trees. There are very few of them in the whole of India. Also, they are fanatically religious people. Therefore, if I am to have success in finding a teacher, I too will have to pretend to be a very religious man.

'No, I am actually not religious. And because of that, I am what you would call a bit of a cheat. I wanted to acquire yoga powers purely for selfish reasons. I wanted to use these powers to get fame and fortune.

'Now this was something the true yogi would despise more than anything in the world. In fact, the true yogi believes that any yogi who misuses his powers will die an early and sudden death. A yogi must never perform in public. He must practise his art only in absolute privacy and as a religious service, otherwise he will be smitten to death. This I did not believe and I still don't.

'So now my search for a yogi instructor begins. I leave Professor Moor and go to a town called Amritsar in the Punjab, where I join a travelling theatre company. I have to make a living while I am searching for the secret, and already I have had success in amateur acting at my school. So for three years I travel with this theatre group all over the Punjab and by the end of it, when I am sixteen and a half years old, I am playing top of the bill. All the time I am saving money and now I have altogether a very great sum, two thousand rupees.

'It is at this moment that I hear news of a man called Banerjee. This Banerjee, it is said, is one of the truly great yogis of India, and he possesses extraordinary powers.

Above all, people are telling of how he has acquired the rare power of levitation, so that when he prays his whole body leaves the ground and becomes suspended in the air eighteen inches from the soil.

'Ah-ha, I think. This surely is the man for me. This Banerjee is the one that I must seek. So at once, I take my savings and leave the theatre company and make my way to Rishikesh, on the banks of the Ganges, where rumour says that Banerjee is living.

'For six months I search for Banerjee. Where is he? Where? Where is Banerjee? Ah yes, they say in Rishikesh, Banerjee has certainly been in the town, but that is a while ago, and even then no one saw him. And now? Now Banerjee has gone to another place. What other place? Ah well, they say, how can one know that. How indeed? How can one know about the movements of such a one as Banerjee. Does he not live a life of absolute seclusion? Does he not? And I say yes. Yes, yes, yes. Of course. That is obvious. Even to me.

'I spend all my savings trying to find this Banerjee, all except thirty-five rupees. But it is no good. However, I stay in Rishikesh and make a living by doing ordinary conjuring tricks for small groups and for suchlike. These are the tricks I have learned from Professor Moor and by nature my sleight of hand is very good.

'Then one day, there I am sitting in the small hotel in Rishikesh and again I hear talk of the yogi Banerjee. A traveller is saying how he has heard that Banerjee is now living in the jungle, not so very far away, but in the dense jungle and all alone.

'But where?

'The traveller is not sure where. "Possibly," he says, "it is over there, in that direction, north of the town," and he points with his finger.

'Well, that is enough for me. I go to the market and begin to bargain for hiring a tonga, which is a horse and cart, and the transaction is just being completed with the driver when up comes a man who has been standing listening nearby and he says that he too is going in that direction. He says can he come part of the way with me and share the cost. Of course I am delighted, and off we go, the man and me sitting in the cart, and the driver driving the horse. Off we go along a very small path which leads right through the jungle.

'And then what truly fantastic luck should happen! I am talking to my companion and I find that he is a disciple of none other than the great Banerjee himself and that he is going now on a visit to his master. So straight out I tell him that I too would like to become a disciple of the yogi.

'He turns and looks at me long and slow, and for perhaps three minutes he does not speak. Then he says, quietly, "No, that is impossible."

'All right, I say to myself, we shall see. Then I ask if it is really true that Banerjee levitates when he prays.

'"Yes," he says. "That is true. But no one is allowed to observe the thing happening. No one is ever allowed to come near Banerjee when he is praying."

'So we go on a little further in the tonga, talking all the time about Banerjee, and I manage by very careful casual questioning to find out a number of small things about him, such as what time of day he commences with his praying. Then soon the man says, "I will leave you here. This is where I dismount."

'I drop him off and I pretend to drive on along my journey, but around a corner I tell the driver to stop and wait. Quickly I jump down and I sneak back along the road, looking for this man, the disciple of Banerjee. He is not on the road. Already he has disappeared into the jungle. But which way? Which side of the road? I stand very still and listen.

'I hear a sort of rustling in the undergrowth. That must be him, I tell myself. If it is not him, then it is a tiger. But it is him. I see him ahead. He is going forwards through thick jungle. There is not even a little path where he is walking, and he is having to push his way between tall bamboos and every kind of heavy vegetation. I creep after him. I keep about one hundred yards behind him because I am frightened he may hear me. I can certainly hear him. It is impossible to proceed in silence through very thick jungle, and when I lose sight of him, which is most of the time, I am able to follow his sound.

'For about half an hour this tense game of follow-the-leader goes on. Then suddenly, I can no longer hear the man in front of me. I stop and listen. The jungle is silent. I am terrified that I may have lost him. I creep on a little way, and all at once, through the thick undergrowth, I see before me a little clearing, and in the middle of the clearing are two huts. They are small huts built entirely of jungle leaves and branches. My heart jumps and I feel a great surging of excitement inside me because this, I know for certain, is the place of Banerjee, the yogi.

'The disciple has already disappeared. He must have gone into one of the huts. All is quiet. So now I proceed to make a most careful inspection of the trees and bushes and other things all around. There is a small water-hole beside the nearest hut, and I see a prayer-mat beside it, and that, I say to myself, is where Banerjee meditates and prays. Close to this water-hole, not thirty yards away, there is a large tree, a great spreading baobab tree with beautiful thick branches which spread in such a way you can put a bed on them and lie on the bed and still not be seen from underneath. That will be my tree, I say to myself. I shall hide in that tree, and wait until Banerjee comes out to pray. Then I will be able to see everything.

'But the disciple has told me that the time of prayer is not until five or six in the evening, so I have several hours to wait. Therefore I at once walk back through the jungle to the road and I speak to the tonga driver. I tell him he too must wait. For this, I have to pay him extra money, but it doesn't matter because now I am so excited I don't care about anything for the moment, not even money.

'And all through the great noontime heat of the jungle I wait beside the tonga, and on through the heavy wet heat of the afternoon, and then, as five o'clock approaches, I make my way quietly back through the jungle to the hut, my heart beating so fast I can feel it shaking my whole body. I climb up my tree and I hide among the leaves in such a way that I can see but cannot be seen. And I wait. I wait for forty-five minutes.

'A watch? Yes, I have on a wristwatch. I remember it clearly. It was a watch I won in a raffle and I was proud to own it. On the face of my watch it said the maker's name, The Islamia Watch Co., Ludhiana. And so with my watch I am careful to be timing everything that goes on because I want to remember every single detail of this experience.

'I sit up in the tree, waiting.

'Then, all at once, a man is coming out of the hut. The man is tall and thin. He is dressed in an orange-coloured dhoti and he carries before him a tray with brass pots and incense-burners. He goes over and sits down cross-legged on the mat by the water-hole, putting the tray on the ground before him, and all the movements that he makes seem somehow very calm and gentle. He leans forwards and scoops a handful of water from the pool and throws it over his shoulder. He takes the incense-burner and passes it back and forth across his chest, slowly, in a gentle, flowing manner. He puts his hands palm downwards on his knees. He pauses. He takes a long breath through his nostrils. I can see him take a long breath and suddenly I can see his face is changing, there is a sort of brightness coming over all his face, a sort of . . . well, a sort of brightness on his skin and I can see his face is changing.

'For fourteen minutes he remains quite still in that position, and then, as I look at him, I see, quite positively I see his body lifting slowly . . . slowly . . . slowly off the ground. He is still sitting cross-legged, the hands palm downwards on the knees, and his whole body is lifting slowly off the ground, up into the air. Now I can see daylight underneath him. Twelve inches above the ground he is sitting . . . fifteen inches . . . eighteen . . . twenty . . . and soon he is at least two feet above the prayer-mat.

'I stay quite still up there in the tree, watching, and I keep saying to myself, now look carefully. There before you, thirty yards away, is a man sitting in great serenity upon the air. Are you seeing him? Yes, I am seeing him. But are you sure there is no illusion? Are you sure there is no deception? Are you sure you are not imagining? Are you sure? Yes, I am sure, I say. I am sure. I stare at him, marvelling. For a long while I keep staring, and then the body is coming slowly down again towards the earth. I see it coming. I see it moving gently downwards, slowly downwards, lowering to the earth until again his buttocks rest upon the mat.

'Forty-six minutes by my watch the body has been suspended! I timed it.

'And then, for a long long while, for over two hours, the man remains sitting absolutely still, like a stone person, with not the slightest movement. To me, it does not seem that he is breathing. His eyes are closed, and still there is this brightness on his face and also this slightly smiling look, a thing I have not seen on any other face in all my life since then.

'At last he stirs. He moves his hands. He stands up. He bends down again. He picks up the tray and goes slowly back into the hut. I am wonderstruck. I feel exalted. I forget all caution and I climb down quickly from the tree and run straight over to the hut and rush in through the door.

Banerjee is bending over, washing his feet and hands in a basin. His back is towards me, but he hears me and he turns quickly and straightens up. There is great surprise on his face and the first thing he says is, "How long have you been here?" He says it sharply, as if he is not pleased.

'At once I tell the whole truth, the whole story about being up in the tree and watching him, and at the end I tell him there is nothing I want in life except to become his disciple. Please will he let me become his disciple?

'Suddenly he seems to explode. He becomes furious and he begins shouting at me: "Get out!" he shouts. "Get out of here! Get out! Get out! Get out!" and in his fury he picks up a small brick and flings it at me and it strikes my right leg just below the knee and tears the flesh. I have the scar still. I will show it to you. There, you see, just below the knee.

'Banerjee's anger is terrible and I am very frightened. I turn and run away. I run back through the jungle to where the tonga-driver is waiting, and we drive home to Rishikesh. But that night I regain my courage. I make for myself a decision and it is this: that I will return every day to the hut of Banerjee, and I will keep on and on at him until at last he *has* to take me on as a disciple, just to get himself some peace.

'This I do. Each day I go to see him and each day his anger pours out upon me like a volcano, him shouting and yelling and me standing there frightened but also obstinate and repeating always to him my wish to become a disciple. For five days it is like this. Then, all at once, on my sixth visit, Banerjee seems to become quite calm, quite polite. He explains he cannot himself take me on as a disciple. But he will give me a note, he says, to another man, a friend, a great yogi, who lives in Hardwar. I am to go there and I will receive help and instruction.'

Imhrat Khan paused and asked me if he might have a glass of water. I fetched it for him. He took a long slow drink, then he went on with his story:

'This is in 1922 and I am nearly seventeen years old. So I go to Hardwar. And there I find the yogi, and because I have a letter from the great Banerjee, he consents to give me instruction.

'Now what is this instruction?

'It is, of course, the critical part of the whole thing. It is what I have been yearning for and searching for, so you can be sure I am an eager pupil.

'The first instruction, the most elementary part, consists of having to practise the most difficult physical exercises, all of them concerned with muscle control and breathing. But after some weeks of this, even the eager pupil becomes impatient. I tell the yogi it is my mental powers I wish to develop, not my physical ones.

'He replies, "If you will develop control of your body, then the control of your mind will be an automatic thing." But I want both at once, and I keep asking him, and in the end he says, "Very well, I will give you some exercises to help you to concentrate the conscious mind."

'"*Conscious* mind?" I ask. "Why do you say *conscious* mind?"

'"Because each man has two minds, the conscious and

the sub-conscious. The sub-conscious mind is highly concentrated, but the conscious mind, the one everyone uses, is a scattered, unconcentrated thing. It is concerning itself with thousands of different items, the things you are seeing around you and the things you are thinking about. So you must learn to concentrate it in such a way that you can visualize at will *one item*, one item only, and absolutely nothing else. If you work hard at this, you should be able to concentrate your mind, your conscious mind, upon any one object you select for at least three and a half minutes. But that will take about fifteen years."

'"Fifteen years!" I cry.

'"It may take longer," he says. "Fifteen years is the usual time."

'"But I will be an old man by then!"

'"Do not despair," the yogi says. "The time varies with different people. Some take ten years, a few can take less, and on extremely rare occasions a special person comes along who is able to develop the power in only one or two years. But that is one in a million."

'"Who are these special people?" I ask. "Do they look different from other people?"

'"They look the same," he says. "A special person might be a humble roadsweeper or a factory worker. Or he might be a rajah. There is no way of telling until the training begins."

'"Is it really so difficult," I ask, "to concentrate the mind upon a single object for three and a half minutes?"

'"It is almost impossible," he answers. "Try it and see. Shut your eyes and think of something. Think of just one object. Visualize it. See it before you. And in a few seconds your mind will start wandering. Other little thoughts will creep in. Other visions will come to you. It is a very difficult thing."

'Thus spoke the yogi of Hardwar.

'And so my real exercises begin. Each evening, I sit down and close my eyes and visualize the face of the person I love best, which is my brother. I concentrate upon visualizing his face. But the instant my mind begins to wander, I stop the exercise and rest for some minutes. Then I try again.

'After three years of daily practice, I am able to concentrate absolutely upon my brother's face for one and a half minutes. I am making progress. But an interesting thing happens. In doing these exercises, I lose my sense of smell absolutely. And never to this day does it come back to me.

'Then the necessity for earning my living to buy food forces me to leave Hardwar. I go to Calcutta where there are greater opportunities, and there I soon begin to make quite good money by giving conjuring performances. But always I continue with the exercises. Every evening, wherever I am, I settle myself down in a quiet corner and practise the concentrating of the mind upon my brother's face. Occasionally, I choose something not so personal, like for example an orange or a pair of spectacles, and that makes it even more difficult.

'One day, I travel from Calcutta to Dacca in East Bengal to give a conjuring show at a college there, and while in Dacca, I happen to be present at a demonstration of walking on fire. There are many people watching. There is a big trench dug at the bottom of a sloping lawn. The spectators are sitting in their hundreds upon the slopes of the lawn looking down upon the trench.

'The trench is about twenty-five feet long. It has been filled with logs and firewood and charcoal, and a lot of paraffin has been poured on it. The paraffin has been lit, and after a while the whole trench has become a smouldering red-hot furnace. It is so hot that the men who are stoking it are obliged to wear goggles. There is a high wind and the wind fans the charcoal almost to white heat.

'The Indian fire-walker then comes forwards. He is naked except for a small loincloth, and his feet are bare. The crowd becomes silent. The fire-walker enters the trench and walks the whole length of it, over the white-hot charcoal. He doesn't stop. Nor does he hurry. He simply walks over the white-hot coals and comes out at the other end, and his feet are not even singed. He shows the soles of his feet to the crowd. The crowd stares in amazement.

'Then the fire-walker walks the trench once more. This time he goes even slower, and as he does it, I can see on his face a look of pure and absolute concentration. This man, I tell myself, has practised yoga. He is a yogi.

'After the performance, the fire-walker calls out to the crowd, asking if there is anyone brave enough to come down and walk on the fire. There is a hush in the crowd. I feel a sudden surge of excitement in my chest. This is my chance. I must take it. I must have faith and courage. I *must* have a go. I have been doing my concentration exercises for over three years now and the time has come to give myself a severe test.

'While I am standing there thinking these thoughts, a volunteer comes forward from the crowd. It is a young Indian man. He announces that he would like to try the fire-walk. This decides me, and I also step forward and make my announcement. The crowd gives us both a cheer.

'Now the real fire-walker becomes the supervisor. He tells the other man he will go first. He makes him remove his dhoti, otherwise, he says, the hem will catch fire from the heat. And the sandals must be taken off.

'The young Indian does what he is told. But now that he is close to the trench and can feel the terrible heat coming from it, he begins to look frightened. He steps back a few paces, shielding his eyes from the heat with his hands.

'"You don't have to do it if you don't want to," the real fire-walker says.

'The crowd waits and watches, sensing a drama.

'The young man, though scared out of his wits, wishes to prove how brave he is, and he says, "Of course I'll do it."

'With that, he runs towards the trench. He steps into it with one foot, then the other. He gives a fearful scream and leaps out again and falls to the ground. The poor man lies there screaming in pain. The soles of his feet are badly burned and some of the skin has come right away. Two friends of his run forwards and carry him off.

'"Now it is your turn," says the fire-walker. "Are you ready?"

" 'I am ready," I say. "But please be silent while I prepare myself."

'A great hush has come over the crowd. They have seen one man get badly burned. Is the second one going to be mad enough to do the same thing?

'Someone in the crowd shouts, "Don't do it! You must be mad!" Others take up the shout, all telling me to give up. I turn and face them and raise my hands for silence. They stop shouting and stare at me. Every eye in that place is upon me now.

'I feel extraordinarily calm.

'I pull my dhoti off over my head. I take off my sandals. I stand there naked except for my underpants. I stand very still and close my eyes. I begin to concentrate my mind. I concentrate on the fire. I see nothing but white-hot coals and I concentrate on them being not hot but cold. The coals are cold, I tell myself. They cannot burn me. It is impossible for them to burn me because there is no heat in them. I allow half a minute to go by. I know that I must not wait too long because I am only able to concentrate absolutely upon any one thing for a minute and a half.

'I keep concentrating. I concentrate so hard that I go into a sort of trance. I step out on the coals. I walk fairly fast the whole length of the trench. And behold, I am not burned!

'The crowd goes mad. They yell and cheer. The original fire-walker rushes up to me and examines the soles of my feet. He can't believe what he sees. There is not a burn mark on them.

'"Ayee!" he cries. "What is this? Are you a yogi?"

'"I am on the way, sir," I answer proudly. "I am well on the way."

'After that, I dress and leave quickly, avoiding the crowd. 'Of course I am excited. "It is coming to me," I say. "Now at last the power is beginning to come." And all the time I am remembering something else. I am remembering a thing that the old yogi of Hardwar said to me. He said, "Certain holy people have been known to develop so great a concentration that they could see without using their eyes." I keep remembering that saying and I keep longing for the power to do likewise myself. And after my success with the fire-walking, I decided that I will concentrate everything upon this single aim – to see without the eyes.'

For only the second time so far, Imhrat Khan broke off his story. He took another sip of water, then he leaned back in his chair and closed his eyes.

'I am trying to get everything in the correct order,' he said. 'I don't want to miss anything out.'

'You're doing fine,' I told him. 'Carry on.'

'Very well,' he said. 'So I am still in Calcutta and I have just had success with fire-walking. And now I have decided to concentrate all my energy on this one thing, which is to see without the eyes.

'The time has come, therefore, to make a slight change in the exercises. Each night now I light a candle and I begin by staring at the flame. A candle-flame, you know, has three separate parts, the yellow at the top, the mauve lower down, and the black right inside. I place the candle sixteen inches away from my face. The flame is absolutely level with my eyes. It must not be above or below. It must be dead level because then I do not have to make even the tiniest little adjustment of the eye muscles by looking up or down. I settle myself comfortably and I begin to stare at the black part of the flame, right in the centre. All this is merely to concentrate my conscious mind, to empty it of everything around me. So I stare at the black spot in the flame until everything around me has disappeared and I can see nothing else. Then slowly I shut my eyes and begin to concentrate as usual upon one single object of my choice, which as you know is usually my brother's face.

'I do this every night before bed and by 1929, when I am twenty-four years old, I can concentrate upon an object for three minutes without any wandering of my mind. So it is now, at this time, when I am twenty-four, that I begin to become aware of a slight ability to see an object with my eyes closed. It is a very slight ability, just a queer little feeling that when I close my eyes and look at something hard, with fierce concentration, then I can see the outline of the object I am looking at.

'Slowly I am beginning to develop my *inner* sense of sight.

'You ask me what I mean by that. I will explain it to you exactly as the yogi of Hardwar explained it to me.

'All of us, you see, have two senses of sight, just as we have two senses of smell and taste and hearing. There is the outer sense, the highly developed one which we all use, and there is the *inner* one also. If only we could develop these inner senses of ours, then we could smell without our noses, taste without our tongues, hear without our ears and see without our eyes. Do you not understand? Do you not see that our noses and tongues and ears and eyes are only . . . how shall I say it? . . . are only instruments which assist in conveying the sensation itself to the brain.

'And so it is that I am all the time striving to develop my inner senses of sight. Each night now I perform my usual exercises with the candle-flame and my brother's face. After that I rest a little while. I drink a cup of coffee. Then I blindfold myself and sit in my chair trying to visualize, trying to see, not just to imagine, but actually to *see* without my eyes every object in the room.

'And gradually success begins to come.

'Soon I am working with a pack of cards. I take a card from the top of the pack and hold it before me, back to front, trying to see through it. Then, with a pencil in my hand, I write down what I think it is. I take another card and do the same again. I go through the whole of the pack like that and when it is over I check what I have written down against the pile of cards beside me. Almost at once I have a sixty to seventy per cent success.

'I do other things. I buy maps and complicated navigating charts and pin them up all around my room. I spend hours looking at them blindfold, trying to see them, trying to read the small lettering of the place-names and the rivers. Every evening for the next four years, I proceed with this kind of practice.

'By the year 1933 – that is only last year – when I am

twenty-eight years old, I can read a book. I can cover my eyes completely and I can read a book right through.

'So now at last I have it, this power. For certain I have it now, and at once, because I cannot wait with impatience, I include the blindfold act in my ordinary conjuring performance.

'The audience loves it. They applaud long and loud. But not one single person believes it to be genuine. Everyone thinks it is just another clever trick. And the fact that I am a conjurer makes them think more than ever that I am faking. Conjurers are men who trick you. They trick you with cleverness. And so no one believes me. Even the doctors who blindfold me in the most expert way refuse to believe that anyone can see without his eyes. They forget there may be other ways of sending the image to the brain.'

'What other ways?' I asked him.

'Quite honestly, I don't know exactly how it is I can see without my eyes. But what I do know is this; when my eyes are bandaged, I am not using the eyes at all. The seeing is done by another part of my body.'

'Which part?' I asked him.

'Any part at all so long as the skin is bare. For example, if you put a sheet of metal in front of me and put a book behind the metal, I cannot read the book. But if you allow me to put my hand around the sheet of metal so that the hand is seeing the book, then I can read it.'

'Would you mind if I tested you on that?' I asked.

'Not at all,' he answered.

'I don't have a sheet of metal,' I said. 'But the door will do just as well.'

I stood up and went to the bookshelf. I took down the first book that came to hand. It was *Alice in Wonderland*. I opened the door and asked my visitor to stand behind it, out of sight. I opened the book at random and propped it on a chair the other side of the door to him. Then I stationed myself in a position where I could see both him and the book.

'Can you read that book?' I asked him.

'No,' he answered. 'Of course not.'

'All right. You may now put your hand around the door, but only the hand.'

He slid his hand around the edge of the door until it was within sight of the book. Then I saw the fingers on the hand parting from one another, spreading wide, beginning to quiver slightly, feeling the air like the antennae of an insect. And the hand turned so that the back of it was facing the book.

'Try to read the left page from the top,' I said.

There was silence for perhaps ten seconds, then smoothly, without pause, he began to read: '*Have you guessed the riddle yet?' the Hatter said, turning to Alice again. 'No, I give it up,' Alice replied: 'What's the answer?' 'I haven't the slightest idea,' said the Hatter. 'Nor I,' said the Hare. Alice sighed wearily. 'I think you might do something better with the time,' she said, 'than waste it asking riddles with no answers . . .'*

'It's perfect!' I cried. 'Now I believe you! You are a miracle!' I was enormously excited.

'Thank you, doctor,' he said gravely. 'What you say gives me great pleasure.'

'One question,' I said. 'It's about the playing cards. When you held up the reverse side of one of them, did you put your hand around the other side to help you to read it?'

'You are very perceptive,' he said. 'No, I did not. In the case of the cards, I was actually able to *see through* them in some way.'

'How do you explain that?' I asked.

'I don't explain it,' he said. 'Except perhaps that a card is such a flimsy thing, it is so thin, and not solid like metal or thick like a door. That is all the explanation I can give. There are many things in this world, doctor, that we cannot explain.'

'Yes,' I said. 'There certainly are.'

'Would you be kind enough to take me home now,' he said. 'I feel very tired.'

I drove him home in my car.

That night I didn't go to bed. I was far too worked up to sleep. I had just witnessed a miracle. This man would have doctors all over the world turning somersaults in the air! He could change the whole course of medicine! From a doctor's point of view, he must be the most valuable man alive! We doctors must get hold of him and keep him safe. We must look after him. We mustn't let him go. We must find out exactly how it is that an image can be sent to the brain without using the eyes. And if we do that, then blind people might be able to see and deaf people might be able to hear. Above all, this incredible man must not be ignored and left to wander around India, living in cheap rooms and playing in second-rate theatres.

I got so steamed up thinking about this that after a while I grabbed a notebook and a pen and started writing down with great care everything that Imhrat Khan had told me that evening. I used the notes I had made while he was talking. I wrote for five hours without stopping. And at eight o'clock the next morning, when it was time to go to the hospital, I had finished the most important part, the pages you have just read.

At the hospital that morning, I didn't see Dr Marshall until we met in the Doctors' Rest Room in our tea-break.

I told him as much as I could in the ten minutes we had to spare. 'I'm going back to the theatre tonight,' I said. 'I *must* talk to him again. I must persuade him to stay here. We mustn't lose him now.'

'I'll come with you,' Dr Marshall said.

'Right,' I said. 'We'll watch the show first and then we'll take him out to supper.'

At a quarter to seven that evening, I drove Dr Marshall in my car to Acacia Road. I parked the car, and the two of us walked over to the Royal Palace Hall.

'There's something wrong,' I said. 'Where is everybody?'

There was no crowd outside the hall and the doors were closed. The poster advertising the show was still in place, but I now saw that someone had written across it in large printed letters, using black paint, the words TONIGHT'S PERFORMANCE CANCELLED. There was an old gatekeeper standing by the locked doors.

'What happened?' I asked him.

'Someone died,' he said.

'Who?' I asked, knowing already who it was.

'The man who sees without his eyes,' the gatekeeper answered.

'How did he die?' I cried. 'When? Where?'

'They say he died in his bed,' the gatekeeper said. 'He went to sleep and never woke up. These things happen.'

We walked slowly back to the car. I felt an overwhelming sense of grief and anger. I should never have allowed this precious man to go home last night. I should have kept him. I should have given him my bed and taken care of him. I shouldn't have let him out of my sight. Imhrat Khan was a maker of miracles. He had communicated with mysterious and dangerous forces that are beyond the reach of ordinary people. He had also broken all the rules. He had performed miracles in public. He had taken money for doing so. And, worst of all, he had told some of those secrets to an outsider – me. Now he was dead.

'So that's that,' Dr Marshall said.

'Yes,' I said. 'It's all over. Nobody will ever know how he did it.'

This is a true and accurate report of everything that took place concerning my two meetings with Imhrat Khan.

signed John F. Cartwright, M.D.
. . . .
Bombay, 4th December, 1934

'Well, well, well,' said Henry Sugar. 'Now *that* is extremely interesting.'

He closed the exercise-book and sat gazing at the rain splashing against the windows of the library.

'This,' Henry Sugar went on, talking aloud to himself, 'is a terrific piece of information. It could change my life.'

The piece of information Henry was referring to was that Imhrat Khan had trained himself to read the value of a playing-card from the reverse side. And Henry the gambler, the rather dishonest gambler, had realized at once that if only *he* could train himself to do the same thing, he could make a fortune.

For a few moments, Henry allowed his mind to dwell upon the marvellous things he would be able to do if he could read cards from the back. He would win every single time at canasta and bridge and poker. And better still, he would be able to go into any casino in the world and clean up at blackjack and all the other high-powered card games they played!

In gambling casinos, as Henry knew very well, nearly everything depended in the end upon the turn of a single card, and if you knew beforehand what the value of that card was, then you were home and dry!

But could he do it? Could he actually train himself to do this thing?

He didn't see why not. That stuff with the candle-flame didn't appear to be particularly hard work. And according to the book, that was really all there was to it – just staring into the middle of the flame and trying to concentrate upon the face of the person you loved best.

It would probably take him several years to bring it off, but then who in the world wouldn't be willing to train for a few years in order to beat the casinos every time he went in?

'By golly,' he said aloud, 'I'll do it! I'm going to do it!'

He sat very still in the armchair in the library, working out a plan of campaign. Above all, he would tell nobody what he was up to. He would steal the little book from the library so that none of his friends might come upon it by chance and learn the secret. He would carry the book with him wherever he went. It would be his bible. He couldn't possibly go out and find a real live yogi to instruct him, so the book would be his yogi instead. It would be his teacher.

Henry stood up and slipped the slim blue exercise-book under his jacket. He walked out of the library and went straight upstairs to the bedroom they had given him for the week-end. He got out his suitcase and hid the book underneath his clothes. He then went downstairs again and found his way to the butler's pantry.

'John,' he said, addressing the butler, 'can you find me a candle? Just an ordinary white candle.'

Butlers are trained never to ask reasons. They simply obey orders. 'Do you wish a candle-holder as well, sir?'

'Yes. A candle and a candle-holder.'

'Very good, sir. Shall I bring them to your room?'

'No. I'll hang around here till you find them.'

The butler soon found a candle and a candle-holder. Henry said, 'And now could you find me a ruler?' The butler found him a ruler. Henry thanked him and returned to his bedroom.

When he was inside the bedroom, he locked the door. He drew all the curtains so that the place was in twilight.

He put the candle-holder with the candle in it on the dressing-table and pulled up a chair. When he sat down, he noticed with satisfaction that his eyes were exactly level with the wick of the candle. Now, using the ruler, he positioned his face sixteen inches from the candle, which was what the book said must be done.

That Indian fellow had visualized the face of the person he loved best, which in his case was a brother. Henry didn't have a brother. He decided instead to visualize his own face. This was a good choice because when you are as selfish and self-centred as Henry was, then one's own face is certainly the face one loves best of all. Moreover, it was the face he *knew* best of all. He spent so much time looking at it in the mirror, he knew every twist and wrinkle.

With his cigarette-lighter, he lit the wick. A yellow flame appeared and burned steadily.

Henry sat quite still and stared into the candle-flame. The book had been quite right. The flame, when you looked into it closely, did have three separate parts. There was the yellow outside. Then there was the mauve inner sheath. And right in the middle was the tiny magic area of absolute blackness. He stared at the tiny black area. He focused his eyes upon it and kept staring at it, and as he did so, an extraordinary thing happened. His mind went absolutely blank, and his brain ceased fidgeting around, and all at once it felt as though he himself, his whole body, was actually encased within the flame, sitting snug and cosy within the little black area of nothingness.

With no trouble at all, Henry allowed the image of his

own face to swim into sight before him. He concentrated upon the face and nothing but the face. He blocked out all other thoughts. He succeeded completely in doing this, but only for about fifteen seconds. After that, his mind began to wander and he found himself thinking about gambling casinos and how much money he was going to win. At this point, he looked away from the candle and gave himself a rest.

This was his very first effort. He was thrilled. He had done it. Admittedly he hadn't kept it up for very long. But neither had that Indian fellow on the first attempt.

After a few minutes, he tried again. It went well. He had no stop-watch to time himself with, but he sensed that this was definitely a longer go than the first one.

'It's terrific!' he cried. 'I'm going to succeed! I'm going to do it!' He had never been so excited by anything in his life.

From that day on, no matter where he was or what he was doing, Henry made a point of practising with the candle every morning and every evening. Often he practised at midday as well. For the first time in his life he was throwing himself into something with genuine enthusiasm. And the progress he made was remarkable. After six months, he could concentrate absolutely upon his own face for no less than three minutes without a single outside thought entering his mind.

The yogi of Hardwar had told the Indian fellow that a man would have to practise for fifteen years to get that sort of result!

But wait! The yogi had also said something else. He had

said (and here Henry eagerly consulted the little blue exercise-book for the hundredth time), he had said that on extremely rare occasions a special person comes along who is able to develop the power in only one or two years.

'That's me!' Henry cried. 'It must be me! I am the one-in-a-million person who is gifted with the ability to acquire yoga powers at incredible speed! Whoopee and hurray! It won't be long now before I'm breaking the bank in every casino in Europe and America!'

But Henry at this point showed unusual patience and good sense. He didn't rush to get out a pack of cards to see if he could read them from the reverse side. In fact, he kept well away from card games of all kinds. He had given up bridge and canasta and poker as soon as he had started working with the candle. What's more, he had given up razzing around to parties and week-ends with his rich friends. He had become dedicated to this single aim of acquiring yoga powers, and everything else would have to wait until he had succeeded.

Some time during the tenth month, Henry became aware, just as Imhrat Khan had done before him, of a slight ability to see an object with his eyes closed. When he closed his eyes and stared at something hard, with fierce concentration, he could actually see the outline of the object he was looking at.

'It's coming to me!' he cried. 'I'm doing it! It's fantastic!'

Now he worked harder than ever at his exercises with the candle, and at the end of the first year he could actually concentrate upon the image of his own face for no less than five and a half minutes!

At this point, he decided the time had come to test himself with the cards. He was in the living-room of his London flat when he made this decision and it was near midnight. He got out a pack of cards and a pencil and paper. He was shaking with excitement. He placed the pack upside down before him and concentrated on the top card.

All he could see at first was the design on the back of the card. It was a very ordinary design of thin red lines, one of the commonest playing-card designs in the world. He now shifted his concentration from the pattern itself to the other side of the card. He concentrated with great intensity upon the invisible underneath of the card, and he allowed no other single thought to creep into his mind. Thirty seconds went by.

Then one minute . . .

Two minutes . . .

Three minutes . . .

Henry didn't move. His concentration was intense and absolute. He was visualizing the reverse side of the playing-card. No other thought of any kind was allowed to enter his head.

During the fourth minute, something began to happen. Slowly, magically, but very clearly, the black symbols became spades and alongside the spades appeared the figure five.

The five of spades!

Henry switched off his concentration. And now, with shaking fingers, he picked up the card and turned it over.

It *was* the five of spades!

'I've done it!' he cried aloud, leaping up from his chair. 'I've seen through it! I'm on my way!'

After resting for a while, he tried again, and this time he used a stop-watch to see how long it took him. After three minutes and fifty-eight seconds, he read the card as the king of diamonds. He was right!

The next time he was right again and it took him three minutes and fifty-four seconds. That was four seconds less.

He was sweating with excitement and exhaustion. 'That's enough for today,' he told himself. He got up and poured himself an enormous drink of whisky and sat down to rest and to gloat over his success.

His job now, he told himself, was to keep practising and practising with the cards until he could see through them instantly. He was convinced it could be done. Already, on the second go, he had knocked four seconds off his time. He would give up working with the candle and concentrate solely upon the cards. He would keep at it day and night.

And that is what he did. But now that he could smell real success in the offing, he became more fanatical than ever. He never left his flat except to buy food and drink. All day and often far into the night, he crouched over the cards with the stop-watch beside him, trying to reduce the time it took him to read from the reverse side.

Within a month, he was down to one and a half minutes.

And at the end of six months of fierce concentrated work, he could do it in twenty seconds. But even that was too long. When you are gambling in a casino and the dealer is waiting for you to say yes or no to the next card, you are not going to be allowed to stare at it for twenty seconds before making up your mind. Three or four seconds would be permissible. But no more.

Henry kept at it. But from now on, it became more and more difficult to improve his speed. To get down from twenty seconds to nineteen took him a week of very hard work. From nineteen to eighteen took him nearly two weeks. And seven more months went by before he could read through a card in ten seconds flat.

His target was four seconds. He knew that unless he could see through a card in a maximum of four seconds, he wouldn't be able to work the casinos successfully. Yet the nearer he got towards the target, the more difficult it became to reach it. It took four weeks to get his time down from ten seconds to nine, and five more weeks to go from nine to eight. But at this stage, hard work no longer bothered him. His powers of concentration had now developed to such a degree that he was able to work for twelve hours at a stretch with no trouble at all. And he knew with absolute certainty that he would get there in the end. He would not stop until he did. Day after day, night after night, he sat crouching over the cards with his stop-watch beside him, fighting with a terrible intensity to knock those last few stubborn seconds off his time.

The last three seconds were the worst of all. To get from seven seconds to his target of four took him exactly eleven months!

The great moment came on a Saturday evening. A card lay face down on the table in front of him. He clicked the stop-watch and began to concentrate. At once, he saw a blob of red. The blob swiftly took shape and became a diamond. And then, almost instantaneously, a figure six appeared in the top left-hand corner. He clicked the watch again. He checked the time. It was four seconds! He turned the card over. It was the six of diamonds! He had done it! He had read it in four seconds flat!

He tried again with another card. In four seconds he read it as the queen of spades. He went right through the pack, timing himself with every card. Four seconds! Four seconds! Four seconds! It was always the same. He had done it at last! It was all over. He was ready to go!

And how long had it taken him? It had taken him exactly three years and three months of concentrated work.

And now for the casinos!

When should he start?

Why not tonight?

Tonight was Saturday. All the casinos were crowded on Saturday nights. So much the better. There'd be less chance of becoming conspicuous. He went into his bedroom to change into his dinner-jacket and black tie. Saturday was a dressy night at the big London casinos.

He would go, he decided, to Lord's House. There are well over one hundred legitimate casinos in London, but none of them is open to the general public. You must become a member before you are allowed to walk in. Henry was a member of no less than ten of them. Lord's House was his favourite. It was the finest and most exclusive in the country.

*

Lord's House was a magnificent Georgian mansion in the centre of London, and for over two hundred years it had been the private residence of a Duke. Now it was taken over by the bookmakers, and the superb high-ceilinged rooms where the aristocracy and often royalty used to gather and play a gentle game of whist were today filled with a new kind of people who played a very different sort of game.

Henry drove to Lord's House and pulled up outside the great entrance. He got out of the car, but left the engine running. Immediately, an attendant in green uniform came forward to park it for him.

Along the kerb on both sides of the street stood perhaps a dozen Rolls-Royces. Only the very wealthy belonged to Lord's House.

'Why hello, Mr Sugar!' said the man behind the desk whose job it was never to forget a face. 'We haven't seen you for years!'

'I've been busy,' Henry answered.

He went upstairs, up the marvellous wide staircase with its carved mahogany banisters, and entered the cashier's office. There he wrote a cheque for one thousand pounds. The cashier gave him ten large pink rectangular plaques made of plastic. On each it said £100. Henry slipped them into his pocket and spent a few minutes sauntering through the various gaming-rooms to get the feel of things again after such a long absence. There was a big crowd here tonight. Well-fed women stood around the roulette wheel like plump hens around a feeding hopper. Jewels and gold were dripping over their bosoms and from their wrists. Many of them had blue hair. The men were in dinner-jackets and there wasn't a tall one among them. Why, Henry wondered, did this particular kind of rich man always have short legs? Their legs all seemed to stop at the knees with no thighs above. Most of them had bellies coming out a long way, and crimson faces, and cigars between their lips. Their eyes glittered with greed.

All this Henry noticed. It was the first time in his life that he had looked with distaste upon this type of wealthy gambling-casino person. Up until now, he had always regarded them as companions, as members of the same group and class as himself. Tonight they seemed vulgar.

Could it be, he wondered, that the yoga powers he had acquired over the last three years had altered him just a little bit?

He stood watching the roulette. Upon the long green table people were placing their money, trying to guess which little slot the small white ball would fall into on the next spin of the wheel. Henry looked at the wheel. And suddenly, perhaps more from habit than anything else, he found himself beginning to concentrate upon it. It was not difficult. He had been practising the art of total con-centration for so long that it had become something of a routine. In a fraction of a second, his mind had become completely and absolutely concentrated upon the wheel. Everything else in the room, the noise, the people, the lights, the smell of cigar smoke, all this was wiped out of his mind, and he saw only the white numbers around the rim. The numbers went from 1 to 36, with an o between 1 and 36. Very quickly, all the numbers blurred and disappeared in front of his eyes. All except one, all except the number 18. It was the only number he could see. At first it was slightly muzzy and out of focus. Then the edges sharpened and the whiteness of it grew brighter, more brilliant, until it began to glow as though there was a bright light behind it. It grew bigger. It seemed to jump towards him. At that point, Henry switched off his concentration. The room swam back into vision.

'Have you all finished?' the croupier was saying.

Henry took a £100 plaque from his pocket and placed it on the square marked 18 on the green table. Although the table was covered all over with other people's bets, his was the only one on 18.

The croupier spun the wheel. The little white ball bounced and skittered around the rim. The people watched. All eyes were on the little ball. The wheel slowed. It came to rest. The ball jiggled a few more times, hesitated, then dropped neatly into slot 18.

'Eighteen!' called the croupier.

The crowd sighed. The croupier's assistant scooped up the piles of losing plaques with a long-handled wooden scooper. But he didn't take Henry's. They paid him thirty-six to one. Three thousand six hundred pounds for his hundred. They gave it to him in three one-thousand pound plaques and six hundreds.

Henry began to feel an extraordinary sense of power. He felt he could break this place if he wanted to. He could ruin this fancy high-powered expensive joint in a matter of hours. He could take a million off them and all the stony-faced sleek gentlemen who stood around watching

the money rolling in would be scurrying about like panicky rats.

Should he do that?

It was a great temptation.

But it would be the end of everything. He would
become famous and would never be allowed into a casino
again anywhere in the world. He mustn't do it. He must be
very careful not to draw attention to himself.

Henry moved casually out of the roulette room and
passed into the room where they were playing blackjack.
He stood in the doorway watching the action. There were
four tables. They were oddly shaped, these blackjack
tables, each one curved like a crescent moon, with the
players sitting on high stools around the outside of the
half-circle and the dealers standing inside.

The packs of cards (at Lord's House they used four
packs shuffled together) lay in an open-ended box known
as a shoe, and the dealer pulled the cards out of the shoe
one by one with his fingers . . . The reverse side of the
card in the shoe was always visible, but no others.

Blackjack, as the casinos call it, is a very simple game.
You and I know it by one of three other names, pontoon,
twenty-one or vingt-et-un. The player tries to get his cards
to add up to as near twenty-one as possible, but if he goes
over twenty-one, he's bust and the dealer takes the money.
In nearly every hand, the player is faced with the problem
of whether to draw another card and risk being bust, or
whether to stick with what he's got. But Henry would not
have that problem. In four seconds, he would have 'seen
through' the card the dealer was offering him, and he

would know whether to say yes or no. Henry could turn blackjack into a farce.

In all casinos, they have an awkward rule about blackjack betting which we do not have at home. At home, we look at our first card before we make a bet, and if it's a good one we bet high. The casinos don't allow you to do this. They insist that everyone at the table makes his bet *before* the first card of the hand is dealt. What's more, you are not allowed to increase your bet later on by buying a card.

None of this would disturb Henry either. So long as he sat on the dealer's immediate left, then he would always receive the first card in the shoe at the beginning of each deal. The reverse side of the card would be clearly visible to him, and he would 'read through' it before he made his bet.

Now, standing quietly just inside the doorway, Henry waited for a place to become vacant on the dealer's left at any of the four tables. He had to wait twenty minutes for this to happen, but he got what he wanted in the end.

He perched himself on the high stool and handed the dealer one of the £1,000 plaques he had won at roulette. 'All in twenty-fives, please,' he said.

The dealer was a youngish man with black eyes and grey skin. He never smiled and he spoke only when necessary. His hands were exceptionally slim and there was arithmetic in his fingers. He took Henry's plaque and dropped it in a slot in the table. Rows of different coloured circular chips lay neatly in a wooden tray in front of him, chips for £25, £10 and £5, maybe a hundred of each. With his thumb and forefinger, the dealer picked up a wedge of £25 chips and placed them in a tall pile on the table. He didn't have to count them. He knew there were exactly twenty chips in the pile. Those nimble fingers could pick up with absolute accuracy any number of chips from one to twenty and never be wrong. The dealer picked up a second lot of chips, making forty in all. He slid them over the table to Henry.

Henry stacked the chips in front of him, and as he did so, he glanced at the top card in the shoe. He switched on his concentration and in four seconds he read it as a ten. He pushed out eight of his chips, £200. This was the maximum stake allowed for blackjack at Lord's House.

He was dealt the ten, and for his second card he got a nine, nineteen altogether.

Everyone sticks on nineteen. You sit tight and hope the dealer won't get twenty or twenty-one.

So when the dealer came round again to Henry, he said, 'Nineteen,' and passed on to the next player.

'Wait,' Henry said.

The dealer paused and came back to Henry. He raised his brows and looked at him with those cool black eyes. 'You wish to draw to nineteen?' he asked somewhat sarcastically. He spoke with an Italian accent and there was scorn as well as sarcasm in his voice. There were only two cards in the pack that would not bust a nineteen, the ace (counting as a one) and the two. Only an idiot would risk drawing to nineteen, especially with £200 on the table.

The next card to be dealt lay clearly visible in the front of the shoe. At least, the reverse side of it was clearly visible. The dealer hadn't yet touched it.

'Yes,' Henry said. 'I think I'll have another card.'

The dealer shrugged and flipped the card out of the

shoe. The two of clubs landed neatly in front of Henry, alongside the ten and the nine.

'Thank you,' Henry said. 'That will do nicely.'

'Twenty-one,' the dealer said. His black eyes glanced up again into Henry's face, and they rested there, silent, watchful, puzzled. Henry had unbalanced him. He had never in his life seen anyone draw on nineteen. This fellow had drawn on nineteen with a calmness and a certainty that was quite staggering. And he had won.

Henry caught the look in the dealer's eyes, and he realized at once that he had made a silly mistake. He had been too clever. He had drawn attention to himself. He must never do that again. He must be very careful in future how he used his powers. He must even make himself lose occasionally, and every now and again he must do something a bit stupid.

The game went on. Henry's advantage was so enormous, he had difficulty keeping his winnings down to a reasonable sum. Every now and again, he would ask for a third card when he already knew it was going to bust him. And once, when he saw that his first card was going to be an ace, he put out his smallest stake, then made a great show of cursing himself aloud for not having made a bigger bet in the first place.

In an hour, he had won exactly three thousand pounds, and there he stopped. He pocketed his chips and made his way back to the cashier's office to turn them in for real money.

He had made £3,000 from blackjack and £3,600 from roulette, £6,600 in all. It could just as easily have been £660,000. As a matter of fact, he told himself he was now almost certainly able to make money faster than any other man in the entire world.

The cashier received Henry's pile of chips and plaques without twitching a muscle. He wore steel spectacles, and the pale eyes behind the spectacles were not interested in Henry. They looked only at the chips on the counter. This man also had arithmetic in his fingers. But he had more than that. He had arithmetic, trigonometry and calculus and algebra and Euclidean geometry in every nerve of his body. He was a human calculating-machine with a hundred thousand electric wires in his brain. It took him five seconds to count Henry's one hundred and twenty chips.

'Would you like a cheque for this, Mr Sugar?' he asked. The cashier, like the man at the desk downstairs, knew every member by name.

'No, thank you,' Henry said. 'I'll take it in cash.'

'As you wish,' said the voice behind the spectacles, and he turned away and went to a safe at the back of the office that must have contained millions.

By Lord's House standards, Henry's win was fairly small potatoes. The Arab oil boys were in London now and they liked to gamble. So did the shady diplomats from the Far East and the Japanese businessmen and the British tax-dodging real-estate operators. Staggering sums of money were being won and lost, mostly lost, in the large London casinos every day.

The cashier returned with Henry's money and dropped the bundle of notes on the counter. Although there was enough here to buy a small house or a large automobile, the chief cashier at Lord's House was not impressed. He might just as well have been passing Henry a pack of chewing-gum for all the notice he took of the money he was dishing out.

You wait, my friend, Henry thought to himself as he pocketed the money. You just wait. He walked away.

'Your car, sir?' said the man at the door in the green uniform.

'Not yet,' Henry told him. 'I think 'I'll take a bit of fresh air first.'

He strolled away down the street. It was nearly midnight. The evening was cool and pleasant. The great city was still wide awake. Henry could feel the bulge in the inside pocket of his jacket where the big wad of money was lying. He touched the bulge with one hand. He patted it gently. It was a lot of money for an hour's work.

And what of the future?

What was the next move going to be?

He could make a million in a month.

He could make more if he wanted to.

There was no limit to what he could make.

Walking through the streets of London in the cool of the evening, Henry began to think about the next move.

Now, had this been a made-up story instead of a true one, it would have been necessary to invent some sort of a surprising and exciting end for it. It would not be difficult to do that. Something dramatic and unusual. So before telling you what really *did* happen to Henry in real life, let us pause here for a moment to see what a competent fiction writer would have done to wrap this story up. His notes would read something like this:

1. Henry must die. Like Imhrat Khan before him, he had violated the code of the yogi and had used his powers for personal gain.

2. It will be best if he dies in some unusual and interesting manner that will surprise the reader.

3. For example, he could go home to his flat and start counting his money and gloating over it. While doing this, he might suddenly begin to feel unwell. He has a pain in his chest.

4. He becomes frightened. He decides to go to bed immediately and rest. He takes off his clothes. He walks naked to the cupboard to get his pyjamas. He passes the full-length mirror that stands against the wall. He stops. He stares at the reflection of his naked self in the mirror. Auto-matically, from force of habit he begins to concentrate. And then . . .

5. All at once, he is 'seeing through' his own skin. He 'sees through' it in the same way that he 'saw through' those playing-cards a while back. It is like an X-ray picture, only far better. An X-ray can see only the bones and the very dense areas. Henry can see everything. He sees his arteries and veins with the blood pumping through him. He can see his liver, his kidneys, his intestines and he can see his heart beating.

6. He looks at the place in his chest where the pain is coming from . . . and he sees . . . or thinks he sees . . . a small dark lump inside the big vein leading into the heart on the right-hand side.

What could a small dark lump be doing inside the vein? It must be a blockage of some kind. It must be a clot. A blood-clot!

7. At first, the clot seems to be stationary. Then it moves. The movement is very slight, no more than a millimetre or two. The blood inside the vein is pumping up behind the clot and pushing past it and the clot moves again. It jerks forward about half an inch. This time, up the vein, towards the heart. Henry watches in terror. He knows, as almost everyone else in the world knows, that a blood-clot which has broken free and is travelling in a vein will ultimately reach the heart. If the clot is a large one, it will stick in the heart and you will probably die . . .

That wouldn't be such a bad ending for a work of fiction, but this story is not fiction. It is true. The only untrue things about it are Henry's name and the name of the gambling casino. Henry's name was not Henry Sugar. His name has to be protected. It still must be protected. And for obvious reasons, one cannot call the casino by its real name. Apart from that, it is a true story.

And because it is a true story, it must have the true ending. The true one may not be quite so dramatic or spooky as a made-up one could be, but it is nonetheless interesting. Here is what actually happened.

After walking the London streets for about an hour, Henry returned to Lord's House and collected his car.

Then he drove back to his flat. He was a puzzled man. He couldn't understand why he felt so little excitement about his tremendous success. If this sort of thing had happened to him three years ago, before he'd started the yoga business, he'd have gone crazy with excitement. He'd have been dancing in the streets and rushing off to the nearest nightclub to celebrate with champagne.

The funny thing was that he didn't really feel excited at all. He felt melancholy. It had somehow all been too easy. Every time he'd made a bet, he'd been certain of winning. There was no thrill, no suspense, no danger of losing. He knew of course that from now on he could travel around the world and make millions. But was it going to be any fun doing it?

It was slowly beginning to dawn upon Henry that nothing is any fun if you can get as much of it as you want. Especially money.

Another thing. Was it not possible that the process he had gone through in order to acquire yoga powers had completely changed his outlook on life?

Certainly it was possible.

Henry drove home and went straight to bed.

The next morning he woke up late. But he didn't feel any more cheerful now than he had the night before. And when he got out of bed and saw the enormous bundle of money still lying on his dressing-table, he felt a sudden and very acute revulsion towards it. He didn't want it. For the life of him, he couldn't explain why this was so, but the fact remained that he simply did not want any part of it.

He picked up the bundle. It was all in twenty-pound notes, three hundred and thirty of them to be exact. He walked on to the balcony of his flat, and there he stood in his dark-red silk pyjamas looking down at the street below him.

Henry's flat was in Curzon Street, which is right in the middle of London's most fashionable and expensive district, known as Mayfair. One end of Curzon Street runs into Berkeley Square, the other into Park Lane. Henry lived three floors above street level, and outside his bedroom there was a small balcony with iron railings that overhung the street.

The month was June, the morning was full of sunshine, and the time was about eleven o'clock. Although it was a Sunday, there were quite a few people strolling about on the pavements.

Henry peeled off a single twenty-pound note from his wad and dropped it over the balcony. A breeze took hold of it and blew it sideways in the direction of Park Lane. Henry stood watching it. It fluttered and twisted in the air and eventually came to rest on the opposite side of the street, directly in front of an old man. The old man was wearing a long brown shabby overcoat and a floppy hat, and he was walking slowly, all by himself. He caught sight of the note as it fluttered past his face, and he stopped and picked it up. He held it with both hands and stared at it. He turned it over. He peered closer. Then he raised his head and looked up.

'Hey there!' Henry shouted, cupping a hand to his mouth. 'That's for you! It's a present!'

The old man stood quite still, holding the note in front of him and gazing up at the figure on the balcony above.

'Put it in your pocket!' Henry shouted. 'Take it home!' His voice carried far along the street, and many people stopped and looked up.

Henry peeled off another note and threw it down. The watchers below him didn't move. They simply watched. They had no idea what was going on. A man was up there on the balcony and he had shouted something, and now he had just thrown down what looked like a piece of paper. Everyone followed the piece of paper as it went fluttering down, and this one came to rest near a young couple who were standing arm in arm on the pavement across the street. The man unlinked his arm and tried to catch the paper as it went past him. He missed it but picked it up from the ground. He examined it closely. The watchers on both sides of the street all had their eyes on the young man. To many of them, the paper had looked very much like a bank-note of some kind, and they were waiting to find out.

'It's twenty pounds!' the man yelled, jumping up and down. 'It's a twenty-pound note!'

'Keep it!' Henry shouted at him. 'It's yours!'

'You mean it?' the man called back, holding the note out at arm's length. 'Can I really keep it?'

Suddenly there was a rustle of excitement along both sides of the street and everyone started moving at once. They ran out into the middle of the road and clustered underneath the balcony. They lifted their arms above their heads and started calling out, 'Me! How about one for me! Drop us another one, guv'nor! Send down a few more!'

Henry peeled off another five or six notes and threw them down.

There were screams and yells as the pieces of paper fanned out in the wind and floated downwards, and there was a good old-fashioned scrimmage in the streets as they reached the hands of the crowd. But it was all very good-natured. People were laughing. They thought it a fantastic joke. Here was a man standing three floors up in his pyjamas, slinging these enormously valuable notes into the air. Quite a few of those present had never seen a twenty-pound note in their lives until now.

But now something else was beginning to happen.

The speed with which news will spread along the streets of a city is phenomenal. The news of what Henry was doing flashed like lightning up and down the length of Curzon Street and into the smaller and larger streets beyond. From all sides, people came running. Within a few minutes, about a thousand men and women and children were blocking the road underneath Henry's balcony. Car-drivers who couldn't pass got out of their vehicles and joined the crowd. And all of a sudden, there was chaos in Curzon Street.

At this point, Henry simply raised his arm and swung it out and flung the entire bundle of notes into the air. More than six thousand pounds went fluttering down towards the screaming crowd below.

The scramble that followed was really something to see. People were jumping up to catch the notes before they reached the ground, and everyone was pushing and jostling and yelling and falling over, and soon the whole place was a mass of tangled, yelling, fighting human beings.

Above the noise and behind him in his own flat, Henry suddenly heard his doorbell ringing long and loud. He left the balcony and opened the front door. A large policeman with a black moustache stood outside with his hands on his hips. 'You!' he bellowed angrily. 'You're the one! What the devil d'you think you're doing?'

'Good morning, officer,' Henry said. 'I'm sorry about the crowd. I didn't think it would turn out like that. I was just giving away some money.'

'You are causing a nuisance!' the policeman bellowed. 'You are creating an obstruction! You are inciting a riot and you are blocking the *en*-tire street!'

'I said I was sorry,' Henry answered. 'I won't do it again, I promise. They'll soon go away.'

The policeman took one hand off his hip and from the inside of his palm he produced a twenty-pound note.

'Ah-ha!' Henry cried. 'You got one yourself! I'm so glad! I'm so happy for you!'

'Now you just stop that larking about!' the policeman said. 'Because I have a few serious questions to ask you about these here twenty-pound notes.' He took a notebook from his breast pocket. 'In the first place,' he went on, 'where exactly did you get them from?'

'I won them,' Henry said. 'I had a lucky night.' He went on to give the name of the club where he had won the money and the policeman wrote it down in his little book. 'Check it up,' Henry added. 'They'll tell you it's true.'

The policeman lowered the notebook, and looked Henry in the eye. 'As a matter of fact,' he said, 'I believe your story. I think you're telling the truth. But that doesn't excuse what you did one little bit.'

'I didn't do anything wrong,' Henry said.

'You're a blithering young idiot!' the policeman shouted, beginning to work himself up all over again. 'You're an ass and an imbecile! If you've been lucky enough to win yourself a tremendous big sum of money like that and you want to give it away, you don't throw it out the window!'

'Why not?' Henry asked, grinning. 'It's as good a way of getting rid of it as any.'

'It's a damned stupid silly way of getting rid of it!' the policeman cried. 'Why didn't you give it where it would do some good? To a hospital, for instance? Or an orphanage? There's orphanages all over the country that hardly have enough money to buy the kids a present even for Christmas! And then along comes a little twit like you who's never even known what it's like to be hard up and you throw the stuff out into the street! It makes me mad, it really does!'

'An orphanage?' Henry said.

'Yes, an *orphanage*!' the policeman cried. 'I was brought up in one so I ought to know what it's like!' With that, the policeman turned away and went quickly down the stairs towards the street.

Henry didn't move. The policeman's words, and more especially the genuine fury with which they had been spoken, smacked our hero right between the eyes.

'An orphanage?' he said aloud. 'That's quite a thought. But why only one orphanage? Why not lots of them?' And now, very quickly, there began to come to him the great and marvellous idea that was to change everything.

Henry shut the front door and went back into his flat. All at once, he felt a powerful excitement stirring in his belly. He started pacing up and down, ticking off the points that would make his marvellous idea possible.

'One,' he said, 'I can get hold of a very large sum of money each day of my life.

'Two. I must not go to the same casino more than once every twelve months.

'Three. I must not win too much from any one casino or somebody will get suspicious. I suggest I keep it down to twenty thousand pounds a night.

'Four. Twenty thousand pounds a night for three hundred and sixty-five days in the year comes to how much?'

Henry took a pencil and paper and worked this one out.

'It comes to seven million, three hundred thousand pounds,' he said aloud.

'Very well. Point number five. I shall have to keep moving. No more than two or three nights at a stretch in any one city or the word will get around. Go from London to Monte Carlo. Then to Cannes. To Biarritz. To Deauville. To Las Vegas. To Mexico City. To Buenos Aires. To Nassau. And so on.

'Six. With the money I make, I will set up an absolutely first-class orphanage in every country I visit. I will become a Robin Hood. I will take money from the bookmakers and the gambling proprietors and give it to the children.

Does that sound corny and sentimental? As a dream, it does. But as a reality, if I can really make it work, it wouldn't be corny at all, or sentimental. It would be rather tremendous.

'Seven. I will need somebody to help me, a man who will sit at home and take care of all that money and buy the houses and organize the whole thing. A money man. Someone I can trust. What about John Winston?'

John Winston was Henry's accountant. He handled his income-tax affairs, his investments and all other problems that had to do with money. Henry had known him for eighteen years and a friendship had developed between the two men. Remember, though, that up until now, John Winston had known Henry only as the wealthy idle playboy who had never done a day's work in his life.

'You must be mad,' John Winston said when Henry told him his plan. 'Nobody has ever devised a system for beating the casinos.'

From his pocket, Henry produced a brand-new unopened pack of cards. 'Come on,' he said. 'We'll play a little blackjack. You're the dealer. And don't tell me those cards are marked. It's a new pack.'

Solemnly, for nearly an hour, sitting in Winston's office whose windows looked out over Berkeley Square, the two men played blackjack. They used matchsticks as counters, each match being worth twenty-five pounds. After fifty minutes, Henry was no less than thirty-four thousand pounds up!

John Winston couldn't believe it. 'How do you do it?' he said.

'Put the pack on the table,' Henry said. 'Face down.'

Winston obeyed.

Henry concentrated on the top card for four seconds. 'That's a knave of hearts,' he said. It was.

'The next one is . . . a three of hearts.' It was. He went right through the entire pack, naming every card.

'Go on,' John Winston said. 'Tell me how you do it.' This usually calm and mathematical man was leaning forward over his desk, staring at Henry with eyes as big and bright as two stars. 'You do realize you are doing something completely impossible?' he said.

'It's not impossible,' Henry said. 'It is only very difficult. I am the one man in the world who can do it.'

The telephone rang on John Winston's desk. He lifted the receiver and said to his secretary, 'No more calls please, Susan, until I tell you. Not even my wife.' He looked up, waiting for Henry to go on.

Henry then proceeded to explain to John Winston exactly how he had acquired the power. He told him how he had found the notebook and about Imhrat Khan and then he described how he had been working non-stop for the past three years, training his mind to concentrate.

When he had finished, John Winston said, 'Have you tried walking on fire?'

'No,' Henry said. 'And I'm not going to.'

'What makes you think you'll be able to do this thing with the cards in a casino?'

Henry then told him about his visit to Lord's House the night before.

'Six thousand, six hundred pounds!' John Winston cried. 'Did you honestly win that much in real money?'

'Listen,' Henry said. 'I just won thirty-four thousand from you in less than an hour!'

'So you did.'

'Six thousand was the very least I could win,' Henry said. 'It was a terrific effort not to win more.'

'You will be the richest man on earth.'

'I don't want to be the richest man on earth,' Henry said. 'Not any more.' He then told him about his plan for orphanages.

When he had finished, he said, 'Will you join me, John? Will you be my money man, my banker, my administrator and everything else? There will be millions coming in every year.'

John Winston, a cautious and prudent accountant, would not agree to anything at all on the spur of the moment. 'I want to see you in action first,' he said.

So that night, they went together to the Ritz Club on Curzon Street. 'Can't go to Lord's House again now for some time,' Henry said.

On the first spin of the roulette wheel, Henry staked £100 on number twenty-seven. It came up. The second time he put it on number four; that came up too. A total of £7,500 profit.

An Arab standing next to Henry said, 'I have just lost fifty-five thousand pounds. How do you do it?'

'Luck,' Henry said. 'Just luck.'

They moved into the Blackjack Room and there, in half an hour, Henry won a further £10,000. Then he stopped.

Outside in the street, John Winston said, 'I believe you now. I'll come in with you.'

'We start tomorrow,' Henry said.

'Do you really intend to do this every single night?'

'Yes,' Henry said. 'I shall move very fast from place to place, from country to country. And every day, I shall send the profits back to you through the banks.'

'Do you realize how much it will add up to in a year?'

'Millions,' Henry said cheerfully. 'About seven million a year.'

'In that case, I can't operate in this country,' John Winston said. 'The taxman will have it all.'

'Go anywhere you like,' Henry said. 'It makes no difference to me. I trust you completely.'

'I shall go to Switzerland,' John Winston said. 'But not tomorrow. I can't just pull up and fly away. I'm not an unattached bachelor like you with no responsibilities. I must talk to my wife and children. I must give notice to my partners in the firm. I must sell my house. I must find another house in Switzerland. I must take the kids out of school. My dear man, these things take time!'

Henry drew from his pocket the £17,500 he had just won and handed them to the other man. 'Here's some petty cash to tide you over until you get settled,' he said. 'But do hurry up. I want to get cracking.'

Within a week, John Winston was in Lausanne, with an office high up on the lovely hillside above Lake Geneva. His family would follow him as soon as possible.

And Henry went to work in the casinos.

One year later, he had sent a little over eight million pounds to John Winston in Lausanne. The money was sent five days a week to a Swiss company called ORPHAN-AGES S.A. Nobody except John Winston and Henry knew where the money came from or what was going to happen to it. As for the Swiss authorities, they never want to know where money comes from. Henry sent the money through the banks. The Monday remittance was always the biggest because it included Henry's take for Friday, Saturday and Sunday, when the banks were closed. He moved with astonishing speed, and often the only clue that John Winston had to his whereabouts was the address of the bank which had sent the money on a particular day. One day it would come perhaps from a bank in Manila. The next day from Bangkok. It came from Las Vegas, from Curaçao, from Freeport, from Grand Cayman, from San Juan, from Nassau, from London, from Biarritz. It came from anywhere and everywhere so long as there was a big casino in the city.

For seven years, all went well. Nearly fifty million pounds had arrived in Lausanne, and had been safely banked away. Already John Winston had got three orphanages established, one in France, one in England, and one in the United States. Five more were on the way.

Then came a bit of trouble. There is a grapevine among casino owners, and although Henry was always extraordinarily careful not to take too much from any one place on any one night, the news was bound to spread in the end.

They got wise to him one night in Las Vegas when Henry rather imprudently took one hundred thousand dollars from each of three separate casinos that all happened to be owned by the same mob.

What happened was this. The morning after, when Henry was in his hotel room packing to leave for the airport, there was a knock on his door. A bell-hop came in and whispered to Henry that two men were waiting for him in the lobby. Other men, the bell-hop said, were guarding the rear exit. These were very hard men, the bell-hop said, and he did not give much for Henry's chances of survival if he were to go downstairs at this moment.

'Why do you come and tell me?' Henry asked him. 'Why are you on my side?'

'I'm not on anyone's side,' the bell-hop said. 'But we all know you won a lot of money last night and I figured you might give me a nice present for tipping you off.'

'Thanks,' Henry said. 'But how do I get away? I'll give you a thousand dollars if you can get me out of here.'

'That's easy,' the bell-hop said. 'Take your own clothes off and put on my uniform. Then walk out through the lobby with your suitcase. But tie me up before you leave. I've gotta be lying here on the floor tied up hand and foot so they won't think I helped you. I'll say you had a gun and I couldn't do nothing.'

'Where's the cord to tie you up with?' Henry asked.

'Right here in my pocket,' the bell-hop said, grinning.

Henry put on the bell-hop's gold and green uniform, which wasn't too bad a fit. Then he tied the man up good and proper with the cord and stuffed a handkerchief in his mouth. Finally, he pushed ten one-hundred dollar bills under the carpet for the bell-hop to collect later.

Down in the lobby, two short, thick, black-haired thugs were watching the people as they came out of the elevators. But they hardly glanced at the man in the green and gold bell-hop's uniform who came out carrying a suitcase and who walked smartly across the lobby and out through the swing-doors that led to the street.

At the airport, Henry changed his flight and took the next plane to Los Angeles. Things were not going to be quite so easy from now on, he told himself. But that bell-hop had given him an idea.

In Los Angeles, and in nearby Hollywood and Beverly Hills, where the film people live, Henry sought out the very best make-up man in the business. This was Max Engelman. Henry called on him. He liked him immediately.

'How much do you earn?' Henry asked him.

'Oh, about forty thousand dollars a year,' Max told him.

'I'll give you a hundred thousand,' Henry said, 'if you will come with me and be my make-up artist.'

'What's the big idea?' Max asked him.

'I'll tell you,' Henry said. And he did.

Max was only the second person Henry had told. John Winston was the first. And when Henry showed Max how he could read the cards, Max was flabbergasted.

'Great heavens, man!' he cried. 'You could make a fortune!'

'I already have,' Henry told him. 'I've made ten fortunes. But I want to make ten more.' He told Max about the orphanages. With John Winston's help, he had already set up three of them, with more on the way.

Max was a small dark-skinned man who had escaped from Vienna when the Nazis went in. He had never married. He had no ties. He became wildly enthusiastic. 'It's crazy!' he cried. 'It's the craziest thing I've ever heard in my life! I'll join you, man! Let's go!'

From then on, Max Engelman travelled everywhere with Henry and he carried with him in a trunk such an assortment of wigs, false beards, sideburns, moustaches and make-up materials as you have never seen. He could turn his master into any one of thirty or forty unrecognizable people, and the casino managers, who were all watching for Henry now, never once saw him again as Mr Henry Sugar. As a matter of fact, only a year after the Las Vegas episode, Henry and Max actually went back to that dangerous city, and on a warm starry night Henry took a cool eighty thousand dollars from the first of the big casinos he had visited before. He went disguised as an elderly Brazilian diplomat, and they never knew what had hit them.

Now that Henry no longer appeared as himself in the casinos, there were, of course, a number of other details that had to be taken care of, such as false identity cards and passports. In Monte Carlo, for example, a visitor must always show his passport before being allowed to enter the casino. Henry visited Monte Carlo eleven more times with Max's assistance, every time with a different passport and in a different disguise.

Max adored the work. He loved creating new characters for Henry. 'I have an entirely fresh one for you today!' he would announce. 'Just wait till you see it! Today you will be an Arab sheikh from Kuwait!'

'Do we have an Arab passport?' Henry would ask. 'And Arab papers?'

'We have everything,' Max would answer. 'John Winston has sent me a lovely passport in the name of His Royal Highness Sheikh Abu Bin Bey!'

And so it went on. Over the years, Max and Henry became as close as brothers. They were crusading brothers, two men who moved swiftly through the skies, milking the casinos of the world and sending the money straight back to John Winston in Switzerland, where the company known as ORPHANAGES S.A. grew richer and richer.

Henry died last year, at the age of sixty-three; his work was completed. He had been at it for just on twenty years.

His personal reference book listed three hundred and seventy-one major casinos in twenty-one different countries or islands. He had visited them all many times and he had never lost.

According to John Winston's accounts, he had made altogether one hundred and forty-four million pounds.

He left twenty-one well-established well-run orphanages scattered about the world, one in each country he visited. All these were administered and financed from Lausanne by John and his staff.

But how do I, who am neither Max Engelman nor John Winston, happen to know all this? And how did I come to write the story in the first place?

I will tell you.

Soon after Henry's death, John Winston telephoned me from Switzerland. He introduced himself simply as the head of a company calling itself ORPHANAGES S.A., and asked me if I would come out to Lausanne to see him with a view to writing a brief history of the organization. I don't know how he got hold of my name. He probably had a list of writers and stuck a pin into it. He would pay me well, he said. And he added, 'A remarkable man has died recently. His name was Henry Sugar. I think people ought to know a bit about what he has done.'

In my ignorance, I asked whether the story was really interesting enough to merit being put on paper.

'All right,' said the man who now controlled one hundred and forty-four million pounds. 'Forget it. I'll ask someone else. There are plenty of writers around.'

That needled me. 'No,' I said. 'Wait. Could you at least tell me who this Henry Sugar was and what he did? I've never even heard of him.'

In five minutes on the phone, John Winston told me something about Henry Sugar's secret career. It was secret no longer. Henry was dead and would never gamble again. I listened, enthralled.

'I'll be on the next plane,' I said.

'Thank you,' John Winston said. 'I would appreciate that.'

In Lausanne, I met John Winston, now over seventy, and also Max Engelman, who was about the same age. They were both still shattered by Henry's death. Max even more so than John Winston, for Max had been beside him constantly for over thirteen years. 'I loved him,' Max said, a shadow falling over his face. 'He was a great man. He never thought about himself. He never kept a penny of the money he won, except what he needed to travel and to eat. Listen, once we were in Biarritz and he had just been to the bank and given them half a million francs to send home to John. It was lunchtime. We went to a place and had a simple lunch, an omelette and a bottle of wine, and when the bill came, Henry hadn't got anything to pay it with. I hadn't either. He was a lovely man.'

John Winston told me everything he knew. He showed me the original dark-blue notebook written by Dr John Cartwright in Bombay in 1934, and I copied it out word for word.

'Henry always carried it with him,' John Winston said. 'In the end, he knew the whole thing by heart.'

He showed me the accounts books of ORPHANAGES S.A. with Henry's winnings recorded in them day by day over twenty years, and a truly staggering sight they were.

When he had finished, I said to him, 'There's a big gap in this story, Mr Winston. You've told me almost nothing about Henry's travels and about his adventures in the casinos of the world.'

'That's Max's story,' John Winston said. 'Max knows all

about that because he was with him. But he says he wants to have a shot at writing it himself. He's already started.'

'Then why not let Max write the whole thing?' I asked.

'He doesn't want to,' John Winston said. 'He only wants to write about Henry and Max. It should be a fantastic story if he ever gets it finished. But he is old now, like me, and I doubt he will manage it.'

'One last question,' I said. 'You keep calling him Henry Sugar. And yet you tell me that wasn't his name. Don't you want me to say who he really was when I do the story?'

'No,' John Winston said. 'Max and I promised never to reveal it. Oh, it'll probably leak out sooner or later. After all, he was from a fairly well-known English family. But I'd appreciate it if you don't try to find out. Just call him plain Mr Henry Sugar.'

And that is what I have done.

The Boy Who Talked with Animals

First published in *The Wonderful Story of*
Henry Sugar (1977)

Not so long ago, I decided to spend a few days in the West
Indies. I was to go there for a short holiday. Friends had
told me it was marvellous. I would laze around all day,
they said, sunning myself on the silver beaches and swimming in the warm green sea.

I chose Jamaica, and flew direct from London to Kingston. The drive from Kingston airport to my hotel on the
north shore took two hours. The island was full of mountains and the mountains were covered all over with dark
tangled forests. The big Jamaican who drove the taxi told
me that up in those forests lived whole communities of
diabolical people who still practised voodoo and witch-
doctory and other magic rites. 'Don't ever go up into
those mountain forests,' he said, rolling his eyes. 'There's
things happening up there that'd make your hair turn
white in a minute!'

'What sort of things?' I asked him.

'It's better you don't ask,' he said. 'It don't pay even to
talk about it.' And that was all he would say on the
subject.

My hotel lay upon the edge of a pearly beach, and the
setting was even more beautiful than I had imagined. But
the moment I walked in through those big open front

doors, I began to feel uneasy. There was no reason for this. I couldn't see anything wrong. But the feeling was there and I couldn't shake it off. There was something weird and sinister about the place. Despite all the loveliness and the luxury, there was a whiff of danger that hung and drifted in the air like poisonous gas.

And I wasn't sure it was just the hotel. The whole island, the mountains and the forests, the black rocks along the coastline and the trees cascading with brilliant scarlet flowers, all these and many other things made me feel uncomfortable in my skin. There was something malignant crouching underneath the surface of this island. I could sense it in my bones.

My room in the hotel had a little balcony, and from there I could step straight down on to the beach. There were tall coconut palms growing all around, and every so often an enormous green nut the size of a football would fall out of the sky and drop with a thud on the sand. It was considered foolish to linger underneath a coconut palm because if one of those things landed on your head, it would smash your skull.

The Jamaican girl who came in to tidy my room told me that a wealthy American called Mr Wasserman had met his end in precisely this manner only two months before.

'You're joking,' I said to her.

'Not joking!' she cried. 'No *suh*! I sees it happening with my very own eyes!'

'But wasn't there a terrific fuss about it?' I asked.

'They hush it up,' she answered darkly. 'The hotel folks

hush it up and so do the newspaper folks because things like that are very bad for the tourist business.'

'And you say you actually saw it happen?'

'I actually saw it happen,' she said. 'Mr Wasserman, he's standing right under that very tree over there on the beach. He's got his camera out and he's pointing it at the sunset. It's a red sunset that evening, and very pretty. Then all at once, down comes a big green nut right smack on to the top of his bald head. *Wham!* And that,' she added with a touch of relish, 'is the very last sunset Mr Wasserman ever did see.'

'You mean it killed him instantly?'

'I don't know about *instantly*,' she said. 'I remember the next thing that happens is the camera falls out of his hands on to the sand. Then his arms drop down to his sides and hang there. Then he starts swaying. He sways backwards and forwards several times ever so gentle, and I'm standing there watching him, and I says to myself the poor man's gone all dizzy and maybe he's going to faint any moment. Then very very slowly he keels right over and down he goes.'

'Was he dead?'

'Dead as a doornail,' she said.

'Good heavens.'

'That's right,' she said. 'It never pays to be standing under a coconut palm when there's a breeze blowing.'

'Thank you,' I said. 'I'll remember that.'

On the evening of my second day, I was sitting on my little balcony with a book on my lap and a tall glass of rum punch in my hand. I wasn't reading the book. I was watching a small green lizard stalking another small green lizard on the balcony floor about six feet away. The stalking lizard was coming up on the other one from behind, moving forwards very slowly and very cautiously, and when he came within reach, he flicked out a long tongue and touched the other one's tail. The other one jumped round, and the two of them faced each other, motionless, glued to the floor, crouching, staring and very tense. Then suddenly, they started doing a funny little hopping dance together. They hopped up in the air. They hopped backwards. They hopped forwards. They hopped sideways. They circled one another like two boxers, hopping and prancing and dancing all the time. It was a queer thing to watch, and I guessed it was some sort of a courtship ritual they were going through. I kept very still, waiting to see what was going to happen next.

But I never saw what happened next because at that moment I became aware of a great commotion on the beach below. I glanced over and saw a crowd of people clustering around something at the water's edge. There was a narrow canoe-type fisherman's boat pulled up on the sand nearby, and all I could think of was that the fisherman had come in with a lot of fish and that the crowd was looking at it.

A haul of fish is something that has always fascinated me. I put my book aside and stood up. More people were trooping down from the hotel veranda and hurrying over the beach to join the crowd on the edge of the water. The men were wearing those frightful Bermuda shorts that came down to the knees, and their shirts were bilious with pinks and oranges and every other clashing colour you could think of. The women had better taste, and were dressed for the most part in pretty cotton dresses. Nearly everyone carried a drink in one hand.

I picked up my own drink and stepped down from the balcony on to the beach. I made a little detour around the coconut palm under which Mr Wasserman had supposedly met his end, and strode across the beautiful silvery sand to join the crowd.

But it wasn't a haul of fish they were staring at. It was a turtle, an upside-down turtle lying on its back in the sand. But what a turtle it was! It was a giant, a mammoth. I had not thought it possible for a turtle to be as enormous as this. How can I describe its size? Had it been the right way up, I think a tall man could have sat on its back without his feet touching the ground. It was perhaps five feet long and four feet across, with a high domed shell of great beauty.

The fisherman who had caught it had tipped it on to its back to stop it from getting away. There was also a thick rope tied around the middle of its shell, and one proud fisherman, slim and black and naked except for a small loincloth, stood a short way off holding the end of the rope with both hands.

Upside down it lay, this magnificent creature, with its four thick flippers waving frantically in the air, and its long wrinkled neck stretching far out of its shell. The flippers had large sharp claws on them.

'Stand back, ladies and gentlemen, please!' cried the

fisherman. 'Stand well back! Them claws is *dangerous*, man! They'll rip your arm clear away from your body!'

The crowd of hotel guests was thrilled and delighted by this spectacle. A dozen cameras were out and clicking away. Many of the women were squealing with pleasure clutching on to the arms of their men, and the men were demonstrating their lack of fear and their masculinity by making foolish remarks in loud voices.

'Make yourself a nice pair of horn-rimmed spectacles out of that shell, hey Al?'

'Darn thing must weigh over a ton!'

'You mean to say it can actually float?'

'Sure it floats. Powerful swimmer, too. Pull a boat easy.'

'He's a snapper, is he?'

'That's no snapper. Snapper turtles don't grow as big as that. But I'll tell you what. He'll snap your hand off quick enough if you get too close to him.'

'Is that true?' one of the women asked the fisherman. 'Would he snap off a person's hand?'

'He would right now,' the fisherman said, smiling with brilliant white teeth. 'He won't ever hurt you when he's in the ocean, but you catch him and pull him ashore and tip him up like this, then man alive, you'd better watch out! He'll snap at anything that comes in reach!'

'I guess I'd get a bit snappish myself,' the woman said, 'if I was in his situation.'

One idiotic man had found a plank of driftwood on the sand, and he was carrying it towards the turtle. It was a fair-sized plank, about five feet long and maybe an inch thick. He started poking one end of it at the turtle's head.

'I wouldn't do that,' the fisherman said. 'You'll only make him madder than ever.'

When the end of the plank touched the turtle's neck, the great head whipped round and the mouth opened wide and *snap*, it took the plank in its mouth and bit through it as if it were made of cheese.

'Wow!' they shouted. 'Did you see that! I'm glad it wasn't my arm!'

'Leave him alone,' the fisherman said. 'It don't help to get him all stirred up.'

A paunchy man with wide hips and very short legs came up to the fisherman and said, 'Listen, feller. I want that shell. I'll buy it from you.' And to his plump wife, he said, 'You know what I'm going to do, Mildred? I'm going to take that shell home and have it polished up by an expert. Then I'm going to place it smack in the centre of our living-room! Won't that be something?'

'Fantastic,' the plump wife said. 'Go ahead and buy it, baby.'

'Don't worry,' he said. 'It's mine already.' And to the fisherman, he said, 'How much for the shell?'

'I already sold him,' the fisherman said. 'I sold him shell and all.'

'Not so fast, feller,' the paunchy man said. 'I'll bid you higher. Come on. What'd he offer you?'

'No can do,' the fisherman said. 'I already sold him.'

'Who to?' the paunchy man said.

'To the manager.'

'What manager?'

'The manager of the hotel.'

'Did you hear that?' shouted another man. 'He's sold it to the manager of our hotel! And you know what that means? It means turtle soup, that's what it means!'

'Right you are! And turtle steak! You ever have a turtle steak, Bill?'

'I never have, Jack. But I can't wait.'

'A turtle steak's better than a beefsteak if you cook it right. It's more tender and it's got one heck of a flavour.'

'Listen,' the paunchy man said to the fisherman. 'I'm not trying to buy the meat. The manager can have the meat. He can have everything that's inside including the teeth and toenails. All I want is the shell.'

'And if I know you, baby,' his wife said, beaming at him, 'you're going to get the shell.'

I stood there listening to the conversation of these human beings. They were discussing the destruction, the consumption and the flavour of a creature who seemed, even when upside down, to be extraordinarily dignified. One thing was certain. He was senior to any of them in age. For probably one hundred and fifty years he had been cruising in the green waters of the West Indies. He was there when George Washington was President of the United States and Napoleon was being clobbered at Waterloo. He would have been a small turtle then, but he was most certainly there.

And now he was here, upside down on the beach, waiting to be sacrificed for soup and steak. He was clearly alarmed by all the noise and the shouting around him. His old wrinkled neck was straining out of its shell, and the great head was twisting this way and that as though searching for someone who would explain the reason for all this ill-treatment.

'How are you going to get him up to the hotel?' the paunchy man asked.

'Drag him up the beach with the rope,' the fisherman answered. 'The staff'll be coming along soon to take him. It's going to need ten men, all pulling at once.'

'Hey, listen!' cried a muscular young man. 'Why don't we drag him up?' The muscular young man was wearing magenta and pea-green Bermuda shorts and no shirt. He had an exceptionally hairy chest, and the absence of a shirt was obviously a calculated touch. 'What say we do a little work for our supper?' he cried, rippling his muscles. 'Come on, fellers! Who's for some exercise?'

'Great idea!' they shouted. 'Splendid scheme!'

The men handed their drinks to the women and rushed to catch hold of the rope. They ranged themselves along it as though for a tug of war, and the hairy-chested man appointed himself anchor-man and captain of the team.

'Come on, now, fellers!' he shouted. 'When I say *heave*, then all heave at once, you understand?'

The fisherman didn't like this much. 'It's better you leave this job for the hotel,' he said.

'Rubbish!' shouted hairy-chest. '*Heave*, boys, *heave*!'

They all heaved. The gigantic turtle wobbled on its back and nearly toppled over.

'Don't tip him!' yelled the fisherman. 'You're going to

tip him over if you do that! And if once he gets back on to his legs again, he'll escape for sure!'

'Cool it, laddie,' said hairy-chest in a patronizing voice. 'How can he escape? We've got a rope round him, haven't we?'

'The old turtle will drag the whole lot of you away with him if you give him a chance!' cried the fisherman. 'He'll drag you out into the ocean, every one of you!'

'*Heave!*' shouted hairy-chest, ignoring the fisherman. '*Heave*, boys, *heave*!'

And now the gigantic turtle began very slowly to slide up the beach towards the hotel, towards the kitchen, towards the place where the big knives were kept. The womenfolk and the older, fatter, less athletic men followed alongside, shouting encouragement.

'*Heave!*' shouted the hairy-chested anchor-man. 'Put your backs into it, fellers! You can pull harder than that!'

Suddenly, I heard screams. Everyone heard them. They were screams so high-pitched, so shrill and so urgent they cut right through everything. 'No-o-o-o-o!' screamed the scream. 'No! No! No! No! No!'

The crowd froze. The tug-of-war men stopped tugging and the onlookers stopped shouting and every single person present turned towards the place where the screams were coming from.

Half walking, half running down the beach from the hotel, I saw three people, a man, a woman and a small boy. They were half running because the boy was pulling the man along. The man had the boy by the wrist, trying to slow him down, but the boy kept pulling. At the same time, he was jumping and twisting and wriggling and trying to free himself from the father's grip. It was the boy who was screaming.

'Don't!' he screamed. 'Don't do it! Let him go! Please let him go!'

The woman, his mother, was trying to catch hold of the boy's other arm to help restrain him, but the boy was jumping about so much, she didn't succeed.

'Let him go!' screamed the boy. 'It's horrible what you're doing! Please let him go!'

'Stop that, David!' the mother said, still trying to catch his other arm. 'Don't be so childish! You're making a perfect fool of yourself.'

'Daddy!' the boy screamed. 'Daddy! Tell them to let him go!'

'I can't do that, David,' the father said. 'It isn't any of our business.'

The tug-of-war pullers remained motionless, still holding the rope with the gigantic turtle on the end of it. Everyone stood silent and surprised, staring at the boy. They were all a bit off-balance now. They had the slightly hangdog air of people who had been caught doing something that was not entirely honourable.

'Come on now, David,' the father said, pulling against the boy. 'Let's go back to the hotel and leave these people alone.'

'I'm not going back!' the boy shouted. 'I don't want to go back! I want them to let it go!'

'Now, David,' the mother said.

'Beat it, kid,' the hairy-chested man told the boy.

'You're horrible and cruel!' the boy shouted. 'All of you are horrible and cruel!' He threw the words high and shrill at the forty or fifty adults standing there on the beach, and nobody, not even the hairy-chested man, answered him this time. 'Why don't you put him back in the sea?' the boy shouted. 'He hasn't done anything to you! Let him go!'

The father was embarrassed by his son, but he was not ashamed of him. 'He's crazy about animals,' he said, addressing the crowd. 'Back home he's got every kind of animal under the sun. He talks with them.'

'He loves them,' the mother said.

Several people began shuffling their feet around in the sand. Here and there in the crowd it was possible to sense a slight change of mood, a feeling of uneasiness, a touch even of shame. The boy, who could have been no more than eight or nine years old, had stopped struggling with his father now. The father still held him by the wrist, but he was no longer restraining him.

'Go on!' the boy called out. 'Let him go! Undo the rope and let him go!' He stood very small and erect, facing the crowd, his eyes shining like two stars and the wind blowing in his hair. He was magnificent.

'There's nothing we can do, David,' the father said gently. 'Let's go on back.'

'No!' the boy cried out, and at that moment he suddenly gave a twist and wrenched his wrist free from the father's grip. He was away like a streak, running across the sand towards the giant upturned turtle.

'David!' the father yelled, starting after him. 'Stop! Come back!'

The boy dodged and swerved through the crowd like a player running with the ball, and the only person who sprang forward to intercept him was the fisherman. 'Don't you go near that turtle, boy!' he shouted as he made a lunge for the swiftly running figure. But the boy dodged round him and kept going. 'He'll bite you to pieces!' yelled the fisherman. 'Stop, boy! Stop!'

But it was too late to stop him now, and as he came running straight at the turtle's head, the turtle saw him, and the huge upside-down head turned quickly to face him.

The voice of the boy's mother, the stricken, agonized wail of the mother's voice rose up into the evening sky. 'David!' it cried. '*Oh, David!*' And a moment later, the boy was throwing himself on to his knees in the sand and flinging his arms around the wrinkled old neck and hugging the creature to his chest. The boy's cheek was pressing against the turtle's head, and his lips were moving, whispering soft words that nobody else could hear. The turtle became absolutely still. Even the giant flippers stopped waving in the air.

A great sigh, a long soft sigh of relief, went up from the crowd. Many people took a pace or two backwards, as though trying perhaps to get a little further away from something that was beyond their understanding. But the father and mother came forwards together and stood about ten feet away from their son.

'Daddy!' the boy cried out, still caressing the old brown head. 'Please do something, Daddy! Please make them let him go!'

'Can I be of any help here?' said a man in a white suit

who had just come down from the hotel. This, as everyone knew, was Mr Edwards, the manager. He was a tall, beak-nosed Englishman with a long pink face. '*What* an extraordinary thing!' he said, looking at the boy and the turtle. 'He's lucky he hasn't had his head bitten off.' And to the boy he said, 'You'd better come away from there now, sonny. That thing's dangerous.'

'I want them to let him go!' cried the boy, still cradling the head in his arms. 'Tell them to let him go!'

'You realize he could be killed any moment,' the manager said to the boy's father.

'Leave him alone,' the father said.

'Rubbish,' the manager said. 'Go in and grab him. But be quick. And be careful.'

'No,' the father said.

'What do you mean, no?' said the manager. 'These things are lethal! Don't you understand that?'

'Yes,' the father said.

'Then for heaven's sake, man, get him away!' cried the manager. 'There's going to be a very nasty accident if you don't.'

'Who owns it?' the father said. 'Who owns the turtle?'

'We do,' the manager said. 'The hotel has bought it.'

'Then do me a favour,' the father said. 'Let me buy it from you.'

The manager looked at the father, but said nothing.

'You don't know my son,' the father said, speaking quietly. 'He'll go crazy if it's taken up to the hotel and slaughtered. He'll become hysterical.'

'Just pull him away,' the manager said. 'And be quick about it.'

'He loves animals,' the father said. 'He really loves them. He communicates with them.'

The crowd was silent, trying to hear what was being said. Nobody moved away. They stood as though hypnotized.

'If we let it go,' the manager said, 'they'll only catch it again.'

'Perhaps they will,' the father said. 'But those things can swim.'

'I know they can swim,' the manager said. 'They'll catch him all the same. This is a valuable item, you must realize that. The shell alone is worth a lot of money.'

'I don't care about the cost,' the father said. 'Don't worry about that. I want to buy it.'

The boy was still kneeling in the sand beside the turtle, caressing its head.

The manager took a handkerchief from his breast pocket and started wiping his fingers. He was not keen to let the turtle go. He probably had the dinner menu already planned. On the other hand, he didn't want another gruesome accident on his private beach this season. Mr Wasserman and the coconut, he told himself, had been quite enough for one year, thank you very much.

The father said, 'I would deem it a great personal favour, Mr Edwards, if you would let me buy it. And I promise you won't regret it. I'll make quite sure of that.'

The manager's eyebrows went up just a fraction of an inch. He had got the point. He was being offered a bribe. That was a different matter. For a few seconds he went on wiping his hands with the handkerchief. Then he shrugged his shoulders and said, 'Well, I suppose if it will make your boy feel any better . . .'

'Thank you,' the father said.

'Oh, thank you!' the mother cried. 'Thank you so very much!'

'Willy,' the manager said, beckoning to the fisherman.

The fisherman came forwards. He looked thoroughly confused. 'I never seen anything like this before in my whole life,' he said. 'This old turtle was the fiercest I ever caught! He fought like a devil when we brought him in! It took all six of us to land him! That boy's crazy!'

'Yes, I know,' the manager said. 'But now I want you to let him go.'

'Let him go!' the fisherman cried, aghast. 'You mustn't ever let this one go, Mr Edwards! He's broke the record! He's the biggest turtle ever been caught on this island! Easy the biggest! And what about our money?'

'You'll get your money.'

'I got the other five to pay off as well,' the fisherman said, pointing down the beach.

About a hundred yards down, on the water's edge, five black-skinned almost naked men were standing beside a second boat. 'All six of us are in on this, equal shares,' the fisherman went on. 'I can't let him go till we got the money.'

'I guarantee you'll get it,' the manager said. 'Isn't that good enough for you?'

'I'll underwrite that guarantee,' the father of the boy said, stepping forwards. 'And there'll be an extra bonus for all six of the fishermen just as long as you let him go at once. I mean immediately, this instant.'

The fisherman looked at the father. Then he looked at the manager. 'Okay,' he said. 'If that's the way you want it.'

'There's one condition,' the father said. 'Before you get your money, you must promise you won't go straight out and try to catch him again. Not this evening, anyway. Is that understood?'

'Sure,' the fisherman said. 'That's a deal.' He turned and ran down the beach, calling to the other five fishermen. He shouted something to them that we couldn't hear, and in a minute or two, all six of them came back together. Five of them were carrying long thick wooden poles.

The boy was still kneeling beside the turtle's head. 'David,' the father said to him gently. 'It's all right now, David. They're going to let him go.'

The boy looked round, but he didn't take his arms from around the turtle's neck, and he didn't get up. 'When?' he asked.

'Now,' the father said. 'Right now. So you'd better come away.'

'You promise?' the boy said.

'Yes, David, I promise.'

The boy withdrew his arms. He got to his feet. He stepped back a few paces.

'Stand back, everyone!' shouted the fisherman called Willy. 'Stand right back, everybody, please!'

The crowd moved a few yards up the beach. The tug-of-war men let go the rope and moved back with the others.

Willy got down on his hands and knees and crept very cautiously up to one side of the turtle. Then he began untying the knot in the rope. He kept well out of the range of the big flippers as he did this.

When the knot was untied, Willy crawled back. Then the five other fishermen stepped forwards with their poles. The poles were about seven feet long and immensely thick. They wedged them underneath the shell of the turtle and began to rock the great creature from side to side on its shell. The shell had a high dome and was well shaped for rocking.

'Up and down!' sang the fishermen as they rocked away. 'Up and down! Up and down! Up and down!' The old turtle became thoroughly upset, and who could blame it? The big flippers lashed the air frantically, and the head kept shooting in and out of the shell.

'Roll him over!' sang the fishermen. 'Up and over! Roll him over! One more time and over he goes!'

The turtle tilted high up on to its side and crashed down in the sand the right way up.

But it didn't walk away at once. The huge brown head came out and peered cautiously around.

'Go, turtle, go!' the small boy called out. 'Go back to the sea!'

The two hooded black eyes of the turtle peered up at the boy. The eyes were bright and lively, full of the wisdom of great age. The boy looked back at the turtle, and this time when he spoke, his voice was soft and intimate. 'Good-bye, old man,' he said. 'Go far away this time.' The black eyes remained resting on the boy for a few seconds more. Nobody moved. Then, with great dignity, the massive beast turned away and began waddling towards the edge of the ocean. He didn't hurry. He moved sedately over the sandy beach, the big shell rocking gently from side to side as he went.

The crowd watched in silence.

He entered the water.

He kept going.

Soon he was swimming. He was in his element now. He swam gracefully and very fast, with the head held high. The sea was calm, and he made little waves that fanned out behind him on both sides, like the waves of a boat. It was several minutes before we lost sight of him, and by then he was halfway to the horizon.

The guests began wandering back towards the hotel. They were curiously subdued. There was no joking or bantering now, no laughing. Something had happened. Something strange had come fluttering across the beach.

I walked back to my small balcony and sat down with a cigarette. I had an uneasy feeling that this was not the end of the affair.

The next morning at eight o'clock, the Jamaican girl, the one who had told me about Mr Wasserman and the coconut, brought a glass of orange juice to my room.

'Big *big* fuss in the hotel this morning,' she said as she placed the glass on the table and drew back the curtains. 'Everyone flying about all over the place like they was crazy.'

'Why? What's happened?'

'That little boy in number twelve, he's vanished. He disappeared in the night.'

'You mean the turtle boy?'

'That's him,' she said. 'His parents is raising the roof and the manager's going mad.'

'How long's he been missing?'

'About two hours ago his father found his bed empty. But he could've gone any time in the night I reckon.'

'Yes,' I said. 'He could.'

'Everybody in the hotel searching high and low,' she said. 'And a police car just arrived.'

'Maybe he just got up early and went for a climb on the rocks,' I said.

Her large dark haunted-looking eyes rested a moment on my face, then travelled away. 'I do not think so,' she said, and out she went.

I slipped on some clothes and hurried down to the beach. On the beach itself, two native policemen in khaki uniforms were standing with Mr Edwards, the manager. Mr Edwards was doing the talking. The policemen were listening patiently. In the distance, at both ends of the beach, I could see small groups of people, hotel servants as well as hotel guests, spreading out and heading for the rocks. The morning was beautiful. The sky was smoke-blue, faintly glazed with yellow. The sun was up and making diamonds all over the smooth sea. And Mr Edwards was talking loudly to the two native policemen, and waving his arms.

I wanted to help. What should I do? Which way should

THE COMPLETE SHORT STORIES

I go? It would be pointless simply to follow the others. So I just kept walking towards Mr Edwards.

About then, I saw the fishing-boat. The long wooden canoe with a single mast and a flapping brown sail was still some way out to sea, but it was heading for the beach. The two natives aboard, one at either end, were paddling hard. They were paddling very hard. The paddles rose and fell at such a terrific speed they might have been in a race. I stopped and watched them. Why the great rush to reach the shore? Quite obviously they had something to tell. I kept my eyes on the boat. Over to my left, I could hear Mr Edwards saying to the two policemen, 'It is perfectly ridiculous. I can't have people disappearing just like that from the hotel. You'd better find him fast, you understand me? He's either wandered off somewhere and got lost or he's been kidnapped. Either way, it's the responsibility of the police . . .'

The fishing-boat skimmed over the sea and came gliding up on to the sand at the water's edge. Both men dropped their paddles and jumped out. They started running up the beach. I recognized the one in front as Willy. When he caught sight of the manager and the two policemen, he made straight for them.

'Hey, Mr Edwards!' Willy called out. 'We just seen a crazy thing!'

The manager stiffened and jerked back his neck. The two policemen remained impassive. They were used to excitable people. They met them every day.

Willy stopped in front of the group, his chest heaving in and out with heavy breathing. The other fisherman was close behind him. They were both naked except for a tiny loincloth, their black skins shining with sweat.

'We been paddling full speed for a long way,' Willy said, excusing his out-of-breathness. 'We thought we ought to come back and tell it as quick as we can.'

'Tell what?' the manager said. 'What did you see?'

'It was crazy, man! Absolutely crazy!'

'Get on with it, Willy, for heaven's sake.'

'You won't believe it,' Willy said. 'There ain't nobody going to believe it. Isn't that right, Tom?'

'That's right,' the other fisherman said, nodding vigorously. 'If Willy here hadn't been with me to prove it, I wouldn't have believed it myself!'

'Believed what?' Mr Edwards said. 'Just tell us what you saw.'

'We'd gone off early,' Willy said, 'about four o'clock this morning, and we must've been a couple of miles out before it got light enough to see anything properly. Suddenly, as the sun comes up, we see right ahead of us, not more'n fifty yards away, we see something we couldn't believe not even with our eyes . . .'

'What?' snapped Mr Edwards. 'For heaven's sake get on!'

'We sees that old monster turtle swimming away out there, the one on the beach yesterday, and we sees the boy sitting high up on the turtle's back and riding him over the sea like a horse!'

'You gotta believe it!' the other fisherman cried. 'I sees it too, so you gotta believe it!'

Mr Edwards looked at the two policemen. The two

policemen looked at the fishermen. 'You wouldn't be having us on, would you?' one of the policemen said.

'I swear it!' cried Willy. 'It's the gospel truth! There's this little boy riding high up on the old turtle's back and his feet isn't even touching the water! He's dry as a bone and sitting there comfy and easy as could be! So we go after them. Of course we go after them. At first we try creeping up on them very quietly, like we always do when we're catching a turtle, but the boy sees us. We aren't very far away at this time, you understand. No more than from here to the edge of the water. And when the boy sees us, he sort of leans forwards as if he's saying something to that old turtle, and the turtle's head comes up and he starts swimming like the clappers of hell! Man, could that turtle go! Tom and me can paddle pretty quick when we want to, but we've no chance against that monster! No chance at all! He's going at least twice as fast as we are! Easy twice as fast, what you say, Tom?'

'I'd say he's going *three times* as fast,' Tom said. 'And I'll tell you why. In about ten or fifteen minutes, they're a mile ahead of us.'

'Why on earth didn't you call out to the boy?' the manager asked. 'Why didn't you speak to him earlier on, when you were closer?'

'We never *stop* calling out, man!' Willy cried. 'As soon as the boy sees us and we're not trying to creep up on them any longer, then we start yelling. We yell everything under the sun at that boy to try and get him aboard. "Hey, boy!" I yell at him. "You come on back with us! We'll give you a lift home! That ain't no good what you're doing there, boy! Jump off and swim while you got the chance and we'll pick you up! Go on boy, jump! Your mammy must be waiting for you at home, boy, so why don't you come on in with us?" And once I shouted at him, "Listen, boy! We're gonna make you a promise! We promise not to catch that old turtle if you come with us!"'

'Did he answer you at all?' the manager asked.

'He never even looks round!' Willy said. 'He sits high up on that shell and he's sort of rocking backwards and forwards with his body just like he's urging the old turtle to go faster and faster! You're gonna lose that little boy, Mr Edwards, unless someone gets out there real quick and grabs him away!'

The manager's normally pink face had turned white as paper. 'Which way were they heading?' he asked sharply.

'North,' Willy answered. 'Almost due north.'

'Right!' the manager said. 'We'll take the speed-boat! I want you with us, Willy. And you, Tom.'

The manager, the two policemen and the two fishermen ran down to where the boat that was used for water-skiing lay beached on the sand. They pushed the boat out, and even the manager lent a hand, wading up to his knees in his well-pressed white trousers. Then they all climbed in.

I watched them go zooming off.

Two hours later, I watched them coming back. They had seen nothing.

All through that day, speed-boats and yachts from other hotels along the coast searched the ocean. In the afternoon, the boy's father hired a helicopter. He rode in it himself and they were up there three hours. They found no trace of the turtle or the boy.

For a week, the search went on, but with no result.

And now, nearly a year has gone by since it happened. In that time, there has been only one significant bit of news. A party of Americans, out from Nassau in the Bahamas, were deep-sea fishing off a large island called Eleuthera. There are literally thousands of coral reefs and small uninhabited islands in this area, and upon one of these tiny islands, the captain of the yacht saw through his binoculars the figure of a small person. There was a sandy beach on the island, and the small person was walking on the beach. The binoculars were passed around, and everyone who looked through them agreed that it was a child of some sort. There was, of course, a lot of excitement on board and the fishing lines were quickly reeled in. The captain steered the yacht straight for the island. When they were half a mile off, they were able, through the binoculars, to see clearly that the figure on the beach was a boy, and although sunburnt, he was almost certainly white-skinned, not a native. At that point, the watchers on the yacht also spotted what looked like a giant turtle on the sand near the boy. What happened next happened very quickly. The boy, who had probably caught sight of the approaching yacht, jumped on the turtle's back and the huge creature entered the water and swam at great speed around the island and out of sight. The yacht searched for two hours, but nothing more was seen either of the boy or the turtle.

There is no reason to disbelieve this report. There were

five people on the yacht. Four of them were Americans and the captain was a Bahamian from Nassau. All of them in turn saw the boy and the turtle through the binoculars.

To reach Eleuthera Island from Jamaica by sea, one must first travel north-east for two hundred and fifty miles and pass through the Windward Passage between Cuba and Haiti. Then one must go north-north-west for a farther three hundred miles at least. This is a total distance of five hundred and fifty miles, which is a very long journey for a small boy to make on the shell of a giant turtle.

Who knows what to think of all this?

One day, perhaps, he will come back, though I personally doubt it. I have a feeling he's quite happy where he is.

Lucky Break

How I Became a Writer

First published in *The Wonderful Story of
Henry Sugar* (1977)

A fiction writer is a person who invents stories.

But how does one start out on a job like this? How
does one become a full-time professional fiction writer?

Charles Dickens found it easy. At the age of twenty-
four, he simply sat down and wrote *Pickwick Papers*, which
became an immediate best-seller. But Dickens was a
genius, and geniuses are different from the rest of us.

In this century (it was not always so in the last one), just
about every single writer who has finally become successful in the world of fiction has started out in some other
job – a schoolteacher, perhaps, or a doctor or a journalist
or a lawyer. (*Alice in Wonderland* was written by a mathematician, and *The Wind in the Willows* by a civil servant.) The
first attempts at writing have therefore always had to be
done in spare time, usually at night.

The reason for this is obvious. When you are adult, it is
necessary to earn a living. To earn a living, you must get a
job. You must if possible get a job that guarantees you so
much money a week. But however much you may want to
take up fiction writing as a career, it would be pointless to
go along to a publisher and say, 'I want a job as a fiction
writer.' If you did that, he would tell you to buzz off and

write the book first. And even if you brought a finished book to him and he liked it well enough to publish it, he still wouldn't give you a job. He would give you an advance of perhaps five hundred pounds, which he would get back again later by deducting it from your royalties. (A royalty, by the way, is the money that a writer gets from the publisher for each copy of his book that is sold. The average royalty a writer gets is ten per cent of the price of the book itself in the book shop. Thus, for a book selling at four pounds, the writer would get forty pence. For a paperback selling at fifty pence, he would get five pence.)

It is very common for a hopeful fiction writer to spend two years of his spare time writing a book which no publisher will publish. For that he gets nothing at all except a sense of frustration.

If he is fortunate enough to have a book accepted by a publisher, the odds are that as a first novel it will in the end sell only about three thousand copies. That will earn him maybe a thousand pounds. Most novels take at least one year to write, and one thousand pounds a year is not enough to live on these days. So you can see why a budding fiction writer invariably has to start out in another job first of all. If he doesn't, he will almost certainly starve.

Here are some of the qualities you should possess or should try to acquire if you wish to become a fiction writer:

1. You should have a lively imagination.
2. You should be able to write well. By that I mean you should be able to make a scene come alive in

the reader's mind. Not everybody has this ability. It is a gift, and you either have it or you don't.

3. You must have stamina. In other words, you must be able to stick to what you are doing and never give up, for hour after hour, day after day, week after week and month after month.

4. You must be a perfectionist. That means you must never be satisfied with what you have written until you have rewritten it again and again, making it as good as you possibly can.

5. You must have strong self-discipline. You are working alone. No one is employing you. No one is around to give you the sack if you don't turn up for work, or to tick you off if you start slacking.

6. It helps a lot if you have a keen sense of humour. This is not essential when writing for grown-ups, but for children, it's vital.

7. You must have a degree of humility. The writer who thinks that his work is marvellous is heading for trouble.

Let me tell you how I myself slid in through the back door and found myself in the world of fiction.

At the age of eight, in 1924, I was sent away to boarding-school in a town called Weston-super-Mare, on the south-west coast of England. Those were days of horror, of fierce discipline, of no talking in the dormitories, no running in the corridors, no untidiness of any sort, no this or that or the other, just rules and still more rules that had to be obeyed. And the fear of the dreaded cane hung over us like the fear of death all the time.

'The headmaster wants to see you in his study.' Words of doom. They sent shivers over the skin of your stomach. But off you went, aged perhaps nine years old, down the long bleak corridors and through an archway that took you into the headmaster's private area where only horrible things happened and the smell of pipe tobacco hung in the air like incense. You stood outside the awful black door, not daring even to knock. You took deep breaths. If only your mother were here, you told yourself, she would not let this happen. She wasn't here. You were alone. You lifted a hand and knocked softly, once.

'Come in! Ah yes, it's Dahl. Well, Dahl, it's been reported to me that you were talking during prep last night.'

'Please, sir, I broke my nib and I was only asking Jenkins if he had another one to lend me.'

'I will not tolerate talking in prep. You know that very well.'

Already this giant of a man was crossing to the tall corner cupboard and reaching up to the top of it where he kept his canes.

'Boys who break rules have to be punished.'

'Sir . . . I . . . I had a bust nib . . . I . . .'

'That is no excuse. I am going to teach you that it does not pay to talk during prep.'

He took a cane down that was about three feet long with a little curved handle at one end. It was thin and white and very whippy. 'Bend over and touch your toes. Over there by the window.'

'But, sir . . .'

'Don't argue with me, boy. Do as you're told.'

I bent over. Then I waited. He always kept you waiting for about ten seconds, and that was when your knees began to shake.

'Bend lower, boy! Touch your toes!'

I stared at the toecaps of my black shoes and I told myself that any moment now this man was going to bash the cane into me so hard that the whole of my bottom would change colour. The welts were always very long, stretching right across both buttocks, blue-black with brilliant scarlet edges, and when you ran your fingers over them ever so gently afterwards, you could feel the corrugations.

Swish! . . . Crack!

Then came the pain. It was unbelievable, unbearable, excruciating. It was as though someone had laid a white-hot poker across your backside and pressed hard.

The second stroke would be coming soon and it was as much as you could do to stop putting your hands in the way to ward it off. It was the instinctive reaction. But if you did that, it would break your fingers.

Swish! . . . Crack!

The second one landed right alongside the first and the white-hot poker was pressing deeper and deeper into the skin.

Swish! . . . Crack!

The third stroke was where the pain always reached its peak. It could go no farther. There was no way it could get any worse. Any more strokes after that simply *prolonged* the agony. You tried not to cry out. Sometimes you couldn't help it. But whether you were able to remain silent or not, it was impossible to stop the tears. They poured down your cheeks in streams and dripped on to the carpet.

The important thing was never to flinch upwards or straighten up when you were hit. If you did that, you got an extra one.

Slowly, deliberately, taking plenty of time, the head-master delivered three more strokes, making six in all.

'You may go.' The voice came from a cavern miles away, and you straightened up slowly, agonizingly, and grabbed hold of your burning buttocks with both hands and held them as tight as you could and hopped out of the room on the very tips of your toes.

That cruel cane ruled our lives. We were caned for talking in the dormitory after lights out, for talking in class, for bad work, for carving our initials on the desk, for climbing over walls, for slovenly appearance, for flicking paper-clips, for forgetting to change into house-shoes in the evenings, for not hanging up our games clothes, and above all for giving the slightest offence to any master. (They weren't called teachers in those days.) In other words, we were caned for doing everything that it was natural for small boys to do.

So we watched our words. And we watched our steps. My goodness, how we watched our steps. We became incredibly alert. Wherever we went, we walked carefully, with ears pricked for danger, like wild animals stepping softly through the woods.

Apart from the masters, there was another man in the

school who frightened us considerably. This was Mr Pople. Mr Pople was a paunchy, crimson-faced individual who acted as school-porter, boiler superintendent and general handyman. His power stemmed from the fact that he could (and he most certainly did) report us to the headmaster upon the slightest provocation. Mr Pople's moment of glory came each morning at seven thirty precisely, when he would stand at the end of the long main corridor and 'ring the bell'. The bell was huge and made of brass, with a thick wooden handle, and Mr Pople would swing it back and forth at arm's length in a special way of his own, so that it went *clangetty-clang-clang, clangetty-clang-clang, clangetty-clang-clang*. At the sound of the bell, all the boys in the school, one hundred and eighty of us, would move smartly to our positions in the corridor. We lined up against the walls on both sides and stood stiffly to attention, awaiting the headmaster's inspection.

But at least ten minutes would elapse before the headmaster arrived on the scene, and during this time, Mr Pople would conduct a ceremony so extraordinary that to this day I find it hard to believe it ever took place. There were six lavatories in the school, numbered on their doors from one to six. Mr Pople, standing at the end of the long corridor, would have in the palm of his hand six small brass discs, each with a number on it, one to six. There was absolute silence as he allowed his eye to travel down the two lines of stiffly standing boys. Then he would bark out a name, 'Arkle!'

Arkle would fall out and step briskly down the corridor to where Mr Pople stood. Mr Pople would hand him a brass disc. Arkle would then march away towards the lavatories, and to reach them he would have to walk the entire length of the corridor, past all the stationary boys, and then turn left. As soon as he was out of sight, he was allowed to look at his disc and see which lavatory number he had been given.

'Highton!' barked Mr Pople, and now Highton would fall out to receive his disc and march away.

'Angel!' . . .

'Williamson!' . . .

'Gaunt!' . . .

'Price!' . . .

In this manner, six boys selected at Mr Pople's whim were dispatched to the lavatories to do their duty. Nobody asked them if they might or might not be ready to move their bowels at seven thirty in the morning before breakfast. They were simply ordered to do so. But we considered it a great privilege to be chosen because it meant that during the headmaster's inspection we would be sitting safely out of reach in blessed privacy.

In due course, the headmaster would emerge from his private quarters and take over from Mr Pople. He walked slowly down one side of the corridor, inspecting each boy with the utmost care, strapping his wristwatch on to his wrist as he went along. The morning inspection was an unnerving experience. Every one of us was terrified of the two sharp brown eyes under their bushy eyebrows as they travelled slowly up and down the length of one's body.

'Go away and brush your hair properly. And don't let it happen again or you'll be sorry.'

'Let me see your hands. You have ink on them. Why didn't you wash it off last night?'

'Your tie is crooked, boy. Fall out and tie it again. And do it properly this time.'

'I can see mud on that shoe. Didn't I have to talk to you about that last week? Come and see me in my study after breakfast.'

And so it went on, the ghastly early-morning inspection. And by the end of it all, when the headmaster had gone away and Mr Pople started marching us into the dining-room by forms, many of us had lost our appetites for the lumpy porridge that was to come.

I have still got all my school reports from those days more than fifty years ago, and I've gone through them one by one, trying to discover a hint of promise for a future fiction writer. The subject to look at was obviously English Composition. But all my prep-school reports under this heading were flat and non-committal, excepting one. The one that took my eye was dated Christmas Term, 1928. I was then twelve, and my English teacher was Mr Victor Corrado. I remember him vividly, a tall, handsome athlete with black wavy hair and a Roman nose (who one night later on eloped with the matron, Miss Davis, and we never saw either of them again). Anyway, it so happened that Mr Corrado took us in boxing as well as in English Composition, and in this particular report it said under English, 'See his report on boxing. Precisely the same remarks apply.' So we look under Boxing, and there it says, 'Too slow and ponderous. His punches are not well timed and are easily seen coming.'

But just once a week at this school, every Saturday morning, every beautiful and blessed Saturday morning, all the shivering horrors would disappear and for two glorious hours I would experience something that came very close to ecstasy.

Unfortunately, this did not happen until one was ten years old. But no matter. Let me try to tell you what it was.

At exactly ten thirty on Saturday mornings, Mr Pople's infernal bell would go *clangetty-clang-clang*. This was a signal for the following to take place:

First, all boys of nine and under (about seventy all told) would proceed at once to the large outdoor asphalt playground behind the main building. Standing on the playground with legs apart and arms folded across her mountainous bosom was Miss Davis, the matron. If it was raining, the boys were expected to arrive in raincoats. If snowing or blowing a blizzard, then it was coats and scarves. And school caps, of course – grey with a red badge on the front – had always to be worn. But no Act of God, neither tornado nor hurricane nor volcanic eruption was ever allowed to stop those ghastly two-hour Saturday morning walks that the seven-, eight- and nine-year-old little boys had to take along the windy esplanades of Weston-super-Mare on Saturday mornings. They walked in crocodile formation, two by two, with Miss Davis striding alongside in tweed skirt and woollen stockings and a felt hat that must surely have been nibbled by rats.

The other thing that happened when Mr Pople's bell rang out on Saturday mornings was that the rest of the boys, all those of ten and over (about one hundred all told) would go immediately to the main Assembly Hall and sit down. A junior master called S. K. Jopp would then poke his head around the door and shout at us with such ferocity that specks of spit would fly from his mouth like bullets and splash against the window panes across the room. 'All right!' he shouted. 'No talking! No moving! Eyes front and hands on desks!' Then out he would pop again.

We sat still and waited. We were waiting for the lovely time we knew would be coming soon. Outside in the driveway we heard the motor-cars being started up. All were ancient. All had to be cranked by hand. (The year, don't forget, was around 1927/28.) This was a Saturday morning ritual. There were five cars in all, and into them would pile the entire staff of fourteen masters, including not only the headmaster himself but also the purple-faced Mr Pople. Then off they would roar in a cloud of blue smoke and come to rest outside a pub called, if I remember rightly, 'The Bewhiskered Earl'. There they would remain until just before lunch, drinking pint after pint of strong brown ale. And two and a half hours later, at one o'clock, we would watch them coming back, walking very carefully into the dining-room for lunch, holding on to things as they went.

So much for the masters. But what of us, the great mass of ten-, eleven- and twelve-year-olds left sitting in the Assembly Hall in a school that was suddenly without a single adult in the entire place? We knew, of course, exactly what was going to happen next. Within a minute of the departure of the masters, we would hear the front door opening, and footsteps outside, and then, with a flurry of loose clothes and jangling bracelets and flying hair, a woman would burst into the room shouting, 'Hello, everybody! Cheer up! This isn't a burial service!' or words to that effect. And this was Mrs O'Connor.

Blessed beautiful Mrs O'Connor with her whacky clothes and her grey hair flying in all directions. She was about fifty years old, with a horsey face and long yellow teeth, but to us she was beautiful. She was not on the staff. She was hired from somewhere in the town to come up on Saturday mornings and be a sort of baby-sitter, to keep us quiet for two and a half hours while the masters went off boozing at the pub.

But Mrs O'Connor was no baby-sitter. She was nothing less than a great and gifted teacher, a scholar and a lover of English Literature. Each of us was with her every Saturday morning for three years (from the age of ten until we left the school) and during that time we spanned the entire history of English Literature from AD 597 to the early nineteenth century.

Newcomers to the class were given for keeps a slim blue book called simply *The Chronological Table*, and it contained only six pages. Those six pages were filled with a very long list in chronological order of all the great and not so great landmarks in English Literature, together with their dates. Exactly one hundred of these were chosen by Mrs O'Connor and we marked them in our books and learned them by heart. Here are a few that I still remember:

AD 597	St Augustine lands in Thanet and brings Christianity to Britain
731	Bede's *Ecclesiastical History*
1215	Signing of the Magna Carta
1399	Langland's *Vision of Piers Plowman*
1476	Caxton sets up first printing press at Westminster
1478	Chaucer's *Canterbury Tales*
1485	Malory's *Morte d'Arthur*
1590	Spenser's *Faërie Queene*
1623	First Folio of Shakespeare
1667	Milton's *Paradise Lost*
1668	Dryden's *Essays*
1678	Bunyan's *Pilgrim's Progress*
1711	Addison's *Spectator*
1719	Defoe's *Robinson Crusoe*
1726	Swift's *Gulliver's Travels*
1733	Pope's *Essay on Man*
1755	Johnson's *Dictionary*
1791	Boswell's *Life of Johnson*
1833	Carlyle's *Sartor Resartus*
1859	Darwin's *Origin of Species*

Mrs O'Connor would then take each item in turn and spend one entire Saturday morning of two and a half hours talking to us about it. Thus, at the end of three years, with approximately thirty-six Saturdays in each school year, she would have covered the one hundred items.

And what marvellous exciting fun it was! She had the

great teacher's knack of making everything she spoke about come alive to us in that room. In two and a half hours, we grew to love Langland and his Piers Plowman. The next Saturday, it was Chaucer, and we loved him, too. Even rather difficult fellows like Milton and Dryden and Pope all became thrilling when Mrs O'Connor told us about their lives and read parts of their work to us aloud. And the result of all this, for me at any rate, was that by the age of thirteen I had become intensely aware of the vast heritage of literature that had been built up in England over the centuries. I also became an avid and insatiable reader of good writing.

Dear lovely Mrs O'Connor! Perhaps it was worth going to that awful school simply to experience the joy of her Saturday mornings.

At thirteen I left prep school and was sent, again as a boarder, to one of our famous British public schools. They are not, of course, public at all. They are extremely private and expensive. Mine was called Repton, in Derbyshire, and our headmaster at the time was the Reverend Geoffrey Fisher, who later became Bishop of Chester, then Bishop of London, and finally Archbishop of Canterbury. In his last job, he crowned Queen Elizabeth II in Westminster Abbey.

The clothes we had to wear at this school made us look like assistants in a funeral parlour. The jacket was black, with a cutaway front and long tails hanging down behind that came below the backs of the knees. The trousers were black with thin grey stripes. The shoes were black. There was a black waistcoat with eleven buttons to do up every morning. The tie was black. Then there was a stiff starched white butterfly collar and a white shirt.

To top it all off, the final ludicrous touch was a straw hat that had to be worn at all times out of doors except when playing games. And because the hats got soggy in the rain, we carried umbrellas for bad weather.

You can imagine what I felt like in this fancy dress when my mother took me, at the age of thirteen, to the train in London at the beginning of my first term. She kissed me good-bye and off I went.

I naturally hoped that my long-suffering backside would be given a rest at my new and more adult school, but it was not to be. The beatings at Repton were more fierce and more frequent than anything I had yet experienced. And do not think for one moment that the future Archbishop of Canterbury objected to these squalid exercises. He rolled up his sleeves and joined in with gusto. His were the bad ones, the really terrifying occasions. Some of the beatings administered by this Man of God, this future Head of the Church of England, were very brutal. To my certain knowledge he once had to produce a basin of water, a sponge and a towel so that the victim could wash the blood away afterwards.

No joke, that.

Shades of the Spanish Inquisition.

But nastiest of all, I think, was the fact that prefects were allowed to beat their fellow pupils. This was a daily occurrence. The big boys (aged 17 or 18) would flog the smaller boys (aged 13, 14, 15) in a sadistic ceremony that took place at night after you had gone up to the dormitory and got into your pyjamas.

'You're wanted down in the changing-room.'

With heavy hands, you would put on your dressing-gown and slippers. Then you would stumble downstairs and enter the large wooden-floored room where the games clothes were hanging up around the walls. A single bare electric bulb hung from the ceiling. A prefect, pompous but very dangerous, was waiting for you in the centre of the room. In his hands, he held a long cane, and he was usually flexing it back and forth as you came in.

'I suppose you know why you're here,' he would say.

'Well, I . . .'

'For the second day running you have burned my toast!'

Let me explain this ludicrous remark. You were this particular prefect's fag. That meant you were his servant, and one of your many duties was to make toast for him every day at teatime. For this, you used a long three-pronged toasting-fork, and you stuck the bread on the end of it and held it up before an open fire, first one side, then the other. But the only fire where toasting was allowed was in the library, and as teatime approached, there were never less than a dozen wretched fags all jostling for position in front of the tiny grate. I was no good at this. I usually held the bread too close and the toast got burned. But as we were never allowed to ask for a second slice and start again, the only thing to do was to scrape the burned bits off with a knife. You seldom got away with this. The prefects were expert at detecting scraped toast.

You would see your own tormentor sitting up there at the top table, picking up his toast, turning it over, examining it closely as though it were a small and very valuable painting. Then he would frown and you knew you were for it.

So now it was night-time and you were down in the changing-room in your dressing-gown and pyjamas, and the one whose toast you had burned was telling you about your crime.

'I don't like burned toast.'

'I held it too close. I'm sorry.'

'Which do you want? Four with the dressing-gown on, or three with it off?'

'Four with it on,' I said.

It was traditional to ask this question. The victim was always given a choice. But my own dressing-gown was made of thick brown camel-hair, and there was never any question in my mind that this was the better choice. To be beaten in pyjamas only was a very painful experience, and your skin nearly always got broken. But my dressing-gown stopped that from happening. The prefect knew, of course, all about this, and therefore whenever you chose to take an extra stroke and kept the dressing-gown on, he beat you with every ounce of his strength. Sometimes he would take a little run, three or four neat steps on his toes, to gain momentum and thrust, but either way, it was a savage business.

In the old days, when a man was about to be hanged, a silence would fall upon the whole prison and the other prisoners would sit very quietly in their cells until the deed had been done. Much the same thing happened at school when a beating was taking place. Upstairs in the dormitories, the boys would sit in silence on their beds in sympathy for the victim, and through the silence, from down below in the changing-room, would come the *crack* of each stroke as it was delivered.

My end-of-term reports from this school are of some interest. Here are just four of them, copied out word for word from the original documents:

Summer Term, 1930 (aged *14*). *English Composition.* 'I have never met a boy who so persistently writes the exact opposite of what he means. He seems incapable of marshalling his thoughts on paper.'

Easter Term, 1931 (aged 15). English Composition. 'A persistent muddler. Vocabulary negligible, sentences malconstructed. He reminds me of a camel.'

Summer Term, 1932 (aged 16). English Composition. 'This boy is an indolent and illiterate member of the class.'

Autumn Term, 1932 (aged 17). English Composition. 'Consistently idle. Ideas limited.' (And underneath this one, the future Archbishop of Canterbury had written in red ink, 'He must correct the blemishes on this sheet.')

Little wonder that it never entered my head to become a writer in those days.

When I left school at the age of eighteen, in 1934, I turned down my mother's offer (my father died when I was three) to go to university. Unless one was going to become a doctor, a lawyer, a scientist, an engineer or some other kind of professional person, I saw little point in wasting three or four years at Oxford or Cambridge, and I still hold this view. Instead, I had a passionate wish to go abroad, to travel, to see distant lands. There were almost no commercial aeroplanes in those days, and a journey to Africa or the Far East took several weeks.

So I got a job with what was called the Eastern Staff of the Shell Oil Company, where they promised me that after two or three years' training in England, I would be sent off to a foreign country.

'Which one?' I asked.

'Who knows?' the man answered. 'It depends where there is a vacancy when you reach the top of the list. It could be Egypt or China or India or almost anywhere in the world.'

That sounded like fun. It was. When my turn came to be posted abroad three years later, I was told it would be East Africa. Tropical suits were ordered and my mother helped me pack my trunk. My tour of duty was for three years in Africa, then I would be allowed home on leave for six months. I was now twenty-one years old and setting out for faraway places. I felt great. I boarded the ship at London Docks and off she sailed.

That journey took two and a half weeks. We went through the Bay of Biscay and called in at Gibraltar. We headed down the Mediterranean by way of Malta, Naples and Port Said. We went through the Suez Canal and down the Red Sea, stopping at Port Sudan, then Aden. It was tremendously exciting. For the first time, I saw great sandy deserts, and Arab soldiers mounted on camels, and palm trees with dates growing on them, and flying fish and thousands of other marvellous things. Finally we reached Mombasa, in Kenya.

At Mombasa, a man from the Shell Company came on board and told me I must transfer to a small coastal vessel and go on to Dar-es-Salaam, the capital of Tanganyika (now Tanzania). And so to Dar-es-Salaam I went, stopping at Zanzibar on the way.

For the next two years, I worked for Shell in Tanzania, with my headquarters in Dar-es-Salaam. It was a fantastic life. The heat was intense but who cared? Our dress was khaki shorts, an open shirt and a topee on the head. I learned to speak Swahili. I drove up-country visiting diamond mines, sisal plantations, gold mines and all the rest of it.

There were giraffes, elephants, zebras, lions and antelopes all over the place, and snakes as well, including the Black Mamba, which is the only snake in the world that will chase after you if it sees you. And if it catches you and bites you, you had better start saying your prayers. I learned to shake my mosquito boots upside down before putting them on in case there was a scorpion inside, and like everyone else, I got malaria and lay for three days with a temperature of one hundred and five point five.

In September 1939, it became obvious that there was going to be a war with Hitler's Germany. Tanganyika, which only twenty years before had been called German East Africa, was still full of Germans. They were everywhere. They owned shops and mines and plantations all over the country. The moment war broke out, they would have to be rounded up. But we had no army to speak of in Tanganyika, only a few native soldiers, known as As-karis, and a handful of officers. So all of us civilian men were made Special Reservists. I was given an armband and put in charge of twenty Askaris. My little troop and I were ordered to block the road that led south out of Tangan-yika into neutral Portuguese East Africa. This was an important job, for it was along that road most of the Germans would try to escape when war was declared.

I took my happy gang with their rifles and one machine-gun and set up a road-block in a place where the road passed through dense jungle, about ten miles outside the town. We had a field telephone to headquarters which would tell us at once when war was declared. We settled down to wait. For three days we waited. And during the nights, from all around us in the jungle, came the sound of native drums beating weird hypnotic rhythms. Once, I wandered into the jungle in the dark and came across about fifty natives squatting in a circle around a fire. One man only was beating the drum. Some were dancing round the fire. The remainder were drinking something out of coconut shells. They welcomed me into their cir-cle. They were lovely people. I could talk to them in their language. They gave me a shell filled with a thick grey intoxicating fluid made of fermented maize. It was called, if I remember rightly, Pomba. I drank it. It was horrible.

The next afternoon, the field telephone rang and a voice said, 'We are at war with Germany.' Within minutes, far away in the distance, I saw a line of cars throwing up clouds of dust, heading our way, beating it for the neutral territory of Portuguese East Africa as fast as they could go.

Ho ho, I thought. We are going to have a little battle, and I called out to my twenty Askaris to prepare themselves. But there was no battle. The Germans, who were after all only civilian townspeople, saw our machine-gun and our rifles and quickly gave themselves up. Within an hour, we had a couple of hundred of them on our hands. I felt rather sorry for them. Many I knew personally, like Willy Hink the watchmaker and Herman Schneider who owned the soda-water factory. Their only crime had been that they were German. But this was war, and in the cool of the evening, we marched them all back to Dar-es-Salaam where they were put into a huge camp surrounded by barbed wire.

The next day, I got into my old car and drove north, heading for Nairobi, in Kenya, to join the RAF. It was a rough trip and it took me four days. Bumpy jungle roads, wide rivers where the car had to be put on to a raft and pulled across by a ferryman hauling on a rope, long green snakes sliding across the road in front of the car. (NB. Never try to run over a snake because it can be thrown up into the air and may land inside your open car. It's happened many times.) I slept at night in the car. I passed below the beautiful Mount Kilimanjaro, which had a hat of snow on its head. I drove through the Masai country where the men drank cows' blood and every one of them seemed to be seven feet tall. I nearly collided with a giraffe on the Serengeti Plain. But I came safely to Nairobi at last and reported to RAF headquarters at the airport.

For six months, they trained us in small aeroplanes called Tiger Moths, and those days were also glorious. We skimmed all over Kenya in our little Tiger Moths. We saw great herds of elephants. We saw the pink flamingoes on Lake Nakuru. We saw everything there was to see in that magnificent country. And often, before we could take off, we had to chase the zebras off the flying-field. There were twenty of us training to be pilots out there in Nairobi. Seventeen of those twenty were killed during the war.

From Nairobi, they sent us up to Iraq, to a desolate airforce base near Baghdad, to finish our training. The place was called Habbaniyih, and in the afternoons it got so hot (130 degrees in the shade) that we were not allowed out of our huts. We just lay on the bunks and sweated. The unlucky ones got heat-stroke and were taken to hospital and packed in ice for several days. This either killed them or saved them. It was a fifty-fifty chance.

At Habbaniyih, they taught us to fly more powerful aeroplanes with guns in them, and we practised shooting at drogues (targets in the air pulled behind other planes) and at objects on the ground.

Finally, our training was finished, and we were sent to Egypt to fight against the Italians in the Western Desert of Libya. I joined 80 Squadron, which flew fighters, and at first we had only ancient single-seater biplanes called Gloster Gladiators. The two machine-guns on a Gladiator were mounted one on either side of the engine, and they fired their bullets, believe it or not, *through* the propeller. The guns were somehow synchronized with the propeller shaft so that in theory the bullets missed the whirling propeller blades. But as you might guess, this complicated mechanism often went wrong and the poor pilot, who was trying to shoot down the enemy, shot off his own propeller instead.

I myself was shot down in a Gladiator which crashed far out in the Libyan desert between the enemy lines. The plane burst into flames, but I managed to get out and was finally rescued and carried back to safety by our own soldiers who crawled out across the sand under cover of darkness.

That crash sent me to hospital in Alexandria for six months with a fractured skull and a lot of burns. When I came out, in April 1941, my squadron had been moved to Greece to fight the Germans who were invading from the north. I was given a Hurricane and told to fly it from Egypt to Greece and join the squadron. Now, a Hurricane fighter was not at all like the old Gladiator. It had eight Browning machine-guns, four in each wing, and all eight of them fired simultaneously when you pressed the small button on your joy-stick. It was a magnificent plane, but it had a range of only two hours' flying-time. The journey to Greece, non-stop, would take nearly five hours, always over the water. They put extra fuel tanks on the wings. They said I would make it. In the end, I did. But only just. When you are six feet six inches tall, as I am, it is no joke to be sitting crunched up in a tiny cockpit for five hours.

In Greece, the RAF had a total of about eighteen Hurricanes. The Germans had at least one thousand aeroplanes to operate with. We had a hard time. We were driven from our aerodrome outside Athens (Elevis), and flew for a while from a small secret landing-strip farther west (Menidi). The Germans soon found that one and bashed it to bits, so with the few planes we had left, we flew off to a tiny field (Argos) right down in the south of Greece, where we hid our Hurricanes under the olive trees when we weren't flying.

But this couldn't last long. Soon, we had only five Hurricanes left, and not many pilots still alive. Those five planes were flown to the island of Crete. The Germans captured Crete. Some of us escaped. I was one of the lucky ones. I finished up back in Egypt. The squadron was re-formed and re-equipped with Hurricanes. We were sent off to Haifa, which was then in Palestine (now Israel), where we fought the Germans again and the Vichy French in Lebanon and Syria.

At that point, my old head injuries caught up with me. Severe headaches compelled me to stop flying. I was invalided back to England and sailed on a troopship from Suez to Durban to Capetown to Lagos to Liverpool, chased by German submarines in the Atlantic and bombed by long-range Focke-Wulf aircraft every day for the last week of the voyage.

I had been away from home for four years. My mother, bombed out of her own house in Kent during the Battle of Britain and now living in a small thatched cottage in Buckinghamshire, was happy to see me. So were my four sisters and my brother. I was given a month's leave. Then suddenly I was told I was being sent to Washington DC in the United States of America as Assistant Air Attaché. This was January 1942, and one month earlier the Japanese had bombed the American fleet in Pearl Harbor. So the United States was now in the war as well.

I was twenty-six years old when I arrived in Washington, and I still had no thoughts of becoming a writer.

During the morning of my third day, I was sitting in my new office at the British Embassy and wondering what on earth I was meant to be doing, when there was a knock on my door. 'Come in.'

A very small man with thick steel-rimmed spectacles shuffled shyly into the room. 'Forgive me for bothering you,' he said.

'You aren't bothering me at all,' I answered. 'I'm not doing a thing.'

He stood before me looking very uncomfortable and out of place. I thought perhaps he was going to ask for a job.

'My name,' he said, 'is Forester. C. S. Forester.'

I nearly fell out of my chair. 'Are you joking?' I said.

'No,' he said, smiling. 'That's me.'

And it was. It was the great writer himself, the inventor of Captain Hornblower and the best teller of tales about the sea since Joseph Conrad. I asked him to take a seat.

'Look,' he said. 'I'm too old for the war. I live over here now. The only thing I can do to help is to write things about Britain for the American papers and magazines. We need all the help America can give us. A magazine called the *Saturday Evening Post* will publish any story I write. I have a contract with them. And I have come to you because I think you might have a good story to tell. I mean about flying.'

'No more than thousands of others,' I said. 'There are lots of pilots who have shot down many more planes than me.'

'That's not the point,' Forester said. 'You are now in America, and because you have, as they say over here, "been in combat", you are a rare bird on this side of the Atlantic. Don't forget they have only just entered the war.'

'What do you want me to do?' I asked.

'Come and have lunch with me,' he said. 'And while we're eating, you can tell me all about it. Tell me your most exciting adventure and I'll write it up for the *Saturday Evening Post*. Every little bit helps.'

I was thrilled. I had never met a famous writer before. I examined him closely as he sat in my office. What astonished me was that he looked so ordinary. There was nothing in the least unusual about him. His face, his conversation, his eyes behind the spectacles, even his clothes were all exceedingly normal. And yet here was a writer of stories who was famous the world over. His books had been read by millions of people. I expected sparks to be shooting out of his head, or at the very least, he should have been wearing a long green cloak and a floppy hat with a wide brim.

But no. And it was then I began to realize for the first time that there are two distinct sides to a writer of fiction. First, there is the side he displays to the public, that of an ordinary person like anyone else, a person who does ordinary things and speaks an ordinary language. Second, there is the secret side which comes out in him only after he has closed the door of his workroom and is completely alone. It is then that he slips into another world altogether, a world where his imagination takes over and he finds himself actually *living* in the places he is writing about at that moment. I myself, if you want to know, fall into a kind of trance and everything around me disappears. I see only the point of my pencil moving over the paper, and quite often two hours go by as though they were a couple of seconds.

'Come along,' C. S. Forester said to me. 'Let's go to lunch. You don't seem to have anything else to do.'

As I walked out of the Embassy side by side with the great man, I was churning with excitement. I had read all the Hornblowers and just about everything else he had written. I had, and still have, a great love for books about the sea. I had read all of Conrad and all of that other splendid sea-writer, Captain Marryat (*Mr Midshipman Easy*, *From Powder Monkey to Admiral*, etc.), and now here I was about to have lunch with somebody who, to my mind, was also pretty terrific.

He took me to a small expensive French restaurant somewhere near the Mayflower Hotel in Washington. He ordered a sumptuous lunch, then he produced a notebook and a pencil (ballpoint pens had not been invented in 1942) and laid them on the tablecloth. 'Now,' he said, 'tell me about the most exciting or frightening or dangerous thing that happened to you when you were flying fighter planes.'

I tried to get going. I started telling him about the time I was shot down in the Western Desert and the plane had burst into flames.

The waitress brought two plates of smoked salmon. While we tried to eat it, I was trying to talk and Forester was trying to take notes.

The main course was roast duck with vegetables and potatoes and a thick rich gravy. This was a dish that required one's full attention as well as two hands. My narrative began to flounder. Forester kept putting down the pencil and picking up the fork, and vice versa. Things weren't going well. And apart from that, I have never been much good at telling stories aloud.

'Look,' I said. 'If you like, I'll try to write down on paper what happened and send it to you. Then you can rewrite it properly yourself in your own time. Wouldn't that be easier? I could do it tonight.'

That, though I didn't know it at the time, was the moment that changed my life.

'A splendid idea,' Forester said. 'Then I can put this silly notebook away and we can enjoy our lunch. Would you really mind doing that for me?'

'I don't mind a bit,' I said. 'But you mustn't expect it to be any good. I'll just put down the facts.'

'Don't worry,' he said. 'So long as the facts are there, I can write the story. But please,' he added, 'let me have plenty of detail. That's what counts in our business, tiny little details, like you had a broken shoelace on your left shoe, or a fly settled on the rim of your glass at lunch, or the man you were talking to had a broken front tooth. Try to think back and remember everything.'

'I'll do my best,' I said.

He gave me an address where I could send the story,

and then we forgot all about it and finished our lunch at leisure. But Mr Forester was not a great talker. He certainly couldn't talk as well as he wrote, and although he was kind and gentle, no sparks ever flew out of his head and I might just as well have been talking to an intelligent stockbroker or lawyer.

That night, in the small house I lived in alone in a suburb of Washington, I sat down and wrote my story. I started at about seven o'clock and finished at midnight. I remember I had a glass of Portuguese brandy to keep me going. For the first time in my life, I became totally absorbed in what I was doing. I floated back in time and once again I was in the sizzling hot desert of Libya, with white sand underfoot, climbing up into the cockpit of the old Gladiator, strapping myself in, adjusting my helmet, starting the motor and taxiing out for take-off. It was astonishing how everything came back to me with absolute clarity. Writing it down on paper was not difficult. The story seemed to be telling itself, and the hand that held the pencil moved rapidly back and forth across each page. Just for fun, when it was finished, I gave it a title. I called it 'A Piece of Cake'.

The next day, somebody in the Embassy typed it out for me and I sent it off to Mr Forester. Then I forgot all about it.

Exactly two weeks later, I received a reply from the great man. It said:

Dear RD, You were meant to give me notes, not a finished story. I'm bowled over. Your piece is marvellous. It is the work of a gifted writer. I didn't touch a word of it. I sent it at once under your name to my agent, Harold Matson, asking him to offer it to the Saturday Evening Post with my personal recommendation. You will be happy to hear that the Post accepted it immediately and have paid one thousand dollars. Mr Matson's commission is ten per cent. I enclose his check for nine hundred dollars. It's all yours. As you will see from Mr Matson's letter, which I also enclose, the Post is asking if you will write more stories for them. I do hope you will. Did you know you were a writer? With my very best wishes and congratulations, C. S. Forester.

'A Piece of Cake' is printed at the end of this book.[*]

Well! I thought. My goodness me! Nine hundred dollars! And they're going to print it! But surely it can't be as easy as all that?

Oddly enough, it was.

The next story I wrote was fiction. I made it up. Don't ask me why. And Mr Matson sold that one, too. Out there in Washington in the evenings over the next two years, I wrote eleven short stories. All were sold to American magazines, and later they were published in a little book called *Over to You*.

Early on in this period, I also had a go at a story for children. It was called 'The Gremlins', and this I believe was the first time the word had been used. In my story, Gremlins were tiny men who lived on RAF fighter-planes and bombers, and it was the Gremlins, not the enemy,

---

[*] 'A Piece of Cake' now appears in *The Complete Short Stories of Roald Dahl: Volume One*.

who were responsible for all the bullet-holes and burning engines and crashes that took place during combat. The Gremlins had wives called Fifinellas, and children called Widgets, and although the story itself was clearly the work of an inexperienced writer, it was bought by Walt Disney who decided he was going to make it into a full-length animated film. But first it was published in *Cosmopolitan Magazine* with Disney's coloured illustrations (December 1942), and from then on, news of the Gremlins spread rapidly through the whole of the RAF and the United States Air Force, and they became something of a legend.

Because of the Gremlins, I was given three weeks' leave from my duties at the Embassy in Washington and whisked out to Hollywood. There, I was put up at Disney's expense in a luxurious Beverly Hills hotel and given a huge shiny car to drive about in. Each day, I worked with the great Disney at his studios in Burbank, roughing out the story-line for the forthcoming film. I had a ball. I was still only twenty-six. I attended story-conferences in Disney's enormous office where every word spoken, every suggestion made, was taken down by a stenographer and typed out afterwards. I mooched around the rooms where the gifted and obstreperous animators worked, the men who had already created *Snow White*, *Dumbo*, *Bambi* and other marvellous films, and in those days, so long as these crazy artists did their work, Disney didn't care when they turned up at the studio or how they behaved.

When my time was up, I went back to Washington and left them to it.

My Gremlin story was published as a children's

book in New York and London, full of Disney's colour illustrations, and it was called of course *The Gremlins*. Copies are very scarce now and hard to come by. I myself have only one. The film, also, was never finished. I have a feeling that Disney was not really very comfortable with this particular fantasy. Out there in Hollywood, he was a long way away from the great war in the air that was going on in Europe. Furthermore, it was a story about the Royal Air Force and not about his own countrymen, and that, I think, added to his sense of bewilderment. So in the end, he lost interest and dropped the whole idea.

My little Gremlin book caused something else quite extraordinary to happen to me in those wartime Washington days. Eleanor Roosevelt read it to her grandchildren in the White House and was apparently much taken with it. I was invited to dinner with her and the President. I went, shaking with excitement. We had a splendid time and I was invited again. Then Mrs Roosevelt began asking me for week-ends to Hyde Park, the President's country house. Up there, believe it or not, I spent a good deal of time alone with Franklin Roosevelt during his relaxing hours. I would sit with him while he mixed the martinis before Sunday lunch, and he would say things like, 'I've just had an interesting cable from Mr Churchill.' Then he would tell me what it said, something perhaps about new plans for the bombing of Germany or the sinking of U-Boats, and I would do my best to appear calm and chatty, though actually I was trembling at the realization that the most powerful man in the world was telling me these mighty secrets. Sometimes he drove me around the estate in his car, an old Ford I think it was, that had been specially adapted for his paralysed legs. It had no pedals. All the controls were worked by his hands. His secret-service men would lift him out of his wheel-chair into the driver's seat, then he would wave them away and off we would go, driving at terrific speeds along the narrow roads.

One Sunday during lunch at Hyde Park, Franklin Roosevelt told a story that shook the assembled guests. There were about fourteen of us sitting on both sides of the long dining-room table, including Princess Martha of Norway and several members of the Cabinet. We were eating a rather insipid white fish covered with a thick grey sauce. Suddenly the President pointed a finger at me and said, 'We have an Englishman here. Let me tell you what happened to another Englishman, a representative of the King, who was in Washington in the year 1827.' He gave the man's name, but I've forgotten it. Then he went on, 'While he was over here, this fellow died, and the British for some reason insisted that his body be sent home to England for burial. Now the only way to do that in those days was to pickle it in alcohol. So the body was put into a barrel of rum. The barrel was lashed to the mast of a schooner and the ship sailed for home. After about four weeks at sea, the captain of the schooner noticed a most frightful stench coming from the barrel. And in the end, the smell became so appalling they had to cut the barrel loose and roll it overboard. But do you know *why* it stank so badly?' the President asked, beaming at the guests with that famous wide smile of his. 'I will tell you exactly why.

Some of the sailors had drilled a hole in the bottom of the barrel and had inserted a bung. Then every night they had been helping themselves to the rum. And when they had drunk it all, that's when the trouble started.' Franklin Roosevelt let out a great roar of laughter. Several females at the table turned very pale and I saw them pushing their plates of boiled white fish gently away.

All the stories I wrote in those early days were fiction, except for that first one I did with C. S. Forester. Non-fiction, which means writing about things that have actually taken place, doesn't interest me. I enjoy least of all writing about my own experiences. And that explains why this story is so lacking in detail. I could quite easily have described what it was like to be in a dog-fight with German fighters fifteen thousand feet above the Parthenon in Athens, or the thrill of chasing a Junkers 88 in and out the mountain peaks in Northern Greece, but I don't want to do it. For me, the pleasure of writing comes with inventing stories.

Apart from the Forester story, I think I have only written one other non-fiction piece in my life, and I did this only because the subject was so enthralling I couldn't resist it. The story is called 'The Mildenhall Treasure', and it's in this book.*

So there you are. That's how I became a writer. Had I not been lucky enough to meet Mr Forester, it would probably never have happened.

* 'The Mildenhall Treasure' now appears in *The Complete Short Stories of Roald Dahl: Volume One*.

Now, more than thirty years later, I'm still slogging away. To me, the most important and difficult thing about writing fiction is to find the plot. Good original plots are very hard to come by. You never know when a lovely idea is going to flit suddenly into your mind, but by golly, when it does come along, you grab it with both hands and hang on to it tight. The trick is to write it down at once, otherwise you'll forget it. A good plot is like a dream. If you don't write down your dream on paper the moment you wake up, the chances are you'll forget it and it'll be gone for ever.

So when an idea for a story comes popping into my mind, I rush for a pencil, a crayon, a lipstick, anything that will write, and scribble a few words that will later remind me of the idea. Often, one word is enough. I was once driving alone on a country road and an idea came for a story about someone getting stuck in an elevator between two floors in an empty house. I had nothing to write with in the car. So I stopped and got out. The back of the car was covered with dust. With one finger I wrote in the dust the single word ELEVATOR. That was enough. As soon as I got home, I went straight to my workroom and wrote the idea down in an old red-covered school exercise-book which is simply labelled 'Short Stories'.

I have had this book ever since I started trying to write seriously. There are ninety-eight pages in the book. I've counted them. And just about every one of those pages is filled up on both sides with these so-called story ideas. Many are no good. But just about every story and every children's book I have ever written has started out as a three- or four-line note in this little, much-worn red-covered volume. For example:

What about a chocolate factory That makes fantastic and marvellous Things — with a crazy man running it?

This became *Charlie and the Chocolate Factory*.

A story about mr. Fox who has a whole network of underground Tunnels leading to all the shops in the village. At night, he goes up through the floorboards and helps himself.

Fantastic Mr Fox.

Jamaica and The small boy who saw a giant Turtle captured by native fishermen. Boy pleads with his father To buy Turtle and release it. Becomes hysterical. Father buys it. Then what? Perhaps boy goes with ~~a~~ joins Turtle.

'The Boy Who Talked with Animals.'

A man acquires the ability to see through playing-cards. He makes millions at casinos.

This became 'Henry Sugar'.

Sometimes, these little scribbles will stay unused in the notebook for five or even ten years. But the promising ones are always used in the end. And if they show nothing else, they do, I think, demonstrate from what slender threads a children's book or a short story must ultimately be woven. The story builds and expands while you are writing it. All the best stuff comes at the desk. But you can't even start to write that story unless you have the beginnings of a plot. Without my little notebook, I would be quite helpless.

The Umbrella Man

First published in *More Tales of
the Unexpected* (1980)

I'm going to tell you about a funny thing that happened to
my mother and me yesterday evening. I am twelve years
old and I'm a girl. My mother is thirty-four but I am nearly
as tall as her already.

Yesterday afternoon, my mother took me up to London
to see the dentist. He found one hole. It was in a back
tooth and he filled it without hurting me too much. After
that, we went to a café. I had a banana split and my mother
had a cup of coffee. By the time we got up to leave, it was
about six o'clock.

When we came out of the café it had started to rain.
'We must get a taxi,' my mother said. We were wearing
ordinary hats and coats, and it was raining quite hard.

'Why don't we go back into the café and wait for it to
stop?' I said. I wanted another of those banana splits.
They were gorgeous.

'It isn't going to stop,' my mother said. 'We must get
home.'

We stood on the pavement in the rain, looking for a
taxi. Lots of them came by but they all had passengers
inside them. 'I wish we had a car with a chauffeur,' my
mother said.

Just then, a man came up to us. He was a small man and

he was pretty old, probably seventy or more. He raised his hat politely and said to my mother, 'Excuse me. I do hope you will excuse me . . .' He had a fine white moustache and bushy white eyebrows and a wrinkly pink face. He was sheltering under an umbrella, which he held high over his head.

'Yes?' my mother said, very cool and distant.

'I wonder if I could ask a small favour of you,' he said. 'It is only a very small favour.'

I saw my mother looking at him suspiciously. She is a suspicious person, my mother. She is especially suspicious of two things – strange men and boiled eggs. When she cuts the top off a boiled egg, she pokes around inside it with her spoon as though expecting to find a mouse or something. With strange men, she has a golden rule which says, 'The nicer the man seems to be, the more suspicious you must become.' This little old man was particularly nice. He was polite. He was well spoken. He was well dressed. He was a real gentleman. The reason I knew he was a gentleman was because of his shoes. 'You can always spot a gentleman by the shoes he wears,' was another of my mother's favourite sayings. This man had beautiful brown shoes.

'The truth of the matter is,' the little man was saying, 'I've got myself into a bit of a scrape. I need some help. Not much, I assure you. It's almost nothing, in fact, but I do need it. You see, madam, old people like me often become terribly forgetful . . .'

My mother's chin was up and she was staring down at him along the full length of her nose. It is a fearsome thing, this frosty-nosed stare of my mother's. Most people go to pieces completely when she gives it to them. I once saw my own headmistress begin to stammer and simper like an idiot when my mother gave her a really foul frosty-noser. But the little man on the pavement with the umbrella over his head didn't bat an eyelid. He gave a gentle smile and said, 'I beg you to believe, madam, that I am not in the habit of stopping ladies in the street and telling them my troubles.'

'I should hope not,' my mother said.

I felt quite embarrassed by my mother's sharpness. I wanted to say to her, 'Oh, Mummy, for heaven's sake, he's a very very old man, and he's sweet and polite, and he's in some sort of trouble, so don't be so beastly to him.' But I didn't say anything.

The little man shifted his umbrella from one hand to the other. 'I've never forgotten it before,' he said.

'You've never forgotten what?' my mother asked sternly.

'My wallet,' he said. 'I must have left it in my other jacket. Isn't that the silliest thing to do?'

'Are you asking me to give you money?' my mother said.

'Oh, good gracious me, no!' he cried. 'Heaven forbid I should ever do that!'

'Then what *are* you asking?' my mother said. 'Do hurry up. We're getting soaked to the skin standing here.'

'I know you are,' he said. 'And that is why I'm offering you this umbrella of mine to protect you, and to keep for ever, if . . . if only . . .'

'If only what?' my mother said.

'If only you would give me in return a pound for my taxi-fare just to get me home.'

My mother was still suspicious. 'If you had no money in the first place,' she said, 'then how did you get here?'

'I walked,' he answered. 'Every day I go for a lovely long walk and then I summon a taxi to take me home. I do it every day of the year.'

'Why don't you walk home now?' my mother asked.

'Oh, I wish I could,' he said. 'I do wish I could. But I don't think I could manage it on these silly old legs of mine. I've gone too far already.'

My mother stood there chewing her lower lip. She was beginning to melt a bit, I could see that. And the idea of getting an umbrella to shelter under must have tempted her a good deal.

'It's a lovely umbrella,' the little man said.

'So I've noticed,' my mother said.

'It's silk,' he said.

'I can see that.'

'Then why don't you take it, madam,' he said. 'It cost me over twenty pounds, I promise you. But that's of no importance so long as I can get home and rest these old legs of mine.'

I saw my mother's hand feeling for the clasp on her purse. She saw me watching her. I was giving her one of my *own* frosty-nosed looks this time and she knew exactly what I was telling her. Now listen, Mummy, I was telling her, you simply *mustn't* take advantage of a tired old man in this way. It's a rotten thing to do. My mother paused and looked back at me. Then she said to the little man,

THE COMPLETE SHORT STORIES

'I don't think it's quite right that I should take a silk umbrella from you worth twenty pounds. I think I'd just better *give* you the taxi-fare and be done with it.'

'No, no, no!' he cried. 'It's out of the question! I wouldn't dream of it! Not in a million years! I would never accept money from you like that! Take the umbrella, dear lady, and keep the rain off your shoulders!'

My mother gave me a triumphant sideways look. There you are, she was telling me. You're wrong. He *wants* me to have it.

She fished into her purse and took out a pound note. She held it out to the little man. He took it and handed her the umbrella. He pocketed the pound, raised his hat, gave a quick bow from the waist, and said, 'Thank you, madam, thank you.' Then he was gone.

'Come under here and keep dry, darling,' my mother said. 'Aren't we lucky? I've never had a silk umbrella before. I couldn't afford it.'

'Why were you so horrid to him in the beginning?' I asked.

'I wanted to satisfy myself he wasn't a trickster,' she said. 'And I did. He was a gentleman. I'm very pleased I was able to help him.'

'Yes, Mummy,' I said.

'A *real* gentleman,' she went on. 'Wealthy, too, otherwise he wouldn't have had a silk umbrella. I shouldn't be surprised if he isn't a titled person. Sir Harry Goldsworthy or something like that.'

'Yes, Mummy.'

'This will be a good lesson to you,' she went on. 'Never rush things. Always take your time when you are summing someone up. Then you'll never make mistakes.'

'There he goes,' I said. 'Look.'

'Where?'

'Over there. He's crossing the street. Goodness, Mummy, what a hurry he's in.'

We watched the little man as he dodged nimbly in and out of the traffic. When he reached the other side of the street, he turned left, walking very fast.

'He doesn't look very tired to me, does he to you, Mummy?'

My mother didn't answer.

'He doesn't look as though he's trying to get a taxi, either,' I said.

My mother was standing very still and stiff, staring across the street at the little man. We could see him clearly. He was in a terrific hurry. He was bustling along the pavement, sidestepping the other pedestrians and swinging his arms like a soldier on the march.

'He's up to something,' my mother said, stony-faced.

'But what?'

'I don't know,' my mother snapped. 'But I'm going to find out. Come with me.' She took my arm and we crossed the street together. Then we turned left.

'Can you see him?' my mother asked.

'Yes. There he is. He's turning right down the next street.'

We came to the corner and turned right. The little man

was about twenty yards ahead of us. He was scuttling along like a rabbit and we had to walk fast to keep up with him. The rain was pelting down harder than ever now and I could see it dripping from the brim of his hat on to his shoulders. But we were snug and dry under our lovely big silk umbrella.

'What *is* he up to?' my mother said.

'What if he turns round and sees us?' I asked.

'I don't care if he does,' my mother said. 'He lied to us. He said he was too tired to walk any further and he's practically running us off our feet! He's a barefaced liar! He's a crook!'

'You mean he's *not* a titled gentleman?' I asked.

'Be quiet,' she said.

At the next crossing, the little man turned right again.

Then he turned left.

Then right.

'I'm not giving up now,' my mother said.

'He's disappeared!' I cried. 'Where's he gone?'

'He went in that door!' my mother said. 'I saw him! Into that house! Great heavens, it's a pub!'

It was a pub. In big letters right across the front it said THE RED LION.

'You're not going in, are you, Mummy?'

'No,' she said. 'We'll watch from outside.'

There was a big plate-glass window along the front of the pub, and although it was a bit steamy on the inside, we could see through it very well if we went close.

We stood huddled together outside the pub window. I was clutching my mother's arm. The big raindrops were making a loud noise on our umbrella. 'There he is,' I said. 'Over there.'

The room we were looking into was full of people and cigarette smoke, and our little man was in the middle of it all. He was now without his hat or coat, and he was edging his way through the crowd towards the bar. When he reached it, he placed both hands on the bar itself and spoke to the barman. I saw his lips moving as he gave his order. The barman turned away from him for a few seconds and came back with a smallish tumbler filled to the brim with light-brown liquid. The little man placed a pound note on the counter.

'That's my pound!' my mother hissed. 'By golly, he's got a nerve!'

'What's in the glass?' I asked.

'Whisky,' my mother said. 'Neat whisky.'

The barman didn't give him any change from the pound.

'That must be a treble whisky,' my mother said.

'What's a treble?' I asked.

'Three times the normal measure,' she answered.

The little man picked up the glass and put it to his lips. He tilted it gently. Then he tilted it higher . . . and higher . . . and higher . . . and very soon all the whisky had disappeared down his throat in one long pour.

'That was a jolly expensive drink,' I said.

'It's ridiculous!' my mother said. 'Fancy paying a pound for something you swallow in one go!'

'It cost him more than a pound,' I said. 'It cost him a twenty-pound silk umbrella.'

'So it did,' my mother said. 'He must be mad.'

The little man was standing by the bar with the empty glass in his hand. He was smiling now, and a sort of golden glow of pleasure was spreading over his round pink face. I saw his tongue come out to lick the white moustache, as though searching for the last drop of that precious whisky.

Slowly, he turned away from the bar and edged back through the crowd to where his hat and coat were hanging. He put on his hat. He put on his coat. Then, in a manner so superbly cool and casual that you hardly noticed anything at all, he lifted from the coat-rack one of the many wet umbrellas hanging there, and off he went.

'Did you see that!' my mother shrieked. 'Did you see what he did!'

'Ssshh!' I whispered. 'He's coming out!'

We lowered the umbrella to hide our faces, and peeped out from under it.

Out he came. But he never looked in our direction. He opened his new umbrella over his head and scurried off down the road the way he had come.

'So that's his little game!' my mother said.

'Neat,' I said. 'Super.'

We followed him back to the main street where we had first met him, and we watched him as he proceeded, with no trouble at all, to exchange his new umbrella for another pound note. This time it was with a tall thin fellow who didn't even have a coat or hat. And as soon as the transaction was completed, our little man trotted off down the

street and was lost in the crowd. But this time he went in
the opposite direction.

'You see how clever he is!' my mother said. 'He never
goes to the same pub twice!'

'He could go on doing this all night,' I said.

'Yes,' my mother said. 'Of course. But I'll bet he prays
like mad for rainy days.'

Vengeance is Mine Inc.

First published in *More Tales of
the Unexpected* (1980)

It was snowing when I woke up.

I could tell that it was snowing because there was a kind
of brightness in the room and it was quiet outside with no
footstep-noises coming up from the street and no tyre-
noises but only the engines of the cars. I looked up and I
saw George over by the window in his green dressing-
gown, bending over the paraffin-stove, making the coffee.

'Snowing,' I said.

'It's cold,' George answered. 'It's really cold.'

I got out of bed and fetched the morning paper from
outside the door. It was cold all right and I ran back quickly
and jumped into bed and lay still for a while under the
bedclothes, holding my hands tight between my legs for
warmth.

'No letters?' George said.

'No. No letters.'

'Doesn't look as if the old man's going to cough up.'

'Maybe he thinks four hundred and fifty is enough for
one month,' I said.

'He's never been to New York. He doesn't know the
cost of living here.'

'You shouldn't have spent it all in one week.'

George stood up and looked at me. '*We* shouldn't have spent it, you mean.'

'That's right,' I said. 'We.' I began reading the paper.

The coffee was ready now and George brought the pot over and put it on the table between our beds. 'A person can't live without money,' he said. 'The old man ought to know that.' He got back into his bed without taking off his green dressing-gown. I went on reading. I finished the racing page and the football page and then I started on Lionel Pantaloon, the great political and society columnist. I always read Pantaloon – same as the other twenty or thirty million people in the country. He's a habit with me; he's more than a habit; he's a part of my morning, like three cups of coffee, or shaving.

'This fellow's got a nerve,' I said.

'Who?'

'This Lionel Pantaloon.'

'What's he saying now?'

'Same sort of thing he's always saying. Same sort of scandal. Always about the rich. Listen to this: "... seen at the Penguin Club ... banker William S. Womberg with beauteous starlet Theresa Williams ... three nights running ... Mrs Womberg at home with a headache ... which is something anyone's wife would have if hubby was out squiring Miss Williams of an evening ..."'

'That fixes Womberg,' George said.

'I think it's a shame,' I said. 'That sort of thing could cause a divorce. How can this Pantaloon get away with stuff like that?'

'He always does, they're all scared of him. But if I was William S. Womberg,' George said, 'you know what I'd do? I'd go right out and punch this Lionel Pantaloon right on the nose. Why, that's the only way to handle those guys.'

'Mr Womberg couldn't do that.'

'Why not?'

'Because he's an old man,' I said. 'Mr Womberg is a dignified and respectable old man. He's a very prominent banker in the town. He couldn't possibly . . .'

And then it happened. Suddenly, from nowhere, the idea came. It came to me right in the middle of what I was saying to George and I stopped short and I could feel the idea itself kind of flowing into my brain and I kept very quiet and let it come and it kept on coming and almost before I knew what had happened I had it all, the whole plan, the whole brilliant magnificent plan worked out clearly in my head; and right then I knew it was a beauty.

I turned and I saw George staring at me with a look of wonder on his face. 'What's wrong?' he said. 'What's the matter?'

I kept quite calm. I reached out and got some more coffee before I allowed myself to speak.

'George,' I said, and I still kept calm. 'I have an idea. Now listen very carefully because I have an idea which will make us both very rich. We are broke, are we not?'

'We are.'

'And this William S. Womberg,' I said; 'would you consider that he is angry with Lionel Pantaloon this morning?'

'Angry!' George shouted. 'Angry! Why, he'll be madder than hell!'

'Quite so. And do you think that he would like to see Lionel Pantaloon receive a good hard punch on the nose?'

'Damn right he would!'

'And now tell me, is it not possible that Mr Womberg would be prepared to pay a sum of money to someone who would undertake to perform this nose-punching operation efficiently and discreetly on his behalf?'

George turned and looked at me, and gently, carefully, he put down his coffee-cup on the table. A slowly widening smile began to spread across his face. 'I get you,' he said. 'I get the idea.'

'That's just a little part of the idea. If you read Pantaloon's column here you will see that there is another person who has been insulted today.' I picked up the paper. 'There is a Mrs Ella Gimple, a prominent socialite who has perhaps a million dollars in the bank . . .'

'What does Pantaloon say about her?'

I looked at the paper again. 'He hints,' I answered, 'at how she makes a stack of money out of her own friends by throwing roulette parties and acting as the bank.'

'That fixes Gimple,' George said. 'And Womberg. Gimple and Womberg.' He was sitting up straight in bed waiting for me to go on.

'Now,' I said, 'we have two different people both loathing Lionel Pantaloon's guts this morning, both wanting desperately to go out and punch him on the nose, and neither of them daring to do it. You understand that?'

'Absolutely.'

'So much then,' I said, 'for Lionel Pantaloon. But don't forget that there are others like him. There are dozens of other columnists who spend their time insulting wealthy and important people. There's Harry Weyman, Claude Taylor, Jacob Swinski, Walter Kennedy, and all the rest of them.'

'That's right,' George said. 'That's absolutely right.'

'I'm telling you, there's nothing that makes the rich so furious as being mocked and insulted in the newspapers.'

'Go on,' George said. 'Go on.'

'All right. Now this is the plan.' I was getting rather excited myself. I was leaning over the side of the bed, resting one hand on the little table, waving the other about in the air as I spoke. 'We will set up immediately an organization and we will call it . . . what shall we call it . . . we will call it . . . let me see . . . we will call it "Vengeance Is Mine Inc." . . . How about that?'

'Peculiar name.'

'It's biblical. It's good. I like it. "Vengeance Is Mine Inc." It sounds fine. And we will have little cards printed which we will send to all our clients reminding them that they have been insulted and mortified in public and offering to punish the offender in consideration of a sum of money. We will buy all the newspapers and read all the columnists and every day we will send out a dozen or more of our cards to prospective clients.'

'It's marvellous!' George shouted. 'It's terrific!'

'We shall be rich,' I told him. 'We shall be exceedingly wealthy in no time at all.'

'We must start at once!'

I jumped out of bed, fetched a writing-pad and a pencil and ran back to bed again. 'Now,' I said, pulling my knees under the blankets and propping the writing-pad against them, 'the first thing is to decide what we're going to say on the printed cards which we'll be sending to our clients,' and I wrote, 'VENGEANCE IS MINE INC.' as a heading on top of the sheet of paper. Then, with much care, I composed a finely phrased letter explaining the functions of the organization. It finished up with the following sentence: '*Therefore VENGEANCE IS MINE INC. will undertake, on your behalf and in absolute confidence, to administer suitable punishment to columnist .... and in this regard we respectfully submit to you a choice of methods (together with prices) for your consideration.*'

'What do you mean, "a choice of methods"?' George said.

'We must give them a choice. We must think up a number of things ... a number of different punishments. Number one will be ...' and I wrote down, '*1. Punch him on the nose, once, hard.* What shall we charge for that?'

'Five hundred dollars,' George said instantly.

I wrote it down. 'What's the next one?'

'Black his eye,' George said.

I wrote down, '*2. Black his eye ... $500.*'

'No!' George said. 'I disagree with the price. It definitely requires more skill and timing to black an eye nicely than to punch a nose. It is a skilled job. It should be six hundred.'

'OK,' I said. 'Six hundred. And what's the next one?'

'Both together, of course. The old one two.' We were in George's territory now. This was right up his street.

'Both together?'

'Absolutely. Punch his nose *and* black his eye. Eleven hundred dollars.'

'There should be a reduction for taking the two,' I said. 'We'll make it a thousand.'

'It's dirt cheap,' George said. 'They'll snap it up.'

'What's next?'

We were both silent now, concentrating fiercely. Three deep parallel grooves of wrinkled skin appeared upon George's rather low sloping forehead. He began to scratch his scalp, slowly but very strongly. I looked away and tried to think of all the terrible things which people had done to other people. Finally I got one, and with George watching the point of my pencil moving over the paper, I wrote:

'*4. Put a rattlesnake (with venom extracted) on the floor of his car, by the pedals, when he parks it.*'

'Jesus Christ!' George whispered. 'You want to kill him with fright!'

'Sure,' I said.

'And where'd you get a rattlesnake, anyway?'

'Buy it. You can always buy them. How much shall we charge for that one?'

'Fifteen hundred dollars,' George said firmly. I wrote it down.

'Now we need one more.'

'Here it is,' George said. 'Kidnap him in a car, take all his clothes away except his underpants and his shoes and socks, then dump him out on Fifth Avenue in the rush hour.' He smiled, a broad triumphant smile.

'We can't do that.'

'Write it down. And charge two thousand five hundred

bucks. You'd do it all right if old Womberg were to offer you that much.'

'Yes,' I said. 'I suppose I would.' And I wrote it down. 'That's enough now,' I added. 'That gives them a wide choice.'

'And where will we get the cards printed?' George asked.

'George Karnoffsky,' I said. 'Another George. He's a friend of mine. Runs a small printing shop down on Third Avenue. Does wedding invitations and things like that for the big stores. He'll do it. I know he will.'

'Then what are we waiting for?'

We both leaped out of bed and began to dress. 'It's twelve o'clock,' I said. 'If we hurry we'll catch him before he goes to lunch.'

It was still snowing when we went out into the street and the snow was four or five inches thick on the side-walk, but we covered the fourteen blocks to Karnoffsky's shop at a tremendous pace and we arrived there just as he was putting on his coat to go out.

'Claude!' he shouted. 'Hi boy! How you been keeping?' and he pumped my hand. He had a fat friendly face and a terrible nose with great wide-open nose-wings which overlapped his cheeks by at least an inch on either side. I greeted him and told him that we had come to discuss some most urgent business. He took off his coat and led us back into the office; then I began to tell him about our plans and what we wanted him to do.

When I'd got about quarter way through my story, he started to roar with laughter and it was impossible for me to continue; so I cut it short and handed him the piece of paper with the stuff on it that we wanted him to print. And now, as he read it, his whole body began to shake with laughter and he kept slapping the desk with his hand and coughing and choking and roaring like someone crazy. We sat watching him. We didn't see anything particular to laugh about.

Finally he quietened down and he took out a handkerchief and made a great business about wiping his eyes. 'Never laughed so much,' he said weakly. 'That's a great joke, that is. It's worth a lunch. Come on out and I'll give you lunch.'

'Look,' I said severely, 'this isn't any joke. There is nothing to laugh at. You are witnessing the birth of a new and powerful organization . . .'

'Come on,' he said and he began to laugh again. 'Come on and have lunch.'

'When can you get those cards printed?' I said. My voice was stern and businesslike.

He paused and stared at us. 'You mean . . . you really mean . . . you're serious about this thing?'

'Absolutely. You are witnessing the birth . . .'

'All right,' he said, 'all right.' He stood up. 'I think you're crazy and you'll get in trouble. Sure as hell you'll get in trouble. Those boys like messing other people about, but they don't much fancy being messed about themselves.'

'When can you get them printed, and without any of your workers reading them?'

'For this,' he answered gravely, 'I will give up my lunch. I will set the type myself. It is the least I can do.' He laughed again and the rims of his huge nostrils twitched with pleasure. 'How many do you want?'

'A thousand – to start with, and envelopes.'

'Come back at two o'clock,' he said and I thanked him very much and as we went out we could hear his laughter rumbling down the passage into the back of the shop.

At exactly two o'clock we were back. George Karnoffsky was in his office and the first thing I saw as we went in was the high stack of printed cards on his desk in front of him. They were large cards, about twice the size of ordinary wedding or cocktail invitation-cards. 'There you are,' he said. 'All ready for you.' The fool was still laughing.

He handed us each a card and I examined mine carefully. It was a beautiful thing. He had obviously taken much trouble over it. The card itself was thick and stiff with narrow gold edging all the way around, and the letters of the heading were exceedingly elegant. I cannot reproduce it here in all its splendour, but I can at least show you how it read:

VENGEANCE IS MINE INC.

Dear ....

You have probably seen columnist ....'s slanderous and unprovoked attack upon your character in today's paper. It is an outrageous insinuation, a deliberate distortion of the truth.

Are you yourself prepared to allow this miserable malice-monger to insult you in this manner without doing anything about it?

673

The whole world knows that it is foreign to the nature of the American people to permit themselves to be insulted either in public or in private without rising up in righteous indignation and demanding – nay, exacting – a just measure of retribution.

On the other hand, it is only natural that a citizen of your standing and reputation will not wish *personally* to become further involved in this sordid petty affair, or indeed to have any *direct* contact whatsoever with this vile person.

How then are you to obtain satisfaction?

The answer is simple. VENGEANCE IS MINE INC. will obtain it for you. We will undertake, on your behalf and in absolute confidence, to administer individual punishment to columnist ...., and in this regard we respectfully submit to you a choice of methods (together with prices) for your consideration:

1. Punch him on the nose, once, hard $500
2. Black his eye $600
3. Punch him on the nose and black his eye $1000
4. Introduce a rattlesnake (with venom extracted) into his car, on the floor by the pedals, when he parks it $1500
5. Kidnap him, take all his clothes away except his underpants, his shoes and socks, then dump him out on Fifth Ave. in the rush hour $2500

This work executed by a professional.

If you desire to avail yourself of any of these offers, kindly reply to VENGEANCE IS MINE INC. at the address indicated upon the enclosed slip of paper. If it is practicable, you will be notified in advance of the place where the action will occur and of the time, so that you may, if you wish, watch the proceedings in person from a safe and anonymous distance.

No payment need be made until after your order has been satisfactorily executed, when an account will be rendered in the usual manner.

George Karnoffsky had done a beautiful job of printing. 'Claude,' he said, 'you like?'

'It's marvellous.'

'It's the best I could do for you. It's like in the war when I would see soldiers going off perhaps to get killed and all the time I would want to be giving them things and doing things for them.' He was beginning to laugh again, so I said, 'We'd better be going now. Have you got large envelopes for these cards?'

'Everything is here. And you can pay me when the money starts coming in.' That seemed to set him off worse than ever and he collapsed into his chair, giggling like a fool. George and I hurried out of the shop into the street, into the cold snow-falling afternoon.

We almost ran the distance back to our room and on the way up I borrowed a Manhattan telephone directory from the public telephone in the hall. We found 'Womberg, William S.' without any trouble and while I read out the address – somewhere up in the East Nineties – George wrote it on one of the envelopes.

'Gimple, Mrs Ella H.' was also in the book and we addressed an envelope to her as well. 'We'll just send to Womberg and Gimple today,' I said. 'We haven't really got started yet. Tomorrow we'll send a dozen.'

'We'd better catch the next post,' George said.

'We'll deliver them by hand,' I told him. 'Now, at once. The sooner they get them the better. Tomorrow might be too late. They won't be half so angry tomorrow as they are today. People are apt to cool off through the night. See here,' I said, 'you go ahead and deliver those two cards right away. While you're doing that I'm going to snoop around the town and try to find out something about the habits of Lionel Pantaloon. See you back here later in the evening . . .'

At about nine o'clock that evening I returned and found George lying on his bed smoking cigarettes and drinking coffee.

'I delivered them both,' he said. 'Just slipped them through the letter-boxes and rang the bells and beat it up the street. Womberg had a huge house, a huge white house. How did you get on?'

'I went to see a man I know who works in the sports section of the *Daily Mirror*. He told me all.'

'What did he tell you?'

'He said Pantaloon's movements are more or less routine. He operates at night, but wherever he goes earlier in the evening, he *always* – and this is the important point – he *always* finishes up at the Penguin Club. He gets there round about midnight and stays until two or two thirty. That's when his legmen bring him all the dope.'

'That's all we want to know,' George said happily.

'It's too easy.'

'Money for old rope.'

There was a full bottle of blended whisky in the cupboard and George fetched it out. For the next two hours we sat upon our beds drinking the whisky and making wonderful and complicated plans for the development of our organization. By eleven o'clock we were employing a staff of fifty, including twelve famous pugilists, and our offices were in the Rockefeller Center. Towards midnight we had obtained control over all columnists and were dictating their daily columns to them by telephone from our headquarters, taking care to insult and infuriate at least twenty rich persons in one part of the country or another every day. We were immensely wealthy and George had a British Bentley, I had five Cadillacs. George kept practising telephone talks with Lionel Pantaloon. 'That you, Pantaloon?' 'Yes, sir.' 'Well, listen here. I think your column stinks today. It's lousy.' 'I'm very sorry, sir. I'll try to do better tomorrow.' 'Damn right you'll do better, Pantaloon. Matter of fact we've been thinking about getting someone else to take over.' 'But please, please sir, just give me another chance.' 'OK, Pantaloon, but this is the last. And by the way, the boys are putting a rattlesnake in your car tonight, on behalf of Mr Hiram C. King, the soap manufacturer. Mr King will be watching from across the street so don't forget to act scared when you see it.' 'Yes, sir, of course, sir. I won't forget, sir . . .'

When we finally went to bed and the light was out, I could still hear George giving hell to Pantaloon on the telephone.

The next morning we were both woken up by the church clock on the corner striking nine. George got up and went to the door to get the papers and when he came back he was holding a letter in his hand.

'Open it!' I said.

He opened it and carefully he unfolded a single sheet of thin notepaper.

'Read it!' I shouted.

He began to read it aloud, his voice low and serious at first but rising gradually to a high, almost hysterical shout of triumph as the full meaning of the letter was revealed to him. It said:

'Your methods appear curiously unorthodox. At the same time anything you do to that scoundrel has my approval. So go ahead. Start with Item I, and if you are successful I'll be only too glad to give you an order to work right on through the list. Send the bill to me, William S. Womberg.'

I recollect that in the excitement of the moment we did a kind of dance around the room in our pyjamas, praising Mr Womberg in loud voices and singing that we were rich. George turned somersaults on his bed and it is possible that I did the same.

'When shall we do it?' he said. 'Tonight?'

I paused before replying. I refused to be rushed. The pages of history are filled with the names of great men who have come to grief by permitting themselves to make hasty decisions in the excitement of a moment. I put on my dressing-gown, lit a cigarette and began to pace up and down the room. 'There is no hurry,' I said. 'Womberg's order can be dealt with in due course. But first of all we must send out today's cards.'

I dressed quickly, went out to the newsstand across the street, bought one copy of every daily paper there was and returned to our room. The next two hours were spent in reading the columnists' columns, and in the end we had a list of eleven people – eight men and three women – all of whom had been insulted in one way or another by one of the columnists that morning. Things were going well. We were working smoothly. It took us only another half-hour to look up the addresses of the insulted ones – two we couldn't find – and to address the envelopes.

In the afternoon we delivered them, and at about six in the evening we got back to our room, tired but triumphant. We made coffee and we fried hamburgers and we had supper in bed. Then we re-read Womberg's letter aloud to each other many many times.

'What he's doing he's giving us an order for six thousand one hundred dollars,' George said. 'Items 1 to 5 inclusive.'

'It's not a bad beginning. Not bad for the first day. Six thousand a day works out at . . . let me see . . . it's nearly two million dollars a year, not counting Sundays. A million each. It's more than Betty Grable.'

'We are very wealthy people,' George said. He smiled, a slow and wondrous smile of pure contentment.

'In a day or two we will move to a suite of rooms at the St Regis.'

'I think the Waldorf,' George said.

'All right, the Waldorf. And later on we might as well take a house.'

'One like Womberg's?'

'All right. One like Womberg's. But first,' I said, 'we have work to do. Tomorrow we shall deal with Pantaloon. We will catch him as he comes out of the Penguin Club. At 2.30 a.m. we will be waiting for him, and when he comes out into the street you will step forward and you will punch him once, hard, right upon the point of the nose as per contract.'

'It will be a pleasure,' George said. 'It will be a real pleasure. But how do we get away? Do we run?'

'We shall hire a car for an hour. We have just enough money left for that, and I shall be sitting at the wheel with the engine running, not ten yards away, and the door will be open and when you've punched him you'll just jump back into the car and we'll be gone.'

'It is perfect. I shall punch him very hard.' George paused. He clenched his right fist and examined his knuckles. Then he smiled again and he said slowly, 'This nose of his, is it not possible that it will afterwards be so much blunted that it will no longer poke well into other people's business?'

'It is quite possible,' I answered, and with that happy thought in our minds we switched out the light and went early to sleep.

The next morning I was woken by a shout and I sat up and saw George standing at the foot of my bed in his pyjamas, waving his arms. 'Look!' he shouted. 'There are four! There are four!' I looked, and indeed there were four letters in his hand.

'Open them. Quickly, open them.'

The first one he read aloud: ' *"Dear Vengeance Is Mine Inc., That's the best proposition I've had in years. Go right ahead and give Mr Jacob Swinski the rattlesnake treatment (Item 4). But I'll be glad to pay double if you'll forget to extract the poison from its fangs. Yours Gertrude Porter-Vandervelt. P.S. You'd better insure the snake. That guy's bite carries more poison than any rattler's."* '

George read the second one aloud: ' *"My cheque for $500 is made out and lies before me on my desk. The moment I receive proof that you have punched Lionel Pantaloon hard on the nose, it will be posted to you. I should prefer a fracture, if possible. Yours etc. Wilbur H. Gollogly.'* "

George read the third one aloud: ' *"In my present frame of mind and against my better judgement, I am tempted to reply to your card and to request that you deposit that scoundrel Walter Kennedy upon Fifth Avenue dressed only in his underwear. I make the proviso that there shall be snow upon the ground at the time and that the temperature shall be sub-zero. H. Gresham."* '

The fourth one also he read aloud: ' *"A good hard sock on the nose for Pantaloon is worth five hundred of mine or anyone else's money. I should like to watch. Yours sincerely, Claudia Calthorpe Hines."* '

George laid the letters down gently, carefully, upon the bed. For a while there was silence. We stared at each other, too astonished, too happy to speak. I began to calculate the value of those four orders in terms of money.

'That's five thousand dollars' worth,' I said softly.

Upon George's face there was a huge bright grin. 'Claude,' he said, 'should we not move now to the Waldorf?'

'Soon,' I answered, 'but at the moment we have no time for moving. We have not even time to send out any fresh cards today. We must start to execute the orders we have in hand. We are overwhelmed with work.'

'Should we not engage extra staff and enlarge our organization?'

'Later,' I said. 'Even for that there is no time today. Just think what we have to do. We have to put a rattlesnake in Jacob Swinski's car . . . we have to dump Walter Kennedy on Fifth Avenue in his underpants . . . we have to punch Pantaloon on the nose . . . let me see . . . yes, for three different people we have to punch Pantaloon . . .'

I stopped. I closed my eyes. I sat still. Again I became conscious of a small clear stream of inspiration flowing into the tissues of my brain. 'I have it!' I shouted. 'I have it! I have it! Three birds with one stone! Three customers with one punch!'

'How?'

'Don't you see? We only need to punch Pantaloon once and each of the three customers . . . Womberg, Gollogly and Claudia Hines . . . will think it's being done specially for him or her.'

'Say it again.' I said it again.

'It's brilliant.'

'It's common sense. And the same principle will apply to the others. The rattlesnake treatment and the other one can wait until we have more orders. Perhaps in a few days we shall have ten orders for rattlesnakes in Swinski's car. Then we will do them all in one go.'

'It's wonderful.'

'This evening then,' I said, 'we will handle Pantaloon. But first we must hire a car. Also we must send telegrams, one to Womberg, one to Gollogly and one to Claudia Hines, telling them where and when the punching will take place.'

We dressed rapidly and went out.

In a dirty silent little garage down on East 9th Street we managed to hire a car, a 1934 Chevrolet, eight dollars for the evening. We then sent three telegrams, each one identical and cunningly worded to conceal its true meaning from inquisitive people: *Hope to see you outside Penguin Club 2.30 a.m. Regards V.I. Mine.*

'There is one thing more,' I said. 'It is essential that you should be disguised. Pantaloon, or the doorman, for example, must not be able to identify you afterwards. You must wear a false moustache.'

'What about you?'

'Not necessary. I'll be sitting in the car. They won't see me.'

We went to a children's toy-shop and we bought for George a magnificent black moustache, a thing with long pointed ends, waxed and stiff and shining, and when he held it up against his face he looked exactly like the Kaiser of Germany. The man in the shop also sold us a tube of glue and he showed us how the moustache should be attached to the upper lip. 'Going to have fun with the kids?' he asked, and George said, 'Absolutely.'

All was now ready; but there was a long time to wait. We had three dollars left between us and with this we bought a sandwich each and then went to a movie. Then, at eleven o'clock that evening, we collected our car and in it we began to cruise slowly through the streets of New York waiting for the time to pass.

'You'd better put on your moustache so as you get used to it.'

We pulled up under a street-lamp and I squeezed some glue on to George's upper lip and fixed on the huge black hairy thing with its pointed ends. Then we drove on. It was cold in the car and outside it was beginning to snow again. I could see a few small snowflakes falling through the beams of the car-lights. George kept saying, 'How hard shall I hit him?' and I kept answering, 'Hit him as hard as you can, and on the nose. It must be on the nose because that is a part of the contract. Everything must be done right. Our clients may be watching.'

At two in the morning we drove slowly past the entrance to the Penguin Club in order to survey the situation. 'I will park there,' I said, 'just past the entrance in that patch of dark. But I will leave the door open for you.'

We drove on. Then George said, 'What does he look like? How do I know it's him?'

'Don't worry,' I answered. 'I've thought of that,' and I took from my pocket a piece of paper and handed it to him. 'You take this and fold it up small and give it to the doorman and tell him to see it gets to Pantaloon quickly. Act as though you are scared to death and in an awful hurry. It's a hundred to one Pantaloon will come out. No columnist could resist that message.'

On the paper I had written: *I am a worker in Soviet Con-*

sulate. Come to the door very quickly please I have something to tell but come quickly as I am in danger. I cannot come in to you.'

'You see,' I said, 'your moustache will make you look like a Russian. All Russians have big moustaches.'

George took the paper and folded it up very small and held it in his fingers. It was nearly half past two in the morning now and we began to drive towards the Penguin Club.

'You all set?' I said.

'Yes.'

'We're going in now. Here we come. I'll park just past the entrance . . . here. Hit him hard,' I said, and George opened the door and got out of the car. I closed the door behind him but I leaned over and kept my hand on the handle so I could open it again quick, and I let down the window so I could watch. I kept the engine ticking over.

I saw George walk swiftly up to the doorman who stood under the red and white canopy which stretched out over the sidewalk. I saw the doorman turn and look down at George and I didn't like the way he did it. He was a tall proud man dressed in a fine magenta-coloured uniform with gold buttons and gold shoulders and a broad white stripe down each magenta trouser-leg. Also he wore white gloves and he stood there looking proudly down at George, frowning, pressing his lips together hard. He was looking at George's moustache and I thought, Oh my God, we have overdone it. We have overdisguised him. He's going to know it's false and he's going to take one of the long pointed ends in his fingers and then he'll give it a tweak and it'll come off. But he didn't. He was distracted by George's acting, for George was acting well. I could see him hopping about, clasping and unclasping his hands, swaying his body and shaking his head, and I could hear him saying, 'Plees plees plees you must hurry. It is life and teth. Plees plees take it kvick to Mr Pantaloon.' His Russian accent was not like any accent I had heard before, but all the same there was a quality of real despair in his voice.

Finally, gravely, proudly, the doorman said, 'Give me the note.' George gave it to him and said, 'Tank you, tank you, but say it is urgent,' and the doorman disappeared inside. In a few moments he returned and said, 'It's being delivered now.' George paced nervously up and down. I waited, watching the door. Three or four minutes elapsed. George wrung his hands and said, 'Vere is he? Vere is he? Plees to go see if he is not coming!'

'What's the matter with you?' the doorman said. Now he was looking at George's moustache again.

'It is life and teth! Mr Pantaloon can help! He must come!'

'Why don't you shut up?' the doorman said, but he opened the door again and he poked his head inside and I heard him saying something to someone.

To George he said, 'They say he's coming now.'

A moment later the door opened and Pantaloon himself, small and dapper, stepped out. He paused by the door, looking quickly from side to side like a nervous inquisitive ferret. The doorman touched his cap and pointed at George. I heard Pantaloon say, 'Yes, what did you want?'

George said, 'Plees, dis vay a leetle so as novone can hear,' and he led Pantaloon along the pavement, away from the doorman and towards the car.

'Come on, now,' Pantaloon said. 'What is it you want?'

Suddenly George shouted 'Look!' and he pointed up the street. Pantaloon turned his head and as he did so George swung his right arm and he hit Pantaloon plumb on the point of the nose. I saw George leaning forward on the punch, all his weight behind it, and the whole of Pantaloon appeared somehow to lift slightly off the ground and to float backwards for two or three feet until the façade of the Penguin Club stopped him. All this happened very quickly, and then George was in the car beside me and we were off and I could hear the doorman blowing a whistle behind us.

'We've done it!' George gasped. He was excited and out of breath. 'I hit him good! Did you see how good I hit him!'

It was snowing hard now and I drove fast and made many sudden turnings and I knew no one would catch us in this snowstorm.

'Son of a bitch almost went through the wall I hit him so hard.'

'Well done, George,' I said. 'Nice work, George.'

'And did you see him lift? Did you see him lift right up off the ground?'

'Womberg will be pleased,' I said.

'And Gollogly, and the Hines woman.'

'They'll all be pleased,' I said. 'Watch the money coming in.'

'There's a car behind us!' George shouted. 'It's following us! It's right on our tail! Drive like mad!'

'Impossible!' I said. 'They couldn't have picked us up already. It's just another car going somewhere.' I turned sharply to the right.

'He's still with us,' George said. 'Keep turning. We'll lose him soon.'

'How the hell can we lose a police-car in a 1934 Chev,' I said. 'I'm going to stop.'

'Keep going!' George shouted. 'You're doing fine.'

'I'm going to stop,' I said. 'It'll only make them mad if we go on.'

George protested fiercely but I knew it was no good and I pulled in to the side of the road. The other car swerved out and went past us and skidded to a standstill in front of us.

'Quick,' George said. 'Let's beat it.' He had the door open and he was ready to run.

'Don't be a fool,' I said. 'Stay where you are. You can't get away now.'

A voice from outside said, 'All right, boys, what's the hurry?'

'No hurry,' I answered. 'We're just going home.'

'Yea?'

'Oh yes, we're just on our way home now.'

The man poked his head in through the window on my side, and he looked at me, then at George, then at me again.

'It's a nasty night,' George said. 'We're just trying to reach home before the streets get all snowed up.'

'Well,' the man said, 'you can take it easy. I just thought I'd like to give you this right away.' He dropped a wad of banknotes on to my lap. 'I'm Gollogly,' he added, 'Wilbur H. Gollogly,' and he stood out there in the snow grinning at us, stamping his feet and rubbing his hands to keep them warm. 'I got your wire and I watched the whole thing from across the street. You did a fine job. I'm paying you double. It was worth it. Funniest thing I ever seen. Goodbye, boys. Watch your steps. They'll be after you now. Get out of town if I were you. Goodbye.' And before we could say anything, he was gone.

When finally we got back to our room I started packing at once.

'You crazy?' George said. 'We've only got to wait a few hours and we receive five hundred dollars each from Womberg and the Hines woman. Then we'll have two thousand altogether and we can go anywhere we want.'

So we spent the next day waiting in our room and reading the papers, one of which had a whole column on the front page headed, 'Brutal assault on famous columnist'. But sure enough the late afternoon post brought us two letters and there was five hundred dollars in each.

And right now, at this moment, we are sitting in a Pullman car, drinking Scotch whisky and heading south for a place where there is always sunshine and where the horses are running every day. We are immensely wealthy and George keeps saying that if we put the whole of our two thousand dollars on a horse at ten to one we shall make another twenty thousand and we will be able to retire. 'We will have a house at Palm Beach,' he says, 'and we will

entertain upon a lavish scale. Beautiful socialites will loll
around the edge of our swimming pool sipping cool
drinks, and after a while we will perhaps put another large
sum of money upon another horse and we shall become
wealthier still. Possibly we will become tired of Palm
Beach and then we will move around in a leisurely manner
among the playgrounds of the rich. Monte Carlo and
places like that. Like the Ali Khan and the Duke of Windsor. We will become prominent members of the
international set and film stars will smile at us and head-
waiters will bow to us and perhaps, in time to come,
perhaps we might even get ourselves mentioned in Lionel
Pantaloon's column.'

'That would be something,' I said.

'Wouldn't it just,' he answered happily. 'Wouldn't that
just be something.'

Mr Botibol

First published in *More Tales of
the Unexpected* (1980)

Mr Botibol pushed his way through the revolving doors
and emerged into the large foyer of the hotel. He took off
his hat, and holding it in front of him with both hands, he
advanced nervously a few paces, paused and stood looking around him, searching the faces of the lunchtime
crowd. Several people turned and stared at him in mild
astonishment, and he heard – or he thought he heard – at
least one woman's voice saying, 'My dear, *do* look what's
just come in!'

At last he spotted Mr Clements sitting at a small table
in the far corner, and he hurried over to him. Clements
had seen him coming, and now, as he watched Mr Botibol
threading his way cautiously between the tables and the
people, walking on his toes in such a meek and self-effacing
manner and clutching his hat before him with both hands,
he thought how wretched it must be for any man to look
as conspicuous and as odd as this Botibol. He resembled,
to an extraordinary degree, an asparagus. His long narrow
stalk did not appear to have any shoulders at all; it merely
tapered upwards, growing gradually narrower and narrower until it came to a kind of point at the top of the
small bald head. He was tightly encased in a shiny blue
double-breasted suit, and this, for some curious reason,

accentuated the illusion of a vegetable to a preposterous degree.

Clements stood up, they shook hands, and then at once, even before they had sat down again, Mr Botibol said, 'I have decided, yes I have decided to accept the offer which you made to me before you left my office last night.'

For some days Clements had been negotiating, on behalf of clients, for the purchase of the firm known as Botibol & Co., of which Mr Botibol was sole owner, and the night before, Clements had made his first offer. This was merely an exploratory, much-too-low bid, a kind of signal to the seller that the buyers were seriously interested. And by God, thought Clements, the poor fool has gone and accepted it. He nodded gravely many times in an effort to hide his astonishment, and he said, 'Good, good. I'm so glad to hear that, Mr Botibol.' Then he signalled a waiter and said, 'Two large martinis.'

'No, please!' Mr Botibol lifted both hands in horrified protest.

'Come on,' Clements said. 'This is an occasion.'

'I drink very little, and never, no, never during the middle of the day.'

But Clements was in a gay mood now and he took no notice. He ordered the martinis and when they came along Mr Botibol was forced, by the banter and good humour of the other, to drink to the deal which had just been concluded. Clements then spoke briefly about the drawing up and signing of documents, and when all that had been arranged, he called for two more cocktails. Again Mr Botibol protested, but not quite so vigorously this time, and

Clements ordered the drinks and then he turned and smiled at the other man in a friendly way. 'Well, Mr Botibol,' he said, 'now that it's all over, I suggest we have a pleasant non-business lunch together. What d'you say to that? And it's on me.'

'As you wish, as you wish,' Mr Botibol answered without any enthusiasm. He had a small melancholy voice and a way of pronouncing each word separately and slowly, as though he was explaining something to a child.

When they went into the dining-room Clements ordered a bottle of Lafite 1912 and a couple of plump roast partridges to go with it. He had already calculated in his head the amount of his commission and he was feeling fine. He began to make bright conversation, switching smoothly from one subject to another in the hope of touching on something that might interest his guest. But it was no good. Mr Botibol appeared to be only half listening. Every now and then he inclined his small bald head a little to one side or the other and said, 'Indeed.' When the wine came along Clements tried to have a talk about that.

'I am sure it is excellent,' Mr Botibol said, 'but please give me only a drop.'

Clements told a funny story. When it was over, Mr Botibol regarded him solemnly for a few moments, then he said, 'How amusing.' After that Clements kept his mouth shut and they ate in silence. Mr Botibol was drinking his wine and he didn't seem to object when his host reached over and refilled his glass. By the time they had finished eating, Clements estimated privately that his guest had consumed at least three-quarters of the bottle.

'A cigar, Mr Botibol?'

'Oh no, thank you.'

'A little brandy?'

'No, really, I am not accustomed . . .' Clements noticed that the man's cheeks were slightly flushed and that his eyes had become bright and watery. Might as well get the old boy properly drunk while I'm about it, he thought, and to the waiter he said, 'Two brandies.'

When the brandies arrived, Mr Botibol looked at his large glass suspiciously for a while, then he picked it up, took one quick birdlike sip and put it down again. 'Mr Clements,' he said suddenly, 'how I envy you.'

'Me? But why?'

'I will tell you, Mr Clements, I will tell you, if I may make so bold.' There was a nervous, mouselike quality in his voice which made it seem he was apologizing for everything he said.

'Please tell me,' Clements said.

'It is because to me you appear to have made such a success of your life.'

He's going to get melancholy drunk, Clements thought. He's one of the ones that gets melancholy and I can't stand it. 'Success,' he said. 'I don't see anything especially successful about me.'

'Oh yes, indeed. Your whole life, if I may say so, Mr Clements, appears to be such a pleasant and successful thing.'

'I'm a very ordinary person,' Clements said. He was trying to figure just how drunk the other really was.

'I believe,' said Mr Botibol, speaking slowly, separating each word carefully from the other, 'I believe that the wine has gone a little to my head, but . . .' He paused, searching for words. '. . . But I do want to ask you just one question.' He had poured some salt on to the tablecloth and he was shaping it into a little mountain with the tip of one finger.

'Mr Clements,' he said without looking up, 'do you think that it is possible for a man to live to the age of fifty-two without ever during his whole life having experienced one single small success in anything that he has done?'

'My dear Mr Botibol,' Clements laughed, 'everyone has his little successes from time to time, however small they may be.'

'Oh no,' Mr Botibol said gently. 'You are wrong. I, for example, cannot remember having had a single success of any sort during my whole life.'

'Now come!' Clements said, smiling. 'That can't be true. Why only this morning you sold your business for a hundred thousand. I call that one hell of a success.'

'The business was left me by my father. When he died nine years ago, it was worth four times as much. Under my direction it has lost three-quarters of its value. You can hardly call that a success.'

Clements knew this was true. 'Yes, yes, all right,' he said. 'That may be so, but all the same you know as well as I do that every man alive has his quota of little successes. Not big ones maybe. But lots of little ones. I mean, after all, goddammit, even scoring a goal at school was a little success, a little triumph, at the time, or making some runs or learning to swim. One forgets about them, that's all. One just forgets.'

'I never scored a goal,' Mr Botibol said. 'And I never learned to swim.'

Clements threw up his hands and made exasperated noises. 'Yes, yes, I know, but don't you see, don't you see there are thousands, literally thousands of other things, things like . . . well . . . like catching a good fish, or fixing the motor of the car, or pleasing someone with a present, or growing a decent row of French beans, or winning a little bet or . . . or . . . why hell, one can go on listing them for ever!'

'Perhaps *you* can, Mr Clements, but to the best of my knowledge, I have never done any of those things. That is what I am trying to tell you.'

Clements put down his brandy glass and stared with new interest at the remarkable shoulderless person who sat facing him. He was annoyed and he didn't feel in the least sympathetic. The man didn't inspire sympathy. He was a fool. He must be a fool. A tremendous and absolute fool. Clements had a sudden desire to embarrass the man as much as he could. 'What about women, Mr Botibol?' There was no apology for the question in the tone of his voice.

'Women?'

'Yes, women! Every man under the sun, even the most wretched filthy down-and-out tramp has some time or other had some sort of silly little success with . . .'

'Never!' cried Mr Botibol with sudden vigour. 'No, sir, never!'

I'm going to hit him, Clements told himself. I can't stand this any longer and if I'm not careful I'm going to jump right up and hit him. 'You mean you don't like them?' he said.

'Oh dear me yes, of course I like them. As a matter of fact I admire them very much, very much indeed. But I'm afraid . . . oh dear me . . . I do not know quite how to say it . . . I am afraid that I do not seem to get along with them very well. I never have. Never. You see, Mr Clements, I *look* so queer. I know I do. They stare at me, and often I see them laughing at me. I have never been able to get within . . . well, within striking distance of them, as you might say.' The trace of a smile, weak and infinitely sad, flickered around the corners of his mouth.

Clements had had enough. He mumbled something about how he was sure Mr Botibol was exaggerating the situation, then he glanced at his watch, called for the bill, and said he was sorry but he would have to get back to the office.

They parted in the street outside the hotel and Mr Botibol took a cab back to his house. He opened the front door, went into the living-room and switched on the radio; then he sat down in a large leather chair, leaned back and closed his eyes. He didn't feel exactly giddy, but there was a singing in his ears and his thoughts were coming and going more quickly than usual. That solicitor gave me too much wine, he told himself. I'll stay here for a while and listen to some music and I expect I'll go to sleep and after that I'll feel better.

They were playing a symphony on the radio. Mr Botibol had always been a casual listener to symphony concerts and he knew enough to identify this as one of Beethoven's.

But now, as he lay back in his chair listening to the marvellous music, a new thought began to expand slowly within his tipsy mind. It wasn't a dream because he was not asleep. It was a clear conscious thought and it was this: I am the composer of this music. I am a great composer. This is my latest symphony and this is the first performance. The huge hall is packed with people – critics, musicians and music-lovers from all over the country – and I am up there in front of the orchestra, conducting.

Mr Botibol could see the whole thing. He could see himself up on the rostrum dressed in a white tie and tails, and before him was the orchestra, the massed violins on his left, the violas in front, the cellos on his right, and back of them were all the woodwinds and bassoons and drums and cymbals, the players watching every movement of his baton with an intense, almost a fanatical reverence. Behind him, in the half-darkness of the huge hall, was row upon row of white enraptured faces, looking up towards him, listening with growing excitement as yet another new symphony by the greatest composer the world had ever seen unfolded itself majestically before them. Some of the audience were clenching their fists and digging their nails into the palms of their hands because the music was so beautiful that they could hardly stand it. Mr Botibol became so carried away by this exciting vision that he began to swing his arms in time with the music in the manner of a conductor. He found it was such fun doing this that he decided to stand up, facing the radio, in order to give himself more freedom of movement.

He stood there in the middle of the room, tall, thin and

shoulderless, dressed in his tight blue double-breasted suit, his small bald head jerking from side to side as he waved his arms in the air. He knew the symphony well enough to be able occasionally to anticipate changes in tempo or volume, and when the music became loud and fast he beat the air so vigorously that he nearly knocked himself over, when it was soft and hushed, he leaned forward to quieten the players with gentle movements of his outstretched hands, and all the time he could feel the presence of the huge audience behind him, tense, immobile, listening. When at last the symphony swelled to its tremendous conclusion, Mr Botibol became more frenzied than ever and his face seemed to thrust itself round to one side in an agony of effort as he tried to force more and still more power from his orchestra during those final mighty chords.

Then it was over. The announcer was saying something, but Mr Botibol quickly switched off the radio and collapsed into his chair, blowing heavily.

'Phew!' he said aloud. 'My goodness gracious me, what *have* I been doing!' Small globules of sweat were oozing out all over his face and forehead, trickling down his neck inside his collar. He pulled out a handkerchief and wiped them away, and he lay there for a while, panting, exhausted, but exceedingly exhilarated.

'Well, I must say,' he gasped, still speaking aloud, 'that *was* fun. I don't know that I have ever had such fun before in all my life. My goodness, it *was* fun, it really *was*!' Almost at once he began to play with the idea of doing it again. But should he? Should he allow himself to do it again?

There was no denying that now, in retrospect, he felt a little guilty about the whole business, and soon he began to wonder whether there wasn't something downright immoral about it all. Letting himself go like that! And imagining he was a genius! It was wrong. He was sure other people didn't do it. And what if Mason had come in the middle and seen him at it! That would have been terrible!

He reached for the paper and pretended to read it, but soon he was searching furtively among the radio programmes for the evening. He put his finger under a line which said '8.30 Symphony Concert. Brahms Symphony No. 2'. He stared at it for a long time. The letters in the word 'Brahms' began to blur and recede, and gradually they disappeared altogether and were replaced by letters which spelled 'Botibol'. Botibol's Symphony No. 2. It was printed quite clearly. He was reading it now, this moment. 'Yes, yes,' he whispered. 'First performance. The world is waiting to hear it. Will it be as great, they are asking, will it perhaps be greater than his earlier work? And the composer himself has been persuaded to conduct. He is shy and retiring, hardly ever appears in public, but on this occasion he has been persuaded . . .'

Mr Botibol leaned forward in his chair and pressed the bell beside the fireplace. Mason, the butler, the only other person in the house, ancient, small and grave, appeared at the door.

'Er . . . Mason, have we any wine in the house?'

'Wine, sir?'

'Yes, wine.'

'Oh no, sir. We haven't had any wine this fifteen or sixteen years. Your father, sir . . .'

'I know, Mason, I know, but will you get some, please. I want a bottle with my dinner.'

The butler was shaken. 'Very well, sir, and what shall it be?'

'Claret, Mason. The best you can obtain. Get a case. Tell them to send it round at once.'

When he was alone again, he was momentarily appalled by the simple manner in which he had made this decision. Wine for dinner! Just like that! Well, yes, why not? Why ever not now he came to think of it? He was his own master. And anyway it was essential that he have wine. It seemed to have a good effect, a very good effect indeed. He wanted it and he was going to have it and to hell with Mason.

He rested for the remainder of the afternoon, and at seven thirty Mason announced dinner. The bottle of wine was on the table and he began to drink it. He didn't give a damn about the way Mason watched him as he refilled his glass. Three times he refilled it; then he left the table saying that he was not to be disturbed and returned to the living-room. There was quarter of an hour to wait. He could think of nothing now except the coming concert. He lay back in the chair and allowed his thoughts to wander deliciously towards eight thirty. He was the great composer waiting impatiently in his dressing-room in the concert-hall. He could hear in the distance the murmur of excitement from the crowd as they settled themselves in their seats. He knew what they were saying to each other.

Same sort of thing the newspapers had been saying for months, Botibol is a genius; greater, far greater than Beethoven or Bach or Brahms or Mozart or any of them. Each new work of his is more magnificent than the last. What will the next one be like? We can hardly wait to hear it! Oh yes, he knew what they were saying. He stood up and began to pace the room. It was nearly time now. He seized a pencil from the table to use as a baton, then he switched on the radio. The announcer had just finished the preliminaries and suddenly there was a burst of applause, which meant that the conductor was coming on to the platform. The previous concert in the afternoon had been from gramophone records, but this one was the real thing. Mr Botibol turned around, faced the fireplace and bowed graciously from the waist. Then he turned back to the radio and lifted his baton. The clapping stopped. There was a moment's silence. Someone in the audience coughed. Mr Botibol waited. The symphony began.

Once again, as he began to conduct, he could see clearly before him the whole orchestra and the faces of the players and even the expressions on their faces. Three of the violinists had grey hair. One of the cellists was very fat, another wore heavy brown-rimmed glasses, and there was a man in the second row playing a horn who had a twitch on one side of his face, but they were all magnificent. And so was the music. During certain impressive passages Mr Botibol experienced a feeling of exultation so powerful that it made him cry out for joy, and once during the Third Movement, a little shiver of ecstasy radiated spontaneously from his solar plexus and moved downwards over the skin of his stomach like needles. But the thunderous applause and the cheering which came at the end of the symphony was the most splendid thing of all. He turned slowly towards the fireplace and bowed. The clapping continued and he went on bowing until at last the noise died away and the announcer's voice jerked him suddenly back into the living-room. He switched off the radio and collapsed into his chair, exhausted but very happy.

As he lay there, smiling with pleasure, wiping his wet face, panting for breath, he was already making plans for his next performance. But why not do it properly? Why not convert one of the rooms into a sort of concert-hall and have a stage and rows of chairs and do the thing properly? And have a gramophone so that one could perform at any time without having to rely on the radio programme. Yes, by heavens, he would do it!

The next morning Mr Botibol arranged with a firm of decorators that the largest room in the house be converted into a miniature concert-hall. There was to be a raised stage at one end and the rest of the floor-space was to be filled with rows of red plush seats. 'I'm going to have some little concerts here,' he told the man from the firm, and the man nodded and said that would be very nice. At the same time he ordered a radio shop to install an expensive self-changing gramophone with two powerful amplifiers, one on the stage, the other at the back of the auditorium. When he had done this, he went off and bought all of Beethoven's nine symphonies on gramophone records; and from a place which specialized in recorded sound effects he ordered several records of clapping and applauding by enthusiastic audiences. Finally he bought himself a conductor's baton, a slim ivory stick which lay in a case lined with blue silk.

In eight days the room was ready. Everything was perfect: the red chairs, the aisle down the centre and even a little dais on the platform with a brass rail running round it for the conductor. Mr Botibol decided to give the first concert that evening after dinner.

At seven o'clock he went up to his bedroom and changed into white tie and tails. He felt marvellous. When he looked at himself in the mirror, the sight of his own grotesque shoulderless figure didn't worry him in the least. A great composer, he thought, smiling, can look as he damn well pleases. People *expect* him to look peculiar. All the same he wished he had some hair on his head. He would have liked to let it grow rather long. He went downstairs to dinner, ate his food rapidly, drank half a bottle of wine and felt better still. 'Don't worry about me, Mason,' he said. 'I'm not mad. I'm just enjoying myself.'

'Yes, sir.'

'I shan't want you any more. Please see that I'm not disturbed.' Mr Botibol went from the dining-room into the miniature concert-hall. He took out the records of Beethoven's First Symphony, but before putting them on the gramophone, he placed two other records with them. The one, which was to be played first of all, before the music began, was labelled 'prolonged enthusiastic applause'. The other, which would come at the end of the symphony, was labelled 'Sustained applause, clapping, cheering, shouts of encore'. By a simple mechanical device on the record changer, the gramophone people had arranged that the sound from the first and the last records – the applause – would come only from the loud-speaker in the auditorium. The sound from all the others – the music – would come from the speaker hidden among the chairs of the orchestra. When he had arranged the records in the correct order, he placed them on the machine but he didn't switch on at once. Instead he turned out all the lights in the room except one small one which lit up the conductor's dais and he sat down in a chair up on the stage, closed his eyes and allowed his thoughts to wander into the usual delicious regions: the great com-poser, nervous, impatient, waiting to present his latest masterpiece, the audience assembling, the murmur of their excited talk, and so on. Having dreamed himself right into the part, he stood up, picked up his baton and switched on the gramophone.

A tremendous wave of clapping filled the room. Mr Botibol walked across the stage, mounted the dais, faced the audience and bowed. In the darkness he could just make out the faint outline of the seats on either side of the centre aisle, but he couldn't see the faces of the people. They were making enough noise. What an ovation! Mr Botibol turned and faced the orchestra. The applause behind him died down. The next record dropped. The symphony began.

This time it was more thrilling than ever, and during the performance he registered any number of prickly sensa-tions around his solar plexus. Once, when it suddenly occurred to him that this music was being broadcast all over the world, a sort of shiver ran right down the length of his spine. But by far the most exciting part was the applause which came at the end. They cheered and clapped and stamped and shouted, 'Encore! encore! encore!' and he turned towards the darkened auditorium and bowed gravely to the left and right. Then he went off the stage, but they called him back. He bowed several more times and went off again, and again they called him back. The audience had gone mad. They simply wouldn't let him go. It was terrific. It was truly a terrific ovation.

Later, when he was resting in his chair in the other room, he was still enjoying it. He closed his eyes because he didn't want anything to break the spell. He lay there and he felt like he was floating. It was really a most marvellous floating feeling, and when he went upstairs and undressed and got into bed, it was still with him.

The following evening he conducted Beethoven's – or rather Botibol's – Second Symphony, and they were just as mad about that one as the first. The next few nights he played one symphony a night, and at the end of nine evenings he had worked through all nine of Beethoven's symphonies. It got more exciting every time because before each concert the audience kept saying, 'He can't do it again, not another masterpiece. It's not humanly possible.' But he did. They were all of them equally magnificent. The last symphony, the Ninth, was especially exciting because here the composer surprised and delighted everyone by suddenly providing a choral masterpiece. He had to conduct a huge choir as well as the orchestra itself, and Benjamino Gigli had flown over from Italy to take the tenor part. Enrico Pinza sang bass. At the end of it the audience shouted themselves hoarse. The whole musical world was on its feet cheering, and on all sides they were saying how you never could tell what wonderful things to expect next from this amazing person.

The composing, presenting and conducting of nine great symphonies in as many days is a fair achievement for any man, and it was not astonishing that it went a little to Mr Botibol's head. He decided now that he would once again surprise his public. He would compose a mass of marvellous piano music and he himself would give the recitals. So early the next morning he set out for the showroom of the people who sold Bechsteins and Steinways. He felt so brisk and fit that he walked all the way, and as he walked he hummed little snatches of new and lovely tunes for the piano. His head was full of them. All the time they kept coming to him and once, suddenly, he had the feeling that thousands of small notes, some white, some black, were cascading down a chute into his head through a hole in his head, and that his brain, his amazing musical brain, was receiving them as fast as they could come and unscrambling them and arranging them neatly in a certain order so that they made wondrous melodies. There were Nocturnes, there were Études and there were Waltzes, and soon, he told himself, soon he would give them all to a grateful and admiring world.

When he arrived at the piano-shop, he pushed the door open and walked in with an air almost of confidence. He had changed much in the last few days. Some of his nervousness had left him and he was no longer wholly preoccupied with what others thought of his appearance. 'I want,' he said to the salesman, 'a concert grand, but you must arrange it so that when the notes are struck, no sound is produced.'

The salesman leaned forward and raised his eyebrows.

'Could that be arranged?' Mr Botibol asked.

'Yes, sir, I think so, if you desire it. But might I inquire what you intend to use the instrument for?'

'If you want to know, I'm going to pretend I'm Chopin. I'm going to sit and play while a gramophone makes the music. It gives me a kick.' It came out, just like that, and Mr Botibol didn't know what had made him say it. But it was done now and he had said it and that was that. In a way he felt relieved, because he had proved he didn't mind telling people what he was doing. The man would probably answer what a jolly good idea. Or he might not. He might say, Well you ought to be locked up.

'So now you know,' Mr Botibol said.

The salesman laughed out loud. 'Ha ha! Ha ha ha! That's very good, sir. Very good indeed. Serves me right for asking silly questions.' He stopped suddenly in the middle of the laugh and looked hard at Mr Botibol. 'Of course, sir, you probably know that we sell a simple noise-less keyboard specially for silent practising.'

'I want a concert grand,' Mr Botibol said. The salesman looked at him again.

Mr Botibol chose his piano and got out of the shop as quickly as possible. He went on to the store that sold gramophone records and there he ordered a quantity of albums containing recordings of all Chopin's Nocturnes, Études and Waltzes, played by Arthur Rubinstein.

'My goodness, you *are* going to have a lovely time!'

Mr Botibol turned and saw standing beside him at the counter a squat, short-legged girl with a face as plain as a pudding.

'Yes,' he answered. 'Oh yes, I am.' Normally he was strict about not speaking to females in public places, but this one had taken him by surprise.

'I love Chopin,' the girl said. She was holding a slim brown paper bag with string handles containing a single record she had just bought. 'I like him better than any of the others.'

It was comforting to hear the voice of this girl after the way the piano salesman had laughed. Mr Botibol wanted to talk to her but he didn't know what to say.

The girl said, 'I like the Nocturnes best, they're so soothing. Which are your favourites?'

Mr Botibol said, 'Well . . .' The girl looked up at him and she smiled pleasantly, trying to assist him with his embarrassment. It was the smile that did it. He suddenly found himself saying, 'Well now, perhaps, would you, I wonder . . . I mean I was wondering . . .' She smiled again; she couldn't help it this time. 'What I mean is I would be glad if you would care to come along some time and listen to these records.'

'Why, how nice of you.' She paused, wondering whether it was all right. 'You really mean it?'

'Yes, I should be glad.'

She had lived long enough in the city to discover that

old men, if they are dirty old men, do not bother about trying to pick up a girl as unattractive as herself. Only twice in her life had she been accosted in public and each time the man had been drunk. But this one wasn't drunk. He was nervous and he was peculiar-looking, but he wasn't drunk. Come to think of it, it was she who had started the conversation in the first place. 'It would be lovely,' she said. 'It really would. When could I come?'

Oh dear, Mr Botibol thought. Oh dear, oh dear, oh dear, oh dear.

'I could come tomorrow,' she went on. 'It's my afternoon off.'

'Well, yes, certainly,' he answered slowly. 'Yes, of course. I'll give you my card. Here it is.'

'A. W. Botibol,' she read aloud. 'What a funny name. Mine's Darlington. Miss L. Darlington. How d'you do, Mr Botibol.' She put out her hand for him to shake. 'Oh I *am* looking forward to this! What time shall I come?'

'Any time,' he said. 'Please come any time.'

'Three o'clock?'

'Yes. Three o'clock.'

'Lovely! I'll be there.'

He watched her walk out of the shop, a squat, stumpy, thick-legged little person and, My word, he thought, what have I done! He was amazed at himself. But he was not displeased. Then at once he started to worry about whether or not he should let her see his concert-hall. He worried still more when he realized that it was the only place in the house where there was a gramophone.

That evening he had no concert. Instead he sat in his

chair brooding about Miss Darlington and what he should do when she arrived. The next morning they brought the piano, a fine Bechstein in dark mahogany which was carried in minus its legs and later assembled on the platform in the concert-hall. It was an imposing instrument and when Mr Botibol opened it and pressed a note with his finger, it made no sound at all. He had originally intended to astonish the world with a recital of his first piano compositions – a set of Études – as soon as the piano arrived, but it was no good now. He was too worried about Miss Darlington and three o'clock. At lunchtime his trepidation had increased and he couldn't eat. 'Mason,' he said, 'I'm, I'm expecting a young lady to call at three o'clock.'

'A what, sir?' the butler said.

'A young lady, Mason.'

'Very good, sir.'

'Show her into the sitting-room.'

'Yes, sir.'

Precisely at three he heard the bell ring. A few moments later Mason was showing her into the room. She came in, smiling, and Mr Botibol stood up and shook her hand. 'My!' she exclaimed. 'What a lovely house! I didn't know I was calling on a millionaire!'

She settled her small plump body into a large armchair and Mr Botibol sat opposite. He didn't know what to say. He felt terrible. But almost at once she began to talk and she chattered away gaily about this and that for a long time without stopping. Mostly it was about his house and the furniture and the carpets and about how nice it was of him to invite her because she didn't have such an awful lot of excitement in her life. She worked hard all day and she shared a room with two other girls in a boarding-house and he could have no idea how thrilling it was for her to be here. Gradually Mr Botibol began to feel better. He sat there listening to the girl, rather liking her, nodding his bald head slowly up and down, and the more she talked, the more he liked her. She was gay and chatty, but underneath all that any fool could see that she was a lonely tired little thing. Even Mr Botibol could see that. He could see it very clearly indeed. It was at this point that he began to play with a daring and risky idea.

'Miss Darlington,' he said. 'I'd like to show you something.' He led her out of the room straight into the little concert-hall. 'Look,' he said.

She stopped just inside the door. 'My goodness! Just look at that! A theatre! A real little theatre!' Then she saw the piano on the platform and the conductor's dais with the brass rail running round it. 'It's for concerts!' she cried. 'Do you really have concerts here? Oh, Mr Botibol, how exciting!'

'Do you like it?'

'Oh yes!'

'Come back into the other room and I'll tell you about it.' Her enthusiasm had given him confidence and he wanted to get going. 'Come back and listen while I tell you something funny.' And when they were seated in the sitting-room again, he began at once to tell her his story. He told the whole thing, right from the beginning, how one day, listening to a symphony, he had imagined himself to be the composer, how he had stood up and started to conduct, how he had got an immense pleasure out of it, how he had done it again with similar results and how finally he had built himself the concert-hall where already he had conducted nine symphonies. But he cheated a little bit in the telling. He said that the only real reason he did it was in order to obtain the maximum appreciation from the music. There was only one way to listen to music, he told her, only one way to make yourself listen to every single note and chord. You had to do two things at once. You had to imagine that you had composed it, and at the same time you had to imagine that the public were hearing it for the first time. 'Do you think,' he said, 'do you really think that any outsider has ever got half as great a thrill from a symphony as the composer himself when he first heard his work played by a full orchestra?'

'No,' she answered timidly. 'Of course not.'

'Then become the composer! Steal his music! Take it away from him and give it to yourself!' He leaned back in his chair and for the first time she saw him smile. He had only just thought of this new complex explanation of his conduct, but to him it seemed a very good one and he smiled. 'Well, what do you think, Miss Darlington?'

'I must say it's very very interesting.' She was polite and puzzled but she was a long way away from him now.

'Would you like to try?'

'Oh no. Please.'

'I wish you would.'

'I'm afraid I don't think I should be able to feel the same way as you do about it, Mr Botibol. I don't think I have a strong enough imagination.'

She could see from his eyes he was disappointed. 'But I'd love to sit in the audience and listen while you do it,' she added.

Then he leaped up from his chair. 'I've got it!' he cried. 'A piano concerto! You play the piano, I conduct. You the greatest pianist, the greatest in the world. First performance of my Piano Concerto No. 1. You playing, me conducting. The greatest pianist and the greatest composer together for the first time. A tremendous occasion! The audience will go mad! They'll be queueing all night outside the hall to get in. It'll be broadcast around the world. It'll, it'll . . .' Mr Botibol stopped. He stood behind the chair with both hands resting on the back of the chair and suddenly he looked embarrassed and a trifle sheepish. 'I'm sorry,' he said. 'I get worked up. You see how it is. Even the thought of another performance gets me worked up.' And then plaintively, 'Would you, Miss Darlington, would you play a piano concerto with me?'

'It's like children,' she said, but she smiled.

'No one will know. No one but us will know anything about it.'

'All right,' she said at last. 'I'll do it. I think I'm daft but just the same I'll do it. It'll be a bit of a lark.'

'Good!' Mr Botibol cried. 'When? Tonight?'

'Oh well, I don't . . .'

'Yes,' he said eagerly. 'Please. Make it tonight. Come back and have dinner here with me and we'll give the concert afterwards.' Mr Botibol was excited again now. 'We must make a few plans. Which is your favourite piano concerto, Miss Darlington?'

'Oh well, I should say Beethoven's Emperor.'

'The Emperor it shall be. You will play it tonight. Come to dinner at seven. Evening dress. You must have evening dress for the concert.'

'I've got a dancing dress but I haven't worn it for years.'

'You shall wear it tonight.' He paused and looked at her in silence for a moment, then quite gently, he said, 'You're not worried, Miss Darlington? Perhaps you would rather not do it. I'm afraid, I'm afraid I've let myself get rather carried away. I seem to have pushed you into this. And I know how stupid it must seem to you.'

That's better, she thought. That's much better. Now I know it's all right. 'Oh no,' she said. 'I'm really looking forward to it. But you frightened me a bit, taking it all so seriously.'

When she had gone, he waited for five minutes, then went out into the town to the gramophone shop and bought the records of the Emperor Concerto, conductor, Toscanini – soloist, Horowitz. He returned at once, told his astonished butler that there would be a guest for dinner, then went upstairs and changed into his tails.

She arrived at seven. She was wearing a long sleeveless dress made of some shiny green material and to Mr Botibol she did not look quite so plump or quite so plain as before. He took her straight in to dinner and in spite of the silent disapproving manner in which Mason prowled around the table, the meal went well. She protested gaily when Mr Botibol gave her a second glass of wine, but she didn't refuse it. She chattered away almost without a stop throughout the three courses and Mr Botibol listened and nodded and kept refilling her glass as soon as it was half empty.

Afterwards, when they were seated in the living-room, Mr Botibol said, 'Now Miss Darlington, now we begin to fall into our parts.' The wine, as usual, had made him happy, and the girl, who was even less used to it than the man, was not feeling so bad either. 'You, Miss Darlington, are the great pianist. What is your first name, Miss Darlington?'

'Lucille,' she said.

'The great pianist Lucille Darlington. I am the composer Botibol. We must talk and act and think as though we are pianist and composer.'

'What is *your* first name, Mr Botibol. What does the A stand for?'

'Angel,' he answered.

'Not Angel.'

'Yes,' he said irritably.

'Angel Botibol,' she murmured and she began to giggle. But she checked herself and said, 'I think it's a most unusual and distinguished name.'

'Are you ready, Miss Darlington?'

'Yes.'

Mr Botibol stood up and began pacing nervously up and down the room. He looked at his watch. 'It's nearly time to go on,' he said. 'They tell me the place is packed. Not an empty seat anywhere. I always get nervous before a concert. Do you get nervous, Miss Darlington?'

'Oh yes, I do, always. Especially playing with you.'

'I think they'll like it. I put everything I've got into this concerto, Miss Darlington. It nearly killed me composing it. I was ill for weeks afterwards.'

'Poor thing,' she said.

'It's time now,' he said. 'The orchestra are all in their places. Come on.' He led her out and down the passage, then he made her wait outside the door of the concert-hall while he nipped in, arranged the lighting and switched on the gramophone. He came back and fetched her and as they walked on to the stage, the applause broke out. They both stood and bowed towards the darkened auditorium and the applause was vigorous and it went on for a long time. Then Mr Botibol mounted the dais and Miss Darlington took her seat at the piano. The applause died down. Mr Botibol held up his baton. The next record dropped and the Emperor Concerto began.

It was an astonishing affair. The thin stalk-like Mr Boti-bol, who had no shoulders, standing on the dais in his evening clothes, waving his arms about in approximate time to the music; and the plump Miss Darlington in her shiny green dress seated at the keyboard of the enormous piano thumping the silent keys with both hands for all she was worth. She recognized the passages where the piano was meant to be silent, and on these occasions she folded her hands primly on her lap and stared straight ahead with a dreamy and enraptured expression on her face. Watching her, Mr Botibol thought that she was particularly wonderful in the slow solo passages of the Second Move-ment. She allowed her hands to drift smoothly and gently up and down the keys and she inclined her head first to one side, then to the other, and once she closed her eyes for a long time while she played. During the exciting last movement, Mr Botibol himself lost his balance and would have fallen off the platform had he not saved himself by clutching the brass rail. But in spite of everything, the concerto moved on majestically to its mighty conclusion. Then the real clapping came. Mr Botibol walked over and took Miss Darlington by the hand and led her to the edge of the platform, and there they stood, the two of them, bowing, and bowing, and bowing again as the clapping and the shouting of 'Encore' continued. Four times they left the stage and came back, and then, the fifth time, Mr Botibol whispered, 'It's you they want. You take this one alone.' 'No,' she said. 'It's you. It's you. Please.' But he pushed her forward and she took her call, and came back and said, 'Now you. They want you. Can't you hear them shouting for you?' So Mr Botibol walked alone on to the stage, bowed gravely to right, left and centre and came off just as the clapping stopped altogether.

He led her straight back to the living-room. He was breathing fast and the sweat was pouring down all over his face. She too was a little breathless, and her cheeks were shining red.

'A tremendous performance, Miss Darlington. Allow me to congratulate you.'

'But what a concerto, Mr Botibol! What a superb concerto!'

'You played it perfectly, Miss Darlington. You have a real feeling for my music.' He was wiping the sweat from his face with a handkerchief. 'And tomorrow we perform my Second Concerto.'

'Tomorrow?'

'Of course. Had you forgotten, Miss Darlington? We are booked to appear together for a whole week.'

'Oh . . . oh yes . . . I'm afraid I had forgotten that.'

'But it's all right, isn't it?' he asked anxiously. 'After hearing you tonight I could not bear to have anyone else play my music.'

'I think it's all right,' she said. 'Yes, I think that'll be all right.' She looked at the clock on the mantelpiece. 'My heavens, it's late! I must go! I'll never get up in the morning to get to work!'

'To work?' Mr Botibol said. 'To work?' Then slowly, reluctantly, he forced himself back to reality. 'Ah yes, to work. Of course, you have to get to work.'

'I certainly do.'

'Where do you work, Miss Darlington?'

'Me? Well,' and now she hesitated a moment, looking at Mr Botibol. 'As a matter of fact I work at the old Academy.'

'I hope it is pleasant work,' he said. 'What Academy is that?'

'I teach the piano.'

Mr Botibol jumped as though someone had stuck him from behind with a hatpin. His mouth opened very wide.

'It's quite all right,' she said, smiling. 'I've always wanted to be Horowitz. And could I, do you think could I please be Schnabel tomorrow?'

The Princess and the Poacher

First published in *Two Fables* (1986)

Although Hengist was now eighteen years old, he still showed no desire to follow in his father's trade of basket-weaving. He even refused to go out and collect the osiers from the riverbank. This saddened his parents greatly, but they were wise enough to know that it seldom pays to force a young lad to work at something when his heart is not in it.

In appearance, Hengist was an exceedingly unattractive youth. With his squat body, his short bandy legs, his extra-long arms and his crumpled face, he looked almost as though there might be a touch of the ape or the gorilla about him. He was certainly mighty strong. He could bend double a two-inch-thick iron bar with his hands alone, and once he had astonished an old carter whose horse had fallen into a ditch by lifting the animal out bodily in his arms and placing it back on the road.

Quite naturally, Hengist was interested in maidens fair. But as one might expect, no maidens, fair or otherwise, were interested in Hengist. He was a pleasant enough fellow, there was no doubt about that, but there is a limit to the degree of ugliness any woman can tolerate in a man. Hengist was well beyond that limit. In fact, his ugliness was so extreme that no female other than his mother would have anything to do with him. This was a great sorrow to the lad. It was also grossly unfair, because no man is responsible for his own looks.

Poor Hengist. Although he knew that every maid and every wench in the Kingdom was far beyond his reach for ever, he continued to long for them and lust after them with unabated passion. Whenever he spied a girl milking a cow or hanging out the washing, he would stop and stare and yearn most terribly to possess her.

Fortunately for him, he was soon to find another outlet for his energies. It had become a habit of his to take long walks in the countryside, through the forests and the glens, to cool his ardour, and over the ensuing weeks he began in some subtle way to fall in love with the landscape of the open air. He would spend his days roaming in deserted places, a silent, solitary, terribly uncouth figure, communing with nature. And thus, gradually and inevitably, he came to learn a great deal about the habits of animals and birds. He also discovered to his delight that he possessed the ability to move so silently through the forest that he could come within arm's length of a timid creature like a hare or a deer before it was aware of his presence. This was not just from practice. It appeared to be a gift that had been bestowed upon him, a rare ability to merge into the landscape and suddenly to emerge again, almost like a ghost, when no man or bird or beast had seen him coming.

His family were very poor and they hardly ever tasted meat or game from one year to the next. Quite understandably, and quite soon, it dawned upon Hengist that he could very easily improve their lot, and indeed his own, by doing a little poaching. He began slowly, with a rabbit or a partridge once a week, but it was not long before the sheer pleasure and excitement of the chase took hold of him. Here, after all, was something he could do extraordinarily well. Poaching was an art. The thrill of creeping up on a crouching hare undetected or of snatching a roosting pheasant from a branch gave him a sense of satisfaction such as he had never known before. He became addicted to the sport.

But poaching was a hazardous occupation in the Kingdom. All the land, all the forests and the streams, were owned either by the King himself or by one of the great Dukes, and although the footpaths on their estates were open to the public for strolling quietly, poaching on these lands was strictly forbidden. Anyone who strayed off the designated footpaths did so at his peril. The undergrowth was strewn with cunningly concealed man-traps whose iron jaws could bite a man's leg to the bone if he stepped on the plate that released the spring. And there the poor captive would remain, pinned to the ground, until a patrolling keeper found him the next day.

In the eyes of the King and the Dukes, poaching was a greater crime than murder. The sentence for murder was simply death by hanging, but the sentence for poaching was far more unpleasant. A convicted poacher would first be weighed on a special balance. Then two leaden anklets would be constructed whose weight had been most carefully calculated by the Royal Mathematician. These anklets would be fastened around the victim's ankles and his hands tied behind his back before he was lowered into the great Drowning Tub that was built of stone and stood permanently in the Market Square of the capital. The man's height had also been measured beforehand by the Mathematician, and a quantity of water had either been added to or taken out of the Tub so that when the man stood on tiptoe on the bottom, the top of his head was just below the surface of the water. The result of all this was that the victim spent many hours, sometimes days, being pulled down by the weight of the anklets, then jumping up again for a quick breath of air when his feet touched the bottom. Finally he sank altogether from exhaustion. The uncomfortable nature of this punishment did much to discourage the population from breaking the law of the land. The hunting of game was the prerogative only of the Royal Family and the Dukes.

But Hengist was not to be intimidated. He had such faith in his powers of stealth that he harboured no fears of the dreaded Drowning Tub. His parents were, of course, frightened out of their skins. Every evening when he went out, and every dawn when he returned with a juicy partridge or a leveret under his coat, they trembled for their son, and indeed for themselves. But hunger is a powerful persuader and the spoils were always accepted and roasted and devoured with relish.

'You *are* being careful, son, are you not?' the mother would say, as she munched upon the tender breast of a woodcock.

'I is always careful, ma,' Hengist would answer. 'That little ole King and them fancy Dooks they ain't never goin' to lay a finger on me.'

Hengist soon became so confident in his powers of poaching that he scorned the cover of darkness and took to going out in full daylight, which was something that only the bravest or the most foolhardy would do. And then one day, on a fine morning in springtime, he decided to have a go at the most protected area in the entire Kingdom, that part of the Royal Forest which lies immediately beneath the walls of the Castle itself, where the King lived. Here the game was more plentiful than anywhere else, but the dangers were tremendous. Hengist, as he crept soft and silent into the Royal Forest, was relishing this danger.

And now he was standing immobile in the shadow of a mighty beech, watching a young roebuck grazing not five paces away and waiting for the moment to pounce. Out of the edge of one eye he could see the south wall of the Royal Castle itself and somewhere in the distance he could hear bugles blowing. They were probably changing the guard at the gates, he told himself. Then suddenly, out of that same eye, he caught sight of a figure among the trees, not forty paces distant. Slowly, he turned his head to examine this person more carefully and, lo and behold, he saw immediately that it was none other than the young Princess, the only child of the King and the jewel in his crown. She was a young damsel of breathtaking beauty, with skin as pure and smooth as a silken glove, and she was but seventeen years old. Here she was then, apparently idling away the morning picking bluebells in the wood. Hengist's heart gave a jump when he saw her and all the old passions came flooding back once again. For a mad moment or two, he considered surprising the damsel by kneeling before her with whispered words of love and adoration, but he knew only too well what would happen then. She would take one look at his terrible ugliness and run away screaming, and he would be caught and put to death. It also occurred to him that he might creep upon her stealthily, coming up behind her unseen then clapping a hand over her mouth and having his way with her by force. But he quickly pushed this foul notion out of his mind, for he abhorred violence of any kind.

What happened next came very suddenly. There was a fanfare of hunting horns nearby and Hengist turned and saw a massive wild boar, the largest he had ever seen, come charging through the trees, and behind it, some fifty paces back, was riding the King himself and a group of noblemen, all galloping full-tilt after the boar with lances drawn. The Princess was right in the path of the running boar and the boar was in no mood to swerve around her. Just the opposite. An angry hunted boar will attack any human who stands in its line of flight. Worse still, it will often swing aside and attack an innocent bystander who might happen to be near. And now the boar had spotted the Princess, and it was making straight for her. Hengist saw the maiden drop her bunch of bluebells and run. Then she seemed to realize the futility of this, and she stopped and pressed herself against the trunk of a giant oak, and there she stood, helpless, with arms outspread as though for crucifixion, waiting for the madly rushing beast to reach her. Hengist saw the boar, the size of a small bull, charging forwards with head down, the two sharp, glistening tusks pointing straight at the victim.

He took off like an arrow. He flew over the ground with his feet hardly touching the earth, and when he realized that the boar was going to reach the Princess before him, he made a last, despairing dive through the air and reached far out with his hands and just managed to grab hold of the boar's tusks when they were within a fraction of the maiden's midriff. Both Hengist and the boar went tumbling over in a heap, but the youth held on to the tusks, and when he leaped to his feet again, the boar came with him, lifted on high by the strongest pair of arms in the Kingdom. Hengist gave a sudden twist with his hands and even the King, some thirty paces distant, heard the boar's cervical spine snap in two. Hengist then swung the massive beast back and forth a couple of times before sending it sailing over his head as easily as if it had been a stick of firewood.

The King reached them first, galloping like mad and reining in his frothing horse right beside his daughter. He was followed by half a dozen noblemen, who all pulled up behind the King. The King leaped from his charger crying out, 'My darling! My little child! Are you all right?' He had witnessed the whole of the four-second drama, and in truth, when he had seen the boar charging straight for his daughter, he thought she was finished. And then he had seen this extraordinary human arrow leaping and flying between the trees and flinging himself upon the terrible boar just in the nick of time. The King was white in the face as he took the sobbing Princess in his arms to console her. Hengist stood awkwardly by, not quite knowing what to do with his hands or his feet or anything else.

At last the King turned to look at Hengist. For a moment or two, the shock of seeing such a spectacularly ugly youth rendered him speechless. But he kept on looking, and as he looked, he found himself liking more and more what he saw. A man is seldom repelled by the malformed features of another man. Quite the reverse. Men, as a whole, take less kindly to other men who are exceptionally good-looking. Women are often the same with other women. Yet, as we all know, good looks do have a profound influence upon the *opposite* sex. This is a fact of life, but as the wise King knew, it caused much disillusionment later on. Yes, the King was telling himself, as he continued to stare at this curious fellow who stood before him, how different he is from the sloppy, effeminate, lecherous young courtiers who surround me at the Castle! This is a real man! He is brave and swift and fearless, and to hell with his looks! It was at this point that a sly plot began to hatch in the King's devious mind.

In his rich royal voice, charged with emotion, he said, 'Young man, today you have done me the greatest service any citizen could perform for his King! You have saved the treasure of my life, the pearl of my Kingdom, my only child, indeed the only child I shall ever have because the poor Queen is dead! I intend to see that you are rewarded in a munificent manner! Pray accompany me to the Castle at once!'

Then the King lifted the Princess up on to his charger and himself got into the saddle behind her. The entourage rode off at a trot, with a rather bemused Hengist running alongside.

As soon as he arrived at the Castle, the King summoned a meeting of the Elders. Ostensibly, these old men were the parliament that ruled the Kingdom, but in reality it was the King himself who decided everything. No man dared gainsay the monarch.

In the Council Chamber the Elders, twenty in all, were assembled in their pews.

Above, on a dais, sat the King upon his throne, and beside him stood Hengist. The latter was not very suitably attired for the occasion. He wore a shirt made from some kind of sacking, his breeches were filthy, and on his stockingless feet was a pair of home-made sandals. The Elders stared at this ugly, ill-dressed creature with distaste. The King smiled. He was a curious man, the King, much given to eccentricities and japes and ingenious practical jokes. For example, at his dining-table, which seated twelve guests, he had twelve little taps concealed under the edge of the table, and if any of his guests, male or female, annoyed him or said something foolish, the King would reach under the table and open the appropriate tap. This would send a powerful jet of water from a tiny hole in the centre of the chair right up the backside of the offending guest.

It had not taken the King long to realize that Hengist, with those terribly ugly features, must be the most sexually disappointed man in the Kingdom. He had actually observed several ladies of the court recoiling and covering their faces as the youth passed by. All this suited his subtle plan very well.

'Learned Elders,' he said, addressing the Council, 'this gallant youth, Hengist by name, has by an act of unbelievable bravery saved the life of the Princess, your future Queen. No reward is too great for him. He shall therefore be granted a stipend of one thousand gold crowns a year and shall be accommodated in a grace-and-favour mansion on the Royal Estate. He shall be provided with servants and a lavish wardrobe and whatever else he desires for his comfort.'

'Hear hear,' the Elders murmured. 'He well deserves it.'

'But that is a mere nothing compared to what other favours I am now about to grant him,' the King went on. 'I have decided that the greatest reward I can bestow upon this valiant and gallant youth is as follows. By Royal Decree, he shall also be granted . . .' Here the King paused dramatically. The Elders waited. 'He shall be granted the absolute right to ravish any maiden, wench, lady, dame, countess, duchess or other female in the Kingdom whenever he so desires.'

There was uproar among the Elders. 'You can't do that!' they cried. 'What about our wives? What about our daughters?'

'What about them?' the King asked. 'You will notice that I have not even excluded the Princess, so why should I exclude your wretched wives or daughters?'

'You mustn't do this, Your Majesty!' the Elders cried out. 'There will be chaos at court! There will be rape in the corridors! The whole place will be bedlam! Our poor innocent daughters! Our dear wives!'

'I doubt your daughters or wives will qualify,' the King remarked drily. 'Only great beauties will stand a chance of

THE COMPLETE SHORT STORIES

being noticed. When a man has his pick, he chooses carefully.'

'We beg you, Majesty!' the Elders cried. 'Do not force us to pass such a law!'

'Nothing you say will deter me,' said the King. 'And, furthermore, I decree that any lady who refuses to submit to the blandishments of Count Hengist – I have just made him a count, by the way – will be put to death in the Drowning Tub.'

The Elders were all on their feet waving their order papers and shouting against the King. 'You've gone too far!' they cried. 'There will be sexual anarchy in the land!'

'Don't be so sure,' said the clever King.

'Sexual anarchy!' the Elders chanted. 'Rape on the ramparts! It's not good enough!'

'Listen,' said the King, beginning to lose patience. 'I'll have the whole lot of you put in the Drowning Tub if you give me any more trouble!'

That shut them up.

'Lastly,' the King continued, 'and you'd better note this carefully, any man, any father or husband or brother, who attempts to interfere with the noble Count in the pursuance of his desires shall also be put in the Drowning Tub. Do I make myself clear?' There was a steely edge to the King's voice, and the Elders sat down and remained silent and sulked. They knew that their ruler, who had the entire army behind him to a man, was all-powerful. He always got his way.

'Draw up the Proclamation immediately,' the King said. 'Have it posted in towns and villages all over the Kingdom. Have the town-criers call out the news in every hamlet! Tell the population that Count Hengist enjoys the freedom of all the women in the realm. And be sure to stress the penalties for disobedience. See also that Count Hengist himself be given a Card of Authority that he can wave in the face of any maiden or wench he may desire.'

Thus, this extraordinary Decree was made law, and Hengist, under the full protection of the King, moved into a mansion near the Castle where servants bathed him and groomed him and taught him how to dress in the style of the court.

At first, the poor fellow was totally bewildered. He wandered awkwardly about the Court, shunned by everybody. The Dukes snubbed him or ignored him. The ladies ran for their lives whenever he hove in sight. And who could blame them? Not even the most lascivious courtesans wanted to go near the poor fellow. He was treated by one and all as though he had leprosy.

But a strange thing had happened to Hengist. His desires seemed suddenly to have evaporated. He knew all about the immense powers he possessed. He was aware that he had the full backing of the King. He could seek out and ravish any maiden he desired, not only at court, but in the towns and villages all over the country. The trouble was, he did not desire them. He felt no urge at all. It was the old story of the forbidden fruit. Make it easy to get and the appetite goes away.

The King, who had been watching all this for several weeks with wry amusement, was strolling one morning on the ramparts with the Princess when suddenly Hengist happened by. 'How goes it, my lad?' said the King, slapping the youth on the back.

'Your Majesty,' Hengist said, 'to tell the truth, I doesn't much care for this thing you 'as done to me.'

'My dear chap,' said the King, 'what on earth is the trouble?'

'Nobody likes me around 'ere,' Hengist said. 'They is all treatin' me like dirt.'

'*I* like you,' said the Princess suddenly.

Hengist stared at her. 'You does?' he said.

'You are the only man in the Castle who does not chase me along the corridors,' the Princess said. 'You are the only decent person in the whole place.'

'Now I come to think of it, my darling,' said the King, smiling a little, 'I suppose you're right.'

'I know I'm right, Daddy,' the young beauty said. 'All the other men around here are totally disgusting. I hate them.'

'Some of them are very handsome, my dear,' the King said.

'That's got nothing to do with it!' cried the Princess. 'I don't give a fig about looks!'

'You mean you likes me a little bit?' Hengist inquired nervously.

'*Like you?*' cried the Princess, flinging herself into his arms. 'I love you!'

The King slipped away, leaving them alone. He was well pleased with the way things had worked out.

Princess Mammalia

First published in *Two Fables* (1986)

When Princess Mammalia arose from her bed on the morning of her seventeenth birthday and examined her face in the looking-glass, she couldn't believe what she saw. Up until then she had always been a rather plain and dumpy girl with a thick neck, but now she suddenly found herself staring at a young lady she had never set eyes on before. A magical transformation had taken place overnight and the dumpy little Princess had become a dazzling beauty. I use the word 'dazzling' in its purest and most literal sense, for such a blaze of glory, such a scintillation of stars, such a blinding beauty shone forth from her countenance that when she went downstairs an hour later to open her presents, those who gazed upon her at close quarters had to screw up their eyes for fear the brilliance of it all might damage their retinas. Even the royal astronomer was heard to murmur that it might be safer to view the lady through smoked glass, as one would the eclipse of the sun.

Ever since she had learned to walk, Princess Mammalia had been much loved around the Palace for her modest and gentle disposition, but she very soon found out that it is much more difficult for a ravishing beauty to remain modest and gentle than it is for a plain girl. She discovered that the kind of extraordinary beauty she possessed endowed her with immense power. In the glittering presence of her new-found image, men became so overwhelmed with desire that they were hers to command. Caliphs and rajas, grand viziers and generals, ministers and chancellors, camel drivers and rent collectors, all of them melted into a froth as soon as she appeared on the scene. They fawned and simpered. They drooled and dribbled. They crawled and toadied. She had only to lift her little finger and they all started scampering around the room in their efforts to please her. They offered her rich jewels and golden bracelets. They suggested lavish feasts in cool places, and whenever one of them got her in a corner on her own, he began to whisper obscenities in her ear. There were also problems with the staff. A servant is just as much of a man as a courtier, and after several unsavoury incidents in the corridors, the King was forced, much against his wishes, for he was a kind king, to order that all male servants in the Palace be castrated immediately. Only the royal chef escaped. He pleaded that it would ruin his cooking.

At first, and with charming innocence, the Princess simply sat back and enjoyed her new-found power. But that couldn't go on. Nobody, let alone a maiden of seventeen, could remain unaffected for long. This was power indeed. It was power unheard of in one so young. And power itself, the Princess soon discovered, is a demanding taskmaster. It is impossible to have it and not use it. It insists on being exercised. Thus the Princess began consciously to exercise her power over men, first in small ways, then in rather bigger ones. It was ridiculously easy, like manipulating puppets.

At this point, the Princess made her second discovery, and it was this. If the power of a female is so great that men will obey her without question, she becomes contemptuous of those men, and within a month, the Princess found that the only feelings she had towards the male species were those of scorn and contumely. She began to practise all manner of droll stratagems to humiliate her worshippers. She took, for example, to going on walkabouts in the city and displaying herself to ordinary men in the street. Surrounded by her faithful guard of eunuchs, she would watch with amusement as the male citizens went crazy with desire at the sight of her blazing beauty, hurling themselves against the spears of the guards and becoming impaled by the hundreds.

Late at night, before retiring to bed, she would divert herself by strolling out on to her balcony and showing herself to the lascivious *polloi* who were wont to gather in their thousands in the courtyard below, hoping for a glimpse of her. And why not indeed? She looked more dazzling and desirable than ever standing there in the moonlight. In truth, she outshone the moon itself, and the citizens would go berserk as soon as she appeared, crying out and tearing their hair and fracturing their bones by flinging themselves against the craggy walls of the Palace. Every now and again, the Princess would pour a pipkin or two of boiling lead over their heads to cool them down.

All this was bad enough, but there was worse to come. As we all know, power, with all its subtle facets, is a voracious bedfellow. The more one has, the more one wants. There is no such thing as getting enough of it, and over the next few months the Princess's craving for power grew and grew until in the end she found herself beginning to toy with the idea of gaining for herself the ultimate power in the land, the throne itself.

She was the eldest of seven children, all of them girls, and her mother was dead. Already, therefore, she was the rightful heir to her father's throne. But what good was that? Her father, the King, who not so long ago had been the idol of her eye, now irritated her to distraction. He was a benign and merciful ruler, much loved by his people, and because he was her father he was the only man in the Kingdom who did not turn cartwheels at the sight of her. What was worse, he was in excellent health.

Such is the terrible corrupting influence of power that the young Princess now began actually to plot the destruction of her own father. But that was easier said than done. It is extremely difficult to bump off a great ruler all on your own without being caught. Poison was a possibility, but poisoners are nearly always apprehended. She spent many days and nights ruminating upon this problem, but no answer came to her. Then one evening after supper, she strolled out on to her balcony as usual, thinking to divert herself for a few moments by driving the crowd of lecherous citizens crazy but, lo and behold, on this night there was no crowd. Instead, an old beggerman stood alone in the courtyard, gazing up at her. He was dressed in filthy rags and his feet were bare. He had a long white beard and a mane of snow-white hair that reached to his shoulders, and he leaned heavily upon a stick.

'Go away, you disgusting old man,' she called out.

'Ssshh!' the old beggar whispered, edging closer. 'I am here to help you. It has come to me in a vision that you are deeply troubled.'

'I am not in the least troubled,' the Princess answered. 'Be off with you unless you fancy a pipkin of boiling lead over your noddle.'

The old man ignored her. 'There is only one way in the world,' he whispered, 'to dispose of an enemy without being caught. Do you wish to hear it?'

'Certainly not,' the Princess snapped. 'Why should I? Yes, what is it?'

'You take an oyster,' the old man whispered, 'and you bury it in the soil of a potted plant. Twenty-four hours later, you dig it up and you squeeze one droplet of its juice, just one droplet, mind you, on to each of the oysters that you are serving to the victim on the following day.'

'Does that fix him?' the Princess asked, unable to conceal her interest.

'It is lethal,' whispered the old man. 'The person who eats those oysters will succumb very swiftly to a terrible paroxysm that will tie his whole body into knots. And after it is over, the whole world will simply shake their heads and murmur, "Poor fellow, he ate a very bad oyster."'

'Who are you, old man, and where do you come from?' the Princess asked, leaning over the balcony.

'I am on the side of the righteous,' the old man whispered, and with that he disappeared into the shadows.

The Princess stored this information away in her head and patiently bided her time. A few days before her eighteenth birthday, the King said to her, 'What do you want for your birthday dinner, my dear? Shall it be your favourite roast boar as usual?'

'Yes, papa,' she answered. 'But let us have some oysters first. I do so love oysters.'

'What a capital idea,' answered the King. 'I shall send to the coast for them immediately.'

On the Princess's birthday, the table in the great dining-room was sumptuously laid and all was got ready for the feast. One dozen fine oysters were put in each place, but before the guests went in to take their seats, the King entered the room alone, as was his wont on special occasions, to make sure that all was to his liking. He summoned the butler and together the two of them walked slowly round the table.

'Why,' asked the King, pointing to his own plate, 'have you given to me the biggest and choicest oysters?'

'Your Majesty always receives the best of everything,' replied the butler, speaking in a high voice. 'Have I done wrong?'

'Today the Princess Mammalia must have the best,' the King said. 'She is the birthday girl. So kindly give her my plate and give me hers.'

'At once, Your Majesty,' answered the butler, and he hastened to change the plates round.

The birthday feast was a success and the oysters went down particularly well. 'Do you like them, Papa?' Princess Mammalia kept asking her father. 'Are they not succulent?'

'Mine are delicious,' the King said. 'How are yours?'

'Perfect,' she answered. 'They are just perfect.'

That night Princess Mammalia was taken violently ill,

and despite the ministrations of the royal physician, she succumbed to a terrible paroxysm that tied her beautiful body into knots.

The next morning the King took from his closet the long white false beard, the long white wig, the filthy rags and the old walking-stick. 'You can burn these,' he said to his valet. 'We can't have fancy-dress parties while the court is in mourning.'

The Bookseller

First published in *Playboy*, January 1987

If, in those days, you walked up from Trafalgar Square into Charing Cross Road, you would come in a few minutes to a shop on the right-hand side that had above the window the words WILLIAM BUGGAGE - RARE BOOKS.

If you peered through the window itself you would see that the walls were lined with books from floor to ceiling, and if you then pushed open the door and went in, you would immediately be assailed by that subtle odour of old cardboard and tea leaves that pervades the interiors of every second-hand bookshop in London. Nearly always, you would find two or three customers in there, silent shadowy figures in overcoats and trilby hats rummaging among the sets of Jane Austen and Trollope and Dickens and George Eliot, hoping to find a first edition.

No shop-keeper ever seemed to be hovering around to keep an eye on the customers, and if somebody actually wanted to pay for a book instead of pinching it and walking out, then he or she would have to push through a door at the back of the shop on which it said OFFICE – PAY HERE. If you went into the office you would find both Mr William Buggage and his assistant, Miss Muriel Tottle, seated at their respective desks and very much preoccupied.

Mr Buggage would be sitting behind a valuable

eighteenth-century mahogany partners-desk, and Miss Tottle, a few feet away, would be using a somewhat smaller but no less elegant piece of furniture, a Regency writing-table with a top of faded green leather. On Mr Buggage's desk there would invariably be one copy of the day's *London Times*, as well as the *Daily Telegraph*, the *Manchester Guardian* the *Western Mail* and the *Glasgow Herald*. There would also be a current edition of *Who's Who* close at hand, fat and red and well thumbed. Miss Tottle's writing-table would have on it an electric typewriter and a plain but very nice open box containing notepaper and envelopes, as well as a quantity of paper-clips and staplers and other secretarial paraphernalia.

Now and again, but not very often, a customer would enter the office from the shop and would hand his chosen volume to Miss Tottle, who checked the price written in pencil on the fly-leaf and accepted the money, giving change when necessary from somewhere in the left-hand drawer of her writing-table. Mr Buggage never bothered even to glance up at those who came in and went out, and if one of them asked a question, it would be Miss Tottle who answered it.

Neither Mr Buggage nor Miss Tottle appeared to be in the least concerned about what went on in the main shop. In point of fact, Mr Buggage took the view that if someone was going to steal a book, then good luck to him. He knew very well that there was not a single valuable first edition out there on the shelves. There might be a moderately rare volume of Galsworthy or an early Waugh that had come in with a job lot bought at auction, and there were certainly some good sets of Boswell and Walter

Scott and Robert Louis Stevenson and the rest, often very nicely bound in half or even whole calf. But those were not really the sort of things you could slip into your overcoat pocket. Even if a villain *did* walk out with half a dozen volumes, Mr Buggage wasn't going to lose any sleep over it. Why should he when he knew that the shop itself earned less money in a whole year than the backroom business grossed in a couple of days. It was what went on in the back room that counted.

One morning in February when the weather was foul and sleet was slanting white and wet on to the window panes of the office, Mr Buggage and Miss Tottle were in their respective places as usual and each was engrossed, one might even say fascinated, by his and her own work. Mr Buggage, with a gold Parker pen poised above a notepad, was reading *The Times* and jotting things down as he went along. Every now and again, he would refer to *Who's Who* and make more jottings.

Miss Tottle, who had been opening the mail, was now examining some cheques and adding up totals.

'Three today,' she said.

'What's it come to?' Mr Buggage asked, not looking up.

'One thousand six hundred,' Miss Tottle said.

Mr Buggage said, 'I don't suppose we've 'eard anything yet from that bishop's 'ouse in Chester, 'ave we?'

'A bishop lives in a palace, Billy, not a house,' Miss Tottle said.

'I don't give a sod where 'ee lives,' Mr Buggage said. 'But I get just a little bit uneasy when there's no quick answer from somebody like that.'

'As a matter of fact, the reply came this morning,' Miss Tottle said.

'Coughed up all right?'

'The full amount.'

'That's a relief,' Mr Buggage said. 'We never done a bishop before and I'm not sure it was any too clever.'

'The cheque came from some solicitors.'

Mr Buggage looked up sharply. 'Was there a letter?' he asked.

'Yes.'

'Read it.'

Miss Tottle found the letter and began to read: 'Dear Sir, With reference to your communication of the 4th Instant, we enclose herewith a cheque for £537 in full settlement. Yours faithfully, Smithson, Briggs and Ellis.' Miss Tottle paused. 'That seems all right, doesn't it?'

'It's all right this time,' Mr Buggage said. 'But we don't want no more solicitors and let's not 'ave any more bishops either.'

'I agree about bishops,' Miss Tottle said. 'But you're not suddenly ruling out earls and lords and all that lot, I hope?'

'Lords is fine,' Mr Buggage said. 'We never 'ad no trouble with lords. Nor earls either. And didn't we do a duke once?'

'The Duke of Dorset,' Miss Tottle said. 'Did him last year. Over a thousand quid.'

'Very nice,' Mr Buggage said. 'I remember selectin' 'im myself straight off the front page.' He stopped talking while he prised a bit of food out from between two front teeth with the nail of his little finger. 'What I says is this,' he went on. 'The bigger the title, the bigger the twit. In fact, anyone's got a title on 'is name is almost certain to be a twit.'

'Now that's not quite true, Billy,' Miss Tottle said. 'Some people are given titles because they've done absolutely brilliant things, like inventing penicillin or climbing Mount Everest.'

'I'm talking about in'erited titles,' Mr Buggage said. 'Anyone gets born with a title, it's odds-on 'ee's a twit.'

'You're right there,' Miss Tottle said. 'We've never had the slightest trouble with the aristocracy.'

Mr Buggage leaned back in his chair and gazed solemnly at Miss Tottle. 'You know what?' he said. 'One of these days we might even 'ave a crack at royalty.'

'Ooh, I'd *love* it,' Miss Tottle said. 'Sock them for a fortune.'

Mr Buggage continued to gaze at Miss Tottle's profile, and as he did so, a slightly lascivious glint crept into his eye. One is forced to admit that Miss Tottle's appearance, when judged by the highest standards, was disappointing. To tell the truth when judged by *any* standards, it was still disappointing. Her face was long and horsey and her teeth, which were also rather long, had a sulphurous tinge about them. So did her skin. The best you could say about her was that she had a generous bosom, but even that had its faults. It was the kind that makes a single long tightly bound bulge from one side of the chest to the other, and at first glance one got the impression that there were not two individual breasts growing out of her body but simply one big long loaf of bread.

Then again, Mr Buggage himself was in no position to be overly finicky. When one saw him for the first time, the word that sprang instantly to mind was 'grubby'. He was squat, paunchy, bald and flaccid, and so far as his face was concerned, one could only make a guess at what it looked like because not much of it was visible to the eye. The major part was covered over by an immense thicket of black, bushy, slightly curly hair, a fashion, one fears, that is all too common these days, a foolish practice and incidentally a rather dirty habit. Why so many males wish to conceal their facial characteristics is beyond the comprehension of us ordinary mortals. One must presume that if it were possible for these people also to grow hair all over their noses and cheeks and eyes, then they would do so, ending up with no visible face at all but only an obscene and rather gamey ball of hair. The only possible conclusion one can arrive at when looking at one of these bearded males is that the vegetation is a kind of smoke-screen and is cultivated in order to conceal something unsightly or unsavoury.

This was almost certainly true in Mr Buggage's case, and it was therefore fortunate for all of us, and especially for Miss Tottle, that the beard was there. Mr Buggage continued to gaze wistfully at his assistant. Then he said, 'Now pet, why don't you 'urry up and get them cheques in the post because after you've done that I've got a little proposal to put to you.'

Miss Tottle looked back over her shoulder at the speaker and gave him a smirk that showed the cutting edges of her sulphur teeth. Whenever he called her 'pet', it was a sure sign that feelings of a carnal nature were beginning to stir within Mr Buggage's breast, and in other parts as well.

'Tell it to me now, lover,' she said.

'You get them cheques done first,' he said. He could be very commanding at times, and Miss Tottle thought it was wonderful.

Miss Tottle now began what she called her Daily Audit. This involved examining all of Mr Buggage's bank accounts and all of her own and then deciding into which of them the latest cheques should be paid. Mr Buggage, you see, at this particular moment, had exactly sixty-six different accounts in his own name and Miss Tottle had twenty-two. These were scattered around among various branches of the big three banks, Barclays, Lloyds and National Westminster, all over London and a few in the suburbs. There was nothing wrong with that. And it had not been difficult, as the business became more and more successful, for either of them to walk into any branch of these banks and open a Current Account, with an initial deposit of a few hundred pounds. They would then receive a cheque book, a paying-in book and the promise of a monthly statement.

Mr Buggage had discovered early on that if a person has an account with several or even many different branches of a bank, this will cause no comment by the staff. Each branch deals strictly with its own customers and their names are not circulated to other branches or to Head Office, not even in these computerized times.

On the other hand, banks are required by law to notify

the Inland Revenue of the names of all clients who have Deposit Accounts containing one thousand pounds or more. They must also report the amounts of interest earned. But no such law applies to Current Accounts because they earn no interest. Nobody takes any notice of a person's Current Account unless it is overdrawn or unless, and this seldom happens, the balance becomes ridiculously large. A Current Account containing let us say £100,000 might easily raise an eyebrow or two among the staff, and the client would almost certainly get a nice letter from the manager suggesting that some of the money be placed on deposit to earn interest. But Mr Buggage didn't give a fig for interest and he wanted no raised eyebrows either. That is why he and Miss Tottle had eighty-eight different bank accounts between them. It was Miss Tottle's job to see that the amounts in each of these accounts never exceeded £20,000. Anything more than that might, in Mr Buggage's opinion, cause an eyebrow to raise, especially if it were left lying untouched in a Current Account for months or years. The agreement between the two partners was seventy-five per cent of the profits of the business to Mr Buggage and twenty-five per cent to Miss Tottle.

Miss Tottle's Daily Audit involved examining a list she kept of all the balances in all those eighty-eight separate accounts and then deciding into which of them the daily cheque or cheques should be deposited. She had in her filing-cabinet eighty-eight different files, one for each bank account, and eighty-eight different cheque books and eighty-eight different paying-in books. Miss Tottle's task was not a complicated one but she had to keep her wits about her and not muddle things up. Only the previous week they had to open four new accounts at four new branches, three for Mr Buggage and one for Miss Tottle. 'Soon we're goin' to 'ave over a 'undred accounts in our names,' Mr Buggage had said to Miss Tottle at the time.

'Why not two hundred?' Miss Tottle had said.

'A day will come,' Mr Buggage said, 'when we'll 'ave used up all the banks in this part of the country and you and I is goin' to 'ave to travel all the way up to Sunderland or Newcastle to open new ones.'

But now Miss Tottle was busy with her Daily Audit. 'That's done,' she said, putting the last cheque and the paying-in slip into its envelope.

''Ow much we got in our accounts altogether at this very moment?' Mr Buggage asked her.

Miss Tottle unlocked the middle drawer of her writing-table and took out a plain school exercise book. On the cover she had written the words *My old arithmetic book from school.* She considered this a rather ingenious ploy designed to put people off the scent should the book ever fall into the wrong hands. 'Just let me add on today's deposit,' she said, finding the right page and beginning to write down figures. 'There we are. Counting today, *you* have got in all the sixty-six branches, one million, three hundred and twenty thousand, six hundred and forty-three pounds, unless you've been cashing any cheques in the last few days.'

'I 'aven't,' Mr Buggage said. 'And what've you got?'

'*I* have got . . . four hundred and thirty thousand, seven hundred and twenty-five pounds.'

'Very nice,' Mr Buggage said. 'And 'ow long's it taken us to gather in those tidy little sums?'

'Just eleven years,' Miss Tottle said. 'What was that teeny weeny proposal you were going to put to me, lover?'

'Ah,' Mr Buggage said, laying down his gold pencil and leaning back to gaze at her once again with that pale licentious eye. 'I was just thinkin' . . .'ere's exactly what I was thinkin' . . . why on earth should a millionaire like me be sittin' 'ere in this filthy freezin' weather when I could be reclinin' in the lap of luxury beside a swimmin' pool with a nice girl like you to keep me company and flunkeys bringin' us goblets of iced champagne every few minutes?'

'Why indeed?' Miss Tottle cried, grinning widely.

'Then get out the book and let's see where we 'aven't been?'

Miss Tottle walked over to a bookshelf on the opposite wall and took down a thickish paperback called *The 300 Best Hotels in the World chosen by Rene Lecler*. She returned to her chair and said, 'Where to this time, lover?'

'Somewhere in North Africa,' Mr Buggage said. 'This is February and you've got to go at least to North Africa to get it really warm. Italy's not 'ot enough yet, nor is Spain. And I don't want the flippin' West Indies. I've 'ad enough of them. Where 'aven't we been in North Africa?'

Miss Tottle was turning the pages of the book. 'That's not so easy,' she said. 'We've done the Palais Jamai in Fez . . . and the Gazelle d'Or in Taroudant . . . and the Tunis Hilton in Tunis. We didn't like that one . . .'

''Ow many we done so far altogether in that book?' Mr Buggage asked her.

'I think it was forty-eight the last time I counted.'

'And I 'as every intention of doin' all three 'undred of 'em before I'm finished,' Mr Buggage said. 'That's my big ambition and I'll bet nobody else 'as ever done it.'

'I think Mr Rene Lecler must have done it,' Miss Tottle said.

''Oo's 'ee?'

'The man who wrote the book.'

''Ee don't count,' Mr Buggage said. He leaned sideways in his chair and began to scratch the left cheek of his rump in a slow meditative manner. 'And I'll bet 'ee 'asn't anyway. These travel guides use any Tom, Dick and 'Arry to go round for 'em.'

'Here's one!' Miss Tottle cried. 'Hotel La Mamounia in Marrakech.'

'Where's that?'

'In Morocco. Just round the top corner of Africa on the left-hand side.'

'Go on then. What does it say about it?'

'It says,' Miss Tottle read, '*This was Winston Churchill's favourite haunt and from his balcony he painted the Atlas sunset time and again.*'

'I don't paint,' Mr Buggage said. 'What else does it say?'

Miss Tottle read on: '*As the liveried Moorish servant shows you into the tiled and latticed colonnaded court, you step decisively into an illustration of the 1001 Arabian nights . . .*'

'That's more like it,' Mr Buggage said. 'Go on.'

'*Your next contact with reality will come when you pay your bill on leaving.*'

'That don't worry us millionaires,' Mr Buggage said.

'Let's go. We'll leave tomorrow. Call that travel agent right away. First class. We'll shut the shop for ten days.'

'Don't you want to do today's letters?'

'Bugger today's letters,' Mr Buggage said. 'We're on 'oliday from now on. Get on to that travel agent quick.' He leaned the other way now and started scratching his right buttock with the fingers of his right hand. Miss Tottle watched him and Mr Buggage saw her watching him but he didn't care. 'Call that travel agent,' he said.

'And I'd better get us some Travellers' Cheques,' Miss Tottle said.

'Get five thousand quid's worth. I'll write the cheque. This one's on me. Give me a cheque book. Choose the nearest bank. And call that 'otel in wherever it was and ask for the biggest suite they're got. They're never booked up when you want the biggest suite.'

Twenty-four hours later, Mr Buggage and Miss Tottle were sunbathing beside the pool at La Mamounia in Marrakech and they were drinking champagne.

'This is the life,' Miss Tottle said. 'Why don't we retire altogether and buy a grand house in a climate like this?'

'What do we want to retire for?' Mr Buggage said. 'We got the best business in London goin' for us and personally I find that very enjoyable.'

On the other side of the pool a dozen Moroccan servants were laying out a splendid buffet lunch for the guests. There were enormous cold lobsters and large pink hams and very small roast chickens and several kinds of rice and about ten different salads. A chef was grilling steaks over a charcoal fire. Guests were beginning to get up from deck-chairs and mattresses to mill around the buffet with plates in their hands. Some were in swimsuits, some in light summer clothes, and most had straw hats on their heads. Mr Buggage was watching them. Almost without exception, they were English. They were the very rich English, smooth, well mannered, overweight, loud-voiced and infinitely dull. He had seen them before all around Jamaica and Barbados and places like that. It was evident that quite a few of them knew one another because at home, of course, they moved in the same cir-cles. But whether they knew each other or not, they certainly *accepted* each other because all of them belonged to the same nameless and exclusive club. Any member of this club could always, by some subtle social alchemy, rec-ognize a fellow member at a glance. Yes, they say to themselves, he's one of us. She's one of us. Mr Buggage was not one of them. He was not in the club and he never would be. He was a *nouveau* and that, regardless of how many millions he had, was unacceptable. He was also overtly vulgar and that was unacceptable, too. The very rich could be just as vulgar as Mr Buggage, or even more so, but they did it in a different way.

'There they are,' Mr Buggage said, looking across the pool at the guests. 'Them's our bread and butter. Every one of 'em's likely to be a future customer.'

'How right you are,' Miss Tottle said.

Mr Buggage, lying on a mattress that was striped in blue, red and green, was propped up on one elbow, staring at the guests. His stomach was bulging out in folds over his swimming-trunks and droplets of sweat were running out of the fatty crevices. Now he shifted his gaze to the recumbent figure of Miss Tottle lying beside him on her own mattress. Miss Tottle's loaf-of-bread bosom was encased in a strip of scarlet bikini. The bottom half of the bikini was daringly brief and possibly a shade too small and Mr Buggage could see traces of black hair high up on the inside of her thighs.

'We'll 'ave our lunch, pet, then we'll go to our room and take a little nap, right?'

Miss Tottle displayed her sulphurous teeth and nodded her head.

'And after that we'll do some letters.'

'Letters?' she cried. 'I don't want to do letters! I thought this was going to be a holiday!'

'It *is* a 'oliday, pet, but I don't like lettin' good business go to waste. The 'otel will lend you a typewriter. I already checked on that. And they're lendin' me their *'Oo's 'Oo*. Every good 'otel in the world keeps an English *'Oo's 'Oo*. The manager likes to know 'oo's important so 'ee can kiss their backsides.'

'They won't find *you* in it,' Miss Tottle said, a bit huffy now.

'No,' Mr Buggage said. 'I'll grant you that. But they won't find many in it that's got more money'n me neither. In this world, it's not 'oo you are, my girl. It's not even 'oo you know. It's what you *got* that counts.'

'We've never done letters on holiday before,' Miss Tottle said.

'There's a first time for everything, pet.'

'How can we do letters without newspapers?'

'You know very well English papers always go airmail to places like this. I bought a *Times* in the foyer when we arrived. It's actually the same as I was workin' on in the office yesterday so I done most of my 'omework already. I'm beginning to fancy a piece of that lobster over there. You ever seen bigger lobsters than that?'

'But you're surely not going to *post* the letters from here, are you?' Miss Tottle said.

'Certainly not. We'll leave 'em undated and date 'em and post 'em as soon as we return. That way we'll 'ave a nice backlog up our sleeves.'

Miss Tottle stared at the lobsters on the table across the pool, then at the people milling around, then she reached out and placed a hand on Mr Buggage's thigh, high up under the bathing-shorts. She began to stroke the hairy thigh. 'Come on, Billy,' she said, 'why don't we take a break from the letters same as we always do when we're on hols?'

'You surely don't want us throwing about a thousand quid away a day, do you?' Mr Buggage said. 'And quarter of it yours, don't forget that.'

'We don't have the firm's notepaper and we can't use hotel paper, for God's sake.'

'I brought the notepaper,' Mr Buggage said, triumphant. 'I got a 'ole box of it. *And* envelopes.'

'Oh, all *right*,' Miss Tottle said. 'Are you going to fetch me some of that lobster, lover?'

'We'll go together,' Mr Buggage said, and he stood up and started waddling round the pool in those almost knee-length bathing-trunks he had bought a couple of years

back in Honolulu. They had a pattern of green and yellow
and white flowers on them. Miss Tottle got to her feet and
followed him.

Mr Buggage was busy helping himself at the buffet
when he heard a man's voice behind him saying, 'Fiona, I
don't think you've met Mrs Smith-Swithin . . . and this is
Lady Hedgecock.'

'How d'you do' . . . 'How d'you do,' the voices said.

Mr Buggage glanced round at the speakers. There was
a man and a woman in swimming-clothes and two elderly
ladies wearing cotton dresses. Those names, he thought.
I've heard those names before, I know I have . . . Smith-
Swithin . . . Lady Hedgecock. He shrugged and continued
to load food on to his plate.

A few minutes later, he was sitting with Miss Tottle at a
small table under a sun-umbrella and each of them was
tucking into an immense half lobster. 'Tell me, does the
name Lady 'Edgecock mean anything to you?' Mr Buggage asked, talking with his mouth full.

'Lady Hedgecock? She's one of our clients. Or she was.
I never forget names like that. Why?'

'And what about a Mrs Smith-Swithin? Does that also
ring a bell?'

'It does, actually,' Miss Tottle said. 'Both of them do.
Why do you ask that suddenly?'

'Because both of 'em's 'ere.'

'Good God! How d'you know?'

'And what's more, my girl, they're together! They're
chums!'

'They're not!'

'Oh, yes they are!'

Mr Buggage told her how he knew. 'There they are,' he said, pointing with a fork whose prongs were yellow with mayonnaise. 'Those two fat old broads talkin' to the tall man and the woman.'

Miss Tottle stared, fascinated. 'You know,' she said, 'I've never actually seen a client of ours in the flesh before, not in all the years we've been in business.'

'Nor me,' Mr Buggage said. 'One thing's for sure. I picked 'em right, didn't I? They're rolling in it. That's obvious. And they're stupid. That's even more obvious.'

'Do you think it could be dangerous, Billy, the two of them knowing each other?'

'It's a bloody queer coincidence,' Mr Buggage said, 'but I don't think it's dangerous. Neither of 'em's ever goin' to say a word. That's the beauty of it.'

'I guess you're right.'

'The only possible danger,' Mr Buggage said, 'would be if they saw my name on the register. I got a very unusual name just like theirs. It would ring bells at once.'

'Guests don't see the register,' Miss Tottle said.

'No, they don't,' Mr Buggage said. 'No one's ever goin' to bother us. They never 'as and they never will.'

'Amazing lobster,' Miss Tottle said.

'Lobster is sex food,' Mr Buggage announced, eating more of it.

'You're thinking of oysters, lover.'

'I am not thinking of oysters. Oysters is sex food, too, but lobsters is stronger. A dish of lobsters can drive some people crazy.'

'Like you, perhaps?' she said, wriggling her rump in the chair.

'Maybe,' Mr Buggage said. 'We shall just 'ave to wait and see about that, won't we, pet?'

'Yes,' she said.

'It's a good thing they're so expensive,' Mr Buggage said. 'If every Tom, Dick and 'Arry could afford to buy 'em, the 'ole world would be full of *sex maniacs.*'

'Keep eating it,' she said.

After lunch, the two of them went upstairs to their suite, where they cavorted clumsily on the huge bed for a brief period. Then they took a nap.

And now they were in their private sitting-room and were wearing only dressing-gowns over their nakedness, Mr Buggage in a plum-coloured silk one, Miss Tottle in pastel pink and pale green. Mr Buggage was reclining on the sofa with a copy of yesterday's *Times* on his lap and a *Who's Who* on the coffee table.

Miss Tottle was at the writing-desk with a hotel type-writer before her and a notebook in her hand. Both were again drinking champagne.

'This is a prime one,' Mr Buggage was saying. 'Sir Edward Leishman. Got the lead obit. Chairman of Aerodynamics Engineering. *One of our major industrialists*, it says.'

'Nice,' Miss Tottle said. 'Make sure the wife's alive.'

'*Leaves a widow and three children*,' Mr Buggage read out. 'And . . . wait a minute . . . in '*Oo's 'Oo* it says, *Recreations, walkin' and fishin'. Clubs, White's and the Reform.*'

'Address?' Miss Tottle asked.

'The Red House, Andover, Wilts.'

'How d'you spell Leishman?' Miss Tottle asked. Mr Buggage spelled it.

'How much shall we go for?'

'A lot,' Mr Buggage said. 'He was loaded. Try around nine 'undred.'

'You want to slip in *The Compleat Angler*? It says he was a fisherman.'

'Yes. First edition. Four 'undred and twenty quid. You know the rest of it by 'eart. Bang it out quick. I got another good one to come.'

Miss Tottle put a sheet of notepaper into the typewriter and very rapidly she began to type. She had done so many thousands of these letters over the years that she never had to pause for one word. She even knew how to compile the list of books so that it came out to around nine hundred pounds or three hundred and fifty pounds or five hundred and twenty or whatever. She could make it come out to any sum Mr Buggage thought the client would stand. One of the secrets of this particular trade, as Mr Buggage knew, was never to be too greedy. Never go over a thousand quid with anyone, not even a famous millionaire.

The letter, as Miss Tottle typed it, went like this:

WILLIAM BUGGAGE — RARE BOOKS

27a Charing Cross Road,
London.

Dear Lady Leishman,

It is with very great regret that I trouble you at this tragic time of your bereavement, but regretfully I am left with no alternative in the circumstances.

I had the pleasure of serving your late husband over a number of years and my invoices were always sent to him care of White's Club, as indeed were many of the little parcels of books that he collected with such enthusiasm.

He was always a prompt settler and a very pleasant gentleman to deal with. I am listing below his more recent purchases, those which, alas, he had ordered in more recent times before he passed away and which were delivered to him in the usual manner.

Perhaps I should explain to you that publications of this nature are often very rare and can therefore be rather costly. Some are privately printed, some are actually banned in this country and those are more costly still.

Rest assured, dear madam, that I always conduct business in the strictest confidence. My own reputation over many years in the trade is the best guarantee of my discretion. When the bill is paid, that is the last you will hear of the matter, unless of course you happen to be able to lay hands on your late husband's collection of erotica, in which case I should be happy to make you an offer for it.

To Books:

THE COMPLEAT ANGLER, Isaak Walton, First £420
edition. Good clean copy. Some rubbing of
edges. Rare.

LOVE IN FURS, Leopold von Sacher-Masoch, 1920   75
edition. Slip cover.

SEXUAL SECRETS, Translation from Danish.   40

HOW TO PLEASURE YOUNG GIRLS WHEN YOU   95
ARE OVER SIXTY, Illustrations. Private printing
from Paris.

Total now due   £995

Yours faithfully,
William Buggage

'Right,' Miss Tottle said, running the notepaper out of
her typewriter. 'Done that one. But you realize I don't
have my "Bible" here, so I'll have to check the names
when I get home before posting the letters.'

'You do that,' Mr Buggage said.

Miss Tottle's Bible was a massive index-card file in
which were recorded the names and addresses of every
client they had written to since the beginning of the business. The purpose of this was to try as nearly as possible
to ensure that no two members of the same family
received a Buggage invoice. If this were to happen, there
would always be the danger that they might compare
notes. It also served to guard against a case where a widow
who had received one invoice upon the death of her first
husband might be sent another invoice on the death of

the second husband. That, of course, would let the cat right out of the bag. There was no guaranteed way of avoiding this perilous mistake because the widow would have changed her name when she remarried, but Miss Tottle had developed an instinct for sniffing out such pitfalls, and the Bible helped her to do it.

'What's next?' Miss Tottle asked.

'The next is Major General Lionel Anstruther. Here 'ee is. Got about six inches in *'Oo's 'Oo. Clubs, Army and Navy. Recreations, Ridin' to 'Ounds.'*

'I suppose he fell off a horse and broke his flipping neck,' Miss Tottle said. 'I'll start with *Memoirs of a Fox-hunting Man, First edition*, right?'

'Right. Two 'undred and twenty quid,' Mr Buggage said. 'And make it between five and six 'undred altogether.'

'Okay.'

'And put in *The Sting of the Ridin' Crop*. Whips seem to come natural to these fox-huntin' folk.'

And so it went on.

The holiday in Marrakech continued pleasantly enough and nine days later Mr Buggage and Miss Tottle were back in the office in Charing Cross Road, both with sun-scorched skins as red as the shells of the many lobsters they had eaten. They quickly settled down again into their normal and stimulating routine. Day after day the letters went out and the cheques came in. It was remarkable how smoothly the business ran. The psychology behind it was, of course, very sound. Strike a widow at the height of her grief, strike her with something that is unbearably awful, something she wants to forget about and put behind her, something she wants nobody else to discover. What's more, the funeral is imminent. So she pays up fast to get the sordid little business out of the way. Mr Buggage knew his onions. In all the years he had been operating, he had never once had a protest or an angry reply. Just a cheque in an envelope. Now and again, but not often, there was no reply at all. The disbelieving widow had been brave enough to sling his letter into the waste-paper basket and that was the end of it. None of them quite dared to challenge the invoice because they could never be absolutely positive that the late husband had been as pure as the wife believed and hoped. Men never are. In many cases, of course, the widow knew very well that her beloved had been a lecherous old bird and Mr Buggage's invoice came as no surprise. So she paid up even faster.

About a month after their return from Marrakech, on a wet and rainy afternoon in March, Mr Buggage was reclining comfortably in his office with his feet up on the top of his fine partners' desk, dictating to Miss Tottle some details about a deceased and distinguished admiral. '*Recreations*,' he was saying, reading from *Who's Who*, '*Gardening, sailing and stamp-collecting . . .*' At that point, the door from the main shop opened and a young man came in with a book in his hand. 'Mr Buggage?' he said.

Mr Buggage looked up. 'Over there,' he said, waving towards Miss Tottle. 'She'll deal with you.'

The young man stood still. His navy-blue overcoat was wet from the weather and droplets of water were dripping from his hair. He didn't look at Miss Tottle. He kept his eyes on Mr Buggage. 'Don't you want the money?' he said, pleasantly enough.

'She'll take it.'

'Why won't you take it?'

'Because she's the cashier,' Mr Buggage said. 'You want to buy a book, go ahead. She'll deal with you.'

'I'd rather deal with *you*,' the young man said.

Mr Buggage looked up at him. 'Go on,' he said. 'Just do as you're told, there's a good lad.'

'You *are* the proprietor?' the young man said. 'You *are* Mr William Buggage?'

'What if I am?' Mr Buggage said, his feet still up on the desk.

'Are you or aren't you?'

'What's it to you?' Mr Buggage said.

'So that's settled,' the young man said. 'How d'you do, Mr Buggage.' There was a curious edge to his voice now, a mixture of scorn and mockery.

Mr Buggage took his feet down from the desk-top and sat up a trifle straighter. 'You're a bit of a cheeky young bugger, aren't you?' he said. 'If you want that book, I suggest you just pay your money over there and then you can 'op it. Right?'

The young man turned towards the still open door that led to the front of the shop. Just the other side of the door there were a couple of the usual kind of customers, men in raincoats, pulling out books and examining them.

'Mother,' the young man called softly. 'You can come in, Mother. Mr Buggage is here.'

763

A small woman of about sixty came in and stood beside the young man. She had a trim figure for her age and a face that must once have been ravishing, but now it showed traces of strain and exhaustion, and the pale blue eyes were dulled with grief. She was wearing a black coat and a simple black hat. She left the door open behind her.

'Mr Buggage,' the young man said. 'This is my mother, Mrs Northcote.'

Miss Tottle, the rememberer of names, turned round quick and looked at Mr Buggage and made little warning movements with her mouth. Mr Buggage got the message and said as politely as he could, 'And what can I do for you, madam?'

The woman opened her black handbag and took out a letter. She unfolded it carefully and held it out to Mr Buggage. 'Then it will be you who sent me this?' she said.

Mr Buggage took the letter and examined it at some length. Miss Tottle, who had turned right round in her chair now, was watching Mr Buggage.

'Yes,' Mr Buggage said. 'This is my letter and my invoice. All correct and in order. What is your problem, madam?'

'What I came here to ask you,' the woman said, 'is, are you sure it's right?'

'I'm afraid it is, madam.'

'But it is so unbelievable . . . I find it impossible to believe that my husband bought those books.'

'Let's see now, your 'usband, Mr . . . Mr . . . er . . .'

'Northcote,' Miss Tottle said.

'Yes, Mr Northcote, yes, of course, Mr Northcote. 'Ee wasn't in 'ere often, once or twice a year maybe, but a good customer and a very fine gentleman. May I offer you, madam, my sincere condolences on your sad loss.'

'Thank you, Mr Buggage. But are you really quite certain you haven't been mixing him up with somebody else?'

'Not a chance, madam. Not the slightest chance. My good secretary over there will confirm that there is no mistake.'

'May I see it?' Miss Tottle said, getting up and crossing to take the letter from Mr Buggage. 'Yes,' she said, examining it. 'I typed this myself. There is no mistake.'

'Miss Tottle's been with me a long time,' Mr Buggage said. 'She knows the business inside out. I can't remember 'er ever makin' a mistake.'

'I should hope not,' Miss Tottle said.

'So there you are, madam,' Mr Buggage said.

'It simply isn't *possible*,' the woman said.

'Ah, but men will be men,' Mr Buggage said. 'They all 'ave their little bit of fun now and again and there's no 'arm in that, is there, madam?' He sat confident and unmoved in his chair, waiting now to have done with it. He felt himself master of the situation.

The woman stood very straight and still, and she was looking Mr Buggage directly in the eyes. 'These curious books you list on your invoice,' she said, 'do they print them in Braille?'

'In what?'

'In Braille.'

'I don't know what you're talking about, madam.'

'I thought you wouldn't,' she said. 'That's the only way my husband could have read them. He lost his sight in the last war, in the Battle of Alamein more than forty years ago, and he was blind for ever after.'

The office became suddenly very quiet. The mother and her son stood motionless, watching Mr Buggage. Miss Tottle turned away and looked out of the window. Mr Buggage cleared his throat as though to say something, but thought better of it. The two men in raincoats, who were close enough to have heard every word through the open door, came quietly into the office. One of them held out a plastic card and said to Mr Buggage, 'Inspector Richards, Serious Crimes Division, Scotland Yard.' And to Miss Tottle, who was already moving back towards her desk, he said, 'Don't touch any of those papers, please, miss. Leave everything just where it is. You're both coming along with us.'

The son took his mother gently by the arm and led her out of the office, through the shop and on to the street.

The Surgeon

First published in *Playboy*, January 1988

'You have done extraordinarily well,' Robert Sandy said, seating himself behind the desk. 'It's altogether a splendid recovery. I don't think there's any need for you to come and see me any more.'

The patient finished putting on his clothes and said to the surgeon, 'May I speak to you, please, for another moment?'

'Of course you may,' Robert Sandy said. 'Take a seat.'

The man sat down opposite the surgeon and leaned forward, placing his hands, palms downward, on the top of the desk. 'I suppose you still refuse to take a fee?' he said.

'I've never taken one yet and I don't propose to change my ways at this time of life,' Robert Sandy told him pleasantly. 'I work entirely for the National Health Service and they pay me a very fair salary.'

Robert Sandy MA, M.CHIR, FRCS, had been at The Radcliffe Infirmary in Oxford for eighteen years and he was now fifty-two years old, with a wife and three grown-up children. Unlike many of his colleagues, he did not hanker after fame and riches. He was basically a simple man utterly devoted to his profession.

It was now seven weeks since his patient, a university undergraduate, had been rushed into Casualty by ambulance after a nasty car accident in the Banbury Road not far from the hospital. He was suffering from massive abdominal injuries and he had lost consciousness. When the call came through from Casualty for an emergency surgeon, Robert Sandy was up in his office having a cup of tea after a fairly arduous morning's work which had included a gall-bladder, a prostate and a total colostomy, but for some reason he happened to be the only general surgeon available at that moment. He took one more sip of his tea, then walked straight back into the operating theatre and started scrubbing up all over again.

After three and a half hours on the operating table, the patient was still alive and Robert Sandy had done everything he could to save his life. The next day, to the surgeon's considerable surprise, the man was showing signs that he was going to survive. In addition, his mind was lucid and he was speaking coherently. It was only then, on the morning after the operation, that Robert Sandy began to realize that he had an important person on his hands. Three dignified gentlemen from the Saudi Arabian Embassy, including the Ambassador himself, came into the hospital and the first thing they wanted was to call in all manner of celebrated surgeons from Harley Street to advise on the case. The patient, with bottles suspended all round his bed and tubes running into many parts of his body, shook his head and murmured something in Arabic to the Ambassador.

'He says he wants only you to look after him,' the Ambassador said to Robert Sandy.

'You are very welcome to call in anyone else you choose for consultation,' Robert Sandy said.

'Not if he doesn't want us to,' the Ambassador said. 'He says you have saved his life and he has absolute faith in you. We must respect his wishes.'

The Ambassador then told Robert Sandy that his patient was none other than a prince of royal blood. In other words, he was one of the many sons of the present King of Saudi Arabia.

A few days later, when the Prince was off the danger list, the Embassy tried once again to persuade him to make a change. They wanted him to be moved to a far more luxurious hospital that catered only for private patients, but the Prince would have none of it. 'I stay here,' he said, 'with the surgeon who saved my life.'

Robert Sandy was touched by the confidence his patient was putting in him, and throughout the long weeks of recovery, he did his best to ensure that this confidence was not misplaced.

And now, in the consulting-room, the Prince was saying, 'I do wish you would allow me to pay you for all you have done, Mr Sandy.' The young man had spent three years at Oxford and he knew very well that in England a surgeon was always addressed as 'Mister' and not 'Doctor'. 'Please let me pay you, Mr Sandy,' he said.

Robert Sandy shook his head. 'I'm sorry,' he answered, 'but I still have to say no. It's just a personal rule of mine and I won't break it.'

'But dash it all, you saved my life,' the Prince said, tapping the palms of his hands on the desk.

'I did no more than any other competent surgeon would have done,' Robert Sandy said.

The Prince took his hands off the desk and clasped them on his lap. 'All right, Mr Sandy, even though you refuse a fee, there is surely no reason why my father should not give you a small present to show his gratitude.'

Robert Sandy shrugged his shoulders. Grateful patients quite often gave him a case of whisky or a dozen bottles of wine and he accepted these things gracefully. He never expected them, but he was awfully pleased when they arrived. It was a nice way of saying thank you.

The Prince took from his jacket pocket a small pouch made of black velvet and he pushed it across the desk. 'My father,' he said, 'has asked me to tell you how enormously indebted he is to you for what you have done. He told me that whether you took a fee or not, I was to make sure you accepted this little gift.'

Robert Sandy looked suspiciously at the black pouch, but he made no move to take it.

'My father,' the Prince went on, 'said also to tell you that in his eyes my life is without price and that nothing on earth can repay you adequately for having saved it. This is simply a . . . what shall we call it . . . a present for your next birthday. A small birthday present.'

'He shouldn't give me anything,' Robert Sandy said.

'Look at it, please,' the Prince said.

Rather gingerly, the surgeon picked up the pouch and loosened the silk thread at the opening. When he tipped it upside down, there was a flash of brilliant light as something ice-white dropped on to the plain wooden desk-top. The stone was about the size of a cashew nut or a bit larger, perhaps three-quarters of an inch long from end to end, and it was pear-shaped, with a very sharp point at the narrow end. Its many facets glimmered and sparkled in the most wonderful way.

'Good gracious me,' Robert Sandy said, looking at it but not yet touching it. 'What is it?'

'It's a diamond,' the Prince said. 'Pure white. It's not especially large, but the colour is good.'

'I really can't accept a present like this,' Robert Sandy said. 'No, it wouldn't be right. It must be quite valuable.'

The Prince smiled at him. 'I must tell you something, Mr Sandy,' he said. 'Nobody refuses a gift from the King. It would be a terrible insult. It has never been done.'

Robert Sandy looked back at the Prince. 'Oh dear,' he said. 'You *are* making it awkward for me, aren't you?'

'It is not awkward at all,' the Prince said. 'Just take it.'

'You could give it to the hospital.'

'We have already made a donation to the hospital,' the Prince said. 'Please take it, not just for my father, but for me as well.'

'You are very kind,' Robert Sandy said. 'All right, then. But I feel quite embarrassed.' He picked up the diamond and placed it in the palm of one hand. 'There's never been a diamond in our family before,' he said. 'Gosh, it is beautiful, isn't it. You must please convey my thanks to His Majesty and tell him I shall always treasure it.'

'You don't actually have to hang on to it,' the Prince said. 'My father would not be in the least offended if you were to sell it. Who knows, one day you might need a little pocket-money.'

'I don't think I shall sell it,' Robert Sandy said. 'It is too lovely. Perhaps I shall have it made into a pendant for my wife.'

'What a nice idea,' the Prince said, getting up from his chair. 'And please remember what I told you before. You and your wife are invited to my country at any time. My father would be happy to welcome you both.'

'That's very good of him,' Robert Sandy said. 'I won't forget.'

When the Prince had gone, Robert Sandy picked up the diamond again and examined it with total fascination. It was dazzling in its beauty, and as he moved it gently from side to side in his palm, one facet after the other caught the light from the window and flashed brilliantly with blue and pink and gold. He glanced at his watch. It was ten minutes past three. An idea had come to him. He picked up the telephone and asked his secretary if there was anything else urgent for him to do that afternoon. If there wasn't, he told her, then he thought he might leave early.

'There's nothing that can't wait until Monday,' the secretary said, sensing that for once this most hard-working of men had some special reason for wanting to go.

'I've got a few things of my own I'd very much like to do.'

'Off you go, Mr Sandy,' she said. 'Try to get some rest over the weekend. I'll see you on Monday.'

In the hospital car park, Robert Sandy unchained his bicycle, mounted and rode out on to the Woodstock Road. He still bicycled to work every day unless the weather was foul. It kept him in shape and it also meant his wife could have the car. There was nothing odd about that. Half the population of Oxford rode on bicycles. He turned into the Woodstock Road and headed for The High. The only good jeweller in town had his shop in The High, halfway up on the right, and he was called H. F. Gold. It said so above the window, and most people knew that H stood for Harry. Harry Gold had been there a long time, but Robert had only been inside once, years ago, to buy a small bracelet for his daughter as a confirmation present.

He parked his bike against the kerb outside the shop and went in. A woman behind the counter asked if she could help him.

'Is Mr Gold in?' Robert Sandy said.

'Yes, he is.'

'I would like to see him privately for a few minutes, if I may. My name is Sandy.'

'Just a minute, please.' The woman disappeared through a door at the back, but in thirty seconds she returned and said, 'Will you come this way, please.'

Robert Sandy walked into a large untidy office in which a small, oldish man was seated behind a partners' desk. He wore a grey goatee beard and steel spectacles, and he stood up as Robert approached him.

'Mr Gold, my name is Robert Sandy. I am a surgeon at The Radcliffe. I wonder if you can help me.'

'I'll do my best, Mr Sandy. Please sit down.'

'Well, it's an odd story,' Robert Sandy said. 'I recently operated on one of the Saudi princes. He's in his third year at Magdalen and he'd been involved in a nasty car accident. And now he has given me, or rather his father has given me, a fairly wonderful-looking diamond.'

'Good gracious me,' Mr Gold said. 'How very exciting.'

773

'I didn't want to accept it, but I'm afraid it was more or less forced on me.'

'And you would like me to look at it?'

'Yes, I would. You see, I haven't the faintest idea whether it's worth five hundred pounds or five thousand, and it's only sensible that I should know roughly what the value is.'

'Of course you should,' Harry Gold said. 'I'll be glad to help you. Doctors at the Radcliffe have helped *me* a great deal over the years.'

Robert Sandy took the black pouch out of his pocket and placed it on the desk. Harry Gold opened the pouch and tipped the diamond into his hand. As the stone fell into his palm, there was a moment when the old man appeared to freeze. His whole body became motionless as he sat there staring at the brilliant shining thing that lay before him. Slowly, he stood up. He walked over to the window and held the stone so that daylight fell upon it. He turned it over with one finger. He didn't say a word. His expression never changed. Still holding the diamond, he returned to his desk and from a drawer he took out a single sheet of clean white paper. He made a loose fold in the paper and placed the diamond in the fold. Then he returned to the window and stood there for a full minute studying the diamond that lay in the fold of paper.

'I am looking at the colour,' he said at last. 'That's the first thing to do. One always does that against a fold of white paper and preferably in a north light.'

'Is that a north light?'

'Yes, it is. This stone is a wonderful colour, Mr Sandy.

As fine a D colour as I've ever seen. In the trade, the very best quality white is called a D colour. In some places it's called a River. That's mostly in Scandinavia. A layman would call it a Blue White.'

'It doesn't look very blue to me,' Robert Sandy said.

'The purest whites always contain a trace of blue,' Harry Gold said. 'That's why in the old days they always put a blue-bag into the washing water. It made the clothes whiter.'

'Ah yes, of course.'

Harry Gold went back to his desk and took out from another drawer a sort of hooded magnifying glass. 'This is a ten-times loupe,' he said, holding it up.

'What did you call it?'

'A loupe. It is simply a jeweller's magnifier. With this, I can examine the stone for imperfections.'

Back once again at the window, Harry Gold began a minute examination of the diamond through the ten-times loupe, holding the paper with the stone on it in one hand and the loupe in the other. This process took maybe four minutes. Robert Sandy watched him and kept quiet.

'So far as I can see,' Harry Gold said, 'it is completely flawless. It really is a most lovely stone. The quality is superb and the cutting is very fine, though definitely not modern.'

'Approximately how many facets would there be on a diamond like that?' Robert Sandy asked.

'Fifty-eight.'

'You mean you know exactly?'

'Yes, I know exactly.'

'Good Lord. And what roughly would you say it is worth?'

'A diamond like this,' Harry Gold said, taking it from the paper and placing it in his palm, 'a D colour stone of this size and clarity would command on inquiry a trade price of between twenty-five and thirty thousand dollars a carat. In the shops it would cost you double that. Up to sixty thousand dollars a carat in the retail market.'

'Great Scott!' Robert Sandy cried, jumping up. The little jeweller's words seemed to have lifted him clean out of his seat. He stood there, stunned.

'And now,' Harry Gold was saying, 'we must find out precisely how many carats it weighs.' He crossed over to a shelf on which there stood a small metal apparatus. 'This is simply an electronic scale,' he said. He slid back a glass door and placed the diamond inside. He twiddled a couple of knobs, then he read off the figures on a dial. 'It weighs fifteen point two seven carats,' he said. 'And that, in case it interests you, makes it worth about half a million dollars in the trade and over one million dollars if you bought it in a shop.'

'You are making me nervous,' Robert Sandy said, laughing nervously.

'If I owned it,' Harry Gold said, 'it would make *me* nervous. Sit down again, Mr Sandy, so you don't faint.'

Robert Sandy sat down.

Harry Gold took his time settling himself into his chair behind the big partner's desk. 'This is quite an occasion, Mr Sandy,' he said. 'I don't often have the pleasure of giving someone quite such a startlingly wonderful shock as this. I think I'm enjoying it more than you are.'

'I am too shocked to be really enjoying it yet,' Robert Sandy said. 'Give me a moment or two to recover.'

'Mind you,' Harry Gold said, 'one wouldn't expect much less from the King of the Saudis. Did you save the young prince's life?'

'I suppose I did, yes.'

'Then that explains it.' Harry Gold had put the diamond back on to the fold of white paper on his desk, and he sat there looking at it with the eyes of a man who loved what he saw. 'My guess is that this stone came from the treasure-chest of old King Ibn Saud of Arabia. If that is the case, then it will be totally unknown in the trade, which makes it even more desirable. Are you going to sell it?'

'Oh gosh, I don't know what I am going to do with it,' Robert Sandy said. 'It's all so sudden and confusing.'

'May I give you some advice.'

'Please do.'

'If you *are* going to sell it, you should take it to auction. An unseen stone like this would attract a lot of interest, and the wealthy private buyers would be sure to come in and bid against the trade. And if you were able to reveal its provenance as well, telling them that it came directly from the Saudi Royal Family, then the price would go through the roof.'

'You have been more than kind to me,' Robert Sandy said. 'When I do decide to sell it, I shall come first of all to you for advice. But tell me, does a diamond really cost twice as much in the shops as it does in the trade?'

'I shouldn't be telling you this,' Harry Gold said, 'but I'm afraid it does.'

'So if you buy one in Bond Street or anywhere else like that, you are actually paying twice its intrinsic worth?'

'That's more or less right. A lot of young ladies have received nasty shocks when they've tried to re-sell jewellery that has been given to them by gentlemen.'

'So diamonds are not a girl's best friend?'

'They are still very friendly things to have,' Harry Gold said, 'as you have just found out. But they are not generally a good investment for the amateur.'

Outside in The High, Robert Sandy mounted his bicycle and headed for home. He was feeling totally light headed. It was as though he had just finished a whole bottle of good wine all by himself. Here he was, solid old Robert Sandy, sedate and sensible, cycling through the streets of Oxford with more than half a million dollars in the pocket of his old tweed jacket! It was madness. But it was true.

He arrived back at his house in Acacia Road at about half past four and parked his bike in the garage alongside the car. Suddenly he found himself running along the little concrete path that led to the front door. 'Now stop that!' he said aloud, pulling up short. 'Calm down. You've got to make this really good for Betty. Unfold it slowly.' But oh, he simply *could not wait* to give the news to his lovely wife and watch her face as he told her the whole story of his afternoon. He found her in the kitchen packing some jars of home-made jam into a basket.

'Robert!' she cried, delighted as always to see him. 'You're home early! How nice!'

He kissed her and said, 'I *am* a bit early, aren't I?'

'You haven't forgotten we're going to the Renshaws for the week-end? We have to leave fairly soon.'

'I had forgotten,' he said. 'Or maybe I hadn't. Perhaps that's why I'm home early.'

'I thought I'd take Margaret some jam.'

'Good,' he said. 'Very good. You take her some jam. That's a very good idea to take Margaret some jam.'

There was something in the way he was acting that made her swing round and stare at him. 'Robert,' she said, 'what's happened? There's something the matter.'

'Pour us each a drink,' he said. 'I've got a bit of news for you.'

'Oh darling, it's not something awful, is it?'

'No,' he said. 'It's something funny. I think you'll like it.'

'You've been made Head of Surgery!'

'It's funnier than that,' he said. 'Go on, make a good stiff drink for each of us and sit down and I'll tell you.'

'It's a bit early for drinks,' she said, but she got the ice-tray from the fridge and started making his whisky and soda. While she was doing this, she kept glancing up at him nervously. She said, 'I don't think I've ever seen you quite like this before. You are wildly excited about something and you are pretending to be very calm. You're all red in the face. Are you sure it's good news?'

'I *think* it is,' he said, 'but I'll let you judge that for yourself.' He sat down at the kitchen table and watched her as she put the glass of whisky in front of him.

'All right,' she said. 'Come on. Let's have it.'

'Get a drink for yourself first,' he said.

'My goodness, what is this?' she said, but she poured

some gin into a glass and was reaching for the ice-tray when he said, 'More than that. Give yourself a good stiff one.'

'Now I *am* worried,' she said, but she did as she was told and then added ice and filled the glass up with tonic. 'Now then,' she said, sitting down beside him at the table, 'get it off your chest.'

Robert began telling his story. He started with the Prince in the consulting-room and he spun it out long and well so that it took a good ten minutes before he came to the diamond.

'It must be quite a whopper,' she said, 'to make you go all red in the face and funny-looking.'

He reached into his pocket and took out the little black pouch and put it on the table. 'There it is,' he said. 'What do you think?'

She loosened the silk cord and tipped the stone into her hand. 'Oh, my God!' she cried. 'It's absolutely stunning!'

'It is, isn't it.'

'It's amazing.'

'I haven't told you the whole story yet,' he said, and while his wife rolled the diamond from the palm of one hand to the other, he went on to tell her about his visit to Harry Gold in The High. When he came to the point where the jeweller began to talk about value, he stopped and said, 'So what do you think he said it was worth?'

'Something pretty big,' she said. 'It's bound to be. I mean just *look* at it!'

'Go on then, make a guess. How much?'

'Ten thousand pounds,' she said. 'I really don't have any idea.'

'Try again.'

'You mean, it's more?'

'Yes, it's quite a lot more.'

'Twenty thousand pounds!'

'Would you be thrilled if it was worth as much as that?'

'Of course, I would, darling. Is it really worth twenty thousand pounds?'

'Yes,' he said. 'And the rest.'

'Now don't be a beast, Robert. Just tell me what Mr Gold said.'

'Take another drink of gin.'

She did so, then put down the glass, looking at him and waiting.

'It is worth at least half a million dollars and very probably over a million.'

'You're joking!' Her words came out in a kind of gasp.

'It's known as a pear-shape,' he said. 'And where it comes to a point at this end, it's as sharp as a needle.'

'I'm completely stunned,' she said, still gasping.

'You wouldn't have thought half a million, would you?'

'I've never in my life had to think in those sort of figures,' she said. She stood up and went over to him and gave him a huge hug and a kiss. 'You really are the most wonderful and stupendous man in the world!' she cried.

'I was totally bowled over,' he said. 'I still am.'

'Oh Robert!' she cried, gazing at him with eyes bright as two stars. 'Do you realize what this means? It means we can get Diana and her husband out of that horrid little flat and buy them a small house!'

'By golly, you're right!'

'And we can buy a decent flat for John and give him a better allowance all the way through his medical school! And Ben . . . Ben wouldn't have to go on a motor-bike to work all through the freezing winters. We could get him something better. And . . . and . . . and . . .'

'And what?' he asked, smiling at her.

'And you and I can take a really good holiday for once and go wherever we please! We can go to Egypt and Turkey and you can visit Baalbek and all the other places you've been longing to go to for years and years!' She was quite breathless with the vista of small pleasures that were unfolding in her dreams. 'And you can start collecting some really nice pieces for once in your life as well!'

Ever since he had been a student, Robert Sandy's passion had been the history of the Mediterranean countries, Italy, Greece, Turkey, Syria and Egypt, and he had made himself into something of an expert on the ancient world of those various civilizations. He had done it by reading and studying and by visiting, when he had the time, the British Museum and the Ashmolean. But with three children to educate and with a job that paid only a reasonable salary, he had never been able to indulge this passion as he would have liked. He wanted above all to visit some of the grand remote regions of Asia Minor and also the now below-ground village of Babylon in Iraq and he would love to see the Arch of Ctesiphon and the Sphinx at Memphis and a hundred other things and places, but neither the time nor the money had ever been available. Even so, the long coffee-table in the living-room was covered with small objects and fragments that he had managed to pick

up cheaply here and there through his life. There was a mysterious pale alabaster ushaptiu in the form of a mummy from Upper Egypt which he knew was Pre-Dynastic from about 700 BC. There was a bronze bowl from Lydia with an engraving on it of a horse, and an early Byzantine twisted silver necklace, and a section of a wooden painted mask from an Egyptian sarcophagus, and a Roman red-ware bowl, and a small black Etruscan dish, and perhaps fifty other fragile and interesting little pieces. None was particularly valuable, but Robert Sandy loved them all.

'Wouldn't that be marvellous?' his wife was saying. 'Where shall we go first?'

'Turkey,' he said.

'Listen,' she said, pointing to the diamond that lay sparkling on the kitchen table, 'you'd better put your fortune away somewhere safe before you lose it.'

'Today is Friday,' he said. 'When do we get back from the Renshaws?'

'Sunday night.'

'And what are we going to do with our million-pound rock in the meanwhile? Take it with us in my pocket?'

'No,' she said, 'that would be silly. You really cannot walk around with a million pounds in your pocket for a whole weekend. It's got to go into a safe-deposit box at the bank. We should do it now.'

'It's Friday night, my darling. All the banks are closed till next Monday.'

'So they are,' she said. 'Well then, we'd better hide it somewhere in the house.'

'The house will be empty till we come back,' he said. 'I don't think that's a very good idea.'

'It's better than carrying it around in your pocket or in my handbag.'

'I'm not leaving it in the house. An empty house is always liable to be burgled.'

'Come on, darling,' she said, 'surely we can think of a place where no one could possibly find it.'

'In the tea-pot,' he said.

'Or bury it in the sugar-basin,' she said.

'Or put it in the bowl of one of my pipes in the pipe-rack,' he said. 'With some tobacco over it.'

'Or under the soil of the azalea plant,' she said.

'Hey, that's not bad, Betty. That's the best so far.'

They sat at the kitchen table with the shining stone lying there between them, wondering very seriously what to do with it for the next two days while they were away.

'I still think it's best if I take it with me,' he said.

'I don't, Robert. You'll be feeling in your pocket every five minutes to make sure it's still there. You won't relax for one moment.'

'I suppose you're right,' he said. 'Very well, then. *Shall* we bury it under the soil of the azalea plant in the sitting-room? No one's going to look there.'

'It's not one hundred per cent safe,' she said. 'Someone could knock the pot over and the soil would spill out on the floor and presto, there's a sparkling diamond lying there.'

'It's a thousand to one against that,' he said. 'It's a thousand to one against the house being broken into anyway.'

'No, it's not,' she said. 'Houses are being burgled every

day. It's not worth chancing it. But look, darling, I'm not going to let this thing become a nuisance to you, or a worry.'

'I agree with that,' he said.

They sipped their drinks for a while in silence.

'I've got it!' she cried, leaping up from her chair. 'I've thought of a marvellous place!'

'Where?'

'In here,' she cried, picking up the ice-tray and pointing to one of the empty compartments. 'We'll just drop it in here and fill it with water and put it back in the fridge. In an hour or two it'll be hidden inside a solid block of ice and even if you looked, you wouldn't be able to see it.'

Robert Sandy stared at the ice-tray. 'It's fantastic!' he said. 'You're a genius! Let's do it right away!'

'Shall we really do it?'

'Of course. It's a terrific idea.'

She picked up the diamond and placed it into one of the little empty compartments. She went to the sink and carefully filled the whole tray with water. She opened the door of the freezer section of the fridge and slid the tray in. 'It's the top tray on the left,' she said. 'We'd better remember that. And it'll be in the block of ice furthest away on the right-hand side of the tray.'

'The top tray on the left,' he said. 'Got it. I feel better now that it's tucked safely away.'

'Finish your drink, darling,' she said. 'Then we must be off. I've packed your case for you. And we'll try not to think about our million pounds any more until we come back.'

'Do we talk about it to other people?' he asked her. 'Like the Renshaws or anyone else who might be there?'

'I wouldn't,' she said. 'It's such an incredible story that it would soon spread around all over the place. Next thing you know, it would be in the papers.'

'I don't think the King of the Saudis would like that,' he said.

'Nor do I. So let's say nothing at the moment.'

'I agree,' he said. 'I would hate any kind of publicity.'

'You'll be able to get yourself a new car,' she said, laughing.

'So I will. I'll get one for you, too. What kind would you like, darling?'

'I'll think about it,' she said.

Soon after that, the two of them drove off to the Renshaws for the weekend. It wasn't far, just beyond Whitney, some thirty minutes from their own house. Charlie Renshaw was a consultant physician at the hospital and the families had known each other for many years.

The weekend was pleasant and uneventful, and on Sunday evening Robert and Betty Sandy drove home again, arriving at the house in Acacia Road at about seven p.m. Robert took the two small suitcases from the car and they walked up the path together. He unlocked the front door and held it open for his wife.

'I'll make some scrambled eggs,' she said, 'and crispy bacon. Would you like a drink first, darling?'

'Why not?' he said.

He closed the door and was about to carry the suitcases

upstairs when he heard a piercing scream from the sitting-room *'Oh no!'* she was crying. *'No! No! No!'*

Robert dropped the suitcase and rushed in after her. She was standing there pressing her hands to her cheeks and already tears were streaming down her face.

The scene in the sitting-room was one of utter desolation. The curtains were drawn and they seemed to be the only things that remained intact in the room. Everything else had been smashed to smithereens. All Robert Sandy's precious little objects from the coffee-table had been picked up and flung against the walls and were lying in tiny pieces on the carpet. A glass cabinet had been tipped over. A chest-of-drawers had had its four drawers pulled out and the contents, photograph albums, games of Scrabble and Monopoly and a chessboard and chessmen and many other family things had been flung across the room. Every single book had been pulled out of the big floor-to-ceiling bookshelves against the far wall and piles of them were now lying open and mutilated all over the place. The glass on each of the four watercolours had been smashed and the oil painting of their three children painted when they were young had had its canvas slashed many times with a knife. The armchairs and the sofa had also been slashed so that the stuffing was bulging out. Virtually everything in the room except the curtains and the carpet had been destroyed.

'Oh, Robert,' she said, collapsing into his arms, 'I don't think I can stand this.'

He didn't say anything. He felt physically sick.

'Stay here,' he said. 'I'm going to look upstairs.' He ran

out and took the stairs two at a time and went first to their bedroom. It was the same in there. The drawers had been pulled out and the shirts and blouses and underclothes were now scattered everywhere. The bedclothes had been stripped from the double-bed and even the mattress had been tipped off the bed and slashed many times with a knife. The cupboards were open and every dress and suit and every pair of trousers and every jacket and every skirt had been ripped from its hanger. He didn't look in the other bedrooms. He ran downstairs and put an arm around his wife's shoulders and together they picked their way through the debris of the sitting-room towards the kitchen. There they stopped.

The mess in the kitchen was indescribable. Almost every single container of any sort in the entire room had been emptied on to the floor and then smashed to pieces. The place was a waste-land of broken jars and bottles and food of every kind. All Betty's home-made jams and pickles and bottled fruits had been swept from the long shelf and lay shattered on the ground. The same had happened to the stuff in the store-cupboard, the mayonnaise, the ketchup, the vinegar, the olive oil, the vegetable oil and all the rest. There were two other long shelves on the far wall and on these had stood about twenty lovely large glass jars with big ground-glass stoppers in which were kept rice and flour and brown sugar and bran and oatmeal and all sorts of other things. Every jar now lay on the floor in many pieces, with the contents spewed around. The refrigerator door was open and the things that had been inside, the leftover foods, the milk, the eggs, the butter,

the yoghurt, the tomatoes, the lettuce, all of them had been
pulled out and splashed on to the pretty tiled kitchen floor.
The inner drawers of the fridge had been thrown into the
mass of slush and trampled on. The plastic ice-trays had
been yanked out and each had been literally broken in two
and thrown aside. Even the plastic-coated shelves had been
ripped out of the fridge and bent double and thrown down
with the rest. All the bottles of drink, the whisky, gin, vodka,
sherry, vermouth, as well as half a dozen cans of beer, were
standing on the table, empty. The bottles of drink and the
beer cans seemed to be the only things in the entire house
that had not been smashed. Practically the whole floor lay
under a thick layer of mush and goo. It was as if a gang of
mad children had been told to see how much mess they
could make and had succeeded brilliantly.

Robert and Betty Sandy stood on the edge of it all,
speechless with horror. At last Robert said, 'I imagine our
lovely diamond is somewhere underneath all that.'

'I don't give a damn about our diamond,' Betty said. 'I'd
like to kill the people who did this.'

'So would I,' Robert said. 'I've got to call the police.' He
went back into the sitting-room and picked up the telephone. By some miracle it still worked.

The first squad car arrived in a few minutes. It was followed over the next half-hour by a police inspector, a
couple of plain-clothes men, a finger-print expert and a
photographer.

The Inspector had a black moustache and a short muscular body. 'These are not professional thieves,' he told
Robert Sandy after he had taken a look round. 'They

weren't even amateur thieves. They were simply hooligans off the street. Riff-raff. Yobbos. Probably three of them. People like this scout around looking for an empty house and when they find it they break in and the first thing they do is to hunt out the booze. Did you have much alcohol on the premises?'

'The usual stuff,' Robert said. 'Whisky, gin, vodka, sherry and a few cans of beer.'

'They'll have drunk the lot,' the Inspector said. 'Lads like these have only two things in mind, drink and destruction. They collect all the booze on to a table and sit down and drink themselves raving mad. Then they go on the rampage.'

'You mean they didn't come in here to steal?' Robert asked.

'I doubt they've stolen anything at all,' the Inspector said. 'If they'd been thieves they would at least have taken your TV set. Instead, they smashed it up.'

'But why do they do this?'

'You'd better ask their parents,' the Inspector said. 'They're rubbish, that's all they are, just rubbish. People aren't brought up right any more these days.'

Then Robert told the Inspector about the diamond. He gave him all the details from the beginning to end because he realized that from the police point of view it was likely to be the most important part of the whole business.

'Half a million quid!' cried the Inspector. 'Jesus Christ!'

'Probably double that,' Robert said.

'Then that's the first thing we look for,' the Inspector said.

'I personally do not propose to go down on my hands and knees grubbing around in that pile of slush,' Robert said. 'I don't feel like it at this moment.'

'Leave it to us,' the Inspector said. 'We'll find it. That was a clever place to hide it.'

'My wife thought of it. But tell me, Inspector, if by some remote chance they *had* found it . . .'

'Impossible,' the Inspector said. 'How could they?'

'They might have seen it lying on the floor after the ice had melted,' Robert said. 'I agree it's unlikely. But if they *had* spotted it, would they have taken it?'

'I think they would,' the Inspector said. 'No one can resist a diamond. It has a sort of magnetism about it. Yes, if one of them had seen it on the floor, I think he would have slipped it into his pocket. But don't worry about it, doctor. It'll turn up.'

'I'm not worrying about it,' Robert said. 'Right now, I'm worrying about my wife and about our house. My wife spent years trying to make this place into a good home.'

'Now look, sir,' the Inspector said, 'the thing for you to do tonight is to take your wife off to a hotel and get some rest. Come back tomorrow, both of you, and we'll start sorting things out. There'll be someone here all the time looking after the house.'

'I have to operate at the hospital first thing in the morning,' Robert said. 'But I expect my wife will try to come along.'

'Good,' the Inspector said. 'It's a nasty upsetting business having your house ripped apart like this. It's a big shock. I've seen it many times. It hits you very hard.'

Robert and Betty Sandy stayed the night at Oxford's Randolph Hotel, and by eight o'clock the following morning Robert was in the Operating Theatre at the hospital, beginning to work his way through his morning list.

Shortly after noon, Robert had finished his last operation, a straightforward non-malignant prostate on an elderly male. He removed his rubber gloves and mask and went next door to the surgeons' small rest-room for a cup of coffee. But before he got his coffee, he picked up the telephone and called his wife.

'How are you, darling?' he said.

'Oh Robert, it's so *awful*,' she said. 'I just don't know where to begin.'

'Have you called the insurance company?'

'Yes, they're coming any moment to help me make a list.'

'Good,' he said. 'And have the police found our diamond?'

'I'm afraid not,' she said. 'They've been through every bit of that slush in the kitchen and they swear it's not there.'

'Then where can it have gone? Do you think the vandals found it?'

'I suppose they must have,' she said. 'When they broke those ice-trays all the ice-cubes would have fallen out. They fall out when you just bend the tray. They're meant to.'

'They still wouldn't have spotted it in the ice,' Robert said.

'They would when the ice melted,' she said. 'Those

men must have been in the house for hours. Plenty of time for it to melt.'

'I suppose you're right.'

'It would stick out a mile lying there on the floor,' she said, 'the way it shines.'

'Oh dear,' Robert said.

'If we never get it back we won't miss it much anyway, darling,' she said. 'We only had it a few hours.'

'I agree,' he said. 'Do the police have any leads on who the vandals were?'

'Not a clue,' she said. 'They found lots of finger-prints, but they don't seem to belong to any known criminals.'

'They wouldn't,' he said, 'not if they were hooligans off the street.'

'That's what the Inspector said.'

'Look, darling,' he said, 'I've just about finished here for the morning. I'm going to grab some coffee, then I'll come home to give you a hand.'

'Good,' she said. 'I need you, Robert. I need you badly.'

'Just give me five minutes to rest my feet,' he said, 'I feel exhausted.'

In Number Two Operating Theatre not ten yards away, another senior surgeon called Brian Goff was also nearly finished for the morning. He was on his last patient, a young man who had a piece of bone lodged somewhere in his small intestine. Goff was being assisted by a rather jolly young registrar named William Haddock, and between them they had opened the patient's abdomen and Goff was lifting out a section of the small intestine and feeling along it with his fingers. It was routine stuff and there was a good deal of conversation going on in the room.

'Did I ever tell you about the man who had lots of little live fish in his bladder?' William Haddock was saying.

'I don't think you did,' Goff said.

'When we were students at Barts,' William Haddock said, 'we were being taught by a particularly unpleasant Professor of Urology. One day, this twit was going to demonstrate how to examine the bladder using a cysto-scope. The patient was an old man suspected of having stones. Well now, in one of the hospital waiting-rooms, there was an aquarium that was full of those tiny little fish, neons they're called, brilliant colours, and one of the students sucked up about twenty of them into a syringe and managed to inject them into the patient's bladder when he was under his pre-med, before he was taken up to Theatre for his cystoscopy.'

'That's disgusting!' the theatre sister cried. 'You can stop right there, Mr Haddock!'

Brian Goff smiled behind his mask and said, 'What happened next?' As he spoke, he had about three feet of the patient's small intestine lying on the green sterile sheet, and he was still feeling along it with his fingers.

'When the Professor got the cystoscope into the blad-der and put his eye to it,' William Haddock said, 'he started jumping up and down and shouting with excitement.

'"What is it, sir?" the guilty student asked him. "What do you see?"

'"It's fish!" cried the Professor. "There's hundreds of little fish! They're swimming about!"'

'You made it up,' the theatre sister said. 'It's not true.'

'It most certainly is true,' the Registrar said. 'I looked down the cystoscope myself and saw the fish. And they were actually swimming about.'

'We might have expected a fishy story from a man with a name like Haddock,' Goff said. 'Here we are,' he added. 'Here's this poor chap's trouble. You want to feel it?'

William Haddock took the pale grey piece of intestine between his fingers and pressed. 'Yes,' he said. 'Got it.'

'And if you look just there,' Goff said, instructing him, 'you can see where the bit of bone has punctured the mucosa. It's already inflamed.'

Brian Goff held the section of intestine in the palm of his left hand. The sister handed him a scalpel and he made a small incision. The sister gave him a pair of forceps and Goff probed down among all the slushy matter of the intestine until he found the offending object. He brought it out, held firmly in the forceps, and dropped it into the small stainless-steel bowl the sister was holding. The thing was covered in pale brown gunge.

'That's it,' Goff said. 'You can finish this one for me now, can't you, William. I was meant to be at a meeting downstairs fifteen minutes ago.'

'You go ahead,' William Haddock said. 'I'll close him up.'

The senior surgeon hurried out of the Theatre and the Registrar proceeded to sew up, first the incision in the intestine, then the abdomen itself. The whole thing took no more than a few minutes.

'I'm finished,' he said to the anaesthetist.

The man nodded and removed the mask from the patient's face.

'Thank you, sister,' William Haddock said. 'See you tomorrow.' As he moved away, he picked up from the sister's tray the stainless-steel bowl that contained the gunge-covered brown object. 'Ten to one it's a chicken bone,' he said and he carried it to the sink and began rinsing it under the tap.

'Good God, what's this?' he cried. 'Come and look, sister!'

The sister came over to look. 'It's a piece of costume jewellery,' she said. 'Probably part of a necklace. Now how on earth did he come to swallow that?'

'He'd have passed it if it hadn't had such a sharp point,' William Haddock said. 'I think I'll give it to my girlfriend.'

'You can't do that, Mr Haddock,' the sister said. 'It belongs to the patient. Hang on a sec. Let me look at it again.' She took the stone from William Haddock's gloved hand and carried it into the powerful light that hung over the operating table. The patient had now been lifted off the table and was being wheeled out into Recovery next door, accompanied by the anaesthetist.

'Come here, Mr Haddock,' the sister said, and there was an edge of excitement in her voice. William Haddock joined her under the light. 'This is amazing,' she went on. 'Just look at the way it sparkles and shines. A bit of glass wouldn't do that.'

'Maybe it's rock-crystal,' William Haddock said, 'or topaz, one of those semi-precious stones.'

'You know what I think,' the sister said. 'I think it's a diamond.'

'Don't be damn silly,' William Haddock said.

A junior nurse was wheeling away the instrument trolley and a male theatre assistant was helping to clear up. Neither of them took any notice of the young surgeon and the sister. The sister was about twenty-eight years old, and now that she had removed her mask she appeared as an extremely attractive young lady.

'It's easy enough to test it,' William Haddock said. 'See if it cuts glass.'

Together they crossed over to the frosted-glass window of the operating-room. The sister held the stone between finger and thumb and pressed the sharp pointed end against the glass and drew it downward. There was a fierce scraping crunch as the point bit into the glass and left a deep line two inches long.

'Jesus Christ!' William Haddock said. 'It *is* a diamond!'

'If it is, it belongs to the patient,' the sister said firmly.

'Maybe it does,' William Haddock said, 'but he was mighty glad to get rid of it. Hold on a moment. Where are his notes?' He hurried over to the side table and picked up a folder which said on it JOHN DIGGS. He opened the folder. In it there was an X-ray of the patient's intestine accompanied by the radiologist's report. *John Diggs,* the report said. *Age 17. Address 123 Mayfield Road, Oxford. There is clearly a large obstruction of some sort in the upper small intestine. The patient has no recollection of swallowing anything*

unusual, but says that he ate some fried chicken on Sunday evening.
The object clearly has a sharp point that has pierced the mucosa of
the intestine, and it could be a piece of bone . . .

'How could he swallow a thing like that without knowing it?' William Haddock said.

'It doesn't make sense,' the sister said.

'There's no question it's a diamond after the way it cut
the glass,' William Haddock said. 'Do you agree?'

'Absolutely,' the sister said.

'And a bloody big one at that,' Haddock said. 'The
question is, how good a diamond is it? How much is it
worth?'

'We'd better send it to the lab right away,' the sister said.

'To hell with the lab,' Haddock said. 'Let's have a bit of
fun and do it ourselves.'

'How?'

'We'll take it to Gold's, the jeweller's in The High.
They'll know. The damn thing must be worth a fortune.
We're not going to steal it, but we're damn well going to
find out about it. Are you game?'

'Do you know anyone at Gold's?' the sister said.

'No, but that doesn't matter. Do you have a car?'

'My Mini's in the car park.'

'Right. Get changed. I'll meet you out there. It's about
your lunch time anyway. I'll take the stone.'

Twenty minutes later, at a quarter to one, the little Mini
pulled up outside the jewellery shop of H. F. Gold and
parked on the double-yellow lines. 'Who cares,' William
Haddock said. 'We won't be long.' He and the sister went
into the shop.

There were two customers inside, a young man and a girl. They were examining a tray of rings and were being served by the woman assistant. As soon as they came in, the assistant pressed a bell under the counter and Harry Gold emerged through the door at the back. 'Yes,' he said to William Haddock and the sister. 'Can I help you?'

'Would you mind telling us what this is worth?' William Haddock said, placing the stone on a piece of green cloth that lay on the counter.

Harry Gold stopped dead. He stared at the stone. Then he looked up at the young man and woman who stood before him. He was thinking very fast. Steady now, he told himself. Don't do anything silly. Act natural.

'Well well,' he said as casually as he could. 'That looks to me like a very fine diamond, a very fine diamond indeed. Would you mind waiting a moment while I weigh it and examine it carefully in my office? Then perhaps I'll be able to give you an accurate valuation. Do sit down, both of you.'

Harry Gold scuttled back into his office with the diamond in his hand. Immediately, he took it to the electronic scale and weighed it. Fifteen point two seven carats. That was exactly the weight of Mr Robert Sandy's stone! He had been certain it was the same one the moment he saw it. Who could mistake a diamond like that? And now the weight had proved it. His instinct was to call the police right away, but he was a cautious man who did not like making mistakes. Perhaps the doctor had already sold his diamond. Perhaps he had given it to his children. Who knows?

Quickly he picked up the Oxford telephone book. The

Radcliffe Infirmary was Oxford 249891. He dialled it. He asked for Mr Robert Sandy. He got Robert's secretary. He told her it was most urgent that he speak to Mr Sandy this instant. The secretary said, 'Hold on, please.' She called the Operating Theatre. Mr Sandy had gone home half an hour ago, they told her. She took up the outside phone and relayed this information to Mr Gold.

'What's his home number?' Mr Gold asked her.

'Is this to do with a patient?'

'No!' cried Harry Gold. 'It's to do with a robbery! For heaven's sake, woman, give me that number quickly!'

'Who is speaking, please?'

'Harry Gold! I'm the jeweller in The High! Don't waste time, I beg you!'

She gave him the number.

Harry Gold dialled again.

'Mr Sandy?'

'Speaking.'

'This is Harry Gold, Mr Sandy, the jeweller. Have you by any chance lost your diamond?'

'Yes, I have.'

'Two people have just brought it into my shop,' Harry Gold whispered excitedly. 'A man and a woman. Youngish. They're trying to get it valued. They're waiting out there now.'

'Are you certain it's my stone?'

'Positive. I weighed it.'

'Keep them there, Mr Gold!' Robert Sandy cried. 'Talk to them! Humour them! Do anything! I'm calling the police!'

Robert Sandy called the police station. Within seconds, he was giving the news to the Detective Inspector who was in charge of the case. 'Get there fast and you'll catch them both!' he said. 'I'm on my way, too!'

'Come on, darling!' he shouted to his wife. 'Jump in the car. I think they've found our diamond and the thieves are in Harry Gold's shop right now trying to sell it!'

When Robert and Betty Sandy drove up to Harry Gold's shop nine minutes later, two police cars were already parked outside. 'Come on, darling,' Robert said. 'Let's go in and see what's happening.'

There was a good deal of activity inside the shop when Robert and Betty Sandy rushed in. Two policemen and two plain-clothes detectives, one of them the Inspector, were surrounding a furious William Haddock and an even more furious theatre sister. Both the young surgeon and the theatre sister were handcuffed.

'You found it *where*?' the Inspector was saying.

'Take these damn handcuffs off me!' the sister was shouting. 'How dare you do this!'

'Tell us again where you found it,' the Inspector said, caustic.

'In someone's stomach!' William Haddock yelled back at him. 'I've told you twice!'

'Don't give me that crap!' the Inspector said.

'Good God, William!' Robert Sandy cried as he came in and saw who it was. 'And Sister Wyman! What on earth are you two doing here?'

'They had the diamond,' the Inspector said. 'They were trying to flog it. Do you know these people, Mr Sandy?'

It didn't take very long for William Haddock to explain to Robert Sandy, and indeed to the Inspector, exactly how and where the diamond had been found.

'Remove their handcuffs, for heaven's sake, Inspector,' Robert Sandy said. 'They're telling the truth. The man you want, at least one of the men you want, is in the hospital right now, just coming round from his anaesthetic. Isn't that right, William?'

'Correct,' William Haddock said. 'His name is John Diggs. He'll be in one of the surgical wards.'

Harry Gold stepped forwards. 'Here's your diamond, Mr Sandy,' he said.

'Now listen,' the theatre sister said, still angry, 'would someone for God's sake tell me how that patient came to swallow a diamond like this without knowing he'd done it?'

'I think I can guess,' Robert Sandy said. 'He allowed himself the luxury of putting ice in his drink. Then he got very drunk. Then he swallowed a piece of half-melted ice.'

'I still don't get it,' the sister said.

'I'll tell you the rest later,' Robert Sandy said. 'In fact, why don't we all go round the corner and have a drink ourselves.'

Roald Dahl

Roald Dahl was born in Llandaff, Wales, on 13 September 1916. His parents were Norwegian and he was the only son of a second marriage. His father, Harald, and elder sister Astri died when Roald was just three years old, leaving his mother, Sofie, to raise her four children and two stepchildren.

At the age of nine, Roald was sent away to boarding school, first in Weston-super-Mare and later in Derbyshire (not far from Cadbury's chocolate factory). He suffered acutely from homesickness and his unhappy schooling was to greatly influence his writing in later life. His childhood and schooldays became the subject of his autobiography *Boy*.

At eigthteen, instead of going to university, he joined the Shell Petroleum Company and after two years training was sent to Dar es Salaam (in what is now Tanzania) to supply oil to customers. However, the outbreak of the Second World War saw him sign up as an aircraftman with the RAF in Nairobi: of the sixteen men who signed up, only Roald and two others were to survive the war.

He detailed his exploits in the war in a further volume of autobiography, *Going Solo*, which included crash-landing in no-man's-land and surviving a direct hit during the Battle of Athens. Invalided out of active service, he was transferred to Washington in 1942 as an air attaché, where an opportune meeting with C. S. Forester, the writer of the *Hornblower* series, set him on a new path.

Roald's first piece of published writing was used to help publicize the British war effort in America. Appearing anonymously in the *Saturday Evening Post* in 1942, 'Shot Down Over Libya' earned him $900. He published several more pieces for the paper, many of which were fictional tales, and these were eventually collected together and published as *Over to You*.

Later stories appeared in the *New Yorker*, *Harpers* and *Atlantic Monthly*. They were widely regarded and he won the prestigious Edgar Award from the Mystery Writers of America three times. In 1953 he married the Oscar-winning actor Patricia Neal and together they had five children.

It was not until the 1960s, after he had settled with his family in Great Missenden in Buckinghamshire, that Roald began seriously to write children's stories, publishing first *James and the Giant Peach* and, a few years later, *Charlie and the Chocolate Factory*. It was not long before his stories were a worldwide success.

After he and Patricia Neal divorced, Roald married Felicity Crosland in 1983. Working to the end on new books, he died aged seventy-four on 23 November 1990.

Now, over twenty years later, Roald Dahl's legacy as a storyteller and favourite of readers around the world remains unsurpassed.

Kiss Kiss

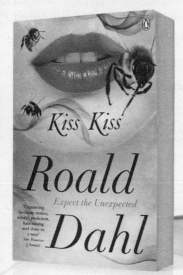

'And it is such a pleasure, my dear, such a very great pleasure when now and again I open the door and I see someone standing there who is just exactly right.'

Eleven devious, shocking stories from the master of the unpredictable, Roald Dahl.

What could go wrong when a wife pawns the mink coat that her lover gave her as a parting gift? What happens when a priceless piece of furniture is the subject of a deceitful bargain? Can a wronged woman take revenge on her dead husband?

In these dark, disturbing stories Roald Dahl explores the sinister side of human nature: the cunning, sly, selfish part of each of us that leads us into the territory of the unexpected and unsettling. Stylish, macabre and haunting, these tales will leave you with a delicious feeling of unease.

'Roald Dahl is one of the few writers I know whose work can accurately be described as addictive' Irish Times

Someone Like You

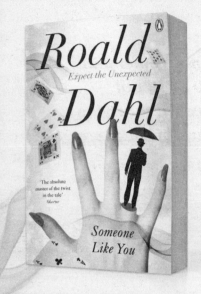

'At that point, Mary Maloney simply walked up behind him and without any pause she swung the big frozen leg of lamb high in the air and brought it down as hard as she could on the back of his head.'

Fifteen classic tales told by the grand master of the short story, Roald Dahl.

In *Someone Like You*, Roald Dahl's first collection of his world-famous dark and sinister adult stories, a wife serves a dish that baffles the police; a harmless bet suddenly becomes anything but; a curious machine reveals a horrifying truth about plants; and a man lies awake waiting to be bitten by the venomous snake asleep on his stomach.

Through vendettas and desperate quests, bitter memories and sordid fantasies, Roald Dahl's stories portray the strange and unexpected, sending a shiver down the spine.

'One of the most widely read and influential writers of our generation'

The Times

Over to You

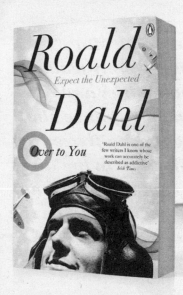

'*I do not remember much of it; not beforehand anyway; not until it happened.*'

Ten terrifying tales of life as a wartime fighter pilot, from the master of the short story, Roald Dahl.

During the Second World War Roald Dahl served in the RAF and even suffered horrific injuries in an air crash in the Libyan desert. Drawing on his own experiences as a fighter pilot, he went on to craft these ten spine-tingling stories: of air battles in the sky; of the nightmare of being shot down; the infectious madness of conflict; and the nervy jollity of the Mess and Ops room.

Roald Dahl brilliantly conveys the banality of a wartime pilot's daily existence, where death is a constant companion and life is lived from one heartbeat to the next.

'*The great magician*'

My Uncle Oswald

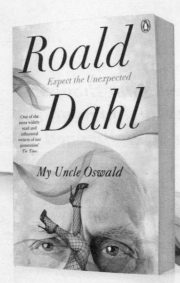

*'My dear, dear sir!
It's a miracle! It's a
wonder pill! It's . . .
it's the greatest invention
of all time!'*

**Meet Uncle Oswald Hendryks Cornelius, Roald Dahl's most
disgraceful and extraordinary character . . .**

Aside from being thoroughly debauched, strikingly attractive and
astonishingly wealthy, Uncle Oswald was the greatest bounder, bon vivant
and fornicator of all time. In this instalment of his scorchingly frank
memoirs he tells of his early career and erotic education at the hands
of a number of enthusiastic teachers, of discovering the invigorating
properties of the Sudanese Blister Beetle, and of the gorgeous Yasmin
Howcomely, his electrifying partner in a most unusual series of thefts . . .

'Raunchy and cheeky entertainment'

Sunday Express

Switch Bitch

*'That's right, I thought.
I want her. I lust after
that woman.'*

**Four tales of seduction and suspense told by the grand master
of the short story, Roald Dahl.**

Topping and tailing this collection are 'The Visitor' and 'Bitch', stories
featuring Roald Dahl's notorious hedonist Oswald Hendryks Cornelius
(or plain old Uncle Oswald), whose exploits are frequently
as extraordinary as they are scandalous. In the middle, meanwhile,
are 'The Great Switcheroo' and 'The Last Act', two stories exploring a
darker side of desire and pleasure.

In the black comedies of *Switch Bitch* Roald Dahl brilliantly captures the
ins and outs, highs and lows of sex.

*'Dahl is too good a storyteller to
become predictable'* Daily Telegraph

The *Wonderful Story* of *Henry Sugar*

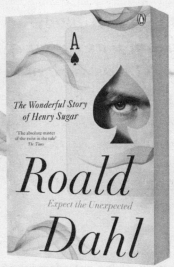

'Men like Henry Sugar are to be found drifting like seaweed all over the world. They can be seen especially in London, New York, Paris, Nassau, Montego Bay, Cannes and St-Tropez.'

Seven tales of the bizarre and unexpected told by the grand master of the short story, Roald Dahl.

Enter a brilliant, sinister and wholly unpredictable world. Here you will find the suggestion of other-worldly goings-on in a dark story about a swan and a boy; the surprising tale of a wealthy young wastrel who suddenly develops a remarkable new ability; and meet the hitchhiker whose light fingers save the day.

'An unforgettable read, don't miss it'

Sunday Times

Ah, Sweet Mystery of Life

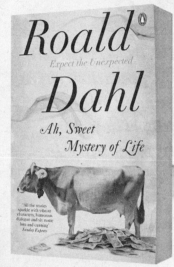

'**Something extremely unpleasant was about to happen – I was sure of that. Something sinister and cruel and ratlike . . . but I had to see it now.**'

The sweet scents of rural life infuse this collection of Roald Dahl's country stories, but there is always something unexpected lurking in the undergrowth . . .

Whether it is taking a troublesome cow to be mated with a prime bull; dealing with a rat-infested hayrick; learning the ways and means of maggot farming; or describing the fine art of poaching pheasants using nothing but raisins and sleeping pills, Roald Dahl brings his stories of everyday country folk and their strange passions wonderfully to life. Lacing each tale with dollops of humour and adding a sprinkling of the sinister, Roald Dahl ensures that this collection is brimful of the sweet mysteries of life.

All the stories sparkle with vibrant characters, humorous dialogue and sly rustic lore and cunning' Sunday Express

Boy

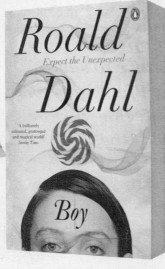

'I was frightened of that cane. There is no small boy in the world who wouldn't be.'

'An autobiography is a book a person writes about his own life and it is usually full of all sorts of boring details. This is not an autobiography. I would never write a history of myself. On the other hand, throughout my young days at school and just afterwards a number of things happened to me that I have never forgotten . . . '

Boy is a funny, insightful and at times grotesque glimpse into the early life of Roald Dahl, one of the world's favourite authors. We discover his experiences of the English public school system, the idyllic paradise of summer holidays in Norway, the pleasures (and pains) of the sweet shop, and how it is that he avoided being a Boazer.

This is the unadulterated childhood – sad and funny, macabre and delightful – that inspired Britain's favourite storyteller and also speaks of an age which vanished with the coming of the Second World War.

'A shimmering fabric of his yesterdays, the magic and the hurt'

Observer

Going Solo

'It isn't often one gets the chance to save a person's life. It gave me a good feeling for the rest of the day.'

'They did not think for one moment that they would find anything but a burnt-out fuselage and a charred skeleton, and they were astounded when they came upon my still-breathing body lying in the sand nearby.'

In 1938 Roald Dahl was fresh out of school and bound for his first job in Africa, hoping to find adventure far from home. However, he got far more excitement than he bargained for when the outbreak of the Second World War led him to join the RAF. His account of his experiences in Africa, crashing a plane in the Western Desert, rescue and recovery from his horrific injuries in Alexandria, flying a Hurricane as Greece fell to the Germans, and many other daring deeds, recreates a world as bizarre and unnerving as any he wrote about in his fiction.

'His account of life as a fighter pilot in the Western Desert and in Greece has the thrilling intensity and the occasional grotesqueness of his fiction' Sunday Times

Roald Dahl's Book of Ghost Stories

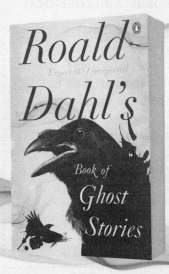

'The best ghost stories don't have ghosts in them. At least you don't see the ghost . . . you can feel it.'

Fourteen ghost stories chosen by the master of the macabre, Roald Dahl.

Who better to choose the ultimate spine-chillers than Roald Dahl, whose own sinister stories have teased and twisted the imagination of millions?

Here are fourteen of his favourite ghost stories, including Sheridan Le Fanu's 'The Ghost of a Hand', Edith Wharton's 'Afterward', Cynthia Asquith's 'The Corner Shop' and Mary Treadgold's 'The Telephone'.

'One of the most widely read and influential writers of our generation'

The Times

THERE'S MORE TO ROALD DAHL THAN GREAT STORIES . . .

Did you know that 10% of author royalties* from this book go to help the work of the Roald Dahl charities?

Roald Dahl's Marvellous Children's Charity exists to make life better for seriously ill children because it believes that every child has the right to a marvellous life. This marvellous charity helps thousands of children each year living with serious conditions of the blood and the brain – causes important to Roald Dahl in his lifetime – whether by providing nurses, equipment or toys for today's children in the UK, or helping tomorrow's children everywhere through pioneering research.

Can you do something marvellous to help others? Find out how at **www.roalddahlcharity.org**

The Roald Dahl Museum and Story Centre, based in Great Missenden just outside London, is in the Buckinghamshire village where Roald Dahl lived and wrote. At the heart of the Museum, created to inspire a love of reading and writing, is his unique archive of letters and manuscripts. As well as two fun-packed biographical galleries, the Museum boasts an interactive Story Centre and is now the home of his famous writing hut. It is a place for the family and teachers and their pupils to explore the exciting world of creativity and literacy.

Find out more at **www.roalddahlmuseum.org**

Roald Dahl's Marvellous Children's Charity (RDMCC) is a registered charity no. 1137409.

The Roald Dahl Museum and Story Centre (RDMSC) is a registered charity no. 1085853.

The Roald Dahl Charitable Trust is a registered charity no. 1119330 and supports the work of RDMCC and RDMSC.

* Donated royalties are net of commission

Roald Dahl

*wrote extraordinary books
for readers of every age*

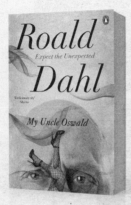

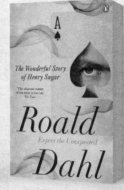

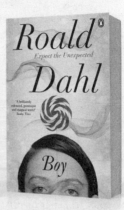

There's a **Roald Dahl**
for all the family

Roald Dahl also wrote some rather popular children's stories:

'Roald Dahl is without question the most successful children's writer in the world'

Independent

He just wanted a decent book to read ...

Not too much to ask, is it? It was in 1935 when Allen Lane, Managing Director of Bodley Head Publishers, stood on a platform at Exeter railway station looking for something good to read on his journey back to London. His choice was limited to popular magazines and poor-quality paperbacks – the same choice faced every day by the vast majority of readers, few of whom could afford hardbacks. Lane's disappointment and subsequent anger at the range of books generally available led him to found a company – and change the world.

'We believed in the existence in this country of a vast reading public for intelligent books at a low price, and staked everything on it'
Sir Allen Lane, 1902–1970, founder of Penguin Books

The quality paperback had arrived – and not just in bookshops. Lane was adamant that his Penguins should appear in chain stores and tobacconists, and should cost no more than a packet of cigarettes.

Reading habits (and cigarette prices) have changed since 1935, but Penguin still believes in publishing the best books for everybody to enjoy. We still believe that good design costs no more than bad design, and we still believe that quality books published passionately and responsibly make the world a better place.

So wherever you see the little bird – whether it's on a piece of prize-winning literary fiction or a celebrity autobiography, political tour de force or historical masterpiece, a serial-killer thriller, reference book, world classic or a piece of pure escapism – you can bet that it represents the very best that the genre has to offer.

Whatever you like to read – trust Penguin.